Breathe

A Glossary and Author's Note are included
at the end of the book.

DOMINICK DONALD

Breathe

HODDER &
STOUGHTON

First published in Great Britain in 2018 by Hodder & Stoughton
An Hachette UK company

1

Copyright © Autolycus House Limited 2018

The right of Dominick Donald to be identified as the
Author of the Work has been asserted by him in accordance
with the Copyright, Designs and Patents Act 1988.

A CIP catalogue record for this title is available from the British Library

Hardback ISBN 978 1 444 77553 2
Trade Paperback ISBN 978 1 444 77554 9
eBook ISBN 978 1 444 77556 3

Typeset in Plantin Light by Palimpsest Book Production Ltd, Falkirk, Stirlingshire

Printed and bound in Great Britain by Clays Ltd, Elcograf S.p.A.

Hodder & Stoughton policy is to use papers that are natural, renewable
and recyclable products and made from wood grown in sustainable forests.
The logging and manufacturing processes are expected to conform to the
environmental regulations of the country of origin.

Hodder & Stoughton Ltd
Carmelite House
50 Victoria Embankment
London EC4Y 0DZ

www.hodder.co.uk

To Diane Turner, physiotherapist, Highworth, Wilts;
Duncan Whitwell and Martin McNally of the
Nuffield Orthopaedic Hospital, Oxford;
Tom Cosker, Neal Jacobs and the late Maz Sutherland,
also of the NOC;
And the surgical teams who helped out on 16 December 2012,
For being really, really good at their jobs.

PROLOGUE

Kensal Rise, London 2 November 1940

First time, a bombed terrace house in Kensal Rise; first soul, a teacher who'd rather stay at home when the sirens went . . .

The house next door was mostly undamaged. The medic stepped over the lintel and squeezed down the little corridor past the lads from Heavy Rescue, stripped to their vests, all grazes and brick dust and faded tattoos. He ducked into the understairs cupboard and through the hole in the party wall into a mirror-image space, but with cushions, tinned food, a lantern, an eiderdown; a shelter the teacher didn't have to share.

But he'd never reached it.

Heavy Rescue had torn out the cupboard's wooden wall and used it to shore up rubble in the corridor beyond. The medic crossed it and scrambled into the tunnel the lads had dug through the rubble of the back room, roofed by a chunk of first-floor joists held up by props. A bugger to sledge in, he thought, with no room to swing and the dead weight of masonry, timbers, furniture all jumbled on top – must have taken most of the night. *Good lads all.* The tunnel jinked left to where the teacher's bed was supposed to be, and there was the Heavy Rescue team leader, bent over, scrambling back – a creak, a moan from old timbers? A jolt to the heart—

'She's sound,' reassured the team leader. 'And the gas is off.' He registered the medic's blue battledress, the armband, the steel helmet. 'You here for him?'

'Aye.'

'Sound as a pound.' He smiled through the brick dust. 'He's alive, unconscious, doesn't seem much marked but he's trapped across the chest. It'll take another four hours, perhaps more, for us to get him out, and we're needed on other jobs. So, is it worth it? Can you do that?'

The medic nodded. 'It'll be rough and ready, chum – I'm no doctor – but I can do his vital signs, perhaps say what's damaged.'

'Can't say fairer.' He replied. 'I'll check on my lads then I'll be by the cupboard, all right?'

The medic let him by, then duckwalked to the end of the tunnel. He found he could stand upright – a patch in the corner of the room perhaps three feet wide where the roof had held and a settee had clotted loose rubble. Another lantern sat in the corner. Props braced an apparently intact wall. A high metal-framed bed jutted from the rubble, one corner embedded in the floorboards. And underneath, sticking out, the teacher's legs – thick woollen socks, bare ankles, grey long johns, and pyjama trousers rucked up to near the knee.

The medic turned on his torch. The angled bed-frame had trapped the man's upper torso, but beyond it his head and arms were still free, sheltered by a big dresser that had been knocked over. *Why's his bed in his back parlour?* He shook his head, aware he was putting off the moment he'd have to stick his head under the rubble. *Time.*

Deep breath. He crawled under the dresser, neck prickling at the thought of the weight of debris piled on top. A pulse from the wrist; weak but steady. Head against mouth to hear breathing; a watery rattle – could be existing illness, but most likely broken ribs and blood in the lungs. He manipulated the right arm. No obvious fractures – he couldn't reach the left without lying across the man's face so left it alone. He moved the chin gently from side to side – upper spine apparently intact – then backed out around the frame to the legs. Stripped him from the waist down: no obvious fractures or signs of internal bleeding. Clothing back up for warmth.

What are his chances? he wondered. Not enough information. He could be bleeding to death in his chest or just have a bad cough – there was no way to tell without examining his upper torso. He nodded. He'd get back to give Heavy Rescue the answer they probably wanted least – no answer at all.

He stood up to rub his lower back.

There was a sickening crack below his feet, like a bone breaking. The bed-frame shifted and dust came down. He started for the tunnel, but the leader was already scrambling through with a four-pound sledge and a couple of props.

'Where was the crack?'

'Underneath.'

'Did the bed shift?'

'Yes.'

'The frame's splitting the floor plate . . . That wall,' he pointed, 'is coming in. When it does, it all comes down. We might not have four minutes, never mind four hours.' He set a prop and started sledging. 'Got morphine?'

Life and death, he thought. 'Yes.'

'Up to you. But might be the best thing.'

Someone was in the tunnel. 'Stan?'

'Everyone out now,' called the gaffer. 'When this goes the party wall may too.'

'Stan?'

'I'll stick with the medic. For a moment or two, anyway.' He turned and offered a wary smile. 'Down to you, chum. The wall goes, so does our escape route.'

'Right.' The medic's throat was dry. Should he walk away? He'd taken no oath – he only picked up his satchel when his day job was done . . . But these lads – Stan might be outside now, having a fag. He had to go that bit further too. He crouched again, stuck his head under the dresser, hearing its creaks above Stan's sledging.

The teacher's eyes were open. The medic jerked up in shock, banged his head, froze. Everything was creaks now.

'Stan?' called the medic. 'Lot of noise.'

'Wall's good.'

The medic was on all fours to scurry out backwards but the teacher's hand on his arm startled him. The lantern showed the man's mouth trying to shape words and his tongue flicked out to wet his lips, iridescent pink in bombsite browns and greys. The medic brought up his water bottle and the teacher lifted his head. A couple of gulps and the head went back, but the eyes stayed fixed on the medic's face inches away.

'My chest hurts.'

'That's because your bed's come down on it, all right?'

'And what's on top of the bed?'

'Well, bits an' bobs an' that.'

'Can you get me out?'

'It might take a bit of time.' The medic was supposed to tell him the truth, but face to face, with the house perched about their ears, it was automatic to lie. 'Back in a jiffy, chum.' He crawled back into the void and pulled his satchel round. Stan's ear was pressed to the wall as his hands ran up and down the crazed plaster, feeling for tremors in the brickwork behind. A chunk near the ceiling dropped onto one of the props. The medic's hands were shaking as he reached in for the syringe and the morphine. He broke the neck off the ampoule cleanly. In with the needle, up with the plunger, repeat with the second ampoule, then the third to be sure. Tap for bubbles, squeeze to lose them. Exactly as in training, only 42 Pardoe Street wasn't the town hall, and this time he was about to take a life.

He was back under the dresser in a moment. 'I've got something for your pain, Mr . . .'

'Torrance.'

'We'll have you back at school in no time. Now, this will take the edge off – let us dig you out quicker, all right?' But the medic could hear the tension in his own voice. He bared Torrance's wrist and squeezed the elbow to bring up the web of veins, nudged the torch-hilt to cast more light, syringe now in his teeth—

'Is this it?'

Left hand pinning the wrist, fingers bridging the vein, syringe down, Torrance's other arm coming up to grab at his right shoulder—

'Is this it?'

Plunger down.

'Yes.' Honesty? Anger at being seen through? Fear? He didn't know. He was looking into Torrance's eyes as he said it, six, nine inches away, and saw a flash of fury in them. Then the gleam started to slip away, the eyes dull, the pupils dilate, breath slacken . . .

Done.

He picked up his torch. Torrance's eyes were closed. If he wasn't dead now he would be in a minute or two, and the medic searched his face, looking for a sign. The mouth had fallen open, and as he stared there was a little click in the throat as if a well-oiled gate had snicked shut, then a puff of breath. His soul, he thought, and reached out to catch it like a child would a bubble, but it was gone, freed, seeping through the rubble to join the chorus of new spirits milling above London.

After a moment he stirred. 'Clear,' he called, crawling out from under the dresser.

Stan was waiting by the tunnel entrance, eyes on the wall, more plaster off, a crack through a patch of bared brickwork. 'Gone?'

The medic nodded.

'Right, off we go.'

The medic scurried into the tunnel, Stan behind him, stumbling along at a crouch until suddenly he was fully upright and in the corridor next door, past the hallway pictures, then into the street, the rest of the lads starting from the front wall where they'd been waiting to lend a hand. 'Keep going!' from Stan, pushing the medic between his shoulder blades, out into the roadway, everyone looking back at 42 Pardoe Street and its crumpled front.

Safe. They clumped together, smokes cupped in hands as a nod to the blackout, watching the two houses, waiting. With its front bay sunken and first floor in, number 42 looked like an old bloke with no teeth, laid out in an open coffin. A couple of the Heavy Rescue lads nodded at the medic as if to say, 'Tough job, well done,' He nodded back. The copper marking the bombsite was off to one side looking no-mates, but suddenly he was heading over, hand out.' The medic would have turned away or steered for the Heavy Rescue van but for a sudden fellowship with everyone in the rescue game. He put his hand out too.

The house fell in with a sigh and a rumble, dust suspended against the three-quarter moon. The policeman had taken off his tin hat and was holding it over his heart. 'His soul has gone to the Lord. May he rest in peace.'

'Rest in peace,' the medic echoed, helmet in his hand. After a moment or two he put it back on his head and fixed the chin strap. He wondered if he would do this again, ever actually feel a soul, feel it slip through his fingers as life turned from light in the eyes to air from the mouth to eternity. He found himself hoping he might.

He didn't know it then, but that was how the Traveller was born.

PART ONE
Dawn

I

The death of the King had emptied the streets. All the way down from Golders Green the buses had been running clear, no one at the stops, no loonies weaving through the traffic, no cabs, no motors, no knots of drinkers outside the pubs because most were shut. Walking down from the terminus at Westbourne Park, Bourton saw that the shops already had black crêpe around their windows, the Royalty Cinema's lights were off, and fewer lads were heading for the night shift at the gas works or Rootes. He supposed everyone was tucked up indoors, welded to their wirelesses, numb at the thought that the shy old man, a sort of stammering rock through fifteen years of war and grey slog, had gone.

He had half an hour in hand by the time he reached the bottom of Notting Hill, even paused for a moment – but he knew that if he ducked into the nick, out of the cold and the soggy air, the other probationers would be chewing over only one subject. He'd had the conversation a dozen times today and he still didn't know what to say. So he headed for Bertram Terrace for a solitary smoke instead.

The terrace was long gone. What the flying bomb hadn't shattered the council had put to the wrecking ball. All that was left were basement-level coal holes tucked under the pavement, many half hidden by debris, with rubble bridges where the houses' front steps used to be. Beyond them, a patch of uneven ground, marked by the odd broken garden wall and clots of grass, ran to the White City railway yards a hundred feet away. But a night like this was all Scotch mist and glistening roofs, the yellow of the yard lights like sulphurous distress flares. If you found the right spot you could almost be a lookout in a crow's nest, bobbing above a fog-bound fishing fleet.

He picked his way to the end of the boundary wall between numbers
11 and 12. He folded his *Evening News*, ready to use it as a cushion,
then remembered the black-bordered picture of His Majesty on the
front. He unfolded the newspaper, might even have apologised, then
rolled and stowed it in his poacher's pocket. He found his stretch of
smooth unbroken wall and scrambled up. As he adjusted himself he
could already feel the cold from the sodden uncapped brick seeping
into the threadbare demob suit he'd bought off a barrow on the 'Bello.
He'd be starting his turn with a dead arse – the price of respect.

Perched on the wall, he was in an island of silence. The first time
he'd come to London, an eighteen-year-old on a weekend pass, he'd
been astonished at the constant din, but here the noise started somewhere else. It might be the Metropolitan Line trains riding the arches
all of a hundred yards away or a brawl outside the Three Horsemen
at the junction with Latimer Road, but in Bertram Terrace, nothing.
Bert Parkin, his supervising officer, who'd shown him the site in his
first week at the Hill, put the silence down to the twenty-odd people
who'd been killed there in 1944 – but Bert'd known some of them
and helped to dig out the rest. For Bourton it was just another bombsite, another hole in a townscape, swept clear of loose debris and
empty until the planners decided what do with it and the council
came up with the money. In the meantime it was a space for lads
playing war, slim pickings for scavengers combing for stray scrap
metal or the knick-knacks of the dead, an occasional somewhere for
courting couples without a roof or tarts aiming to roll a mark. In the
meantime, come darkness, it was a bubble of quiet, almost of privacy.
He'd had precious little of that since 1939.

Bourton lit a Capstan, drew the smoke into his lungs and looked
across the yards at the dark squat terraces of Shepherd's Bush. That
was someone else's ground – the yards marked Notting Hill nick's
boundary – and it meant nothing to him. He was only three months
a policeman, three months a probationer walking the Hill's twelve
beats, yet he'd completely identified with his ground. Or part of it:
Notting Dale, the division's scruffiest end. He turned on the wall to
face his patch. On misty nights it almost disappeared, the dense,
shoddily built streets smothered by the sagging smoke from the Great
Western Railway line or factories on higher ground. But he'd walked

every street, introduced himself to every shopkeeper during the early turn and every publican during the night, learned about the tarts, the pubs, the rackets. Three months in and the Dale – poor, creaky, full of minor villainy and generations of grudges – was where he was learning to be a civvy.

Twenty-six seemed a bit old to be growing up.

A snatch of music came from the end of the street. After a moment or two he realised it was the National Anthem, probably coming from the Three Horsemen. A bunch of petty thieves, gyppos and local hard men, trying out the strangeness of 'God Save the Queen' with the help of the pub's plinky joanna. There was a long pause at the end of the first verse, probably while they all worked out that they didn't know the second, then the music began again. *They'll be repeating it all night. And selling booze to miserable patriots long after closing.*

He checked his watch, complete with hands that glowed in the dark – GI officer issue, swapped for half-inched Hong Kong Police badges. 21.20 – time to be moving. He slipped off the wall, brushed damp brick dust from his trousers and started across the rubble, focusing on the ground in front of him; woolgathering on bombsites after dark could get you a broken leg. His Capstan wasn't helping his night vision so he pinched it out, returned it to the packet and picked up his feet, looking for the rubble bridge between the coal holes. There it was, a patch of light between two grey-black pits, just past the shoe pointing at him from the rubble.

Shoe? He went down on one knee, picked it up and turned it to catch the indifferent light. New, solid, cleat on the heel, polished toecap, fresh scuffs on the uppers. A shoe this good wouldn't be thrown away, not in 1952 London with leather in short supply, not in the Dale. Its twin would be somewhere nearby. Chances were its owner was still in it. He put the shoe down, roughly where he'd found it, and started walking along the edge of the coal holes, trying to see in. But the light was too poor – he'd need a torch—

Idiot. The shoe had been pointing away from the coal holes, which meant its owner had probably come from them, and was either looking for a rubble bridge to get back to Latimer Road or was heading for the railway yards. A would-be suicide? Someone who'd fallen into the coal hole, hurt himself, was staggering around half-conscious? Or some professional type, rolled by his bit of rough and trying to find his way home?

Bourton started to walk down the garden of number 12. And within five paces he found the shoe's owner, partly hidden by a clump of grass and nettles, face down, bare headed, in shirt sleeves, sleeveless pullover, sodden and very still.

The man's left arm was outflung. Bourton lifted the wrist – thick, slick with rain, no watch – and felt for a pulse. Was there something? He wiped the wrist dry with his handkerchief and tried again. *Weak, irregular, but definitely there. But in this cold and wet, perhaps not for much longer.*

What now? Think. It might have been a training problem at Peel House. Off-duty officer finds unknown man, unknown injuries, near death; public house with violent reputation and criminal patrons only fifty yards away; no telephones for two hundred yards, other than in said public house; no police box for four hundred yards. It would be unwise to move the injured man, for fear of worsening his condition. It would be unwise to leave him: if he has been attacked his assailants may return; if it is the scene of a crime, it may be disturbed in the officer's absence, and the officer's assistance may save the man's life. A call for assistance is unlikely to be heard over the National Anthem being sung in the public house and the activity in the nearby railway yards. Which left . . .

Thank you, Bert Parkin. First day in the Dale the old bloke had said, 'You're never off duty, never. Buy a spare whistle, string a lanyard through it and put it on when the uniform comes off – it might save your life one day. Or someone else's.' Bourton clamped the whistle between his teeth and blew, SOS in Morse. Meanwhile he checked the man's mouth – open, apparently clear, breathing OK – then his back: no apparent wound, what felt like a thick, diamond-shaped scar just above his belt, otherwise slick and very cold. He shrugged off his coat and jacket, tugged the jacket underneath the body, rucked the man's sodden clothing up around his neck and wiped his back dry with the *Evening News*. Then he put his hat on the man's head, opened his shirt, and lay across him, wrapping his coat around them. Skin on skin, warmth on cold. Not much, but all he could do.

It was starting to rain again. What were his chances of being heard?

Probably only one of the two closest beats was being walked by the late turn, and if it was one of the old blokes he might even be back in the nick. Perhaps a Good Samaritan would hear, and investigate, or try the police houses on Treadgold Street, or use the police box on Sirdar Road, or even pop into the Dale nick. Though helping the Old Bill wasn't exactly the Dale way.

He paused in signalling while another Metropolitan train went by. Someone was still hammering the Three Horsemen's joanna. The train had pulled in at Latimer Road station; he started repeated short blasts, hoping people stepping onto the platform would hear it. Looking along the body, he could see the man's trousers had ridden up his legs, showing GI socks. He felt a sudden pang. Where did you get those, mate? The stalls? Or Germany – Korea, even? Come on, you bastards, come on!

A window sash banged, back of Evesham Street. A head appeared, looking around the ruins of the terrace. Bourton let the whistle fall and yelled, 'You there! In Evesham Street! This is PC Bourton, Notting Hill! I have an injured man here! Please run to the police box for assistance!' Another head materialised in the same window.

He thought he caught 'Dick Barton, Special Agent!' and a laugh.

'This is not a fucking JOKE!'

Someone belted across the junction with Latimer Road. Bourton jammed the whistle back in his mouth and blew SOS again. Here, half-wit, here! The man swung back around the corner and stopped, head cocked, as he looked towards the bombsite. 'PC Bourton! In the garden of number twelve!'

The man started running. By the time he'd reached the coal holes, Bourton had recognised him as a lanky Notting Hill DC he'd seen around but didn't know. He stood up, shouted that he needed an ambulance, then got back to sharing body heat. 'You might just make it, mate,' he told the body. You might just make it . . .

★

By the time the ambulance turned into the terrace, bell clanging, two lads from the late turn had joined him, Leakey helping to keep the body warm while Hitchcock searched for the man's hat and coat, perhaps some identification. The ambulancemen were followed across the rubble by a straggle of drinkers from the Three Horsemen, muttering and curious. They laid their stretcher down beside the body and used Leakey's torch to check the man for wounds. When they lifted Bourton's hat everyone could see blood matted in the silver-blond hair. 'Accidental?' asked Leakey.

An ambulanceman took a closer look. 'Hard to tell,' he said. *Which means you don't know.*

'Hair like that, he's foreign,' said Leakey. 'Scandiwegian or something.'

'Foreign or not, he's a tough bugger,' said one of the ambulancemen, 'still to be alive in this cold.' They wrapped him in a couple of blankets and buckled him onto the stretcher. Leakey led the way with his torch, stopping after a few paces – 'Hat here, Bourton, you marked it?' – then leading the procession across the rubble bridge. Hitchcock's head appeared out of the coal hole and Bourton reached down to pull him up.

'There's a coat and a jacket down here,' he called to Leakey. 'The only identification I can find looks like it's French.'

Bourton stuck his hand out and Hitchcock paused, probably dubious about the probationer getting first dibs, then handed it over. He shone his torch obligingly as Bourton opened the card folder on a photo of a square-jawed man with a broken nose in a wide-lapelled suit. 'Jonas Sarunas Senkus,' read Bourton. '*Né* – born – Lithuania, 1914. He's a *blessé de guerre*, war wounded.' It seemed to be some kind of French veteran's card. 'A Paris address. Nothing British? No National Registration card?'

'Nah. But then half London's stopped carrying them. Not much point,' said Hitchcock. They were being withdrawn in two weeks, and no one would be prosecuted for going without in the meantime. 'But if he's Lithuanian they might know him in the hostel on Ladbroke Grove.'

'Oi! Steady!' The other coppers turned at Leakey's voice to see him by the ambulance, hands outstretched, trying to protect the crewmen loading Senkus into the back from a knot of angry boozers, but a couple had got behind him and were tugging at the stretcher from the rear step. Bourton and Hitchcock sprinted across the rubble bridge to help.

An ambulanceman slipped and fell, while a man in a pinstripe jacket bellowing 'Froggie cunt!' struggled over him to get at the straps on the stretcher. Leakey had pulled his stick and was jabbing it at the chests of three or four others, all yelling, but two more had climbed onto the rear step and were dragging the ambulanceman out by his boots. Bourton grabbed one around the shins and yanked hard; the man lost his grip and jackknifed onto the step, wrist and face hitting the steel with a smack. More men seethed around Senkus, one kicking the other ambulanceman huddled on the ground.

'What's this about?' Bourton yelled to Leakey, as he grabbed a collar and tried to drag the man out of the wagon.

'Disrespect,' shouted Leakey, 'us, the casualty, God knows. And you, Tommy Lee,' he bellowed at one bloke, 'GET OFF HOME!'

Sudden silence. A man stood under the wagon's interior light, brandishing Bourton's paper and drawing every eye. Oh, hell, thought Bourton. It must have got stuck to the body. 'Look!' shouted the man. 'His Majesty King George the Sixth! Our king! Our *late* king! And they were using him FOR A RAG!'

A moment's pause while the drunks filtered the insult and the coppers snatched for their sticks, then Leakey disappeared under flailing arms, Hitchcock blew for help and men jostled Bourton through the door and onto a spare stretcher. He lashed out, kicking, clawing, biting at a hand that tried to hold his head down. He could see Senkus, blanket stripped off, pale and still, an ambulanceman kneeling beside him, fastening the straps. Then the vehicle jerked forward. The attackers lost their balance and tumbled out of the rear doors.

Bourton swung to his feet. Pinstripe backed away, bumping into another drinker unhooking a first aid bag from the wagon wall, and Bourton pushed them both out the back. The wagon was clear, rumbling along slowly, bell clanging, the ambulanceman wrapping blankets around Senkus.

'Is he still with us?' asked Bourton.

The ambulanceman nodded. 'Don't know how.' He'd lost his collar button and there was brick dust on his tunic. He saw the direction of Bourton's gaze and looked sour. 'Bloody Dale,' he said. 'You could lob a shell into that corner and no one would miss 'em.' Under the harsh yellow light Bourton could see he had to be in his fifties, with smoker's skin and a mouth puckered from keeping false teeth in place. Too old for nights like this. 'Thanks for clearing them out,' he added. 'I owe you one.'

'Get him there alive and we're evens,' said Bourton. 'Somewhere, sometime, I think he's done his bit. He deserves better than killing himself in a coal hole.'

2

22.20. Bourton stood in the vehicle yard, arse numb, feeling the scrapes from the scuffle as he set his cape against the drizzle. He smiled obligingly at a couple of late-turn probationers taking the mickey. *Twenty if they're a day and not a ribbon to their names.* He adjusted his helmet – *Nah, bonnet* – strap. *Ah well – if you can't take a joke . . .*

'Bourton.' He snapped to attention. The sloping-shouldered silhouette of Inspector Adams – the guv'nor – stood in the nick doorway, the lanky figure of the DC from the bombsite in a pool of light behind him. 'DC Athill's handling your Froggy. Care to assist?'

'Yes, sir.' He knew he sounded take-that-hill eager, but a sniff of CID, something he'd otherwise wait years for . . .

'I'll square it with Sergeant Harbison. Call in when DC Athill's done with you and the sergeant will reassign you. Understood?'

'Sir.'

'Come on then, Marconi,' said Athill, trotting past, seeming to jam on his hat, light a Player's and button up a mack all at the same time. 'Army?'

Bourton nodded at the guv'nor and followed Athill. 'Yes, Mr Athill. Middlesex Regiment, mostly. Though—'

'Thought as much,' said Athill, ducking out of the nick's yard. 'Your Morse is shit.'

★

22.30. Bourton stood on a broad front step, waiting for his knock to be answered. But the huge terraced house on the corner of Ladbroke Grove stayed dark. It had once been the Lithuanian embassy, but in 1940 the country had been gobbled up by the Soviet Union and the diplomats, probably worried they'd be gobbled up too, had stayed on. Now Lithuania was part of the USSR and the old embassy was a sort of cultural club and hostel for Lithuanians who didn't want to go back – or had been too chummy with the Nazis to risk it. Bourton wasn't sure where Lithuania was. He banged again.

'I heard you ask for the Dale beats,' said DC Athill, a skinny six-footer, who stooped as he drew on the Player's cupped in his hand. 'Altitude getting to you on the Hill?'

Bourton smiled. Notting Hill was only a hundred feet higher than the lowest point of the Dale but it might as well have been another country – big, ornate, stucco-fronted statements of Victorian prosperity, home to professionals and widows in genteel decline. 'At least in the Dale we've got canaries to tell us if the air's unfit. What do you use here? Old dears?'

'Must be joking – never get a decent brew. No, probationers. No use for anything else. Surprised you ain't been tapped for it.' Athill picked a stray shred of tobacco from his tongue. 'Of course, the gen is you don't think you're a probationer. Never got the signal.'

'Bad ears,' said Bourton. Christ, did everyone in the nick know? 'Was in mortars for a bit.'

'That would do it,' said Athill. 'That and being a smart aleck.' He stepped back to look at the still-dark building. 'Give it another thump.' Bourton complied. 'I heard you got into it with the Three Horsemen,' said Athill.

'If you could call it that. I think they were too tipsy to do any damage.'

'No bottles? No knuckles?' Bourton shook his head. 'You were lucky then.' Athill turned to watch a van crawl up Ladbroke Grove. 'Of course, they'll think they've given you a kicking. Lunchtime, evening tomorrow, they'll be the terrors of the Metropolitan Police in general and PC Bourton in particular. You might need to do something about it if you want to keep walking that beat – show them what you're made of.'

'Thought I might have a get-out-of-jail-free card.'

'They'd nick it from you if you did.' A tiny flame flickered behind a ground-floor bay window. 'Do you think they've got electricity?' asked Athill. 'Or did Uncle Joe take that too?'

A hallway light went on and the front door opened a crack, revealing a sliver of a middle-aged woman in a nightcap and a chief petty officer's coat reaching well below her knees. She was holding a candle. 'Yes, gentlemen?'

Athill removed his hat and stepped into the light pool on the front step. His cigarette had disappeared. 'I'm Detective Constable Athill, ma'am, and this is Police Constable Bourton. We're making enquiries about an incident involving a Lithuanian man earlier this evening in Notting Dale. Would you know a Jonas Senkus?' The woman stepped back, her hand to her mouth. 'Is he a member, a resident, a—'

She was nodding, the nightcap tassel bobbing. 'A room – he shares— What happened? Where—'

'Can we come in, Mrs . . .?'

'Hill – yes.' Her accent was a foreign one Bourton didn't know. He felt a slight surprise. He thought he'd more or less heard them all.

She ushered them into a brown hallway with bubbled wallpaper and scuffed parquet leading to a sweeping staircase. She stepped past it to open a door and press a light switch. A low-watt chandelier revealed a formal parlour with heavy dark furniture and a large, empty fireplace. 'Please, take a seat. I will fetch Dr Kalvaitis.' She pecked up the stairs in little paces, showing much-darned socks below the yards of Royal Navy barathea.

Athill stood in the hallway, hat in hand, back to the stairs, ignoring the parlour. He was probably in his early thirties but had a spiv's moustache that somehow made him look older. 'Did you notice anything about her?' he asked. Bourton shook his head. 'You done much of this?'

Bourton shook his head again. 'Bert Parkin's still got me recceing the ground.'

'All right. Well. Her reaction. The doorstep – now that was normal, but immediately running for the head . . . You interested in CID?' Bourton was surprised and showed it. 'Course you are. It's where the smart alecks go. Though if you don't learn to talk like a probationer you won't get the chance.'

Either Athill's nosy, thought Bourton, or I've really pissed off the other uniforms. 'Received and understood,' he said.

'Believe it when I see it,' said Athill, lightly.

There was silence for a minute or so, until Athill took pity on him. 'It's different from when I joined. Then the Met was short of young blokes. There were lots of us who'd done five, six years in the forces and the old 'uns weren't going to gyp us for a little backchat. Now we're the old blokes and the probationers are twenty and you stick out like a sore thumb.'

'Thanks,' said Bourton. The reassurance prompted him to chance a question. 'What mob?'

'RN. Petty officer telegraphist.' He peered at a photo of a group of gloomy men in frock coats and Ruritanian uniforms. 'Corvettes and then an escort carrier. Atlantic, Russia, Malta convoys. Five years of it. Put me off the sea for life. The missus mentions boating on the Serpentine of a Sunday and I call the DI for work. What does "Middlesex mostly" mean?'

'A year with the Glosters, then seven with the Die-hards. Though I was in the Merchant Navy for about ten minutes in 'thirty-nine.'

''Bout nine too long, I reckon,' said Athill. 'Poor buggers. Must have been good to shoot back for a change.'

There was a creak from the stairs and they turned to see a thin, grey-haired man slowly descending the last flight, fastening a field-grey overcoat with purple velvet lapels. 'Officers, I am Dr Kalvaitis, the director of Lithuania House.' He halted on the bottom step. He had dramatically sunken cheeks under a bushy drooping moustache; it looked like a squirrel's tail stapled to a skull. 'May I ask why you are calling on us at this late hour?'

'A routine matter, sir,' said Athill, blank-faced, warrant card out. 'We understand from Mrs Hill that a . . .' this time he had to check his notebook '. . . Jonas Senkus lives here?'

'Stays here,' said Kalvaitis, pulling wire-rimmed glasses from a hip pocket. 'He has only recently arrived from France. He is here until he finds a room of his own. We help Lithuanians in his position – jobs, references, a bed. Has something happened to him?'

'What does he do, sir?'

'He is a mechanic, I think. He has just started at Rootes on Barlby Road. A good job, a good wage – I think he will soon have his deposit and will be leaving us. Is he injured?'

'Does he have family here, sir?'

'No one – where is he?'

'In France?'

'I don't know— I don't think— Mrs Hill— Where is he?'

'When did he come to Britain, sir?'

'Three weeks ago. Are you going to tell me where he is?'

'Which are you more interested in, sir – his whereabouts, or his condition?'

Kalvaitis was silent. He started blinking rapidly, then closed his eyes and rubbed them hard, the specs' wire rims bobbing on his thumb and middle finger. 'We – I – guaranteed him. He is our respon-sibility. If he is in trouble . . .' His hand came down and his eyes opened. 'We are guests here. We cannot have one man risk that. If we are sent back it will be to the gulag or the Lubyanka.' Athill gazed at him impassively. 'Concentration camps,' Kalvaitis added. 'The secret police headquarters. They shoot people in the basement—'

'I read the papers, sir.'

'Of course.' An awkward smile. 'I am sorry. I should be helping you with your enquiries. Is that the phrase?'

Where had his concern gone? wondered Bourton. And why was Athill pushing so hard over what was probably an accident on a bombsite?

'What do you need to know?' Kalvaitis asked.

'Could we have a look at his room, sir?' asked Athill.

'Of course,' said Kalvaitis. He brushed past them to the top of a staircase leading down to the basement, pressed on an old bell-push light switch, then paused. 'Is Senkus in trouble?'

'His room, sir?'

'Sergeant—'

'Officer.'

'I have been toyed with by policemen for forty years, Officer. Most of them could make me disappear.' Kalvaitis looked weary, angry and perhaps worried all at the same time. 'So please, English policeman, be kind enough, when I ask a question, to answer it or say, "I will not answer." Don't play training-school games, yes?'

'Just doing my job, sir,' said Athill, evenly.

'Damn your job,' said Kalvaitis.

'Shall we start again, sir?' Athill's tone didn't change. 'Where would we find Mr Senkus's room, sir?'

'Down here.'

It was a former boot room or even cold store, a freezing box off the basement corridor, with whitewash over bare brick, a tiled floor and a small barred window. There was a single bed made up with taut patched blankets, a school desk with a straight-backed hall chair, and two neat stacks of belongings, one on a battered suitcase, the other on a knapsack, tucked in a corner. It felt like a guardroom cell.

'He shares it,' said Kalvaitis, gesturing at the two stacks. 'With Mr Brazauskas. Mr Brazauskas works nights, Mr Senkus days, so . . . Excuse me.' A couple of men had ducked out of rooms further down the corridor; Kalvaitis spoke quickly in foreign and they disappeared. Athill was already going through the pile of belongings on top of the suitcase and jerked his head for Bourton to do the same with the knapsack. Kalvaitis returned. 'May I ask what you are looking for?'

Athill looked up. 'Anything that might help us know more about Mr Senkus and what happened to him, sir.'

'He is dead?'

'Badly injured, sir.'

'He was attacked?'

'I'm sure we'll find out when he wakes, sir.'

'He is unconscious?'

'In the Hammersmith, sir,' said Athill. 'Perhaps when we're done here someone would take him some essentials. Toothbrush, ration book, night clothes.'

'Of course,' said Kalvaitis. He stood in the doorway, moustache working, apparently thinking through what he'd heard. Then he excused himself and disappeared.

'Get after him,' Athill told Bourton. 'See what he does with that gen.'

Bourton nodded. The corridor was empty so he tried his luck with the stairs. As he reached the top he could see light down the passage to the left. He headed for it, hoping his boots wouldn't squeak or clump. *Eavesdropping at a doorway – there's detection for you . . .*

'Officer?' He turned. Mrs Hill was in the hallway, surprised at seeing him where he wasn't supposed to be. Inside the room he could hear Kalvaitis ask an operator to connect him to Whitehall 2422. *Who is he going to call about Senkus at this time of night?*

'Mrs Hill,' said Bourton, as if he belonged, but blushing. He knocked on the door and pushed it open. Kalvaitis was standing at a desk, telephone in hand, mouth open.

'Excuse me, Dr Kalvaitis,' said Bourton, 'we would like to see Mr Senkus's immigration paperwork, if you please.'

3

22.55. 'Anything from the kit, Mr Athill?' asked Bourton, on the front step, the drizzle doing little to cool the windburn of having been caught.

'Nah,' said Athill, reaching for his Player's. 'Travel light, these blokes. Poor bastards. Wouldn't be surprised if that's all he has in the world. Forty, and he can carry his life in a knapsack.' He lit up. 'His messmate might be all we've got.' He took his first pull. 'Paypacket says he's paid out of the old Great Western offices at Paddington.'

Two hours later they were stepping across railway tracks towards a clump of navvies huddled smoking under a signal-box gantry. A daisy chain of managers had led them to a gangmaster at Westbourne Park depot and a cutting two hundred yards from West Ealing station. As Bourton stepped into the pool of light from the navvies' work lanterns, bonnet and cape signalling Law's here, he saw a couple of men pinching out their cigarettes and turning away with unease. *Dodgy papers? A pub glassing?*

'It's all right, lads,' said Athill, taking off his hat as he stepped over the last rail and past the picks and sledges left out in the wet, 'no one's in trouble. We just want a chat with a feller about his mate. Who's Buzzy?' Glances pointed Athill to a man in his mid-twenties only partly covered by the gantry, sucking hard on his cigarette as if it would proof him against the rain. New to the gang so doesn't qualify for a dry spot, thought Bourton. Close to, he could see that 'Buzzy' Brazauskas was more like a hunt jockey than a navvy, a lean five foot eight or so, with dark hair under one of the flattish peaked caps he'd seen on German railway workers and Dutch bargees.

Brazauskas nodded. 'I'm Buzzy.'

They found partial shelter under a brick overhang in the embankment wall away from the rest of the gang. Buzzy brought his pick under its old waterproof shroud – 'I leave it, they take it, give me rusty pick.' He lit another smoke from his stub and put them both in one corner of his mouth. 'Something happen to Senkus?' he mumbled.

'What makes you think that, sir?' replied Athill.

Buzzy pinched the end of the stub and flung it away. 'Police are here, he is my London room man. Stands to reason. So what happens to Mr Hero?'

'Mr Hero?'

'He fights the Russians, he fights the Chinks—'

'Chinks?' asked Bourton.

'France Chinks, Indo-China Chinks. He was in the Légion Étrangère. He have the scars but he is mechanic, *fighting* mechanic. He has nine-millimetre monkey wrench?'

'You don't like him much, sir?'

'Like?' Brazauskas paused. 'Probably he is OK, but the boys in Lithuania House, we are in the same boat. We go to the pub, the footy – not he. The great Vejas, so mysterious—'

'Vejas?'

'Ah, partisan name, means – oh, like "wind". Not like "fart".' Grinning. 'He was this great partisan, fighting the Russians to make Lithuania free again. Apparently. Although maybe he was only a small partisan and the bigger ones got dead.' He retrieved a flask from the hip pocket of his waterproof. 'But I am probably not fair. I have known him for three weeks and . . . No. I am fair.' He uncapped his flask. *You always this chatty or are you talking to keep out the cold?* 'Two Sundays ago, we were drinking in the park. His flask is in a round bullet . . .' He outlined what looked like a webbing belt at his waist and shoulders.

'Pouch?' asked Bourton.

'For PPSh?'

'PPSh?' repeated Athill.

'Soviet submachine gun,' Bourton slipped in, 'circular drum magazine.' To Buzzy, 'Magazine pouch?'

'So, PPSh magazine pouch. The flask has some design – he hides it but he doesn't, you know? I'm supposed to know it? I spend the war on farms and a Germany radio factory. We talk about home, the war, after the war, and he says things with such – ah, *bedeutung*, ah, importance, like I know the code and understand he is telling me so much more. All the time he has this secret smile, like "The stories I could tell you if only you were top secret like me . . ." He was arse-hole.'

'Was? What makes you think he's dead?' asked Athill.

Buzzy screwed the lid back on his flask. 'Don't you say?' Athill shook his head. 'Oh, OK.' Admittedly the light was poor, but Bourton didn't think Brazauskas seemed worried by what sleuths might think was an inadvertent admission of murder. 'So I can't pinch his shoes. Nice shoes. No good for work but nice shoes . . . What happened to him?'

Athill told him and asked what Senkus might have been doing in Bertram Terrace. He had to explain where it was. The man shrugged. 'He liked holes. He told me that. Probably hiding a lot as partisan. He has no friends here, does not like London. Perhaps he finishes his shift, finds nice hole to have a drink in. Funny fellow.'

'What time does his shift finish?'

'Four. Was it accident?'

'Is there any reason why you think it couldn't have been?' asked Athill.

Buzzy shrugged again. 'He had a pistol. A little one. A woman's suicide pistol. The Russians are coming, save my honour . . . In his PPSh pouch. Perhaps he thought someone want to accident him? Or perhaps he shows off.' Brazauskas took the waterproof off his pick and nodded at the gang leaving the shelter of the gantry. 'I must—'

'In a moment, Buzzy,' said Athill. 'Would anyone have wanted to "accident" him?'

Brazauskas tapped the pick head on a rail to check its seating and thought. 'He is here three weeks – long enough to be not popular, not to make enemies.'

So perhaps, thought Bourton, he'd brought them with him.

'Is there anyone we should notify? Anyone he talked about?'

Buzzy shook his head. 'No one here, I think. He talks of a woman in Paris – Diana. Wife of another partisan, I think, but . . .'

There wasn't much more that Brazauskas could tell them. They clumped across the tracks to the bridge by the station and clambered up the embankment, over the parapet and onto the road. They squeezed into the pre-war Morris Ten Athill had signed out earlier, Bourton slinging his cape into the back before he settled happily into the passenger seat. He'd sat in a car perhaps six times since he'd left the army, and never on duty; being driven around by a superior officer was an even bigger bonus. He toyed with a cheeky thought. 'You navy?'

'What did I tell you?' Athill pressed the starter motor.

'Thought as much. Your weapons knowledge is shit.'

The engine caught on the third try. 'Now that, smart aleck,' said Athill, 'is why, come the end of your probationary period, you'll be looking for another job.'

4

03.30. 'Guns and partisans.' Athill turned onto Portobello Road, the heart of Notting Hill, and the market where all paths crossed – the fraying genteel pawning their silver, young couples buying bric-à-brac for their lodgings, the skint pecking through the fruit and veg to pad out their coupons. Now it was silent, shrouded in mist, with street-lamps and pawnbrokers' balls popping up like range markers in the gloom. 'I can see your cogs whirring, a whisper of mystery and it's attempted murder. But six years of coppering have taught me that between dull and exciting, it's dull that happens.' He slowed to a crawl. 'He could just be a man of mystery who got sloshed and fell over. Happens. Either way, we won't know much for sure until daylight and we can get a good look at where he came a cropper.' He pulled into the kerb and turned off the engine. 'But first . . .' he turned to Bourton '. . . you know what good coppering's all about?'

Bourton suspected all his Peel House answers would be wrong. 'No.'

'Sources. People who know stuff. Different stuff. Different worlds. Perhaps they're in a position to bend some rules, perhaps they just know something you don't. Sources.'

'Yes, Mr Athill.'

'Enough of the oil. Rex, for Pete's sake, for tonight, anyway.'

'Rex.'

Athill nodded. 'Let's start you off.' He opened his door. 'Time to talk to the ladies at the telephone exchange. Nice clean heads there, too.'

★

Eunice Hooper was a tired-looking brunette in her mid-thirties, blocky in Land Army serge and wan without makeup – 'So no one thinks

I'm a tart on me way to work.' She had something of a Pennines mill town in her accent and a smile that hid her teeth. She walked Bourton around the shift at the switchboard, introducing him to the women free to slip off their headsets, and when Athill returned from the khazi ushered them into a supervisor's cubby smelling of paper and the carbolic on the DC's hands. She shut the door on the din from the switchboard.

'What was the number?'

'Whitehall two four double two,' said Bourton.

She unlocked a wall cupboard and pulled out a thick directory. 'Hands out, love,' she instructed Bourton. She rested the *GPO Reverse Directory Greater London* on his palms and flicked through towards the end. 'Whitehall, Whitehall . . . The twos are government, I think.' Another page. 'So . . . two two is Air, and Housing, First Supplemental, two three is Pensions, two four Colonial. All of the two fours.' She looked up. 'Got what you need, love?' she asked Athill.

'Never know till you find it,' said Athill. 'That's the fun of this detecting game. Thanks, Eunice.'

'Don't mention it.' She returned the directory to its cupboard. 'Nice to meet you, Dick.' She made chivvying motions. 'Now, let me get back to me girls.'

★

'Colonial Office my arse,' said Athill. They were back in the Morris, with drizzle somehow working through the closed window to plop onto Bourton's left shoulder. 'What would a bunch of Lithuanians have to do with the Colonial Office? Lithuania was never painted pink.' He raised a warning finger. 'And before you get ahead of yourself, Dick Bourton – our Frog may be something secret, but that's only half the story.'

Bourton nodded. 'He's one thing, what happened to him is another. The two aren't necessarily related.'

'Every one a coconut,' said Athill, approvingly. 'Smart aleck.' He checked his watch. 'Ten to four. Perfect. Kalvaitis should be back in the Land of Nod. I can't make him disappear but I can wreck his kip.'

They drove the two hundred yards to Ladbroke Gardens – the luxury of it! – and parked halfway down the street. As Bourton closed his door he looked automatically at Lithuania House's big dark bay window. There was a sudden glow from deep, a little ember in the clinker, that as suddenly died. *A cigarette? But why—*

'Rex,' he called quietly. Athill halted and turned. 'They've got a sentry, sitting well back in that parlour, where he can look both ways and no one can see him.'

'How could you?'

'He just took a puff.' Athill walked on and Bourton, niggled at being ignored, trotted to catch up. 'Obviously his sergeant never told him a light'll get you killed.'

'Or he did and this bloke knows he isn't in Korea any more.' Athill stopped again. 'Look, Dick Barton . . .' He paused, apparently trying to find the right words. 'You want everything to mean something, like in your radio show. But it doesn't. Six years of coppering, I've never known a mystery. Never. That Evans lad, off St Mark's Road, killed his wife and kid, couldn't remember where he'd put them? Stupid as a yard of two by four. Neville Heath, bit and whipped that woman up in Pembridge Gardens, killed another girl in Bournemouth? Liked it vicious. This bloke, he could be a sentry, or he could just be one of the lads from the basement having a fag. Everything means nothing. It's just – the sea. It isn't from anywhere, it isn't going anywhere, it's just there.' He sighed. 'God save me from probationers. You're all like bleedin' puppies.'

5

This time Kalvaitis himself opened the door, dressed in a dark blue pinstripe suit and a collarless shirt. 'Sergeant?'

'Still a constable, sir,' said Athill. 'Still work for a living, thank you. We've got some more questions, if you don't mind.'

Kalvaitis stood back and they moved into the hallway. The door to the parlour was open and Bourton registered a hefty man in a faded boiler suit with a shock of white hair standing in the middle of the room, diffident, as if they'd interrupted his quiet smoke behind the kitchen block. Bourton nodded at him and he smiled, then turned away.

'I understand Mr Senkus has a lady friend, sir, in Paris,' said Athill. 'A Diana something. Wife of a partisan. Would you happen to know how we can get hold of her?'

'No,' said Kalvaitis.

'Are you sure about that, sir?'

'Yes.'

'Because you clearly know about her.'

'I do not have her address.'

'Ah. Bit early for an appointment, isn't it, sir?' Athill gestured at the suit.

'Four o'clock is when policemen often call.'

'But you don't get up in your best for them, do you, sir?'

Athill and Kalvaitis were niggling each other nicely so Bourton stepped into the parlour. The hallway light revealed an enamel mug on the mantelpiece and an upright chair askew against the wall. 'Good observation post you've got here, mate,' said Bourton, taking off his bonnet. The man in the boiler suit smiled again. The room smelt of rough tobacco. 'Nice seat, a cup of tea, a smoke . . . Course, hall light would ruin your night vision.'

The man shrugged. 'I keep the door closed.'

'So would the cigarette.'

The man smiled. 'Make-believe.'

'So what are you looking out for, then?'

'Soviet tank army, coming from Holland Park. Of course, if they come from Paddington direction where I cannot see them . . .' His thumb slit his throat theatrically. 'Kalvaitis is a silly old woman.' He nodded at the ribbons on Bourton's chest. 'Army?'

Bourton nodded. 'You?'

The man shrugged. 'A different one.' *Which means the Germans. Army? Waffen SS? Or something really nasty, like the camp guards or police battalions?* He pulled a pack of Caporal from his chest pocket and shook one out for Bourton. 'Still, all the same side now. Poniak.'

'Bourton.' He took the cigarette and Poniak's matches, wondering if the Lithuanian had his blood group tattooed on his upper arm; he still wasn't easy fraternising with former enemies. 'French smokes?'

'Vejas brought a carton.' Poniak examined his cigarette. 'For him, but . . . For Lithuanians, this is civilisation.' *For which, read, you all raided his kit while he was at work.* 'Diana Geravicius, the partisan wife? She lives in Neuilly. Cleans house.'

Bouton asked him to spell the name and he jotted it down. 'Does Kalvaitis know?'

'He has the address, he sends her pension. He doesn't like your friend.'

'I think he feels the same.'

'I'll get the address for you, tell you.'

'Thanks.' Bourton drew in the Caporal smoke and held it in his chest, feeling the old coarse tickle in the tubes and throat. He closed his eyes to savour it.

'Where are you?' asked Poniak.

Bourton smiled. *Clever bugger.* He opened his eyes. 'France. 'Forty-four. You?'

'Home. Before.'

'I'm sorry.'

'I learn to smoke with these. I steal them from my brother.'

'So nothing's changed, then?'

Poniak laughed. 'Nothing.'

Bourton took another drag. 'Thanks for the smoke. And the help and that.'

Poniak shoved his hands deep into his pockets, a local league goalie trying to keep warm at half-time. 'Why not? I can choose, so I help. Besides, most British, they think Communism is the newsreels. You have seen it. You know it. Not here,' he tapped his head, 'but here,' his gut. 'Even Kalvaitis does not know it. Sitting here, in London. Your secret police say "please".'

'How do you know I do?'

'You're the Korea copper. Famous. In Notting Hill, at least.'

Great, thought Bourton. The nick thinks I'm a smart aleck and the Hill thinks I'm Pathé stardust. 'Were you in the Legion too?'

'No. Different things, but never the Legion. I would not be here if I had been Legion.' Bourton nodded. He'd be in France – the Legion might be rough, but at least they gave you a passport after . . . *But what about Senkus?* Bourton excused himself, nipped the end of the Caporal and joined Athill and Kalvaitis in the hallway.

'Dr Kalvaitis, sir, why did Mr Senkus come to Britain?'

Kalvaitis stiffened. 'He wanted to.'

'But he's a French national. It says so on his ID card. And he's got a girl there – no one here. Why leave France?'

'I don't know. When he wakes up, ask him.' Kalvaitis's eyes flickered towards the parlour and Bourton's followed suit. Poniak had stepped into the bay so his front was out of sight, but the back of his head appeared to be moving slowly from side to side, and suddenly he was walking to the hall, putting on an impersonal smile. He said something foreign, nodded at the coppers, then disappeared downstairs. Kalvaitis seemed distracted. *What?*

'Excuse me, sir,' said Bourton, ducking through to the parlour. He stood in the bay and cast around, and there, ten, fifteen yards away, was a huddle of bodies against the railings. A man pounded towards them from Lithuania House and stepped in, draping an arm over his shoulder. Two figures backed away and turned before they reached the streetlamp, leaving two others struggling towards Lithuania House, one in a boiler suit, the other with bandages, and both with thickets of mayflower hair.

'Blow me,' said Bourton. 'It's Senkus.'

*

'This is stupid,' said Bourton, half of Senkus's near-dead weight hanging from one shoulder. 'He belongs in a hospital. Six hours ago he was mostly dead.'

'We can look after him here,' said Poniak, pushing open the door to a room with an unmade bed and embers still glowing in the fireplace.

'Bollocks,' said Bourton, as they lowered Senkus, eyes half open and muttering in foreign, onto good sheets. One of the men from the basement appeared with a coal scuttle. 'Kill him, more like.' Mrs Hill lifted Senkus's head to drape a cloth over the pillow. 'Why not leave him there?'

'He wants to come back,' Poniak said. 'So we can look after him here – Mrs Hill, she was a nurse, we keep him warm.'

'Till you kill him.'

'This is not my idea,' said Poniak, looking as if he didn't think much of Senkus's chances either.

'Whose is it?' Bourton nodded at Senkus. 'His? If he's got any ideas he should be given Bovril an' a pat an' told to shut up. Or the boss?' He jerked his head towards Kalvaitis on the landing. 'Just obeying orders, are you?' Poniak wore a heard-it-all-before half-smile but the tension in him said the jab had hit. 'This is London, not Lithu-bloody-ania. I saved his life, and now you're going to kill him for nothing.' He looked back and forth, from Mrs Hill in her fraying flannel nightdress, hair impressed from sleep, to Poniak, stiff and diffident beside what Bourton now realised must be Kalvaitis' dressing-table, a collar perched on the veneer. 'Bunch of fucking idiots.'

*

'What's he doing walking out of hospital?' asked Athill, back in the car.

'He never did. He was brought back,' said Bourton.

'What?'

'Two blokes who didn't want to be seen. Poniak signalled them from the window, saying don't come in. Then he ran out the basement to get Senkus an' the others legged it.'

'What?' Athill was clearly puzzled. 'Why not go out the front door?'

'Because we'd follow him. This way he's got Senkus before we can see anything.'

'But Pontiac was waiting when we arrived. So – they were expecting him?'

'Must have been.' *But then* . . . 'No. If they had been they'd have got rid of us. Or if they couldn't, sneak Poniak out earlier. No, he must have been watching for something else.'

'And why come back?' Athill had moved on. 'He's much safer at the hospital.'

'They can't protect him there, on a ward . . .' a sudden insight '. . . but they can here.'

'But who brought him? And who are they protecting him from?' Athill shook his head. 'It's been too long a turn for this.'

'Sounds like a mystery, Mr Athill,' Bourton said lightly.

The DC stared at him. 'If I was tricky, Bourton, I'd note that down, and at the end of the turn, when your guv'nor asks how it went, I'd say, "That Bourton is a right arse, get rid of him." And he'd say, "I'd heard that too, and we will."' He lit another Player's. 'Earlier you were asking Kalvaitis about Senkus coming here. Why?'

Bourton heard no niggle in his tone so took the question at face value. 'Immigration.' Athill's smoke glowed. 'My fiancée, she's stateless, right of residence in Hong Kong but stateless. White Russian refugee, all her life in China, though she's more French than Russian, brought up in the French zone of Shanghai, French convent school . . .' Athill was making hurry-up gestures. 'Right. Now she's coming here – she's been given right of residence like him, but it took letters from the Colonel, General Horrocks, General de Guingand.' Athill raised his eyebrows. 'We flogged the Korea nag up hill and down dale, the generals kicked up a fuss, said they'd guarantee her . . . Six months. How long would it have taken Senkus? Immigration are really shirty – they'd just say, "No ties in Britain, French national, stay in France." Someone's got to be pulling strings for him. And quickly – he'll have got his discharge from the Legion last year at the earliest. The basic hitch is five years and they didn't let DPs join up before 'forty-six.' Athill was smiling so Bourton pressed on. 'And another thing. Anna – my fiancée – says that citizenship is like Oz for people like her. Any country as long as it isn't Russia. Senkus has a French passport and a girl in France, why come here?'

Athill chuckled. 'Who's learning the ropes now?' Another pull. 'You've got the makings, you know. You notice, you listen, you push. Get confirmed and you'll be in civvies in a year or two.' He shrugged. 'But if you don't keep your trap shut . . .'

'Mr Athill.'

'And remember – questions don't mean there's a mystery. There's no such thing, not in real policing. The answers are out there. Like America, for Columbus.' He took a long pull. 'We just haven't discovered it yet.' Bourton sensed he was smiling. 'And you know what? Until Senkus is in a fit state to answer questions, this bit of America is none of our bleeding business.' He pressed the starter. 'Time for char and a wad.'

6

06.10. Bourton stepped out of the nick into the vehicle yard where he'd begun his turn. The mist had turned into fog and he breathed deep to test it. There was already an acid tang at the back of his throat. By noon, visibility would be down to a hundred yards; by nightfall he'd be spitting green-black phlegm into his handkerchief.

'Still here?'

Bourton turned to see Athill in the doorway. 'On my way.'

'Best get off sharpish,' said Athill. He wet a finger and stuck it in the air. 'Shouldn't be a bad one. Not cold enough. Still, they might choose to cancel leave.'

'I'm in a section house,' said Bourton. 'They'd get me anyway.'

'Bachelor quarters?' Bourton nodded. 'Best sort something out for your fiancée, then, before she gets here. You applied for married?'

'No joy,' said Bourton, ticking off the accommodation officer's verdict on his fingers. 'Probationer, not married, and she doesn't exist.'

Athill snorted. 'What a load . . . So, you're looking for rooms, then?'

'Easier said on my pay. And as soon as you find out about them, places . . .' He looked at the end of the Caporal he'd cadged from Poniak. ''Sides, I'm not sure what she'd like.'

Athill looked at him. 'She's going to marry you, isn't she?'

Bourton nodded, thinking as he often did, Nineteen months and counting. Will either of us look, sound, feel the same?

'Four walls, a floor, and a cot for a baby nine months down the line. That's what she'll want.' Athill pulled on his Player's. 'When does she arrive?'

'Twenty-third.'

'Better get a move on, then. Half the windows on the Hill got signs in them. Landlords be glad you're not a blackie.'

'Bit steep.'

Athill shrugged. 'Be her funeral.' He took a last puff and ground out his smoke. 'So what did you think of your turn?'

'Interesting. An education. A laugh.' Athill snorted. 'Thank you for the chance.'

'Beats walking for a living.' Athill made way for someone stepping into the yard. 'Ray.'

'Rex.'

Athill gestured towards Bourton. 'Ray, this is Dick Bourton – Dick, Ray Martin.' *Blimey, I'm one of them.*

'Mr Martin.'

'Bourton.' Martin, a blocky Brummie, reached out with one of his builder's mitts and grabbed Bourton's cigarette. 'Froggie smoke? Got another?'

'No, I pinched it.'

'An' if I weren't picky I'd pinch this one.' He handed it back. 'You the Korea one?'

'I was there for a bit, yes.' The two DCs laughed.

'I heard that,' said Martin. *More rumour mill.*

'What've you got?' asked Athill.

'Midnight flit, Elgin Terrace. Maybe theft as well.'

'Dr Crippen, eat your heart out.' They laughed again, then Athill stiffened. 'Oy, Dick Barton, you've got time. Nip into your uniform and pop along to – where, Ray?'

'Thirty-four.'

'Thirty-four Elgin Terrace. Off duty, mind. Go along, say hello.' Bourton nodded, puzzled. Athill smiled. 'There'll be a room free. And who better as a tenant after a bit of thieving than a copper?'

★

'I must be honest with you, this is a cold house.' The landlord, Colonel Suchanek, waved a tweedy arm at the full-height picture window on the landing, with a view over huge bare gardens and the ornate backs of another row of houses. 'But I refuse to board these up, as they were when I bought it. And,' another floor, another picture window, 'the room is a little large for the fireplace. But I am sure a little cold is of no concern to someone who walks the beat in all weathers.'

'In fact, sir, it makes you appreciate a bit of snug.' Two more floors, two more picture windows; a sheer drop to what looked like a couple of vegetable patches and a neat little shed. 'And it'll be my fiancée who'll be here first, until we're wed – and she's coming from Hong Kong. So London cold will be a bit of a shock.'

'I'm sure she will get used to it. And will you be here much before you are married?'

Bourton was flustered. 'She's a nice girl, sir.'

'I'm interested in your uniform, not her morals.' Very much Colonel Suchanek now, rather than the landlord of a terraced house at the foot of Notting Hill with peeling paint and battered stairs. 'See her often and wear your uniform to and from the house and perhaps we could knock a few bob off the rent.' He stopped. 'Here we are.' The fourth-floor landing was small and blank-faced with four doors off. Servants' rooms, thought Bourton, stuck under the eaves. 'I'm afraid I shall have to change the locks.' He beckoned Bourton into a room at the front of the house with two dormer windows and a damp, pervasive chill. 'It shouldn't be as cold as this. I suspect Mr Hearn hasn't lit the fire for a while. The furniture stays. Next door,' he pointed at a wall, 'is Miss Lewis, a teacher in Hammersmith. The rear room this side is empty – the chimney needs repairing. Across the landing is the bathroom. Please, look around.' He stepped out of the room.

It was perhaps three hundred square feet, a truncated L with well-worn floorboards, mismatched furniture and competing wallpaper. The open wardrobe and scraps of paper on the floor were evidence of Hearn's flit. Bourton ran his hands around the window frames – no draught; along the wallpaper – no damp; over the fireplace – the trap worked and he could feel the acrid draught when he opened it. The alcove beside the chimney breast housed a makeshift kitchen cupboard, three shelves half hidden by a little curtain on a string, with a two-ring gas burner resting on top. He checked the connection beside the fireplace – no smell of gas. The single bed looked lost on the expanse of floor but the mattress didn't seem to have any stray springs and the fabric headboard was appropriately feminine. Bourton sat in an armchair in the corner. The room was better than most he'd seen but he still felt clueless, unable to link a place with Anna, Anna and him, the life they were supposed to share. In Hong Kong they'd have taken what they could get and made it work – but after nineteen months, a war, the end of the army for him and the east for her, everything either of them knew, he wasn't sure he had a picture of what he and Anna should be. Trying to find somewhere to live just made him ever more aware that he really didn't know her at all.

Ah, well, he thought. It's not as if I can tell her to get off the troopship.

He turned to look out of the window. The other side of the street was a mirror image – dormer windows, patchy stucco, cheap post-war concrete tiles, squads of chimneys. And sky. Nothing above the roof-line, no factory chimneys or rooftop shacks or laundry-shrouded tenement blocks, just sky. Her own patch of sky . . .

'Mr Suchanek?' he called. 'I'll take it.'

The Traveller rang the doorbell, then lowered his head deferentially. She'd be a while – the women always were, smoothing down their dresses, primping their hair – but she might be looking through a judas or a chink in the parlour curtain, and a bit of humility helped 'em decide they were doing the right thing.

He could hear high heels on tiles and instinctively stood up straighter. He sniffed for acid in the air, then exhaled through his teeth, watching the plume. It isn't cold enough, he realised regretfully. This one will be gone by midday tomorrow. So, let's see if we can fit another in tonight. There's that old bird Stoke Newington way . . .

The door opened six inches or so. 'Mr Higgins?'

Her name flew from his head so he raised his hat, said, 'Ma'am,' a pleased laugh.

'Oh, none of that, please. I'm not the Queen.' Her hand shot up to her mouth as she realised what she'd said, a gasp, a cough catching in her chest.

'We're all sorry for her trouble, I'm sure,' he said, suddenly itching to get off the front step, 'and wishing our monarch a long and glorious reign, I know.'

The door was wide open now, light shining past him down the tiny path onto the street, and he could see she was in her Up West finery, all for him. She was trying to say something more but the cough had taken over.

'Ma'am? Let's see about that air, now, shall we?'

She was already stepping aside, nodding, her other hand searching for the hanky she'd probably refused to bring to the door. He was in. He closed the door behind him and stood politely in the hall, eyebrows together in concern, the caring doctor making his rounds, a hand gesturing at his case. 'Everything we need is in here. If you would just show me where to go?'

7

20.55. The temperature had dropped while Bourton was off duty. Biting cold meant thickening fog; visibility was down to thirty yards, the traffic was playing dodgems, and there'd already been an assault in Talbot Road. 'Bunch of lads, it sounds like,' said Leakey, on the way up to CID where there was a radio and a sporting chance of hearing Winston wave off the King. 'Chased him from Ladbroke Grove tube. No knuckles or anything, but the victim took a knocking.'

Winston came on at nine p.m. Stuck outside the doorway to CID, Bourton couldn't hear many of the words but he recognised the gloomy burden-of-history tone Winston always used for bad news. It took him back to his mum's kitchen, and Mrs Fortin's front room, and a barrack hut at Micheldown Camp – places where he could remember hearing Winston try to make something out of the leaden misery of the fall of France, or Tobruk, or Singapore. And do it too long and too richly, like the Technicolor half of a double feature. And that took him back to the Alhambra on Nathan Road in Kowloon, and 'In The Good Old Summertime', Anna in her *cheongsam*, blue-grey eyes above the tight scarlet-trimmed silk, Western curves beneath, of China, Russia, nowhere . . .

'God Save the Queen,' finished Winston, echoed respectfully in the room and slightly more awkwardly outside it. Bourton said nothing. He was hard inside his trousers and it seemed somehow disrespectful.

Back in uniform he made his way to the roll-call room, heaving with a double turn swapping fog stories. 'Winter of 'forty-eight,' said Stratfull – a probationer, then, thought Bourton, doing the sums – 'some days then you couldn't see ten yards.'

'Had its good side, though,' said Bourton. 'On guard at the Palace no one could see you put down your rifle, scratch your bits, stamp and clap a little.'

'Dick Barton, special sentry,' said Norris, another probationer, to snorts.

'PC Norris, special kipper,' said Bert Parkin, from the rear row. Rumour had it Norris's SO had caught him catching forty winks in the police box on Westbourne Grove – the kind of pugging-up that was clever in a veteran and skiving in a probationer. 'Must be nice to finally find something you're good at.'

The laughter was much wider, with a lot of the older blokes joining in, and Bourton was surprisingly gratified to get the support – even if it only meant they disliked Norris more.

''Ten-shun!' They all snapped to attention as the guv'nor and Sergeant Harbison wormed their way to the front. Bert reached forward and prodded Bourton in the back. 'Now,' he said, 'let the fun begin.'

★

'A proper fog, 491 Bourton,' said Bert Parkin. 'First pea-souper of the winter. Last month's, December's, those were more like mucky mists, but this one,' he smacked his lips, 'you can feel it on your skin. And nights like tonight, they all come out.' They were waiting outside the nick for their lift up to the top of Ladbroke Grove, Bourton to walk Beat Ten, Parkin to stand on the bridge over the Great Western lines, where the fog would be thickest, waving a lantern and untangling motorists. 'Apart from the prossies. Burglars, cosh artists, spivs shifting wholesale. Car thieves. Con-men even, 'cos everyone's at home and susceptible to a hard-luck story on a foggy night. Rapists.' He tested the fit of his gloves. 'Chummy, chummy everywhere and every one for clink.'

'So what do I look for on Ten, then?' Bourton asked.

'Double up on the pawnbrokers on Golborne Road. Look in on McKenna's – it's the kind of night they'd take delivery of off-the-ration meat. Check the Princess Louise has arrangements in place for the nurses going off duty. Check Rootes's – they may have cancelled the night shift. Take a proper turn around the Memorial Park in your early-hours walk-by, stop any drunks freezing to death – they'll get you some time off your feet too. If you can't get a couple of drunk-and-incapables on a night like this, you're no kind of copper.

Oh,' an afterthought, 'and don't get worried by bangs from the railway lines – those'll be the crow-scarers by the signals, let the drivers know they've changed.

'The thing I like about foggy-night policing,' said Bert, happily, 'more happens. A week's worth of policing in one night. And everyone is more or less a villain. Can't beat it.'

The area car dropped them at the railway bridge. They separated to get the handover summary from the blokes they were relieving, Bert tipping him to walk slow ('an' Chummy will only hear you when you nick him'). Looking over Dan Hennessey's shoulder as he talked through some argy-bargy at the Cobden Club, catching a glimpse of Bert as he stooped to hear what his dismount had to say, Bourton felt a rush of affection for the man, a relief at being out of Athill's world and back in Bert's – solid, not over-bright, but pretty wise, and resolutely un-fly, no one would ever mistake Bert Parkin for a spiv. A lighthouse maybe, Bourton thought, seeing him standing tall and dense with his lantern. A spiv, never.

★

23.40. Once the pubs had emptied, the beat was an undertaker's back room. He'd done the rounds of Golborne Road, checking the doors were locked and the pawnbrokers' shutters secure. McKenna's yard was empty and the lights off. He'd got the all-clear from the caretaker in the convent at the top of the Portobello – the nuns belonged to an enclosed order and wouldn't come to the door. Halfway to the Cobden he heard scuffling in an alley, thought he might have stumbled on a bit of criminality, stopped and aimed the torch – but it was just a couple having a knee-trembler, too excited to be ashamed or embarrassed by the beam, her teeth in his shoulder, both of them silent as if Nan was in the same room. He clicked the torch off and turned away. Apart from them, the streets were as empty as the night before. *If all manner of crooks are out, they're on someone else's beat.*

He crossed the entrance to Bewley Street and stopped. He wasn't sure through the haze but there might have been a bloke, something watchful in the set of his head, standing in a front garden partway down. Bourton checked his stick and cuffs and fixed his chin strap, just in case he had a bit of sprinting to do. He was about fifteen yards away before the man, staring straight at him, seemed to register his presence.

'Can I help you, sir?' Another five yards.

'Oh, Officer, she's in the back.'

'Who is, sir?' Close to, the man was old – in his sixties at least – and agitated. If he was in the mood for running, Bourton thought his chances of catching him were good.

'Gladys. Mrs Hartham. I called—'

'Who, sir?'

'The police, an ambulance . . . She's very still.'

'Can you show me, Mr . . .?'

'Potter, Ernest Potter.' He turned and led Bourton through the handkerchief garden to the front door. 'She has bad lungs, see, and when it's foggy I look her up.' Through the doorway and past a narrow staircase. 'She keeps the ginnel door unlocked.' He went into the back room. 'I knocked but it was so quiet . . .'

A woman of Potter's age was sitting in a heavy armchair by the fireplace, head against one of the wings, eyes closed, mouth open. She was obviously dead. There was a tinge of blue about her lips and her cheeks seemed to have fallen in over empty gums. She was in a blue dress with a synthetic sheen, an embroidered cardigan and her best shoes. He felt her wrist. Nothing. There was a mug of what looked like cocoa on the mantelpiece and the curtains were drawn. *So, it's after dark, she's all ready to sit down, drink her cocoa, listen to the wireless, when bang, lights out . . .*

A clanging ambulance or police bell crawled down Bewley Street and he ushered Potter out into the front garden as a marker. When the ambulancemen appeared, Bourton was unsurprised to find that one was the older bloke from the night before.

'No hurry with this one,' Bourton said. 'Well gone, I'm afraid.'

'And her fancy man's not going to be giving us trouble, either.' They smiled.

'What was it?'

'Heart attack, probably,' said the other ambulanceman, stooping to look at the woman's face. 'Or perhaps she choked on her teeth. They seem to be at the back of her mouth.' He stood up. 'One for the police surgeon, any road. Where can I call from?'

8

00.20. Bourton checked both ways before crossing the Grove. The fog played tricks with sound: there'd be wafts of traffic noise but no vehicles, front doors closing but a street staying still. Back in '48–9 the trickiness had given London a fun cowboys-and-Indians edge. Now he had to will away the feeling that a battalion of Chinese infantry would pop up from the pavement.

'All right, Dick?' He turned. Bert had conjured himself from the gloom of the houses at the end of Kensal Road, lantern swinging low. 'Piss stop. One of the pleasures of age. You know the lock-ups?' Bourton shook his head. 'Through a ginnel, middle of the terrace. Good pugging-up spot, border of two beats. Very convenient. And well out of view.'

'No one can see anything tonight, Bert.'

'The church harpies round here got those X-ray eyes, particularly if a bloke wants a widdle. Something kept you?'

Bourton smiled. 'Expecting me, were you?'

'Course. Hoped you'd spell me on the bridge, to be honest, but it got that bad . . .'

'Old lady, Bewley Street.' They walked onto the bridge over the railway lines. 'Older 'n you, even. Cup of cocoa, sat down, lights out.'

'What she die of?'

'Don't know – relieved before the surgeon come. Ambulance lads said happen her heart, happen she choked on her teeth. Her fancy man said her lungs were bad, he'd check on 'er in the fog.'

'Carries a lot of 'em off, bad fog,' said Bert, cheerily. 'Wonder more of 'em don't move away.' He turned to Bourton, suddenly curious. 'Her teeth? Who has their cocoa with their teeth in?'

'She hadn't drunk it yet. It was on the mantel, and she was in her chair.'

'Fair enough. You cover her?'

'No.'

'Dick, Dick . . .' Bert stuck the lantern on the bridge parapet and looked up and down the Grove. 'Old lady, got her standards – won't want the world tramping by, her in her slippers and housecoat. Bit of respect, now.'

Bourton wanted to say, She's dead, and it's just the surgeon and the ambulance lads, but he knew that wouldn't wash, so he stood up for himself. And opened Pandora's Box . . .

'But she wasn't in her slippers. Or housecoat. Best shoes, best dress.'

'Best shoes? By her feet?'

'No, on 'em.'

Parkin glanced at him. 'You have your cocoa in your boots?' Bourton shook his head. 'Me neither. Well, perhaps she had a caller. Two mugs?'

'Only one.'

'Well, perhaps just seen 'em out. You need to keep an eye open for that sort of thing, young Dick. Little things. All right?'

'Bert.'

'Good lad.'

Bourton smiled and waited for Bert to detect something, but his SO was clearly done. *Why does her outfit matter? Or the cocoa? Why don't you explain?* He shook his head. *I swear, between you and Athill, the coppering world is all oddity and no mystery. And that makes no sense at all.*

★

01.05. Barlby Road: the lights of the Rootes factory glowing half-left; the darkness of St Mark's Road to the right; the fog lifting down to the Memorial Park. One o'clock call done; next the park, Princess Louise's, then up the Grove. The odd spectral footfall, but otherwise empty streets. *Bert Parkin, your pea-souper policing is letting me down.*

Police whistle – hard, insistent through the murk. *But where from?* He took his bonnet off, closed his eyes, focused. *The Grove. Upper end. By the Great Western bridge . . .*

He pounded up the street, jamming his whistle between his teeth, blowing every few paces, past Rootes, Harben's yard, *The cavalry's coming, Bert,* the Pall Mall Depository, the girders of the bridge, into the Grove, lantern on the pavement, abandoned Vauxhall 14, front doors open, two figures wrestling on the bonnet, Bert's voice, 'Come on, lad,' and a bass moo of anguish, 'I'm sorry, Chriiiiiisss . . .'

The lad was face down, flailing and wriggling as Bert tried to get a grip, so Bourton went low, grabbed a kicking ankle and pushed towards the radiator. The knee pain brought the lad's torso up and suddenly Bert had his arm in a lock and was pulling him to the ground, cuffs emerging as he pinned him with his weight. 'Blaggers, jeweller or pawnbroker,' Bert said, as he drew deep to steady his breathing, 'bag in the front,' nodding at the car, 'suspect, about eighteen,' breath, 'maybe five ten, eleven stone,' breath, 'long dark coat, went onto the tracks,' breath, 'western side.' Bourton nodded and ran to the bridge rail. He could hear someone scrambling across hard core.

'He's running along the rails. Where can he come out?'

'Get after him,' breath, 'you idle beggar, and find out.'

Bourton waved, sprinted to the end of the bridge, scrambled over, hung, dropped onto the embankment wall, gathered, dropped again, parachute roll onto the track bed, blessed his boots – *He'll have been lucky not to break his leg* . . . He listened. Hard core quiet, thrumming rails, engine pulling slowly from Paddington way, click of a signal changing, steam whistle sounding from down track . . . A clang, a curse? He lay down at track level where the fog was wispy, cast the bright beam of the beat lantern both ways, and saw turnups north side, no more than fifty feet away, a hand reaching down, retrieving something from the rails, then the feet turning and limping for the other embankment . . . *How far are the trains?* A single yellow light each way, giant's eyes, the rails juddering like a drill, but no engine noise, gobbled by the fog . . . Up, then suddenly a bang, sharp, clear – a shot? – face to the hard core, lantern off, hands over the bonnet – *Fucking stupid, the bonnet's more protection than flesh and bone. Where is it from? No whine to go with the bang so it didn't come close.* He raised his head gingerly. Another bang – flinch, smack down, face against the rock. A clang as rails switched. Head up slowly. *No one's shooting at you – it's those fucking crow-scarers by the signals. Which means the train is close. But which track of ten? Fuck it.*

He stood. *Where the hell's the lantern? Sod it.* He hurled himself head down across the lines, boot against a sleeper, stumbling onto the rails, a rush of sound from the left, a yelp from ahead, a black mass powering by a few feet from his nose— *Fuck! Where did that come from?* He looked right. Light still there. *No idea which track. Best not to think about what-ifs.* He picked his way across in the train's wake and crouched by the north embankment wall, unbuttoning his cape and pulling out his torch. Looking along the track bed, he caught the villain's legs, hobbling west. *Wants a way up he can manage with his limp – only it's bricked up ten, fifteen feet, a regular tunnel wall. But further down the south side it's waste ground, back gardens . . .* The feet started climbing into the murk – *He must have found some steps.* Bourton hurried to follow, found brick stairs and started climbing, torch in hand, Bert's whistle carrying from the bridge.

'Fuck off, copper.'

Bourton halted and clicked the torch off.

'That won't help you.'

At the top of the steps?

'I've got a gat, see, an' I'll use it. Now fuck off.'

'All right, chum.' *What's a gat?* 'Chris, is it? I'm going down the steps, OK?' He scraped the soles of his boots on the brick then stood still. After about thirty seconds he could hear the robber along the top of the embankment, dragging his foot, breathing hard. *He won't be able to hear much.* Bourton climbed the steps, onto a narrow path.

The sound was gone. He paused to be sure but the shuffling had stopped and he trotted along the path, right hand tracing a high brick wall, left gripping his torch, a train on the nearest track, a rough edge to the brickwork then a void, bend down—

Flash in his face, shot beating the air beside his head, legs away in shock, falling, falling, right hand clutching the broken brickwork, *If I drop I'm done for,* left dropping the torch and scrabbling for a hold, *He fucking shot at me! Will he do it again?* Hanging, arms pulling. *Can't do this for long.* Heave, legs onto the path, roll sideways. He wriggled back to the cover of the high wall, and lay still as the train filled his ears and the smoke filtered into his lungs, eyes closed, holding in the cough, waiting waiting waiting . . .

So that's what a gat is. Should have told me.

He lay there for what felt like hours. The muzzle flash had taken his night sight and the train his hearing, so he hugged the top of the path, thinking through the villain's choices, waiting for his brain to give him the all-clear. *Bastard probably aimed to kill, only I bent down. No follow-up shot. Legged it? Or can't see me 'cos I've dropped the torch.* He shook his head. *Lost two lights in thirty seconds. Signed for them too.*

What now? Report to Bert? Or track the villain? He's got a gun but in this fog, it's just a point-blank weapon. Though lethal. So, search for him, but keep your distance ... Bourton stood, took off and rolled up his cape, then dropped it through the hole in the wall. It made a soft thud as it hit the ground. No shot in reply. Bourton slipped over the broken brickwork and crouched on damp, low-grassed ground. *Gardens of Kensal House flats.* No light from the building. He checked his stick, picked up his cape, a heavy oilskin sausage over four feet long, and swished it in front of him a couple of times. Bert Parkin's crowd-control weapon of choice. *Might come in handy.*

What will the little bastard do? With a gammy leg, the easy choice – Ladbroke Grove, where he can flag down a car, and use his gun to keep coppers at bay ... Bourton worked his way along the side of the block of flats, cape out, *So much for a quieter life,* and peered over the hedge lining the front path. A pool of light, no movement. Bert's whistle from down the road, Bourton's in response, then a creak, a metal-framed window opening above, murmuring.

'You! On the first floor! Have you got a phone?' An old head shaking, handkerchief over the mouth, white hair in clumps. 'Has anyone else?'

'Porter.' A woman's croak.

'Please telephone for the police. Tell them PC Bourton, Notting Hill, reports an armed man near the northern end of Ladbroke Grove. He has already tried to kill one police officer. Ask them to send assistance. Police, PC Bourton, armed man, assistance. Do you understand?'

The woman nodded, then closed the window. He was partway down the path when it opened again and she called, 'Look out for yourself, dear.'

He paused. *I'm chasing someone who has tried to kill me. I'm equipped with a cape, a stick and the majesty of the law. What I wouldn't do for a Sten and a couple of Mills bombs.*

Slowly north up the Grove, over the canal bridge, visibility about twenty yards in the streetlight. High wall of the cemetery on the left, terraced houses with postage-stamp gardens on the right, rattle of a black cab coming south, a shape emerging from behind a garden wall and hobbling into the road, the cab braking, a thump as it jerked to a stop and the figure slid over the far side of the bonnet. Bourton started running but the figure was up again, yelling at the cabby, who piled out and started jinking down the road, old training kicking in, the villain coming round the cab and into the driver's seat, interior light showing incomprehension, babyish frustration, *He can't drive . . .*

'Chris,' called Bourton, ten yards away, cape held wide, *No threat, me,* 'you're not going anywhere, chum.' Bert's whistle sounding perhaps a hundred yards off, Chris staring at Bourton, face hard and weak, as he brought up a small automatic pistol behind the driver's door glass. 'Lose the gun now, chuck it in the canal – I won't say a word. It's just the loot.' Bourton took his bonnet off. He felt cold, hollow. 'You led me a merry dance, chum, well done, leg an' all. An' well done on that jump, proper paratrooper, you.' The words welled up without conscious thought. 'Chuck it now, before other officers come, while it's just us.' Chris was opening the door and stepping out, pointing the gun from his waist where he couldn't hit a bloody thing.

Then a piercing whistle from the north and Chris spinning, a Harrow Road PC barrelling out of the fog. 'Gun!' yelled Bourton, the copper stumbling to the deck, another lad behind him, civvy trousers, uniform shirt, trying to pull up, bang from the weapon, onto his arse. 'Chris!' Spinning back, pistol shaking, hand pulling back the slide, *Fucked extractor,* Bourton stepping away, arms wide, 'Stop there, chum,' the villain running across the road for a hole in the cemetery wall, all three coppers up now, Bourton tracking him to the south. 'No one's hurt, a good brief—'

The pistol came up, up. Everyone stopped. Chris pointing the weapon at Bourton, ten yards, the muzzle shaking, Chris looking along the barrel, bare head, angry eyes, Chris walking at him, Bourton backing away, no foresight on the muzzle, flinching.

'Cape!' yelled Bert, puffing up behind.

Bourton flung it and ducked, bang, looked up when he realised he hadn't even heard the round go by, and Chris was through the hole, the coppers piling after and going to ground.

Darkness. Chris had already disappeared amid the headstones and high grass. To Bourton's left was the off-duty lad, his white uniform shirt a mark in the gloom. Bourton crawled over. 'He'll be able to see that.'

'Was thinking that myself.'

'Might not hit it, though.'

'Reassuring.'

'Listen, he can't climb the wall – he's only getting out through a gate. Why don't you run up to the first entrance and see if you can help keep him in? Should be guns here soon.'

'What about you two?'

The Harrow Road copper was peering between a couple of head-stones to Bourton's right. 'Don't know about you, chum,' said Bourton, 'but I'm keeping my distance.'

'An' I'll be right behind you.' He reached over. 'Maurice Prentice.'

'Dick Bourton.'

The off-duty lad popped back through the wall. Bourton and Prentice scrambled up and threaded between headstones, pausing every few paces to listen, Bourton making some noise so they didn't surprise the little bastard into firing another round or two. Within a minute or so they heard scuffing gravel as Chris hobbled across a path. He cut short a sob. *You'll be telling yourself it's your leg or lack of puff, but I know it's because you're a whiny little bastard who wants his mum. Well, wait a few minutes and you'll have plenty to cry about.*

The scuffing stopped. Bourton waved Prentice down and went on alone, placing his boots carefully, reckoning the grass and soft ground would deaden his footfall. And there Chris was, sitting on a bench in the glow of a gas lamp, hands around his head, looking wet and miserable and ten years old. *What? Didn't know criminal glory would be like this? A sprained ankle, no loot, a foggy cemetery, and an un-automatic pistol?*

Bourton lay down on the damp ground a row back from the path, protected by a black headstone, broad and Victorian, topped with a pair of droopy figures. After a couple of minutes he could hear Prentice stalking up, not too noisily, and beckoned him onto his bed of what felt like grass, nettles and dead fern. 'We watch,' Bourton whispered slowly, though Chris was sniffling so hard he wouldn't hear them if they chatted, 'and wait for the guns. At my signal, we blow,' tugging out his whistle, 'OK?'

'Wilco,' Prentice whispered back. 'If he moves?'

'We follow – under cover.'

'All right.' Prentice snatched a look around the headstone. 'Ask him to surrender? He looks all in.'

'I've tried twice. Each time he's tried to kill me. You can have a go.'

Prentice thought for a moment and shook his head.

So they watched instead. Chris put his head back in his hands for a bit, wiped his nose on his coat, fiddled with the slide on his pistol, rubbed his right ankle, at one stage stood up and sniffed the air, God alone knew what for. After a while he slumped back on the bench, gun between his knees, head hanging low. The guns are coming, chum, thought Bourton, and then you'll get your shootout.

Area car bells along Harrow Road. Chris jerked to his feet as if hoisted by a puppeteer's strings, cast about, then stepped off the path, out of the gas lamp glow, and was gone.

'Fuck,' whispered Prentice, 'what now?'

Earn our pay. 'Keep him penned in. You cross the path about twenty yards that way,' he pointed east, 'me twenty the other. Then take cover, listen, move back if he comes towards you, run if he threatens you. Blow when you hear the guns. OK?'

Prentice nodded but made no attempt to move. Bourton smiled encouragingly but Prentice was rooted, a replacement who wouldn't leave his veteran oppo. *I can't really make him, and don't really want to. And it doesn't matter anyway.*

'No,' offered Bourton, 'safer if we stick together. Less chance of getting shot by our lads. Follow me, OK?'

Prentice nodded. Bourton scrambled up, silently counted off his twenty paces, and when he crossed the path outside the gas lamp's glow Prentice was on his shoulder. They reached the grass and Bourton stumbled on stone coping and fell against a flat-topped tomb. No shooting. *So either he didn't hear us or he couldn't work it out in time . . .*

They crouched with their backs to the worn sooty stone, heads under the bruised lip of the top slab, and listened. Silence. Which meant the area cars had stopped, and the guns were out, dividing up. They'd be coming through the first gate, acres to search, could be flailing around all night – and the villain had either stopped himself sniffling or was too far away to be heard. *How far is the gate? A hundred yards? Two? Ah, well . . .*

He stuck his whistle between his teeth, Prentice doing the same, waiting to signal kick-off. Intake of breath, piercing blast, echo from Prentice, a bang through the din, the two of them taking it in turns, one constant screech, ears sore, echoes from down the gravel path, and while he was drawing breath yells from close, 'Come out, you bastards!' Head up, muzzle flash from ten yards away, back down, cursing, *Bastard should be running*, Prentice popping up—

Prentice: 'It's jammed!'

'No, it's single shot.' Bourton was reaching for him, but Prentice was already round the tomb, stick out, Chris uncoiling as he racked the slide forward and spotted the copper, head up in triumph, bang and a yelp, Bourton starting after, Prentice still going, and it was Chris who was falling away under the upraised stick, down, down, down . . .

'Fuckin' 'ell,' gasped Prentice, standing over the body. 'I thought it was fuckin' jammed, fuckin' cunt,' a vicious prod, 'shoot me, you bastard.' He looked around, caught Bourton's eye, pointed at the gunman, pushed him to the ground with a jab in an injured shoulder, 'You should kick him an' all.'

Bourton moved the weapon away with his boot. He heard voices on the path and called them over, pistols out, uncertain moving into darkness. 'He's on the ground and disarmed,' before they fired at a shadow, 'and I think he's shot himself.'

They huddled around Chris as he gripped his left leg and shrank away from a torch beam.

'Should have waited a minute or two,' said one of the coppers. 'We could have done it for him.'

'And finished the job.'

'That was him,' Bourton nodded at Prentice. 'Light Brigade, that bloke.'

'I'm hurt,' said Chris.

'Not enough.'

'My leg.'

'Got two of 'em.'

'I'm bleeding.'

'So's Bert Parkin,' said a new arrival, Sergeant Harbison from the voice, 'and if he dies your neck'll be sore an' all.'

'Bert? What? How?'

Prentice started kicking the villain, a Harrow Road copper trying not too hard to hold him back.

'Bourton? That you?' Harbison.

'How bad?'

'In the thigh. Hit the artery. He's lost a lot of blood. May not make it. If he does it's down to a cabby. Where were you?'

Oh, Bert, thought Bourton. I never thought to check. You didn't make a sound. I thought that bullet had just— *When I froze, you— Oh, God. You took my bullet, chum. You took my bullet.*

9

06.00. At the Hammersmith Hospital, with only the brick dust and blood on his uniform trousers, the lead in his boots, the grit behind his eyes to tell that the games were over: his coppering world had changed. Bert was old, and unfit, and probably dying, and there was fuck-all Bourton could do about it.

There was a knot of glow-worms outside the entrance, sparking through the gloom, and as the fog eddied he could see a clutch of coppers, from the Hill and Harrow Road, uniform and mufti, huddled and murmuring. A couple turned to him as he clumped up and Prentice proffered a fag.

Bourton shook his head. 'How's he doing?'

'Not good,' said a bloke from the early turn. 'They think he had a heart attack after.'

'Ah, bollocks,' said Bourton, threading his way through.

'Where were you, then, while he was bleeding to death?' Norris stepped out from the cover of the crowd. 'Trying to get yourself in the papers?'

Bourton wasn't in the mood. 'And where were *you*? No one shot at you tonight.' He pushed past, heading for the doors, only to hear Prentice call his name. He turned to see that the Harrow Road copper had stuck his hand out.

'Thanks, chum.'

'For what?' asked Bourton. 'I nearly got you shot.'

'Nah,' said Prentice. 'That was me.' He pushed his hand forward. 'Thanks.'

Bourton shook, diffidently returning the other man's nod. 'Yes, well . . . Next time, let's stay further away.'

★

A cordon of coppers fidgeted, aimless, outside the doors to Bert's ward. The guv'nor shook his head as Bourton approached, arms wide as if to keep a gawker away from a traffic accident. Bourton halted and the fence came down.

'They're not letting anyone in in case we infect him, Bourton, so here is as far as you go.'

'Sir.'

'They've repaired the artery and filled him back up with blood, so now it's Parkin's battle. But he's very weak and it might not go his way. We need to be prepared.'

'Sir.'

'Have you given your statement? In full?'

Adams was looking at him hard, as if Bourton was supposed to read something into the question, but reception was bad – he could almost feel mental static fizzing behind his eyes – so he just said, 'Sir.'

'Well done.' Adams smiled approvingly. 'And the Incident Book?' Bourton nodded automatically, then was still, unsure. *Did I write up Gladys Hartham or not?* 'Well, if you haven't, before the late turn will do.'

'Sir.'

'And well done on getting Granger.' *Granger?* 'The suspect. Tenacity is a very good quality for a policeman.'

'Thank you, sir.'

'Though it might have been better to let the armed officers get to him first. Criminals who try to kill policemen are bad news, and this one's too young to hang.'

He thought of explaining but he was drained, and the old soldier in him said Adams didn't really want to know, so he fell back on 'Sir.' It covered a lot of ground.

'Given that Prentice is the arresting officer, I think it's appropriate that he does the reading over.' Bourton nodded, not really following. 'Though if you wish you can attend as well.' A querying eyebrow. *Oh – the overtime of the magistrate's court as a reward . . .*

Bourton shook his head. 'He earned it, sir. An' be good to get my head down.'

Adams nodded. 'Night like that. How was your turn with DC Athill? Whet the appetite for CID?' For a moment he had no idea what Adams was talking about, but then it came to him in snatches, images from another time.

'Yes, sir.'

'And DC Athill says he couldn't have got as far as he did without you.'

'Well, thank you, sir.'

'Don't thank me, thank DC Athill. Buy him a pint or something. He says you might make a possible for CID at some point, if you can . . . rein in a little.' Beneath his weariness there was a spark of pleasure at the thought that CID might be attainable. He realised Adams was speaking.

'Of course, you'll want to see how Parkin is doing. I'm sure you can have a look through the glass.'

'Does Mrs Parkin know?'

Adams nodded. 'She's down in the canteen, if you want to . . . er . . .'

Pay my respects? But Bert isn't dead yet. 'Sir.' Though looking through the porthole in the swing door you'd never have known he wasn't. His bed was nearest the nurses' desk, on the edge of the glow from its downlight. He was slack as a fresh corpse and cut off at the midriff by the bedclothes, blankets taut over the cradle protecting his leg. Stretched out under his drip stand he looked still, pale, sunken, old. *But even eighteen-year-olds look like Methuselah as they die . . .*

★

The canteen was empty but for a table near the counter. Vera Parkin perched on the edge of a chair, shapeless in what she'd flung on – coat over her housecoat, some kind of blue hat still jammed on her head – holding the hands of two women as a brew cooled in front of her.

'Vera? Mrs Parkin?' She looked up, no recognition in her eyes. 'Dick Bourton. Bert's probationer. He brought me . . .'

She nodded, nothing in the eyes to say whether his words meant anything at all. 'Hello again, dear.'

'Hello,' he replied. He was ready to trot out 'They're doing all they can. He's strong,' but realised she'd faced a parade of coppers offering soggy nothings, needed someone to tell her something solid.

'He saved my life tonight. When the suspect pointed his weapon at me I froze. He told me what to do.'

'And did you do it, dear?'

'Yes.' He looked hard into her face, drawn and weary. 'And he got shot as a result.'

Silence. Vera's expression hadn't changed. She nodded again, and suddenly Bourton wondered if she'd been given something to calm her down, or just couldn't take in anything new.

'It was a ricochet, they said.' Her voice was surprisingly flat. 'So it wasn't meant for anyone at all. Was it? And whatever it hit first slowed it down. And if he hadn't done whatever he did, you'd have been killed. And you're both still around. Aren't you?'

'Yes.'

'So it wasn't you, dear. And it wasn't him. It was Christopher Granger – and he should hang.'

10

He woke, sweating, after dark. Streetlight was seeping through the threadbare curtain. He was surprised to see his wrists weren't wired together. *I was back in the culvert. This has to stop.* He wiped his face with his dirty uniform shirt. *Section House. Hendon. Got another night turn.* He checked the clock: 19.05. Three hours in hand. He relaxed. *Eleven hours of kip – Kunu-ri can only have wrecked an hour or two of it. Not bad going, really. Particularly as I nearly got shot last turn.* He shook his head. *But Bert wasn't enough to bump Korea from my dreams.*

Three or four evening newspapers had been jammed under his door and he had to nudge them aside to open it. The bathroom mirrors showed grazes he couldn't feel patterning his arms and legs, and he'd acquired bags under his eyes overnight.

Back in his room he had a look at the papers. His turn had made it onto the third page. 'Bobby Shot By Thug,' declared the *Evening News*. They'd even got most of it right. Apart from his name, under-lined in thick pencil, which seemed to be Barton.

Tea was bready sausages and soggy chips in the canteen downstairs. For once he was grateful that the rebuilding of the Hill section house had seen him banished to Hendon, because none of the other coppers were from his nick. And that meant they owned no part of his turn – so no blow-by-blow, no pats on the back from blokes sharing the drama of a turn they'd slept through, just 'You all right? SO going to make it? Let's hope the little bastard cops it,' before they moved on to the football, or coppering in the smog. Is last night *my* coppering in the smog story? wondered Bourton, as he heard about the thief who'd tried to pinch an area car with a copper pugging on the back seat – the night I lost my oppo?

★

20.40. He made it in an hour early in case his uniform needed needlework, to find Station Sergeant Filkins penning Roger Leakey in a
corner of the locker room, waving his finger at him, Leakey in his
shirt tails nodding obediently, hands trapped in half-buffed boots.
Bourton halted, ready to back up the stairs, but Filkins turned and
saw him. Suddenly the finger swivelled, like a coaxial machine gun.

'Goes for you, too, Bourton,' said Filkins. 'No talking to the papers.
Clear?'

'Of course, Sergeant.'

'Not another word.'

'Haven't spoken to them at all, Sergeant.'

'How'd they get your name?'

'I didn't give it to them, Sergeant.'

Filkins's top lip puckered around his dentures, the sure sign he
was about to say something sarky, so Bourton beat him to it. 'If I had
they'd have spelled it right.' *That came out smart-aleck.* 'Will be that
old dear in Kensal House, I bet, Sergeant. I gave her my name. Or
one of the Harrow Road mob, no one from Notting Hill, anyhow.
After all,' *Lay it on thick for Filkins's foggy mind,* 'you run the tightest
nick in F Division. That's what they told me at Peel House.'

Filkins was nodding. 'And you won't get the chance to forget it.
Either of you. Clear?'

'Clear,' they choroused.

They waited for Filkins's cleats on the flagstones at the top of the
staircase before breaking the silence. 'Bloody Met fossils,' said Leakey.
'You'd think they'd know we've been yelled at by the pros.' Bourton
snorted. *So being in a fight with a senior bloke makes me a little more
equal.* 'Oh, the Ladbroke Arms is out of bounds. Filkins's orders.'

'Can he do that?'

'Thinks he can. Too many journalists, he says. As if they won't just
follow the lads off turn.' He started buffing. 'You been down the Three
Horsemen since the other night?' Bourton shook his head. 'Tommy
Lee – gyppo totter, used to have a line in cigs, I had to give him a
smack or two about the ribs. When I stuck my head in on the late
last night he said they were looking forward to you coming by, give
you another welcome. You get any licks in?'

Bourton inspected his trousers. 'The odd punch.'

'Well, looks like they think you didn't, so you probably need to give them the evil eye – once they think they've got the edge . . .'

'Understood.' Athill had said the same. The Dale was that kind of place.

Leakey cleared his throat. 'You ever been down the Ladbroke Arms, Dick?'

'No. Any good?'

Leakey shrugged. 'It's where the lads go. Might be worth it. You being bunked separate. And not turning out for any of the teams. Just . . . Show willing.'

'When would I?' asked Bourton. There was a tear in the right knee – if he backed it with black cotton he might bluff parade . . . 'I'm on nights. Before turn?'

'The other probationers do – four, five in the afternoon, after the early comes out. Get some tea, dead sober come ten.'

'Four, five o'clock, I'm still kipping, chum. I need my eight hours.'

'Weekends? Off-duty days? Might help.'

'Help with what?'

'Oh, come on.' Old chickenpox scars puckered on Leakey's brow as it furrowed in annoyance. 'Old news, but you're not one of the lads. You might be if you were down the Ladbroke Arms of an evening, buying rounds.' He pointed his shoe brush. 'You should get a gong for last night, and instead you'll be lucky if you're given the time of day.' He turned away. 'Oh, and they say you're lying about the Imjin.'

'What about?' Bourton was baffled. 'About *not* being there?' Leakey looked puzzled. 'Listen, when the Imjin happened I was about to get on a troopship. Nearest I ever got to that battle was a shameful parade a month on when all the odds and sods, like me, who joined after it, got all the credit, when the blokes who'd earned it were dead or starving in some shit-hole.' Suddenly Bourton joined some dots. 'I don't keep quiet about the Imjin because I'm modest but 'cos I weren't there.' *Broad Gloucester. Must be angry.* 'And another thing. I don't go to the pub 'cos I spend my off-duty time either trying to get my girl into this country or trying to find her somewhere to live when I do. And I've had to stay off the booze since shit-fly fever laid me out last year,' he lied. And, he didn't add, because the people he'd have to talk to were arseholes.

'Yeah, well, tell it to the Ladbroke. Take a bloody megaphone.' Leakey would probably have smiled if Bourton hadn't pissed him off. 'Only make sure there's no reporters around. Also, no Filkins. Or anyone who might rat on you to Filkins.'

'Which, from what you say, is more or less the whole nick.'

Leakey nodded. 'Good plan, eh?'

'A peach.' Bourton closed his eyes and let some of the anger out with his breath, so he could think about what Leakey had said. But all that came to mind was whether Anna would still love him and Bert would live. The rest just couldn't get a look-in.

'You know what, Rog?' If he were calmer he wouldn't have risked the intimacy. 'Right now, I got some other stuff on my plate. I'm spending most of my weekend at the Middlesex. Want to join me?'

I I

Monday, mid-afternoon, and Tottenham Court Road was still, the second-hand car dealers shuttered, crowds in mourning bands lining the street five and six deep, cordoned by coppers in vast blank capes. There was a smell of wet wool and silence in the biting cold but for the occasional cough and sniffle and, from the Euston Road end, the muffled rhythmic tramp of the escort bringing the coffin from King's Cross. The sky was a solid belt, mist and cloud and rain with no beginning or end, leaching the colour from the advertising hoardings and the odd bright coat, and blending it all into the backdrop of blackened brick.

A ripple of hats being doffed on the other side of the road, and as Bourton braced, the escort marched into view, the sodden grey coats and bearskins of the Grenadiers, horse gunners in gold frogging tugging their animals' heads down, and finally the gun carriage with the coffin, a high and solitary offering, trundling by at a businesslike pace. There was a collective sigh behind him, and as the procession moved on towards Westminster and the lying in state, with the Duke of Edinburgh and the brother who wasn't dead or a deserter – Gloucester? – brisk and hatless behind, he could see the heads opposite stayed bare for minutes, with only occasional glances at neighbours or the shuffling of numbed feet to indicate that the main attraction had been and gone.

There was a patch of damp on the knee of his No. 1 trousers. Inspecting his cape as they formed up to return to the nick, he found a hole he could shove a finger through. So he nearly got me after all, he thought, skin prickling. Ah, poor Bert.

It was still only 11 February, five days after the King's death, three after Bert's shooting, and Bourton felt that this month would never end.

★

16.10. 'Hello, Dad.' His father stood in front of the house in Elgin Terrace, by a great box wrapped in a tarpaulin, shivering slightly in a patched sou'wester – probably the one Bourton had been sent to sea with when he was fourteen, as if a boy steward stood deck watches.

'Officer.' The oilskin covered an old Ike jacket with a frayed hem and holes in the cloth where the insignia had been removed. He looked like a survivor from a sunken troopship. He jerked his head towards the end of the street. 'Brothers are having a pint.'

Bourton nodded at the box. 'How we getting that up to Hendon? Take up half the bus.'

'It's for Miss Anna.' He rapped on its top. 'Poor girl's travelled around the world without a stick. Least we can give her is a chest for her trousseau. Nice bit of ash. Russians are partial to ash, I hear.'

Bourton smoothed the tarpaulin as if he were rubbing the grain of the wood. 'How long did it take you, Dad?'

'Ah, the odd day.' He pulled the sou'wester close around his face. 'Your mother's made a cushion for the lid. Bit previous, perhaps – says "Anna Bourton 1952" on it. So you got ten months.'

They must have been working on it all winter and never a word. His mother would have unpicked something she loved for the wool, and his father would have turned down paid job after paid job as he obsessively worked the wood. Bourton didn't know what to say.

'She's a great girl, Dad,' he finally offered. 'You'll love her.'

'Just so long as you do.' He stood at one end of the chest. 'Let's get it up and out of the rain.'

★

The chest was a smooth, pale Aladdin's cave of curtains and cushions – 'She can send 'em back when she's done her own' – and Sunday best. Bourton took his brothers' suits down to the Suchaneks' kitchen to give them a press, and returned to find patches of colour dotting the barren room, like wildflowers in a fallow field. 'Paper the windows,' said Bob, his eldest brother, 'bank the fire for the night before, and half the chill will go. Though it'll still be damn cold. Tell you what, those picture windows need bricking up.'

They crowded into the bathroom and took turns at the basin,

keeping up a constant chaffing back and forth, and Bourton had a snapshot of evenings they'd never had, all getting ready for a dance or the pictures – never had because the war had grabbed them all up and scattered them, miles from home; a family life amputated, never to grow back.

They dressed in the glare of the unshaded light: his father in his weddings-and-funerals, made before the war for someone with more fat and flash; Bob in the demob he'd been issued in '46, tiddied up nicely – the navy had made him a dab hand with a needle; Ted in a decent bit of worsted from a Gloster Aircraft trip to uncouponed America; and Bourton in best battledress – he felt a fraud or a scruff in anything else. They pinned on mourning bands and medals, inspected each other in the mirror, all the jollity gone. Bourton's father nodded with satisfaction and opened the door. 'You'll do him credit.'

*

The line snaked around Parliament Square, over Westminster Bridge and along the Embankment in front of St Thomas's – patient, purposeful, sober, the bowed heads humming quietly despite the sleet and patchy light. As their group shuffled forward and the line grew behind, Bourton wondered again at what had brought people here, to wait until the early hours to see the sealed coffin of a man they'd none of them met, who'd never been short of clothes or food or work or shelter. A pensioner from Edgware said it just seemed fitting. Bourton agreed, though he still couldn't work out why.

'Corporal Bourton?' A man his own age, six foot or so, holding his hat, with a limp and red hair and a coat that said Officer. Bourton started to stiffen, then realised the tone had been wrong – tentative, deferential, junior. 'Private Marling. Tony Marling. From Ten Platoon. I was beside you when you were hit in Holland.' Holland – a month after he'd joined the Die-hards – Marling, Marling . . . Nice lad, posh, failed officer selection, guileless and new and—

'You were hit at the same time.'

Marling smiled. 'They had to take the foot off. Looks like they let you keep your head.' He waved forward his father, taller, skinnier, with an awkward smile, fifty quid of coat and hat, and a shooting stick he probably hoped his son would use. As the line stumbled forward Bourton could see that the shy, keen lad of '44, unhappy in his own skin, had turned into an easy individual with no side and a talent for joining in.

'What game are you in now, then, Tony?' asked Bourton.

'I'm a solicitor. Old ladies' wills, that sort of thing.'

'He's being modest,' said his father. 'He also sits as a councillor in Kensington.'

'Well, there you go,' said Bourton's dad breezily. 'Dick's a police officer in Kensington. He can arrest you when you're caught being funny with your expenses.'

They all laughed, Marling senior more abruptly, a laugh with an edge, as if Arthur Bourton had offended him. You want more deference, Bourton realised, but you're too polite to say so. He couldn't help remembering his childhood, the lean years, and his father tugging his forelock for fag-ends, a few floorboards here, a day's joinery there, anything to keep body and soul together. *He's earned his right to say what he likes. So have the rest of us. And you're just going to have to get used to it.*

★

Words stopped at the gates. Hats came off and backs straightened, even though there were probably twenty more yards of sleet before shelter, and the only sounds were shoe leather through slush and a couple of umbrellas being shaken out under the awning. Steps up, a narrow doorway, a bare, high-walled cavern of shadows – and on a candle-lit dais, Life Guards and Beefeaters at its corners, swathed in the royal standard with the crown at its head, the coffin, almost too small for the space, too frail for the weight of veneration. Somewhere in there, thought Bourton, as he snapped to attention and saluted, under all this hoop-la, is a man – a good bloke who did his best with a burden he hadn't asked for. Small man, big job, and it killed him. *That's* what I think about this.

12

Bert seemed fairly perky for a man the *Evening Standard* had said was hovering near death, though that might have been because of the cake on his lap – glossy with ration-defying quantities of eggs and butter – or his nursery of get-well flowers colonising every bedside table in the ward. His skin was still pale after a week in hospital but at least he'd expanded to fit it. He waved Bourton to a chair – 'Might still be warm from the commissioner's arse' – and sat up. 'As your SO, young Dick,' he said, 'it is my considered opinion that getting shot has its compensations. Vera's even had someone offer her a refrigerator. How about that?'

'Where would you put it?'

'Ethel's room.'

'And where would you put Ethel?'

'Kitchen table.'

Bourton smiled. They both knew he'd turn down the refrigerator even if he had room for it.

'I heard you been by while I was asleep. Thanks for that.'

'Well, thanks for saving my life.'

'Ah, did nothing of the sort.' He closed his eyes for a moment and shifted in the bed.

'How is it?'

'Will be fine. With lots of rest. Lots of cake. No visitors.' He closed his eyes again. 'You know, while I've been lying here two things have been on my mind. One is, what happened with that old girl? Had her cocoa in her best shoes.'

Who? Oh, Bewley Street – Gladys. 'Had her teeth in,' Bert nodded. 'Don't know.'

'Find out, would you? Odd one, that, an' it's the little things . . .' Bourton nodded indulgently. 'Ask that Rex Athill for a bit of help, if you like. After all, you ain't a DC yet.'

'Bert.'

'An' the second is, you been down the Three Horsemen?' Bourton shook his head. 'I hear some of the natives are a bit uppity, asking when you're coming back for round two.'

'I haven't been ducking it, Bert, it's just—'

'Longer that goes on, harder it'll be to set right. You can't police the Dale if they think they've got the edge on you. Get down there one night in civvies, take someone to watch your back, pick someone you can beat an' beat 'im. An' check hands – no coins, no knuckles. Use some of that army boxing.' He pretended to bob and weave in the bed.

'I'll sort something out.'*But I was a sod-awful boxer – what the hell will I do?*

★

Two nights later, on Beat Ten for the first time since the shooting, it seemed only fair for Bourton to fulfil one of the no-longer-dying man's not-quite-last requests. The houses on either side of Gladys Hartham's were dark, but light shone through the etched-glass panels on Ernest Potter's front door, so Bourton gave it an exploratory rap.

'Mr Potter?' The door opened on its chain. 'Mr Potter, it's PC Bourton from Notting Hill. I was the responding officer when—' The chain was released and the door swung open.

'Have you found him?' Potter spoke over his shoulder as he stowed an entrenching tool in an umbrella stand.

'Who, sir?'

'Whoever was with Gladys before she died.'

'And who was that, sir?'

Potter stared at him, as if he was pulling his leg. 'That's your job, isn't it? Whoever she'd got dressed up for.' He stepped to one side to usher Bourton in.

'I'm sorry, sir, I can't – I'm walking my beat.'

'So why are you here, then?'

'I came to find out what the situation was with Mrs Hartham.'

'Situation? We buried her day before yesterday. Doctors wouldn't even give her a post-mortem, said she could have gone any time.' He shook with anger or cold. 'But she wouldn't have dressed up unless she had a visitor, an' if she had a visitor, they should have post-mortemed her. Stands to reason.'

'I see, sir.' *Annoyed she might have had someone else? Or genuine suspicion?*

'An' you should be finding out who that visitor was. Going door-to-door, like when the policeman got shot the night Gladys died. You did it for him. Why not for her? Eh? Why not for her?' Suddenly Potter pushed the door shut. 'Sod off, Mr Policeman,' he yelled through the glass panes. 'You're all just looking out for yourselves.'

Blimey, we've pissed him off. Or – a blink of empathy – he's a lonely old man who's just lost his happy old age. And is furious at being ignored. He started back up towards Portobello Road. *Has someone put the wind up him? Why else answer the door with that entrenching tool? In a respectable street?* He settled into his slow beat gait. *Still, should check with the surgeon, keep Bert happy. And see if the neighbours spotted a rival for his Gladys's affections.* All things he'd have to do on his own time – and with Anna due in a week . . .

He turned onto the railway bridge on the Grove. He'd expected to feel a shiver of recognition, a few frames of that night's drama spooling out behind his eyes, but it was just a bridge carrying a road over a railway line, smoke drifting above the ironwork and evening traffic pounding along the tarmac. He was quietly pleased. He had enough skeletons waving their arms at him in his dreams without acquiring a new crew.

★

The night turn was footsore and grumpy but they still had to march the two miles to the funeral route, through silent streets, past shuttered shops, an empty Hyde Park. They filtered through mourners stamping their feet in the chill, murmuring, respectful, with hours to wait until the cortège passed by, then formed up on the tarmac to march between the servicemen lining the route – riff-RAF at ease in sky blue and REME mechanics in improbably clean battledress – towards Marble Arch and their section of the cordon. And suddenly the mechanics had given way to Glosters, his old battalion – Major

Whitcombe talking to CSM Gannon, so that was probably A Company, then the familiar faces of B, with Phil Spivey looking up from his inspection of 4 Platoon to do a classic double-take, 'Dick Bourton?' And there was 6 Platoon, his boys for all of eight weeks but his for ever, their heads turning to catch sight of him. Suddenly Bourton knew how he was going to handle the Three Horsemen.

13

18.25. Two hours of catch-up in the Bramley Arms with lads he'd last seen crowding the bed as the medics strapped him up for the train – his blokes, in a way that the night turn weren't and never would be. The pints were free – anyone with a 'Gloucestershire' flash had to fight to buy a round nowadays – so the lads were nicely warmed up by the time they pushed into the Three Horsemen for the business of the night. Medals had been removed and belts loosened, but they still looked much too parade-shiny for the public, all chipped varnish and cheap etched glass, with weak lighting leaching yellow through the lamps' thick nicotine film. A listless gaggle of old boys made room at the bar, and Gant the landlord came through from the snug to offer a round on the house, trailing cronies like the smear left by a wormy dog dragging its arse. I hate this place, thought Bourton. It's enough to turn a bloke teetotal.

'Not sure I've seen you since Bert brung you in,' said Gant, mild offence on his bland slab face. 'Though o' course I been 'earing about your trials and tribulations. The 'ooligan shooting at you, that business the night His Majesty died. Must be wishing you was safe and warm back in Korea.'

'Garn,' said Bourton. 'Chinks and Gooks are tough little buggers – make your lot look like ponces and queens.'

'King George the Sixth!' called Phil Spivey, glass up, challenging the public to make some noise, and a satisfying roar came back.

'My lot?' asked Gant.

'Yep,' said Bourton. 'Last time I saw him,' pointing at a bald bloke in his forties with a long thin face and a nose like a hatchet blade, 'he was trying to pull a dying war hero out of an ambulance.' Joe Malley from 6 Platoon put his arm reassuringly around Baldy's shoulders. 'And that git,' Bourton nodded at a man in tank-crew coveralls slipping into the saloon, 'I owe him for a few free punches. Yeah, cowards and chancers the lot of 'em.'

'Now, don't cause any trouble, Mr Bourton,' Gant said uneasily, probably working out how much damage the Glosters could do to his joinery, 'not today. Not on my premises.' He nodded at the Glosters. 'A riot could cost my licence.'

'Wouldn't want that,' said Bourton. 'Wouldn't know where to find the criminals.'

'Try Bertram Terrace,' Gant pressed on.

'And have you lock us out? No. You and I,' Bourton grabbed his shoulder, 'will go out to your yard. Those two, then anyone else who wants a go, come out one at a time. Fair fight. My mates will stick around, make sure nothing out of order happens. All right?'

Gant nodded reluctantly. 'But I'm turning off the taps.'

'Bad idea,' said Bourton. 'After the day they've had the lads are thirsty. Can turn 'em off when we've gone. Now, do you tell your muckers or do I?'

★

The yard smelt of piss, mould and puke. It was no more than nine feet wide, with old barrels stacked under the blackened acid-worn walls and a cat sleeping in a rusty three-wheeled pram. Light didn't seem to reach below waist level. Bourton and Phil Spivey cleared an area at the end. There'd be no room for fancy footwork. Which suited Bourton fine.

Gant brought out Baldy, and Spivey checked his hands. Three inches on me and the reach of an ape, thought Bourton, as Gant inspected his own fists. *Better find a plan.* 'You got a name?' he tried, hoping to slow things down.

'Course,' said Baldy, and stepped in before Gant was clear with a looping right that wandered over Bourton's shoulder. Without thinking, Bourton thumped Baldy as hard as he could in the gut. The older man collapsed on his knees and vomited beer across the yard. Spivey had to skip clear to keep his parade-bulled boots intact.

'You gettin' up again?' asked Bourton contemptuously, thinking, Hope not. Baldy's head shook very slightly as he retched again. 'Thought as much. Coward.'

'You proud of yourself?' asked Gant, stooping to help Baldy to his feet. 'Beating up a bloke twice your age?'

'Well, the bloke he could've killed can't, so, yes.' Bourton realised he meant it. 'Bring out your next champion.'

The man in the tank coveralls was a different proposition – shorter, wider, a decade younger, almost bouncing on his toes with eagerness to get another free punch at a copper. Bourton had barely got his fists up before Tanky had hustled in and tattooed his elbows with short hard jabs to bring down his guard, then landed a glancing blow to Bourton's cheek with a right cross. Tanky skipped backwards and lowered his fists. 'Who's a coward now, then?' he called, teeth bared.

Bollocks, thought Bourton, heart suddenly echoing in his chest. An old boxer. *But he doesn't know what's on the ground . . .* He moved a couple of feet towards the wall, as if trying to cancel the skill advantage by hemming the fight. Tanky brought his fists into a low guard, already confident in his edge, skipping in, shoulders shimmying for a repeat, slipped on Baldy's vomit, pitched forwards only to be brought up by Bourton's left maw clutching him around the throat, three hard punches to the face with the right. As Tanky tried to bring his head down to his chest and his arms up, Bourton gave him a hard sort-of-uppercut under the ribs that drove the breath from his lungs in a spatter of blood and spit. Bourton stepped back. Tanky was still standing, arms around his middle as he tried to fill his lungs, but the Three Horsemen wasn't somewhere you showed mercy, so Bourton banged in an ugly right cross to the nose. Tanky curled up on the ground and coughed.

A commotion at the pub's back door. I hope this one's no good too, thought Bourton, because he'd cut his right on Tanky's teeth. But it was someone with a thicket of blond hair, squareish – surely not Senkus? – dragging a bald man bent almost double.

'Hey, Korea copper, it's Poniak,' said the sentry from Lithuania House.

'All right, chum,' said Bourton, thinking, Trouble now. 'Phil will check your hands.'

Poniak laughed. 'I do not fight – no one else will fight, I think. Everyone is on good behaviour.' He pulled his cargo upright. Baldy. 'Is true they try to pull Senkus from the ambulance? When he is knock out?' Bourton nodded. 'This one?'

Bourton nodded again. 'And this one.' He pointed at Tanky.

'Fine,' said Poniak. He stepped away from Baldy and unleashed a ferocious punch to the face that drove the man down like a fence-post under a sledge. 'For Vejas.' He bent down to help Tanky to his feet, but as soon as he let go the man sagged sideways to the paving. 'Hey, landlord,' he gestured at Gant, 'you hold him up.' Gant shook his head and Bourton thought Poniak might make something of it, but he just said, 'OK, is worse for him, then.' He crouched and his fist flashed down into the shadows. Bourton thought he might have heard something break. 'Also for Vejas,' he said, as he stood. He looked from Tanky to Baldy and back, surveying his handiwork. 'They will live.' He turned to Bourton. 'So, we finish here?' He gestured at the Three Horsemen's damp, buckled walls. Bourton nodded. 'Then let's go to good pub and tell kill-Communists stories.'

*

Bourton wasn't sure that the Walmer qualified as a good pub, but the kill-Communists stories were real. '*Waves* of 'em, chum,' Ted Hipkins – one of the forty or so blokes to make it back from the Imjin – muttered into his glass. 'Nah, *swarms*. Shadows, stinky Chinky shadows, all around.'

'Night?' asked Poniak.

'Always,' said Hipkins, boozily inaccurate. 'No artillery an' air, see.'

'Artillery,' said Poniak, 'the Russians had. Wheel to wheel.' He lined up empty glasses in a row. 'Katyusha. Rockets. Day, night – hours. Then tanks, waves of tanks, men on tanks, between tanks—'

'Never see 'em,' said Hipkins. '*Sense* 'em. Shadows. Bugles—'

'I seen 'em,' said Bourton, eight pints giving him the right to jump in, 'up near Kunu-ri, November the twenty-ninth, nineteen fuckin' fifty.' He grabbed a smoke from the ashtray, dropping ash along the table. 'Sitting on the road in my jeep,' pint on the trail, 'mouth o' the pass,' ashtray at the end of it, 'hills on either side,' glasses a gauntlet, 'over the ridgeline an' down they come. Full moon. Thousands. Ant-streams. So *fast*. An' that,' he banged a pint into the ashtray, 'were that. No one were gettin' out o' that fuckin' pass.' He had a sudden snapshot of the Yanks in their int tent, baggy unshaven tramps but savvy enough, earnestly listening to the word from on high that they didn't know what they were talking about: 'There are no Chinese in Korea. They will not cross the border in force. There are no Chinese near Kunu-ri . . .' *Steady lads all, and all dead, most like.* He scooped up the pint standing in for his jeep. 'Friends.'

The conscious ones struggled upright. 'Friends.' Glasses banged down.

'Happen you killed some of our friends,' Des Small, sounding innocent, 'all friendly, like.'

'Do you have Communist friends?' Poniak jabbed back. 'I killed only Communists.'

'Steady.' Phil Spivey was up, masking Poniak from Small, and a couple of other lads with dignity somehow pricked through sloshing beer. 'Not today, lads, the King—'

'A good man!' called Poniak, suddenly a diplomat. 'And I was his servant!'

'The King!' bellowed Joe Malley.

'The King!' they bellowed back, the pints jerky and deliberate. 'The King!'

Phil Spivey was pantomiming at Bourton, who realised he'd missed a cue. 'Come on, Poniak, me old Commie-killer.' He stood up and put his hand on the Lithuanian's shoulder. 'Let's get a breath.'

Outside, they leaned against the Walmer's bowed front, puffing away, bareheaded in the drizzle, letting the wet and the smoke cut through the fuzz.

'Don't know where my hat is,' said Bourton, after a while. 'Do you?'

'No. But I have my shoes.' Triumph. 'Drunk and no shoes – that is problem.' His smoke flopped from his lip to the pavement. Bourton handed over a Capstan. 'You know, Korea copper,' eyes closed for the first puff, 'you are a good man. Like your king.' He nodded. 'Also good man. It is good to serve a good man. I have serve some bad ones.' He pushed out a steady stream of smoke. 'Now I serve no one.' He opened his eyes. 'So this I tell you for free. Before you came in, that night? My make-believe OP?'

'Yep.'

'Kalvaitis is a snob. He does not dress up for a low person. And perhaps,' he took another puff, 'an important person wants Vejas to be safe.' He stuck a forefinger in front of his mouth. 'No questions, Korea copper, that is all.' Suddenly he pushed himself away from the wall. 'So, Dick Barton, do we go in and not start another fight?'

PART TWO

Daylight

14

23 February: Anna Day. Bourton paused in the doorway to check what she would see. Odds and ends: makeshift curtains – patchwork on threadbare cotton sheets – tacked onto the window frames; a balding armchair with his mum's cushions as a toupée; a cornflower bedspread out-fading a nasturtium headboard; a newish Ekco wireless in well-buffed Bakelite, squatting in the centre of the kitchen table . . . The only thing of love was his father's ash chest sitting below one window, his mother's cushion message-down on its lid, and it wasn't even from him. He shook his head. *She's travelled ten thousand miles for this.*

★

Watching the *Empire Dee* dock, buffeted by the women and old folk sidestepping to catch sight of darling Jimmy at the rails, Bourton didn't feel anticipation, but the queasy gut and chilled skin of fear. *Four months, that's all we had. Four months of heightened feelings, senses – a lightning romance, a strange city, a city on the edge. How can nineteen months apart and Southampton in a wet winter not pop that bubble?* He realised he hadn't felt as nervy since D-Day and his baptism of fire. *Must be something about the sea.*

The stream of khaki started down the gangplank. Single blokes, kitbags and rifles, faces alight, home where there were no leeches or ambushes or tarts with penicillin-proof clap; then married men bringing wives and families back from garrison, bulging cardboard cases banging the sidechains, kids shivering at a cold they'd forgotten. The stream trickled out and there was no sign of her. A couple of military policemen hustled up the gangplank, making way at the top for a brace of deckhands off to sample the Saturday fleshpots. *If they're letting the crew off . . . where is she?*

'Sergeant Bourton?' He turned to see an immaculate old man, bright eyes, long face, tweed cap over silver hair. 'Brian Horrocks.' He stuck his hand out, forcing Bourton's arm to change course just before the snap in an automatic salute. 'It's a pleasure to meet you at last.' *Old Jorrocks, a military legend, and he's here – for Anna . . .* Bourton had never shaken a lieutenant general's hand before – he hadn't even saluted that many – but old Jorrocks seemed to think it was the thing to do, so . . . 'We appear to have a difficulty. Would you like to follow me?'

But the redcaps had already re-emerged on deck, a splash of colour between them – Anna in a scarlet coat, ash-blonde hair escaping from her Shanghai astrakhan hat, spots of fury as bright as her lips on her creamy skin, each policeman with fingers buried deep above her elbows in the let's-not-cause-a-scene hold, her voice, cold fury, 'I have never been detained before, not even the Japanese—'

'Anna!' Bourton thrust the flowers at Jorrocks and started up the gangway, jabbing his finger at the redcap corporal. 'You have no authority to hold her! She is not a dependant so does not fall under the Army Act!' As he reached the deck, fury expanding him so he felt his suit would split, the two redcaps stepped back, one sticking out a hand to pacify, the corporal reaching for his baton. 'I am a proper police officer.' Bourton pointed at the corporal. 'This is unlawful detention, and if you try to use that on me I will take it off you and throw you overboard,' now in his riot-stopping bellow, 'and nick you when you're fished out. Is that perfectly clear?'

'Anna Yermakovna Timofeyeva,' said Jorrocks, smoothly, 'I am Brian Horrocks. What a delight to meet you at last. The Orient has clearly lost its brightest pearl. These, I believe, are for you.' The junior redcap had snapped to attention, star-struck, freeing Anna to reach for Bourton's flowers and, God help her French Concession schooling, curtsy. *The grace of her.* 'Corporal.' Jorrocks was all command now. 'Sergeant Bourton is correct. You have no authority to detain Miss Timofeyeva. Who ordered you to do so?'

The corporal was silent, out of his depth, and Bourton wanted to reassure her, bring her eyes to him, but he didn't want to break Jorrocks's hold – Jorrocks got things *done* – and she could only stare ahead, bristling with humiliation.

Suddenly, another voice: 'Corporal, get that bloody woman off this ship.'

Jorrocks turned, raising an arm slightly to instruct Bourton to keep back. It had the authority of an artillery battery. An army officer emerged from the companionway, tired, clearly harried, hat back, hands on hips, 'R Berkshire' flash on his shoulders. 'Chop chop.'

'To whom do I have the pleasure of speaking?' asked Jorrocks, smoothly.

'More to the point, who are you?' The officer turned to the redcap. 'Take her—'

'One of "that bloody woman"'s guarantors,' said Horrocks, his tone still light. 'That bloody woman, Captain . . .'

'Napier.' Grudgingly, hands disappearing behind his back.

'. . . is a former Hong Kong police auxiliary. She is the fiancée of a Metropolitan Police officer, who before learning all about the laws of the United Kingdom spent nine years with the colours, was wounded three times, and clearly absorbed much more of King's Regulations than have you. He would be acting lawfully if he were to arrest you for wrongful imprisonment, and unlawfully, but thoroughly reasonably, if he were to thrash you for insulting her so.'

Napier breathed deeply to contain his anger, but it dribbled out anyway. 'With all due respect, sir, whoever you are, I am Adjutant Troops, and she refused an instruction.'

'Which was?'

'To wait to be escorted ashore.'

'So you had the MPs drag her to the quay like a criminal?'

Napier blinked.

'No.' Anna's purr had an edge, like a torch singer seeing off a heckler. 'He called them when I told him that his was the only regiment to get a battle honour for running away.'

Jorrocks laughed admiringly. 'She knows regimental history and can do a court curtsy. Where did you find her, Sergeant Bourton?'

'A NAAFI tea wagon in the New Territories, sir,' answered Bourton, made literal-minded by his fury.

'Matchmaking with your brew? Excellent.' He turned back to Napier. 'Now, Captain Napier, if you'd looked at Miss Timofeyeva's paperwork you would know who I am, inasmuch as I am not General de Guingand, who is her other guarantor. As her guarantor I will now escort Miss Timofeyeva to her meeting with a charming man from Immigration, who does not abuse his authority when balked.' Horrocks stepped close to Napier so neither his voice nor the steel in it would carry to the redcaps. 'I will be lunching with General Dempsey next week. I will not mention to him that we have met and in other than ideal circumstances.' Napier had migrated to attention now. 'I suspect that Constable Bourton would not see the need to arrest or thump you if you were to bring his fiancée's possessions and documentation ashore. Straight away.' He lifted his tweed cap. 'Good afternoon, Captain Napier.'

Bourton turned to Anna, her fury goading Napier back into the accommodation, an angry flush still in her cheeks, crushed flowers someone else had had to give her clutched in her fist like a club. Their reunion had been wrecked before it had even begun. He was aware his lips were trying to frame an apology, but as she turned to him her eyes were warm, delighted, victorious, and all he could think of to say was 'Hello, love. Will you marry me?'

Suddenly her eyes filled with tears and she stepped into his arms with a force that pushed him back. 'The answer is still the same, Richard.' She snuffled into his collar. She smelt of carbolic and lavender and felt like home. And when she looked up to kiss him, her make-up smeared and her hat askew, her body trembling like after a nasty little action, all he could think was *This is my future.*

★

They were carried through the bureaucracy on a tide of Jorrocks's charm – 'Does she really need to fill in that part? Couldn't we do it, Mr Hargreaves, once the lovebirds have gone?' All the time they could see a thicket of berets and flat caps gathering outside the office window, with the occasional head bobbing up to see if the great man – 'Monty's greatest commander, chum' – was really there. When they were done Jorrocks passed the forms to Hargreaves and smiled. 'I feel like a padre who's just got the register signed. You may kiss the bride.'

Bourton wasn't sure he wanted to, not in this room with this audience, but it was all part of Jorrocks's sense of theatre, and Anna was smiling with an eyebrow raised, so he reached across, aiming to signal, Job done, but she pulled him in for something noisy but somehow chaste – 'We are nearly legal, now, Richard.'

'Well, you are at least, Miss Timofeyeva,' said Hargreaves. He handed over her card pulp passport, the temporary document that had always shouted, 'Temporary person', open on the page with the new stamp. 'To all intents and purposes, you are no longer stateless. You won't be able to get full citizenship until you're married or you naturalise, but from now on you have a home in the United Kingdom of Great Britain and Northern Ireland.'

Anna looked at Hargreaves, then back at Bourton, clearly trying for what she always called British blankness, already aiming to fit in, but her eyes showed hope and uncertainty and the need for reassurance.

'It's true, love,' said Bourton. 'You heard the man. Welcome to Oz.'

Anna's fingers crept over the stamp as if she were reading Braille.

'Take an Act of Parliament to get you out of the country,' continued Hargreaves. 'That, or an issue with these.' He touched the small pile of signed forms. 'So there you are.'

She buried her face in Bourton's shoulder. He smoothed her hair, kissed her crown and muttered nonsense in her ear.

'Right.' Horrocks picked up his hat. 'Memory Lane awaits. Mr Hargreaves – many thanks.'

'Been an honour, sir.'

'Before you go, sir,' Bourton's words seemed to be colliding in his mouth, 'thank you. I never heard of anyone doing the like, and without you and General de Guingand I don't know that I'd have got Anna in. Letters are one thing, standing guarantor . . . But coming down here – and on a Saturday – I don't know if we'd have got through all this without you or even if we'd have stayed out of the cells. So thank you.'

Jorrocks smoothed his hair, then donned his hat. 'Least I could do, Sergeant Bourton. You did more than your duty and, in return, the army made an utter hash of things. What else is rank for? Besides, no one listens to me in my new job.' He smiled. 'Black Rod may sound impressive, Sergeant Bourton, but no one in Parliament does a bally thing I tell them to. And you gave me an opportunity to finish some business. Anna Yermakovna?' She emerged from Bourton's shoulder, back straight, face set in polite determination. He gave a little bow. 'I wish you every happiness. Sergeant Bourton is a fortunate man. And the next time you write to your father, please send him my warmest regards. He may not remember Captain Horrocks, from Ekaterinburg, in 1919, but I remember him. I regret I could do nothing to help him, or chaps like him, get out then, and am delighted to have been able to assist his daughter now. I wish him quiet times. Good day to you both.'

15

He'd pictured a crowded compartment, steamed windows and excited chatter about home, with him and Anna snuggled up, bridging nineteen months with the nothings they'd missed. But the train was mostly empty and Anna didn't want to talk. 'This,' she nestled under his arm and rested her head on his chest, 'is what I have longed for.'

They woke at Waterloo. She carried the bruised flowers; he hefted her cases, cardboard with a Chinee patch-up, one still wearing the stencil of an RAF wife in quarters at Kai Tak. They were arm in arm all the way, through two noisy bus journeys and chatty streets; her scarlet coat glowed like a solitary slow tracer bullet bumping off rocks. At one point – knees touching, top of the bus, Oxford Street unrolling below – he asked if it all seemed drab after the colour and spark of Hong Kong. She shook her head. 'Manchuria is drab. This – this is dark, Richard. It just needs light.'

They passed a boarded-up bombsite. 'And a bit of a rebuild,' he added.

She squeezed his arm reassuringly. 'Perhaps a little. But what is underneath is good – all it needs is a good clean.' She laughed. 'This is my home, now, Richard. I will see and say only nice things about it.'

She was all wonder as they walked down the Grove from Holland Park Avenue. 'The road is so wide and the houses so big . . . Who lives here, Richard?'

'Professors. Doctors. Professional people, mostly. Their widows – lots of old dears.'

She stood on the broad front step of the Suchaneks' house as he opened the door. 'This big house, Richard?'

'It's just a room, love.'

'In this big house?' He nodded. 'We can find something less grand – you don't—'

'This is fine, love. It's right for you. Besides,' he smiled, 'I tried for something less grand, but it wasn't there.'

'You can afford it?'

When we're wed, and paying for one place, not two, and with rent assistance, and perhaps a second pay packet . . . 'Yes.'

'Then show me.'

He led the way with the cases and paused outside the room. She was gazing out of the huge picture window. 'Do they not have electricity?'

'Who, love?'

'The people out there. Where there is no light.' She was pointing at the black void behind Elgin Terrace.

'It's gardens, love.'

'Gardens?' She giggled. 'Gardens? Where are the squatters?'

He realised she was still in Hong Kong, where the open spaces in towns were covered with squatters' shacks. Every answer would make her feel foolish so he opened the door and turned on the light. 'Look, once we're married – I mean, we can find somewhere . . .'

'Is all this mine?' She was standing inside the doorway, scanning the room, and he stepped past her to the nearest window.

'I'm sorry about the curtains, but there's some fabric and that in this chest my dad made for you, some things my mum put together, and in the morning you'll see it's just the houses opposite and a lot of sky—'

'Is all this mine?'

'O' course.' Her face gleamed with joy. 'I'm sorry it's so cold,' moving to the fireplace, 'you might need your hat,' he squatted and struck a match, 'until she catches—'

'All this is mine?' Her eyes were running around the walls, as if checking for the cracks that would explain her luck.

'It's a bit rough and ready, and even the landlord says it's a cold house—'

'Richard, it is . . . perfect.'

'Well, it's not, you know.' The newspaper caught. He stood and wiped his hands on his hanky. 'I'd hoped for more.'

'And I had expected less. Is it rotten? Is there a family of eight next door? Will the rent double tonight?' He shook his head. 'Richard, when you were away, the places I looked at for us, no light, no water, hens on the landing, pigs in the khazi, and I would do it because we would be together. So this – this is perfect. And tomorrow we make it home.'

She stood beside him, gazing at the coal struggling to catch, and raised her palms to the fireplace as if it were giving off real heat. 'Will you stay tonight?'

Everything slowed. 'Well . . .'

'My first night in England?' She'd turned to him but he couldn't read her expression.

'If you want me to. I'll take the chair.'

She shook her head. 'We'll share the bed. It is small but it is a cold night. We will need to cuddle.'

'Yes.'

She smiled. 'Poor Richard. Do you ask? Or do you not?' She draped her arms around his neck and stood on tiptoe, body at polite dancing distance, to kiss him with a whisper of tongue. He put his hands on her waist, wondering if he could steer her close to feel how hard he'd become. 'You will have the sweets, Richard. But not tonight. Tonight, I just want you to stay close.'

'That's fine, love.'

Suddenly she clutched his cheeks. The teasing in her eyes had been replaced by vulnerability and perhaps regret. 'Stay close from now, Richard. I have had enough of letters and wars and somewhere else. From now on, no separations. Understand?' He nodded. 'From now, we are together.'

The Traveller threaded down the ginnel behind the houses and then the path past the privy, Gladys's spare keys in one hand, his case in the other – bit late to be out with it, but no risk, no fun . . . The back door opened easily enough. *Someone must be oiling the locks.*

Inside, the house felt like death. Or perhaps that was his imagination, him not having been in any houses after the fact, as it were. Which reminded him that he shouldn't be in this one, so he needed to shake a leg.

Once his eyes had adjusted to the darkness he walked carefully to the back parlour. He closed the door behind him, laid his case down, opened it and took out the torch by feel, then moved to the window, closed the curtains and clicked on the beam. *A photo will do. Rats won't eat them, not like the slippers.* He needed her as an old lass, really – he wouldn't recognise her in her youth, particularly if he was looking at her photo in a year or two's time. And what was the use of a memento if it didn't make him remember?

There, on the crowded mantelpiece. Her and another old biddy on a seaside promenade, holding hats on their heads as they brandished ices. That would do fine. Would fit easily in his poacher's pocket, too. He knelt down beside the fireplace, found a couple of old *Daily Express*es, took a few sheets, wrapped the picture, slipped it inside his coat, then rearranged the photos to cover the gap. Torch off, curtains open, out through the kitchen, down the path, into the ginnel, past the backs of the other houses to the huge double doors at the end and the wicket gate onto Bewley Street. Job done.

Build a cabinet? Keep the vermin out?

He stepped through the wicket gate into a pool of light from a streetlamp and a hard look from a spry old bloke walking past. The Traveller touched the brim of his hat, a bit of old manners that shadowed his face, then headed off to his hide and his mementos.

16

March 1952

'Nothing has been bombed, Richard.' Anna at the window, the pair of them jammed together on a mostly empty bus, holding hands, watching Cirencester go by. He realised the only England she'd seen in daylight was London and Southampton Docks. 'And it isn't black.'

'Reckon it weren't important enough for the Luftwaffe. And no industry to make it mucky.' *Or provide real jobs.* 'Could still do with a good scrub, though.'

'That's the army speaking.' He'd forgotten the hold of her captivating smile, which dimpled her cheeks and crinkled the corners of her eyes. 'You are a mucky civvy now. Let everything be dirty.'

The bus bumped beyond the town's patchwork of brick and Cotswold-stone terraces to open fields glimmering under frost and knots of buildings sending smoke signals straight up into a clear sky. 'It's gorgeous, Richard,' she whispered. 'The colour and the light – the pictures just don't show it.'

'It is.' He felt a little hot-water bottle of love and pride in his middle. 'Bloody hard, though. Glad I'm in the big city. Warmer, and everything don't smell of shit.'

The bus slowed. Two figures stood by a dog cart at the Cerney Cross stop, the pony inspecting the verge. Bourton got up, smiling. 'This is us, love.' He took her case – *What's in this, the Tsar's gold?* – and his day pack, and stumbled along the aisle. He helped her down, and when he turned his father was there, warm smile on his face and flat cap in one fist, his mother a couple of paces behind in her church coat and good shoes, stiff and shy.

'Dad, Mum, I'd like you to meet my Anna, Anna Timofeyeva. Anna—'

'Miss Anna?' His father made an odd sort of bow and stuck his hand out. 'I'm Arthur Bourton. It's an honour. Welcome to Ampney St Mark.'

Anna bobbed in a half-curtsy as she shook hands, grand enough to be Princess Margaret Rose meeting a foreman. 'Mr Bourton. Thank you for inviting me to your home.'

'Life wouldn't have been worth much if I hadn't,' he said, keeping hold of her hand. 'He would have arrested me and there's no knowing what his mother would have done.'

'Miss Timofeyeva,' the syllables rolled out of his mother's mouth as if she'd been rehearsing them, and she grabbed Anna's hand as his father let it drop, wearing a smile she'd give the wife of a new vicar, 'welcome to Ampney St Mark.' She realised she'd echoed Arthur and dropped Anna's hand in embarrassment.

'You hobble the pony, Dad?' asked Bourton.

'Nope,' he said, eyes on Anna. 'Partridge is too old to wander. You know what, Miss Anna?' She was smiling awkwardly, shivering, and Bourton realised she was nervous – the girl who stuck her chin out and dared life to break her stride. 'He never said you was a corker.'

★

Ridge Cottage: red brick, two up, three down, as Cotswolds as kippers, set back behind its vegetable patches and low stone wall, with chipped paint on the window frames and brickwork needing pointing. *Hard wet winter.* And for the first time in Bourton's life he felt nothing on seeing it. *It's just a house.* He turned back to the dog cart, the women perched on the bench seat, hands in laps, smiling gamely as Partridge pulled them resentfully up the lane. He realised his mother didn't much like his fiancée, and didn't care. *She's my life now.*

Bags; brew; then the dog cart up to the vicar's. Kettley was new to Ampney, old, and polite until he'd heard Anna's account of where she was from, which he greeted with a chill that said 'adventuress' or even 'tart'. Then he was all obstacles: they must wed in her parish, if that was no longer Hong Kong then her new one in London, if she had not been in London long enough to establish residence then perhaps a register office might do. If they were set on a church then

Unitarians or even Methodists did not ask too many questions. Or, of course, they could wait – unless time was an issue . . .

Anna squeezed Bourton's hand to keep him down. 'Time is an issue, Mr Kettley, but not because I am up the duff.' The vicar flushed. 'The padre of Richard's battalion was to marry us on the fifth of August 1950. But on the third of August Richard was sent to Korea, where he was wounded. When he was evacuated, unconscious, near death . . .' a catch in her voice; Kettley to his credit looked ashamed '. . . in June 1951 he was sent back to Britain, not to me, in Hong Kong. We were only reunited at Southampton Docks a week ago – a year and a half after I waved him off to war. So you see,' her searchlight smile, 'ours is a love story that would have been consecrated by the Church of England long ago – if Richard had not been risking his all against godless Communism.' After that Kettley's obstacles disappeared.

All the way to the stables at the big house Anna was silent, absorbed, Bourton wishing the vicar had just kept his trap shut. The unhitch-unharness-rub-down drill was harder than eight years before, his fingers more awkward, his mind on her, but when he returned from the tack room she'd stepped out of her gloom. 'You really are a country boy, Richard.'

'My cousins are. Tough as old boots, snare a rabbit in a hiccup. I just got brung up here.' They pushed the dog cart against the wall. 'Though some country habits . . .' He grabbed her round the waist and pulled her close. 'I bet these stables haven't seen hanky-panky for years.' He bent down to kiss her and her mouth opened, her arms wrapped round his neck and her legs whipped round his waist and suddenly they were tottering to a wooden partition wall. Her coat was open and she ground herself against him. Then, as he started hoicking up her skirt, she lifted herself away to make it easier, a hand fumbling at his fly. But then her nails dug at his wrist.

'Someone will come—'

'No, they never go out—'

'Not like animals.' She broke free.

'Better 'n not at all.' He was suddenly furious with her teasing. 'So when will we?'

'It is hard to seem angry, Richard,' she stifled a giggle, 'with that sticking out.'

He looked down. His cock had escaped and was pointing at her. 'You got it out.'

'Or perhaps you burst the buttons?'

'Don't laugh.' She giggled anyway. 'It's not right.' He tried to put himself back in his trousers but he was too hard.

Anna cast a theatrical look over her shoulder before stepping in close. 'Oh, Richard,' she grabbed his cock, 'what will I do with you?' She dropped to her knees and brought it close to her mouth. 'I think you need some help.'

⋆

His mother ignored their spooniness as she plied them with well-mashed tea and scones and a month's rations' worth of butter and jam. He tried to tell her that she shouldn't have, but the butter was from College Farm, the damson was the last of the autumn jars, the flour was from Filey's in return for some of his dad's joinery . . . True? Perhaps, so he left it.

'What did the vicar say?' she asked.

'Soonest would be four weeks,' said Bourton.

'Then that's what we'll do.'

'Just family, Mum, sandwiches and kegs in the village hall. Let's keep it small.'

'We will, Dick love, we will. But Miss Timofeyeva's come so far and it's been so long and we're going to do it right. All right, dear?'

Anna nodded. 'All right, Mary – Mrs Bourton.'

'Anna, Mum, please. She's not the Princess of Muck.' They all laughed but he could see his mother thought Anna was quality, with her perfect skin and foreign clothes and easy curtsy, would have hosted them in the parlour, except it would have been too formal for her son . . . *Either a tart or a duchess.* 'What happened to princesses in Shanghai, love?'

'When the money ran out, they died. Or they found a . . .' Consternation.

'Friend,' suggested Bourton. 'Tell 'em what your dad did before China.'

'I think you would say he was a carter. In Irkutsk, in Siberia. He had twelve carts at one point, built it up from nothing. Then the war destroyed the economy, the Revolution came, he ran away . . .'

'And ended up in Shanghai. Tell 'em what he did in Shanghai, love.'

'He was a doorman at a club. Also,' she added helpfully, 'a spy.'

'Which got them to Hong Kong – a thank-you from His Majesty for services rendered, as it were. So not exactly mates of that Tsar, then.'

His parents were speechless. His father rallied first. 'Mary's from Ampney. Her dad, his dad, all the Packers, all Ampney. I'm from Poulton, up the road. My dad was from Poulton. My mum was from Bristol, but she's been forgiven. Not great movers, us.'

'Will your father come for the wedding?' tried his mother.

'They would not let him in. Besides, he – we – cannot afford it.'

'And he's happy sending you away to the other side of the world?'

'He thinks the Communists will take Hong Kong,' nodding, 'and he wants me to be safe.'

'But – but when will you see him again?'

'Perhaps never,' said Anna flatly. 'Richard is my life now.'

'Oh, my dear,' said Mary. She seemed on the verge of tears but shrank away when her husband reached for her shoulder, offering top-ups instead. 'And your mother?'

'She ran off with a Chinese general when I was seven. She took my brother. I think they are on Formosa.' Anna covered her cup. 'I won't have any more tea, thank you, but please may I have another scone?'

*

'And I screamed, screamed, "Richard, that staircase is moving," and he said "Get on it, girl, and you'll move too."' Anna's audience – a clump of cousins, Joan Packer's fourteen-year-old Violet with eyes wide as if she were an ambassador from Hollywood – howled. Bourton blushed with pride. *Playing the innocent so she don't scare them. That's my girl.*

His mother was in the parlour doorway, looking intently at Anna, a smile on her lips but her eyes cold, beyond-the-pale judgemental.

Simple dislike? Or were princess tarts and Chinese generals too much? 'Great tea, Mum,' he tried. 'Done yourself proud there.'

'Just rabbit stew. Thank your cousins. They bagged 'em.'

'Well, it was smashing. Don't get none of that in London.'

'You wouldn't. Rats is all the game they got.' Her eyes softened. 'You happy, Dick?'

'What do you think, Mum?' She nodded. 'And she's why. She's a great girl, Mum. She's just been through stuff that people in England don't.' He suddenly felt the urge to make her understand. 'Never had a real home, always a foreigner. Born a refugee. Had to up sticks and run twice because of the Reds. Went to school with a knife and brass knuckles, just in case her mum had her kidnapped. Grew up in the middle of a civil war. Lived under the Japs for four years, for God's sake, no food, no money, the secret police picking up her friends, her dad . . .' *Enough.* 'And she's come out of it loyal and honest and true. Everything you'd want from a daughter-in-law. Might even get some decent-looking grandkids out of her.'

'But . . . but . . .' She was searching for words, trying not to offend. 'Her family . . .'

'Father's the family she knows and he's salt of the earth. Picked himself up and started again three times. They think the world of 'im out there.'

His mother clearly didn't think much of 'out there'. 'Does she love you?'

'Of course.'

'And she's not taking advantage?'

'Mum,' lightly, 'Hong Kong's got about fifteen thousand white blokes and ten white girls. She could have found an officer, some taipan, could have Dear-Johned me in Korea or any time after. The wonder is she chose me at all.' He raised his hand to stop the oblig-atory any-girl-would. 'She's the tops, Mum. She's just a bit foreign. All right?' He turned without waiting for a response, to get another look at Anna – face alive, her mouth a scarlet barometer of animation. He smiled, remembering the stables. *What a girl* . . .

A nice girl had never done that to him before.

17

'She like the place?'

'Loves it.' Bourton's bulk displaced enough of the early-evening tide in the Earl of Uxbridge to give him and Athill pint-lifting room. 'Course, in Hong Kong you reckon you're doing well if you haven't got squatters on the landing and pigs in the khazi.'

'So Elgin Terrace looks good. Whereas Mile End . . .' Bourton laughed as Athill raised his pint. 'Cheers.'

'Cheers.' They drank. 'And thank you. Your word with the guv'nor.'

Athill shrugged. 'Did a good job. Pain in the arse, of course, but a couple of years on the beat will knock the bounce out of you.' He shook out a couple of cigarettes. 'Don't get yourself killed first, of course.' He lit them. 'You're about to be a married man. First duty? Come home at the end of the turn.' He took his first pull. 'End of the lesson.'

'Mr Athill.' Bourton drank. 'Know who I ran into down at the Three Horsemen?'

Athill grinned. 'Don't tell me you took on Primo fucking Carnera, too?'

'You heard about that?'

'Come on, chum, this is our ground.'

'Yeah, well. Remember that sentry in Lithuania House? In the boiler suit?'

'Pontiac.'

'That's the bloke. Poniak. Was at least Wehrmacht, probably something more – police battalion, Waffen SS . . .' Athill was motioning for him to hurry up. 'Yeah, well, we got matey an' he told me something interesting. He said, about the second time we called, that Kalvaitis would only get into number ones for an important person, and that an important person wanted Senkus to be safe.'

'O' course.' Athill didn't seem surprised. 'He had a visitor. You remember what he was wearing? Suit, shirt, no collar. Four in the morning? He'd be in a pully over his nightshirt, perhaps old clothes.'

'His collar was on the dressing-table,' remembered Bourton, 'the bed was unmade, there were embers in the grate.'

'Yep. He woke up, got togged up for Mr Big. Who came in, had the chat, Kalvaitis starts to get undressed again, takes the collar off, then we turn up.' He flicked his filter to shake off the ash. 'And then Mr Big's muckers deposit Senkus on their doorstep. You know, I badgered them for a week at Lithuania House to question Senkus about what happened, an' each time it's "He's recovering, perhaps in a few days." Eight days on, I knock on the door, say I've come for that chat, an' he's gone. No forwarding address. All balls, of course. But if there's no Senkus, we can't get stuck in, and if we don't get stuck in, then whatever they don't want us digging up stays well buried.'

'But what would that be?' asked Bourton, baffled. 'I mean, it's not like they've got a racket or a string of tarts. They're just blokes with bugger-all English, working their arses off.'

'For them to know, and us never to find out,' said Athill, sounding philosophical. He nodded at Bourton's glass. 'Drink up or you'll never get the next round in.'

★

Standing in the bathroom, preparing for the first day at Tours and Trains, *Strange that an advertisement should say 'Fluent French' as if this is an extraordinary thing . . .*

Things to do:

Make some warmth for the room, a man's room, cold, bare; some colour. Mary Bourton's cushions were a lovely gesture but not enough, and in any case 'Anna Bourton 1952' was face down, so as not to put a wicked spell on a status she had yet to win. A good woman, probably, Mary Bourton, but country, suspicious. It would work in the end, but it didn't matter – they would not be living in her pocket.

Enough stray thoughts. Finish the dress, put up curtain rails, find backing for the fabric from the market, turn it into curtains – perhaps that army blanket, give it a trim? Perhaps get a sewing machine on the never-never? Or was that for really big things you couldn't afford? Finish the dress.

A snapshot of a day to come: at the altar in that cold church full of people in old clothes, smelling of mothballs and cigarettes; the mean-minded priest, her in the dress and the Astrakhan – no, a too-practical touch, it did not belong – and Richard, beaming with pride and happiness, bamboo-blond hair stuck to his forehead, eyes gleaming, lighting a little pocket-warmer in her tummy, the two of them a patch of light in that faded chilly place . . .

That was why she needed to do things: to make a home he could move into. Their home, their life.

A new bed? It was small for two. But where would they get a new one? Anyway, single bed, they would have to cuddle. Also, she hoped for a lot of sex. She liked that he was so keen. It was a good sign.

She coughed. Two weeks she'd been here and the cough wouldn't go – a little thing, her breath would catch occasionally, but it lingered, as it had in Shanghai. *There must be something in the London air, some metal or sulphur or something that comes from chimneys. Like in Harbin.*

She shivered and put Manchuria away.

She looked up into the bathroom mirror, centred the cultured pearls. *Formal, feminine, ready to go.*

'You ready, love?' Richard, knocking on her door. She stuck her head onto the landing. He'd just removed his helmet and his fair hair was sweaty, tufty, stubble already showing on his chin, strong nose smudged with oil. He looked massive in his uniform, solid, like the trunk of a tree sawn off at five feet ten, and she suddenly felt wet. Not now . . . Back in the bathroom she closed her eyes and conjured up Imanishi-sensei's face to push the urge away. No uniform, no cold hands carrying the aura of the dead, no view of chimneys and barrack blocks and wire, she did not want to depress herself – just the face . . . And, poof!, the feeling was gone.

'In here, Richard.' He knocked on the half-open door and came in. 'How do I look?'

He inspected her from head to toe as if she were about to go out on parade. Finally he smiled. 'Ready to knock 'em for six.' He gestured at the pearls. 'Might want to leave them behind, though. Most girls here are much more dowdy in the office – they save that for the evening. All right?'

★

Riding home after her first day in a new job in a new land; lower deck of the number 15, shopping wedged between her calves, coat modestly covering her knees, another Londoner in a city of strangers.

The 'girls' of Tours and Trains have single syllable names – Vi, Re, Mag – and titter at her nun's French. But they seem good-natured, and kind when she found herself coughing ('It's the air, An, you'll get used to it'), admire her taste in men ('He can arrest me!'), though unsure whether to envy her wardrobe or dismiss it ('They make clothes in Hong Kong, do they? Oooh, that didn't come from Macclesfield'). And the rest of her day sailed along once she'd taken Tor's handset at about noon and told Monsieur Georgieff from the Wagons-Lits – yelling in Russian because he wasn't getting the answer he wanted – that not even Stalin would use language like that to a woman he had never met, and that she was not sure if the crackle she could hear was the line or Georgieff scratching off his syphilis scabs; and Vi had gone out with her at lunchtime to help with the shopping ('Anything that'll boil well – you can't fry, not unless you want to use up all your butter or dripping, and that's a waste, and if you don't have an oven . . .'). And Mr Pattison had said that her 'slightly old-world' French was just right for a certain kind of letter, and could she draft something to Monsieur Maille, the manager of the Hôtel Bristol?

But as they turned into Edgware Road, and bumpy vegetables shifted in her soggy canvas bag, she realised that in a life of strange arrivals – the Concession, the camp, the comfort house – she had felt more foreign in that office than ever before.

★

Home just before six, Richard on the step, waiting in mufti, washed and shaved and ready for his turn; then three hours together, tea – fish and chips, a celebration – and vinegary hanky-panky, lights off so no silhouette on the threadbare curtain, clothes folded first to avoid grease stains. Afterwards – he seemed happier about not going all the way, after he'd come a couple of times – she traced the new scars, the pits in the right leg from the mortar fragments, the rings on his wrists from the wire cuffs, then reminded herself of the old, the dents in the thigh and the lash down the back from the machine-gun bullets, the puckered scalp from the piece of tank, thanking God that now he had a safe job and would come home to her every evening.

★

So for the next three weeks, as Richard worked every night to stock up leave time, a new routine. Wake to his footsteps just past six, breakfast, wash and dress, then tuck him in and trot to Tours and Trains; home at half five, tea, a little play, then send him out the door at nine fifteen and settle in. Two hours, perhaps more, wrapped in a blanket in the armchair, fire damped to make the coal last, listening to band music and arched-eyebrow comedy and sewing, sewing, sewing, the curtains but mostly the dress. Not out of notions of chiffon and magic. Instead she worked for the beginning of something, for better or worse, because until it began she was in limbo, away from what she knew, not yet part of what she didn't, outside an identity waiting to be put on. Somehow it seemed appropriate that her last act before the future was to hang her unfinished curtains on the rail Colonel Suchanek had put up – something to begin their married life with, to shelter them from the outside world, but incomplete. The past is not yet done, she thought, as she closed the door behind her. Perhaps the future will be more neat.

She took the train on her own, so Richard would not see the gown, and was met by Joan Packer in the College Farm van, dress hitched above the knees so she could fight with the pedals. Later, a viewing of the gown in the box room that Violet had moved out of for the night, which seemed to involve most of the women in the village and perhaps from other Ampneys too, and offers of shoes, and make-up, and howls of open, happy envy ('Oh, that's *silk*, a yard of it! I haven't seen silk since – oh, I can't remember'). And endless cups of tea, and history swaps, and bald questions once the little ones had been shooed away ('You done it yet? Ain't too late – hop round now, quick one against the woodshed'). Later, a delegation of the groom's guests, Die-hard friends, including Bill Nickerson, the best man, younger and happier than in Hong Kong; a snapshot of an old-slippers past, dances and picnics and China-innocents wide-eyed in Kowloon. And work that mattered ('A nose for Reds, she 'ad, kid you not, and when she speaks that Chinese – hingle bingle wong wang wing'). Glowing with scrumpy and goodwill as she rolled into Violet's lumpy bed, she realised, I may be a city girl but it's with people like this that I feel at home.

★

Morning. A typhoon of primping, and when the women let her out there were two Packers – Joseph? Stanley? – to carry her down the path that the hordes of visitors had turned to bog. Alone on the dog cart, holding her white heather bouquet, impervious to the edge in the air as Joan took pictures, she suddenly missed her father – a sharp pain, a rib breaking – who'd take up most of the bench seat, wrap a strong arm around her to keep her on, nod at the strange English instead of pointing, and send her down the aisle, as he'd seen her off on the *Dee*, to be happy, his life's work done. 'We'll send him the photos, my dear,' said Joan, passing up a hanky from her sleeve. Arthur hopped up to take the reins in his hand; and Partridge bumped down the lane, grumpy under her magnolia coronet.

At the doors Anna thought, I have no idea what happens now. I am a guest at my own wedding. But then they opened, and as her eyes adjusted she saw Richard standing at the end of the aisle, in an unfamiliar suit, neck white above the old tan where the razor had shorn him, and she realised she *did* know what happened now: they were to be joined. Which she had wanted for two years, since the third, fourth time at the tea wagon. She smiled and stepped over the threshold as the organ played.

The Traveller headed up the Great Western Road, past the bus depot, to the bridge over the Grand Union – *Should give Mrs Faccini a little time to make her preparations* – and put down the case. *The nervous type. Won't do to rush her.* He shook out a Senior Service, lit up and leaned against the ironwork. *Odd night, tonight: no wind, but the fog eddying, patch of clear here, solid blanket there. This one won't last. And there may not be any more until autumn – winter's well gone. So, the old bloke down the Elephant tomorrow night?*

'I know you.' The Traveller turned, automatically bringing his hand up to pull his hat brim low. A lean old man in a tweed jacket with turned-up lapels was no more than a couple of yards away, nodding at him, finger wagging. *How come I didn't hear him?* 'I know you. I saw you come out the station and I thought, I know that man, an' I seen the case, an' I knew it.'

'You must be thinking of someone else, chum,' said the Traveller, reaching for the case. 'I've never seen you before.'

'Bewley Street. Was you came out of the ginnel, couple of weeks ago. With that case an' all. But you're not local. I know you're not.'

When he'd been getting the trophy. 'Look, chum . . .' A group of coloureds was walking up from the bus depot after their shift, other side of the road. *Don't want them crossing.* '. . . I don't know where Bewley Street is. I'm never round here—'

'How do you know it's around here?' Almost a screech. A couple of the coloureds were looking over.

'I just guessed, chum. Look,' an eddy in the smog and suddenly the coloureds were gone, 'I've never been in Bewley Street in my life. I've come up, calling on an old navy chum, an' I'm early, he won't be back yet, so I'm standing here having a quiet smoke. All right? So I'd be thankful if you'd leave me be. Here,' he took his Senior Service out of his pocket, 'have a smoke, keep the fog away.'

'What's in the case?' The old man was pointing at it. 'Sid Horne said a bloke with a sample case had been calling on my Gladys.' *Gladys? The soul in Bewley Street? How—* 'So what's in it? What were you doing in the ginnel behind Gladys's house?'

Of all the luck. He could hear an engine coming down from Harrow Road. *Go now.*

He grabbed the old man by his lapels and lifted him, back against the ironwork, hands flailing at his ears, tipped him, head below the parapet, legs scissoring up, then let go. He heard a yelp and a splash, but he had already picked up the case and started walking north, the engine turning into a Ford van crawling south in second, driver's window down. With a bit of luck he'd be long gone by the time the old bloke got out of the water. He lengthened his stride, mind working. *Can't do Faccini, not now, too close, can't do anyone, need a bus, and my hide, and to wait out the fuss.*

What fuss? His stride slowed. *Nothing linking me to Bewley Street, the old bloke doesn't have my name, once he's out of the water he can't see twenty yards, I'm free and clear.* He hefted his case and smiled. *And with all the work I put in on the Edgware fairy, Mrs F, the Papist bint Marylebone way, shame to waste it . . .*

18

They rode back to London on a slow train, cuddly, content, bruised and weary from too much sex, shifting in tacky clothes – there wasn't much you could do over five days in a Weston boarding-house in April but fuck and forget to dhobi. Bourton had apologised a couple of times for the wind off the Bristol Channel and the closed fairground rides on the pier, but Anna took every damp, chilled outing as an excuse to get inside, warm and sticky, and after six weeks of No he couldn't believe his luck.

Now he itched to get back to the job. Ever since Anna had arrived he'd been marking time, walking turns with his head at the Hammersmith and his heart on Elgin Terrace. But seeing Bert limping in at the wedding, somehow thinner and fatter at the same time, he remembered that he actually enjoyed coppering, that Rex thought he might eventually be good at it. Most of all he had the sense, coming back to London, that him-and-Anna, coppering, the city were one. A proper life. And he was going to give it a proper go.

★

Anna opened the door to the room with an air of occasion and stepped back. He put down the cases and scooped her off her feet. She yelped. 'What are you doing?'

'Carrying the bride across the threshold.' She looked offended and surprised. He was puzzled. 'Not a Russian custom, then?'

Theatrical contempt. 'I am a Cossack, Richard. Our custom is to kidnap the girl with a lot of shooting, then put her in a hut with her mother-in-law and the smell of horse piss.'

He slung her over his shoulder and patted her rump proprietorially. 'You're as Cossack as scrumpy.' He crossed the threshold and dipped his shoulder to lower her to the cornflower counterpane. He'd expected to see a little 'Ravish me' in her eyes, but mostly there was flatness, perhaps disappointment. What did I muck up? he wondered. What did I miss? He paused, but couldn't ask, and Anna didn't seem disposed to say.

★

Cuffs on his locker, ribbing at roll-call – for the first time in months Bourton was one of the lads. And he had Beat Eight, his favourite, the heart of the Dale, Bertram Terrace and the Three Horsemen where, as Sergeant Harbison put it, 'For reasons unknown PC Bourton has a new reputation as a cross between John Wayne and Joe Louis.' Back in the saddle and beginning to fit in, suddenly he was the copacetic copper.

Walmer Road: the pub where Poniak had gone all confidential, the scrubby park that whiffed of slurry after a few days' rain, the old kiln that was almost the last relic of the Dale's beginnings as a back-garden brick factory and piggery a century before. Then bleak-faced houses opening straight onto the street, the Methodist chapel, the Rugby Mission club, where lads were still working the punch bags gone ten, Pitney's panel-beating shop, the bombsite on the corner with Silchester Road – small figures hopping over the rubble—

'Now then, lads,' he called. 'Ain't it a bit late to be out?' Instead of scattering, the figures filtered through to the pavement and the light. Close up, he could see they were little 'uns, eleven, twelve, in dusty shorts and threadbare shirts and jumpers. 'After dark's one thing, lads, but twenty past ten . . .'

'When else you goin' to practise a night engagement?' asked the boy on the left, excited eyes below a pudding-basin cut. 'You're Dick Barton, intcha? We 'eard about you.'

'Good,' said Bourton. 'Makes it easier to walk you home.'

'No, it don't,' said the boy. 'That's a non-sequitur.'

What the hell is that? wondered Bourton.

'You not 'avin' to do something else, bein' available to walk us 'ome – now that would be logical.'

'All right, how about . . . the fear and respect in which the Metropolitan Police is held makes it easier to walk you home and not have you run off?'

'That's better,' said the boy. 'I'm over in the prefabs on Latimer – Don and Terry, they're halfway up Silchester.' They formed around him. 'Only you're not to take us to the door, all right? Walk us 'ome an' we'll scramble in the way we came out.'

'Now now,' said Bourton. 'Your parents need to know you've been out.'

'No, they don't,' the boy said. 'Look at it this way. We run off, you won't catch us an' we can be out all night. You don't snitch on us, you know we're safe an' sound. All right?'

Bourton smiled. 'You learn negotiating on the stalls?'

'Nah,' said the boy, 'it's just growin' up, innit?' He seemed to weigh if Bourton was worth a confidence. 'I'm Derek Jeffrey.' Hand out to shake, as if Bourton had come to call.

They walked up Silchester Road, the boys quizzing him about Korea ('Did they, like, come in waves, like I read?') and D-Day ('You must 'ave seen *something*') and the army ('I'm goin' to be a para-trooper.' 'Nah, tanks – they are so *big*'). Questions tripped over answers, Derek taking the lead with Don an eager echo and Terry waving his arms and gurning, hamming to get noticed amid the torrent of words. He suspected they might be primary-school chums separated in secondary – Derek was bright enough to be at the local grammar. Bourton lifted Don over his back garden wall and had Terry sit on his shoulders to prise open his first-floor bedroom window, jammed shut by the wind. Then it was down to the prefabs, temporary homes on a cleared, resurfaced bombsite in the lee of the Metropolitan Line that had permanent-looking gardens and house-proud front doors. Derek's house was dark – 'Mum an' Dad are at the pictures, late show at the Royalty' – as they made their way to the concrete front step.

'You'll 'elp us, won't you?' asked the boy.

'Help you do what?' asked Bourton.

'Train.'

'For what?'

'The army.'

Bourton looked at him. 'You're what – twelve? You got six years.

An' with your non-sequitur, perhaps you'll want to go to college. The army'll train you when it trains you.' He gestured at the front door. 'In you go.'

Derek pushed it open and switched on the hall light, then turned as if an idea had occurred to him. 'If you're Dick Barton,' he said, 'can I be Snowy?'

'Nah. You can be Jock, always wanting to get stuck in.' Bourton turned away. 'Good night, Derek. And go to bed.'

★

His eleven o'clock call-in sent him to the British Legion club behind Ladbroke Grove tube station, where Norris had responded to a wake that had turned into an old blokes' brawl. But Bourton found the other copper on the pavement, bonnet off, checking his jaw like an extra outside a western saloon, as yells collided inside. Bourton bent down.

'You never – *never* – sit out on the public thoroughfare in that uniform, looking like you been bested. Understand? Tit.'

Bourton jammed his whistle into his mouth, opened the door and blew as hard as he could. Eyes slitted against the sudden glare, he sensed shapes duck away as if an errant firework had shot under the lintel. As the curses ricocheted he let the whistle drop.

'I'm PC Bourton, late sergeant in the Die-hards,' he called, in a muster-parade baritone, hands on his hips. 'I will be coming in in ten seconds. Anyone who attempts to strike me will be arrested and will spend the night in the cells with drunks and ponces, will get breakfast from the Salvation Army, and then will go in front of the magistrate and get their names in the paper. So sort yourselves out.' He closed the door. Norris was now at his shoulder. 'Stay here. You go in, someone will belt you 'cos he'll know you're an arse. An' if they don't, I will.' Bourton loosened his stick, wishing he had his cape rolled and ready to go, then took a deep breath and opened the door. *Pity it doesn't swing.*

'Now then,' he called, 'what have we here?'

What he had was beer, some broken glass, chairs now more or less upright, and old blokes in blazers with ties at half-mast, many not trusting themselves to get to their feet. He got the odd nod from the innocent and smile from the brass-neck guilty. Scanning the faces he wasn't sure much damage had been done – probably booze, old arguments and sloppy punching. *Trust Norris to be the only bloke marked in a clawless cat-fight.*

'Sergeant Bourton.' A small man, five-two perhaps and eight stone in dripping clothing, RN badge on his blazer pocket and a pint in a surprisingly big fist, was in his path with his hand out. 'John Collins.' They shook. 'We're sending off an old friend.' He nodded at a framed picture sitting intact on a pristine table – a young leading seaman and his girl, holding hands against a cloth backdrop of Brighton's Royal Pavilion. His parents had its twin on the mantelpiece. 'Would a Die-hard drink with some old matelots?'

Bourton removed his bonnet. 'Father and brother were navy and the RN always got me home, so be honoured, Mr Collins, but should probably be back to my beat.' The pint was full, probably for him, and he realised that some little gesture might screw the lid down on whatever had boiled over. 'But I'd be pleased to toast the killick,' he nodded at the photo, 'thank him for his service and send him on his way.' He took the pint. 'To?'

'Ernie Potter,' said Collins, reaching for a glass from a nearby table. Everyone stood, some with the help of blokes or furniture, and a chorus of variations on Ernest Potter rippled around the room as the glasses bobbed up and down.

Ernest Potter? He knew that name – dead common, of course, but . . . 'Did Mr Potter live in Bewley Street?' Collins nodded. 'I met him. I was the responding officer when his – a lady friend of his, Gladys Hartham, passed away.'

'That was terrible for him,' said Collins. 'He was that keen on her.'

'He certainly seemed very cut up.' Bourton remembered his anger the second time they'd talked, on his doorstep. 'But he seemed healthy as a horse. What happened?'

'Drowned,' said Collins. 'Got sunk on the old *Daisy* in the Great War, swum around the North Sea for hours on end, an' goes an' drowns in the Grand Union.'

'How?'

'Don't know. Stone cold sober. They reckon he went in off the bridge on the Great Western Road, an' it was cold, and dark, and he couldn't pull himself out. Or he didn't want to.' Collins bent in close. 'A couple of blokes say he jumped, because he was that keen on his Gladys.' Collins shook his head. 'But that's not him. He was a tryer, old Ernie. Just kept on keeping on.' He lifted his glass once more. 'Ernie Potter, gamest of the game.'

Bourton clinked, sipped, then put the pint down before he got caught drinking on duty. *I know that bridge. It's all girders and lattice-work – it's not the kind you fall over, even if you're drunk, let alone sober.* And suddenly he remembered Potter's entrenching tool, his insistence that Gladys had had a visitor, his anger that nothing had been done – jealous anger, but perhaps stemming from something deeper. *And I still haven't checked what happened to the widow – not properly, the way Bert asked.*

He nodded at the old blokes and made for the door. *Something else to get on with.*

19

Come 06.10, back in mufti, he was thumbing through the incident book, finding the name of the police surgeon who'd pronounced Gladys Hartham dead, and by eight he was outside the man's surgery on North Pole Road, getting in the door ahead of his patients.

Frayed shirt cuffs and a surgery more like a bedsit suggested Dr Vaughan wasn't prospering, but he was helpful enough once reminded. He'd noted nothing immediately suspicious about her appearance – heart attack due to lung function being suppressed by the smog, was his guess – and notified her GP, Dr Reid, who would have certified her. His surgery was on Talbot Road. Did Bourton want him to call first?

So off across the Grove. Even with the call Reid kept him waiting forty minutes. He was brisk and defensive. Gladys Hartham had had bad lungs for years, and a weakened heart, and every winter he'd treated her he'd told her to move out of London or she'd be gone by spring; and each time she said Hitler hadn't shifted her and, besides, she was still there, wasn't she? He was surprised she'd lasted that long. So he'd examined her body before morning surgery, determined that her heart had failed suddenly, perhaps as a result of a coughing fit – there were indications she had been unable to breathe – checked with the coroner, then certified her. And there'd been no post-mortem because coroner's rules called for one only in the case of sudden death or the patient not having seen a doctor recently – and he'd paid a house call on her a couple of days before her death, which, while sudden, was down to something she'd been dying of for years.

Bewley Street. Bourton realised he'd never seen it in daylight before. It looked smaller and meaner than he'd thought it was, and the scrubbed steps and postage-stamp gardens more defiant. But every parlour he was shown into was pristine. Most of the people he talked to had no difficulty remembering 6 February – that was the day the King died, and we were heartbroken, weren't we, listening to the wireless, that poor girl, the burden – but the seventh meant nothing to them. Of course Gladys had died that day, but, you know, two months ago, anything other than that? Mrs Agostini, Gladys's next-door neighbour, a very handsome woman of about thirty back from a morning's shopping, said she didn't know anything about a visitor, but if Gladys was in that blue dress with the crêpe collar, she only wore that for special occasions, like weddings, christenings, trip to the Palladium. Maggie Sims, other side of Gladys's, she'd know, her and Gladys were thick, but she wouldn't be back from work till six, maybe later . . .

He came out of Mrs Agostini's to see two figures by a garden wall halfway up the other side of the street, talking to an old dear – Mrs Marks? She made a good brew – on her doorstep. Her finger came up in an accusatory point, straight at Bourton. He felt a childish impulse to run. As the two figures approached he saw that one was a fortyish woman with a big belly, whom he'd chatted with half an hour before, and the other a lad, thirteen? fourteen?, squat and pimply with a front lick that swooped upwards like the lid of a badly opened tin.

'Constable Bourton?' She was puffing slightly. 'This is me youngest boy, Jem, he might have something for you. Go on, lad.'

'Hello, Jem,' said Bourton, getting out his notebook. 'All right, lad, so?'

'Well, I was coming home from school—'

'What day was this?'

'Seventh, so—'

'How do you know?'

'They kept us late – they needed to make up time for ending early when the King died so they kept us on two hours extra the next day. I was walking back, would have been about six o'clock, right foggy night, and as I passed Mrs Hartham's—'

'How did you know it was hers?'

'Got the unicorn doorknocker – they didn't want it for Spitfires.'

'How could you see through the smog?'

'Weren't that thick – you could see length of a cricket pitch, easy.'

Of course, it will have got worse over the evening – it would have been clearer at six than when I mounted at ten. 'Anyway, Mrs Hartham opened her front door, and there was a bloke there, on the doorstep. He took off his hat—'

'How did you see him?'

'She had her hall light on. That's why I looked, suddenly a bit of light when everything else was dark.'

'Can you describe him?'

'He had a mack on. Sort of khaki, I suppose. Old bloke. But that's from his back. Sort of felt like an old bloke.'

'What kind of old? Stooping old?' The boy shook his head. 'Same age as . . .'

'Dad,' said Jem.

'Who's fifty-one,' offered his mother.

'I'd say he was a bit shorter than you, and normal build, really.' Jem seemed to think he should be doing better. 'He had a case, though. A boxy kind of case.'

'Suitcase?'

'No, not as big as that. Like a really thick attaché case. Like you see the travelling salesmen carry,' he added happily. 'With their bits in.'

'A sample case?' asked Bourton.

'Yes. Like a salesman.' Jem made a little deductive leap. 'Which would be pretty strange, wouldn't it, a traveller calling at six of an evening?'

*

18.20. Stout, late fifties, in a wide-shouldered coat, Mrs Sims looked like a rugby coach in smart two-inch heels. Every surface of her front parlour had its complement of photos. By the time she returned from putting the kettle on he'd worked out that she was a widow (chief engineer, Merchant Navy, tankers) with five grown-up kids (Canada, Australia, three sets of anonymous terraced housing somewhere in Britain) and at least a dozen grandchildren. Close, but scattered.

Maggie and Gladys had been neighbours and friends for nearly thirty years, sharing stories, recipes, rations, patterns – even holidays after Don Hartham died in '48. Maggie had collected Gladys's shopping and pills when her chest was weak, nursed her when she was ill, though Ernie Potter had helped a bit with that, last couple of years, and done much of her scrubbing (Gladys had housemaid's knee). She'd even dressed her for her laying-out – 'Not a job for a man never knew her' – and helped sort out her effects. If Gladys had had an appointment on the day she died, she certainly hadn't mentioned it. Nor did she have a diary – 'What would she put in it? The bingo?'

'Who would she have worn that dress for?'

'A man.' The answer was automatic. 'Not for a woman – well, short of the lady mayoress, or the Queen. And for big occasions out.'

'What would she wear for her cocoa?'

'Pinny.'

'On her feet?'

'Slippers.'

'Jem . . .' he checked his notebook '. . . Horne, across the way, said he saw Gladys letting in a salesman, about six on the evening she died.'

'Six o'clock?'

'Yes. Did you get a card, a sorry-you-were-out slip, anything like that?'

'No.' Her brow creased. 'Six o'clock?' She paused. 'You're not asking for no reason. What are you after?'

'I don't know,' said Bourton. 'I'm just dotting *i*s, really.' He tried a conspiratorial smile. 'But this salesman is a bit rum.'

She waved a hand dismissively. 'I don't know anything about any traveller. All I know is she had bad lungs, and it was only Mackeson's stout and proving Dr Reid wrong kept her going all these years.' She stood up. 'Now, Mr Bourton, you got time for a cup of tea before you go?'

20

Bourton was still stuffing his notebook into his demob pocket as he stepped out of the police box and into Rex Athill's arms.

'Oi-oi,' said the DC. 'What you about, then? Playing smart aleck off duty?'

Bourton shook his head, thinking, Spot on, and then, You must have seen me go in and waited. 'A favour for Bert. Wanted to know about a suspicious death.'

'Because?'

'Curious?' Bourton shrugged.

Athill's face was blank, clearly disbelieving. 'And?'

'Coroner's lady says I should talk to DC Brown.'

'Mancini's.'

'Mr Athill?'

'George Brown. We'll find him in Mancini's, Bramley Road.' He smiled. He looked like a vulpine Zorro before he impaled someone. 'I'm going to listen to Dick Barton at work. Who knows? Might even be able to give you a tip or two.'

★

'Mr Athill.' They walked into Mancini's to be greeted by a clerky bloke in specs and a stained suit, half rising behind a table but somehow drooping as he did so, smiling weakly as if he hoped to be recognised but had no expectation of it.

'Mr Christie,' said Athill, with a polite nod.

'You know him?' asked Brown, dark and wiry and new to Bourton, fizzing with energy even in his chair. Behind his head was a picture of old Alf Mancini in his ring days, all bounce and steel in long shorts and title belts, and Bourton could have sworn there was a resemblance. 'He's been nodding at me like the Dale idiot.'

'Remember Evans? Hanged a couple of years ago? Killed his wife and baby?'

'Yeah. Searched the drains outside his house for the nipper.'

'His landlord.'

'The bloke Evans said did it?'

'The same. Ex-copper, would you believe it?' Brown looked surprised. 'I know. Hardly fills you with hope for after the job.'

Brown gestured at his table. 'In for a brew?'

'Not really,' said Athill. But Ma Mancini was already banging down a mug. 'On the other hand . . . Nah, Dick Barton, Special Agent, has a couple of questions for you. Thought I'd look in, see how it's done.' He turned to Bourton. 'Off you go, Sherlock.'

'Ernest Potter, Mr Brown.' Bourton smiled nervously.

'Grand Union Canal.'

'That's the bloke. Coroner's clerk says you're looking into how he ended up there.'

'Yep.'

'What happened?'

'Why d'you want to know?'

'Bert Parkin was asking. Death-bed request.' Brown was looking puzzled. 'I'm a probationer, Mr Brown,' said Bourton. 'I do what my SO asks.'

Athill snorted.

'Not what I heard,' said Brown. His fingers tattooed on his mug. 'All right. Will Stratfull saw some lads on the Great Western Road bridge, looking at something in the canal. Went down, helped to pull Potter out. No obvious marks on him, other than his fingertips, which were torn up. Probably tried to claw his way up the brick sides of the canal but kept falling back – his age, the cold, weight of his sodden clothes . . .' He took a swig. 'Canvassed in the Grand Union pub just over the bridge, and half a dozen of the houses backing onto the canal, nothing seen or heard – though he went in on a foggy night.'

'How do you know?'

'From doing my job,' said Brown, with an edge. 'So perhaps his cries didn't carry. Couple of Jamaican drivers on their way home from the bus depot mentioned seeing a bloke who could have been Potter on the bridge, would have been about quarter past six in the evening when they'd come off shift, talking with another bloke. So it looks like Potter entered the water from the bridge.'

'Because?'

'There's no access to the towpath from there and there wasn't enough current or breeze for him to have drifted more than a few yards.'

'Jump, fall or push?'

'First two. I talked to his neighbours. They mentioned he had this lady friend, this . . .'

'Gladys Hartham.' Brown looked suspicious. 'I responded when she died.'

'OK, so some of the neighbours said he was very cut up when she died. Perhaps he jumped. On the other hand, others said he was angry, not suicidal. PM said he drowned, a couple of bruises on his back. Could have been the parapet on his way over, or something in the water when he fell – there's always scrap in there.'

'Did the Jamaicans hear what Potter and the man were talking about?'

'Nah. They said they could have been arguing, but the tricks fog plays, could have been a row from Maida way. Frankly, when I write it up I'll be saying there's nothing to point to anything other than an accident or suicide – or, given the fingers, a suicide where he changed his mind too late to save himself.'

'Not an easy bridge to fall off,' offered Bourton.

'No, but it can happen – daft things happen all the time. If you'd had more than fifteen minutes on the job you'd know.' He opened his hands and shrugged his shoulders. 'Show me the cosh bruise on the head or the punches and scratches as he was pushed over and we can talk about murder. But short of that, it's accident for the family, and suicide for the rest of us.'

*

'First things first.' Athill led them down Latimer Road, past a totter swinging a bag of rags onto his cart and Father Hall from St Francis of Assisi doffing his hat on a doorstep. 'Death-bed favour, you say. But Bert was up and about – what, three, four weeks? – before Potter died. If you weren't an upstanding officer of the law I'd say you were lying.'

'More like stretching things a little, but . . . yes.'

'That's a good start.' Pulling out his smokes. 'So what's the truth you're stretching?'

'Bert wanted me to look into Potter's fancy woman.' Athill clicked his fingers, trying to summon the name. 'Gladys Hartham. Bert said there was something rum about Mrs Hartham's death and wanted me to check what had happened. Mr Potter felt the same.'

'How do you know?'

'I spoke to him in February. He was sure we weren't doing enough. Then the other night I got called to a brawl at Potter's wake –'

'I heard about that.'

'– and apparently his death wasn't clear-cut.'

'And what did you find?'

'I should talk it over with Bert.'

'Well, we're here now. Go ahead.'

So Bourton laid it out, anomaly building on anomaly: Gladys's dress, her teeth, her cocoa, her visitor with the sample case, Potter's suspicions, and then his fall from a bridge you couldn't fall from – nothing to Brown, but when seen in the light of everything else, something solid and suspicious and screaming for action.

'How come you're the bloke finding all this out?'

'Don't know.'

'You're not telling me something.' He lit his Player's. 'What did she die of?'

'Her doctor said heart failure induced by the smog.'

'Did he think it was suspicious?'

'No.'

'Did the police surgeon?'

'No.'

'So you've got a woman who died of natural causes, a grief-stricken old man who drowned, and a salesman.'

'Rex, it's—'

'Nothing.' He offered a cigarette but for once Bourton said no.

'Did anyone even want her dead? Someone needs their inheritance? An old grudge?' A deep pull. 'Look, Dick Barton . . . we've both seen enough to know, death, it just happens. Wrong place, wrong time, no meaning, no reason why.' He shoved his hands into his pockets, leaving his cigarette welded to his lip – a spiv poster-boy. 'You want to be Sherlock, there's got to be something there. And this time there isn't.'

'Mr Athill.'

'I know that voice,' unsticking his fag, 'I got copyright on it. It's the I-understand-what-you're-saying-sir-but-you're-full-of-it" voice.'

'Rex, it fits.'

'Only 'cos you want it to.' Bourton felt offended, as if someone had stamped on his den, and it must have shown. 'All right,' said Athill, resetting his hat. 'I'll do this. I'll go and think and see if there's some way we can dig a little deeper, find that something. All right?'

'Thanks.'

A small smile. 'This job isn't about theories, you know. It's about stuff. Stuff you can put in front of a bonehead jury and say, "This is it." No stuff, no theories.' He turned to face Bertram Terrace and took another deep pull. 'You been doing some asking around, haven't you?'

Bourton nodded, puzzled. 'How else d'you find stuff out?'

'Most probationers,' a plume of smoke, 'can barely ask for directions.'

'Honest?' asked Bourton, properly surprised. 'What use is that?'

Athill smiled broadly. 'In case you hadn't noticed, probationers are tits on a mule. You'll never guess who I just heard from. Indirectly, of course.'

'No idea.' The DC gestured deliberately at the bombsite. 'Still no idea.'

'Kalvaitis. The old bloke from Lithuania House. Yesterday DI Knox says he's had a request. Doesn't say who from. He asks me to look into what happened to Senkus that night. When I've got a spare moment. Not an investigation, o' course. Just a little rummage around. Now I can't talk to Senkus, 'cos he's legged it an' anyway he can't remember what happened. Or so the guv'nor says. And chances are there's nothing to find, two months on. Still, someone wants to know – did he fall or was he hit? And if he was hit, was it 'cos he's a

Lithuanian, or a git, or just wrong place wrong time? In other words, do they all have something to worry about, or just him?'

'How do you find out?'

'God knows. Something else I have to think about.' He lit another smoke from the embers of the first. 'I could do with a uniform who knows the Dale.' His smile was slightly humouring, as if he were offering Bourton a chance to trip himself up. 'Who knows how to ask questions. Want to help?'

21

Asleep on their bed, sheet tangled around his hips, head under a bunched pillow as if he'd started to stifle himself but changed his mind, Richard was oblivious to the daylight. She decided not to wake him. He sweated and shifted his way through sleep. She didn't know how often he slept through it.

This is a strange life we are starting for ourselves, sharing a bed we do not sleep in, sharing time but not a rhythm. But I will be a proper police-man's wife. I will learn the words, and how to live around the shifts (no, 'turns', apart from the early one, which is the 'worm'), and I will make us a home of this big cold room in the sky, with pigeons cooing in the gutters and the draughts from the chimney, the fabrics that do not match each other, the weather, us . . .

And he will know that he is loved.

She lit the fire and diced the vegetables for the soup. She looked unhappily at the neat little piles. *I am a good cook, I know I am, but how do you cook with no oven, two rings, and hardly any fat? Millions live like this. Is it an English trick I should know, like understatement? Or do they eat and not taste? Perhaps I can do something with the fire, get a baking tray, bake food that tastes of coal . . .*

He woke after six, while she was in the armchair, the curtain draped across her knee and a needle in her hand but her attention on the wireless: *The Archers*, supposedly country people but wooden, with none of the life or worldliness of the Bourtons and Packers, but interesting nonetheless – *Do the English sit in their canteens and dream of being country people?*

'I love you so much, Anna Bourton. You know that, don't you?' His tone was wistful, regretful, even, as if love might not be enough.

'That is a nice message to hear.' She stuck the needle into the arm of the chair and walked over to the bed to kiss him. The bedclothes were tented above his erection.

'So, not just the morning.'

'No,' said Bourton, unveiling it, 'just most of the time, really.'

Anna dropped her trousers and trotted half naked to the ring, turning off the heat under the soup, then turned to take off her jumper and blouse. She could have sworn his cock twitched as she unclasped her bra. 'Make me warm, Dick Bourton. Nice and warm.'

★

He left at nine fifteen, glowing as always with cheery yesness, the first thing she'd noticed by the tea wagon two years ago. 'That looks good.' He beamed, pointing at her new name on the cushion on the chest, and she knew he meant them, not the needlework. 'No escaping me now.' But the vein of unhappiness she'd sensed making love was still pulsing gently. It wasn't her – he had woken with it, like a film of sweat – and she did not think it was the dreams, because he had been undisturbed at the end. *So, something at the station. I'll get him to talk in time.*

Now he had gone she could do the jobs he should not see. First she cleared and washed up – doing this around him seemed indecent, like letting him see her soiled underwear. Then she banked up the fire, to bury the embers; he would like it to glow all night, build up a warm fug for morning, to keep this cold snap, this last gasp of winter, at bay, but the coal was too smoky, and in any case it would be a waste. Finally she sat down with the form, and decided on her lies and evasions.

'Application to become a Citizen of the United Kingdom of Great Britain and Northern Ireland'. *So far, so true. I want to be a citizen, and now I am Richard's wife I am entitled.* And for much of it she could write confident truths: date and place of birth, current address, last address, occupation, name and occupation of spouse, date and place of marriage, and so on. But what of 'Current and/or previous nationality/nationalities'? Just the Nansen passport? (Which is, of course, no nationality at all.) Or the El Salvadorean passport her father had bought to protect his stateless daughter? A document to which she was not entitled, not being a citizen, so need not be mentioned, particularly as it condemned her to . . . the Yu Yuen Road Civilian Assembly Centre, which really should not be entered under 'Previous addresses not in the United Kingdom, its Dominions, Colonies or Dependencies', if only because of what had come after it. *After all, Richard does not know of these places. Why burden the Home Office?*

Sins of omission. Just like the omissions from the medical history form she'd given that nice Mr Hargreaves. She smiled. *Still following Daddy's advice: 'Don't tell officials what you don't have to.'* She sat up straighter. *So why tell them anything at all?* She flung the form on the fire and riddled the coals so that it caught. *Fool. Say nothing. Citizenship can wait.*

★

Later, once the paper was ash and she knew she would not sleep, she put on her scarlet overcoat, her father's doorman's brass knuckles and cosh in either hip pocket, and her Astrakhan, and trotted down to the street. A strange night: the feel of winter – biting cold, still, clammy air, a fog with a whiff of metal, rotten eggs – but in April. *Sunlight and long days soon.* She jammed her hat low and crossed the Grove to take a turn through Notting Hill at night – Richard's world. Friday-night drinkers, happier, richer, readier to forget; tonight couples heading back to lodgings; unattached men circling knots of women, others straggling home, cash gone, weekly ritual complete, snatches of songs – 'This two-funnelled baaaarstard, Is getting me daaaahn' – hanging in the air. She got two offers as she walked up the Portobello – the red coat, she hoped – and two Negro men lifted their hats to her appreciatively, an innocent compliment she could tell, even though she could not read Negroes yet, so unknown to her. There was a scuffle outside the Star and she skirted it, right hand on the sap, up to Westbourne Grove.

The Caccia Café perched on a corner opposite a bank, a hard yellow glow through its long front window, stray night birds gazing at a street too dark for them to see. She opened the door. The dumpy old Italian woman behind the counter nodded her to a table. She ordered coffee – the café served proper coffee and awful, awful tea – and picked up a brown-ringed *Evening News*. 'Coshing Gangs Stalk the Fog.' A Gaumont actor arrested. Why is it only American dances that take the dance halls by storm? *We should go dancing at weekends* ...

'Excuse me, miss, I'm sorry, but . . .' She looked up. A man at the next table – fifties, long face with a martyr's expression, high forehead, glasses – was leaning across. Did he want the paper? A light? 'Are you Mrs Bourton? The wife of PC Bourton?' She nodded, surprised. 'I thought so. I'd seen the two of you around, up St Mark's Road and its purlieus, and of course I knew – well, knew of – him, what with having been a police officer myself. I always look out for them, and then him being in the papers—'

'The papers?'

He nodded. 'Oh, yes, when that officer got shot on Ladbroke Grove, your husband helped to nick the bas— oh, excuse my French, little tyke who did it.' He smiled. 'He hasn't told you, has he?' She shook her head despite herself. 'There's your beat bobby for you – modest, every man jack.' He moved back to allow the Italian woman to put Anna's coffee on the table, then leaned across once more. 'I'm sorry, I should have introduced myself. Reg Christie. Late of Harrow Road nick.'

'Anna Bourton.'

A life story in the space of a brew. A proper school, two wars, wounds, civic responsibility – but a past-glories life story meant to inspire confidence, sympathy, even admiration; the kind of monologue one could provoke on any bus, with any Londoner who had an eye to be caught and a need to explain. We mattered once. London – like Shanghai – was full of it.

The door opened as a night bird walked out – a girl returning to her pitch? – and the sudden blast of air caught in her throat. She coughed, a couple of little catches, almost sneezes, then something tickled in her chest and she was rummaging in her coat pocket for the hanky beneath the sap – *Not again.* A watery rattle in her lungs, and suddenly her diaphragm was spasming, driving mucus up her throat – *It had gone!* – and into the cotton. Her eyes were watering but she could see his hand reaching over to pat her back and shook her head. After a few seconds the spasm stopped and she wiped coffee grounds from her lips. Christie was looking ahead as if to avoid embarrassing her. She closed her eyes and placed her hand on her chest, sure she could hear her lungs crackle. *It had gone.*

'I got gassed,' said Christie, quietly, 'in the Great War. It drove me out of the police. And it troubles me still.' He took his glasses off and wiped his eyes. 'There are days when I don't think I can make it up the stairs.' Glasses on. 'But then I take a puff of my special apparatus and it clears the bronchial tubes, the aioli,' a pause as if the word was significant, 'and I can carry on.' He turned to face her again. 'Without it I think I'd have died years ago.' He tucked his handkerchief inside the top pocket of his coat, a bizarre attempt at soigné. 'Winter's always hard, particularly when the fog comes in, settles on the Dale for days on end . . .' He smiled, a shy, awkward, vulnerable effort. 'Something I put together with my medical training. It's been a help for many, I can say.' The smile waned, as if he was about to ask her out, knowing she'd refuse. 'I can give you a dose or two of it some time, if you like.'

22

Bertram Terrace was transformed by spring, the rubble fringed with a patchy rainbow of gorse, cow parsley and forget-me-nots, and greenery that would be feet higher and flowering hard come July. It was a sorry sort of day, with a tired sun and heavy air, but Bourton could hear the thrum of bees.

'You ever see the scene in daylight?' Athill asked.

Bourton shook his head. 'Haven't been back since that night.'

'No one else examined it either.' Athill nodded at the bombsite. 'All right, off you go.'

Bourton showed him where he'd found the shoe and Senkus's body, then they scrambled down to number 11's coalhole. An arched space ran under the packed rubble and they ducked in. It ended in a slope of loose masonry and chunks of stucco, hiding what would have been a little door into the basement of the house to allow the housemaid to fill the scuttles without getting wet. The little tunnel was about five feet high, with a low shelf two bricks deep along one wall.

'Could be any of the better holes I knew in the war,' said Bourton. He perched on the shelf, knees up to his chest. 'Covered from rain and mortars, rig a groundsheet across the entrance,' he pointed, 'light a fire, dry your feet, make a brew.' He smiled. 'Just seeing it makes me want to light up.'

'Would Senkus have felt at home here?'

'God, yes. Can just see an old soldier like him – take the weight off, get out the Caporals and the flask, think of other times, other places, old oppos . . .'

'How would he know about it? He'd only been local for three weeks. Not as if it's on the way to and from Rootes.'

'Someone from Lithuania House?'

'Didn't mix,' said Athill. 'Remember that Buzzy?'

Bourton nodded. 'He said Senkus was always happy in a hole. Perhaps he was always looking for one.'

'Why?'

To visit his ghosts. 'It's like hiding in your shed with a bottle. You don't know anyone who came back and does that?'

There were scribbles on the walls and ceiling, men's and women's bits, something that might have been Latin, bollocks about the Mancinis being wop spies. Bourton leaned his head against the wall and breathed deeply. Damp, broken concrete, his sweat, someone else's piss . . . Suddenly he was seeing not the tunnel but the culvert, dawn revealing the hapless Yank cuffed and cold, skull caved in where the Chink had chosen to save ammunition and beat him to death, the rest of them bound and shivering, waiting for the bastard to come back . . .

Bourton stood up, banging his head on the ceiling, and the images were replaced by the ground inside the tunnel – brick dust, scorching from a fire, weeds emerging from the cracks, a used rubber johnny. 'See if you can find something to write with,' he said to Athill stooping over the rubble slope. 'It's time Kilroy was here.'

'Won't be much, chum,' said Athill. 'It's all broken brick, fragments.' He was turning a half-brick in the weak light. 'Though this has got a bit of colour.' He held it up at eye level, a hunchback examining pawn. 'That's a bloody hair.' He duck-walked out and turned it in full daylight. 'He had that white hair, didn't he?'

'Like mayflowers.'

'Mayflowers,' he grinned, 'white, chum, white. You couldn't be more Glaaahster if you tried.' He showed Bourton two or three white strands caught in a crack between the brick's face and old mortar. 'Which might make this blood.' Happily, pointing at blotches and smears the colour but not the pattern of rust stains. 'It'd last, wouldn't it?' Bourton nodded. The bloodstains in the barn in Oostergaat were there a whole winter after the Germans had stuck the farmer's family against the wall. 'But if you fell on this you'd never get so much blood – a little cut, then you'd roll off. This is from a solid whack.'

Bourton scrambled out of the hole and tried to think it through. 'So Senkus is sitting in his dugout with a drink and a smoke and a memory or two. Someone's with him. A chat turns into a row. The row turns into a scuffle. Senkus is bashed. He staggers out, clambers up to reach safety. Shoe comes loose as he stumbles, groggy, a few more paces, and over.'

'That could work.' Athill climbed out with spidery ease. 'Let's have a look at the others.'

Number 10's tunnel had collapsed, rubble part-filling the coal hole to within three, four feet of the surface. Number 9 had been swept fairly recently and there was candle wax on the brick step. Number 8 could have been the twin of the tunnel where Senkus had been hit – rubble, graffiti, weeds, stucco fragments everywhere, the remains of a fire. And cigarette butts. Bourton reached down to pick one up but found himself reaching for a stucco fragment instead. Because it wasn't stucco but cigarette paper – curled and misshapen, yes, but the tear was still clear where someone had field-stripped the stub. Bourton inspected a few more fragments. All the same. *An old soldier, back in the line, waiting to do his rounds, sipping from his flask, smoking and swapping lies with his oppos, stripping the smokes as he finished them so the traces blew away.* A bit of graffiti caught his eye. 'Lietuva' something. He remembered that word from Lithuania House. This was where Senkus had come to meet his ghosts.

So what had he been doing in the other hole?

23

'Why you askin' now?' Waite was more interested in his office view – the Rootes floor and a vehicle yard full of Humber armoured cars – than the two coppers. Short, mid-fifties, with graphite eyebrows and thick grey hair, his fingertips were so ingrained with oil and metal filings he should have left a speckled slick every time he pushed back his fringe.

'His memory started coming back,' Athill extemporised. 'He remembered he'd been hit, just not who hit him.'

'He all right, then?'

'Yes.'

'Good,' said Waite. 'He wor a good hire. Had a few other Poles through before an' they're the same – turn their hands to anything, really.'

'Was that where he said he was from?' asked Athill.

'Aye,' said Waite. 'He worn't?'

'Lithuania,' said Athill.

'Where's that, then?' asked Waite.

Bourton shrugged.

'What did you know about his background?' asked Athill.

'Nothing,' said Waite. 'To be honest, worn't interested. Know what he'd worked on, though. Said he'd learned his trade on aero engines, then tanks, half-tracks, lorries – Hanomag, Škoda, Chrysler, bit of everything.'

'He get on with the other lads?'

'No idea. Never heard that he didn't. Mind you, he worn't here long.'

'Did he have any mates?'

'No idea.'

'You mind if we ask?'

'Before their break, I do. Distract them. Most of these sods'll take any excuse.'

'What time did he clock out that day?'

Waite examined the time card sitting on his desk. 'Two thirty-four.' He tapped the card. 'Double shifts an' overtime since November, but that day we shut down at half two out of respect, or he'd have been here gone six. Good worker, that. An' he got stuff done,' he added. 'Any arse can sit on a production line, but we're overhauling here as well as assemblin', an' that means mechanics. An' Jonny is a mechanic.'

★

'He coming back?' A stringy lad in RAF coveralls, his black hair in a ponce's quiff, standing in the front row of the crowd around the two coppers. It was growing all the time as workers came through with their brews. Bourton watched their faces, as Athill had asked, but most of them wore the smiles or openness that said this was a happy ship.

'Dunno. I'll ask when I see him.' Athill scanned the huddle. 'He have an oppo, a mate?'

'Can't you ask him?'

'He can't remember.'

A chorus of sympathetic muttering. 'He kept himself to himself, really,' said the gaffer. 'Did his shift, his overtime, then off.'

'Anyone he had a gripe with?' A man with an enamel mug promptly looked down.

'Had a falling out with Mikey Brady,' said the foreman, nodding at the man still looking at the floor.

'Because he called him "gimpy".' That was the ponce in RAF coveralls.

Senkus limped? First I've heard of it.

'"I am gimpy and you are stupid,"' said one of the others, in a Bela Lugosi voice. '"I earn gimpy. Do you earn stupid?"'

'An' then 'e 'oisted 'im up in a chain,' the gaffer, 'an' went off for 'is brew.'

'Seems a bit much,' said Athill, lightly.

'Nah,' said the ponce. 'He ain't the first bloke not to get one of

Mikey's little jokes.' None of the others seemed to think the humiliation had been out of order.

'And no one called him gimpy again,' said the gaffer.

'So what time did you get off on the sixth of February, then,
Mikey?' asked Athill. 'Day the King died.'

'Was in Nottingham, wasn't I?' Brady was wearing a one-up grin.
'Two weeks.' He waved his mug at Waite's office window, where the
man was making get-out-of-it gestures at the coppers. 'Check me
card.'

They did just that, Waite delighted to help if it got them out of his
factory. 'He wor in the Blakely Street plant. Nottingham. Third to the
fourteenth.' He handed over the card. 'Perhaps they needed someone
who wor useless.' He shook his head. 'Londoner. Give me Poles any
day.'

★

'How long d'you reckon Senkus had been on the ground before you
found him?' Athill asked, outside the gates, as he passed Bourton a
smoke.

Bourton turned towards Bertram Terrace a mile away, as if he could
see it through the Memorial Park, Silchester Baths, the streets of
smoke-blackened brick. 'He was dead cold. And sodden, front and
back, though it was only drizzling and the ground wasn't wet.' He lit
up. 'Couple of hours at least. Three?'

'Prob'ly as close to an answer as we'll get.' A long pull. 'So he was
hurt at six, seven thirty.'

'Unless he was hurt earlier, collapsed in the tunnel, woke up, tried
to get out . . .'

Athill nodded. 'Four, five hours is a long time to be sitting in a
hole in the ground in winter.' His thumb stabbed over his shoulder
at Rootes. 'They say he didn't mix, he got along, he could look after
himself. And he wasn't around long enough to piss off anyone new.
So whatever happened, happened,' he pointed his cigarette at the
Dale, 'down there.'

★

14.50. They started their canvass at the time Senkus would have made it down to the Dale, with the houses opposite Bertram Terrace – three storeys, Victorian, given over to bedsits and damp. Room after room, with nothing like a number or a linking corridor to say you were knocking up a complete home or part of one. Householders of all ages, both sexes, most shades of white and two of black, with little in common but poverty. Some rooms would have done credit to a Grenadier Guards kit inspection; others had mould on the walls, scabbed or bubbled plaster, and the feeling that TB seethed in the brickwork and the rafters. And Bourton noted it all down: 'Number 140, first floor right, Hornung, widower, French polisher, 6 Feb job in Regent's Park; first floor right rear and rear, Kelly, warehouseman, Mrs Kelly, char, out.' Then on to Stoneleigh Street, some whole houses, others proper flats; owners not tenants, salaried not occasional, with sets of furniture, parlours, even the odd car. And all – even the kids hopscotching in the street – confirmed what the coppers already knew or had guessed.

Everyone used Bertram Terrace as a playground. Punters from the Three Horsemen, pissing games on the wall above the White City yards; classes from St Francis of Assisi, nature watch in the rubble-strewn gardens; mates on a budget, chatting and smoking without having to stand a round; courting couples; kids milling around after school, hide and seek and D-Day up and down the gardens; a gaggle of wives from Rifle Place, stringing washing lines between the walls in good weather and gossiping over each other's smalls. And no one had seen anyone come out of Bertram Terrace that night, at least until the ambulance came; we was all indoors, weren't we, listening to the wireless . . .

Which Bourton instinctively believed. He remembered the streets that night: the emptiness that had knocked half an hour off his bus journey, and left him blowing for help from non-existent passers-by.

'Can't be the washerwomen,' said Athill, as they stepped into the street of prefabs in the lee of the Metropolitan Line, 'not in February. Can't be the kids – they'll have had school or tea.' Of the fourteen prefabs they got responses in only two. 'All families, you see,' said Mrs Patch in number 9. 'Most of the mothers work and the kids are at school.' Including the Jeffreys. 'Nice family, they're all nice families, really. He's Scotch, a driver, he's away a fair amount. Beryl, she's in pay up at Vanguard, and that Derek, be a doctor or a judge one day, he's that sharp. Beryl doesn't know where he gets it from.' But she, too, had nothing useful, so they crossed the road and started back towards Bertram Terrace.

The rough edge of the Dale: a façade of three-storey stucco and, behind it, short streets of back-to-back two-up-two-downs, some close to slipping sideways onto the District Line tracks, and the odd semi-derelict warehouse or corner factory. The doors were opened by women in housecoats or ill-fitting hand-me-downs, frayed fabric behind grey aprons, hair coarse and hands like navvies', and everything smelt of piss, bleach and damp. After a while Bourton realised they were getting less and less, as if cooperation declined with the quality of the brickwork. 'Why?' he asked in Freston Road.

'Shame.' Athill looked as if he'd been the one on his feet for thirteen of the last eighteen hours, with little sleep in between. 'You've never done a full canvass, have you?' Bourton shook his head. 'We knock on their doors with our pensions and housing allowances and we listen to their answers and we judge them.' He seemed to be in a ruminative mood so he reached for his smokes. 'Half the time, we suspect someone based on what we see and sense as much as hear.' He popped a cigarette into his mouth and told Bourton, 'Smoke your own, you cadging monkey.' He lit up. 'Three years ago, missing girl up Talbot Road. Fifteen years old. Go to the flat, mother's worried but keeping it in, father's at work, and I look at the pictures on the mantelpiece, and the happy snap of the parents is mostly hidden by one of Dad with his arm around the daughter's waist, girl in a cotton dress that's too small for her, pointing her tits at the camera. And I just knew, day is long, he was screwing her, and she'd run away.'

'Did you find her?'

'Brighton did. Holding her for soliciting.' He drew deep. 'I looked at her mother and I thought, This is three rooms, how could you not know? Judging her. From two pictures on a mantelpiece.' He exhaled. 'If I were them I'd want us to leave them alone too. Half the time I want to do just that.'

In daylight the badly painted signboard outside the Three Horsemen seemed to show three wolfhounds with jockeys up. Athill led, doffing his hat to Gant and telling him – oh-so-politely – that he'd be asking a few questions. Bourton sensed a certain respect in the nods and smiles that rippled around the public bar as he loitered by the door. Daylight showed up the chips and stains on the joinery, the nicotine film on the glass. The drinkers were mostly off six a.m. to two p.m. shifts, he reckoned, with a few old 'uns with old pints in the mix; they clocked on at the Three Horsemen as regular as they did at work. They'd have been here on the day the King died, and they used Bertram Terrace as their khazi – surely they'd seen something.

Only they hadn't. Gant's self-serving explanation rang true. 'No one was out, Mr Athill. Everyone who came in, all day, said the same. Streets were empty all afternoon. O' course there's a bunch of blokes you won't have seen – lots of places let out early that day, out of respect, so lots of blokes popped in here early an' all. We'll put the word out, one o' them might have something, but everywhere was dead, Mr Athill, dead – no offence meant, o' course.'

'Two months on,' Athill grumbled, as they stepped back onto the pavement. 'Might as well never have happened.' He stuffed his hands into his pockets. 'Get on home, get a cuddle and some kip. I'll do the south stretch,' nodding up St Ann's Road towards Holland Park and the gentry, 'for an hour or two.' Bourton thanked him. He suddenly needed to be off his feet. Athill sighed. 'Let's try again tomorrow afternoon. And tell you what, why don't you bring old Pontiac along?'

24

Anna woke him at seven for root vegetable soup with bacon bits and, once scoffed, a foot bath. 'You need to watch these, Dick Bourton,' separating his toes, an unsettling move, intimate, invasive, 'find a sitting job. Or only walk eight hours a day rather than fourteen. Or these will give up on you. Or your legs.'

'Done worse.' Sounding grumpier than he meant.

'I know, but you don't have to. Stop volunteering. You're a civilian now.'

'And if more civilians volunteered then perhaps the country wouldn't be so bloody miserable and we wouldn't be living in one room.' He flushed. He knew he couldn't make sense of what he'd just said, even if it was logic through and through.

'It's a lovely room,' she knelt like a geisha and gazed steadily into his eyes, 'a lovely married home. You are a good man for earning for it, and a good man for carrying burdens that others will not.' Her hands were on his knees now and while her voice had softened it was yet more emphatic. 'But when you volunteer it affects me and us. It has brought you illness and kept us apart. It has nearly killed you. So please listen to me, Dick Bourton, when I tell you it is someone else's turn now.'

*

Roll-call. A rash of counterfeit fivers, nastiness between ponces likely as the Maltese vice gangs expand west, Cohen's schmatter shop cleaned out last night. And a Crown Court date for Christopher Granger, charged with the attempted murder of PCs Parkin, Prentice and Bourton, namely 2 May. 'So some of you will be needed as witnesses,' said Harbison. 'You'll be early worm for the duration, and the rest, be aware – there will be press.'

Granger . . . Bourton hadn't forgotten him, exactly, just put the memory of him in a part of his brain where he'd not be needed, alongside stuff like, say, how the Union Castle shipping line wanted its second-class crystal buffed. And now he was going to have to get out a lint-free cloth.

Only later, on Beat Three, walking up to the Cock in Bottle to make sure they didn't have a lock-in, it hit him. Anna: he'd never said a word of it to her, but in ten days' time, there he'd be, steps of the Bailey, Pathé cameras rolling: 'Here are the three officers whose heroism brought this desperado to bay: PC Parkin, recovering from the terrible wound he suffered that night; PC Bourton, attacked twice by Granger; and PC Prentice who, armed only with a truncheon, brought the gunman to the ground' – and Anna still thinking coppering was bunions, checking doors and helping old dears across the road. What the hell was he going to say? More to the point, when?

*

He certainly didn't say it the next morning: guilt made him dilly-dally after his turn to ensure she'd left for work by the time he got home. He slept solidly for seven hours, too tired to toss and turn, but had time for a quick wash and shave before joining Athill at Mancini's.

The detective talked through the morning's canvass as Bourton gobbled sausages and mash. The Rifle Place laundry club didn't convene until spring. There were lads in Bertram Terrace most afternoons after school, or throughout the day, off and on, over spring and summer, but not so much in winter or after dark. The coal hole under 9 Bertram Terrace was the preserve of a Michael and Teresa Platt – wed two years but rooming with her mum on Sirdar Road – who'd meet for some energetic hanky-panky two, three times a week.

'Who told you that?' asked Bourton, surprised that anyone would know.

'The mum.' They considered the strangeness of that domestic arrangement. 'Probably sends them out the door with a wink.'

'Teresa gets pregnant, she becomes a housing priority.'

'See?' said Athill. 'Judging again.' And no one had seen anyone around Bertram Terrace that day. 'Have you noticed everyone can remember that day, but no one can remember seeing anyone else?'

'Might be a mystery, Mr Athill.'

'Watch it.'

They found Poniak waiting for them at Bertram Terrace, leaning against a wall, smoke in hand, white thatch above the turned-up collar of his patched tweed jacket, making hand-me-downs and debris look exotic, as if he were an advertisement for a continental cigarette. 'Hey, Korea copper,' he raised his cigarette in an abbreviated salute, 'and other copper, you annoy any Lithuanians lately?'

'I got plans,' said Athill, sticking his hand out.

'Good to have plans,' Poniak shook, 'and cigarettes.'

'Mr Senkus still alive, then?'

'As far as I know,' said Poniak. 'But what I know?' He smiled. 'Senkus know nothing too. So, show me this writing.'

They dropped into the coal hole in front of what had been number 8 and Bourton steered Poniak into the little tunnel. He scanned the brickwork. 'Ah, this, ah . . . "Lithuania lives." And this – this is names, dead dates, not full names, like code names partisans choose so their families are not killed.' Bourton nodded, remembering Buzzy saying something similar. 'Senkus is Vejas, wind, this one bear-killer, this one eagle . . .' He scanned the walls. 'He does a lot of writing here. This French, army writing. This . . . this is a Lithuanian song, old song, a girl, her boy leaves the village for the winter. Strange song for Senkus.' He looked at them over his shoulder. 'It is very *girl.*' He returned to the brickwork. 'This is about free fish, English, some other man write, strange. So, Senkus again, he does not like the MGB, wants to make a bonfire of them, burn alive. Him and every Lithuanian.'

'MGB?' asked Athill.

'Soviet secret police. Only they have an army too.'

'Why's he doing all this?' asked Athill, offering a smoke. Poniak came out of the tunnel to take it and light up.

'His place? He does not have anywhere else.' He shrugged. 'Perhaps, also, he is being a partisan again. Most of the time they live in holes in the ground, in the woods. For years.'

'Years?'

'Years. Since 'forty-four, some of them. Of course, most are dead or in gulag.' A cynical smile. 'Our history, you do not know. The Russians come in 'forty, out in 'forty-one. When they come back in 'forty-four, some people fight, hoping Britain, America will come and help. And keep fighting. Some may be fighting now. Though Britain and America did not come. Doing other things.' The two policemen said nothing. 'So perhaps that hole is a kind of home. Someone like Senkus, he is not good with soft things any more.'

'Who are you afraid was trying to kill him?' asked Athill.

'MGB,' Poniak said evenly, as if the question had been expected.

Which it probably had, thought Bourton. *With Poniak being author-ised to say so much. And being a bolshy beggar, saying more . . .* 'Why?' he asked.

'They hunt people down.'

'Senkus?' Athill's disbelief was genuine. 'He's hardly bloody Trotsky.'

'He's famous, in a little way.' He smiled. 'Really. He beat them. He walked out. Last year. Most of his unit was killed or captured but he walked out. All free Lithuanians know about Vejas' long walk.'

'Through the Iron Curtain?' asked Athill, unconvinced.

'Some places,' Poniak said, 'the iron is rust away.'

★

'Balls,' spat Athill, once Poniak had ironically tugged his forelock and left. 'I may not be a secret agent but if the Russians were going to kill him they wouldn't bash his head in with a brick off some rubble pile. They'd come prepared, some kind of assassin – push him out the window if they didn't want anyone to know, ice-pick if they did. Yes?'

'Sounds right.'

'MGB? Rot. And if Senkus hadn't climbed out and you hadn't found him, he might've been there for weeks. What use would that be?' He scanned the Dale as if a suspect might conjure himself from the streets. 'Whatever happened to Senkus happened down here, for reasons got nothing to do with spies or partisans. He got into his hole, started drinking and thinking about his mates, and at some point that afternoon he either got into that other hole and got bashed, or he got bashed on his own turf and the brick got dumped. Either way, the Red Peril got nothing to do with it. And unless we talk to every single bugger who uses this bombsite, we haven't a prayer of finding out who or why.'

Suddenly he smiled. 'Tell you what, though.' He fished out his smokes. 'In the meantime you can get down there with your notebook and copy all those scribbles.'

'All of 'em?'

'All of 'em.' He lit up. 'First rule of detecting, get a lackey. Off you go. I got work to do.' He pointed his smoke. 'And if you find any bones, leave 'em be. Kids found a skull in a bombed-out house on St Mark's Road in 'forty-nine, give me no end of trouble.'

25

The connections in Bert Parkin's brain . . .

'You seen a picture called *The Blue Lamp*?' The two of them at attention in front of the grey-stippled mirror in the Old Bailey's latrines, inspecting each other for lint and exhaust smuts, Bourton still slightly awed by his first time amid the stonework, the gowns, the milling press.

'Can't say I have.'

'Came out a couple of years ago. Some of it was filmed in the Dale – well, North Pole way.'

'Still no.'

'Got that Derek Bogarde in it.'

'Nope.'

'Copper gets shot in it.'

'Nope.'

'Well, Vera says I look just like him. The actor.'

'Dirk Bogarde?'

'No. The copper. Dixon.'

'Oh, right. Should look it up.'

'Wouldn't take Anna to it. Dixon gets killed.'

'Right.'

'You tell her yet?'

'What?' Bourton was now thoroughly lost.

'About the shooting and that.'

'Oh. Sort of,' said Bourton. 'Told her about the trial and being a witness and so on.'

'Mention guns at all?'

'Well, the one that shot you.'

Parkin smiled. 'Hoping she won't add two and two?'

'Hoping she won't hear about two and two. She does, I'll be branded with fours.'

'In marriage honesty comes with coupons, that's what I say,' said Parkin. He nodded at himself, pleased either with his turnout or his philosophy. 'Give 'em a little bit at a time.'

★

Sitting alone on the bench – Bert already torturing Court Number Three with his logic – Bourton thought, She'll find two and two, it's a cert. Never mind the newsreels, the papers will have a field day. Six weeks into marriage to a woman he felt he'd known for ever and he didn't know what he could tell her and when. Typical of Bert to declare you had to ration honesty, then not to reveal which bits were off the books. Wise, and at the same time no bloody use at all.

'491 Police Constable Richard Arthur Bourton!' He stood, gave his tunic a tug, his boots a cursory glance, and walked to the doors. Here goes, he thought. Keep it simple . . .

★

Looking back on it later, it got jumbled, Crown and defending counsel and even Anna afterwards reduced to snapshots randomly reshuffled.

Defending counsel, 'Could it not have been one of the fog running charges, set off by a train?' and to the first titters, 'Not unless it had a muzzle flash and was fired from waist height twenty feet above the tracks'; and then later, 'But it was a dark night, a foggy night, and a very small bullet. How did you know where it went?' In reply, fed up with the man's efforts to make Granger look like a lad on a lark, 'Because I've been shot at before,' to laughs, including from the judge, 'in 1944, 'forty-five, 'forty-six, 'forty-seven, 'fifty and 'fifty-one. I'd been hoping 'fifty-two would be a year off,' the laughs a chorus now, the public gallery looking like the circle at the Palladium.

Anna, patient but unhappy, head framed against the Lyons Corner House window: 'But I knew, Richard.'

'How?'

'Through a strange little man called Mr Christie.' The second time he'd heard that name. 'I see him around. He says he knows Rex Athill.'

The Crown: 'So you believe Granger tried to kill you three times?'

Pause, while he weighed his oath against gainsaying the Crown (jowly, plummy, extravagant hand gestures), and opted not to break the law. 'No, twice, sir. By the railway line and on Ladbroke Grove. In the cemetery he was trying to kill PC Prentice. I was just holding his coat.'

But no matter what order the snapshots from that day got shuffled into, the final picture, the one he always came back to, was Granger's mother: outside the Bailey when the day was done, him and Bert lighting up by the railings, Maurice Prentice in the doorway smiling gormlessly for the newspapers, and the woman emerging from a huddle of Sunday best. 'I'm Mrs Granger, Christopher's mother.' He nodded, wondering what he would say to her apology. *Not a lot, probably.* 'Why were you saying those things?' Both hands white-knuckled on her bag so she wouldn't point, because pointing would be rude. 'He wanted you to stop chasing him, no more, he never meant to hurt you, either of you.' Then silence, her mouth working as she emptied herself of excuses his brain chose not to hear, until he stuck his hand out, as if she were a motor nudging into traffic.

'Mrs Granger, you need to find whoever sold your boy that gun and thank him. Because if he hadn't sold him a dud, I'd be dead, PC Parkin would be dead, PC Prentice would be dead, and your boy would never have made it out of that cemetery alive. The only thing,' getting a head of steam, 'between him and his maker is a broken extractor. And you can put that in your church hat and smoke it.'

26

Another doorstep, grey plaster, cracks in the brickwork, paint peeling around the letterbox, watching Athill bang the knocker and wait. Blimey, ain't you a patient man, thought Bourton. A turn here, another there, where theft or assault or a counterfeit-coupon ring would allow, Bourton joining him now and again, footsore in civvies, the pretend detective at his master's shoulder, the two of them banging across the Dale like a fly butting window panes, trying to find out everyone who'd used that bloody bombsite, been mentioned in its graffiti, so they could talk to them. Everyone in the Dale must know they were looking at the terrace – they had to, 'cos no one was using it any more: they'd all been scared away. The coppers never seemed to get any nearer what they needed, but still Athill did his bit. And Bourton didn't know how.

'Where d'you go in your head,' he asked him, by a front gate in Avondale Park Gardens, birdsong and weeds and unpointed brickwork, 'when it's not going anywhere?'

'Everywhere,' said Athill, 'nowhere. Run through old drills. Remember what Dot wants me to get done.' He walked up to the door and knocked. 'Anything important gets in the way. Finding it hard?' Bourton nodded. 'You'll get used to it.' He stepped back to peer in the front window. 'No one about.' He checked his watch. 'Besides, it's not usual to get so little return.' He turned and gestured at the street. Bourton held the gate for him. 'Mind you, it's hardly usual to be asked by no one in particular not to investigate an attack on someone you're not allowed to talk to, happened three months ago.' He banged the gate shut behind him. 'Waste of time. In fact, I may be about to disappoint you, but the whole thing's a waste of time, and it's time no one in particular got told. Let's get a brew.'

Betsy's behind the drill hall was full, give or take, Athill getting careful nods as they threaded their way through to the back. 'Fatty

Romero, holding court,' said Athill, jerking a thumb at the huddle of men in jackets and mackintoshes, no concessions to the May mugginess, across three tables in the centre of the room. 'Bookie's runner from the Bush. I think he collects for a bloke White City way. Didn't know this was his patch now.' He stirred his brew with a spoon tethered to the wall by a tea-stained string. 'You been thinking about your old girl at all? Bewley Street way?'

Gladys Hartham. 'I thought you were going to see if there was another way at it.'

'I did say that.' Athill took off his hat as he stirred. 'Scout's honour, what do you think happened?'

'Someone killed her. Someone she was expecting and dressed up for.'

'Why?'

'Don't know.'

Athill took a sip, steam or sweat beading on his moustache. 'How did he do it?'

'Don't know.'

'But the doc says it wasn't murder. It was what dozens of old dears die of every fog.'

'He probably wasn't looking very hard.'

'Agreed,' said Athill. 'But he probably knew what he was looking at.' He took a long swig of tea. 'Let's say the visitor is a wrong 'un. If the doctor says it wasn't murder, then the visitor's a thief, or a conman, or a rival for your old bloke in the canal, but he isn't a murderer.' He sounded certain but tentative, trying not to offend. 'Why are you sure he is?'

'Because . . .' As he lined up the anomalies he realised they'd already been dismissed more than once and weren't what the DC wanted to hear. Suddenly he knew that Athill wanted something else entirely, the spark that turned anomalies into certainties, the primal trigger that stood hairs on end – the untouched gramophone in the half-empty cellar, loose gravel on cobbles in a *pavé* street, the hawthorn bough in a laurel hedge . . .

What is it?

'It's the fog. He doesn't call on her in daylight. When it's clear. When she opens the door she's the only one can see his face.'

'Perhaps that's the only time . . .'

Bourton shook his head hard. '*No.* A traveller who calls after tea? People are at the pub or listening to the wireless.' But more was needed. 'It's that . . .

'No. Right. War story. Korea. November 'fifty, way up in the north, pushing to the Chinese border. I'm in an American regimental HQ, we've got their supply route and I go up to see their dispositions, pick up any int. And they're having the dickens of an argy. They think the Chinese are coming into Korea and they're exposed, stuck out in the mountains on their own. They want to pull back to somewhere safer. But command in Japan won't listen. MacArthur's won his war, he's said there are no Chinks, lo and behold, his Int people say, No Chinks. Where are their vehicles? Where are their fires? These GIs are imagining things. The only threat is what's left of the North Korean army and they've had it. So everyone will stay put.

'But the Chinks haven't got any trucks, they're doing without fires. They're crossing the border, hundreds of thousands of 'em, carrying everything they need. They eat cold food, sleep under bushes during the day, move at night. The evidence that MacArthur says proves there are no Chinks in Korea proves there are. And when 14076868 Sergeant Bourton RA says, "I've bloody *seen* Chinks in Korea – I've spent six months in Hong Kong watching them buggers other side of the wire, I *know* what they look like, we killed a bunch of 'em Friday last, did for one myself", do they listen? Do they heck. MacArthur's a genius, he knows his business, There Are No Chinks In Korea.' He banged the table for emphasis. 'Two nights later, Chinks come down in their thousands and cut them off, and before the week's out, most of those lads are dead, and I'm a prisoner with a hole in my leg and my wrists wired together.' He wiped away the spittle at the corner of his mouth. 'That's why I think he did it.'

'Blimey,' said Athill. 'Someone touched a nerve.' He looked around the room, avoiding Bourton's eye. 'So, no proof is proof, is that right? CID should be a shoo-in for you.' He turned to the bottom of his mug for inspiration. 'All right,' he said, finally looking up. 'Got a name? Got a company? Got a description? Got a "Meet the 'cyclopaedia man at eighteen hundred"?' Bourton shook his head. Athill stuck his hands out palm up – Cheap at half the price, chum! 'Surely you can see that you can't prove it. Can you? In fact, not only can't you prove it, you don't even have anywhere to start. Even if you're right, someone you got no description of, no name, has killed her for a reason you don't know, in a way that don't show, leaving no evidence, and stolen away in the fog. Jesus Christ, it makes Senkus look open and shut.' He reached for his cigarettes. 'Leave it.'

'Rex—'

'*Leave it*. There's nothing there. For God's sake, you've got a knockout wife, it's spring . . .' Bourton's smile was grudging. 'Perhaps something will come along – perhaps, I don't know . . . But in the meantime,' shaking out a smoke, 'why don't you make a baby or two?'

27

'Puffed up like pigeons,' muttered Stratfull, as a super and chief inspector Bourton had never seen before swaggered to the front of the roll-call room, every copper in the nick filing in behind to find space around the walls. 'Something's up.'

'Atten-shun!' called Adams, and everyone stood as upright as they could. 'Silence, please, for Superintendent McGee.' So that's the divisional commander, thought Bourton. Sharp eyes, jutting chin, looks like he thinks he's a Leader of Men.

'You will all be aware of the events surrounding the arrest of Christopher Edward Granger for the attempted murder of PCs Parkin and Bourton of this station and Prentice of Harrow Road, and for robbery and assault occasioning at Phelan and Rose, pawnbrokers of Praed Street.' Whispers and nudges. 'Many of you will I am sure share my dissatisfaction at the fact that the ultimate penalty was not available to Mr Justice Hoban in this case, that the attempted murder of a police officer, let alone three, is not an automatic capital offence, no matter the age of the culprit.' Mutters of 'Hang 'im.' Granger had got three life sentences. 'However, there is one aspect of this case that is much more satisfactory, and of more than passing interest to this station.' He cleared his throat theatrically. 'Her Majesty the Queen,' utter quiet, 'has graciously approved the award of the George Medal to PCs Parkin,' a roar, Bourton joining in, and heads turning to cheer Bert, mouth hanging open, 'and Prentice, as well as a number of other awards.'

Other awards? For me? thought Bourton, appalled at a flash of envy even as he yelled his respect, Is there something for me?

McGee was making quieten-down gestures with his hands, and the sound dropped to a happy rumble. 'Now, I will not embarrass PC Parkin' – *If he's moved on there's nothing for me* – 'who I had the pleasure of guarding Lots Road with in 'twenty-six – yes, he goes back that far!' A cry somewhere of "Allo, Granddad!' and Stratfull's 'That'll be "Granddad GM", to you' – 'I won't embarrass him by reading out the citation. All I will say is that it reflects only a fraction of his worth.' *A nice touch – almost makes up for the reminder that 25 years in, Bert's still a PC* ... 'We all know, and Her Majesty now knows of PC Parkin's courage that night. What the citation does not make clear is that Granger and his accomplice would have escaped scot-free if PC Parkin had not spotted, on a foggy night, in a dark car, that they looked suspicious. So very well done, PC Parkin. You are an example to all of us.' He waved a piece of paper. 'The collective citation will be on the station notice-board.' The room was a cheery mob before the VIPs reached the door.

Bourton managed to grab Bert's sleeve, 'Well done, Bert,' genuinely happy for him, 'you earned it,' but he wasn't sure Bert heard him amid the to and fro.

'There a pension with that?'

'You'll get to meet the Queen, chum.'

And from Bert, dazed, slightly appalled, 'What'll Vera wear? You can't meet the Queen on coupons . . .'

Bourton struggled through the crowd towards the door, wearing a smile that felt more like a wound, Good old Bert. He found himself waiting beside Leakey for a blockage in the doorway to clear.

'Told you,' said Leakey. 'You deserve that gong, not him. He just got shot.'

'He saved my life, most like,' said Bourton, sharply. 'I reckon that'll do. 'Sides,' realising that his anger was with himself for thinking the same ungenerous thing, 'I've been shot before, three times,' *if you count mortar and tank fragments as bullets*, 'and if that's what it takes to get a gong, he can keep it.'

★

He sat on their bed, boots off, the citation in his fist, watching Anna busy herself with a brew, legs bare beneath the old army shirt whose spare button had branded her thigh in her sleep. He felt a bit awkward – never won anything before, just his stripes, and those he'd earned through hard work, competence, and other blokes copping it, whereas this . . .

'You know that night Bert got shot?' She turned and nodded severely; she'd derived an Old Testament satisfaction from Granger's fate. 'Well, the Queen's giving him a medal for it. A big one. Like the DCM, for civvies.' She nodded. *Good girl, knows her gongs.* He held out the sheet. 'This says why.'

She wiped her fingers and took the paper. 'So, George Medal, Police Constable Albert Edward Parkin . . .' She cast down the page, then started. 'But it mentions you, Richard, "Queen's Commendation for Brave Conduct". Her Majesty is giving you a medal?'

'Well, a little one. Like a mention in despatches – I get a leaf to sew on.'

'I will sew it on.' She sat beside him and held his hand. '"Constable Bourton followed the man across the tracks . . ."' She gripped more tightly. 'He shot at you . . . "Constable Bourton pursued the man onto Ladbroke Grove . . . The man stopped a taxi at gunpoint . . ."'

'Not quite right, that bit,' Bourton offered helpfully. 'Taxi sort of ran him over, really.'

'"The man pointed his gun . . . Constable Bourton warned the other officers . . . Constable Parkin ran at the man, warning Constable Bourton . . ."' Not sure that can be right, thought Bourton, Bert not being a runner as such. '". . . and was seriously wounded. Mr Jaggs, despite the risk . . ."'

'He saved Bert's life, that cabby, game old bloke.'

She looked into Bourton's eyes. 'This is you, Richard, all you. The big medals for everyone else, but you—'

'I didn't try to take him on. Bert, Maurice Prentice – read on, he had a go, Maurice, lucky not to cop it – even the first lads through the wall into the cemetery, they were taking him on, sticking their necks out. Me, I was just winding it in.'

'So you're learning.' She'd dropped the citation to the floor and was holding both his hands in her lap. 'Like Rex says, you come home at the end of the turn.' She suddenly reached forward and kissed him hard, a particularly insistent full stop. 'I am so proud of you, Richard Arthur Bourton, Queen's Bravery Man. And I am most proud that you do not have the George Medal, like Bert, or the British thingummy

Medal, like Mr Jaggs. Do you know why?' Bourton shook his head, knowing it was a woman's question no man would answer right. 'Because there is no future for men with medals. And you I married because I wanted a future.' She lay down awkwardly and pulled him over to spoon beside her. 'Let's cuddle, my Bravery Man.'

So they spooned, her breasts hard against his back, hips cupping his wide dray-horse arse, the body that could drag him urgent from the deepest sleep somehow reassuring and calming, absorbing his disappointment. He could feel himself getting used to things. He smiled. She could probably get him used to almost anything.

A few minutes later, as he was about to drop off, something occurred to him. 'Sorry I can't get you to meet the Queen,' he offered. 'Only the medals do that.'

'I am glad,' said Anna. 'You would stare at her *tétons*.' He looked back at her in puzzlement. 'Tits, Richard. You like tits. And she has great tits.'

His jaw dropped. 'That's the *Queen*.'

She laughed her dirty laugh, a huge bass burst of glee. 'And you think she doesn't do this?' She sat up, pulling the shirt over her head, and pointed her breasts at him like headlamps. 'Trousers off. We have twenty minutes for riding school.'

★

She closed the front door, turned, sniffed the air and, poof!, their interlude was gone.

The May mist was different. Yes, things were obscured – the buses on the Grove were just red boxes labouring up the hill, the people Monet smudges. But it was grey not yellow, with no sulphur, no metallic tang, no clamping cold. It wasn't a kind mist, like the spring haze up in the Territories away from the reek of the harbour, moisture with a hint of grass and wild garlic, or even a sea mist, laced with half-burned oil from the *Dee*'s bunkers – but it wasn't a cruel one, either. It didn't make her cough, like that April fog . . .

Her eyes passed over the plate outside Dr Reid's surgery, and once more she felt the urge to step in, mention that the fog had troubled her in April and could he listen to her chest? But Dr Reid worked for the government – not socialist any more, no longer the atheists who stole what they could, but still a government, that made rules, and took notes, and talked to itself, department to department, letters and meetings about which one never heard, until one day they led you to a room smelling of sweat and vomit to show you your lies . . . What if Dr Reid found out that her cough was an old one? A gift from before she answered the health form's 'Do you suffer, or have you ever suffered, from a respiratory illness?' with 'No'? Then he would tell, and the officials would talk and meet, examine her forms, and invite her into that room to tell her they were sending her back . . .

She shook her head. *Melodrama! Next I will be conjuring up a sick-bed with blood-spotted linen and a doomed lover flitting around my feet* . . . But melodrama or no, London's winter fog, the little she'd seen of it, had made her cough – a cough like the one she'd taken from Harbin, that condemned girls to the chimneys, without even a last visit to the stirrups to see if they were still clean, girls who had become evidence so must turn into ash . . .

What do others do against the fog? Masks? Pills? A backstreet man, a Monsieur Chen or Docteur Tsang, with home cures? Like Mr Christie, confusing his lungs with garlic mayonnaise . . . She shook her head again. How much could she ask without giving too much away? And who did she ask?

She sidestepped around a girl in a light striped cotton dress, wrong for the weather, wrong for her thick waist and sideboard legs. But the girl didn't care: she had a smile on her face, a long, powerful stride, and two, three men turning to watch her solid buttocks eat up the pavement. *British defiance, in clothes – wearing it is a mistake, but I will wear it, and it will work.*

Merde, thought Anna. *I will not surrender to the melodrama. I will ask the questions when I need to. And November is another country* . . .

Now that the end of winter had stopped play, the Traveller had more time to think.

Often enough he'd turn to the war. And miss it. He tried to remember call-outs from start to finish – the minutes between the siren and the telephone bell, as the lads would fidget, joke, check loads, smoke; the drive through blacked-out streets backlit by fire, around rubble, ruptured mains, holes where roadway used to be; and the tunnel or ladder or splintered rafters that led him through a bombsite to a casualty needing hand-holding, splinting, easing into a harness, or the freeing of their soul. But he had no memento of the smell of those days – of explosives, rubble, gas, sweat, fear, blood, sewers. Even his bombsites – old favourites he'd visit in the hope that rubble and darkness would bring back the rescue game whole – were as false and lifeless as a museum. So all he had were snapshots: jokes around a card-table, a botched drill, bodies coming back after a cave-in, a gaffer holding back the rubble as he'd pulled out one of his lads. And the faces of casualties – when they knew what he was and, sometimes, when they knew what was to come . . .

More often, though, he'd sit in his little den, when the outside world allowed, and he'd hold a ring, or a watch, a scarf with a last whisper of scent, and dwell on the soul who'd owned it, and how he'd set it free. A word in the street or on the bus, courting chats, and then, as the air turned acid and the city half blind, liberation – a ticking clock in a still parlour, the smile or nod that let him begin, the eyes as the penny dropped, the electric moment as flesh lost will and the soul soared free. Sometimes he suspected he might be putting a face, a voice, a room with the wrong memento, remembering something that didn't quite happen. But then he'd console himself that in any case the soul was freed, and resolve that, come the winter, his new trophies would signal soul, place and time.

It always paid to prepare.

PART THREE
Twilight

28

'Korea this 'ot, then, Sergeant Bourton?' Don Flett from Silchester Road, bony little shoulders jutting from his vest, a dhobi-grey handkerchief knotted round his forehead, hair bristle-short for the nits or the summer.

'Yep,' said Bourton, looking round his semi-circle of a dozen recruits, fidgeting in excitement, eyes eager; and at their heart Derek Jeffrey, shrouded in a threadbare army singlet, sweating under a cap comforter – probably aiming to look like a Commando, or even (touching, this) British-Army-in-Korea. The boy was too keyed-up to grin, but he still hummed with cat-got-cream for having finally lassoed Bourton to run through some drills. 'And you know what it smelt of, this hot?' The boys shook their heads. 'S-h-i-t.' Faces twisted in disgust. 'They use it as fertiliser. There we'd be, advancing across some field' – overegging it: Bourton hadn't really advanced anywhere, unless by jeep – 'and you'd pass the old blokes in funny hats, spreading it on their cabbages.'

'What about that Palestine?' asked Derek, showing ownership by knowing Bourton's career better than his paybook.

'Even hotter. And you know what it smelt of when it was hot?' They all shook their heads expectantly. 'O-r-a-n-g-e-s.' A groan of disappointment. 'Orange groves everywhere. Right!' He stood up theatrically and the boys followed suit. 'Let's start with section attacks.'

Two hours of scrambling up and down the rubble was enough to give everyone a shot at section 2ic, or gunner or loader on Pete's mum's broomstick that served as a Bren; the boys were marked with barked knees, brick dust, nettle-stings and reddened shoulders, chaffed each other, and glowed. They swigged warm water from Bill Nickerson's canteens, replayed the battles of the morning, and told lies, just like real infantrymen. Bourton stood in the shade and smiled. *Could be on Salisbury Plain.*

'Right, lads!' Heads swivelled. 'Next we're going to do a little field-craft. I'll walk you over the rubble, show you what makes a sound, what doesn't. Then we're going to team up and try to creep up on each other. All right?' They nodded. 'With a bit of luck you'll slink like Chink or spook like Gook, filtering through those Yank lines. So, Corporal Jeffrey,' Derek as organiser had hogged section command for himself, 'allocate oppos, please.'

★

Another hour and they were played out, sitting against a shaded broken wall, eyes closed, mouths open, grime tracks down their chests and the odd muscle twitching from exhaustion. Sergeant Bourton felt a wicked urge to get them up, run a last exercise, but they were only twelve. *Still, you want to play soldiers, that's what it's about.*

The boys drained the canteens, staggered upright, tried out their salutes and clumped stiffly home to their dinners, Pete with the broomstick across his shoulders, hands looped over it like a real Bren. Bourton would have idled his way home but an idea had hit him while they were practising knifing sentries and he walked Derek, Don and Terry to the prefabs instead. The boys were too exhausted to say much, and when he stopped opposite Bertram Terrace, no more than a hundred yards from Derek's front door, they seemed glad to creak to a halt. Bourton nodded at the bombsite.

'You ever play there, Derek?'

The boy paused to let the question filter through. 'Mum won't let me.'

Bourton smiled. 'And you haven't tried to change her mind? Or ignored her?'

Derek shook his head. 'She knew 'em. Family in number thirteen. She charred for 'em when she was a girl. Says it's haunted.'

Bourton looked at the other two and they seemed uneasy. 'And what about you?' Terry looked at Derek, who nodded. 'Weeeell . . . when I was little.' *Says a twelve-year-old.* Terry jammed his hands in his pockets and looked away guiltily.

'Terry,' quietly, 'I'm asking as the law, son.' Derek had tensed. 'You can say.'

Terry shrugged in apology. 'An' about a year ago.'

'Terr—' Derek, surprised.

'I walk past it every time I come down,' more to his friend than his interrogator, 'every day for years, an' I thought, Well, let's see.' A touch defiant. 'An' no one came out. There's no ghosts. Just rats. Sorry.'

'It's all right,' said Derek. 'I think.'

'You've not played there since?' A mulish shake of the head – a little Dale defiance of the law. 'You're sure?'

Terry nodded. 'It's not as if I got that many mates.' *And Derek's friends don't go to Bertram Terrace . . .*

'But all over the Dale people say boys play there,' said Bourton. 'Who then?'

'Dunno.' Derek. *Ignorant or unhelpful?* 'But not us. An' not no one who's real Dale,' he offered. 'The Caseys all suffocated an' Mrs Tarrant drowned in 'er cellar.' He braced as if about to defy the Gestapo. 'An' anyone who's Dale knows that's not a place you play.'

★

Three weeks of baking heat had recast the city – every street a parade of net curtains and opened windows, every front garden a patch of seaside, deckchairs and glasses of beer and pasty winter skin. Londoners wore smiles and the wrong clothes and the smell of sweat. And there was a wave of daytime burglaries and night-time argy-bargy, as the sticky and sleepless aired old grudges and magicked up new ones.

If front gardens were a patch of seaside, then the Thames foreshore was an ailing resort. Families, the old, kids with parents on weekend shifts, flirty lads and girls hoping for a little exposed flesh – all sorts had camped out at the high-tide mark, claiming patches of whiffy mud with cardboard or newspapers laid among the debris, hoping for a waft of cool air from the water. The occasional tough soul splashed in the river, until defeated by gluey mud or a jab from something sharp. And in the meantime the river's business carried on: coal barges chugging upstream to feed Battersea or Lots Road, scrap metal heading downstream to some Essex smelter, a River Police launch trawling for suicides and waving the odd swimmer away from Tower Bridge's lethal eddies.

And in the foreground, cool, intelligent profile alert to the whole show, Anna – sitting upright on a mat of cardboard, legs tucked under, glorious *tétons* silhouetted by sunlight through her Hong Kong cotton blouse, glowing with hereness and curiosity and fun. Bourton looked at his thick legs and padded middle. *I'm the dray horse and you're the show pony. How did I catch you? And what's keeping you with me? Richard Arthur Bourton, the plodding provider? Or your loyalty, and generosity, and gumption?*

She leaned back on straight arms. 'They should build a pier. Or put fairground rides on Tower Bridge. Then we would really be on holiday.' She turned to him. 'This is very strange, yes? This really doesn't happen often?'

He shrugged. 'I'm no more a Londoner than you, love.'

She shook her head. 'Can't be. There would be fish-and-chip shops, or little shellfish stands.' Three bare-chested lads on the strand, with mud-spattered shins, changed direction, eyes on Anna's cleavage. She rolled onto her front and rested her hands on the mud. 'Your recruits.' Blank. 'Playing soldiers.' He nodded. 'Was that just playing soldiers?' His confusion must have shown. 'You weren't doing a little detecting, too?'

He looked away. 'Well, I mean . . . Just at the end. It weren't the idea,' he said hastily, 'it just came to me, you know, at the end . . .'

She was nodding. 'That I believe. You are not – *guileful*, Richard. A secret motive and those boys, bombsite boys, they would not have come.' Her give-and-take smile, new to him since marriage – a teaspoon each of concession and expectation. 'Please, don't make it a habit, my love. I like our crazy life – no, I love it. Starting when you end, our evenings, our weekends, making love at strange times, this,' she jerked her head at the scene behind her, 'the beach before your turn . . . It's our marriage.' A wholly French shrug. 'It is what we have made. And when you go detecting your mind is always elsewhere, and you are tired, and sore.' She waved a mock naughty-boy finger. 'And unpaid. When you are on the clock you are theirs. When you are not, you are mine.' She patted his knee. 'Keep me happy, Richard.

I am a very simple girl, you know.' He snorted and her eyebrows climbed in surprise. 'No, really, I am. Love, sex, food, laughter. Everything else – *everything* else – it's just . . .' she shrugged '. . . pffft.'

'Pffft?'

'Pffft.' She was smiling again. 'Sometimes English is very shit.'

29

September 1952

They'd caught the last of summer, even if brown leaf-tips warned that autumn was near. They'd started in Ampney St Mark for Dave Packer's snares and his dad's fruit and veg and hiked east, to see the Thames before the factories and cities had their say. They found a private reed-patch just outside Lechlade, swam naked through chest-deep water with a bottom current streaming cold around their shins, and dried off in a muddy crouch; then after his mother's corned-beef sangers they walked through the town, Anna looking like a water-nymph clothed to please the censors, and headed across the flood plain, through a wheat haze.

A mile or so out of Faringdon they knocked on a farmhouse door, negotiated bivvy rights, morning milk and eggs, and camped in a stand of willows above a stream. They had bread and cheese and his dad's cucumber and tomatoes for tea, and found that lying down to try to tickle the fish, hip to hip, brought other things to mind. Then the midges started hovering, and his Yankee Deet came out to deter them, and the second and third times they made love there was a sweet acid overlay to her scent of sweat and musk and woodsmoke – a cocktail he knew would be in his brain when he was seventy and ga-ga. *Anna Timofeyeva Bourton, you are my all.*

They were woken in the morning by the dairyman moving the herd, and made love with muted giggles as he passed not ten yards from their heads. Afterwards Bourton collected the food and milk, still warm in the bottle, and they gorged themselves on eggy bread and a fried egg apiece, and hard-boiled the last three in the kettle; their tea had poached egg-white bobbing through the leaves. *For the first time since you got here, girl, you haven't had to stint.* He felt proud.

They washed in the stream, enjoyed a little hanky-panky, packed up and swung slowly south-east across the Vale, the Berkshire Downs a haze-set bump in the flat ground. They ate lunch on a knoll under a lightning-blackened hornbeam, tomatoes, apples, the last of the bread and cheese, and gloried in the view: to the south the Uffington White Horse a hesitant slash on the wavy green face of the Downs, to the north Folly Hill, with the tower standing sentry, and below it the hum of the Swindon road, the traffic dots and dashes of muted colour across the signalpad of the Vale. Then over the railway line and the dry ditch of the old canal, and by half three they were at Burleaze Farm, where he'd learned the land wasn't for him.

Madge Leitch was in the kitchen, shorter, squarer, muscled red arms scrubbing a sheet in the sink. She squealed obligingly when he appeared in the doorway – 'Dicky Bourton! Ain't you the sight!' – and then when she'd looked him up and down and measured his width, 'An' if we'd known you'd turn out like this we'd have kept you an' sold the tractor!' They sat down for a brew and a chat: the farm – 'We got another fourteen acres, but finding the labour . . .'; her girls – 'Joanna wed last year, David Horrobin, nice lad, surveyor, they're in Witney now, an' Eleanor, well, she's training to be a teacher, up in Birmingham – would you credit it?'; Anna – 'I swear, my dear, you could do a lot better than him'; and London – 'It's like Sixpence Quarry, that place, everyone dives in an' never comes back.' Then she led them to the first floor and her pride and joy, a bathroom – 'Put it in three year ago, I swear I'd live here if I could' – with a big cast-iron tub squatting under jerry-rigged pipework. They shared a near-scalding bath, sweating through the steam, dressed in clean clothes and walked down to the copse by the spring to pitch their camp, Bourton chuffed he could remember the way: he'd crossed a lot of fields since 1941.

A proper supper at the farmhouse: a saddle of roast hogget, a ration-busting statement of honour, and because the Leitches weren't minded towards leftovers, and they were all eating two hours after their custom, most of the meat was gone by half eight. Bob Leitch – browner, leaner, but still with grey wire-wool hair and subsiding-tombstone teeth – delighted in the extent of Bourton's hopelessness as a farm labourer. 'He learned how to drive a tractor, an' fit the right attachment, fair's fair. But bless him – one day I asked him to start on the barley, just the one field that year, it was the war so everythin' given over to wheat – so off he goes, I come down to the nine-acre twenty minutes later an' I can't find him, an' where is he? Over in the horseshoe, mowin' down the wheat, rat-a-tat-tat. An' it weren't even ripe!'

'To be fair,' said Bourton, 'in my head I were leading a tank charge up the Downs.'

Their bivvy was amid a trio of sycamores on the edge of the copse, where ivy bound the trees and some self-seeded elder into a windbreak, and midges searched for the spring. They slapped on his Yank insect-repellent and slept a long, Deet-tinged sleep, untroubled by bad dreams of east Asia.

*

Summer stayed for the week; freckling limbs, chaff in boots, and nights so warm he'd wake with only Deet between him and the stars. They'd sleep until they woke, ate when they were hungry and went where their feet or a lift could take them: White Horse Hill, the Lambourn gallops, the earthen forts that dotted the edge of the Downs.

They were like Borstal kids on a spree. On the Tuesday they marked White Horse Hill with a quick one in a deep ditch, her inhibitions about rutting outside like animals exploded in a moment, and after that Anna seemed bent on anointing every sight with a legover. They trespassed, engaged in public indecency, even pinched a couple of cobs of corn; they goaded each other to pee in the open, getting her bottom nettle-stung and his socks sodden when a walker's Springer interrupted. Often their mouths were purple from brambles and pockets stuffed with eaters from the branches jutting over garden walls.

Time without a shift change and skies without a roofline meant space to think, learn, understand. Anna's fascination with the idea that the land could provide was entertaining, then puzzling, until he remembered that, thanks to the Chinese civil war and then the Japs, she'd barely stepped outside the French Concession for eight whole years: food came from carts or gutters or ration points, not a field.

And he understood her devotion to the snares much better when she reminded him that in starving Shanghai even rats had had a price.

For the first time he also understood that there were limits to what she could accept about him. She couldn't fathom why he'd leave this idyll, couldn't see the other side, of hard winters, low pay, no other jobs when your first one went, no secrets, no fun. Nor would she accept there were limits to his country skills. When the snares stayed empty it was the fault of his cousin Dave – who even at ten had been the richest lad in the Ampneys from all the rabbit skins he sold for RAF flying jackets – not Bourton, who suspected he hadn't grasped the finer points of where the traps should go. Bourton knew he could strip a Bren, remember the rules of evidence, quell small disturbances with voice alone. What he couldn't do was be a countryman. Far as he was concerned, he was a Londoner who'd been born in the wrong skin. Far as she was concerned, he was the Last of the Gloucestershire Mohicans.

What if that was why she loved him?

The last morning she did the rounds of the snares at a sprint and he heard her whoops before he'd even left the copse. The rabbit was a big bugger, nearly the size of a hare, quivering with fear, right foreleg cinched by wire, rear right thumping the ground in some strange tic. It was staring towards the trees, ignoring Anna, hands on her hips and grinning as if she'd caught it with its paws in the biscuit tin.

'Watch it, Richard!' she ordered, pointing at it, then cantering back into the copse. *Poor devil. Least we're not a cat.* She was back within a minute, naked, glowing, eyes glistening, her right arm by her side. It must have taken him a full five seconds to speak.

'For Christ's sake, love, someone'll see you!'

'*Débrouillez-vous*, Richard,' beaming to split her face, '*débrouillez-vous!*' His old pattern bayonet emerged from beside her thigh. 'Make do,' she waved the blade, her right breast moving in sympathy, '*on se débrouille!* And you want me to thumb a lift, covered in blood? Or in wet clothes?' She had reached the rabbit. 'Be practical, Richard!' She pulled the rabbit's head back and slit its throat with a single hard slash that went through the spine. She held the head, bemused, as blood arced away, then dropped it, grabbed the body by the thrumming hind legs and pressed the stump of neck against the grass. 'We drain it, yes?' He nodded, not trusting himself to say anything. 'For how long?'

'Well, he's not a very big animal,' he tried, shocked. 'Probably, er, a minute will do.'

'OK.' Her cheeks glowed beneath the blood paintbrush-flicked across her face. One hand held the rabbit against the ground while the other loosened the snare. 'And then?'

'Well, take off the paws.'

Impatient, she laid the rabbit on its back, hacked and sawed at the feet in turn till they were mostly off, then put the bayonet down, wormed her fingers under the skin at the neck and pulled, the pelt easing off like a sea-boot. Then up with the bayonet, point on the sternum, a gentle lean forward and the ribcage split open with a snap, releasing a puff of steam from the innards. She cut clumsily at the mess of lights in a soup of blood, bone-chips like pearl barley on the surface of a broth. 'Blade is too long, I think,' she muttered, intent.

'Meant to give reach to a short rifle.' Surprise made him literal. 'Now, for gutting—'

'*Et voilà!*' She held up the rabbit by its hind legs, ribs open like the doors on a box of bloody keepsakes. 'My first rabbit!' She wiped something off her top lip, smearing blood and what might have been a fleck of liver across her cheek, and smiled with innocent accomplishment, scarlet streaking her ruddy arms and freckling her breast. 'We borrow a pan with a lid from Madge and we have our lunch.'

November 1952

Days like today . . .

The fog was in, but damp sat in the air, a rain that wouldn't come, and the Traveller could feel it seeping into the joints as if his bones were salt crystals soaking up the wet, the cold an extra edge, numbing, slowing . . . The water sat on his chest, bringing on the cough, a good clean cough, thick green slur with never a trace of soot, but enough to slow him, make him sorry for himself, want a fire and his Bovril instead of a stranger's front parlour and another soul flying free – and that cough would never do for freeing souls. What would he have to sell?

Days like today, he wondered if he was too old for the game, if he was being warned his time might soon be done, like a miner with the shivers or bloody lung. What would he do? Retire from a trade no one knew he'd had, like a knocking-shop needle-man? Or be found in harness, slumped over some old 'un, two souls climbing, invisible untethered balloons? Days like today might make a party think of his mortality, and that wasn't right at all.

His calling was to think of others'.

30

Roll-call. A new subdued relief. At the desk, Sergeant Tullow – severe, dark, cadaverous, not much warmth; different faces in the room. *And off we go.* Break-in last night, flat in Talbot Road backing onto the communal gardens; check for suspicious behaviour in the other communals dotting the ground. Rape on Barlby Road about 1900 hours, victim dragged into waste ground adjoining the railway line; suspect five foot eight, Scotch accent, khaki mackintosh, dark hair, seemed to know the turf. Trouble outside the Calypso Drinking Club on All Saints' Road at about 2000 hours; might be English lads against Caribbeans; move on any gatherings of young men in Portobello area. And as of 2040 hours, the Hill had its own coshing gang: a pedestrian assaulted on Bonchurch Road, no attempt to rob, with the assailants disappearing into the fog.

Tullow closed his muster book and scanned the room. 'You'll all have heard about the murder of PC Sidney Miles in Croydon last night. He was shot while trying to apprehend two armed men on a factory roof. He had twenty-two years' service; three commendations; and a wife. It appears he was first through the door onto a roof where the two suspects had already been firing at other officers for some time. He was shot between the eyes and killed instantly.' Pause. 'What you may not have heard is that the shooter is apparently sixteen.' A murmur of anger. 'So, like our Mr Granger, he won't hang.'

He came out from behind his lectern. 'Much in this incident is familiar for us. But we were lucky – our villain had a defective firearm. Anyway . . . It's easy to let something like this change how you deal with the public. To think they don't deserve it. Or that the next chap you talk to has a gun. Or, like the papers, that every lad who hasn't had his call-up yet is a little bastard coshing people in the fog.' More murmuring. 'Don't. No rough words, no hanging back. We do our jobs tonight like we did last night and the night before. Nothing's changed. Nothing.' A last dose of the sergeant's eye, then a nod. 'There's a collection for Mrs Miles on the station sergeant's desk. Dismiss.'

★

06.10. Home after a foggy turn, quiet as a Monday belfry, to find Anna in the armchair, encased in his winter sleeping bag, a brew in one hand and colour in her cheeks. 'You all right, love?' he asked. 'Here, let me light the fire.'

She shook her head. 'Please, no need – this is very warm.' He moved to the grate but she waved him away. 'But this thing, Richard, it smells so bad of – of sweat, and something very . . . khazi and *rifle oil*. How can it smell of rifle oil?'

'Korea,' cheerily, 'so cold you slept with your weapon. Only way to stop it freezing solid.' He nodded at the bag. 'Lost a barrel nut for my Sten in there. Let me know if you find it.' He smiled. 'You must be cold to take refuge in that.'

'Now I think I might be too warm.' She pulled the bag away to reveal underwear and laddered nylons and the blue print blouse that put light in her eyes, and a skin so goosy her nipples were like buttons on servants' bells. She saw his gaze, made a noise of foreign disgust starting low in the throat, and scampered to the heavy woollen skirt laid out on the bed. 'Check me for oil and *merde*, Richard, please. If you have made me filthy . . .' She buttoned her scarlet coat over the summer jacket that didn't go, crammed the Astrakhan down hard, and only then turned to her ear-rings. As she cocked her head to work the studs, eyes elsewhere to focus, he realised her cheeks were pink.

'Since when have you worn rouge, love? Thought you was peaches and cream.'

'Ah, Richard,' she tsked, 'it's a winter blush.' She started work on the second stud. 'The beginning of winter in Shanghai, I'd get the coughs, the colds . . . I haven't had a proper winter since then.' The ear-ring went in. 'Proper winter. I've never had a proper winter, of course, not like a proper Russian.' She stepped in and kissed him. 'Get into that warm bed, Richard Bourton, and rest. How can we be naughty in the back row if you doze off in the middle of the main picture?' She wiggled her fingers at him in goodbye as she crossed the lintel. 'Bioscope at six, *à l'heure!*'

She was most of the way down the stairs before he realised she'd left a full hour earlier than usual. And as he pulled his boots off, even with the sound tricks the haze played, he could have sworn it was her cough he heard slowly marking distance, like an echo-sounder, the length of Elgin Terrace.

★

A 'winter blush'. Enough to convince him? Because I need him to ask no questions. Because questions will either push me to a doctor, who can find out my cough is old, or force me to explain why I cannot see a doctor. And either way the conclusion will be: She is a liar – a liar who has lost her right to be in Britain, perhaps even to be his wife. He will not discover my sins of omission – but he will know that they have been committed . . .

So I must manage things. If the first fog of the winter is enough to awaken the cough that had gone I must be able to manage life within it, to conserve strength for the second, the third, the fourth. So:

Leave home an hour early, before daytime fires are lit and the fog has its edge. Keep a fine handkerchief over the mouth, to filter the air and contain the coughs. Walk slowly but normally where they know me, and with mouth-closed small steps, like a good Chinese wife, where they do not. Take the buses if they run, as far as they will take me. Hide inside the office all day, hanky tucked away, trying not to talk, then offer a something-is-coming-on cough to prompt Pattison into sending me home. The girls say the air is always worse by dusk, so buses all the way; a few paces, then a seat, and the hope of a nap through the stop-start crawl, until the Grove and the short walk home, already hiding the handkerchief of the day and its soot, blood, mucus, matter like liver scum, at the bottom of my bag where Richard cannot see it, and wait until he swims off to work, breathing the air as if it is the stuff of life, to pull it out and soak the evidence away.

And if the fog is too thick for the buses to run? Leave home even earlier, to cover the three miles on foot, Chinee-paces and hanky-breathing all the way; the tube is much too dear for An-the-saver so would signal something is wrong and, besides, An-learning-London-and-loving-what-she-sees would treat a pea-souper as more local colour. So, up the Grove, Notting Hill Gate, into Hyde Park and Marlborough Gate, to recharge among fountains and pools and empty benches, then leave the park by Speakers' Corner and step across, through Mayfair to Soho Square and benches where I can sit or lie, eyes closed, letting tears wash away the acid, coughing up the soot, and when I am ready to be seen, walk into the office, bright-eyed An, vigorous and unmarked by the walk, comparing fogs like a real Londoner. And in the evening I will do it all again, two hours, door to door, and climb the Elgin Terrace stairs with three or four hankies speckled with grit, soot, matter, jammed at the bottom of my bag.

And the ultimate distraction for this husband I love but lie to? Normal married life. Which tonight means fish and chips and a double feature, with cigarette smoke and smog furring the film, and three hours of thinking, Can I keep control? And then, happy married time done, we can walk down to the station, and I will kiss him on the steps and send him in, and go home to soak the handkerchiefs, then hide them among my dirty smalls, and go to bed hoping that, overnight, something will change.

31

'Halfway there,' called Bert, 'an' you ain't been rumbled yet!'

'Halfway there!' the other coppers chorused and raised their glasses. Bourton nodded, took a swig, and smiled.

He hadn't wanted to mark the first year of his probation – he'd been a near-pariah for most of it – but Bert had been keen, and saying no to him was like turning away Father Christmas. Now he was pleased he'd buckled. Because a year down, he was beginning to fit in. He could feel it in the chit-chat, the bodies jostling close, the fact that, bar his Peel House chum Dave Timmons, everyone in their corner of the Ladbroke Arms – Rex, Rog Leakey, Maurice Prentice, Will Stratfull, Brian Hitchcock, even some old mucker of Bert's with wattles and a broken nose – was a confirmed, time-served copper. The commendation helped: it said that people could rely on him, and when things got hairy he wouldn't be found pugging up in a doorway, or volunteering some other poor beggar. Whether that would be enough to get him confirmed in twelve months' time – who knew?

★

John Foley, the old copper with the wattles, was an oppo of Bert's from A Division in the 1920s who fancied himself a comedian. 'I deal,' his cod-scary expression suggesting he might have been trying for Bela Lugosi, 'in the dead.'

'As a copper?' asked Bourton, surprised rather than shocked.

'Aye. Coroner's officer. Down in Kennington.'

'Business must be good,' Bourton said, 'what with the smog and all.'

Foley shrugged. 'We get the odd traffic accident, a pedestrian who's been knocked down, but even then . . . Everyone slows down, you see, in the smog, so less damage is done. You'll find winter mortality is about thirty per cent higher anyway, and of course there are the suicides who realise it'll be dark until April. But apart from that,' shrugging again, 'not so's you'd notice.'

'But everyone says the smog carries them off – the old, the chesty.'

Foley was looking at him as if he were a fool. 'That old nonsense? It kills 'em, for sure. But not for weeks.'

Bourton's stomach sank and all over his skin, hairs he didn't know he had were upright, chilled. 'It kills them after?'

Foley nodded. 'A month, perhaps six weeks.'

Bourton's mouth was dry. 'And what kills them? Heart failure?' He was willing the pub to silence, and perhaps it worked, or his hearing was just acute, because the answer came through clear as a triangle in a school band.

'No,' scoffed Foley, even more superior. 'You need to find some new London fairy tales. Chest infections. They call it bronchitis, but something gets in the lungs, and before you know it, no matter how much penicillin you pump in, it worsens and worsens and that's that. Heart failure?' He shook his head. 'O' course, there's lots that do have dicky hearts – you might get an old 'un with both heart and lungs on the fritz – but it's the lungs that do 'em . . .'

*

John Foley was a listeners-need-only-nod kind of talker, which Bourton was happy to be. For through the Irishness that grew as the booze went down, the life story ('I'd helped my da lay them out so the dead didn't worry me'), the ghoulishness ('She'd melted to the chair!'), and the Clever Me ('Puzzles are my fort-ee and every body is a puzzle'), Bourton had one thought that stopped him saying anything at all: *She was murdered. And somehow I'm going to prove it.*

32

'Let's have your hypothesis, then.' Foley's arms were crossed defensively, even though Bourton and Parkin were his guests, and the big panelled room in the Kennington coroner's offices lined with ledgers was his empire.

'Mr Foley.' There was something petty about a sober Foley that suggested first names would send them back empty-handed. 'On the seventh of February I was called to the body of a Gladys Hartham. It was a foggy night and she had suffered from a weak heart and lungs for years. Her GP certified her death as natural causes, namely,' from notes now, '"congestive heart failure accompanied by coronary atheroma and hypoxia (chronic bronchitis)". In layman's terms, apparently, that means her weak heart stopped while her ill lungs were short of oxygen due to the smog. However, Bert noticed irregularities about the conditions in which she was found.'

'I never saw her myself,' Bert distancing himself from the whole project by looking at pictures, 'just from what Dick here reported.'

'A subsequent canvass revealed that she had an unknown visitor at about six p.m. on the night she died. She is believed to have died between about five and eight p.m. This visitor could not be seen clearly or identified. He is described as looking like a travelling salesman, but the fact that he called at an unusual time for travellers, and that none of the neighbours appear to have been called on, seems suspicious. My hypothesis,' trying out the word, 'is that the visitor killed her, for reasons unknown, taking advantage of the fog in some way to gain access to her house and avoid identification. Her doctor assumed that the fog had killed her, because that was what he'd been warning for ages, and certified natural causes. My hope,' aiming for deference, 'is that your expertise will either prove or disprove my hypothesis.'

'Very well,' said Foley. 'Sounds thin, but every case starts some-where. Furthermore,' censorious now, 'everyone who's been near that final disposition is full of it. The doctor just threw it all in. Heart and hypoxia don't generally get put together.' Foley grabbed a huge bound 'Kennington' ledger and laid it on the wide oak table. 'This is what we call the Daily Book. It's the contemporary record. It has nothing to do with inquests or any rulings: those are legal judgements. And it has nothing to do with death certificates – that's the business of the registrar. It is merely a chronicle of the reporting of a death and the medical determination of its cause.'

'And it's in chronological order?'

Foley nodded. 'Of reporting.'

'So if we're to get a feeling for how unusual it is for someone to die like Mrs Hartham?'

'This is your best bet.'

'But you don't list by cause of death?'

'No.'

'What if someone wanted to know how many people across a district, or a city, died of a given illness? Or a type of accident?'

'He or she would have to go to the district health officers or the registrars.'

'So how do you know about people dying because of the smogs?'

'Strictly speaking, of course,' Foley was smiling, 'we don't *know*. The fog isn't an official cause of death. But we know that in Kennington we have about four thousand deaths a year. That works out as thirteen or fourteen deaths a day from mid-October to mid-March, and eight or nine a day during the other months. We know there are no smogs in the summer and that certain causes of death fall off or stop entirely during those months, whereas at certain times in winter and spring you're writing some COD more often than others, sometimes three or four names in a row. The clumps'll start in December, end in – what? – May. Each time you'll have sixteen, seventeen deaths a day. It's something the family doctors talk about – a couple even report deaths as fib or fizz.'

'Eh?'

'Fog-induced bronchitis and fog-induced seizure. Those aren't formal, you won't see them in the registers, it's a shorthand.

Between colleagues, you might say. Like CRD for suicides on railway tracks.'

'CRD?' Bert asked, interest piqued.

'Corporeal redistribution,' said Foley.

'Right.' Bert stirred, a big animal emerging from hibernation. 'Makes sense. Had a bloke who jumped in Hackney. His leg wound up in Thetford.'

'That's nothing.' Foley grinned. 'Bill Gregson in King's Cross had everything but the head, and that got all the way to Blair Atholl. Found it in the coal wagon.' They both laughed and Bert immediately launched into a spry pantomime, an astonished fireman finding a head on his shovel. *Two fifty-year-old men . . .*

'So you can tell which names in the register were killed by the smog?'

'Yes,' Foley, still snorting, 'not all, but – yes. Two main clues. The first is "hypoxia" as a COD.' He opened the ledger. 'According to the doctors, it's the people with serious cardiovascular and pulmonary diseases who are most at risk from the fog – that is, conditions such as coronary atheroma, hypertension, bronchitis, emphysema.' Bourton nodded, not really knowing what the first two were. 'Now, most people who die of these conditions die without the help of the fog. Their final dispositions – the medical statement, after due deliberation, of COD – will state they died of these conditions alone. So,' a finger went down the page of the opened ledger, 'here we are, first of February, a fifty-five-year-old man, COD coronary thrombosis – heart attack. And on the sixth, seventy-two-year-old woman, emphysema.' He looked up from the ledger. 'But for many people already suffering from these conditions the fog turns a manageable illness lethal. For those patients, the final disposition will often put hypoxia first, to show that the underlying condition wasn't actually that bad. The fog just suddenly made it worse.' He smiled, not too patronisingly. 'Is that clear?'

Bourton nodded. 'And what's the second clue?'

'Timing. We get noticeable bumps in mortality with similar CODs from about four weeks after a pea-souper.' He turned a few pages. 'Right, we had a big one middle of November last year, so let's examine the week before Christmas.' Looking up: 'Mortality's ordinarily down then – everyone hangs on till the New Year – so should be obvious.'

Bourton moved to his shoulder and followed his finger down a column. 'See, here we are.'

'What's "preliminary disposition"?'

'The initial opinion by the police surgeon or doctor responding to the report of a death. There'll be an element of hedging bets. The disponent will probably not know the patient, but even if he does he won't want to commit himself. For your purposes, "final" is where the codewords come in, perhaps after further examination – the younger ones, for instance, might have been post-mortemed.'

'The others aren't?'

'No.' Foley straightened. 'These people have been ill for years and dying for weeks, with their doctors in and out the door. What's to find out?' He bent down to the ledger again and ran his finger across the page. 'Here we are. "Acute bronchitis" becomes "hypoxia (acute bronchitis)". Not from a PM, just more information. In this case, the deceased died from a lack of oxygen, the cause of which was his acute bronchitis. More precise, if you will. Take a look.'

Bourton scanned the page. Most of the dead were old, fifty-five or more, and had been carried off by the kind of things you'd expect – cancers, heart disease, liver failure, pneumonia – with two multiple injuries from road traffic accidents, blood loss from a severed brachial artery, peritonitis, and a coal-gas suicide to spice up the mix. And then a clump – four names out of six, all hypoxia, three broncho-pneumonia, one purulent bronchitis. One was seventy-four, another a five-year-old. He turned the page. Four more names, all hypoxia, two purulent bronchitis, one broncho-pneumonia, and a pertussis.

'Pertussis?'

'Whooping cough.' The victim was a nine-month-old baby.

'It's a hell of a thing, this,' said Bourton, feeling subdued, 'all these deaths. Books of them.' He turned to Foley. 'And it doesn't, you know, make you blue?'

'No,' he said lightly. 'In fact sometimes it does the opposite. Death is a kind of disorder. There's a lot of satisfaction to be had from ordering it.' He pulled out his watch. 'I'm due in the mortuary. Are you all right here for half an hour?'

★

'I'm still not clear what you're after, Dick.' Bert was leafing through an inquest ledger, offering up silly names, or bizarre ends, like strangely shaped marrows at a fête.

'Somewhere to start. The doctors say her death is commonplace. But here's a Daily Book that will be just like our coroner's. And so far it hasn't had a single entry of heart and hypoxia, which are supposed to have killed her. We've got dozens of other deaths, and not one of hers. If that isn't a sign that her death is suspicious, I don't know what is.' Bert was looking bored. 'Tell you what.' Bourton felt like he was trying to busy a child. 'Why don't you see if you can find a brew?'

*

He shouldn't have been so down, so fourth-day-in-sodden-foxhole miserable – but he was. Two words, and his whole project was kaput. *What were you thinking? That you'd show up a couple of doctors? Discover and solve a puzzle that the clever bastards didn't even know existed?* That would have been worth Anna's disappointment at his detective-ing. But as it was . . .

'Which cat got your cream?' Bert, a brew in each fist, and Foley, both glowing with the cheer of drunks on payday. 'You shouldn't take this so serious, Dick my boy, else you'll get all gloomy and dull. Here, John,' Bourton moved the ledger out of sloshing range just before the mug came down, 'tell him Christmas is around the corner.'

'What have you got, then?' asked Foley. He followed Bourton's finger. '"Twenty-ninth of March, Frederick William Slingsby, Hampton Street . . . Heart failure."' His hand stopped at the final disposition: '"Hypoxia/congestive heart failure (chronic bronchitis)"?'

Bourton didn't want to offend Foley but Bert, typically, didn't care. 'That's like Mrs H.' He sipped his tea. 'So it was natural causes. Can we go home, then?'

'It makes no sense.' Foley looked genuinely puzzled. 'We don't put hypoxia and congestive heart failure together. Hypoxia and bronchitis, pneumonia, something to do with the lungs – yes. But heart and hypoxia – no.'

'Happen it wasn't the smog that killed him,' suggested Bourton, hopefully.

'It was the smog.' Foley was very certain. 'That's what "hypoxia" means. It's the code word.' He stepped back as if the ledger might hit him. 'The preliminary disposition is the doctor's best guess. So, Slingsby had heart disease, heart disease is lethal, he is dead, heart failure killed him. If further investigation confirmed it, the final disposition would be heart failure, nothing more. If investigation suggested something else, heart failure would disappear. Understand?' Bourton nodded. 'Now "chronic bronchitis" does not belong in that book – it's a persistent condition, not a lethal one. It. Does. Not. Belong.' He shook his head. His wattles wobbled indignantly. '"Hypoxia" belongs, but with a life-threatening condition. Which heart failure is, but it doesn't get put with hypoxia.' He put his hands on his hips. 'It's as if, once they looked at him, they weren't sure what killed him, so they decided it was the smog, then put down anything that might work as an underlying condition.' Back to the ledger. 'No PM. And Dr Baigent as disponent.'

He looked old, preoccupied, shorn of fun. After a few moments he offered a small, apologetic smile. 'Would you mind leaving me, gents? I think I have some work to do.' He headed for the investigation files, face fallen in – as if he'd not only been in that wet foxhole, he'd got a Dear John too.

★

Two days on.

'Here's where we are.' Foley had a coarse brown-card folder open to reveal half a dozen pieces of paper and pages from a policeman's notebook lined with neat pencilwork. 'Frederick William Slingsby, seventy-two, was found dead on the evening of the twenty-ninth of March in his house on Hampton Street, near the Elephant. By his half-brother, Michael Reeves, sixty-eight, of 12A Motcombe Road. The police surgeon said he had died about a day before. According to Dr Baigent, he had been suffering from heart failure for several years and acute bronchitis for about two. He showed the classic hypoxia symptom of patches of bluish tissue. He also had tiny broken blood vessels in his face, probably from a coughing fit – he tried to draw breath, it caught in his throat or chest, he started coughing and couldn't stop. The strain caused the blood vessels to rupture. Meanwhile his weak lungs and heart meant he wasn't getting enough oxygen – that's the hypoxia – and they killed him.'

'Both of 'em?' asked Bert. 'Normally isn't it one thing or the other?'

'Yes.' He folded his hands, clearly uncomfortable and wary of showing it. 'But no PM was carried out so we don't know which. The smog killed him. There we are.'

'But did it?' asked Bourton, fishing for something solid amid the medical gobbledegook like a refugee tracking meat in soup. 'I mean, from what you were saying, nothing he had was bad enough to mean he'd run out of air. Because it's the ones with really bad lungs who're carried off, isn't it? Not just bad lungs?'

'It appears so.' Foley reached for the notes, a sudden, useful prop. 'What we do know is that he was not the only one.'

'Eh?' said Bert, finally reverting to yards off the pace.

'I've been consulting some of my colleagues,' said Foley. 'Mr Slingsby and your Mrs Hartham are not alone.'

Foley looked up to make sure they'd noticed the rabbit he'd pulled from his hat, but all Bourton could think was, Damn. More Gladys Harthams make her death commonplace, natural causes. 'Now, I've spoken to the coroner's officers in Westminster, the City, Marylebone and Southwark. I chose them because I trust them, they're all good fellows, and I was asking them to examine if there's been a failure of procedure.' Foley was now looking intently at them both, as if about to share a secret. 'There has been.'

'A failure?' asked Bert.

'Yes,' said Foley, nodding. 'Between us we have four cases this year where individuals died of unclear, but smog-related, causes. Two were hypoxia and heart failure. One was from acute bronchitis (phosgene), one from heart failure and tuberculosis. In all four cases, there was no PM, no inquest, and the final determination was not one we would ordinarily put down as a cause of death. In all four cases the deceased died suddenly, and during a smog.'

'Well, they would,' said Bert. 'They died of smog-related causes.'

'But the causes are false, Bert,' said Foley, quietly. *Is that the strain of 'failures of procedure' or does he mean it?* 'Granted, what we have,' he patted the paper, 'doesn't tell us if they died suddenly because of a smog or, like most of them, a month or six weeks after the smog that set them off – and in the middle of another one. That we don't know. What we do know is that the causes are wrong.' His light tone couldn't hide that he was stricken.

They sat in silence for a moment or two, Bourton wondering if Bert's slowness was rubbing off on him because he wasn't sure he was keeping up. But, looking at Foley, he knew that the older copper's world was no less damaged than when they'd left him two days before. In the meantime, he'd just got used to it.

'All right,' said Bert. 'I'll take your word for it.' He looked puzzled but he was clearly gripped – his brew, like theirs, was untouched. 'But why tell us?'

Suddenly Bourton's skin tingled to a something-bad-is-coming chill. He could have been back in that ditch near Suwon, face down and bleeding, sensing the Chinks swarming across the field. 'You think something terrible has happened,' he said slowly, all of it clear as a well-lit map, 'and that your ledgers have hidden it.' Foley blinked as if 'hidden' were a slap. 'And the coroner's officers can't make sure because it's a coroner's problem.'

'Oh, arseholes.' Bert shook his head.

'And CID won't look at it yet because, as a DC I know says, there's nothing there.'

Foley seemed to be relaxing, his face settling into a sort-of-smile, even as Bert started murmuring, 'No, no, no, no, no.'

'But we can,' said Bourton. 'Right?'

'John Foley, you got no business—'

Foley was nodding, relieved, looking only at Bourton, ignoring Bert's 'He's a lad, you bastard.' He closed the folder. 'Right,' he said. He offered it to Bourton.

'That's bloody poisoned and all,' scoffed Bert, pointing at it as if it would give you Delhi belly or itchy balls. 'Don't you touch it, Dick Bourton. Don't you dare.'

Bourton looked at it: cheap austerity card, filled with paper so poor ink would splodge, and information no one wanted to touch.

'You game?' Foley asked.

I am, thought Bourton, reaching, but he never got the chance to say it. Bert snatched the folder. 'You don't need an SO, you need a mother.'

33

Outside, Bourton felt as if the world were moving at a different pace, on the other side of a barrier – sounds through a filter, light from another sun. He'd walked into that office looking for evidence that one woman hadn't died of natural causes, and left it with four other names he'd never heard of. This wasn't someone taking advantage of the smog to kill Gladys Hartham. This . . . This . . .

'Why?' he heard himself say. 'Why would someone kill five people?'

'Keep your voice down,' said Bert. 'And no one's killed anyone at all.'

'But he thinks they have,' said Bourton, the barrier dissolving, 'and we're to prove it.'

'We prove nothing. This,' he waved the envelope holding the folder, 'is one of those messages they shoot the messenger for.' He jammed on his mangy tweed cap. 'I leave you to it an' you'd be holding this bomb when the music stops. An' that is why,' he looked more obey-me than he ever had before, 'you are going to do what you're told. We are *not* going to find out who killed Gladys Hartham. But we might find something that will tell someone else how to.'

★

A front garden in Motcombe Road – a blackened terrace of three-up-three-downs tucked off Kennington Lane. Michael Reeves was round-bodied, skinny-faced and younger than his years; he strained his Home Guard battledress even when resting on his spade. He offered inside and a brew but, for the first time since Bourton had met him, Bert was operating at the double, and they stood by the veg patch, hands jammed in pockets, watching their breath spool through the air, three allotment cronies chatting about onions.

Reeves had looked in on Fred a couple of times a week, more to keep him entertained (he was a widower, didn't get out much) than out of worry (Mrs Rosser over the way at 94 looked out for him). They'd play cards or dominoes, perhaps go down the Crown and Anchor, but Fred wasn't that strong – he was seventy-two, for God's sake – and when it got cold and foggy he wasn't up to a walk. So that day – couldn't even remember which it was – he'd knocked on the door about four p.m., no answer, let himself in and found Fred, on his bed, eyes open, gone.

'What was he wearing?' asked Bert.

Reeves was silent for a few seconds, eyeing them both. 'Woolly, old shirt and trousers. Weren't dressed for bed, if that's what you mean. The doctor said he'd have been feeling like something was wrong, probably lay down for a rest, had a coughing fit . . .'

'Had he been ill?' asked Bourton.

'No,' said Reeves. 'But he was seventy-two. Dicky heart, Dr Baigent said, his lungs were rough, and then that air . . .' He shook his head.

'Had you seen him during that fog at all?' asked Bourton.

'Dunno,' said Reeves. 'How long was it? I hadn't seen him for a few days.'

'Anyone else? Mrs Rosser? A visitor?'

Reeves shrugged. 'Don't know. Could ask her.' He looked hard at Bourton. 'No sign of a visitor, if that's what you're after.'

'Not really,' said Bourton. 'Just wondering if anyone saw him during the fog, to know if he was in distress.' Reeves nodded. Bourton wasn't sure he was convinced.

He watched them down the path, hands folded on the spade handle, chin propped on top, radiating suspicion.

Bert waited until they were fifty yards off before he spoke. 'I'm not sure there was much seriously wrong with that bloke till the moment he died.' He pulled out his cheap fob watch. 'Let's push on, find something lets us dump this an' go.' He must have seen Bourton's scepticism. 'I'm not going to tell a bunch of doctors they're idiots.' The watch went back into his waistcoat pocket. 'And for as long as I'm your SO, you won't neither.'

★

Bénédicte White, sixty-seven (final disposition: congestive heart failure and tuberculosis), had been found dead at her home in Lisson Grove by her friend and near-neighbour Helen De Marco. Mrs De Marco lived in a three-storey house north-east of Marylebone station that looked across the road to a blank brick wall and the railway lines beyond. She was tanned or foreign, well turned out, and looked ten or fifteen years younger than the sixty-four in Foley's notes. She ushered them into a formal parlour full of heavy dark furniture and garish popery, Christ brooding from a painting on the wall behind her sit-up-and-beg chair. From the expression on his face he was sitting on his crown of thorns.

Mrs De Marco had found Mrs White on Sunday, 30 March – Bourton's first full day as a married man – when she'd called to pick her up for ten o'clock mass, as usual. There was no answer to her knock, and she knew that Bénédicte got a bit ill when the fog was bad – she'd had half a lung removed because of TB, was in that sanatorium for eighteen months – so got her spare key and went in. And found her lying on her sofa in her drawing room, already cold; lips blue, tongue out, eyes open, a terrible sight, as if someone had ripped out her last breath.

'Why d'you say that?' asked Bert.

'Because that is what she looked like.' Slowly, as if baffled she'd say anything else.

'So you don't think someone killed her?'

'What? Oh, no, no. Who?' asked Mrs De Marco, her puzzlement obvious now. 'She lived on her own. And why? She was just a widow woman.'

'What was she dressed for?' asked Bert.

She shook her immaculate mane. 'For . . . for . . . Not for bed,' she tried. 'She was dressed for, well, Saturday, to go out, I mean not for inside – to perhaps call on friends, clothes that were perhaps a little sensible, a little smart, her blue Warwick House dress, the shoes for Princess Elizabeth's wedding. It was so long ago,' apologetic, 'really, I'm not sure . . .'

'And the front door,' asked Bourton, 'was it properly locked when you went in?'

'What?' Mrs De Marco shook her head. 'Oh, you think . . . No, it was so long ago, I do not remember.' Now she was upset. 'The Lord took her. It is enough.'

They left her on the doorstep, Bert bustling, Bourton tagging along feeling that she might start crying as soon as she was hidden from the street. At the end of the road Bert looked both ways, indecisive, a sure sign of unease: placid certainty was how he met the day.

'You see that picture of Our Lord?' Bourton nodded. 'Staring at me throughout.' Bert shivered. 'Enough to give anyone the willies.'

'Should we try her neighbours, in case they saw anything?'

'Six months on? What would we find out?' He turned to Bourton, suddenly looking suspicious. 'We're enquiring, remember? Don't think you can make me do more on the sly.'

'Bert.' *Even my SO thinks I'm tricky.* 'But how do we find out something,' slowly, wanting an answer but wary of pushing, 'if we don't talk to anyone?'

Bert looked worried now, almost henpecked. 'Sometimes finding out something gets you sat on.' A big dhobi-grey hanky came out, the tweed cap came off and he mopped at his scalp – a summer day-tripper's gesture bizarre in a dusky November street. 'I'm a charlie as your SO, you know,' he offered wearily. 'You've got clever questions and I never have any answers.' The hanky was folded and put away. 'But some things can kill your prospects sure as those tykes killed Sidney Miles.' He nodded as if he'd decided something. 'Least I can do is stop you rushing through that door.'

34

Constance Dean (seventy) had lived on the fourth floor of an amputated block of Corporation flats in a courtyard off Mincing Lane in the City. More than ten years after the Luftwaffe had called, bricked-up doorways and tattered wallpaper still scarred the stump. She'd been found dead in her sitting room on the afternoon of 9 January, by a City policeman, a PC Partridge, summoned by a neighbour, a Mrs Rose Burrell, worried that Mrs Dean's morning paper had still been folded on her mat at lunchtime, her habit being to read it over breakfast. According to the police surgeon, she had probably died in the early evening of 8 January. Preliminary disposition had been heart failure; final disposition hypoxia (heart failure).

Mrs Burrell was probably around seventy herself, a wiry woman with sharp eyes and a small chin. Mrs Dean had had bad lungs, though Mrs Burrell thought she overegged it; she'd cough outside Mrs Burrell's door, often had a hanky to her mouth when she knocked, could be heard hacking away in her living room when she knew Mrs Burrell was moving around. And it was a coughing fit that had killed her. 'Just goes to show.'

Mrs Dean'd get a fair number of visitors – she had a canasta evening every week, Thursdays, friends from all over. She'd tried to get Mrs Burrell in at the beginning but she'd never liked cards, really, thought they weren't right, all that gambling. And then Mrs Dean's daughter Evelyn would come up from Southwark. She's in the flat now, took on the lease when her mum died. No Mr Dean – killed in the Great War – no gentleman admirers that she knew of, surprising, really, a very *familiar* party . . .

They heard Mrs Dean's front door bang and made their excuses. Even the cold, damp air on the landing was preferable to Mrs Burrell's fog of spite.

If Evelyn – Mrs Newley – was any measure, then Constance Dean had probably been a nice old bird. Fortyish, slightly chubby, with heavy eyebrows and a severe bun of grey hair, she apologised for her pinny, the shopping, the clutter, nothing proper in, before seating them in her parlour where she plied them with a decent brew and biscuits made with real butter, and talked about her mother: the cards, the choral society she'd sung with for twenty years, and before that the confectionery shop she'd kept going after Father was killed until the thirties had busted her and the debts had taken her house in Croydon. Yes, she'd had problems with her lungs, but mostly she was old and wouldn't slow down, and her death may have been sudden, horrible, but she didn't think her mum would have reckoned it unfair – she'd had thirty-five years her husband never got.

They left knowing not much more. Yet as they headed for the Monument and the tube home for their early mount – eight p.m., top of the Grove, some half-arsed plan to sweep for coshing gangs – Bourton found that death after death, these old 'uns with their lives shrunk to the odd visit and what they could busy themselves at, wore him down.

'Bugger me,' said Bert, stopping halfway down the steps to the platform, Londoners concertinaing around them. He turned to Bourton. 'You know what these old ladies and gents have in common?' *The answer will come quicker if I say nothing.* 'They all lived alone. Gladys Hartham, Mr Slingsby, Mrs White, Mrs Dean. All lived alone. One, yes, but all? What are the odds?'

'Small,' breathed Bourton, staggered both by the simple intelligence of the observation and that Bert had made it. 'Very small.' Bert nodded, smiling. But Bourton couldn't enjoy his SO's insight because he'd already made the next leap.

'But that means someone's choosing them,' Bourton said slowly, 'stalking them, even.' Bert was shaking his head now, turning away. 'How else does he know?'

★

06.45 the next morning, Crawford St W – spiffy mansion blocks just east of Edgware Road. Bert was grumpy – the sweep for gangs had been an utter waste of time, and neither of them had had time to change. He took one look at Crozier Mansions – a curved-fronted vision of newly painted brick and concrete, with brass handrails escorting the front steps and cast-iron sconces from a Sherlock Holmes picture – and put his on-duty brassard on his sleeve. 'Rich-flat porters,' answering Bourton's unasked question, 'won't give us the time of day else.'

The head porter, Mr Hildreth, enthroned behind a gleaming mahogany counter in the red-carpeted hallway, looked as if he'd have been happier if at least one of them had been a sergeant. Michael Walsh, the junior porter who'd found Captain Thomas Bradford (fifty-three) dead on 28 March, was stoking the boilers in the basement. He was forty if he was a day, narrow-shouldered, brilliantined hair, with a black chin, a pressed brown porter's coat strangely free of coal dust, and a thick Irish accent that probably determined his status.

Twice a week Captain Bradford had had groceries delivered from Whiteley's, and twice a week Walsh had taken them up. At eleven a.m. on 28 March he'd entered the apartment through the scullery door as usual, gone into the kitchen to leave the boxes, and found Captain Bradford in the doorway to the corridor beyond, on his back, eyes open, mouth blue, cold and dead. It was hardly a surprise: he'd been gassed in the Great War (final disposition; acute bronchitis [phosgene]) and the fog always took him hard. But he'd loved London – loved the shows, the Wigmore Hall, the park, hadn't tired of it, hadn't tired of life, though if he'd gone to Switzerland . . . Walsh shrugged.

'He live alone?' asked Bert, hopefully.

'He was married,' said Walsh, 'but, mostly she— Yes.' In fact he'd seen her around more after the captain's death – apparently she was contesting something in the will so the flat hadn't been sold or handed on. He had a key if they wanted a look.

Bradford's flat was stuffed with cushions and carpets and things in velvet, Eastern-ish articles on tables and mantels, walls of books that hadn't come from a station Smith's, and pictures that might be expensive. The photos of the captain as a second lieutenant of light infantry looked like they'd been left behind by a former owner. Walsh showed them where he'd found Bradford, in an old dressing-gown over suit trousers and a collarless white shirt. The kitchen had been clear, with dry crockery in the draining rack and no sign of food being prepared. Given Foley's notes said Bradford had probably died no later than 2300 hours on the twenty-seventh, he'd either copped it after lunch and before he'd started preparations for his supper, or after clearing up his evening meal.

They walked out through the front door and stood in the hall while Walsh locked it behind them. He nodded at Bourton's chest. 'What's that leaf thing, then?'

'Nothing much,' said Bourton, to Bert's grin. He pointed at Parkin. 'Should ask him what the red and blue ribbon is.'

But Walsh wasn't listening. 'I ask 'cos I've seen it before,' he said, 'a guest – well, a something of Captain Bradford's.' *A 'something'? Was Bradford a, well, a fairy?* Bourton had never been in a fairy's house, thankfully never had anything to do with them, though he'd heard they had artistic statues, pictures of pretty boys, and he'd seen none of that. 'In a blue uniform, with a medical armband and a satchel, with one of those things,' he pointed at Bourton's commendation, 'bang on his chest. You know why I noticed?' Bourton smiled encouragingly. 'You seen a girl with a new engagement ring? Sticking her hand out? Well, that was him, only it was his chest. Just asking for you to notice.'

'Like you, then,' said Bert, nodding at Bourton.

'Fact, that was the last time I spoke to him,' said Walsh, 'day before I found him cold. Rang up to ask if he wanted to see the feller. An' sure enough he did.' Walsh sighed as he reached the stairs. 'Rich, educated man like that, wanting to see his sort . . .'

★

Bert led them down the stairs while Bourton did the quizzing. Accent, obsequious manner, skin, all said the guest didn't fit Bradford's life – a tradesman, not an equal, but oozing the knowledge he'd not be turned away. 'Like rough trade,' called Bert over his shoulder. Fiftyish, said Walsh, and looked like he'd lived every year of it. 'Rough trade,' said Bert emphatically. And then there was the uniform: a soldier's battledress, but blue, with a medical armband and no badges that the porter could recall. Who wears dark blue BD? Bourton asked himself. *Navy beachmasters, I think, and there's no need for them off Edgware Road. Air-raid wardens, and they haven't been around since 'forty-five.* 'Didn't Winston have a blue battledress?' called Bert. 'Or was it one of them boiler suits? Perhaps it was the prime minister.' *Not navy medics: they wear regular rig, bell-bottoms and all, not the serge and puttees. And this bloke was too old to be a matelot junior rate, anyway. And a satchel? What kind of satchel?* Bourton couldn't help thinking, It's got to be our bloke, got to be. Fourth, fifth victim, lives alone, gets a visitor—

'It's not our bloke,' said Bert, as he headed for Hildreth – the man was hailing him – 'if we have a bloke at all. This is just someone in fancy dress.'

'Fancy dress?'

'Didn't the ARP wear blue BD?' He took the piece of paper Hildreth held out. 'Though why you'd dress up as one of them . . .' He picked up the porter's phone and placed a call to Kennington. 'Mind you, bloody ridiculous, half of them.'

It's our man. Bourton punched his other palm with the certainty of it as Bert muttered, listened, muttered. *It's our man.*

Bert replaced the receiver, thanked Hildreth and beckoned Bourton towards the door. He halted by one of the sconces on the steps and stuck his hand out. 'Got a smoke?' A strange smile hovered on his face. *Tension? Relief?* Bourton shook out a Capstan. Bert took it with one hand, removed the on-duty brassard with the other, nodded at Bourton to do the same. Bourton complied, though he still thought it was daft – either you were smoking in uniform or not.

Bert lit up. 'We're off the hook, young 'un. There's been a woman found. In Kennington. A smog death, with no life-threatening illness. Died day before yesterday. And you know what?'

'What?' asked Bourton, ashamed that he regretted being lifted off the hook.

'She had a caller. A traveller. With a sample case. Evening of day before yesterday. Just like Gladys Hartham.' Bert took a huge draught of relief. 'And John Foley thinks he can go to the Murder Squad . . . Can't believe we've dodged the bullet.'

Oh, hell, thought Bourton, feeling as if a wave had dumped him on his arse and driven seawater up his nose. This was mine. *This was mine.*

'And the Murder Squad!' Bert was shaking his head, probably out of pleasure and disbelief. He pointed his cigarette at Bourton. 'All down to you. Not bad for a probationer, Dick Barton – not bad at all.'

35

The Murder Squad lived among the same nicotine stains and jumble of furniture as the rest of CID, but these were the matinée idols of British coppering – faces from the newsreels, names from the papers. His notebooks open, Bourton was ashamed of his big jerky handwriting, the odd doodle – the marks of a man without a school certificate, unused to anything so precise as a pen. And he was ashamed for Bert, relegated by his lack of answers to old-bloke-in-a-chair, waiting out a turn somewhere warmer than a beat. So Bourton talked through all he had and tried to ignore the feeling that DS Lloyd – sharp as a shell splinter and as easily distracted – might notice there wasn't much.

'You going to get a PM on the woman in Kennington?' he asked at one point.

'We'll see,' said the DS. 'If we think there's a need.'

'They all lived alone,' more emphatic than he had any right to be, 'and all died in the evening,' an insight he'd had as he'd laid out what he knew, 'all of them dressed, none ready for bed. What are the odds? Doesn't it shout that someone killed 'em?'

'If they did, Bourton, we're the ones to find out.'

*

Lloyd brought Bourton back over the same ground several times, always from different places in the story. *But you had everything I got first time out.* And Lloyd seemed to know it.

'OK, last time,' he said. 'This salesman.'

'I never saw him,' said Bourton. 'All I got is the lad. Jem Horne.'

'I know,' said Lloyd. 'We'll be talking to him. But, nine months on, his memory may be poor. And what he remembered after two months – well, perhaps it's the best we'll get.'

'Bloody hell,' said Bourton, catching up. 'You've got nothing useful from the Kennington killing, have you?'

A neutral smile. 'Fifties. Raincoat. Trilby. Sample case. That's about it.'

'Then try this Walsh bloke. The porter. Captain Bradford, Edgware—'

'The bloke in blue battledress,' Lloyd nodded, 'but was he carrying a sample case?'

'No,' said Bourton. 'A satchel or something.'

'And we don't know if Captain Bradford is a victim. Or even Enid Chirk,' a shrug, 'but, like Gladys Hartham, she was dressed for visitors, her death isn't right, and she got visited by a traveller. So we start with what we know.'

'But it's the same bloke, has to be, same sort of deaths, same time, all alone.' Still pushing this rock uphill. 'A strange visitor. He was just in a disguise or something, that's all. Besides,' it struck him, 'you can trace him. Send someone down to the PRO and you can trace him.'

'How?' asked Lloyd, finally looking curious.

'He's got one of these.' Bourton pointed at his silver leaf. 'Look through the *Gazette*. He's in there somewhere.'

'Good idea, Bourton.' Definitely condescending. 'We'll certainly do that, unless, of course,' a professional smile – *You've had enough of me*, 'he was dressing up as an air-raid warden, in which case there isn't much point.' *Arsehole*.

'Nice one, sir, put me in my place.' He was fed up now. 'Which is apparently spotting murders you haven't.'

'Possible murders.' Tone quiet, a teacher thinking of a putdown. 'Done now?'

'Yeah.' Surprised at himself. 'You got what I got two hours ago.' He grabbed his bonnet from Lloyd's desk. 'Thank you very much for your time, sir, an' I hope you catch him.'

★

Tullow was on the desk, and as soon as he saw them enter the nick he jammed his thumb up at the ceiling. 'Guv'nor wants a word.'

'Skipper,' said Bert, leading the way to the stairs.

'You're on Eight,' to Bert, 'and, Bourton, you're on Four. No handover. You'll just have to make it up as you go.' Deliberate pause. 'Should be used to that.'

They waited outside the guv'nor's office for ten minutes – probably the commander's niggle to make them ponder their sins. But Bert was too time-served to fret – once he'd told Bourton to leave the talking to him, he just whistled perkily – and Bourton dozed on his feet. *I've been carpeted by bosses who could give me thirty days' cells. Amateurs . . .*

'Parkin. Bourton.' Not Inspector Millett, the commander of Tullow's relief, but Adams, who must have come in special, just to give them grief. His face was cold, hard, flat, the scar on his upper lip glowing red underneath the 'tache; the wait might have been theatre but the anger was real. 'I do not expect to be told what my officers are doing by the Murder Squad. I expect them to tell me. Why didn't you?'

'We were going to, sir,' said Bert, in a purr Bourton had never heard before, 'soon as we had something to show.'

'When would that have been?'

'When we had evidence, sir. Or so much coincidence it couldn't be.'

'You're CID, all of a sudden?'

'Police officers, sir,' sharper now, 'doing our duty.'

'In your own time? Like Humphrey Bogart?'

'If we'd asked to do it during our turn, sir, it wouldn't have got done.'

'Suddenly you're full of answers. Has Bourton turned you into a smart aleck?'

'He's turned me into a better copper, sir,' said Bert, 'which is not how it is supposed to work.' *Blimey, where did that come from?* 'If he hadn't dug away, no one would know this murderer was even out there. So I'm very sorry for your embarrassment, sir, but I am not sorry for what we done.'

'You should be.' He pointed at Bourton. 'Up until this point there was a sporting chance you'd come off nights. You won't. When your probation is up we will decide if the Metropolitan Police will dispense with your services.' Now the finger jabbed at Bert. 'And you're going to join him. Whenever he's on nights, so are you. Every time you get cold and sore and forget what your wife looks like, you can remember the importance of keeping your guv'nor informed.'

'Sir,' said Bert, sounding like it was a good idea.

'As for both of you,' standing now, 'you need the Murder Squad to find something to investigate. If they don't, I'll find a way to put you on the dab. Understood?'

'Sir,' they chorused.

'Now get to your posts.'

*

They paused on the front steps to pull on gloves, check buttons, taste the Grove. It was a soggy night, cold droplets of moisture in the air, but strangely clear, without a whisper of mist. 'Rain by dawn,' offered Bert, no sign he'd just kicked his copper world off its axis – told his own guv'nor that the man would have kept a murderer free; that this bobby knew better than his boss; and that he wouldn't, wouldn't, wouldn't, eat crow for what he'd done. Bourton hadn't been a copper for long, but he still knew that what he'd just heard was unheard of. Coppers of Bert's generation took the stick, shut the trap and moved on. *Perhaps Adams was too angry to notice. Either way, we're better off out of the building.*

'You ever said anything like that before?' he asked.

'Never been in that situation before.'

'Of the guv'nor being wrong?'

Bert snorted. 'Of the guv'nor being daft wrong. I mean, you can't dab a copper for finding a murderer, stands to reason. He tries it on, he'll look a right twerp. He can't even keep me on nights for long. I'm a hero bobby. I read it in the *Express*.' He turned to Bourton. 'Won't do it, you know,' he said, probably referring to the disciplinary action.

'I know,' said Bourton.

Bert laughed. 'What makes you so confident?'

'They'll find something,' said Bourton. 'The Squad. Somewhere out there, this traveller's killing for who knows why. An' they'll see it.' He set his bonnet square and fitted the chin strap. ''Sides, he's a decent stick. He's not going to dab someone for doing too much policing, even if he ain't a hero. I just humiliated him, that's all.' He shrugged. 'Sorry if I mucked you up.'

'Garn,' said Bert, 'what can he do? Can't promote me, can't demote me, an' I'm still getting free drinks at the Uxbridge.' He clasped his hands behind his back. 'As for you, I'm sure come a year's time he'll forget.' He laughed. 'Probationers don't make it 'cos they got no authority, or they're idle, or they're arses. Not you.' His laugh turned into a chesty wheeze. 'Annoying the guv'nors *and* spotting a murderer. Dick Bourton,' he raised an arm in salute as he clumped down the steps, 'you're an education.'

36

A round of hellos as Anna shut out the cold, a clammy compress around the bones. *In winter, this is a city for things with oil and feathers, not people with joints and lungs.* The half of the office from south of the river not in yet, as if the Thames bridges had checkpoints, soldiers jabbing bundles with bayonets . . .

She hung up the Astrakhan and her coat, shivered, and threaded through to her desk. There was already a stack of letters and another of envelopes waiting for her – reminders of the new sterling limits to go out to the Christmas tours. Pattison disappeared down the passage to make his morning brew, so she picked up the handset from her telephone, placed it on her chair, and sat on it, to warm up the Bakelite. *London in winter* – a sudden pang of disloyalty – *cold, damp; short of money, clothing, butter, light, heat; the gloomy, thrifty hub of an empire of sunshine and plenty. Who wouldn't leave?*

*

Out at lunch to try the new greengrocer. She needed fruit for stewing, but she resented buying it when two months ago she'd been gorging on it for free. Yet he had some nice winter cabbages, and those crumbly soup potatoes, and the parsnips weren't wooden, and after a few minutes she'd softened enough to half fill her just-in-case bag, topped up with a couple of pounds of cookers she might sweeten with a dash of milk.

That idyll happened to some other girl. Someone hopeful, future-ish, free. Now winter had come, taking the light, the horizon, and soon enough the air. She remembered this gnawing uncertainty from being selected in the Yu Yuen Road camp, climbing into the truck, knowing something bad would happen but not what or when. *Oh, Richard, I am sorry that I do not share your joy in this place, at this time, but I remember that cough, and I am afraid.*

In the porch outside Fogden's hardware shop, shuttered since his death, there was a woman behind a table and a small crowd in front, listening to her pitch. 'So we've impregnated the muslin – very fine muslin, remember – with our special formula—'

'Smells like carbolic,' said a hard London voice.

'Not an ounce of carbolic in it,' she insisted. *Educated voice, half will buy on the strength of that alone.* 'Devised by a pharmacist, to catch the particulars that the muslin misses. So you have the double protection. The fine muslin catches the coal dust, the formula bonds with the sulphur – and, as we all know, it's the sulphur particulars we want to keep out – and holds it in the mask. Put it on and within an hour it'll be black with the particulars it's kept out of your lungs.' She waved a band of whitish fabric with string loops at either end. 'Five bob apiece.' Oohs and aahs, a matron saying at that price you'd wash it out and re-use it next day, but the hawker was shaking her head. 'You'd wash away your protection, swirling down the drain.' She held it up with both hands. 'Five bob, ladies and gentlemen, a pound for five – enough to get you through the worst pea-souper.' *A day's wages!* 'For anyone with a cough, weak lungs, anyone old. It might just save your life.'

It might. Anna's hand shifted towards her purse, a reflex response to a future threat, like checking a pistol's magazine, but then halted, clamped by her father's voice, his wisdom – 'Where will this woman be when the smog comes? Where you cannot remonstrate . . .'

My God, I miss him. A new life, a new man, a new country, and she was as honest as she could afford to be, as true as the Pole Star. But Richard came from a clear world where there was no need for lies and no difficult choices, and sometimes she felt too young, or stupid, or alone, to make those choices or shape those lies herself. *Or perhaps too frightened.* Fear blinkered you, blocked out reason and will, until you walked down the gauntlet of bayonets despite knowing it funnelled you to death. But Yermak Timofeyev had walked through the unclear world, made choice after choice, told lie after lie, and they had survived; and even when his decisions went wrong, condemned her to a captivity that should not have been hers – as if El Salvador would declare war on Japan! – he had acted, not surrendered. And done it for her. Now, in this at least, she was alone. And, no matter what she did, the world she had joined, the choices she had made meant that someone – her, her husband, her father, even old Jorrocks – would be betrayed.

She looked at the faces humming past, set, animated, intent, adrift, juggling home, love, family, money, but certain that the things here yesterday would be here tomorrow. British faces, untroubled by foreign uncertainty, making choices about fripperies: paint not shelter, ingredients not calories – choices that did not compromise or devour. A black and white world, with black and white choices – choices that trap someone coming from the world of grey. This is not my world, she realised, with a slashing pain across her middle as if laid open by a *katana*, and never will be. She felt the urge to scream.

Instead she took a firm grip of her just-in-case bag, wiped her eyes with a hanky, and stepped smiling through the office door.

Lately he'd come to think of after-fogs as recruiting season. When did you get the lads all keen? When there was a whiff of glory in the air: a campaign won, a dragon slayed, the heroes home for parades, cooing girls and free beer – that was when you set up your stall and waited for the boys to bite. It might take a week or two of exotic places and sloe-eyed bints, but you'd get them in the end. They'd got him, after all. And his game weren't that different. The chosen had already been primed. The pain of the pea-souper just past was a ghost in the lungs, the diaphragm still stiff from coughing, and the fear of the next one growing in the gut like an ulcer. And along comes yourself, reassuring, capable . . . understanding. If his recruits thought about it properly, weighed up for and against, there'd be little sense in a body like him. But just like the lads who never thought wars killed or crippled, never thought because they'd heard the call, his volunteers never really thought about the sense of someone like him because they'd felt the fear.

So the days after, he'd set out his stall. The days of recruiting on his doorstep were long gone. Instead he'd ride the buses, walk the pavements, search for those with the look – fear, relief, vulnerability, resolve. And of these four, the most important was resolve. For without the determination to carry on, there was little he could sell, and if there was little he could sell, there was nothing he could take.

And, like the boys taking the King's shilling, his recruits wouldn't come straight away. Like the recruiters, he had to coddle them a little – make them feel that he knew, understood them and what they went through. And he was well past the stage where he would push. Let them come to him, was his philosophy now. He'd rather wait and have them join in their own time than get the wibbles and shy away.

Patience is the key. He stepped back and allowed a couple of elderly ladies to step onto the bus's rear platform ahead of him. *And turnout. No one trusts a scruff.* He stepped onto the platform and through to the lower deck. There was an old man with a hanky across his mouth on one of the bench seats. He nodded at him. *And so it begins . . .*

37

'You missed Monty, you know.' Tony Marling took a first swig. 'If you'd stuck around in hospital a little longer, you'd have seen the man himself. "Hewwo, hewwo, don't wowwy, get another cwack at Jewwy," lobbing Player's onto the beds. As soon as he left, the nurses were sent down the wards to pick them up. The CO said it was bad for our health.' They both laughed. Telling the maimed not to smoke, thought Bourton. 'Bloody army.' It turned into an impromptu toast.

'Why'd you leave it?' Marling, curious but cautious, as if it might be tricky ground.

Bourton glanced across the table at Anna and Marling's fancy woman, Dorothy Mottram – the women Marling's idea, to bridge the distance. But Dorothy was a thirtyish divorcée, chilly snobbery and a glancing handshake – not Anna's type at all. 'Thought it was time to start something else. Anna coming along. And you get to feel you're chancing your arm a bit.'

'Those?' He nodded at the scars around Bourton's wrists.

Bourton opened his mouth to take offence, then realised how petty it would sound. *I got his foot cut off, after all.* 'Per'aps. Longest twelve hours of my life. Nothing like that to make you see the virtues of Civvy Street.' He paused. 'We saw so many skeletons with their wrists wired together, Yank prisoners they'd murdered, when they do it to you . . .' He could see sympathy and confusion competing on Marling's face. *Give him something.* 'Oh, the Chinks stowed the prisoners who couldn't run to collect later. Only the Die-hards came up first.' He smiled. 'My PoW story. Twelve hours in a culvert with a sore leg, feeling sorry for myself.' Marling smiled in support. 'Besides, I'd never been a civvy, really. Thought it might be worth a go.'

'And the police is being a civilian?'

Bourton smiled. 'Not far wrong, there. They do like telling you what to do.'

'And you didn't think of doing something where they don't?'

Bourton shrugged. 'I don't listen to 'em, anyway.' Astonishment stopped Marling's glass halfway to his mouth. 'Honest. Half the time you just ignore 'em, get on with what needs to be done.' He took a swig of his own bitter.

'And they don't mind?'

'Turns out they do. So perhaps I should start looking for something else.' Saying it hurt less than expected. 'Thing is,' looking around at the Holland Park Hotel bar's brass and mahogany, the etched mirrors, the gilt, 'I think I decided years ago that London was the most exciting place in the world, and that a copper got to see it all. Besides, what kind of London job can an infantry sergeant get? Not as if I've got skills. Or a School Certificate. I still want to do it. Question is whether they still want me.'

'With your commendation? Come on. You're straight as a die, Dick. You were as a soldier.'

'Was I?' Bourton felt he could see, touch, smell 1944 any time he chose – the road he'd been shot on, the wheat he'd tried to hide in, the hedgerows he'd dreaded crossing, the dead he'd known or helped to make. But memory had turned nineteen-year-old Dick Bourton into a cipher in green serge. 'Have to take your word for it.'

'And you will be as a copper, I know. Chin up.' Marling raised his glass. 'They can't make you pregnant.'

★

The women didn't get on. Dorothy sneered and kept her distance and Bourton was minded to jump in, explain Anna had dressed for the pub, not this empire of chiffon and pearls, somehow set the bitter woman straight, but then he saw Anna's polite barbed expression and smiled. This was a battle she'd win on her own.

But it made him wonder – *What does Marling see in her? Is a snobbish cast-off all a young cripple can get for a screw? Or is she what passes for normal in his world?* Whichever, she wasn't a nice woman, and they wouldn't do this again.

The Marling part of it, though . . . Tony could get a man talking. He had an innocent, interested quality, an open face, perhaps an air of having been knocked down a few times that made you want to confide, if only to include him. But there was also a sharp brain, confidence, a strip or two of anger. Bourton suspected he was the type you'd take for innocent and harmless until he whipped a razor blade from his hatband and slit your patronising throat. And then underneath some kind of exaggerated respect for Sergeant, formerly Corporal, R. A. Bourton. Bizarre, given they were the same age, and Bourton was a probationary plod with a fourteen-year-old's schooling, while Marling was a nob in Savile Row stitching with a solicitor's ticket and a nodding acquaintance with the great and good. Is it just 'forty-four? wondered Bourton. *Am I his section commander, his immediate God, until he dies?*

'. . . but it's Civil Defence that takes up most of my council time.'

Bourton climbed back into the conversation around the table, rather than in his head. 'Didn't know we had any.'

'We don't, really. Which is the point.'

'Of what?' asked Bourton. 'I mean, if the Russians drop the bomb we're all goners. Who needs rescue squads and air-raid wardens?'

'I can see why you'd think that.' A well-rehearsed line. 'But that's not what we need. We need shelters, and we need to stock them. We need trained personnel who can organise and conduct the exercises, coordinate police, and fire brigade, and medical services, works departments, electricity board, sewerage. The assumption is there'll be some warning, time enough at least to get the sinews of government and society under cover. So since Winston got in again we've been putting Civil Defence back on its feet.'

'I haven't heard anything about it.'

'No one wants to make a noise. Everyone might start asking about shelters, and fallout, and how much room there might be.'

Bourton nodded. 'So what's it got to do with you?'

'It's a council job – like it was in the war. And I volunteered myself to be Mr Civil Defence for the Royal Borough, its Pharaoh of Fallout, its Shah of Shelters.' He emptied his third pint. 'I chair the CD committee. We meet every month, all the departments and services. Of course no one takes it seriously.' *Can't blame them: sounds dull and pointless.* 'Which is great for someone like me. Even the Pharaoh of

Fallout at the LCC can't be bothered – he relies on me instead. Do you know how the Bolsheviks seized control of the Russian Revolution?'

'Shot everyone?'

'Well, yes, though that's not an option open to me.'

Bourton laughed. 'Ambitious, then, are you?'

'Of course. Wills are a living but council meetings are a ladder. Old dears, property disputes, sewage, street lights – to hell with them!' He wiped his mouth. 'Pardon my French,' in clipped, passable Lahndon, the false gentility of a Die-hard NCO. 'No, the Bolshies grabbed control of their party by going to all the meetings, controlling all the committees, taking over the admin – all the crap no one else would deal with.' A bang from the ladies' end of the table: Anna appeared to have dumped her knuckleduster and sap beside the ashtray. Dorothy's eyes were wide, her mouth half open. The women *really* weren't getting along. 'Then they shot everyone,' said Marling. He stood up, one hand pinching the rims of their glasses, the other raised in a sort-of-Lenin pose. 'First, London CD, next the world!'

★

'That bitch.' Anna put her arm through Bourton's at the second try. 'God!' She wrapped herself around his arm and rested her head on his shoulder, so heavily he thought it would fall off if he stepped away. 'That was not just me, was it?' Her booze-breath was sweet on his face. 'I mean, yes, I'm a Russian bint, only a little better than a whore –'

'Love—'

'– but I am a good wife, married to a good man, I am British too, and what does she have? A man she can't keep, an education she can't use?' She swung round to face the way they'd come, pushing against his arm. 'You shit like me!' she yelled down the street.

'Anna, love—' He was restraining her now.

'You piss like me! You fuck like me! Or not!' She ground her hips, an unbelievably lewd gesture in the open street – Lambourn Terrace, his ground, while the nibs were having their tea. 'Bet you couldn't get this one, all limbs, all man!' An image popped up, of the brothel protest in 'forty-five, the Bremen whores' fury at the enforcement of the no-fraternisation order, tarts in mufti, fucking the air outside the camp, soldiers not as shocked as they should have been – only this was Anna, his love.

'You showed her, Anna, love,' shepherding her out of the light, 'cold cow. Poor old Tony, be like screwing the dead.' He started her towards Holland Park Avenue, her against the ill-lit walls, him on the kerb side in the damp yellow glow of the streetlights. 'Come on, girl, I need to get some chips on board before my turn.' He laughed, knowing it sounded forced. 'Remind me to get some stodge down you first, next time we go for a drink or two. That gin goes straight to your head and no mistake.' His hand on her waist pulled her in tight, hips bumping, proprietorial and safe. 'My girl.'

She was sniffling. 'Three gin and tonics – a Cossack drinking gin? – and I am sloshed. And I let that cold cow live. I shame my father!'

He laughed. 'Looked like you had her thinking you'd kill her for a moment there. Sap! And knuckleduster! In the Holland Park Hotel! What were you thinking?'

She half stumbled and waved her free hand dismissively. 'She was on about the war, about manning, womaning, a radio in the riff-RAF. A radio. *Merde* . . . I told her that if she thought that was action, she should try China after the Japs surrendered, where killing a soldier here, a bandit there, it's the price of a ticket home.' The brighter lights of the Avenue in front of them brought her head up, as if she could smell the fish-and-chip shop already. 'So, which way?'

'Across the road and to the right. We'll cut through.' But only part of him was focused on getting to the chippy. Most of him was thinking – hairs on end, a tingle in the fingers – Why were you killing people to get home? I thought you spent the war *at* home. What happened to a quiet time in the French Concession in Shanghai?

★

All through his turn her drunken words kept jumping into his head. He'd think, It doesn't matter. She didn't mean it. I'm getting the wrong end of the stick. But then he'd remember the rabbit on their last day at Burleaze Farm, how she'd cut its throat without hesitation, and her surprise when the head had come off – almost as if the last throat she'd cut had been much, much thicker. They hadn't been the actions of the city girl he'd believed her to be. The city girl she'd told him she was. Much of the time he reran her account of her war, an account he could neither forget nor change: four years stuck in the Jap-occupied Concession, poor, hungry, powerless, shunted from building to building, with occasional schooling, occasional work, and the constant fear of randy victors or their secret police – but at least not behind barbed wire in one of the disease-ridden camps where the vicious little bastards had put their enemies' civvies; for once, statelessness had had its uses. And no matter how he tried, he couldn't match up this account with killing bandits and soldiers just to get home.

Then just after the three o'clock call-in he had a thought – one that knocked away the battens shoring up a bulkhead he hadn't known was ready to fail.

Anna was a wrong 'un. He loved her so much that he'd never noticed – no, allowed himself to accept – what their marriage had revealed. When it came to sex, Anna wasn't right.

She'd been different in Hong Kong. A peacetime courtship, in a hot, humid, smelly version of London: pictures, noodle shops, tea in Victoria House amid the old British papers and charity ladies. And in the dark they'd kissed, fumbled, talked about the future, hoped that there was one – a respectable British courting, save for the sweat, cockroaches, rickshaws and jabber, and the half-million Red troops on the border waiting to invade. Innocent, even when she was tossing him off; innocence with the worst type of girl – a good girl, a future girl, who'd remind you of what you couldn't have until you got home.

And then there was the romantic past he'd pieced together over noodles, bad beer and brews beside the tea wagon. A vigilant father, determined to keep her from the Shanghai Russian traps of good times, bad men and easy money. Schooling by nuns: high walls, low hems, and looking away when the boys went by. The Japs, who'd grab, fondle, drag, particularly in the evenings – enough to keep you indoors. The Russian dances, lines of dampened-hair boy aristos, fake airs and Japanese cash. Hotel *soirées* of the uninterned, smooth older Germans, dashing Italians, swaggering Japanese, all offering an apartment, a wardrobe, cash on the dressing-table. Then love: the respectable fiancé, Éric Varenne de Something, the silk buyer who'd swept her off her feet after the Jap surrender, got his hands on her before the big day and dropped dead of blood poisoning before 'I will.' Then, after the Red victory in the civil war and flight to Hong Kong, suitors galore: military, a junior taipan after only one thing, a couple of policemen – all at arm's length. Then a NAAFI wagon in the New Territories, and a ploddy sweating corporal with a big smile and a big heart, followed by eighteen months of pining for the man who would not return.

A Shanghai girl who knew something, enough, about sex – but less than most. Yet in England she behaved as if a barrier had simply been chucked away. Sucking him off in the stables. Christening every site on their holiday outside. Grinding outside the hotel last night. Taking charge in the bedroom, even starting the fun. She was too *familiar* with sex, or what went with it, to be a good girl. Another inconsistency. *What does it mean? Do I love her any less? Are these things I have to know?*

Eight months married, and suddenly he was uncertain for the first time about the most certain thing in his life – his wife. He cursed silently as he turned back to his beat. Why, my love, did you have to get drunk?

38

'I told yer!' Friday night at the Bush Bop, a new dance hall conjured from an old 'chute factory, the trumpet leading the band – Negro airmen down from Bedfordshire – through 'Chattanooga Choo Choo' in about double time, and Bill Nickerson itching to get onto the floor. 'It's those bleeding Yanks!' He clicked his fingers, not quite in time. The rest of him seemed to be writhing like a snake fed a speed-laced mouse. 'Jen?' He grabbed his girl's hand and found a gap in the crowd.

'I'd forgotten just how he danced!' called Anna in Bourton's ear, her dense perfume – a customer's thank-you – cloying as a Hong Kong summer. *I'll have to get used to it. Another thing I can't mention, like you being a liar and a – a – a libertine?* She laughed as Jenny's auburn head suddenly bounced above the throng, a sheep jumping in a crowded flock, surprise then glee as she came down and the air flared her skirt.

Anna was glowing as if she'd come and then been handed a pound of off-ration butter. Her colours had intensified, Judy Garland waking up in Technicolor: blush on peach cheeks, scarlet rosebud mouth, eyes of garnet-set turquoise, hair of varnished ash. Not a whisper of knowledge about how she'd kicked away his certainties.

'Still not a patch on you!' She flung against him, head to toe, arms round his neck. He could feel her nipples through his shirt and his hands went straight to her arse. She settled in them for a moment, then grabbed them and led him to the floor. 'Let's boogle!'

But Bourton found the music relentless, too fast for his feet – the Yanks played around with melodies too much – and after five or six numbers he led the way to a corner table where it was almost too dark to see what they were drinking. Bill and Jen – small, animated, a twentyish typist from Acton, starry-eyed at her grown-up swain – had taken their jackets off and were pulling sodden cotton away from their skin. Bourton was happy for him. His Hong Kong squeeze – a Chinee dancer-who-wasn't – had wanted a ring and a passage home, and nagged, and made him feel like a mug; the news they were going to war had cheered him up no end. And Lucy Wing had probably found another mark before they'd been away two weeks.

'The young 'uns,' Bill brought Bourton and Anna into his chat, 'they get it, but the old buggers, they're still tryin' waltzes an' foxtrots.'

'Nothing wrong with a waltz,' said Bourton, who'd waltz to anything. 'Slow, dignified.' Bill and Anna laughed. 'The dance of empires.'

'Dance of grannies,' snorted Bill, 'whereas this, this is all swing, sunshine, *sexyyyy*.' Jen grabbed his arm and sort of sputtered behind her hand, suggesting she might not take him entirely seriously. 'Negro music.' He took a big swig. 'You need to get me down one of those calypso joints your way. Bet the music's hoppin'.'

'He won't be,' Anna puffing out her cheeks and stamping heavily and deliberately, a fat man trying to nail a cockroach, 'one – two – three—'

'I do not dance like that,' said Bourton, to a chorus of hysterical laughter, 'I will have you know.' *Did you screw good dancers, and keep your knees clamped for bad ones like me?* 'And furthermore,' full height, shoulders back, 'you are all under arrest.'

She has no idea. Looking at her rapture at the crowd, the company, the music, *life*, almost unable to stand because of the fun, wrapping herself around his arm and making his heart blush treasonably when he wanted to feel cold, he knew she didn't have any idea of what she'd said and done. And he would never have the courage to tell her – or be cruel enough to pick apart her lies. He wanted to tear off his clothes, stand on top of the Empire State like King Kong, and howl.

★

Saturday. Day turn: Loftus Road – Queen's Park Rangers versus Coventry City – and Bourton and Parkin, standing with their backs to the pitch and eyes on the stands, watching thirty thousand people – two infantry divisions – play out a tribal rite. And when the final whistle blows, thought Bourton, they'll all disperse within half an hour. *You're not in Ampney any more.*

'You heard from John Foley at all?' Bert asked, partway through the second half. The chat had been desultory, perhaps because they'd ordinarily be asleep, and Bourton had to rummage to remember who Foley was.

'No.' *Now there's a thing: a week ago this killer was all I could think about.*

'Or the Squad?'

'No.'

'Oh, well. Still, no one's dabbed you yet so could be worse.' Bert was nodding as if he'd solved the riddle of the sphinx. 'Of course, being old mates and such, I have heard from John, a snippet here, another there, when the Squad chat to him, or he puts something together.' *Oh, he's been sprinkled with magical intelligence dust. He'll be swearing me to confidence next.* 'So this goes no further,' Bert's face was contorted to permit a surreptitious stage whisper, 'as it were.'

'Mum's the word,' said Bourton, out of the corner of his mouth.

'Excellent.' Bert did the bobby's bob, forward onto the balls of his feet, up and then down, three, four times, ordering thoughts, trying to look as if he had nothing dramatic to divulge, or just numb legs. 'So, John.' Bob. 'He tells me that the Squad are looking at travelling salesmen whose routes cover more than one of the potential victims. So far they're still collecting and eliminating.' Bob. 'But they're certain they'll get there in the end. They've even got a nickname for him.'

'So they're certain he exists?' Bert nodded. 'How many victims, then?'

'Perhaps two,' said Bert, 'perhaps three.'

'But that's daft. We probably found four or five.' He turned to face his SO. 'What are they playing at?' Bert tapped the side of his nose and looked sagely at the stands, blank-faced and silent. 'Well?'

'Oh.' Bert covered his mouth, an old dear gossiping about her host. 'The Traveller.'

'What traveller?' asked Bourton. 'I thought they were tracking down travellers?'

'*The* Traveller. That's what they're calling him.'

'Oh, for God's sake,' angrily, in broad Gloucester, ignoring Bert's shushing motions, 'bloody nicknames! They just need to catch him. We've already had one fog since we gave him to them.' Bourton quietened. 'If he's killing, then . . .' He shook his head. 'Two victims. *What* are they playing at?'

'They know their business, young Dick, they surely do.' Bert nodded, riddle solved again. 'You ought to give them some thought, you know, when you're confirmed. Could be an aide to CID straight off, play your cards right, and then CID itself – a different do from my day. The young 'uns, like Athill and Brown, well, they're almost honest men, I'd say.' A glimmer ran across his happy, impassive face. 'A few years in CID and then the Murder Squad.' As if confirmation, plain clothes, the Squad were all dead certs. 'Could be right up your street.'

★

Saturday night at the pictures, *The Greatest Show on Earth*, men in tights looking indecent, and Dorothy Lamour, his pin-up of '44, taken to Normandy in his kitbag, sultry under palm trees across a couple of pages of *Picture Post*. There was nothing like her in Cirencester. But now Dorothy was showing her age, and beginning to resemble the madam at the Alexandria knocking-shop he'd visit off the night run from Jerusalem. Still, Anna liked the tights, and the spectacle, and the Royalty was warm, and he could think in the dark.

Whatever wasn't right about Anna and sex, it wasn't sex for money. Because if Anna was a word, it would be Joy – like now, eyes wide, immersed in the magic of the screen, no hint that she knew the seat covers were burned, the hinges glued by wartime gum, and insects scuttled across the patchy carpet when the lights went down. No one could get caught up in a thing like her. And if he'd seen anything in the eyes of whores, on duty or off, it was that what they did never left them.

Which was reassurance, but not help. Which was why on Sunday, after lunch and a cold walk in the park – a bit of hand-holding and breath-watching and ducks and drakes on the Serpentine, the water not sure if it should ice over – he kissed her as they reached the station, told her he'd be home in an hour or so, in part to see the hurt, then trotted up the steps to catch Rex Athill before he ended his turn.

39

'Stone the crows, a visitor.' Athill smiled and gestured at the paper on his desk, a jumble of pages torn from coppers' notebooks, tip reports, letters and phone message slips. 'You like detecting, you want to deal with any of this? What must be an old dear,' he rummaged, 'says her neighbour, a "blackamoor", been kidnapping cats, putting them in his cellar. Another one says Commies are behind the coshing gangs – good British boys wouldn't do such a thing. So I'll be off to Party HQ, then, ask them to hand the lads over.' He waved a message slip. 'Even the educated are going mad – Dr Vaughan, North Pole Road, claims someone's hanging around outside his surgery, offering some kind of breathing apparatus.' He looked at the message slip again. 'Suppose Vaughan isn't obviously insane.' He leaned back in his chair and put his hands behind his head. 'So what brings you to my dull door on a day off?'

Bourton sat down on one of the hard chapel chairs set aside for visitors. He leaned forward, elbows resting on Athill's desk. 'Advice.'

Athill nodded. 'Is it this thing with the Murder Squad?'

'You heard about that?'

'Suspect the whole station's in the know.' Athill smiled, the grin of someone enjoying a grief that wouldn't touch him. 'So, talk to Uncle Rex.'

★

'So what's the problem, then? Sounds like the Squad have got it well in hand.' Athill had tipped his chair back so his head was resting against the wall. 'And if they haven't got anyone yet – well, this isn't your usual. This one'll take time.'

'Which is the point.' Trying to be patient. 'Far as we know, this bloke kills in pea-soupers. If he isn't caught before another one, per'aps he'll kill again.'

'Which the Squad will know full well,' said Athill, sounding a little strained himself. 'Sounds to me like they're working with what they've got.'

'But they're not.' Bourton, fraying a little. 'They're working *two* bodies, *two* grounds, not five or six. They're ignoring most of what's there.'

'Dick Barton. We've been here before. In an inquiry, you deal with what you've got, not what might be.' He unearthed his smokes from beneath one scattering of papers and a hammered-brass ashtray, probably the base of a Bofors shell, from another. 'I tell you about this bloke Evans, off St Mark's Road? Hanged for killing his wife and baby daughter?' Bourton remembered that lecture back in February, about Evans and Neville Heath and how things were simple really. 'He walked into a nick in South Wales saying he'd killed his wife and buried her under the manhole outside his house.' Athill pulled some matches out of his jacket pocket and lit up. 'So we looked. But she wasn't. Eventually we found both of them in the wash-house. When we got hold of him, he couldn't get his story straight, decided his landlord had done it, this ex-copper called Christie, some backstreet abortion gone wrong, only the PM showed she hadn't— Ah,' waving inconvenient narrative away, 'thing is, if we'd followed him down those rabbit holes we'd never have got out. In the end we just had to focus on the solid stuff. A confession, motive and opportunity, which no one else had. All that confusion, it just boiled down to him being thick as a yard of two by four. See?' An elaborate shrug. 'They're just doing what I'd do, starting with what they've got – a salesman calling on old ladies in the smog, and the ladies ending up dead. If the rest of what you found out is as weak as the stuff you had *before* this other woman died in Kennington, there isn't much else they can get a handle on.' He offered Bourton a Player's. 'Understand?'

Bourton took the cigarette. Ignoring all those other dead dented his pride: no me, no victims. But it also missed something. There was a loose thread there which, if he could just find and tug it, would cause the whole Squad investigative woolly to fall apart.

'What if they're wrong?' he said suddenly.

Athill was looking at him calmly, clearly trying to work through what Bourton was saying. 'Then there'll be no case,' he said slowly. 'No victims, no murders.'

'I don't mean that,' said Bourton, impatiently. Athill's eyes narrowed as if he wasn't going to put up with much more. 'What if looking only at those two takes them off course? What if what matters isn't the traveller's get-up but the medic's? Then as soon as the fog starts they're looking for the wrong thing, and people start getting killed.'

'But last time we had this chat you thought it was a traveller,' said Athill, irritated and confused. 'What's going on? Dick Barton has to disagree?'

'It's not the outfit as such,' knowing he was losing him, 'it's about being wrong.'

'Dick,' said Athill, carefully, 'I'm going to say this an' I'll ask you not to take it hard.' He drew deeply on the cigarette so the smoke puffed out with his words, like the traces of a fire below decks. 'You're a probationary PC – an unusual one, but still. You have never conducted a murder inquiry. You're not even supposed to have conducted *any* kind of inquiry. You've put two and two together along the int line, but never investigated a murder. Now, so far,' he tapped off the ash, 'you may have proved lots of people, including me, wrong. But now,' he took another pull, 'there is a murder inquiry under way and you have to trust that the people doing it know what they're up to. Because they do. And you,' he breathed out a plume of smoke, 'do not.'

Bourton put his hands up. 'Fair cop. I don't. But what if this is all they do and it's wrong?'

Athill was shaking his head, clearly unsure if he understood. 'But what else can they do? It's an investigation, not a ouija board. They got to investigate, based on something. And you have to accept that they know what they're doing.'

'No.' Bourton saw tobacco threads on his fingers from where he'd just snapped the cigarette in two. 'Last time a bunch of people told me that – told me that the evidence of my own eyes wasn't real, that I hadn't a clue, an' the experts had to be trusted,' broad Ampney now, 'a Chinese army came crashing out the hills an' killed thousands and thousands of good blokes. Among them, very nearly, me.' He stood up. 'An' I got the scars an' nightmares to show for it.' Athill was still, wary, tense, and though Bourton knew he must be oozing argy he didn't give a damn. 'Bugger that for a game of soldiers.' He stabbed the desk with his index finger. 'I'm not doing that again.'

PART FOUR
Night

40

4 December 1952

The passengers waited in clumps around black-smutted snow, bent in their coats against the hard chill, breathing puffs that Anna expected to form crystals and tinkle to the pavement. The snow had a light yellow cast, as if the clouds had been stocked with summer pee. She remembered that first bus trip through London nine months ago, when bomb damage had looked romantic and she would see and hear only good things about her new home. *Where did I lose those innocent happy glasses?*

She was changing. London was hurting her and she could not love it the same way. Nine months ago the smoke rising straight into the still, frozen air would have been signposts to happy families huddled around glowing fireplaces beneath. Now it just piled up above the city, ready for the fog, whenever it came – the fog it would bind to, to make air of ground glass. And that knowledge stripped the smoke of any innocence. Stand at the top of the hill, look into the Dale or down the Grove, and she could be back above a Chinese floodplain, every puffing chimney becoming a torched village or hamlet and a danger she must walk through if she was going to make it home.

Richard was changing too. Sometimes she saw a sort of assessment in his eyes, a film of calculation on *his* happy glasses, so that he saw questions where previously he had known only enthusiasm, openness. Could it be marriage, or the distance of their lives, work? Or the real Anna, familiar tits and stories, all mystery gone? Or perhaps he was thinking about her in ways he must not. If she were wiser she would understand that film and peel it off, like an unwanted map overlay. But she was foreign, and frightened, carrying lies she could not share, shadowed by choices she did not want. Perhaps they could only find their happy glasses if they were somewhere else.

Ah, Richard, my love – she might even have said it under her breath – *why did we go away? Could we not have stayed here and made the most of what we had?* But neither of them had known that paradise was only paradise if, later, you lost it.

'Mrs Bourton?' A man in a thin coat with a balding nap, high forehead under a brown, too-small trilby, and glasses with a taped arm. He lifted the hat briefly. 'Reg Christie.' Deferential, almost obsequious. 'I've had the honour a time or two.' His hands were chapped, blotched red and blue from the cold. 'I have also had the honour of meeting your husband, I believe.' She realised he thought he was unrecognised so she nodded. *How is your garlic mayonnaise?* 'I had been hoping for the opportunity to say, as a former police officer myself, who also had the honour to serve and suffer for King and country, many congratulations to your husband on his decoration.' His hands went back into his coat pockets. 'I was commended several times myself, and I know how hard it is to come by these little distinctions.'

'Thank you, Mr Christie. I will be sure to pass on your congratulations.'

There was silence, so Christie filled it, as British people did, with the weather. 'This cold is a terrible thing,' he offered. The others at the bus stop were pretending not to listen but catching every word. 'A person is grateful for no wind – the wind where I come from, it finds the gap in your clothes and burrows through. Which is why we Yorkshiremen place such emphasis on our clothes,' he seemed to stand straighter – to show off his coat? – 'because it matters so. But still, this cold. Of course, you being a young one, Mrs Bourton, you wouldn't know, but this cold, it's terrible on the sciatica, I might say. Terrible on the joints.'

There was a murmur of agreement from a spherical old woman sitting on the bench. Then the others started shifting, picking up bags or standing up. He stepped closer and took off his hat, as if he was moving in for a kiss, and Anna shied away. His eyes widened, a flash as a boiler door opened and immediately slammed shut, before his face slipped back to blandness. 'And on the lungs. Every breath . . .'

The other passengers were stepping around them now and she looked up, a 15, gestured at it with her hand, as if to say, 'Yours?' but he was shaking his head '. . . like breathing over broken glass.'

He touched her arm and Anna havered, moved from foot to foot, uncertain whether to brush him off, shake his hand, board the bus – so unBritish of him, they had no intimacy, no knowledge, nothing shared. But the broken glass – he *knew*. 'It seems you might have shaken off that cough, if you don't mind my saying.' She did, and she decided: she stepped back with a formal, severing nod, but he wouldn't stop and followed, trilby back on, that uncertain you're-about-to-shun-me smile skimming across his face, 'but if it should return, ten Rillington Place. That's where I, and my breathing apparatus, can be found. Every evening.' The bell went on the bus and she turned to jump for the platform. His hat came up again as the 15 pulled away. 'Rillington Place, Mrs Bourton,' he called, then suddenly looked left and right, as if appalled by being loud. 'Good day.'

41

'Bourton? DS Lloyd. Anything come to mind?'

Finally, the Squad deigns to answer. 'Ah, sir, thank you very much for talking to me, sir.' Bourton retrieved his notebook from a tangle of Mrs Suchanek's knitting. 'This is the landlord's phone so I'll try to keep it brief.' He found a blank page. 'Fact is, sir, I was rather hoping you might have something for me.' He paused but there was so little to hear he might have been talking into dead space. 'Some news.' He stared at one of the Suchaneks' photos, of twirly-moustached gents in feather-adorned trilbies brandishing rifles and resting their feet on dead wild boar. 'Anything you might pass on if we met in the canteen or something, just a snippet —'

'You think I'd say something in the canteen, do you?'

'Actually, sir, I think you would.' He didn't, but it was worth a try. 'The way you'd talk to anyone who'd started something you had the run of. Sir.'

Silence. *Probably shaking his head.* 'Probationers are supposed to defer to a DS. But you sound like you're talking to someone under your thumb. Got many of them, Bourton?'

'Well, I'm a probationer who's likely for the chop and I've got a wife of strong opinions, so the answer is no, sir.' A snuffling noise that might have been a suppressed laugh. 'Seriously, sir, if I'm going to be kyboshed by this, I'd at least like to know something's coming of it.'

'And what would you do if I didn't tell you?'

Honesty. 'Look for some other way of finding out. Prob'ly get myself into more trouble.'

An audible laugh. 'Wouldn't be surprised. On either count.' Warmer now. 'Wait a mo.' Lloyd laid the phone down. Bourton heard his chair go back, the murmur of voices, and pictured the room, battered, nicotine-brown and humming with purpose.

The phone was scooped up. 'Right, this is what I can tell you. We're concentrating on two deaths – your Gladys Hartham and Enid Chirk in Kennington. Canvasses have given us travellers working their streets and we've got four, believe it or not, who do both. We're running them down. Separately, we've canvassed around several of the other deaths to get descriptions of visitors before they died, including Captain Bradley.'

'Bradford.'

'Bradford, but it was so long ago nothing – nothing – has come out of it. And then we're trying to find a link between Mrs Hartham and Mrs Chirk, some common reason for their murder, but we're not having much success.'

'So at the moment it's the travellers who're the best bet?'

'Yes.'

'And do you have a motive yet?'

'No. Wait a mo.' Lloyd put the phone down again, turned some pages beside the handset, then scooped it up. 'Mrs Chirk's daughter says a brooch is gone, but that's the kind of thing could have been lost for a while without her knowing – she's in Redditch, didn't see her mother much. Mrs Hartham's possessions were boxed up in March and sold off or passed on so there's no way of knowing if anything was pinched there. No big cash withdrawals before death by either lady. We know too little about Mrs Hartham's estate to say whether she left what she should have. Mrs Chirk's executors, on the other hand, claim everything's in order there. So it doesn't look like robbery, and if not that . . .'

'Could be anything or nothing.'

'Yes.'

'So it's the travellers.'

'Yes. We've got these names – we didn't think we'd get any – and we think we should have a suspect sharpish.'

'That's excellent, sir,' said Bourton. 'But what happens if the travellers don't pay off? If they're a dead end?'

Silence. *Have I pissed him off? When this is the question that matters . . .* Then something hard went down on the desk at Scotland Yard and Lloyd breathed in. *Just lit a smoke.* 'Then we do what we always do, go back to the beginning and start again.' Another silence. *But this one sounds tactical, while he gets his wording right.* 'Of course,' he said slowly, 'the Traveller might kill someone else. And if he does,' another puff, 'chances are he'll tell us something that the other killings couldn't. Don't worry, Bourton,' the detective's attention had clearly been pulled elsewhere, 'we'll get him. You just concentrate on keeping your head down.'

★

'Does she always carry around knuckles and a cosh?' asked Marling. He laid a silver cigarette case open on the table; Bourton took one of the neatly penned smokes, only good manners stopping him stowing a pair in his breast pocket and one more behind each ear.

'Yep.' *To fight off all those bandits she's never supposed to have come across.* 'Shanghai was a tough town. She used to carry a knife with a spring blade to school.' Marling snorted as he lit their smokes. 'Mind you, half of it was her dad, I think. Her mum ran off with a Chinese warlord when she was a girl, took her brother – would've took her, too, only the nuns wouldn't let her out of school. He was always worried she'd send someone to fetch her.'

'Bloody hell,' said Marling. 'Did she?'

'Don't think so.' Bourton eyed the clean-shaven young men in tweeds and ties and gleamy-eyed girls in pullovers and imitation pearls who seemed to be the pub's home team. Nurses from the Campden Hill Road hostel, he assumed, and students from Queen Elizabeth College next door. *Would have been nice to be one of them.* 'Per'aps they got word.'

'Bloody hell,' again.

'Yep,' Bourton took a swig. 'A long way from Dorothy's gin and pearls.' It suddenly struck him that Anna might have opened Marling's eyes, made him aware of other possibilities – possibilities he'd never explored. *Too shy and posh for girls when he had both feet, too shy and crippled when he hadn't.* Making him easy prey for the Mrs Mottrams of this world. 'Lots of different kinds of girl out there, old mucker,' a deliberate khaki echo that made Marling blush happily, 'happen I can introduce you to one some day. If your Dorothy,' he nodded like the roué Marling probably wanted him to be, 'isn't around. Or even,' inspired, this, 'if she is.'

'Good show!' Unconscious self-parody, his glass raised for a toast. 'Other girls!'

'Other girls.' Bourton took a swig. *Only if they're my wife – secrets or not.* 'But first, I want to pick your brains.'

★

'The same uniform?' confirmed Bourton.

'The same,' said Marling. 'Blue battledress and a tin hat,' sounding proud enough to have paid for the kit himself, 'and a beret, now, with a CD badge – half of them don't know how to wear it, of course. They just want the caps they wore to beat the Kaiser. But,' he brought out his cigarette case again, 'it looks less dramatic than a tin hat – which is useful, given people might be alarmed if CD were swanning around in helmets in peacetime.'

'So they wear uniform in public? It's just that last time you said the whole thing was keeping a low profile.'

'Figure of speech.' He offered a smoke, which Bourton took. 'They're in uniform to and from drill nights, the odd exercise which takes them onto the streets – that sort of thing.'

'And do they make house calls?'

'Not really,' said Marling, uncertainly. 'Do you mean knocking on doors, asking if everyone's all right, like the ARP wardens used to?' Bourton nodded. 'No. They might go to a building to inspect it, say we're thinking of putting an ob on the roof, but otherwise no.'

'So it would be odd if a CD bloke called on someone in their flat for the job?' Marling nodded as he lit both their smokes. 'And are any of your blokes medics?'

'Yes. Two to every station – well, that's establishment. We haven't got there yet.'

'And they wear your normal Red Cross brassard?'

'Yes.'

'So if a bloke in blue battledress with a brassard calls on someone during the daytime, he's not necessarily in fancy dress.'

'Fancy dress?' Behind the aromatic smoke Marling looked offended. 'What? No, of course he could be CD, going about his business. But it would be a bit unusual.' Now he looked curious. 'Has this visitor, this medic – done something?'

'Tony, my old chum,' said Bourton, 'I wish I knew.'

★

He laid out some of it – number of suspicious deaths, Mr CD Battledress as last known visitor to one of them, detectives looking elsewhere – because he knew what he wanted, and suspected giving too much might not deliver. And Marling obliged.

'When all's said and done,' he sat back on his chair, a languid man of the world with his elbow on the table, legs crossed like a five-year-old trying not to wee, 'you want to find this chap. Whether he's your man or not, he visited one of the people with dicky lungs on the day he died, so in the ordinary scheme of things you'd chat, yes?' Bourton nodded. 'Then let's find him.' Marling smiled triumphantly. 'Huge fun. Actually that's the beer talking,' he took a puff, 'because I suspect it will be deathly dull, but it can certainly be done. You say he has a Mention-for-civvies?' Bourton nodded again. 'Then it should be pretty straightforward. We ring each head of district and ask if they've got a chap with a silver leaf. Town hall, eleven hundred hours tomorrow.' He banged his hand down on the table. 'Done.' A boozy, innocent grin. Bourton would have felt a little guilty if he hadn't known that Marling wanted to feel useful – perhaps just like his old Great War veterans in their cockeyed berets.

'Thanks, mucker.' Marling's grin widened. Bourton stood up. 'Eleven hundred it is.'

★

Home for tea before his turn, Anna so delighted that – in her eyes – Bourton had agreed to find an alternative to the awful Mrs Mottram that she sent him out of the door with a warm, wraparound, pump-priming kiss to tell him he'd done well. Still, he felt a touch guilty as he trotted down the stairs. *Might not be so pleased with me after a day or two of illicit detective-ing.*

But perhaps one lie deserves another.

Bert was on the nick steps ready for his turn, working his hands tightly into his gloves and sniffing the freezing air in anticipation before going back in for roll-call. 'With a bit of luck, Richard my lad,' he said, without preamble, 'it'll stay still a while longer. 'Cos with this cold, for this long, soon as there's a bit of moisture in the air, we could have the pea-souper of pea-soupers. And as you know,' Bourton could see his teeth gleam in the weak lantern light, 'I love a bit of foggy policing.'

'And the Traveller?' Bourton paused beside him. 'Won't it just mean he comes out? And,' he nodded at Bert's vast blue torso, 'what about chasing those bloody coshing gangs, then? You really think foggy policing is it, with them around?'

'I,' Bert said lightly, 'will not be chasing anyone – which means the gangs leave me unmoved. Like Caesar's wife. As for the Traveller,' he lowered his voice, 'it's no longer any concern of mine or yours. You and me, we've done our bit. It's time for us,' he turned on the step to go back in for roll-call, 'to have some fun.'

5 December 1952

Say what you like, the Traveller told himself, taste was the only way to know . . .

Nothing told you more about the day to come than how it felt on your tongue the hour before. So, up with the larks and the milkmen, out of the door in duffel coat over jumble, hand on the smokes kept for coppers and nosies, the buggers who might bother him on business – 'You know how it is, Officer, sometimes you just can't sleep . . .' Early streets: empty pavements, guttering streetlamps, post vans from the mail trains, lorries for the garrison, the guardsmen kipping straight-backed, nodding on their seats . . . Then into the square of tall white houses with big shuttered windows, and a private garden behind railings, to which he has the key . . .

Push the gate to and down the path to the lawn, so grassy it could only belong to the rich – his own little weather station, with himself as all the instruments in a shabby mufti box. He feels the grass – brittle with frost – and lies down, face to the stars blinking beyond the city glow, a kind of still salute to the souls seething above the rooftops, and then rolls over to his front, cold grass blades against stubble, closes his eyes, parts his lips, then sticks out his tongue, just a touch, enough to lick a stamp, and tastes . . .

Moisture. It sparkles on his tongue, a dew already bonding with the acid in the air. He smiles. All over London there will be a blanket of damp draped over the ground, cooling as it meets the frozen earth. Now that he has tasted the air he lights a cigarette, securely cupped so it cannot blink, takes a pull and breathes it out, oh-so-deliberate, to see where it will go. Straight up. A smog signal. Moist air, cold ground, no wind, stars above, and a week or more of

Londoners shivering around their grates, emptying their hearths into a still blue sky – that's how you make pea-soupers that will last . . .

Goosebumps. Because with this much cold, this little wind, this fog could be close and sharp and long, laying London out like a sweetshop – limitless souls in jars like gobstoppers, waiting for him to remove the lids. He feels the tingle of performance – the chance to do something special . . .

Tongue still out, he closes his eyes to think through his day. *Start west, with the old girl in Braybrook Street. Catch her soul by half six, she won't say no – 'It'll be a tough one, Mrs Whatnot, and I knew you'd want to be prepared . . .' Then around the corner to East Acton, hop the Central to Holborn and the lady with the boarding-house near Russell Square. Free her, then Tottenham Court Road and the Northern going south, to Tooting Bec, for the old publican by Streatham Cemetery . . .*

Half the skill in freeing souls was ordering your rounds, getting souls in sequence so none went unfetched – a skill that was tested as fog stopped traffic and slowed a fellow down. Get it right and a man could reap four, perhaps even five a day; wrong and he's stranded while some sickie's pining. Or he's out when he shouldn't be, out after time, when no excuse is a good one, and the smokes are no distraction.

He opened his mouth and drew deep, tasted sulphur on the tongue and the prickle of acid in the throat, drew deeper, and there it was, the speckles of sharpness on his lungs, a tingly sparkler winking in his chest, and he knew – knew – there was too much in this air for a mere breeze to blow away. This was going to linger, a Scottish winter night of a fog, not going even when it had gone. *Days of it. Days and days and days of it, eight, ten, twelve souls, free to soar away . . .*

He stood up. *Time to prepare.*

42

06.15. Anna was still in bed, a picture in a children's book, where the printer's ink allowance ran to little splotches of pure colour – ash-blonde fan of hair, creamy skin, pool-blue eyes, scarlet blush. The bedclothes were pulled up under her chin. All that was missing was a wolf in a bonnet.

'Thought you'd be at the day, love.' He pulled off his boots. 'Not like you to be abed.'

'Ah, this room is an icebox,' rooting around under the bedclothes, like a dog in its basket, 'and it is Friday and I think they can wait a little for their continental travel,' her hands suddenly appearing on the turn-down, 'and if you get in here you will find I have been waiting for my husband.' He threw off his jacket and trousers and slipped in half dressed. 'At least take off your socks.'

'Why?' She'd grabbed his hand and guided it between her legs. 'I'm not going to wait for my wife.' She was extraordinarily wet. 'Not sure she's been waiting for me.'

'Preparation time,' she opened her legs wide and grabbed him by the waist, 'is never wasted.' Her nails dug into his padding and pulled him into her and he didn't have time to wonder why. She came immediately, a long hard wailing orgasm that wrapped her legs around his waist and drummed her heels on his buttocks. 'Ah, just keep going,' she murmured, as she steadied her breath, her pelvis slipping into rhythm, hands on his hips. 'Just don't stop.'

*

She washed quickly – by the sound of it a squat-and-splash in the bath, a reminder she was some parts Chinese, even if her blood was Russian – knocked on Sylvia Lewis's door to tell her the bathroom was clear, and trotted back in towel and dressing-gown to find Bourton lighting the fire. 'What are you doing?' she asked sharply, heel hooking the door shut behind her.

'You're cold, love. I thought a fire would help.'

'Now? For ten minutes?' She put her coat over her dressing-gown and shimmied to let the towel drop. 'Then you'll be asleep.' She stepped into her underwear and fastened her suspender belt. 'And if not, put on some more clothes.' She sat, back to him, to roll on her stockings. 'Too many fires. Everyone says this is why the air is so bad. Fewer fires, Richard,' sharply, 'that is what London needs.'

'It's a fire, love,' he tried, 'not the butter ration going a-wasting.'

'I'm sure everyone says that. As if it doesn't matter.'

'But does it?' asked Bourton, puzzled but gentle because he'd clearly crossed a line he couldn't see. 'I mean, why shouldn't they just light fires?'

'Richard,' standing, a goose-bumped vision in unmatching underwear, 'do you not see the people in the streets with the hankies on their mouths? The – the . . . *spivs* selling masks?'

'But that's London, love,' he offered. 'That's how it is.'

'And it's right?'

'But a fire is wrong?'

'When it is not needed?' Staring, blouse and skirt untouched on their hangers, as if dressing would give him permission to disagree. 'Yes.'

'But . . .' he was threading gently through the unmarked minefield of her feelings '. . . what are people supposed to do? And what about the power stations? Have you seen the coal barges? What's a fire in our grate compared to that?'

She'd turned her back. He stood by the fireplace, hands open and coal-dusted, no idea what to say or do, as she finished dressing.

'Jewellery, love?' he asked, as she reached for her scarlet coat.

'In my bag,' she said shortly, picking it up from beside the bed and heading for the door. She turned suddenly at the threshold. 'What's it like out?'

'Oh.' He cast his mind back to his turn. 'Cold. Bit o' damp. Still.' He smiled. 'Plume-o'-breath weather. I always like that.' He nodded, a peace-offering in a war he hadn't started, but her face was suddenly hard, eyes flat as if she'd be back with a shotgun to right some wrong. His skin prickled.

'*À bientôt*, Richard,' voice light as she closed the door behind her. He looked at the smudges on his hands and wondered what the hell he'd walked into.

★

10.45. His plume-o'-breath weather had become something else. Night had been supplanted by, at best, a sort of day draped in a yellow haze. The weak sun had barely made it past the Knightsbridge roof-line, probably lighting Hyde Park and the Palace but struggling to do more than show up the sulphur cast to the mist in the streets beyond. Rounding the corner to Kensington Church Street's final straight stretch, Bourton could see that the fog thinned as it climbed, so that Barker's shop windows were blurred by murk while the upper floors were solid and insistent. He made a mental note to pop along to Derry & Toms and see if the store's roof garden was above the fog – Anna might take the smog a little different if she were standing amid the tropicals, looking out on a city of chimney-stack stepping-stones jutting from a gorse-yellow lake. *Not a natural sight, but probably a great London one for all that.*

He showed his warrant card to the town hall porter and headed up to the attic where they'd banished Civil Defence under the banner of 'Preparedness'. Tony Marling was already tucked behind one of the two desks. 'Morning, Dick,' breezily, 'got it all to ourselves,' a guileless schoolboy smile, 'which is very helpful and entirely accidental, our Secretary, Preparedness having decided that the fog's too bad to come in. Most likely the weekend's too close and she's chancing her arm. Which is exactly,' he banged his shoe, prosthetic foot and all, onto the desktop, 'the kind of third-rate individual banished to CD.'

'And it's pukka for you to be doing it? With work and all?'

'Oh, yes.' He was rubbing his hands with excitement at all the investigating they were about to do. 'The partners took one look at the weather forecast and legged it for the country. As for clients,' he waved a hand dismissively, 'they don't have anything that won't wait.' He patted a ring-binder sitting on the blotter. 'All we need. Grab Mrs

Carver's chair,' he nodded at the other desk, 'and join me. What are we asking about?'

★

Twenty-eight boroughs and the City of London. Marling kept the enquiries general, as Bourton wanted: a CD member may have been a witness to a serious crime and Marling had agreed to help track him down; did the section concerned have someone on its nominal roll who wore the silver oak leaf of a King's Commendation for Brave Conduct on his uniform? When the head of section was answering he usually didn't have that information to hand, but would promise to check the personnel files and ring back when he could – though with many of them, it sounded like that wouldn't be very soon. By one o'clock two boroughs (Chelsea and Islington) had said no, another two (Southwark and Finsbury) had rung back, and fourteen were, apparently, consulting their files. Which left another ten boroughs plus the City yet to be approached. 'This could take a while,' said Bourton.

'Mostly it's a matter of waiting,' offered Marling. 'They'll ring in time.'

There wasn't much for Bourton to do, as Marling insisted on making all the calls himself. So he had a lovely slap-up lunch – sausages, mashed carrots and chips, then stewed fruit and fake custard – in the canteen, a warm, half-panelled vision of officer country, with a highly polished parquet floor and framed pictures of the Borough before the Blitz. Bourton took his time while flicking through a gravy-stained *Express*. His belches afterwards even tasted of meat. *Warm, well fed and no one shooting at me. Heaven.*

Back in Preparedness he relieved Marling on the phones – 'Take calls only,' strict instructions, which for once he decided to follow – and scanned the notes Marling had taken. 'Hasn't speeded up any,' said Marling, fastening his foot. 'Got through to twenty-two of the twenty-nine, responses from eighteen.' He pulled up his sock over the strapping. 'No joy in any. There's a good half a dozen with Mentions, some proper gongs – a CGM in Deptford, a DCM in Camberwell, a couple of BEMs. I have to say, I'm a bit bloody impressed – but not a sausage.' He stood up and grabbed his *Daily Telegraph*. 'Just take the

calls, Corp'l Bourton,' the officer he'd never been, 'while I pop down
to the mess.' He smiled, enjoying the turnabout. 'Carry on!'

★

Marling was only three, four minutes gone when the telephone rang,
startling Bourton's thoughts from his brain like pheasants from a
hedgerow. He had to wait for them to come jostling back before he
lifted the receiver to his ear. 'Secretary, Preparedness Kensington,
Constable Bourton speaking.' John Meikle, head of section, Battersea,
returning Mr Marling's call, information pertaining.

'We got a feller. Good lad, good lad.' Bourton felt the start of a
tingle. 'Harold Openshaw. Team leader, Rescue.' Meikle's words came
out in a Jock accent so thick that lumps of sound were fighting to get
out – fast and flat, a tearing burst of syllables, like a German MG 42,
rip, pause, rip. A tiny part of Bourton's brain was telling him to duck.
'He's got a King's Commendation, right enough. Awarded in 'forty-one,'
puff, 'for a rescue in the City, the May Blitz – ye mind it?'

*Light a smoke and perhaps you can keep the excitement from your
voice.* 'I was still a lad, Mr Meikle,' he pulled out his Capstans but his
shaking left hand tossed half a dozen across the desk, 'working on a
farm.' He shepherded them back onto the blotter. 'Afraid I got no
closer to the Blitz than the newsreels.'

'Ye were well out of it, son,' avuncular. 'Anyway, he was on the
squads, north of the river somewhere. One kidney, forces widnae
touch him, disnae stop him.'

'Excuse me for asking, Mr Meikle, how are you organised? I mean,
are you all part time, or full time, or—'

'Heads of section are full time,' another abrupt burst, 'then the
Preparedness people, they're just regular council staff, seconded to
Civil Defence, as it were. Blokes like Harry, they're part-timers, just
like the TA. Thursday nights, day after the TA, as half the time we're
using the same drill halls, Sat'day mornings. Good trainer is our Harry,
doin' well wi' 'em.'

'Do you know his day job, Mr Meikle?'

'Clippie on the buses.' *Shift work, then. Could be at Bradford's block
of flats of an afternoon, Bewley Street at six p.m., depending on the roster.*

'Does he have any medical duties at all? Wear a Red Cross armband?'

Meikle snorted. 'Not him. He's a rescue man through an' through.'

Though he could just stick the brassard on any time he chose. 'How old is he?'

The rustle of paper came down the line. 'Thirty-four.'

Thirty-four? But Walsh said the man going up to Captain Bradford was an old 'un – fifty or more. But perhaps – one kidney, with a hard life and, say, no teeth . . . 'He – er – could he pass for fifty?'

'Twenty-five, more like. No' even any grey in his beard, lucky beggar.'

Hardly fifty and clean-shaven. This is just wilful. You'll be telling me he's a Chinese dwarf next. 'Don't suppose the beard's new?'

'He's had it for as long as I've known him,' a lighter clicked in Battersea, 'which is, eeh, November o' fifty-one, a year, more, aye.' A snort, perhaps a sneeze. 'Am I right in thinking you're looking for a fifty-year-old wi' a clean chin?'

Bourton nodded, for all the good it would do. 'I am.'

'Could be me,' said Meikle, 'if only I was brave.' The lighter clicked again. 'Sorry I couldnae be more help.'

★

That was the closest they got to a suspect all day. They managed to speak to twenty-seven of London's twenty-nine Preparedness departments; twenty-three replied. But after about four thirty the traffic was one way. Marling dialled again and again with never an answer or an incoming call, the whir of the dial all too often accompanied by a 'Bloody weather,' or 'Idle bastards.'

'They've all gone home,' he said, as he waited for Preparedness in Stoke Newington to pick up the receiver. He looked slightly ashamed. 'Alas, local government doesn't really have the same dedication as the Met.'

'So what's our next step?' Bourton asked, as Marling put a cover over the telephone.

'Bright and early,' said Marling, folding a couple of sheets of notepaper and slipping them inside his breast pocket. 'Saturday is Drill Day, across all CD. If we get all six unresponsives before fifteen hundred hours we might even catch our chap in uniform, silver leaf and all.'

'We can't telephone?' Bourton asked, thinking of what zigzagging across London would do to Marling's stump but hoping he sounded idle instead.

'The chaps are keen as mustard even if Preparedness aren't,' said Marling, flatly, checking his strapping. 'No one'll answer. They'll all be running their drills.' He looked out of the window, where the darkness had a yellow edge. 'But if we're going to catch them all we may need to have the weather on our side.'

43

London had gone. As he stepped through the wicket, a dry smoky chill puffing over the lintel, everything that made the city – skyline, city signs, crowds, scarlet double-deckers – had disappeared, lost in the murk. *I can't see the kerb, for God's sake, let alone Barker's across the road.* He looked both ways, the chill crawling down his neck, resisted the urge to kneel, cock his Sten, listen for Gooks. *Coshing gangs will love this. And our man. But we're on your trail, sunshine.* He raised his hat to Marling, locking up behind. *Tomorrow we nab you.*

Just don't kill anyone in the meantime.

The walk home was like dancing through a power cut. Bodies emerged from the murk, braked, sidestepped, lost their nerve, so he stayed slow and off the side streets and listened for the coughs. Sometimes he found himself in a sudden concertina of bodies, like in a column on the march. Come Notting Hill Gate, crossing points were marked by clumps of murmuring Londoners waiting for nerve, pecking left and right before a blind dash across, sometimes holding hands, or – once – in the lee of a bloke facing the traffic, pulling on his smoke to make it glow like a beacon, and waving his arms to chivvy the timorous. When Bourton turned into Elgin Terrace he was surprised he could see the luminous hands on his GI watch, and that he'd left Marling seventy minutes before. *This turn will be a bugger.*

The room was dark and had the bite of chimney long cold. He turned on the switch to see Anna in bed, on her side, facing away from the door, knees tucked up and head barely visible above the turn-down; he half expected to see her thumb in her mouth. She didn't stir as the light came on, or as he apologised and turned it off.

'Are you sickening, love?' he whispered, on the off chance she was awake.

'Turn on the lamp,' she said clearly. 'Tea's on the ring, bread and marge under the plate. I hate margarine.' He worked his way to the table and turned on the lamp. Her eyes were scrunched shut, her face grudging and sour, and even though her hair was mussed and her cheeks blushed, as if she'd just slipped off him, she still managed to look ugly. 'Do not look too closely at the marge. There may be soot in it.' He took a couple of steps towards the bed but she waved him off without opening her eyes. 'I am fine, Richard, just cold and tired. And I do not like the fog. It reminds me of Harbin.'

'Fair enough, love.' Her early childhood there – chimneys, utter poverty, extraordinary cold – must have been misery enough. But if that was really what bothered her she'd have mumbled it into her pillow, nudging him to pull it out, not announced it to the room. *Ah, bollocks.* He turned to light the gas and heat his *ragoût* – French stew, but still stew, just with hope and class. *Does coppering make you read your family too?*

He gulped his food despite the soot gritting the marge – after all he'd had rations laced with flies in Palestine, drains in Holland, shit-whiff in Korea – and managed two hours' hot-eyed kip, barren and thin, spooned behind her as she looked away. He woke, went for a piss, returned. *Not a speck of affection.* He sullenly pulled on his boots. *Not a kiss, a cuddle, even a kind word; just stewing there, Her Grumpiness.* 'I'll be out early in the morning,' he told her, as he knotted the laces, unsure whether she was awake to hear, 'a little job with Tony.' With her in this mood he'd be happy if she were asleep. 'Why don't you stay in bed tomorrow?' And frig yourself chirpier, he chose not to say. *Chirpier, and truthful.*

Grumpy wife and I've no clue why. Must be an old married bloke now . . .

★

'Been here before,' said Bert, standing on the nick steps and scanning the Grove.

Bourton nodded. 'Try not to get you shot this time.'

Bert was puffing through pursed lips, trying to make breath rings in the chilly acid air. 'Just so long as it ain't fatal.' He pulled his bonnet brim down low. 'Got attached to all that cake.' He nodded at the area car pulling up at the corner and picked up his lantern. 'Looks like your lift's here.' He smiled. 'Off you go, 491.'

'No words of wisdom?'

He shook his head. 'No, you know what you're doing. After a fashion.' He ambled down to the pavement, turned left to head up to his lighthouse turn on the corner of the Grove and Holland Park Avenue, then paused. 'These coshing gangs.' He turned back. 'You come up against 'em, it's stick, all right? They got brass knuckles and there's lots of 'em. Get in among 'em an' it's cape in the left but stick in the right. Cut, not jab. Head down and keep moving. Fat bugger like you might make 'em fall.'

'Bert.'

'I mean it.' His voice had a weighty this-matters about it that made Bourton feel awkward. 'I got a feeling that sometimes you might just be a bit *nice*. Affable. And with scum like that, nice can get you killed.' He nodded for emphasis. 'Smoke that one, 491.'

44

6 December 1952

Beat Two: a mix of shops up Westbourne Grove, whores at either end, a local for the Maltese gangs and – a hundred yards apart – one each for proddy and papist navvies. And Friday night, pay night, was usually good for brawls, bustle, backchat. But the fog seemed to have driven everyone home early and kept them from going out after – even Maggie Oddplod, the cold-proof Polish tart, seemed to be taking the night off. A night that cold the bus windows should be fogged from the huddle, but the lower decks were empty in the weak tobacco-yellow glow and the uppers might just as well not exist. The lack of traffic coming back from the pubs suggested people might not have ducked in in the first place. The gaggle of couples leaving the late picture at the Rank on Queensway were complaining the cinema had been mostly empty, with the screen only visible from the front ten rows, and from his call-ins the rest of the ground was no busier. And his first pass by the cabbies' shelter showed it dark and locked – too few fares for them to be out. Which meant he'd have to fall back on the Caccia for his break, and pay for it. *A night like this, with everyone in, even the coshing gang won't be out – where will they find someone to hurt?*

He was wrong. One o'clock call-in, the box on Westbourne Grove by Colville Terrace, he came out with a Resume Normal Pattern and straight away caught a whistle – hard, sharp blasts, well spaced as if the copper were moving hard – sitting in the air like a magic carpet. He closed his eyes as he'd done that night in February, knowing there'd be no repeat even if his accelerating heart said otherwise. The sound was north, Talbot Road way, and moving east, perhaps towards Westbourne Park station – his beat.

Tin in his teeth, blowing hard and sharp in acknowledgement, doubling up to Ledbury Road, eyes on the paving, acid air catching like three-inch mortar smoke, waving him on, bayonet fixed, *Those little bastards could do with some cold steel* . . . Ground bouncing past even at his stodgy canter, dropping a pace to hawk up gritty green stuff and spit it on the pavement, then into Westbourne Park Road, roof of the bus station a tin Chinaman's hat above the murk, listening past his thumping heart . . . Voices, feet; a laugh or two. *They must be close, heading for the warren north of the canal, fewer straight open streets to follow them down –* and behind them the whistle again, from Grove way, *Bri Hitchcock on Beat One, a right greyhound.* He drew his truncheon, pondered the cape but he wanted a hand free, and moved into the junction to block the route north.

They backed out of an eddy fifteen yards away, four of them, loose-limbed and confident, almost egging on a catcher they couldn't see. He hefted his truncheon, stood stock still. *I'm behind you.* The nearest was only five yards away now. *Just a few more steps.* He reached out with his left hand.

The boy turned. Underneath the stocking on his face and the cap comforter on his head – *He's come dressed for a trench raid –* he was slight, five foot and a few, 'Fuck – Old Bill!' coming out in a falsetto shriek. The others turned as the boy sprang back, and he could see the glint of metal in their hands and off a club of some kind. That was all he had eyes for as the tallest one – his height or more – ran in, wood up. *Nails!*

He parried the club with his stick, knocking it aside, trying to jab but the boy had slipped past, another behind pattering his back with weak knuckle punches, jacket and cape absorbing the force. He turned, sweeping the truncheon with his right and clutching at cloth with his left, then hit the tarmac on his left knee as it buckled under a blow to the back of the leg. His left hand grasped something soft, and as he tugged he could feel the body come with it and as the knuckles came in on his shoulder he looked up to see anger, then fear catch fire in the eyes under the comforter, and that was enough. *I'm a police officer and a sergeant of British infantry, and boys or not this isn't fucking on.* He scythed the stick behind him, caught someone at hip level, felt his right leg buckle as someone deadened it with a kick, yanked the boy in as he jabbed up with bonnet brim and caught him across the bridge of the nose. Then Bourton registered the club cutting down and let go of the lad in time for the nails to skate down his forearm, laying the cape sleeve open to his jacket, numbing his forearm but not breaking the bone. Two, three quick hits on the bonnet, and by the time he was looking about him again the figures were bolting out of view. He wasn't going to catch them and he didn't try.

'Dick!' Hitchcock, brought up in surprise. 'Thank God. I heard the shouts, chum.' *There were shouts?* 'I thought it would be a civvy.' Hitchcock looked down the street and then up towards the canal and the bridge that had been the end of Ernie Potter. 'Which way?'

'North,' the pistons beginning to move, 'and you might get to follow them. Little one with brass knuckles, I bust his nose.'

'Teach 'em to tangle with the Bill.' Hitchcock was gone.

Bourton tested the rent with his fingers as gingerly as a real wound. The tear went through the jacket sleeve, perhaps even the shirt – the skin that the club hadn't numbed felt cold. *They're not a coshing gang, they're a murder-charge-to-be.* He stood up and dusted his knees, tried out his dead leg, shook his half-dead arm, set his bonnet, and suddenly pictured Hitchcock, on his own, bloodhounding the trail beyond the Harrow Road, looking down until the moment all four ran in to batter him senseless. 'Bri? Bri?' he called, as he stumbled north, battered mouth of the bus-station tarmac on the right, blackened yellow brick of the tube-station entrance on the left, remembering the whistle and scrabbling for it, fingers slow, breathing deep to blow only to see the other copper stranded by a streetlamp on the canal bridge, scanning the pavement with an indignant peck.

'You see anything?' called Hitchcock. 'Try over . . .' jerking his thumb at the other side of the street. 'I think the little bastard's using a hanky.' *Criminal mastermind.*

'Fucking hell, Dick, what happened to you? You got holes in your bonnet you could shove your fist in. And your arm!' Bourton oblig-ingly presented the sleeve for inspection. 'What did they use? A razor and a sledge?' Hitchcock looked into Bourton's eyes, his brow furrowed, showing the most concern of a year of serving together. 'You all right, then?' He decided something. 'You're not all here, chum.' Bourton wasn't sure he disagreed. 'We need to get you to a doc.' Hitchcock shook his head. 'You, 491, are a bleeding bargy magnet.'

★

He spent most of the rest of the turn on a bunk in the nick basement. He gave his statement, DC Hume took pictures of the damage, and Hitchcock wrote it up in the Incident Book. The guv'nor had a police surgeon look in on his way back from a declaration on Grenfell Road to pull at his eyelids, tut at his arm and clear him for kip. He dreamed that a patrol of Chinks, stockinged faces and rags around their boots, grabbed him from his room behind the int shed above Suwon and dragged him to the Silchester Road baths, but then Anna took them into a thruppenny booth, and afterwards they came out, smiling, to let him go.

He woke with the clumping of the early turn, to strange brickwork, a jumble of men's voices, a camp-bed, the smell of fags, the sense of resting up after shock, and for a few moments he thought he was in a corner of some company HQ, sleeping off a brewed-up Bren carrier. Then his eyes fell on his kit lined up beside the camp-bed – condemned bonnet, cape and jacket gaping like wounds on a washed corpse, everything stinking of smoke, acid, sweat. *I'm a civvy. I've got a home, a bed, a wife. I don't have to feel like this. Perhaps I should look for a safer line of work.*

The thought was well gone by oh six thirty, when he stood on the landing in Elgin Terrace, forearm swollen and raw scalp glowing, determined to lie to his wife of eight months. But she was asleep – real shut-eye, no sulk, didn't even stir when he pulled his tin trunk from under the bed – so there were no lies to tell. He had a slice of curling bread and gritty marge, dug out the GI parka from the bottom of his Korea kit, left a note on the back of a brown OHMS envelope propped against her Singer, and was out of the door well before seven and the prospect of her waking up to carpet him about – well – anything.

But trotting down the stairs, doffing at Suchanek leaving the front hallway, shaking out a smoke on the front steps, he still felt fragile, thin, a threadbare sheet fresh off the line clean, and shipshape and ready to rip. The hand with the match shook. I wasn't like this in February, he thought, and I got shot at. Call yourself a Die-hard?

45

Urgency in the smog . . .

'The weather's agin us.' Tony Marling, outside the town-hall wicket, heavy dark wood walking stick in one hand, fancy smoke in the other, a silvered 'CD' in the buttonhole of a thick tweed suit and a Die-hard tie underneath. With the old gas mask case over his shoulder containing their sandwiches – meat paste and onion, all his cupboard ran to – he looked ready for the hills; only the chrome barrel of the huge torch jutting from his hip pocket pointed to a December day in the capital of the British Empire. It was daylight – the haze had a ghostly glow the night had been without – but the fog screened the sun and sopped up half its light. They'd make little progress above ground. 'Won't even be any local trains this afternoon,' said Marling. 'The tube's our only bet.' He gave a brisk, unconvincing, officer-like smile. 'The game's afoot!'

*

By the GI watch, 14.10. A morning of trudging across a hidden, depopulated city, mostly at Marling's uncertain pace. St Marylebone, St Pancras, Stoke Newington CD sections down – each in its own way a bust. And no time to see more than one more section before CD did what every Brit in uniform, any uniform, would do on a day like this: bunk off early for their tea. So they plumped for the nearest of the three remaining sections – Poplar. Where the smog would always hit first, worst and last.

First stop, Highbury tube station, courtesy of a lift in Stoke Newington CD's Morris van. Even with all lights on and a brace of old blokes on the running boards wielding Coleman lanterns, it took twenty-five minutes to cover a mile and a half. The old grocer's van, the running-board retreads with the lights calling like lookouts in drift ice, the driver's frizz jutting out under his beret – it all smacked to Bourton of Abbott and Costello, not a last-reel chase. *Somewhere out there is a bloke who kills in the smog – and we stagger after him with the broken and the used-up and the still-useful-for-something-else stitched together in a Frankenstein's search.* Making do wasn't such a virtue when it let people get killed.

The Northern Line to Moorgate, then the southbound Metropolitan. Bright, empty, strangely mute, the tube seemed to have been laid on for a newsreel, with only fag butts and scraps of newsprint to say there'd once been other passengers too. When they got off at Shadwell no one joined them.

Outside the station doorway's saucer of light, they stepped into – under? – a shroud so dense it draped the street, buildings, sky, and wiped out everything past their fingertips. Silence from the railway line above, a burst of chat as a pub door opened, birdsong from what must be trees somewhere unseen – *Probably think this strange low glow means it's dawn.* Otherwise nothing – in Cable Street, which on Saturday should heave with barrows, gossips, life. Bourton cast around. Either the streetlamps were off or the fog had swallowed the light. And there'd only be coppers with lanterns at the odd major junction. So no light, no visibility, unknown ground, and a mile and a half to the Missions to Seamen hall on the West Ferry Road, with the bridges over the dock entrances, the brick-faced basins, the river . . . Bourton halted. He had to call Marling back, parade-voice to cut through the fog, and beckoned him into the booking hall where there was light enough to plan every stride. Trusting to paper, pencil, the accuracy of the *A–Z* and some basic infantry skills to keep them from a fall into a sheer-sided dock or the river's freezing scummy whorls . . .

Bourton led, with Marling's blackthorn to white-stick in his left hand, and the torch beaming glassily from his right. First steps, straight away feeling the tug from Marling's fist on the tail of his parka – a drill learned to thread through gaps in wire on boiler-black nights, not to cross a major East End thoroughfare on a Saturday afternoon. 'Step up now,' as Bourton found the opposite kerb. 'Wheeling,' as he turned, then – steered by the blackthorn tracing the pavement edge – they started their march. *Eight hundred paces down Cable Street until the turn.* Bourton called the count every fifty and Marling responded with the waypoints, reassuring him every time the kerb disappeared for a junction or a warehouse ramp and his country uncertainty told him to turn. Now and again they'd catch a sound – a train on a viaduct, a football on a tenement staircase, a lorry coughing by – from something they'd never see, almost as if it had been carried on radio waves.

Nine hundred and sixty-two paces, not eight hundred. *My dead leg stepping short? Or sloppy patrol plan? Progress, anyway.* Down Love Lane, seventy paces – *Oil-laced breeze, the river. No mud-stink so high tide* – and then turn left onto The Highway, staying on the north side, away from the Thames. *Swap hands, stick right, torch left, find the kerb edge, place the blackthorn, check Tony – stride still strong – and start the count.* Four hundred paces, marching at a good lick, into the swing, the early twilight so still that the slosh of water on the brickwork, the moan of fenders bumping a dock, a foghorn towards Limehouse Reach, all carry. *Halt. Right wheel. Cross. Left wheel. Swap hands. Kerb. March . . .*

They followed the kerb down to Narrow Street. At least eight hundred paces, more likely a thousand, with the Thames below and to their right. Puffs of cleaner river air occasionally pushed through the fog to uncover railings, perhaps a lifebelt, the fog beyond. And popping up sudden as rabbits, streetlamps, two cars, a couple fraternising against the railings. For fifty yards or so they matched strides with a quavering-voiced old dear walking her dog, until it retched. Different railings, cleaner, clammier air from both sides – *Bridge over the first dock?* Just past the bridge, nearly five hundred paces down, Marling's stride started losing its rhythm. Bourton lost the kerb with his stick, slowed, Marling's shoulder took him in the back, legs tangled, down they went. *Can feel every one of last night's bruises now.*

'Damn.' Marling's voice came up from the kerb. 'Torch OK?'

'Bugger the torch,' said Bourton, checking it anyway. 'How are you?'

'Rolling to victory,' Marling said lightly.

'The foot?'

'It'll do,' a little edge, 'at least until I get home.' An eddy revealed Marling's face, looking up. 'You think this chap's your man, don't you?' Bourton shrugged. 'Balls.' Marling stood up with a slight wobble, his legs still concealed. 'You're after him. Very "push on".' His smile was surprisingly bright, all teeth and sparkle – probably delighted to have something real to push on for. 'Let's find him then.'

46

West Ferry Road. 'Half a mile to go,' Bourton called, as the air changed – the chill of water both sides, an all-points breeze, which meant the huge West India Dock opening up on the left, a chasm across the neck of the Isle of Dogs guarded by huge cranes and warehouses he couldn't see. He listened for the squeak of derricks, the clang of hatch covers, the voices of gaffers calling away pallets, but caught only the slap of the water and silence where the stevedores and warehousemen should be earning time and a half. *Taking the weekend off.* Their steps were claps in the emptiness, plod patter plod pause bump – Marling walking heavy on his stump: *Might not have much more in him.* Bourton sniffed the air, but instead of the exotics supposed to hang over the docks, fruit, spices, the unknowable, he got oil, rubbish, drains, wet metal, and the smell-badge of smoggy London: coal smoke.

'Sun's gone,' Marling said, grit in his throat. He was right; the over-the-horizon glow, a barrage on a near-ish battlefield, had been gulped by the fog god. The light must have been ebbing for a while and Bourton hadn't noticed. Now it was gone, at least an hour early, and twilight seeped down from above, thinned royal blue on a coarse yellow blotter. Bourton turned on the torch. 'Let's up the pace,' said Marling. *To get there in time.*

Bourton obliged. Straight away Marling's stride lost its beat as his fake foot dragged, and every other pace Bourton's parka jerked low and left as he pulled himself straight. Bourton didn't dare look over his shoulder, at a set, slack, sweaty face that would blush or tighten in shame or anger the moment it was seen. He just upped the rate, focused on the blackthorn and the count, hawked up phlegm when the grit was wrapped – *Finally a pace that pulls in enough acid air to need spitting.*

Footsteps, men's voices.

'Mind your front!' warned Bourton, as a flat cap and greatcoat surged into the torch beam, twisted away with a laugh, and was gone.

'You there, Parky?' A strong bass voice, pure Cockney.

'Gone past me, chum,' Bourton called across his front, halting, Marling bumping and grabbing his hip through the parka to stay upright.

'Thanks.' The voice went with a beard and a barrel torso swathed in a naval duffel. 'You lost or something?'

'Not yet.'

The Cockney laughed.

'The Missions to Seamen hall?'

'Fifty yards, chummy.' The breath from the beard could have cleaned spark plugs. 'You'll find it if you don't fall in,' a laugh, 'but lights are off. Just been by.' A nod and he was gone.

'Check anyway,' said Marling, voice tight and shirty.

'O' course,' said Bourton. 'By the left, quick march.'

The hall was on its own on the river side of West Ferry Road, rough-edged brick, what might be big chapel windows, double oak doors up a fan of good stone steps. It was locked and dark and cold enough to have been that way for days. 'Try the sides,' suggested Marling, as he sat, face to the street, voice light now he was resting and the ship had sailed. *Think I'd thought of that on my own.* Bourton walked around, torch in his right, tracing the building with his left, hoping for no booby-traps – basement light wells or sheer river drops – where the beam couldn't go. He found three more doors, all locked. The building couldn't even summon the vaguest glow of light, let alone a piece of paper directing section members somewhere else. Poplar CD were long gone, if they'd ever been there at all.

'See, it's our patch.' A voice from the steps, loaded with the fake reason of someone set on harm, carrying like a pneumatic drill. 'An' you're on it.'

'Now, lads, I'm restin',' Marling in passable London to soften his posh, 'so I'd be grateful if you'd let me,' but his grammar was still proper.

'How much those duds cost?' another voice, as Bourton reversed the torch. *Need a bit of impetus.* He summoned a trot from wooden thighs – *Can risk a stumble, what is it about this fog?*

'Ai'd be grateful . . .'

'Didn't get those off a barrow.'

'Lookin' for sailors, is yer?'

'So you got to pay a tax.' The first voice, from above. *They're backing him up the steps, three, four of them, a day of ghost streets and now there's argy?* 'A membership, yeah.' A couple of sniggers. *Three, four of them, knives, coshes? And I'm wire-tight, beaten, had enough – but Tony, ah, bollocks, Tony.* He found a spark for his legs.

'Got a nice watch or summink?'

'Hands off.' Marling's voice – polite, reasonable, but higher-pitched, tense.

'Good for a few quid, so spiffy 'n' all.'

'No, I'm not.' Having a conversation – *Where the hell are those steps?* 'His bleedin' nibs.'

'Taking the mick.' *It'll start any moment.*

A smack of hard on soft and a yelp, a sudden chorus of fury, muffled blows and commands. Bourton's weight carried him stumbling from the first to the third step and he slowed, hefting the torch, fourth. *They must be within reach.* A jab of thigh pain and a leg returning to the murk, then a body surging up, just a torso, butchered by night and fog, 'Who's that?' from waist level, then a choked cough as Bourton jabbed hard at the torso with the torch butt and stamped once, twice, something soft, following with a stay-down half-kick into nothing that hit bone, then up to the scuffle, torch beam first, switch on – *Please, God, no knives.*

A heap of three bodies, perhaps four, brown battledress on top punching into the darkness with both fists. Bourton bent and drove off his back leg, right fist clutching serge and tugging the body free of the ruck. His fist opened automatically but the man kept going, impetus tossing him into the gloom. Another figure leaped in as if it was his turn now, pummelling on tweed – Marling's back? – and then, as Bourton banged him hard in padded ribs with the torch, a current of pain through the coshed forearm, the man's shoulders came up and back, getting distance for harder punching.

Time to get stuck in.

He put the torch down, beam on, stepped in and stamped down as hard as he could in the small of the back, driving the heel through

– *Thick clothes should stop the spine breaking* – and as the man reared
back screaming Bourton scragged him, right hand into the seat finding
his balls, left up to the head clutching hair – *Sergeant Bourton will
now demonstrate the hair and testicle hold!* – and swept through again,
hurling him like a hay bale, but he let go too soon with the man's
head still down and heading for something hard, and Bourton stood
listening, shocked at his clumsiness, for the smack of head on stone
that would see him—

Thump. *Soft landing*. Sobbing. *Out of action.*

Keep it in check, chum.

A sharp smack and a shout of pain from the huddle, but without
the torch there was nothing to see. 'Dick?' yelled from below as he
stepped in, caught the whir of something long, hard – *Tony's stick?*
– snap past his head and down, then another bark of pain. 'Dick!'
Bourton's arms flailing ahead, hitting slick cloth, *A mack?* and
clutching, the stick coming down weakly on his left shoulder, *Stop
bloody clubbing me, you bastards!*, snatching with his right, tearing it
out of a hand, then hacking two-handed, two, three, four times at
waist height or lower, catching legs or hips, curses, shrieks of proper
pain, and then the stick was slashing at empty air.

'Tony?'

'Took your time,' said Marling, from his shins. 'I hate to think what
they've done to my suit.'

'I think I got three,' trying not to sound narked, 'which isn't bad.'

'Why didn't you just shout, "Police"? They'd have scarpered.'

'They wouldn't.' Bourton started feeling along the top step for the
torch. 'Would have been an opportunity to hit a copper free and
gratis. They'd have took it.' His left found the barrel of the torch.
'Would all have jumped on me, 'stead of me on them.' He checked
the lens – intact. 'Know the secret of a good barney?'

'Brass knuckles?'

'Enemy looking the other way.' He pointed the torch in the direction of Marling's voice, found his legs, moved the beam up. 'Why
you still down? You hurt?'

'Not that I can feel. Bet I'll be sore tomorrow, though.' The beam
found his face; scrapes, puffiness by one eye, a huge grin: he seemed
to have enjoyed it. 'No, I've got one of them for you to arrest.' Marling

shifted to allow the beam onto his prisoner's face – bloody nose, mouth, forehead, eyes closed, skin slack. *Oh, Christ.* 'Though we might need to carry him.'

'You haven't hurt him, have you?' He knelt and aimed the beam at the man's eyes. Eighteen perhaps, skinny neck. *Probably skinny everything, not much opposition for a grown man in a ground fight.* 'Can't afford to hurt anyone. Collar them, neither.'

'Why?' Offended, probably at the thought of giving up his prize.

'Questions,' said Bourton, aiming for a mysterious full stop, as he found the boy's strong pulse and cupped his beery breath. *Not going to die on us.*

'Oh.' Bourton could sense that he was thinking, a sort of static in the air. 'You really are privateering.' A pause. 'And your bosses really don't like you.' Marling sat up. 'How on earth did you manage that?'

Like to know myself. 'A knack.'

'Oh, balls,' said Marling, patting the ground as if looking for his specs.

'What?' asked Bourton.

'I've lost my bloody foot.'

47

How many lies in a single sentence?

'On a job with Tony, love, back at tea-time.'

A job? Paid? Or duty? Or a hobby? And 'love'? When he should be here, holding me? Off-duty time, Saturday time, doing this not-a-job instead of the pictures or the pub of normal people, or spooning, even arguing, this is love? And 'tea-time'. There will be tea? I don't want to make it, not for this not-at-home not-husband. And he won't be back, anyway, another lie . . .

The illness, making you mean. Or the lies. Or fear. No one is nice with fear.

She laid the note on the table, fingertips confirming the slick on the Formica, gritted with soot and sharper black stuff, a film covering every hard surface like grease in a coolie noodle-house and stretching out of the room, down the stairs, across the Hill, west London, the areas she knew and the tube-map places she did not, as far as the hills and heaths outside London's chimneys and the clammy river's reach. A film borne by the very air, which windows and doors could not keep at bay, that kissed and draped whatever one wiped or cleaned, that speckled, scalded, stretched the skin and must sit in every breath, planted crystals of malice deep, to be wrenched from blighted lungs in blood-laced phlegm . . .

More melodrama. She put on the kettle, deciding to ignore the slimy handle, to be a proper English person, taking refuge in tea and denying the awkward and true. *So, the everyday: plan tea, which you will cook after all, because of love, and duty, but also because it is something to do. Being English is so easy when you try . . .* The roofs across the way were still visible. *So perhaps the fruit and vegetable stalls are still up, and if I wear the thin pullover and the cheap slip underneath I can point at Dawson and get a couple of rashers thrown in with whatever is left after everyone has showered their coupons on their weekend splash. So liver, bacon and onions, with luck, and mashed root vegetables and potatoes for fuel, all just needing reheating whenever his 'job' is done. Then dhobi hankies, and after, perhaps turn to the Singer, something crude, so that coughs and itchy eyes do not crazy up a trim . . .*

She shivered. *Stop being angry and you start being cold. Still, no fire, not yet. Wait until the shopping is done, time enough for a good glow for Richard's return, when he will want warmth to go with his food – and to know that I have been warm too, to assuage—*

The coughs erupted, a razor-fingered fist clutching at her lungs, doubling her over, and as she grabbed for the hanky in her pocket another spasm hit, opening her mouth at the sudden stab, spitting matter on her teeth, her tongue, and even, oh, God, on the table, scarlet specks spattered across the Formica that she just *knew* were pieces of her. She moaned, despair as much as pain. *Thousands of miles, a passport and a new life, and still you are a White Russian girl in a garret with bad lungs, trading tits for food and a man, meat for opera if there were coupons for costumes—*

The coughs took over, ground glass in her chest and a fist clenching below, and she grabbed hold of the table, bent double, unable to think beyond, How do I make this stop?

★

They didn't find the foot. Half an hour of Bourton's fingertips inching across slick, gritty, freezing stone, while Marling watched his prisoner and sat sentry in case the boys came back. Nothing. Cigarette butts, sodden oily newspaper smelling of fish and chips, coat buttons, but no fake foot, shoe, sock, leather strapping. At one point Bourton thought he heard voices, scuffing feet, wondered if the boy's mates had come for him, but the noise passed, if it had ever been there.

'I'll hop,' said Marling, very perky. Bourton's silence said, Bad idea. 'If I can rest on you, use the stick as a little crutch, we should be able to make Commercial Road, get a cab – might take a while.' *An hour? More? His good leg will give out and I'll have to carry him.* 'I hop all the time.' *From the bath to bed?* 'Very attainable.'

Just for once, let's not die hard. One foot, no crutch, docklands in the dark, a bashed-up Cockney on our tick, his mates gathering as we hobble home. This is the retreat from Moscow. But then it's his pain, his pride: he should say what he bleeding likes.

'Want something for your leg?' asked Bourton. 'My gloves might fit.'

'No need,' said Marling, bright enough to be leading a desert expedition away from its broken vehicles. 'I've got my French stockings. Just the thing.'

Bourton shrugged and hefted the boy in a fireman's lift. *Ten stone, with fourteen pounds of that being clothes.* 'Wait here a mo,' he told Marling, and started briskly down the steps, knowing their width now he'd traced them with his fingertips. A few strides, jolt down onto tarmac, careful paces, up onto the kerb, straight ahead. Brick wall. Right turn, the flare-in-water glow of a streetlamp high left, and his fingers found a corner, crumbling nibbled brick obvious even through gloves, inching around, left hand tracking more brick, cold slick glass with a chink of light behind, and a door. He knocked hard, waited, again, and again.

'Yeah?' An old man's head, bright hallway haloing fronds of hair on his scalp, no sign on his face that opening up to a brick outhouse with a body over his shoulder wasn't normal. *Isle of Dogs.* 'Whashu wan'?' *No teeth?*

'I'm an off-duty police officer,' his foot was ready as the geezer tried to push the door closed, 'and I found this lad unconscious in the street. Is he local?' He lifted the boy down, leaned him against the lintel, pointed his chin.

'Whassi' to you?'

'Nothing,' said Bourton, shortly. 'I don't want to collar him or anyone else. I just want to make sure he doesn't die. All right with you?'

'Bera?' the old man called down the hall as Bourton sat the boy on the doorstep and walked away. 'Is this . . .?' The name was lost in the fog.

Marling was fiddling with his stump. It was thin, tapering, yellow and patchy in the torchlight, like a chipped-varnish leg from a cheap kitchen table. First sight, and it made Bourton want to cry. He took the torch, watched him fold over hankies, fasten them with a sleeve suspender, *Right dandy*, then double over the stocking, hold it all in place with a garter and the second sleeve suspender, *Must think his clothes all want to fall down.* Then he laid his notebook in the bottom of his empty gas mask case, stuck his stump into it and lengthened the strap. When he looked up he was smiling. 'Had a better idea. Might not need a shoulder after all.' He stood, holding the strap just below his hip. 'See? New foot.' He took a clumping couple of paces, a tweedy squire at a fête trying out a new partner for the three-legged race. 'I'll miss that shoe, though.' He took the stick in his other hand. 'Shall we?'

This time Bourton's fist kept them bound, gripping a handful of hip-height tweed as the weakening torchlight led them back the way they'd come. Even with the stick and the notebook, Marling sank every other step, like a coffin with a stand-in pallbearer. *Nine hundred paces to the turn.* After fifty or so Bourton realised the clipped 'sh' he'd been hearing was Tony's breath pushing through his teeth every time his stump hit the notebook. Effort or pain, it wasn't a good sign, so Bourton started singing to take Marling's mind off it. They lurched behind the little yellow glow, Bourton trying to read their path through his feet as he half-heartedly rumbled through the snatches of music that came to mind and kept an ear for the scuffles that might mean trouble.

'If you sing "Abide with Me",' said Marling, clearly, 'I will fucking deck you.'

Bourton laughed. 'What was I giving you?'

'"Roll out the Barrel". I thought the end must be bloody nigh.' Marling snorted – a normal peeved noise that put a little fizz in Bourton's veins. 'And you're not to hang out the washing on the Siegfried Line, either.'

'"White Cliffs of Dover"?'

'If those bloody bluebirds come near me, I'll shoot.'

'"A Nightingale Sang in Berkeley Square"?'

'Have you ever heard any kind of bird sing in Berkeley Square?'

'Not my end of town.'

'I've heard tarts there,' reflective, 'though they seemed to caw. Like rooks.'

Over cross streets, ramps, cobbles, moving so slowly they glanced off obstacles – a brick wall, an unlit lamppost, a Baby Austin – and lurched on. Voices came and went, snatches of chatter hanging in the air, with Bourton and Marling halting, silent, just in case. At some point after four hundred paces the box-foot got wedged in the jaw of a storm drain and Marling pitched forward, hitting the ground with a smack, and sat there eyes closed, stump crossed, sweaty skin leached paler by pain, while Bourton freed the mask case and tried to brace its buggered cardboard bones – make-work that gave Marling the breather he wouldn't ask for. After ten, fifteen minutes Bourton announced he'd failed, and handed over the box-foot for Marling to stuff his leg into, hoisted him upright, and they were moving again. Only this time Marling would hesitate at the end of the dip, put more weight through the stick, bounce back to his good foot with the help of the compressed-air 'sh' through his teeth. His stump's in trouble, thought Bourton, even if it's only post-halt blisters on the end. *Looks like you'll be carrying him soon enough . . .*

An engine, low, almost idling, seemed to hover behind them. Bourton turned, willing it by. Headlights, a couple of voices, one calling – *The boys, coming back for more, in Dad's old motor.*

'Me!' shouted Marling, so close and loud Bourton flinched. 'I have!'

'For pity's sake,' whispered Bourton, hefting the torch, 'they'll—'

'Over here!' Marling was waving the stick now and Bourton grabbed his arm to bring it down. *Not that anyone could see it.* 'Right here!' He shook off Bourton and stepped towards the lights and the hard-edged creak of a handbrake. 'It's mine!'

What is? Bourton followed, took station on his shoulder, reversed the torch, a sudden hand from the darkness, on his forearm, the other holding—

A foot, in a shoe. From the gloom: 'This yours, then, mate?'

*

The arms belonged to Vic Spencer, forty or so, stubble, high shoulders, jungle pallor. His apologies – *What for?* – seemed to block each other in his mouth. He led them to his lorry – 'Michael! Turn on the light an' get that door open!' A creak of metal, a head-height glow, and then a pool of light on a door. 'Park yourself there.' Hand out to Marling, as if helping the Queen ashore. 'Turn, that's right, sit.'

Marling held up the foot to inspect it. 'Where'd you find it?' asked Bourton. The other door opened and he registered a brown-clad figure disappear from view.

'On the street outside our gaff,' said Spencer, 'an' I knew, said to the missus, "That ain't local,"' but Bourton was already following the lorry bed to the tailgate, torch off and hefted, 'so we thought, there's a bloke in trouble, probably done 'is bit, how else is he getting off the Isle? An' 'ere we are.' A layer of false cheer.

'Got any bruises, then, Michael?' Bourton clicked on the torch, beam head-height, catching a tall figure, over six foot, hunching shoulders, turning away. 'Oi, switch it off, chum.' Bourton stepped in, grabbed his collar and pinned him to the bodywork. And in the torch beam he saw a stick-weal on the forehead, scrape on the chin, torn coat.

'You got some good licks in on this blighter, Tony,' called Bourton.

''Ere, now,' Spencer was at his shoulder, 'they was just 'is friends.'

'Four-against-one kind of friends,' said Bourton. 'Run-away-when-the-odds-halve kind of friends.' He turned to Spencer, bobbing by the tail light, probably wanting to free his lad and knowing he shouldn't, and Bourton's desire to punish someone was gone. *At least he brought the boy to fix the damage, instead of staying at home, or hunting us down.*

'You, Mr Spencer,' Bourton nodded at him, 'are driving us home. Kensington. Put your ration to good bloody use.' Spencer bit off a protest, then nodded. 'An' Michael,' he banged the boy's body against the lorry, 'is riding in the back, where it's cold an' there's no one to talk to.' From the angle of his head the boy was looking at the ground. 'But first,' Bourton's grip shifted to the throat and he started bumping him towards the cab, 'you got some apologising to do.'

*

Spencer was a talker. Three of them on the bench seat, Bourton straddling the transmission housing, Marling asleep against the door pillar and Spencer hunched forward as if the extra six inches would pierce the gloom. He chatted to keep silence out, but once he lost the urge to excuse or apologise and Bourton to knock him back, they got by. They could see the road just ahead but little else and ambled in first gear, occasionally in second when visibility lifted, steering by the glowing streetlamps and the bumps when they hit the kerb. Often they'd halt while Michael, summoned by a fist on the cab wall, took a torch to find a street sign, and then Bourton would check in his *A–Z*, make an estimate of distance and directions, and banish him to the back. They could see five yards by the City border, twenty yards along Victoria Embankment, then down to ten from Birdcage Walk on. The route seemed mostly deserted, apart from the occasional scarlet pinpricks of smokers, and knots of swankies in furs and ulsters gliding towards the Albert Hall. By the time Bourton handed Marling over to the care of his building's porter ('Sore leg, chum. Drink and a bath should do it') he thought the Spencers had paid off their debt and wouldn't have raised his voice if they'd inched off in the dark. He was surprised when he left the building to see the lorry still there, engine hiccuping, Michael at the cab with his torch to show him the way.

The boy was contrite and questioning even before he'd straddled the transmission – 'Was it the war, then? That Mr Marling?' And before Bourton could answer, 'Proper toff, that – wasn't giving up, nohow.' So as the Bedford trudged up Campden Hill Road in first, visibility good enough to register empty pavements and shutters locked, Bourton gave them version two, rehearsed and mostly pain-proof, civvies for the use of . . .

South Holland, October '44: the push for the Maas, a typical Dutchy village, four blokes, a forward observer team for the mortars and medium machine guns – 'Vickers, you know 'em, only long-range' – looking for a room with a view to support the next hop. Across the road is a big old house with windows looking out across roofs, fields, two farms to the next village. A bit obvious, Jerry will have registered it; but the baseplates are down, the Rifle Brigade company's already at the start line, a greenjacket's waving them the all-clear for booby-traps, there's no time for anything better. Gather opposite in a looted haberdasher's, waiting for a lull in the harassing fire – heavy machine guns, mortars, the odd shell – reaching into the square, bracing them-selves for the dash. Thumbs-up from the greenjacket corporal sheltering in the house doorway, another burst of heavy fire, and then – Christmas! – a Sherman nudges up, stop-starting, commander a bump out of the turret hatch scanning with his binos. Cover. The sprint to twenty tons of steel, Barry Gwatkin stumbling on rubble and steadying himself on the hull, and the moment his arm comes down there's the sound of a huge metal mallet and the tank rocks back brews and blows, all in an instant. A scythe of metal that kills Barry Gwatkin and two greenjackets, and crushes Marling's foot. 'Yankee metal, British foot. That's the modern battlefield for you.'

Silence. For a moment Bourton saw, felt, moments of that morning, paper-thin slices of a big bitter cake. The engine cover punting Barry's head high; clang-thump-lights-out as the rivet hit; that hollow-gut dread before, leaning against the shop shelves, shielded by four walls and shadow, staring at the house opposite across a chasm of light. And he remembered his hand on a webbing strap, serge, and a sharp-edged shoulder-blade – the shove he'd given Marling, willing, clueless, first-action Marling, to get him across the cobbles to the tank that would take his foot. Poor young Marling, as old as Bourton but infinitely more innocent, recovering from the shove, opening up into a loose, stooping stride, his last ever, the moments before he suddenly became weak, creaky, prey for meal-ticket divorcées . . .

A blink and Holland was gone. Spencer was shaking his head and murmuring something; Michael was clenching his hands, pressing them between his knees, as if he'd otherwise hit himself from guilt. *Clearly not such a bad lad after all, if Dad can keep his collar un-felt.* The acid air in the cab seemed laced with a different kind of deference, too, a hint of the forelock trimming the Lest We Forget. Bourton couldn't help but smile. *They probably assume Tony was giving the orders. It's a different Britain, chums.* He stepped down into Elgin Terrace and shut the lorry door. *It's time you found that out.*

'It's about the bronchioles, you see.'

Last call of the day, and rather than dash for the old Jew in Hendon ripe for the catch and risk a chat with a copper when caught out late, here he is, converting this old precious off the A40: widow, asthma, haze in the parlour and soot sparkling on the sill, eyes awash with nerves . . .

She nodded behind the purple hanky clutched over the lower half of her face, like a huge port-wine stain she couldn't hide with her hand. *Probably borrowed from some purple best.* She'd been coughing, he could tell – acid-stung eyes, pink capillaries above the glowing hanky, scarlet skin – and he began to feel the tingle on his tongue, from the tang in the air that seeped inside but mostly the knowing, instinct, her soul to his, I'm ready, ready ready ready, just show me how. He smiled. *Always the way with the true pea-soupers. Every hack is a puff on the embers of fear, a cry for help, for a soul to be free . . .*

'That's what troubles asthmatics, ma'am.' Another name he couldn't remember; perhaps it would come with the trophy. 'As you know, it's a disturbance of the mechanism controlling the fibrous tissue and the muscles in the bronchioles, such that the oxygen flow to the lungs is interrupted.' *Such that. Thank you, Dr Petty . . .* 'The fog, of course, acts as a further disturbance. Hence your current distress, as it were.' She was nodding hard now. 'And this is where my device has been of so much help to so many.' He nodded too. 'It soothes.' Hand showing a flat calm. 'And inflates.' The other making and pumping half a bellows. 'Soothes. And inflates.'

Her hanky came away: purple lips, as if stained by the rag.

Bruises from clamping the hanky to the mouth, or a proper lack of air, a taste of what's to come. 'You're very knowledgeable, Mr Straw.' She was trying to smile.

'Taught by the best,' he said. 'Surgeon to His Late Majesty, God rest his soul, an' Surgeon to the Fleet. Can't get better than that.' Brown-coat talk not white, none of the professional man of confidence needed to convert the lettered or posh. But the air on his tongue and the flush in her face told him she was on the hook. Only telling her the truth could possibly push her away.

'So how does it work, Mr Straw?' She didn't need the sell. There was a sudden fear in her eyes – a spasm coming? – and she wasn't interested in niceties any more.

He reached down and opened his case. 'It's very simple, ma'am. Think of it as a kind of trip down Memory Lane.' He smiled, a small hello to her soul. 'One of those air-raid drills we all used to love.' He pulled out the apparatus, the mask, the box, the straps, and presented it as if to place it on her head. 'You put it on. I've rubbed it over with my special preparation, smells a little like Vicks, take away that mask smell, and wrapped the edge, softened it, for a more comfortable fit. So you put it on, like,' slipping from white-coat chat into Yorky, word and voice, as her soul came near . . . He lifted up the crown strap, looking for a signal, and she nodded, so he moved in, gentle, confident, trusted, blood thick, skin prickling, sound half-distant – the emancipator's first kiss . . . 'Put it on. Close your eyes. Breathe.'

48

'Hello, darling!' A fire, the smell of cooking, stodgy British band on the wireless, gorgeous wife waving from the armchair. He seemed to have walked into a Sunday-paper advertisement for a furniture set – though the wives in the papers weren't dressed for a sergeants' mess Christmas skit in a cap comforter, scarlet coat, oil-stained sleeping bag. He felt a surge of love and strode for the chair. 'I'm not kissing,' knitting up as a barrier, 'because I've got some horrible cough. This pea-soup, it must carry germs as well as soot and the soot goes *everywhere.*' Her cheeks had a scarlet glow and her smile seemed a little brittle. 'Tea's in the pans, just warm it up. I hope the lids have kept the soot out. Dawson didn't have any bacon but he said the liver was lamb's and he might even be right.'

'You eaten, love?'

'I have, thank you.' An inspection eye. 'Did you go out that mucky, Richard?'

'Nope, but Tony fell over down in the docklands and I had to help. Should see his suit.'

'And was the job a success?'

'Sort of,' said Bourton, lighting the rings and putting the pans on. 'Didn't find what we were looking for, but it sort of narrowed the field. Next time should be easier.'

'And will there be a next time?'

'O' course.' He hung up the parka and turned, braced for the stare of stone, or more of yesterday's strangeness about the coal. Instead he saw her forehead and the cap comforter as she bent over her knitting. *No sign that I've been doing exactly what she said had to stop. Next she'll be saying—*

'That's nice, darling.'

Where the hell has my wife gone?

Or – a treacherous thought, this, as he scoffed the liver – *Is this some kind of ambush in preparation? A sweet 'yes' now, to prepare the ground for a knockout 'no' later?*

Nah. He shook his head, looked up to be sure she didn't think he was scorning her soot-free scoff, but she was still clacking away. *She's not like that. But why did I think she was? And why am I even minded to think it?*

An insight stopped a forkful of orange mash and gravy halfway to his mouth. *Something's disordered, off-kilter, like a late dawn, no birdsong, empty streets in daylight – disordered in her, this, us. Something is wrong. And I don't know her, love her, well enough to sense what it is.* He touched her knee with his left hand to say, 'I'm trying but not very well,' and she looked up at the contact, with an immediate warm smile, honest, deep, and he felt a glow in the middle of his chest as if she'd placed a smoke against the centre of a paper target.

'Food all right?'

'It's grand, girl. Silk purses.' Her smile became settled, expected, less real. *We'll get there, love,* he told himself, *even if I don't quite know how.*

★

Turn time.

Tullow at the desk and a roll-call for any late turn, any time of year. Bootle Borough Police, assistance with a kiter, blah-blah, Worcestershire Constabulary, counterfeit petrol coupons, blah-blah, this division, affray outside Loftus Road, blah-blah . . . As for the fog – no word on the coshing gang, the Traveller, the helpless and old carried off by their coughs. *Why bring in the extra bodies, pay the bleeding overtime, if we're just going to chase cheque-kiters?*

A lighthouse turn at the bottom of the Grove. The odd voice, bursts of chat, giggles, perhaps a song, but the fog was too thick for any of it to turn into real people. *Might as well be on the Goodwin bleeding Sands.* Every ten minutes, shutter the lantern, shoulders back, chin up. 'Ladbroke Grove, follow the light! Ladbroke Grove, follow the light!' Open lantern, swing across his front, to and fro, to and fro. About face, call, shutter, swing, swing. Close shutter, left turn. 'Holland

Park Avenue, follow the light! Holland Park Avenue, follow the light!'
Open lantern, swing, swing. About face, call, shutter, swing, swing.
And repeat, both streets, perhaps introducing a little clockwork stop-
start to pep up the task, knowing no one can see and wouldn't believe
it if they did. *Which dorf in Germany had those marionettes, bloke and
his nagging wife, came out of the clock tower to peck at each other on the
hour? Hellendorf, Papendorf, Dorfendorf? And who was the bloke in C
Company shot her nose off with a Bren?* Then nine minutes of stamping,
listening and looking for the unusual when nothing can be seen,
nothing's normal, and nothing's going by.

And because there's so little job to do, think about stuff. The hunt,
on a Sunday. *Give up on Poplar? And is Tony up to trying the other two
sections?* The Traveller: *What's he after? And is he finding it? Is he killing
as I stamp, shout, daydream on Met time?* The future: *What do I do if
I get the copper's boot?* And, above all, Anna – *What's knocked our
compass off? And if I don't find out, what then?*

Turn time . . .

49

7 December 1952

Hours of eye-on-clock fretting, surges of hysteria. *He will be back at six twenty and I must be serene.* The driving question: how to live with it?

Try different spots in which to breathe. Sit high on the chest, lower in the armchair, lowest on the bed; stand in the doorway, at the bedhead, on the tabletop. Try out filters (hanky, dishcloth, Richard's musty gas mask) to keep the grit at bay. Put spot and filters together to find a lighter sting, smaller fish-hooks, a breath starting below the neck . . . And all the time read the paper, or knit coal-flecked wool, or listen to the trill of the wireless, propaganda from a world where people breathe; a drumbeat of the everyday to distract from the clots and bloody grit and heavy eyelids and bruise-seized ribs and leaden bones begging for bed – a bed you cannot take to for fear you'll never wake. But then you cannot be at the end of your tether, Anna Bourton, she told herself past midnight, cannot really face death. You know that standing on a table wearing woollies and a gas mask and reading the *Express* through the blurry pane is absurd. *And when you are truly lost nothing is absurd, it merely is, reduced to flat existence the moments before it ends. Ergo, you are not hopeless – not yet.*

So to bed, hoping to hide from the everywhere fog, or the failure to escape it, or the fear, the lies, and where they've got you. And because it is cold you slide down, toes jammed at the foot, staying straight because the foetal curl of despair might press on the lungs. You tuck the gritted bedclothes over your head to block winter's bite, close your eyes, breathe in, out, in, out, breath warming the cocoon and the mind slipping back to rue Tai Wo winters and the glory of your coat-draped bed . . . And realise after time that there's no acid in the fug, no particles, no sting; the lungs rumble but do not catch; the diaphragm and ribs press up, down, a controlled steady bellows puffing air into this cave, as if a calisthenics instructor has just demonstrated how to breathe and you are slowly discovering you were born to it.

I can breathe.

Of course, it is carbon dioxide now, not oxygen, but is it any worse than the ground glass? Because everything can function, be, while thoughts slow and eyes rest. And of course I will have to let in some air some time, to take oxygen with my grit, but for now, for the first time in days that feel like weeks, for now, I have ease.

★

Bourton noted the light under the lintel, *Anna will be up*, tried the doorknob, unlocked the Banham when the door didn't budge. And stepped into disarray: a jumble sale of clothes on the bed, odd-angled armchair, table wonky to the wall, gas mask on the Formica, *Express* pages scattered on the floor, hankies draping the Singer, the chest, the pan-handle, for Christ's sake. His Reserve kit had been gutted with green cloth innards flopped on the floor. And no sign of Anna. If he didn't know her better he'd assume she was in the pub or had done a flit.

He stepped in, picked up a pair of woollen stockings, a mucky hanky she must have wiped liver-hands on, *Not the gyppo cotton, girl, we got rags for that*, walked around the end of the bed, noticed the fire was out, the grate full. *If she's up surely she'd be laying it for the day?* and kicked a suitcase, empty, open on the floor beside the wardrobe as if waiting for everything on hangers to be swept in and the lid to be jammed shut. *Surely not.* He opened the wardrobe door, the drawers beneath; her clothes were still there. *So she hasn't started packing. Not that she'd go – something's off with her betimes but a good girl, no reason.* He shook his head. *Flapping about because of a bit of mess.*

His left hand fell on the foot of the bed, and beneath an army towel, her red coat, bedclothes, something solid. A foot. He sensed her body hidden beneath the wool and cotton, a burial barrow turfed over with jumble. He smiled with relief and love at the thought of her bundled in, *A nice warm fug in there and all,* and draped his parka on the jumble, whipped off his boots stork-legged, pulled back the bedclothes as he sat and swung his legs.

'Morning, love!' Her face at rest, pale, creased, blush around the mouth and hanky below her chin. Then her eyes opened, something crackled, she jackknifed and coughed hard, long and wet. He pulled out his own hanky but she was shaking her head, teeth clamped shut, and then a spasm hit. Her mouth opened in pain and his hand was suddenly laced with mucus, blood, purple grit, a ribbon of it dipping from her bottom lip as she moaned, and then another cough spattered matter on his clothes as if she'd taken a bullet through the lungs, and he flinched, sat back. He wiped, registered blood on the hanky, reached out as the coughs didn't stop. Tears trickled down cheeks pink from coughing. *You are sick, girl. How long have you been like this and never said a word?*

'Anna, love . . .' An edge in his voice. *If you die because you didn't want to trouble me, I will never forgive you,* but the anger fell away at her distress and what he knew was his fear. He moved down and cradled her head with one arm and her back with the other. 'It's all right, love, it's all right,' more softly, 'all right.' He lay there feeling useless, flat-footed, knowing anything he said would come out wrong but that it wasn't in him to stay silent, even if he should. 'We'll sort it out, just you see.' He tentatively stroked her back and it brought her forehead against his upper chest. She burrowed under his chin. 'Nothing to worry about. Just a horrible cough, after all.'

*

'We'll get you out of town.' An hour on, tucked in, Anna's eyes closed as her breath took on the rhythm of sleep, Bourton's open but seeing little in their fetid little cavern, their closeness and concealment making every word a hushed conspiracy. 'Send you to Ampney, air's clear there. I mean, there's fog, particularly down Lechlade way,' blathering, head and hands tucked in reminding him of Yanks bayonetted cocooned in their sleeping bags, 'but it's good clean Gloucestershire fog, bit o' woodsmoke, o'course, the wind'll blow it away.'

'I have to work.' Every consonant a tiny cough.

'If it's soupy tomorrow office'll be shut. An' you'd be a sickie anyway.'

'Your mother doesn't like me.'

'Doesn't know you. Besides, ain't for long. An' I'd rather you was down there arguing than up here coughing.'

'What about doctors?'

'Doctors there same as the doctors here. Three, four in Cirencester.'

'I don't have clothes.'

This was getting silly. 'Perfectly good ones, love. Like your red coat. They loved that, first time we went down. First colour of the spring.'

'But what will I do?'

'Rest.' As gently as he could. 'Sleep. Get well. Breathe some proper air, get that cough out of your lungs.' He smiled at what would win her. 'Eat Mum's scones with butter off the ration, her raspberry jam, damson if the raspberry's gone.' *Which it will be now.* 'Get Dave to nab you a pheasant or two. You can go out, snare some rabbits. Do you good to get out on the heath.' Her shoulders had relaxed. She must be warming to the notion. 'Set up shop by the parlour fire. Finish that scarf somewhere you can see what you're knitting.'

'I'm not going for that long.'

'O' course,' keeping the triumph at her acceptance out of his voice, 'just what you need to wait out the fog, clear the lungs, no one to look after but yourself.'

She raised her head so that for the first time since he'd come in the door she was actually looking at his face. 'But what about you? Who'll look after you?'

'Can feed in the canteen – can *débrouille* like the best of 'em. Managed for a while before you come along, though not as well. Might even lose a bit o' weight.' He tried for a reassuring tone. 'I can look after myself, love. It's you who really needs it.'

His eyes must have adjusted because he could see her smile, brow unknotted, face softened. *Job done. Get her in the country, breathing clear, and perhaps we can talk about what it might be. TB?* His stomach lurched. *Then he— She couldn't go down to his mum's. But it can't be TB. The Proctors, they all had that dry cough, gravel in a bowl, and she doesn't – and TB means surgery, isolation hospital, the churchyard above Stroud . . .*

'We're supposed to stick together,' she whispered.

'It's days, love, nothing more.' *Please, stay until it's gone.* 'An' I can come down on the train at weekends, can come down this weekend, bring you home, no time at all. Just to clear the lungs. Like a little cure. A spa. Switzerland, only in Gloucestershire.'

'I can stay here.'

'But you're ill, love.' Gripping her shoulder hard. 'This fog, it's clearly got something in it, doesn't agree. You need to get away from it. Wait it out, give your lungs a rest.'

'The fog will pass.'

'An' kill you.' She blinked as if he'd slapped her, but the realisation had popped into his head and he wasn't going to take it back. 'You know how many people these fogs kill? Thousands. Every time. I've looked at the death books an' every borough, every time, people die. Old, young, babies, people with weakened lungs, they start off with a cough, something in the air doesn't agree, infection sets in an' suddenly there's nothing they can do. Penicillin don't kill it, the infection builds, an' a month or two later they're dead.' Her face was still and suddenly he felt the urge to smack her with it. 'You think it couldn't happen to you? Half the people I've heard about say the same thing, an' six weeks later they're dead just the same.'

He'd hoped for shock, pain in her eyes, but all he got was assessment. 'How do you know this?'

'I've been looking. Off an' on, for months an' months, helping out, like. These jobs for Rex,' remembering he'd told her it was semi-official, not an off-duty jaunt away from his brand new wife, 'looking for people who've died in the fogs. An' you know why it's hard to find the ones we need?' She nodded, blankly, probably not getting the whole story but he didn't have the energy to join dots. 'Cos there are so many of the ones who just die. They've got a lung problem, asthma, bronchitis, bit of pneumonia –'

'But I have none of those.'

'– or a cough. You've got a cough, right?' She nodded. 'From what the coroner's officers an' the doctors say, it starts as a cough, something gets in, an' a month or two later they're drowning in pus, drowning in their own lungs.' He reached across. 'An' you,' kisses between the words, 'have a cough. So let's get you dressed and down to Paddington, love. 'Cos you really shouldn't be in the Big Smoke.'

50

He waved her off on the nine-ten, in her best because Mum would be spiffy for church; a snapshot of her eyes, a clapped hanky and the Astrakhan up against the seat-back, staring ahead like a hostage waiting to be shot. *I'm trying to save you, love, not deport you.*

'You're not with her?' Fred Packer, in the hallway of College Farm Lodge, a sword fight with broomsticks echoing down the phone line. 'She's poorly an' you're not bringin' her down?'

'The Met don't notice Sundays.' *It never occurred to me.* 'I got some CID aide work to do afore my turn, an' they cancelled leave for the fog, so I'm not going—'

'What's wrong wi' 'er?' Joan, snatching the receiver. 'Not morning sickness, is it?'

'Christ, Joanie, leave off. It's the fog, it's given her a shocking cough.'

'Not up the duff yet?'

'An' she needs to rest so she can recover, get her lungs an' spirits up.'

Silence at the other end. 'Lungs? She's not poorly poorly?'

'It's this cough, the soot in the fog, gets in your throat.'

'An' you're not bringing her down?'

Am I the only one didn't think of it? 'Look, Joanie,' guiltily, civil-testy, 'coins'll run out in another minute or so. Anna'll be fine – she just needs a little break, all right?' He could hear breathing down the line but not much else. 'Look,' warmer, 'could you let Mum know, or my dad if she's up the house, an' get her met off the nine-ten, Ciren Town? Trains are that slow she won't be in afore eleven.'

After a moment or two: 'All right, Dick.' Her hand went over the receiver, then she was back. 'Is she OK? I mean, her and your mum, we could put her up, but if the kids . . .'

He closed his eyes at the thought that he'd put Typhoid Mary on the Cirencester branch line. 'I think so, Joanie. She says it's just a cough, but she's in a right flap.' But he couldn't leave it there. 'This fog, Joanie, it can turn a cough into an infection an' an infection . . .' Twin tears were poised at the top of his cheeks. 'Look, could you just make sure she's settled in? I'll be down soon as the fog's done, take a day, or in lieu, all right?'

'All right, Dick.' She was silent – *Feeling my worry, gesturing at Keith, picking her nose, God knows.* 'An' you look after yourself. Weren't you nearly shot in a fog?'

The pips weren't coming to save him so he had to answer. 'Never poke my head out of my shell now,' he tried. 'Say hello to everyone.'

★

Bourton felt liberated, as if he'd put his pontoon winnings in the ship's safe and could leave the troopdeck without worrying about light fingers nicking them. *You'll be all right, girl.* A thought – wish? – shot into the ether. *Sleep, air, decent chow, they'll do it for you.* He tried to lock up the thought that this was a cure for exhaustion, not illness.

Out of yet another echoing tube station into another familiar other-worldly street. Barker's had its shutters down as if it was closed for the duration of something long. And if Kensington High Street's other buildings were showing lights, they weren't reaching through the fog. Kensington Court, on the other hand, glowed like a liner entering harbour. Last night's porter, probably pulling a double shift, walked Bourton up to Marling's flat. Carpets, brass banisters, a well-oiled lift smelling of wood polish, everything gleaming despite the smog. Either the porter had a tireless elbow or mansion flats got a different class of pea-souper.

'Dorothy keeps calling.' Marling swung away on crutches, plush old dressing-gown billowing, across a long squire's corridor of old rugs and hunting prints. Bourton thought he caught a shimmer of nylons on the stump. 'She thinks Saturday nights are hers.' He shouldered open a swinging door into a white-tiled kitchen with a small Formica table under windows onto fog. 'Honestly, she's got marvellous tits but it really isn't worth the vinegar.' He propped the crutches against the wall and, in a slow, precise PT demonstration, lowered himself one-legged onto a chair. Bourton could see corduroys and a collarless shirt under the gown – a ginger Basil Rathbone in a Sherlock picture. 'Proper mash in the pot.' He indicated a big home-knitted cosy on the table. 'Cups in that cupboard.' Bourton pulled one out. 'Do you think the vinegar comes with the tits, as it were? Eventually it all sours in the bottle?'

Given the way Anna's been lately, perhaps. But Bourton wasn't going to say as much. 'Was Dorothy ever – nice an' that?'

'Noooo.' A couple of sips while he thought it over. 'Wanted to fuck, though, right from the off.' Happy, direct, guileless, Watson not Sherlock, behind the plot, about to look a fool. 'Counts for a lot in my book.'

'Would in anyone's,' said Bourton, pouring a dark brew. The steam smelt of tea not dishwater and it took discipline not to close his eyes and cup the scent. *Wonder if he needs a valet – can iron with the best of them* . . . A slurp. *A proper mash.* He couldn't help closing his eyes after all.

'Anyway,' Marling fished his cigarette case out of his pocket, 'let's do things differently today. We're going to borrow a council car.'

A refuge when your leg gets gyppy – I can see that. He nodded. 'Can you drive it?'

'No, you will.'

'But . . .' Bourton saw any number of disasters, most of which meant jail, or his pay being docked for damages until he was fifty, or both. 'Won't we get nicked?'

'Us? A policeman and a pillar of the Conservative Party?'

'Can't we just phone the sections?'

'No one'll be in.'

'We can't burgle them, I'm an officer of the law.'

'So am I.'

'I can't break into places.'

'So I will.'

'But I'd be an accomplice.'

'For God's sake,' a little leader-of-men steel, 'do you want this chap or not?'

★

The only vehicle fuelled was the mayoral Humber, £500 of gleaming toff-trolley, with a coat of arms on the rear door. Can't see much and my feet are lead, thought Bourton; that vehicle's not coming back in one piece. Yards of gear clashes across the town-hall tarmac and Marling was clearly thinking the same. He stared at Bourton's feet as if there were four of them. 'Like you'll do any better,' Bourton growled. 'It'll come back to me.' He thrust his *A-Z* at him. 'Map-read, Long John. Kidderpore Avenue, page forty-two, by way of Finchley Road, west side of Regent's Park, Baker Street, Oxford Street, Park Lane, I reckon. Straight shots.' They jumped forward. 'Anyway, this was your idea.'

Turn onto Kensington High Street. No point in waiting. Can't see any headlights, hear any engine over the Humber – just pull out, as gradual as beat legs and feet will allow. The white lines and left kerb were visible, but a mustard glow had papered over buildings, traffic lights, street-lamps.

'Speed and distance,' said Bourton, his words as tight as his hands clamped to the wheel. 'If you can't see, measure distance, speed, time. Speed, call it fifteen, distance to Hyde Park Corner two miles, check watch. If we run over a PC on lighthouse, it's Queen's Gate, perhaps Knightsbridge.' A sudden frozen white O of shock – an old dear with a lead and, presumably, a dog, gone before he could brake. 'Fuck.' They slowed to a crawl. *No bumps so we didn't hit her or the animal.* He flexed fingers, clammy in gloves. 'Speed ten.'

'Mile and three-quarters,' said Marling. 'Seven minutes at fifteen m.p.h., ten and a half at ten m.p.h.' Leaning over the dashboard to scan wide through the windscreen. 'Roughly.'

'I look out,' abruptly, 'you check your watch.' A swinging light. A copper on lighthouse snapping to attention as they passed. *Does the mayor get this all the time? Lighthouse means this must be* . . . 'Queen's Gate.'

'OK. Nine minutes at ten m.p.h.'

Marling called each minute, Bourton's eyes flicking between windscreen, speedometer and mirror. A waving light in the road two minutes in. Hard halt. A figure appeared by the bonnet, torch waist-high, a glowing cigar in the mouth, 'Thanks, old man,' a hand waving a clutch of coats over to the park, then tapping the bonnet, standing aside, a voice calling, 'Morning, Charlie!' as they pulled past.

'Your mayor called Charlie?'

'Yours too,' said Marling. Then, realising the question had a point, 'Yes.'

'We might just have met one of his friends.'

'Hell,' said Marling. 'Three minutes.' Then, 'Chelsea have a Humber too.'

Five and a half minutes in, a swinging lantern – *Old Brompton Road?* – and then another, further back, eight, ten feet up. He braked again: a copper on lighthouse, touching the brim of his bonnet. The high lamp moved in, borne by something solid, black, besieging the car – a horse, a mounted PC in his tent-like cape, bending in the saddle, then straightening to bellow, 'Honours!' Almost immediately, 'Eyes . . . left!' and chestnut legs, gleaming black boots and glowing harness paraded past the car, as a troop of Household Cavalry saluted a former sergeant and private of infantry of the line. If Bourton hadn't been terrified one would shy and kick a hole in the panelwork, he'd have laughed.

A steady ten, burning braziers, *Hyde Park Hotel*, doormen in long coats and toppers on the pavement to keep out the riff-raff. 'You been in there?' Marling asked. 'Do a great cocktail. Dorothy—'

'Watch,' said Bourton.

'Oh, for God's sake, we'll know when we hit Hyde Park Corner. It'll be full of cars.'

It was. Window down as they ambled in, hard by the kerb to declare their neutrality, Bourton could hear an echo of engines, revved low enough to cough, sitting in the fog. Headlights head-high, a horn blaring as a huge Scannell pushed in, swerved, stalled, was lost in the vapour as Bourton bumped onto the pavement in panic. 'Pedestrian!' shouted Marling, a wrench of the wheel and a jolt down to the tarmac, a blink of brake lights. *Slow.* A taxi in the rear-view leaned on its horn, another lorry from the right inched towards Park Lane. *Let it go.* The driver's mate leaned out of his door to offer a toothless thumbs-up, a string of lights and shapes nudging out of the fog in surprised succession. Bourton halted.

'We're stuck for the duration,' said Marling. Hooting from behind the taxi in the rear-view. 'Trick might be not to stop.' Bourton started easing forward, but the taxi behind had swung out and was butting into the traffic, the cabby leaning on his horn and yelling. A motorbike let him in, he turned to cross Bourton's front, jolted and stopped as a Bedford lorry radiator crunched his passenger compartment.

'Fuck,' said Bourton. 'I hope he doesn't have a fare.'

'There's a gap!' shouted Marling. 'Bugger the fare! Drive!'

The cabby was out, arms and voice suggesting paintwork, not a threat to life, so Bourton edged forward, jolted as Marling hit his thigh – 'Faster! Oomph!' – then followed rear lights as they arced left, either into Park Lane or Apsley House, back up to a steady ten with his foot hovering over the clutch, lights disappearing as the car ahead speeded up. Away. 'Like dodgems,' said Marling, 'only with consequences.'

'An' blindfolds,' said Bourton, raising his arms in a half-cluck to unstick his pits.

'What they need there,' said Marling, 'is one of those policemen with lanterns.'

'Traffic ate him,' said Bourton. 'Now do the maths for Park Lane an' points north.'

Kneeling by the armchair, holding down the hands of the accountant's widow who stayed in Brondesbury to be close to the grandchildren who never came: *Home for half-past ten in time to greet the wife, change for chapel, service tie, the good shoes taken from the fairy off Edgware Road, perhaps his jacket too – 'Mr Gittins's son,' I'll say. 'You'll remember I mentioned him and how grateful he was. He gave it to me now his dad's passed on.' Then leave her at the hall for her Sunday sandwich and mild, hurry back, supposedly to duty – 'I must not let them down, my dear' – and the chance of three, perhaps four souls, if the cabby off Southwark High Street, the frightened Polish lass in Borough, the greengrocer off the New Kent—*

The pulse had gone. He looked at her eyes behind the mask's eyepiece but they were closed, and her body had the slump of death. He'd missed it. He'd been thinking instead of watching and truly feeling, and her soul had escaped, ungreeted, unwelcomed. He shook his head. Her soul deserved better than that, even if she hadn't; it deserved a man with open hands, an open heart, flinging it into the sky, like a pigeon with a once-damaged wing. He stood, his left hip creaking, some kind of nick in his back. The pains always popped up with his disappointments. He reached stiffly for his apparatus, removed it from her face, and put it back in its box on the parlour table. He wasn't very interested in her now that he'd mucked up the emancipation, decided he wouldn't even look for a memento – what about the consultation was worth remembering? He gave her hair a cursory brush down with his hands, stuck her tongue back in her mouth, laid her hands on the chair arms, and walked down the corridor to the kitchen. He lit the gas, put the kettle on, and climbed the stairs to her bedroom to find something for his joints. A pint of tea or Bovril and perhaps a good embrocation would put some spring in his step.

51

Hampstead Civil Defence lived in a church hall near Parliament Hill, where the air was better and a glimmer of sun reflected off the murk. Worthies were handing out tea to the congregation from ten o'clock, and summoned the head of section while Marling and Bourton tried the brew. It had the colour of Bourton's cheese-squits from Palestine.

Samuel Rosen looked like a bruiser but was a philosophy lecturer at the University of London with perfect Berlitz English. He was far too savvy to buy what they were selling. 'So you're looking for someone,' to Bourton, 'and you are the point of entry,' to Marling. Bourton nodded. 'And why do you want this chap?'

'Can't say,' said Bourton, flatly.

'So you suspect him of something. And you want one of my men.'

'No,' said Bourton. 'We're trying every CD section in London, looking for a man with a King's Commendation.'

Rosen laughed. 'Just the two of you, in this fog?'

'The phone helps,' said Bourton. 'And the section heads. They've lent a hand.'

'Have they?' Flat, neutral, unimpressed. He shrugged. 'It's moot, anyway, as I don't have anyone. Frank D'Agostini has a Mention – that won't do?' Bourton shook his head. 'So you've come all this way for nothing.'

'No's good, sir. Narrows it down.'

'How many more have you got?'

'Two. Poplar weren't at home and Wandsworth—'

'Poplar,' he pulled out a cardboard-covered address book, 'tend to drill in an empty warehouse they've borrowed from a fruit company. I can call their head of section, Stanley Chinn, for you, if you like.'

'Don't suppose you know Wandsworth, too, while you're at it?'

'No,' reaching for the phone, 'it's south of the river. Haven't got round to coordinating with them yet.'

Let's hope the Thames'll block radiation, then, thought Bourton. Might be filthy enough.

★

Poplar CD's offices were behind the town hall, an island of Georgian perfection in what felt – from the eddies in the air and the smell of broken brickwork – like acres of bombsite. Chinn reigned from behind a desk big and black enough to have been hewn from Nelson's flagship. Pale, thin, bald, in layers of clothing under a blue boiler suit, he looked like a revolutionary who'd just shot the desk's last owner and was secretly enjoying his warmed-up chair.

'PC Bourton.' Chinn's hands were flat on the desk, his shoulders braced, defensive, and Bourton felt a tingle. *I'm getting close.* 'What do you want to know?'

Bourton was nonplussed. 'Well, I explained on the phone.'

'A fiftyish man with a King's Commendation. I got all that. So 'ere I am.' Bourton was still confused. 'Catch up, Bourton.' Sharp, dismissive. 'The only man in the section who fits your bill is me.'

★

Bourton might have been flicking through his notebook like a real copper giving evidence but he didn't feel in charge. And Chinn could tell. ''Aven't done this much, 'ave you, Bourton?' He had a Cockney accent with clipped edges, like the cabby who followed that car in the pictures, and right now sounded as if he'd been accused of losing it.

Peel House Rule 1: Do not allow a suspect to establish an ascendancy. 'No. Most of the people I talk to are biddable after resisting arrest.' A hard smile, nice and fake. That's enough talking down to me, sunshine. Chinn blinked, offered a tiny nod, as if he'd got the message. 'What do you do, Mr Chinn?'

'Clerk of works at St Bart's.'

'Which means?'

'I run maintenance.'

'Keep you busy?'

'Yep.'

'Pull you Up West at all?'

'Not so's you'd notice.'

'Stockwell?'

'No.'

'North Kensington?'

'No.'

'Marylebone Road?'

'No.' Chinn shook his head. 'Dunno what kind of crook I'm supposed to be, but Bart's keeps me busy ten hours a day, weekends when we've got works.'

'You wear your CD uniform much?'

'No. Home to drill and back, East India Dock Road.'

'Which section were you in before you became the gaffer?'

'Borough engineer's department.'

'But you must pick up a bit of medical knowledge, working in a hospital.'

'I'm an 'andyman,' Chinn sat forward, diction slipping, beginning to feel the needle, 'in charge of other 'andymen. I've got nothing to do with the doctors.'

'Where were you on the evening of February the seventh?'

'What?'

'Day after the King died. Where were you?'

'What? 'Ow do you expect me to know what I was doing one day in *February*? Do you know?'

'Yes.'

'What?'

'Finding the woman you might have killed.' Chinn was still for a few seconds, then he blinked. 'So I'm not mucking around. What were you doing, evening of February the seventh?'

'I thought you was interested in something a bit bent.' Chinn pulled out a card-bound ledger with 'Duty Roster' stencilled on the cover from the desk. 'What day was it?'

'Thursday.'

He opened the ledger. 'We didn't 'ave anyone on that evening.' He looked up. 'I might have gone to the lying in state.'

'Didn't start till the eleventh.'

'Ah, bollocks. What time do I need to 'ave been busy?'

'What would you have been doing?'

'Up at 'alf five, work at 'alf seven, clock off at 'alf five, 'ome at quarter past six, then just me an' the missus for the evenin'. Day after 'Is Majesty,' shaking his head again, 'most like at 'ome, listening to the wireless. Not much of an alibi.'

But one easily checked, with the hospital, and if he was telling the truth, then on that night, in that fog, he couldn't have made it to Bewley Street from Smithfield before six thirty – half an hour after that lad saw the Traveller on Gladys Hartham's doorstep. Bourton nodded. 'You're right.'

'Should have kept my trap shut.'

Why didn't he? Would never have known about his commendation, otherwise. Guilty man's bravado, wanting to dare the copper to pinch him? Or the brass neck of an innocent one with the opportunity to play the police?

'Perhaps,' said Bourton. 'Still, we'll see.'

52

He isn't sleeping.

Richard hadn't slept in their bed since Friday evening. He couldn't have, because she was there. Thirty-six hours without sleep. And Friday was just a nap. Vi or Re would say, 'He's warming someone else's bed,' but Richard, so guileless, would give himself away in an instant. No, he was walking his beat all night, doing his Rex job all day, becoming beaten and weary and sore, and needing warmth, sex, food, love, a hot bath. And he needed meals with real meat, and no questioning, no disagreement, just 'Yes, my love, you are so clever, and brave, and big.' *And instead he comes home to a mess and a whining, selfish woman who shouts at him for wanting to build a fire, does not ask properly what is taking his time.*

And she had not yet washed the evidence, scattered around the room. Klaxon-calls of her despair – flung clothes, the mug she'd spat in, two days' worth of bloody rags . . .

The train slowed. Now they were beyond the fog and her breath came regularly again, a little crackly and with coughs, but little coughs, blood and grit reminders, but that was what you would expect. Now she was out of London and did not worry about whether the next breath would come, she could think clearly, widely, not the blinkers of obsession, of fear. She could make decisions.

The window moved past pillars, a roof, figures on a station platform, a sign – Reading – as the train lost momentum, the brakes squealed, and a tinny announcement echoed outside, unclear through the carriage wall. She stood, grabbed her Kai Tak case, moved to the window and pushed it down, stuck her head out onto a world with a horizon, and was gripping the door handle even before the train had come to a halt. Richard Bourton needed a wife. And she knew how to make it possible again.

★

She crossed a footbridge, found the booking hall, changed her ticket, pocketed the refund. She sat in the buffet over a cup of terrible tea, case at her knees, breathing slowly and deeply, watching the station go by. The air tasted of wet serge, mothballs, cabbage, cigarettes.

Two hours of thinking it through, threading between the pillars of what she knew, the way she had found clarity in the jeremiads and evasions of coolies and spies.

One: she could not go to the doctor. They were the government: they would report her to ministry men, who would check her forms and see that she had lied. And then? The right of residence stripped, with her guarantors no defence. Which meant deportation, perhaps even prison. Where would that leave poor, honest, loving, loyal Richard?

Two: no one must determine what was wrong with her – because if it was what she thought, a gift from some Japanese laboratory, carried on the hands of a man who caressed the dead, it might mean banishment to a sanatorium, even detention, and questions.

Three: Richard could not find out she had lied on the forms; he would see her true, hate her, but stay loyal because he could do no other – and go under with her.

Four: Richard could not find out about the full level of her fear. For his clever brain would ask, Why is she so frightened? and eventually find the answer: Because of something she has concealed. Which would lead, inevitably, to: She is a confection of lies.

Five: her place was by his side. *He is doing something which takes his hours, his normal life, his sleep, which is driving him, which matters. And I worry about washing and hiding hankies, guarding untruths, instead of finding out the thing he is trying to change or stop, and leading him through it, hand in hand.*

So, the five pillars – fact or subjective argument, who cares? But they lead inevitably to: going home. Whether it is a choice of reason or emotion.

Two hours of thinking it through, three brews. Two hours and her chest had reached a kind of equilibrium: sparkles inside, like phosphorescence on water, pins and needles of the lungs, and tickles down the tubes that could catch the breath, but a kind of order inside that made her feel composed, even serene. *See? This is all it takes. No melodrama, just a brief respite. Or help . . .*

And determination. Standing on the platform as the train pulled in, she was aware of the moment of an act of will, the way she'd felt on that ridge – in Hebei? Or further north? – looking down on the baking valley with loose threads of smoke leading up to the sun. She had a choice, of staying where she was, or walking into who knew what, apart from pain and fear. But just like then, this was a theory choice, not a practice choice. In practice, there was no choice at all.

★

She had walked past the street entrance innumerable times, registering the sign, the small entryway, the single row of houses with the blank wall opposite, and above it the tube line, skimming people above the grubby Dale. She had not registered how poor the houses were. Even with eyes red and smarting from the fog, through dust-speckled eyelashes and gritty tears, she could see the patchy plaster, sagging pediments above the windows, cracks in the brickwork with shrubs growing out of them, makeshift curtains. Nor had she registered how small Rillington Place was – small enough to see its full width, despite the fog. She paused as she walked down the pavement, arm's length from the rotting window frames and patches of damp, thinking, This cannot be. But then she was back in her stride: *London is poor, the Dale is poor, and Monsieur Fung and his remedies lived down a street where the ground never saw daylight, with pigs foraging, laundry that never dried, earth that stank of spilled piss from the tanner's tubs. And Monsieur Fung could work miracles . . .*

She knocked on the door of number 10. The wood sounded hollow, rotten, and left a flake of paint on her knuckle. She reached for her hanky and saw a doughy bespectacled face, hip height, parting the makeshift curtain in the shallow bay. It fell again. She heard a bitter voice cawing from the room. It might have said 'whore'. There was an exchange, then the curtain parted again: another ill-defined face, but harder, masculine, glasses being adjusted over the nose. The man blinked, nodded with a deferential smile and dropped the curtain. The voices moved to the space behind the door. Anna caught the words 'respectable woman'. The door half opened to show Christie, in his suit, as if about to step out.

'Mrs Bourton.' She nodded behind the fog mask she'd bought at Paddington and he bobbed deferentially. 'An honour.' An undertaker's smile. 'To what do I owe this pleasure?'

She lifted the mask away from her mouth, wafting what smelt like a spoonful of Vicks straight up her nose and sneezed, breathed in sharply to do it again and grit stirred in her throat. The first cough came before she had her hanky up or her lips closed and spat matter on the door, and she turned away immediately before the fit drove Christie indoors. But even as it passed and she pulled the mask over her mouth, she was aware that he hadn't moved from the doorway, saw that his smile was still on his face, and thought, He has seen all this before, and was grateful.

'This is a terrible one indeed,' he said, 'worst I've known in years. Difficult, for people like us.' He was assuming something shared, as he always did, but this time it seemed frivolous to object.

'It is,' she said, making to pull the mask away but he shook his head.

'I can hear you perfectly well, Mrs Bourton.' Undertaker's smile again. 'Live and fight in a gas mask, Mrs Bourton, and you get quite used to the muffled voice. Acute hearing, like they always said. Came in handy in the second war. The number of times I'd be head in the rubble, listening for the cries of the poor souls.'

'Invaluable, I'm sure.' He was turning her into Miss Bountiful again, and she felt she had to add something to tone it down. 'I'm sure many people had reason to be thankful.'

'That they did. Though many was the time you'd hear nothing at all. Or,' he looked down, 'hear the cries stop before the rescue squad could get to them.'

Enough civilities. 'Mr Christie, you mentioned a special breathing apparatus?'

He nodded. 'I did.' He pulled the door a little tighter to him. 'And I would be delighted to administer a treatment – there's been some call for it over the last few days, as I'm sure you'd understand. Unfortunately I cannot do so immediately,' professionally apologetic, 'as I have some Sunday business to conclude.'

'Of course.' The mask helped hide her disappointment. 'Perhaps later today?'

'Oh, of a certainty.' Emphatic, eager. 'In three-quarters of an hour? It's only my weekly talk to the Boys' Brigade at Redemption Hall.'

Anna smiled so widely that acid air seeped into her mouth. Forty-five minutes, and she would have a lifeline to tomorrow.

'The Brigade and Methody, Mrs Bourton,' said Christie, as he stepped back from the doorway. 'Made me what I am.'

★

She walked home so deliberately she was aware of every heel strike, the roll of her foot, the push in her calf. The room felt as if she'd left it ship-shape and squeaky and come back to find it turned over by burglars or squatters or Japanese police. She put the Kai Tak case under the bed without unpacking, picked up the bloody hankies, washed off the grit from the sink bowl, and put them in to soak. The white ones were ruined, but the army green rags she'd run up on the Singer . . . She picked up, folded and put away the clothes she'd scattered in her panic, wiped down the Formica, put the armchair back at its angle to the table and the table against the wall, then straightened and folded down the bed. *See? Order – skin deep, but at least not disorder, weakness, evidence of despair.* She looked at the table, where she'd stood to gasp at the ceiling air just hours before, and smiled to herself. *Just the possibility of an answer boxes up the fear, and the lies, pushes away hysteria.* There were specks, dark, blood, perhaps matter, on the sheet turn-down. She stripped off the bedclothes, folding the blankets and draping the counterpane over them – *I'll make it when I get back from Christie's and can breathe* – then took the sheets to the bath to scrub out the marks. Back to the room to find a scrap for a note to Sylvia Lewis, to apologise for the bathroom – though she hadn't seen her since Friday. Perhaps she was away. Anna realised she'd be late for Christie, for clear lungs, for feeling free. What was she doing scrubbing and folding when she could be breathing deep?

53

'Mr Christie.'

'Mrs Bourton.' He stood back to let her in. The corridor was narrow and the front door seemed to stick, so even though he leaned away her shoulder brushed his chest and her leg his thigh. He seemed to smile apologetically but the corridor was dark and she might have been mistaken. 'Please go straight ahead,' a spectral hand – long, white, large on a skinny wrist – pointing down the ill-lit corridor, 'to the kitchen. Mrs Christie prefers that I do not hold my consultations in our parlour. Alas, so great is the need for housing that we decided to do our bit and let the room I would otherwise have used.' She walked through the smell of rotting wood, damp, patchy wallpaper, carbolic, past two closed doors. She paused by the third, facing the staircase, with a fourth, clearly external, at the end of a tiny lobby to her right. He walked around her, keeping his distance, and opened the third, the kitchen door. She stepped in as he turned on the light switch. Window on the right, onto a dark brick return, with a door beyond it; two or three wallpapers; a little Belling cooker; a worn worktop; and a sink on the wall opposite the window. She'd been in half a dozen kitchens just like it over the past nine months. It had the chill of somewhere unheated for a decade.

'Now, Mrs Bourton,' closing the kitchen door, 'the consultation fee is ordinarily a pound.' *A day's wages!* 'However, I think in this case I can offer a police officer's discount,' he was wearing his obsequious smile again, 'of twenty-five per cent, so fifteen bob it is.' Her hand kept her bag firmly closed. 'I would dearly like to be in the position to charge less, but alas, so efficatous does my apparatus prove to be that there is often little need for subsequent consultations.' He licked his lips.

Ah, well, I came here for this. It would be foolish to haggle. 'I quite understand, Mr Christie.' Miss Bountiful again. 'A fee is a fee.' She turned away from him to get out the cash and lay it on the worktop. 'Now, how shall we proceed?'

He brought out a chair two-handed from below the end of the counter. 'This is my incline chair.' He put it in front of the cooker. 'It allows the patient to lie back, upright enough so that even the worst afflicted can draw breath, shallow enough that the vapours can reach even the furthest aioli.' It looked like a fold-up deckchair from the park, but with netting instead of canvas. 'The patient lies back in the chair, and I administer the treatment.' He inspected her clothing. 'You will want to remove your coat, and perhaps your pullover, and either fold down the collar of your blouse, or tuck something over it – a handkerchief, something of that sort.' His nervous smile, just like that first time in the café, as if admitting to a little failure. 'The unguent around the edge of the apparatus has been known to stain clothing.' She nodded, emptied the hip pockets of her coat into the pockets of her skirt, and handed it to him to hang on the door. The panel edges were oily black, and she stretched out as he reached up to the hook to try to stop the cloth brushing against the muck, but the coat was up now and any damage done. Christie turned, saw her arm still raised, and the professional smile returned. 'Is there something more you wish for from your coat?'

'No – well,' patting her hip pockets to sustain his misunderstanding, 'no, I have what I need, thank you.' She smiled her thanks and turned away to remove her jumper, wondering if there was some English code she was missing – a way of responding to all these mannerisms supposed to whisper, Respectability, but instead calling, Look how far I think I have fallen!' She felt a pang of sympathy for the man. *All of us have fallen. Or will fall.*

She passed the jumper to Christie to drape over her coat and his eyes went to her breasts, with another of his smiles, one she couldn't read. 'Thank you,' he said. Eyes up. 'You will of course need to remove the mask, but I quite understand if you wish to do that when in the chair. Many of my patients like to retain their aids until the last moment.' He indicated the chair. 'Please make yourself comfortable while I prepare the apparatus.'

She crimped a clean hanky around her collar and moved to the chair. She locked her knees together and dipped into the netting, hands on the struts, and immediately sank, her bottom seeming only inches from the floor. Her bag dropped off her shoulder and she grabbed for it but the strut was in the way. Christie scurried from the door – he'd been watching her move, perhaps hoping for a knees-open treat – and picked up the bag, handing it over. 'I will need to put it safe to one side, Mrs Bourton, when you are ready, perhaps when you have put the aid away.' She nodded, thinking, How do I sit? *Feet flat, knees high, body squashed forward as if ready to spring.* She rested her bag on her knees, rooted for another hanky, and unhitched the mask from her ears. Straight away she felt cold air seep between the cloth and her lips. She paused, panic spiking as Christie watched her. 'We all love our aids, Mrs Bourton.' Low, sympathetic. 'They make it possible for us to brave the day.' Another smile, this one a rictus in a blank white face, sweat on his upper lip. *Is he in severe pain?* 'But the particules from your aid will not go deep, Mrs Bourton, will not pass the epiglottis; they are not your breath itself. Whereas with my apparatus,' patting a card gas-mask box on the counter, 'the particules are the breath itself. You close your eyes, you breathe, and within minutes my special preparation is exploring the aioli and bronchioles, seeking out the soreness and soothing the pain and fear. If you put your aid aside now, Mrs Bourton, you will not need it later.' Colour had come back to his face but he still looked tense – a back spasm? – as she removed the mask, wrapped it in the hanky, and put it at the top of the bag. She could reach for it when he was done.

'Now,' from behind her head, 'you will need to sit back and relax, to incline,' a proud smile in his voice, 'close your eyes, and be still.' She heard opening, extracting, fixing noises, and as she lay back, before her body sagged and her neck hit the top bar, glimpsed him in his shirt-sleeves pressed against the cupboard, arms on the counter working on something out of view.

'So, how does your apparatus work, Mr Christie?' Cracks in the wall led up to glitters on the ceiling – smog specks in spiders' webs, a thought that did not make her want to cough. *It's working already.*

'It is based upon the standard box respirator.' She sensed him reaching along the counter behind her head. 'Filters in the mask keep

out the particules of smog. My special preparation in the box laces
the pure oxygen with unguent. So,' voice tense, 'you breathe in filtered
air,' a couple of thumps, 'improved with pure oxygen, and my preparation; a blend that soothes and invigorates.' She heard the oven door
open and smelt gas. 'I must heat the preparation for a moment to
ensure it is mixed through.' He was standing beside the chair, pale,
sweating from his fiddlings, smiling hard, eyes wide. *He must be in
a lot of pain.* 'Now, this works best if you rest your arms on the side
of the incliner,' raising his shoulders, 'which brings your shoulders
up, opens the lungs. We can put the bag to one side,' taking it from
beneath her compliant hands and putting it on the edge of the counter,
'and you can have the use of it when the treatment is done. Arms
up,' he took her hands, his palms cold and moist, and laid them on
the struts, 'and shoulders in, excuse me,' then pushed her shoulders
so they lay inside the netting. 'Settle into the seat so your posterior
is low and your feet off the floor, your legs hanging off the edge of
the chair.' She rested her calves on the bottom strut, immediately
feeling the bite of the narrow frame. 'And you close your eyes.' The
oven door opened behind her and Christie put something on the
counter. 'In a moment the treatment can begin.' He was standing
beside the chair now, still pale, wide-eyed, sweaty, but smiling reassuringly. 'I must apologise for the smell of gas. My wife swears by
this cooker, but sometimes it does not burn off everything from the
nooks and crannies.' Anna nodded. He looked at the counter. 'I will
prepare the apparatus.'

She closed her eyes. Within moments she felt her eyelids settling
for sleep, slumping on her cheeks as her body drooped in the strange
framed hammock. *In a minute or two he won't need his apparatus. I
shall drift off on the back of my silly nights, my fretful days, the worries
about the lies and the laundry and the air, and I will wake in an hour
or two, with Christie fifteen bob richer, thanks to his magic deckchair, and
I will saunter home with a girlish bounce, ready to leap into song, like
Judy Garland on the trolley in St Louis, and then wait for my husband
with a real smile, an I-love-you smile, not the brittle Please-do-not-look-
too-hard-or-ask-too-much . . .*

'I am applying the apparatus.' She opened her eyes to see Christie
putting a gas mask over her face, fitting straps behind her head as

she breathed out against the medicinal rubber, *Yet more Vicks, British winter runs on Vicks,* and everything clouded through the mask's yellowed visor. 'Breathe for me, please, Mrs Bourton, to make sure that the filters are working,' she breathed in, more Vicks, 'nod if you are receiving air,' she nodded, 'and now I will turn on the valves.' She could see his arm and shoulder as he reached past her to the counter, saw his hand as it came down to the mask, felt the tug as he adjusted something on the snout, and closed her eyes to settle in. 'And breathe.' A first tentative sip. 'Let's breathe deeply, Mrs Bourton,' a strong pull, Vicks, something hedgerow-flavoured, of course the gas, her chest still rising as her lungs swelled, the vapour sliding past the grit and rawness, then out, 'and again,' not even the whisper of a cough, so she let her diaphragm press flat to make room for a bigger breath, then slowly let the bellows rise, sucking warmer air laced with balm into the mouth, the throat, the chest, 'and out.' Another three or four breaths and she was into a rhythm, the pacing, the sweetness of the balm, Christie's hypnotic chant, her tiredness all making her feel drowsy, light-headed, a tingle in the fingers, the oven door must have swung open because the gas was strong—

She opened her eyes to Christie's face a foot from the visor, eyes huge, mouth open, lips drawn back, blink blink as his hands clamped on her wrists. His body came down on hers in the netting, she bucked weakly but he absorbed it, tried to kick but his weight was on her thighs, tried to thrash her hands but all his strength was holding them down as hers ebbed. *He is killing me!* Suddenly her left slipped off the frame, a flash of hope, but he shoved it through the netting, and flattened his body on hers as she wriggled like a fish a minute out of water, without the breath to make 'No!' more than a whisper. His free hand grabbed a fistful of breast, his pelvis pressed into her torso, and she could feel his old man's balls in her lap, a slug in his trousers hardening as he ground against her, and he put his face against the panel, no specs to hide his eyes or yellowed skin as his breath fogged the visor, and said very clearly, 'Die, you bitch, die.'

Will Richard ever know? she thought with the last of her air as she twitched in the netting. Fight fight fight, and I die in a web. Oh, Richard, I am so sorry . . .

She coughed, a little tickle in her flattened lungs, but it caught in the throat and tripped some other reflex, because suddenly she was retching into the mask, drops spattering back on her face as she automatically inhaled gas and acid. Christie pulled back, and her left hand, trapped in netting, hit the floor. Her arm straightened, and as she vomited in the mask and he jerked away, the chair toppled sideways, pitching them onto their sides on the linoleum, face to face, the frame and her deadweight trapping his left arm. She reached up, ripped off the gas mask, whipped vomit from her mouth and breathed, choked, coughed, spat all at once, breathed again as his free hand came up to her throat. She pulled the sap from her right pocket, and as he squeezed, his thumb crushing cartilage, sparking stars, rolling her head back, freeing him to climb on top of her, hardening on her belly, *I can't see, the end is near,* she twitch-flailed the sap and felt the jolt in the wrist as she caught something. Suddenly his hands and his body were gone, his bony lower legs flailing on her thighs as she breathed, coughed, breathed, gradually aware that he was shouting, *I can hear now too,* breathed, breathed, *Can see, must not stop.* She flailed again with the sap at his shins, his legs retracted and she had air, *Face him to fight him,* onto her left side to see him on his side near the door, hands on his balls, staring at her with red-eyed fury. *Finish him.* Her feet found purchase and she was up with half the broken deckchair hanging from her left hand, netting snagged on her wrist. She paused to breathe, lift the wreckage to get at her left-hand pocket and pull out her father's knuckles, but he was struggling upright. *I cannot have caught him properly,* the fury turning to calculation, and she realised she could not close with him, she was too weak, too one-handed, the sap would not be enough—

'Look at you now, bitch.' His accent, manner, voice all rough now, the bedside professional dumped like a truss. 'Miss Hoity. But you were a whore all the time.' He was standing slightly bent over in front of the door so she had to move him if she was going to get out. She stuck the half-chair in front of her as a barrier. 'All your airs and the weapon of a whore. Husband know you're whoring, does he?'

'Does your wife,' voice croaky, she coughed but kept the sap hand low – *He is weak, a little clever, so win time, talk* – 'does she know you attack young women?'

His mouth turned down in contempt. 'Whore.' She looked at him hard, to show she was not afraid, knowing somehow that fear would kill her. 'Nah. Women nag all the time, and do you know when it stops? When you're dead.' He glanced at the drawers under the counter. *Looking for a weapon.*

'You can't use a knife.' His eyes came back, calculating. 'Ever used a knife? I have. Blood, everywhere. You can't clean it all up. Your fat wife will see it. People in the house will see it.' She hefted the cosh. 'And I will hit you, a few times, face, hands – bones will break. Other people will see it. Your wife will see it. You cannot use a knife.'

'Use it properly,' a rigid smile, 'no blood at all. Drops. Slide it in, between the ribs, reach up to the heart—'

'I will fight. I am not some grey English girl.' She spat, French contempt so scathing that he flinched. 'You think you can find the heart, with me fighting for my life? You think you have a *knife* that can find my heart in your house? Your oven doesn't work. Your chair doesn't work.' She shook the remains of it on her knuckle hand. 'You don't work.' His eyes widened. 'I felt you, old man, rubbing against me, only getting a little hard when I was a little dead, a young woman, and all you can do is *frotter* until she is still, and *then* you are a stallion with your old hangy balls—'

He grabbed the chair frame and yanked hard, pulling her off balance and in. His left came up in a fist, her heels jerking across the floor, and suddenly she stopped resisting, cannoned into his middle with the frame, the knuckles bouncing off somewhere low, and as his angry eyes widened in surprise and his left swung a mistimed punch she rapped with the cosh, a couple of times. He yelped and went down on his left knee, and suddenly she was half past him looking down at his pallid face, his left hand scrabbling up her front for her throat. She rapped him on the shoulder and his hand came down, *Finish him,* she swung the cosh wide to take him in the side of the head with all her might but suddenly she was on the floor, head numb, legs scrabbling, flailing again with the cosh and the trapped knuckle-hand and pistoning her knees, anything to keep him off, everything shrouded in scarlet as he threw her coat over her head. She hooked it off with the knuckle-hand, the chair frame jabbing her chest, and saw Christie aiming a frying pan at her head. She swung the knuckle-hand again and the chair frame took Christie's legs out and he went over. She scrabbled away from him, the door, safety, and stood.

'You're not walking out of here, whore.' He hauled himself up with the help of the door-handle, his right gripping the pan.

'You think? Mr Droopy? You and your wife's pan?'

'Come and get it, whore.' He raised the pan as if receiving a tennis serve. Her eye fell on a length of tubing snaked across the chipped worktop from behind the Belling, one end hanging down towards the floor. *Must have come out of the gas mask when I pulled it off.* The respirator box sat on its own, connected to nothing. *So not even the pretence of science – just Vicks in the mask and coal gas in the tube. What a fool . . .*

Use your brain.

'I know what you are thinking, Mr Christie.' He blinked at the courtesy. 'You are thinking, I cannot let her go, she will run straight to the police, or tell her husband. But I won't. You think I want people to know I came to your house? That I was such a fool? My husband, he thinks I'm in the country. He need never know.' She could see she had him thinking beyond the simple kill-or-be-killed, and she picked up speed. 'I walk out of here, I go home, I change, I go to Paddington, I get on the train for my cure, and in a week he comes down, my bruises have faded, the ripped clothes have gone, there is nothing – *nothing* – to tell him what has happened here.' She paused. 'If you step aside.'

He smiled, vicious, satisfied, not what she'd expected. 'No one knows you're here, whore.' He raised the pan and stepped in. 'You're mine.'

She gasped at her stupidity and as he swatted aside the shattering chair-frame and her shrouded wrist and moved in for the kill her throat caught, a cough that made him flinch and triggered a spasm, pulling blood and grit from deep in her lungs, and a thought into her conscious: *He flinched when I spat too.* She gobbed everything at his mouth. He leaned his head back so far his wattles tautened, and she hawked and hawked as his free hand left her throat and swept at his face, and she stepped back, two, three paces. Out of range.

'TB,' she said flatly. 'Now you'll get it too.'

He screamed, an extraordinary wail of anger and frustration, scrabbled at his pockets, wiped at his mouth with his shirt-sleeve, then realised it wasn't enough and pushed past for the sink, left hand out to hold her at bay. But she didn't have the strength to finish him; her steps to the worktop were stilt-like, her chest rumbling, and when she grabbed her handbag with her knuckle-hand, no chair-frame now to hold it back, there wasn't enough strength in her arm to stop the bottom thumping on the floor. The water was running and Christie was rinsing his mouth as she walked back to the door, facing him all the way, to pick up her coat and then her pullover, crumpled in the corner. He took a bite out of a bar of soap and rubbed it around his gums. She grabbed the door handle.

'You can't tell.' He was standing full on, mottled hands flexing, foam around his mouth, his face red with anger, his eyes narrow with hate. 'Can't tell your yokel husband, can't tell the police.' He jabbed at her with his right. 'Cos I know about you, whore. You got something you don't want knowed. Else you'd have told your husband. That nice Mr Christie offered to help my cough.' She must have blinked because there was triumph in his face too. 'He don't know about your TB, do he? An' you don't want him to know.' She could almost see cogs turning. ''Cos there's something about your TB,' sounding deliberate as if each word was a new step in logic, 'wouldn't be normal TB, you wouldn't want to infect him, no. You've got something else. And you've told some big lie about it. Some foreign lie.' He was smiling now as she stepped into the doorway. 'I got the measure of you, whore.'

For some reason she felt she could not leave him with the last words, even if they were inadequate, given that, if she had just a little more strength, she would be beating his skull in right now. 'And I have the measure of you, Droopy Man.' If her fingers hadn't been wrapped around a knuckleduster and a cosh she'd have dangled a pinky or two. 'Good day.'

She backed down the dark corridor, Christie still under the weak kitchen bulb, his cold knowing smile seeming to say she was wrong. And even when she'd lost sight of him, and knew he was on the other side of the front door that she hadn't the strength to pull to, that smile stayed with her, a lethal Cheshire Cat that sat in the fog and reached down into her chest, cold and sharp. Only when she'd turned out of Rillington Place and into St Mark's Road, when she was two hundred yards or so nearer home, did the smile leave her, popped by the needle of a coal-lorry's horn. And at that moment her legs gave way, dumping her in a tangle on her backside, and she vomited, once, twice, a gruel as acid as the air, and started to shiver. She didn't have the strength to move. So she sat on the filthy pavement with her eyes closed, left fist still shrouded in netting and her right clutching the cosh, vomit dampening her lap and drying in her hair, and sobbed and coughed uncontrollable tears.

54

Another dead end. Bourton paused on the doorstep of Wandsworth's head of section, in a web of three-up-three-downs off the York Road, and tried to summon up What next from his gluey brain. 'Well, that was the last,' said Tony Marling gently. 'Perhaps your man isn't in CD.' *He must be.* 'You need some shut-eye.' Marling's voice was gentle, as if aware their failure might leave him tetchy. 'If you can get the mayor's charabanc back to the garage, I can promise you a bed and some scoff.'

★

Sitting in the bath, as she scrubbed and scrubbed; *He'd done that before.* She stopped scrubbing, shocked at the thought. *That chair, that mask, it was all practised.* It was such a terrible thought that her schooling tried to dismiss it. *Perhaps he hadn't done it all together before. The mask was practised, but the chair didn't work, did it? But the chair didn't work because of me, not it, or him.* She looked at the hand that an hour or so before had tipped the chair and saved her life. There would be bruises from the netting, the broken wood. *Although he did not work.* She stood up, her shocked body ahead of her thoughts. *He got excited as I became still. He was not hard when he put the mask on. I would have seen or sensed it. Though he is old, perhaps it would take time . . .* She shook her head. *The weaker I was, the harder he got. He was excited by the idea of my being still.*

'No no no.' She kicked the end of the bath to squash the thought and the memory, of lying still on the futon in the comfort house, trying to be what Imanishi-sensei needed because it would keep her alive, but despite the powder, the ice-chilled skin, her limpness, and the cold medicinal horror of his pathologist's hands, being too warm, sensate, vital, to make him hard. The memory was gone, popped by another thought: *He did not look at me like other men look at me. I don't know how I know this, but I do.*

She shivered. *Of course Christie has done this before. He likes his women dead.*

And because he is clever he will know that I will know that I am not the first. And that means I must die too.

★

Bourton managed three and a half hours' kip, on a small bed in Marling's spare room, his feet hanging over the end and his hair probably staining the button-backed headboard. He woke to find Marling had summoned up gammon and two veg – probably from the dumb waiter in the kitchen: there was no evidence of cooking.

He headed up the hill to the station with eyes that opened and legs with spring.

Roll-call in CID, taken by a detective inspector Bourton had never seen before, with a crackpot plan for a cordon and sweep to nab the coshing gang before the normal working week began. He pointed to the arrows and neatly chalked street names on his blackboard, and all the PCs wrote things down carefully in their notebooks and looked excited. Bourton did some quick arithmetic. At least a hundred yards of front per bloke; visibility in the night and fog, ten yards maximum; percentage of frontage unseen at any one time, eighty. He raised his hand.

'Sir.' The DI turned to him. 'Bourton, sir. We'll be spread thin, sir. Sweeps gobble up blokes – we'd allow a battalion a mile in Palestine, sir, an' that was in daylight. If we halved the frontage, concentrated where the gang ain't struck yet, west of the Grove . . .'

'Or we can stake you out as the decoy, Dick.' Bri Hitchcock from the back. 'If there's trouble in the fog, it'll come to you.'

'Just don't stand too close when it happens,' a genial rumble from Bert, and the room erupted, Bourton laughing with them, the DI smiling obligingly, waiting to shoot him down. Sergeant Tullow, on the other hand, was shaking his head at him. *That's me told, then.*

But it turned out Tullow was just looking out for him. 'It's all bollocks,' he told Bourton later, as he dropped him off at his point in the cordon. 'We both know it. But it shows we're trying.' Tullow smiled. 'Sergeant I-done-this-for-real-you-nana Bourton.' He stepped back onto the area car's running board. 'By the way, they probably don't attack in the Dale 'cos that's where they live. Catch 'em tonight, prove me right, and make me feel happy all over.' He tapped the roof of the car and it headed on into the soup.

★

I cannot be debilitated, not now. Anna fished out her mask and dressed to fight – heavy shoes, old trousers, a silk blouse that would tear, her reclaimed jumper with the low neck. And she spent the rest of the day and all night locked inside, weapons carefully distributed – knuckles and cosh on the Formica table, German bayonet under the chest cushion, metal-edged webbing belt down the side of the armchair, big pan by the further window, sharp kitchen knife beside the head-board, the hot kettle on the ring, the long Chinese bayonet always by her right hand. When she had to go to the lavatory she went armed, each time convinced he would be waiting behind whichever door she must open. She ate some bread and margarine for supper, with barely appetite for that. And when she went to bed, still wearing her shoes, with the knuckles and Nazi bayonet under the pillow, she cried and cried, hating her weakness and her fear, waiting for Richard to come home.

★

8 December 1952

Four hours of it. The occasional pedestrian, the odd vehicle, but no gang, no whistle blasts, no shouts even from offstage, just plod, plod, plod. By the time the sweep was called off at two thirty and Bourton was allocated a beat to walk, he was convinced that of all the time-wasting he'd done as a bobby, the past four hours had been the most pointless, if only because they'd been so stupid.

Only at the end of the turn, after four more hours of sweet FA, when he was settled on the bench, boots off, scrunching life into his feet – the benefit of the gammon and shut-eye was long gone – did he hear the news. Half two, one of the area cars came across a bloke weaving down Lancaster Road, bent double over busted ribs, cold, bloody, clearly concussed, with a gashed and probably broken arm; coshed at about nine o'clock, before they'd even mounted their turn, he'd fallen into a basement and lain there, unconscious, for hours. Lucky to survive in this cold, thought Bourton. 'And the skipper' – John McGahern speaking, a keen, whippet-like Scouser with a weak blue chin – 'Tullow says there were two attacks, western edge of Paddington ground, other in Maida Vale, beginning of our turn, sound like our boys.'

'Done our sweep the other direction,' said Will Stratfull, 'might have caught 'em.'

'Anyway,' McGahern again, 'Lancaster Road bloke, this is from Vic Dexter in the car, Lancaster Road bloke just kept saying,' he got out his notebook, 'like it meant something . . .'

'A clue, per'aps.' Bert, very slowly.

'Yeah, one of them, he said, "Spoo likes glue," over and over.'

'What the hell does that mean?' A day-bloke, at the door.

'It'll mean something to him.' Bert again, sounding wise and obvious.

'A girl you stick to.' McGahern, to a couple of chuckles.

A sudden chill came over Bourton and his hands came off his feet. He shoved his socks and boots back on and threaded through the crowd.

Tullow was in the skippers' room on the second floor, brew in hand, feet on the desk, darning on display. 'What can I do for you, Bourton?'

'Have you got what the coshing victim said, Sergeant?'

Tullow reached along the desk and picked up a statement form. He scanned the page. '"Spoo likes glue, sling likes ching."' He looked up. 'Mean anything to you?'

'Per'aps.' Bourton cast around for where to begin. 'When I was in Korea—'

'Oh, Christ,' pointing at a chair, 'if it's war stories you'd better take the weight off.'

Bourton sat. 'When I was in Korea a Yank corps we were attached to ran a patrol school. I got sent. Chief instructor was this lunatic, thought he was the reincarnation of Hiawatha or someone. He also thought our enemy could teach us a thing or two about fieldcraft.' He remembered the clump of grass he'd stood on in October '50, which happened to have a rucksack and a Chinese soldier underneath it. 'Anyway, he had this phrase, to gee us on. "Ah'm gonna make yuh slink like Chink an' spook like Gook." Gooks, that's the North Koreans—'

'Nowhere near Notting Hill, yet.'

'Sorry, skipper. Anyway, it became a catchphrase, sort of. So, there's this group of lads in the Dale, kept on at me to give 'em a bit of army training, an' in the summer, I spent a morning running 'em up and down a bombsite, bit of fieldcraft. An' I used that phrase. A fair bit.' Bourton paused. He was having difficulty swallowing. 'Turn it around an' it could sound just like "spoo likes glue, sling likes ching."'

Tullow reached for his notebook. 'Names.'

'They can't be the gang, skipper. The lads who attacked me, they were older, their voices had broken – the Dale boys, they were all twelve, thirteen at a pinch. And the coshing gang didn't know me. All those boys, after that morning, they knew me. Friday, when the gang came out of the fog and saw me, they said, "Old Bill," not "Dick Barton."'

'But they may have older brothers or mates.' He pushed over his notebook. 'Names, addresses if you've got them, any info you might have on these boys.' He gave Bourton the inspection once-over. 'Then get your head down. I don't know which candles you're burning at both ends, but you look all in.'

55

'Bourton, we're not your landlady.' Station Sergeant Filkins, behind his desk, waving a couple of message slips. 'Tell,' he looked at the top one, 'Mrs Packer that she is not to call this number or use this station as a message service.'

Joanie? Bourton apologised, then took and read the slips. Yes, must be, a Mrs Packer, at half ten and quarter to twelve last night. Anna had never arrived in Ciren – was she OK?

Christ. He ran up to the phone box by the Scarsdale, still in his shirt, goose-bumping from premonition as much as the cold, and gave the operator the number at College Farm.

'Joan?'

'Ow!' Cross muffled words, then 'Dick? Dick? Keith,' voice away from the receiver, 'start your breakfast.' Clattery echoes in the hallway. 'Dick, she never came. I was there until one. The trains were running fine. I couldn't stay longer an' I asked Mr Turpin at Ciren Town, gave him the number here, left a message on the board for her, tried your Mr Suckerneck when I could after four when she didn't turn up – I even tried the railway police.'

'You hear anything?'

'Not a word. No one like Anna. There was an old bloke took ill at Didcot—'

'An' you didn't manage to speak to Suchanek?'

'I spoke to his missus but she hadn't seen her—'

'Joan.' He'd heard the worry in her voice, practical Joanie now guilty and fret. 'Joanie, look, I haven't been back to our place in twenty-four hours. Chances are she's there, tucked up with a brew.'

'She got on the train?'

'I put her on. She waved at me as they pulled out.' *Or would have done if she hadn't been so grumpy.* 'Chances are she felt better, got off, came back an' has been sleeping it off.'

'But she never phoned.'

'I may not have told her you were picking her up.' Silence while she presumably thought he was stupid and he realised he was: his brain was gummy from strain and lack of sleep, and he couldn't remember what he'd said to who, when. 'Look, Joanie, I'll go round our place now, see what's going on.' His mouth saying it but his heart thumping. 'I'll ring you back, all right?'

He rested his forehead against the panel above the phone, trying to order his thoughts, or just get the whole creaky apparatus of his brain moving.

Anna, Anna, what are you playing at? Why not just stay on the train?

★

He ran his hand over the bedclothes, heart thumping fast, hoping for an Anna-shaped bump and finding it. He sat down in relief. *So at least you're here. Now all we have to do is get you away again.*

A cough from under the bedclothes – she must be cocooned as before. He took off his boots, warned her he'd be lifting the blankets, slipped in and wrapped himself up too. There was something hard under the pillow and damp clots on top. *She's been bleeding,* a jolt of fear, *a lot,* but realised the consistency, the smell, were wrong. Wet hankies, he realised, moving them away. She'd been crying them sodden.

'You all right, love?' Her hair brushed against his face as she nodded. 'Wanted to be home?'

'Wanted to be with you.'

A little glow started in his chest. He smiled. 'Well, you got me, Anna Bourton.'

'I do.' Her arms reached around him and pulled him in hard for a cuddle but his weight against her chest made her cough and she slipped her hands back to cover her mouth. He lay on his side and held her loosely, left hand cupping her head, waiting until the spasm had passed.

'You been all right, then?' She nodded. He could feel some kind

of string looped behind her ear and realised there was a whiff of
something medicinal – Vicks? *Some kind of mask. Ah, well, whatever it
takes.* 'Sounds like that cough might be a little easier.' She nodded
again. 'That's good. What's it like out there beyond the fog?'

'Different,' she murmured.

'I'll bet. Not sure I can picture it, really.' He started stroking her.
'Gets so you think it covers the whole world.' Her back spasmed and
a hanky came up, but this time sobs not coughs, her head burrowing
hard. 'It's all right, love.' *It isn't.* 'There there,' more neutral, 'I'm here.'

She was speaking, sounds he couldn't decipher, and only when her
fists came away could he understand her. 'I don't deserve you, Richard.'

'What's that gammon?'

'I don't. I don't, I don't.' She rested her head in his shoulder. 'Could
we stay like this for a while?'

'Of course, love.'

'Thank you.' Her arms pulled him in once more. She wrapped her
legs around him, the heels of her shoes – *Shoes?* – digging into his
calves. 'And then, when I awake,' her voice had already acquired the
blur of sleep, 'you take me to College Farm.'

★

They slept. Bourton woke sweaty and lost amid the shards of a dream,
something with the fog, and old ladies, and the Chinese soldier from
the culvert carrying a sample case, blood and hair and brain stuff
smearing the corners. *France was right hard, and Belsen was a nightmare,
so why do I dream Korea?* It must be day, or what passed for it, because
there was just enough light in the cocoon to see Anna's eyes staring
at him.

'We make a pair,' she said.

He was awake enough to realise she probably meant something,
but too cobwebbed to take it any way but straight. 'What kind?'

'Stiff-upper-lip kind. Me and my cough, you and your dreams.
Everything-is-fine kind.' She coughed. He could hear a crackling in
her throat but the spasm didn't catch. *Coughs but no crisis. Where's the
panic, the despair, of yesterday?*

'Much better, see?'

'I'm glad.' He said no more, for fear she'd use agreement as reason to stay.

'And when you are properly awake, *chéri*, we can go to Paddington.' She hadn't changed her mind while they'd slept. *But why is she ready to go to Ampney today when she refused to yesterday? Is she just calmer? Or is it something else?* 'I am all packed, all ready. We can go off to see the Wizard.'

A talker. The Traveller knew it the moment she ushered him into the front parlour. A tea tray on a dark side table; two cups and saucers, a sugar bowl with a silver spoon sticking out of a month's worth of Tate & Lyle, and some home-made biscuits on top of a stack of three little plates. He turned to see her in the doorway, hanky to her mouth but cheeks creased in a smile. *She isn't desperate for air, just lonely and wanting to chat.* He almost walked out. But his feet were sore after two days and eight souls, and his body was stiff from three nights' hard lying, and he could do with a brew, and her happy soul could do with being set free. So he nodded when she asked if he would like a cuppa, and sat where she suggested, and closed his eyes while she clattered in the kitchen.

He was woken by her voice as she placed the teapot on the tray. 'How did you come to develop your apparatus, Mr Straw?'

It took a few seconds for the cobwebs to part. He sat up, mustering his professional smile. 'I had the great good fortune, ma'am, to study with the Surgeon to the Fleet, and His late Majesty's household surgeon, Sir Cecil Wakeley, while he was working at Haslar.'

'Oh, Sir Cecil.' She was smiling encouragingly.

'One of the conditions we studied was the effects of gas inhalation, particularly chlorine, which is a peril faced by submariners. In developing an amelia for this affliction we ascertained that our preparation could be used to ease the symptoms of all of those suffering from the effects of a caustic on the throat and lungs – which, as I am sure you are aware, is the mode of operation of the smog on these vital tissues. I therefore determined that there was great assistance to be offered to those who suffered through

London's pea-soupers, and used Sir Cecil's ideas, and preparation, to create an apparatus worthy of the task of bringing relief. And I may say that it has proven completely effective.'

'Milk and sugar, Mr Straw?'

'Yes, and one spoon, ma'am. You are extremely generous.'

'You are my guest, Mr Straw. We must always look after our guests.' She smiled and he did the same. 'When were you at Haslar, Mr Straw?' She handed over the cup. 'You may have come across my late husband, John Travers.'

'I don't recall the name, ma'am.'

'You would probably have met him with Sir Cecil. He was his chief writer for three years, and would have gone with him to Civvy Street if his illness had not set in. In fact,' she gestured at the bookcase beside the mantel, 'we have a little shelf of Sir Cecil's publications, inscribed to my late husband.'

He felt a jab of fear. *One more minute, one more minute of questions, and she will know that everything I have told her is a lie. Distract and think.*

'Indeed you do.' He saw a familiar spine – his Bible, the Red Cross's *Elementary Anatomy and Physiology Manual* – in the parade of pamphlets on the shelf. 'I see you have the Red Cross *Manual*.' A nod towards it. 'Many is the class I have taught using that text.'

'Oh, yes.' She smiled. 'Greek to me. John typed Sir Cecil's foreword for that. He always said it was the only one of Sir Cecil's publications he could ever understand.'

'It is very clear. An excellent training aide.' He smiled again, hoping she'd have moved on from her husband, but she picked up a framed photograph of a smiling man in CPO's rig from the mantel. He stood. 'Is that Chief Travers?'

'It is. You'd have known him a little older. That was taken in 'thirty-seven, when he was appointed to Barham and was off to the Med.'

'Indeed. A balder man, the chief,' a guess based on the broad bare forehead under the cap, 'and very punctualous. Very particular.'

'Ever so,' she smiled, 'a flagship man, my John. All the admirals loved him.'

'Sir Cecil was lucky to have someone with his experience.' He smiled, his mind ratcheting through choices. *How do I kill her? She doesn't need the apparatus, she's probably strong enough to survive it, anyroad. And if we keep talking she won't have the trust to try it on. But if I use my hands, a kitchen knife, a cushion, it will be murder plain as day, and the police will be asking about visitors before the neighbours can forget . . .*

He lifted his teacup, jerked his arm and slopped half its contents down his shirt.

'Oh, Mr Straw . . .' She waved her hands weakly, ready to pat him dry with her palms.

'It's nothing, Mrs Travers.' *Must be her name, doesn't seem the remarrying type.* 'A cursed twitch, an old friend from 'forty-one, but could I trouble you for a cloth?'

'Of course.' She bustled out, unaware he was a couple of paces behind, and there was a moment in the corridor when he nearly turned left for the kitchen, to drown her in her sink or stifle her and lay her head in the oven. Instead he turned right, to the front door, opened it swiftly and stepped onto the passage, hustling into the fog towards Horseferry Road, her voice bewildered on the doorstep and echoing around the brick-faced central courtyard, the Traveller thinking, Four days in, and the magic is gone, gone, gone . . .

56

Side by side on the nine fifty-two, holding hands in her lap, her head on his shoulder, a smile on the face of the old dear opposite. *I hope Anna's noticed. She's always partial to being love's young dream.* Silence, apart from the dear's knitting needles, Anna's cough and occasional snuggling noises, and Bourton's 'Bugger me! Mind my French,' when, blink, the fog was gone and the world appeared outside the windows, chimneys and tin roofs and patches of green, a slide inserted in a pier-end viewfinder.

The old lady left them at Reading. Bourton stuck his leg across the compartment door after her to stop anyone else climbing in. *This is how it should have been yesterday: her, me, us. Sorry, my girl.*

'Thank you for coming with me,' said Anna, quietly. The mask was off now that London was behind them. Her lips had the scent and gloss of Vicks and Vaseline.

'Should've done it yesterday. Should've put you on it on Friday or Saturday. Should have noticed you were having difficulties. Should have looked to my wife. Should have—'

'Should have, should have. That's enough "should have". The world is full of "should have". It stops us from . . . everything. Just do, Richard. That's what. We just do.'

Suddenly she sounded immeasurably older than him, voice aged by the cough – a firm, soft-edged bleakness, granny telling Billy why he had to eat his friend. He wasn't sure if she actually meant it. 'There's got to be some "should", love, some rules an' that.'

'Ah, Richard, you'd be a policeman if there were no police.'

'But you've got to have rules. You've seen, I've seen what happens when you don't.'

'You think that was about no rules? It was all rules. New rule, one nationality goes in a camp another does not. Break the camp rules and you go up a chimney. New rule, everyone goes up the chimney. Rules.'

'But those were bad rules. You got to have good rules.'

'Which is "should", I know.'

She was supplying his own argument and it niggled. 'Those bastards in Belsen were what happened when the rules didn't have "should".'

'And the ones in the stripes? They survived by "should"? They threw it away to survive. That's how they lived to see you drive through the gate.'

Now pinching his experience, too. 'How do you know?' Meaning, You weren't there.

'I was a refugee, Richard.' A wave of her free arm dismissing it. 'It's the same thing.' She sat up and away, a physical signal of a different kind of chat. 'You take the work you can find, legal or not, you lie and cheat, you blow with the wind. Rules and "should" – that's the British Liberation Army, coming through the gate. Do – that's the person the rules are done to. We both know which we are.'

'But you don't need to be that any more.'

She laughed, a surprisingly joyful sound, no edge at all. 'What a lovely thought.'

Lovely, as in 'All that is behind me'? Or lovely, as in 'You stupid man'? Bourton smiled because he thought he ought to. *Some ways I know you well. Others, I haven't a clue.* 'Glad to brighten your day.'

'Ah, Richard,' turning to face him, 'have I offended you?'

'Per'aps a bit.' A patient I-won't-tell-you-off smile. 'You're a lot cleverer than me, love. Easy for you to make me feel simple. Straw in my hair.'

'That's schools, not you. What did the CO say? "Might be too clever for a platoon." So he makes you the intelligence sergeant. There's a clue.' She shifted so their bodies touched again and took his hand. 'Peace offering. What's my clever man been doing?'

And so the editing began, each strand of his day-and-night job pared to an Anna core.

The coshing gang: 'So these lads been attacking people in the fog, vicious attacks, a couple of them been lucky to survive. Anyway, they used one o' my Korea phrases, you know, "Slink like Chink" –'

'Horrible phrase.'

'– an' hardly anyone knows it, so it got me worried that per'aps the gang's linked to my boys, you know, Derek and Don and Terry, the boys I did the drills with in the summer, 'cos I used the phrase with them, a lot. One o' the reasons I'm glad I'm here, love,' squeezing her hand, 'otherwise I'd be knocking on their doors, leading 'em to finger their brothers . . .' And so on. No mention of the club with the nails, the scrapes and bruises she'd yet to see, the bonnet with a hole in it the size of a heavyweight's fist.

Tony Marling: 'He's been helping out with this Rex job. There's a link to Civil Defence and he's big in CD.'

'Tony?'

'Yeah, he may only be my age but he's got plans, he has. So he's Mr CD, in Kensington anyway. It's been strange, being with this posh bloke, a councillor – it's as if he's still a rifleman in Holland an' I'm still his corporal, but now I'm a probationary copper an' he hobnobs with chief supers.' No mention of the fight, the wild-goose chase across the capital or the reason for it, the laws they'd probably bent to do what the Met didn't want done.

The "Rex job": 'So this Gladys Hartham, she couldn't have died of natural causes, 'cos the people carried off by the smog, it takes four, six weeks. So we been looking through the books, find the people who've died of one of these smog CODs. But at the time, in the middle of it – 'cos if they take weeks to die, why they dying during the fog that's supposed to kill 'em two months hence?'

'Because of an earlier smog?'

Her bloody logic. 'We made allowances.' *Did we?* 'An' we found a few. So the Murder Squad got brung in an' they found that some of the victims had a visitor just before they died, like Gladys Hartham did. A bloke, looked like a salesman, carrying a sample case.'

'Selling what?'

'Don't know. The Squad are tracking down salesmen working the areas where these people lived. Though I wonder if he's a salesman, I got to admit. Who's going door-to-door after six p.m. in a fog?'

'Someone late on his round? Working on commission, desperate for any sale?'

'Per'aps. But would the householders open the door? All of these people, they had lung trouble, chest trouble, always struggled in the smog. Just opening the door would set them off. Can't see them doing that for a traveller, not unless he had something they needed.'

'Cleaning products.'

'Eh?'

'Haven't you noticed? It leaves a – a coating, a film, everywhere. And it smarts. Think what it could do to your silver, your good wood, if you don't clean it off.'

'Do you worry about cleaning if you're coughing your lungs up?'

'Perhaps. People do strange things in distress.' She sensed he wasn't convinced. 'It's possible.'

'Yes, it is.' Nodding, a concession. 'So then, Miss Fog, what else are they going to need?'

'Anything they can't get to the shops for, that isn't rationed. Perfume? Magazine subscription? Music, a radio, if they're shut indoors? Something medical – a balm, an ointment?'

Outside the window were the muted colours of a clear country winter; a dhobi-faded sky, the toffee of bare hawthorn hedgerows, frost-peaked furrows in a ploughed field – no haze, or walls, or masks. 'What they really need, o' course,' said Bourton, 'is fresh air. Just like you. Bit o' country in the lungs.'

Anna stiffened. 'Air. He could be selling air.'

'Can't buy it,' said Bourton, shaking his head.

'Not air, really.' He had the sense of cogs whirring. 'I mean breath.'

'What do you mean?'

'People sell masks, people buy them, even if they think they won't work. Why not sell breath?'

'How?'

She shrugged, but her shoulders and neck were tense, as if the action had been ordered at gunpoint, and she suddenly had a pallor to match. 'You hear things.'

'What things?'

'Where to go. If you need something. Get rid of a baby. Get strong pain medicine.'

'And who do you go to for breath?'

'I've met a man. Said he had a breathing apparatus if ever I needed help.'

'A breathing apparatus?' *That rings a bell, back of the head, some dusty corner.*

'Said it had helped him,' *A roll-call, recent, Harbison or Tullow.* 'He'd been gassed in the first war,' *no, not the muster room,* 'devised it with his medical knowledge,' *somewhere with windows, desks, empty, in daylight,* 'or so he said, though what knowledge . . .' *couldn't be the skippers' or guv'nors' rooms, too small. It was CID, Rex Athill, back in November.* 'Anyway, you know him, or he knows you. He introduced himself because he said he had a commendation too.' *That Sunday he had the divisional detective's duty, leaning back against the radiator, waving a busybody's letter from a doctor, somewhere local, complaining about someone bothering his patients with some remedy.* 'Horrible man, Mr Christie,' *Christie, Christie, Christie,* 'the one who used to be a policeman,' *from Mancini's café, back in the spring or summer, when asking DC George Brown about Ernie Potter; the shabby diffident man,* 'or so he says, though he is no advertisement for your force, Richard,' *and Rex knew him, he was linked to one of his cases. Yes, the simpleton off St Mark's Road, killed his wife and baby. Christie was the landlord.* 'He's someone who offers an apparatus. Try him.'

Something she'd said finally filtered through. 'Medical knowledge?' She nodded stiffly, pale enough to puke, and he knew it was strange, knew he should ask what was going on, but he had a sniff of the fox and he wasn't going to let it go. *Surely not Christie. But a copper gets the basics of first aid, would have had to use them in the war.*

And then, pushing aside the past: 'Commendation?'

'That's what he said.' Goosebumps. *It could be him.* 'Or something like it. But I am not sure that he is . . . an honest man. Perhaps he made everything up.'

'Why?' Sharply, wanting it all to be true.

'To look important?' She tapped him on the knee. 'Come to London as a foreigner and you realise everyone is telling about themselves, making themselves look important, more than drab, all the time.' A lumpy shrug. 'Like Shanghai. Everyone was someone before. In Russia.'

'Where is he?' Sharper still, but she didn't bridle – just blinked, eyes neutral.

'Rillington Place. I've been past, a little street, ten houses perhaps. You can find him.'

'They'll know at the nick.' *Rex, or someone else in CID, the Incident Book.*

'Be careful, Richard.' Her eyes had softened, her colour returned. 'If he is your man, he will be dangerous.' She reached for his hand and this time the gesture felt warm, natural. 'You are a strong man so you think you are safe. But what is it you always said about fights?'

'Watch the nobodies. They'll have knives.'

'Watch the nobodies.' Suddenly she was up on one knee and leaning in, head in his shoulder and arms around his neck, her weight pushing them over until he braced his arm on the window-frame. 'He's a nobody, Richard. Watch him.'

★

I can't take it back. Burrowed into his shoulder, teetering with every bump over the rails, Anna knew she'd started something, a line of thought that he'd worry until he pulled it in or it escaped. *But what else could I do? I think Christie has killed before, and Richard thinks the same of this traveller. He is selling breath and so, perhaps, is this traveller. And he could kill again – and so, thinks Richard, will this traveller.*

What will Richard find out? Not much. He will not be alone, it will be police business, and Christie knows saying anything about me will incriminate him. Unless, of course, he needs to tell, for fear of something worse – such as being hanged as this traveller man, when he might be innocent and I might be his alibi. She held Richard tighter. *Don't do this thing I've given you. Who knows where it will lead?*

In Shanghai this would be so easy: tell someone he is the enemy and wait for him to flow past the Bund. But this is England. There are no gangsters killing gangsters or Reds killing Nazis or Whites killing Reds. There is Police Constable Richard Bourton, honest, clever, true – and unable to kill in cold blood, even a man who so clearly needs killing.

The tears started to return, *Weak, weak, weak,* but she couldn't help it. *I get us together, time with each other for the first time in weeks, and I end it.* He'd already left, she could tell. He was in some police room or shabby house, talking to the people who would lead him up the string, or perhaps he was tucked up inside his head, asking himself questions to decide where he went when he returned to London.

'It's all right, love,' he said. She felt a rush of warmth at the thought that he didn't even know why she was distressed. *And it will probably always be this way – I do not tell him, and he loves me just the same.* His big hands on her back lifted her onto his lap, to cuddle her like a fretting child, but the simple male strength of it made her wet and she found herself fiddling at his flies – need, love, gratitude, she wasn't sure.

'Love . . .'

'Quickly.' He was immediately hard.

'But someone—'

'Between stations.' His cock twitched at her touch.

'But your trousers—'

'I'll take them off.'

'Can't hide.'

'I'll pull them up if someone sees.' She stood up, yanked everything down to her knees and climbed on, need pushing her all the way down, past the tightness and discomfort. He was looking out of the window, probably trying to work out how long they had, contained nearly-bliss on his face. 'Besides,' she settled her bottom and pulled her clothes further down her legs, then off one foot, releasing her knees, 'you probably won't last until . . .?'

'Swindon.' His eyes were closed now. 'Just passed through Shrivenham. Prob'ly about five minutes, ten if we're held.'

'As if you'll last ten.' She started moving, little more than a wriggle, to get him used to her, and closed her own eyes. She had a flash of the time in the stables, before they were married, when she was being a nice girl. *You've come a long way since then, Anna Bourton.* She started pushing up, heels through thighs to hips, again and again, wallowing in the thought. And then another thought, hard and cold, withering her arousal – *And yet you have come no distance at all. The lies that could destroy us in February are still ticking away today.* She opened her eyes to see Richard's still closed, face still enraptured, unable to notice that her movement was now mechanical, a transaction, aimed at getting him done.

57

14.35. The fog is my friend. A thought at the top of the Grove, looking north to sights he couldn't see, tucked behind a yellow twilit shroud. *The same fog as this morning – same smart on the skin, same prickle in the throat – but this time it's my friend. Because it's as London as buses that don't stop, fake Cockneys, sharp practice on the stalls – the other side of the London coin. And I am a London copper.*

And as the fog swallowed the clip from his boots, *And he can't see me coming.*

Up the nick's front steps, Anna's knuckles and cosh weighing down his parka pockets. *What a girl.* A nod to DC Martin in the hall, there-there-ing an old bloke in a boiler suit sagging on the bench. He took the stairs to CID three at a time. *She's put a spring in your stride.*

'Rex is on an ob in Paddington, if you're looking.' DC Brown, typing four-fingered; the rest of CID was empty. 'Lord knows what he'll see.' Bourton didn't leave so he looked up. 'What is it?'

'A few Sundays ago CID handled a complaint from a family doctor that someone was hanging around his surgery offering a breathing apparatus. Anything done with it, d'you know?'

'Got the date?' Bourton nodded. 'Daily actions, filing cabinet nearest the door, date order.' He turned back to typing. 'Anything else?'

Worth a go. 'You know that bloke Christie, ex-copper, landlord of Evans, hanged for his wife and baby?'

'And?'

'You know where he lives?'

Pause. 'Rillington Place.' Another. 'Only house with a big manhole outside. Last one in the street, by the wall.' He looked up. 'You like him for something?'

'Dunno yet.'

'Fair dos.' He rearranged himself inside his trousers and nodded at the filing cabinet. 'Go.'

Bourton found Athill's summary in the November file, clipped to a letter from Dr Vaughan of North Pole Road. *The one pronounced Gladys Hartham dead.* He described the man loitering outside his surgery as middle-aged, five ten, thin, bald, with glasses. Bourton closed his eyes, tried to bring to mind the face and build of the man behind the table in Mancini's, but he couldn't really remember him at all.

'We got a photo of Christie?'

'Doubt it. Ain't a villain so if we have it'll be in the filing cabinet with the pervs and Commies.' He stood up and marched through his guv'nor's open door, returning with a board-cover scrapbook. 'Or here. The bosses have kept clippings on CID pinches ever since Acid-Bath Haigh. Perhaps the papers took an interest during Evans. Have a look. Make sure your hands are clean.'

Two Maltese pimps free with their razors; a Glasgow armed robber nabbed on Hill ground; Christopher Granger – *Thought I nicked him, not CID*; Evans trial, January 1950. And there, sure enough, was a picture of Christie, in *Daily Express* newsprint, hardly of int quality, but showing a bland-faced middle-aged man in glasses and a hat. *Could well be him. Gaunt face suggests he could be skinny.* He read a couple of the surrounding articles. Defence counsel had tried to suggest Christie might have had a hand in the death of Evans's wife and baby, though the judge was having none of it – served throughout the Great War, impeccable record as a policeman, of unblemished character, blah-blah-blah. Bourton paused. *What if he is the Traveller? Is anyone going to want to hear it? If the nobs and guv'nors have decided he's salt-of-the-earth . . .* And then: *What about Evans? If Christie's a suspect, Evans's briefs will be sure to yell, 'Miscarriage of justice!' and Hill CID will pull up the drawbridge.* He scanned the clippings to be sure. Detective Chief Inspector Pitts had led the interrogation, assisted by DI Knox. *Balls. Head of Hill CID.* He shook his head. *First things first. Let's see if he flies as a suspect.*

He put the scrapbook on Brown's desk and returned to the file to see who had followed up on Dr Vaughan's letter. DC Hume: 'I/v w comp 30 Nov 52, nfip, nfar.' *So he spoke to Vaughan, who provided no further information, and no further action required. More or less what any copper would do – if they didn't know someone was murdering sick people in the smog.*

He closed the filing cabinet. 'Got what you need?' asked Brown, still typing head down, but somehow pulsing, Give me something.

You're too clever and cover-your-arse. I give you anything and the guv'nors will have me. 'A start,' affably. 'I need to talk to a bloke, see if it flies. Thanks for the help.'

He fished out the Murder Squad number and trotted down to the phone box on the Grove. A DC Nunn answered almost immediately. Bourton gave his name and nick, asked for Lloyd – 'It's about the Traveller' – and heard some back-and-forth: 'Who's Bourton?'

'Dunno.'

'Why's he want the skipper?'

'Traveller.'

'Why?' Then, directly, 'Why do you want DS Lloyd?'

'I was hoping for a little gen on how you're doing with the Traveller. Your first victim,' flattering them, 'Gladys Hartham, I was the responding officer when she was found.'

A hand was over the receiver, hiding nothing. 'Says he responded on Gladys Hartham.'

'Sound like he's off the farm?'

'Sounds like he ate it.'

'Look like a pill box with a whitewashed lid?'

'Can't hardly tell over the phone, can I, then?' To Bourton: 'What do you look like?'

'Pill box with a whitewashed lid.'

Silence, then from somewhere else in the Squad, 'Skipper said he's a lippy bugger.'

'Sounds right,' said Nunn to the room. 'All right,' to Bourton. 'DS Lloyd is out so you'll have to try your luck with me. What do you want to know?'

Say nothing and try Lloyd when he gets back? But the DS might not say more than Nunn – might even say a lot less. And all the time the Traveller will be out there.

Ask. 'You got a suspect?'

'Custody? No.'

'A name?'

'Yes.'

'Is he a traveller?'

'Yes.'

'What's he in?'

'Er . . .' *Holding back.* '. . . electrical goods.'

'Does he sell anything on the side?'

Silence, then: 'What? Under the counter? Johnnies or something?'

'Not sure.'

Another silence. 'If you got something, Farmer Giles, you tell us. That's how the Met works. You pass it up. We investigate. *Comprenez?*' A good French accent. 'Send.'

Hand over Christie, no evidence, on the phone, to a stranger who hasn't been softened up? I won't get the time of day.

'Not sure what I got, really.' *Hold him off.*

'Well, if you don't tell, you don't get anything. Speak now or for ever hold your peace.'

Deal straight. But first step, get him to listen.

'I'm not a detective, let alone Murder Squad, but I was an int sergeant, I done a share of trying to put things together. Different line, similar job.' *He's listening.* 'And so I ask questions. How is he choosing these people? Why are they opening the door to him if it will make them ill? What's he selling that makes them want to buy then, there, when they're desperate?'

'And what answers do you get?'

'It's all about the fog. When does he kill? The fog. Who does he kill? People made ill by the fog. He's choosing them *because* they're ill. And they open the door *because* of the fog – because they're at their last tether and he can make it better. He isn't just a murderer using the fog to kill without being seen, with his sample case giving him the excuse to get in the door. The fog is at the heart of it.'

'So what you're saying,' distracted, 'is that you don't think we've got the right man.'

Balls. 'Not that, no.'

'It's some kind of fog wraith instead.' Laughs down the line. 'At the moment I'm hearing a gypsy act. Is there any actual information here? Or did your unit have to rely on veils and crystal balls?'

'There's a man been reported around Notting Dale doctors' surgeries, offering a breathing apparatus.' Silence. *Got you.* 'A bloke doing that could meet people who are ill. Come the smog they're going to need him so they'll open the door.'

'They would.' Silence. 'Anything on the apparatus man?'

'Description.'

'Which is?'

If it doesn't match their man? 'Sketchy.'

'Let's have it.'

'Five ten or so,' each word slow and reluctant, 'thin. Glasses.'

'Age?'

'Not very clear.'

A silence that said, 'Speak.'

'Middle-aged.'

'Any leads to him?'

'Perhaps.' And before Nunn could turn the screws for not telling, 'It's early days. I've only just added two and two.'

'Right. Wait a mo.' The receiver clanked. He pictured them huddled around a desk, smokes in hand, dissecting his few nuggets, dismissing them the way he'd dismissed those of keen patrol commanders so many times before. *I hope I was nicer than they'll be with me.* Nunn came back on the line. 'Right, we'll talk to the guv'nor when he checks in.' *Not a bad start.* 'This apparatus man stuff is a bit thin. Can you find out more?'

I bloody can. 'Yes.'

'Do we need to tell your guv'nor?'

Without thinking, 'Best not to, Mr Nunn. I'll do it on my own time.' Silence. *More needed.* 'I'm not top of the bill with my guv'nor.' More silence. 'I think this Gladys Hartham business made 'em look bad. It comes up again, I'm for the dab, per'aps the drop.'

'Fair enough. Call when you have something. All right?'

58

15.00. One of these days, Richard Arthur Bourton, you'll switch your brain on before pressing the speech starter.

If he was going to talk to Christie, and Christie was the Traveller, he needed to go with a Met grown-up, to cross *t*s come a trial. But his automatic reply to Nunn had committed him to doing it under the guv'nor's radar. That meant he needed someone who'd keep his mouth shut in a good cause. And inasmuch as he had blokes he could ask – Hitch, Rog Leakey, Bert, Rex – his half-hour trudging through the nick, or the Scarsdale, or even the Uxbridge, turned up none of them. *Looks like you're on your own, wooden-top.*

The entrance to Rillington Place was narrow, blank-faced, more like the entrance to a vehicle yard than people's homes. He could hear a Metropolitan Line train stuttering along the viaduct, close enough for the driver to spit out his window and hit a front door. He paused, taking advantage of the fact that he was in civvies to light a smoke, lean against the wall and, as Bert would say, cog-i-tate.

What kind of chat was this going to be? Depended. If Christie was different from Dr Vaughan's description and salt-of-the-earth? Then it would be about his breathing apparatus. Just like Dr Vaughan described, and a wrong 'un? Then push a little, without letting on about the Traveller, or the sample case, anything that might set him destroying evidence or running for the hills. Simple, really. Play it by ear.

He pinched and stowed the smoke, then checked his pockets for Anna's going away presents. *Nobodies have knives. Better be ready, just in case.* But there was no spine-tingle saying, Danger, nor a sense that a puzzle was about to be solved. *Alone, in civvies, brought by coincidence and prejudice. Hard to believe I'm about to cross swords with a murderer.*

The street was miserable, even for the Dale, barely one level above

drunks in dripping basements sharing their TB – probably rooms by
the week for new arrivals shaking off northern soot or Caribbean
dust, knowing they'd do better soon. *And Christie's lived here at least
since '49.* Now Bourton's puzzle-sense perked up because the threadbare street reminded him of the threadbare man in Mancini's, beaten
by the world, an elderly show-pony used to an arbitrary whip. And
tallish, thinnish, with specs – as Vaughan had described. *Traveller or
not, you're up to something.*

The only house with a big manhole cover outside was number 10,
as chipped and sagging and rotten as the rest of the street. There
were shrill voices in the front room, and he paused before knocking,
knowing sound would carry through one-brick-thick walls, ill-fitting
doors, thin window-glass in rotten frames. Sure enough he could hear
a woman upbraid someone for collecting his cards, in a high, cutting,
breathy voice; he claimed he'd always provided in the past, and as an
educated man would find a position in no time. Apart – her voice
richer, stronger, more vicious now – from the time he went away. A
slap. *Eavesdropping over.* Bourton knocked hard on the front door,
feeling the centrepiece give under his knuckles. *This house is held
together by habit.* Silence for a moment or two, then theatrical whispers
he couldn't catch. He knocked again. The curtain over the upper sash
parted and a face appeared – man, thinnish, fifties, featureless, glasses
going over the eyes and then a moment of shock before the drape
dropped again. Christie. Bourton knocked a third time. He thought
he heard the woman call, 'And where do you think you're going?'

He couldn't be scarpering, could he? He banged the centrepiece again
and called, 'Mr Christie!' The door opened on a short fat woman in
a pinny, dark-framed specs the only features on a doughy white face,
trying to stand aside. 'If you're looking for my husband, he's gone
down the back.' Flat, Yorkshire, neutral, the tone of a wife used to
fobbing off bookies' heavies or angry husbands. Bourton could see
no evidence of the slap.

'Thank you very much, Mrs Christie,' pushing past into the smell
of damp, dust, drains, 'PC Bourton, Notting Hill,' down an ill-lit
passage beside the stairs to a door. As he reached for the knob he
heard a slam at the back of the house. He opened the door on a
grubby kitchen – *No Christie* – and at the end, beside a window onto

the return, another door. He tried it; unlocked but jammed shut. He retreated, then took a run up to hit it with his shoulder and full fifteen stone, and it came down in a shell-burst of plaster, dust and rotten wood – *Christ, I hope I don't collapse the back of the house* – to rest against the blank wall of the return, Bourton sprawled on top. He fished Anna's cosh from his pocket, jogged down the return, turned left, past a wash-house and a dilapidated privy, door ajar, a low wall beyond marking the beginning of the garden, an unkempt bed with vegetable canes just visible on the right, and behind it a patchwork of upstairs lights – *Back of Lancaster Road houses?* – glowing suspended in the fog. No sign of Christie. *Should have brought a torch.* He walked down a hard-surface path, keeping the privy well to the left, cosh still in his right hand. *These gardens back onto terraced houses, no way out, where would he go? I suppose he could hop over garden walls until he finds a house to run through.* He stopped and listened. A dog barking, sounded like St Mark's Road; digging in a Lancaster Road garden, two, three houses over; engines turning over in the bus yard to his right. And suppressed breathing, somewhere close – in the privy, or behind it? *A nobody, Anna had said. And nobodies carry knives.*

'Mr Christie?' The breathing was held. 'Mr Christie, this is Richard Bourton, from Notting Hill. We never met, but I saw you once, in Mancini's, when I was with Rex Athill. I only want a word.' *Just get him out where I can see him.* 'I can put my warrant card out here, on the path, so you can have a look. Then we can talk, one officer to another.' He fished it out with his left, laid it on the paving, and stepped into the bed. 'I came looking for some insights.' Low and Gloucester, aiming for simple-minded reassurance. 'My wife, who I think you know, she said you'd be the man to talk to.' Arms wide, even though Christie almost certainly couldn't see the gesture. 'All I'm here to do. Talk.'

He waited, a minute, perhaps two, listening to the rhythm of the three streets on a winter Monday, middle of the city's worst smog. *Why run? 'Cos he's the Traveller? Or something else? His missus needled him about doing time. Salt-of-the-earth, my arse.*

'So you spoke to your wife.' Soft, Yorkshire, nervous; from the privy.

'I did. She mentioned a couple of chats you'd had.'

A pause. 'Chats.'

'Yes, chats.' Silence. 'About how you've been offering to help people.' The breathing was audible again. 'Look, shall we talk in the open?'

'And you just want to talk?'

'I just want to talk.'

Bourton stepped back and braced himself, knuckles in the left hand, cosh in the right. *If he's the Traveller he'll want to get close and I've had enough of being knocked about.*

'So talk.'

He's not coming out. 'Very well, Mr Christie.' Relaxing a little. 'Why did you run, may I ask, soon as you laid eyes on me?'

'There have been some . . . misunderstandings at my place of employment.'

'Money?'

'Some accounting disagreements. A payroll chap's hazard, I'm afraid.'

'They sacked you?'

'No.' Emphatic. Blustery. 'I will not remain where I am neither trusted nor believed.'

'So you collected your cards.' *But he panicked when he saw me – ran away and hid. Would he do that for a little petty theft?*

'And will be looking for new employment once this fog has passed.'

'Be tough before Christmas.'

'I do not expect any difficulties.' Silence. 'I'm a grammar-school man, Mr Bourton,' almost plaintive now, 'that always stands you in good stead.'

'I got a brother clever enough for the grammar,' *make him feel superior,* 'all they could do with me was put me on a ship or hitch me to a plough.'

'We all find our own path.' A squeak of unoiled hinges. *He's coming out.* 'And you've found other means of distinguishing yourself. Serving King and country. Nicking that Granger tyke.'

'Never did the trenches, though, Mr Christie, not like you. And from what I hear at the station,' straightening, slipping the cosh up his sleeve, *If I'm on my guard he'll clam up,* 'you've had commendations of your own.'

'They mention that, do they?' Christie took shape in the murk, collarless shirt and braces, as if he'd popped out to do a bit of digging before tea.

'They do, Mr Christie. CID always say you're a man to rely on.'

'One does one's bit.' They nodded at each other, man to man.

'I'm going to be honest with you, Mr Christie. It's what you deserve, after all.'

'It is, Mr Bourton.'

'We had this report, back in November. And I'm ashamed to say we're only now following it up.'

'By means of a probationary officer in civilian clothes?'

Whatever he might be, he isn't stupid. 'It's all hands to the pump, Mr Christie. Four days of fog, everyone's on double turns, sweeps at night for this coshing gang, door-to-door in the Dale during the day for information. You know what it's like. Must have been the same for you in the Blitz. Fitting the policing around the raids.'

'It was certainly busy.'

'An' the blackout – just like the smog, no visibility and suddenly everyone's at it.'

'Looters.'

'B and E.'

'Tarts.'

'Black market.'

'Courting couples.'

'I swear, this job, see more knee-tremblers than you get.' Christie laughed. *Softening nicely.* 'So you know the drill.'

'I do, Mr Bourton.' He shivered and stuffed his hands in his pockets.

He must be relaxing – he's suddenly feeling the cold. 'Want to go inside, Mr Christie? It'll be a lot warmer.'

'I'd rather not. Mrs Christie and I were having – well, an altercation when you knocked, and it's best.' A couple of paces forward, hands still in his pockets, and Bourton had to lock his wrists to stop his weapons coming up. 'Would appreciate a smoke, though, if you have one.'

'O' course.' Bourton put his hand into his right hip pocket, let the cosh drop in, rummaged ostentatiously for his Capstans, then plucked the packet and matches from inside his parka. He offered them to Christie and studied his face as he bent in for his light – bland, pale, watchful eyes behind specs, suspicious and wary rather than fearful. *Why has the fear gone? Because he's bought the deference act? Or because I've accidentally told him that whatever he feared won't happen?* With Christie's first puff his cheeks sank beneath the bones – a mummified skull blowing a kiss.

'Thanks for this, Mr Bourton.' Christie held his smoke in the old soldier's grip, cupped so the glow was shielded by his palm. 'Met still come down on smoking in uniform?' Bourton nodded as he lit his own cigarette. 'Bet you're glad of your civvies, then.'

'I am that.' They both puffed away. 'So, this report. End of November. A local doctor reported someone standing outside his surgery, offering patients some kind of breathing device. Now, the description – five ten, fifties, thin, bald, glasses – would fit a lot of people but I notice it also fits you. And when I tell the wife I've been shanghaied and why, she says, "Oh, that nice Mr Christie, he's mentioned a breathing apparatus to me more than once, to help me with my cough and that." So you're my first port of call. Do you have an apparatus?'

'It wouldn't be illegal if I did.'

There's a guilty answer. 'Depends what you do with it, Mr Christie, as you know.'

'Indeed I do.' *Defensive, even arrogant?* 'I do not charge anyone for using it, and do not represent it as anything more than a personal remedy. I do not advertise myself as any kind of medical practitioner, or the holder of any medical certification other than my St John's. It is something I devised to assist my breathing during pea-soupers, when I found that the effects of my gassing in France were exacerbated by the sulphur and coal particules in the air. I know that others suffer during these fogs, so offer the assistance of my device at no charge to those I think might benefit.'

'And how do you decide who might benefit?'

'People I know who are clearly suffering.'

'And how do you know them?' Tone light, to avoid the appearance of an interrogation.

'How does one know anyone? Neighbours, although it is a very low kind of crowd here, Mr Bourton. People one knows, from church, from former employment, from public houses. People one meets in cafés, like Mrs Bourton. Old comrades, in the British Legion.'

'And do you do house calls?'

'No.'

'Why not?'

'My apparatus is not very portable.'

'Because?'

'It works through an oxygen cylinder, which is very heavy.'

'And where do you get that?'

'Lee's scrapyard. He does some cutting with oxy and gives me the nearly empties.'

'Why?'

'He's a friend, Mr Bourton. Been a friend for over twenty years.'

'Could I see your device, please?'

'I'm afraid not. A chum is fitting a new length of hose. I tore it yesterday.'

'That's a pity. What about the oxygen tank?'

'I returned my most recent one after the mishap yesterday.'

'So how will you get through this pea-souper?'

'With difficulty. Yesterday's interrupted application has done some good, but should the fog last into Wednesday, I am afraid things will become much harder for me.'

'Why Mrs Bourton?'

Silence. Christie pulled deep, his gaze shifting, then settling on his house. 'You've seen my wife, Mr Bourton. She is not an attractive woman. And until today I worked in a haulier's. All men, Mr Bourton. You will not be surprised to hear that the people most in need of my apparatus are old, and ill.' He turned to face Bourton. 'Your wife is very young and very beautiful, Mr Bourton. Being of help to a lady like that – it brings colour into the life of someone like me. And nothing more.' He was gazing intently at Bourton now. *Sincerity? Or selling a lie hard?* 'She is a respectable woman, Mr Bourton, and the wife of a police officer. Even if I were the kind of man who would exploit a device of this kind, which I am not, I would never think of doing so with someone like her.'

'Of course not,' cheerily, thinking, Why is he making so much of this? 'So you wouldn't have been offering this apparatus to patients at a surgery on the twenty-eighth of November?'

'I would not. I was not.'

'Thing is, Mr Christie,' lying now, 'we've got a witness, was in the surgery on the twenty-eighth, knew you and identified you by name. First patient I tried says, "Oh, it was that Mr Christie." Never knew police work could be so easy.'

'But I haven't done anything illegal.' *As good as a confession.*

'The Crown might say otherwise. Loitering outside a surgery, preying on the sick, who knows what motive? Would you want putting under the microscope?'

'For a little chit-chat outside Dr Vaughan's?'

'Who I never mentioned?' Silence. *Gotcha.* 'Anyway, perhaps we'd want to talk about more than Vaughan's.'

'But you said . . .'

'You're an old copper, Mr Christie. Do you think I'd be talking to you now, run off our feet as we are, because of a little complaint like Dr Vaughan's?'

'You promised honesty, Mr Bourton.'

'I've been honest. I just haven't told you everything.'

'If you think I'll stand for being monkeyed about—'

'I know you won't, Mr Christie. That's why I'm talking to you on your ground.'

'I've been law-abiding—'

'By and large.'

'What does that mean?'

'What it says.'

Christie stepped back, a finger in a jabbing point. 'If that bitch,' casting around – *For a weapon?* – 'if she's been talking, well, I can tell—'

'She just spoke a little loudly, that's all.' Hands wide again – Look! No weapons! 'Walls are thin.'

'Bitch with her lies.' He'd retreated to the privy door. 'Her word against mine.'

'And your criminal record.' Christie had paused. 'It's there, even if the Hill CID don't advertise it. Another little financial misunderstanding.' A shot in the dark. 'It's the kind of thing that can play badly, fellow copper or not. With the Crown, with us.' Silence. Christie's back was turned now, tense, looking everywhere but at Bourton, as if he couldn't decide to fight or run. 'If you don't help me now, Mr

Christie, you'll have to help someone else later. And that chat will be neither friendly nor respectful.'

Christie snorted. 'There's nothing respectful about this conversation,' indignation, but somehow false, 'insulting a man in his own home, a former colleague.'

'No offence meant.'

'It was rendered, nonetheless.'

'Then I apologise.'

'Thank you.'

Why did the mention of the jail term turn him on his wife? Or was 'that bitch' someone else? And is he calm now 'cos he's under control, or 'cos I was close to something, and am now miles away? 'Smoke, Mr Christie?' He proffered another Capstan as a peace offering. Christie turned back, but the air must have caught in his throat and before he could take the cigarette he was doubled over coughing, a rich phlegmy sound only partly contained by his fist. He hawked matter onto the path and then the spasms started again.

He's not the Traveller. Bourton suddenly knew it in his bones. *The Traveller moves through the smog, lives it, breathes it, it's his element – he's not going to be brought up short by a puff of sulphur. And because it's his element, if he sees a solitary copper turn up on his doorstep he's going to run, knowing he can get away – or he'll kill the copper in the fog, when no one can see, and bury him deep. After all, when you're facing several death sentences, what's one more? But Christie didn't fight or flee – he shut himself in the privy as if hiding from Dad's strap. And if he's up to something with his apparatus, his stamping ground must be local – if he could prowl outside the Dale, why risk Vaughan's?*

Christie's coughs had stopped. He walked over, hand outstretched for his smoke. Bourton lit the cigarette. 'I hope you don't mind, Mr Bourton,' first pull, 'if I indulge in a little exercise. You are making a point of telling me nothing about the issue of which the Vaughan complaint is a part. I quite understand. I too would try to avoid revealing anything if I were in your shoes. However, I have the advantage of having once been a police officer for longer than you have been one. And thus I have discovered much of what you are trying to protect.'

Very superior. 'Such as?'

'You are looking for a man who offers a breathing device to ill people at their own homes. His apparatus, unlike mine, is very portable. And because it is you here, rather than a couple of DCs or even a full PC in plainclothes, this man is suspected of something more than petty larceny and less than murder. Would this be correct?'

Not only is he not stupid, but I am cack-handed. 'I can't say, Mr Christie.'

'Of course.' He took another pull and stepped in until he was no more than two feet away. Suddenly Bourton had lost command and he didn't know how.

'Now, Mr Bourton, you've not been entirely honest with me – which I understand – and you've not been particularly respectful of me. Which I regret.' *Where was the world-beaten nobody of Mancini's?* 'But you have asked me to help you, and I am always willing to assist my former colleagues, to justify the good opinion of the Hill CID. What would you say if I told you that I knew of a man such as the one you are looking for?'

What's he playing at? 'I'd say, "Please tell me all you know."'

'Which, alas, is not too much. But it might be a start. And when I am done, will you please go?'

'Mr Morris?' Red-rimmed eyes and a muslin mask around the door. 'It's Mr Straw,' said the Traveller, 'with your balm, sir. Please let me in.' *A little abrupt on the doorstep*. But he was still out of sorts after the chief writer's widow, not yet back in his rhythm, joints still a little grumpy despite a nice dry hour on the Northern Line. The door pushed to, the chain was released. Morris walked away, shrouded in a fur coat, muttering, 'Bloody man, get a telephone. How can I call for help otherwise?'

The Traveller closed the door. 'I have my rounds.' *Sour old Jew*. 'I wouldn't be by the phone even if I had one.' No need for pleasantries, this was an ill-tempered soul, almost beating against the rib-cage, pleading to be set free to play with happier companions.

Morris turned into a back room set out as a little study. 'Here. We'll do it here.'

No ceremony. No need for reassurance or the medical professionalism that set his work apart. Suits my mood, thought the Traveller. *Quick and hard, never mind the bruising.* Morris was already sitting in an upright chair by a desk. 'Let's get on with it.' He took off the muslin mask, hawked into his mouth and then into a bowl spittoon on the leather inlay, a wet rumble in the chest, as the Traveller laid the sample case on the desk, opened it with the lid masking the contents, and took out the apparatus.

'It's like a gas mask, Mr Morris.' The furrier was reaching for it and the Traveller pulled back. 'I'll fit it, if you don't mind.' Morris gestured at him to hurry up. Crown strap, fit the mask, ensure a seal, step back—'

He punched Morris as hard as he could below the ribs, driving the breath out of his lungs and into the mask, and held the rubber to his face as he tried to suck in pure oxygen and found only crystals of pain. The furrier's arms came up to tear away the apparatus but the Traveller grasped his wrists, held the hands down against the thighs, all his weight pressing the dying man to his chair as the coughs opened the gates for his soul. There was too much muck inside the mask for the Traveller to see through the vision panes and catch the moment in the man's eyes, but he felt it in his wrists and thighs and smelt it in his trousers. He fancied he could see the soul slip out of the study window, like smoke finding a draught, and smiled. *I've got my rhythm back.*

Then he went upstairs to find a clean shirt – perhaps a monogrammed one as a memento: the Yid had been a showy bugger. He couldn't make another house-call with the widow's tea still staining his front.

59

16.05. 'Which one, Barton?' The Murder Squad's administrator sounded like a BBC announcer. 'DS Lloyd or DC Nunn?' Her tone softened. 'I will ensure the relevant officer receives any message.'

I need to talk, explain. Ring back when they're in? But time is against us. If I leave a message they may have the savvy to see where it could lead. 'DC Nunn.' *At least he knows what this is about.* 'Message reads: "Subject of 30 Nov complaint is John Reginald Halliday Christie, 10 Rillington Place, London W. He states his apparatus is not portable. No proof provided. Christie states that he knows of an individual with a portable apparatus who has been offering it to the sick. This individual is Arthur, no last name, formerly a medic with Paddington Civil Defence during the war."'

'Message ends?'

'Ends. Look,' before she cut him off, 'will he get it soon, act on it soon? Because if he's caught up there are things I could do.'

'Of course he's caught up. He'll get the message. Goodbye, Barton.' Gone.

'Bugger.' Cheering from downstairs. Fidgety and distracted, he covered both ears and stood up to think as questions jostled in his head. *When would Nunn get the message? He might not check in for hours. Would he read it right? She called me Barton, perhaps he won't recognise the name, won't bother reading it. Would he act on it? Would the Squad be ready to listen?*

He'd picked up the phone humming with excitement, thinking, We're on your tail, you'll be nicked before morning. But now he couldn't get people to do what he saw needed to be done. *Been here before, chum.* 'The Supreme Command is clear. There are no Chinese units in Korea.' *And those nice scruffy blokes wouldn't accept the truth, let alone act—*

'Bourton!' Harbison in the doorway. 'Why are you standing in the middle of CID with your hands over your ears? Trying to hear no fucking evil?' He shook his head. 'Lunatic. Follow me.'

Down the stairs, through the hubbub in the hallway to the first of the interview rooms. John Absalom, an avuncular fortyish PC with a badly scarred cheek, was minding a lanky lad, fourteen, fifteen, trying to look cocky, Adam's apple bobbing with nerves.

'Oi, Slattery.' Harbison. 'Say it.'

'It's the Old Bill.' Surprisingly deep.

'Sound familiar?' Bourton shook his head. *So that's what the fuss was about. They think they've got the coshing gang.* 'Then let's try in here.' Next interview room, and a filled-out older version of the first lad, sneering at McGahern. 'Pittaway!' The lad's eyes dismissed Harbison and widened as they passed over Bourton. There was bruising across his nose and under his eyes and what looked like ink across his forehead. 'Say it!'

'It's the Old Bill.' Again, deep, unfamiliar, with a good dose of mockery.

'Don't know him,' said Bourton.

'Probably the one you nutted,' said Harbison, happily. 'The bruise across his nose fits a bonnet peak perfectly, and we've managed to roll a print of a Met badge off his bonce. Must have given him a good whack.' He stepped back into the corridor. 'Two more to try.'

'Who are they?'

'Barry Flett, your Don's older brother. He's the link.' Harbison led the way to the stairs. 'His mates Pittaway and Slattery are cousins. Bennett is Pittaway's neighbour. All Dale.' The third suspect sat in the middle of the canteen, minded by a tall, sour-faced copper called Timpson. Five two, six stone, dripping wet, looking doomed, as if Timpson might eat him. *And he's been crying. Just a lad. But happen nearly lethal.*

'Got the paper, Bennett?' The boy looked up at Harbison, swallowed and nodded. 'Say it, then.' A pause. 'Out with it.'

'It's the Old Bill!' A fractured shriek, part treble, part falsetto.

Bourton nodded. 'That's him, near as I can tell.'

'Spiffing,' said Harbison. 'Flett's down here if you want a shufti.' He led the way towards the cells.

'How did you get 'em, skip?'

'Timpson was talking to Don Flett up in his house when Pittaway came to the door and asked for his brother. Timmo saw the nose, sneaked after him on the off chance. Pittaway went into a bombsite. Timmo heard a few voices and rustled up the cavalry. Caught them warming up for more GBH. They had themselves a nice little club-room all set up, a little campfire, mess-tin a-brewing. Very dyb-dyb-dyb.'

'They say anything about why?'

'Not saying anything at all.' He picked up the ring of cell-block keys from the custody desk. 'Apart from name, rank and number from that Pittaway joker. They seem to think they're fucking Commandos or something.'

Campfire, campfire . . . The coal holes. 'Bombsite wouldn't be Bertram Terrace, would it, skipper?'

'It would.' Harbison unlocked the door to the cells. The nearest one was open. 'Know every bombsite in the Dale, do you? This,' he gestured at a stretched version of Don Flett with a ghostly moustache and jiggling legs, 'is Barry Flett, getting a whiff of home for the next ten years.'

'An' who are you?' asked Flett.

A bloke you could have killed. Bourton turned away and walked out of the cell block.

'You remember an incident, Sergeant,' as Harbison locked the cell-block door behind them, 'back in February, night the King died? I found a Lithuanian bloke bashed over?'

Harbison paused. 'We gave you a turn with Rex Athill, see what you could find.'

'Skip,' in agreement. 'He had a little refuge, a sort of club-room in Bertram Terrace too. Way Mr Athill worked it out, this Senkus got bashed with a brick by someone chewing the fat with him, climbed out groggy and collapsed on the rubble.'

'Well, there's a thing,' said Harbison. They stood at the foot of the stairs while he thought it through. 'Right now,' musing, 'all we've got is the bruises and the weapons, and a good brief could make a soupy jury wish those away.' He smiled. 'But they won't have worn balaclavas if they were chewing the fat with the Lithuanian, will they?'

60

00.10. His body must have decided four hours' kip wasn't enough because he woke after seven, already two hours late for parade. He sneaked into the nick via the vehicle yard to avoid the station sergeant's desk and minimise the strafe. He nodded at Len Green, warming up his area car, and ducked into the locker room where Norris was sitting on the bench, smoke in hand, dressed for the beat.

'Lord Bourton deigns to join us!'

Bourton felt like asking him what he was doing sitting smoking two hours after the turn had begun, but he wasn't going to be baited, not tonight. 'Yup.'

'You're for it.'

'Yup.' Bourton opened his locker.

'Coppering too menial for you?'

'Yup.' He laid his tunic on the bench, then turned back to check his uniform trousers.

'Talking to me too menial for you?'

'Yup.' *Trousers will serve.* He hung up his parka, unlaced his boots and removed them, his civvy trousers and shirt – *He's quiet. Probably takes a while to think of something to say* – and bundled the lot into the bottom of the locker.

'Oh, well,' said Norris, 'I'll leave you then.'

'Yup.' Buttoning his shirt as Norris slipped past. On with the heavy blue trousers, braces up, feet into boots. He turned to the tunic, gave it a last once-over. There was a cigarette burn, right in the middle of his new Korea ribbon.

Norris.

Out of the locker room, look left to the stairs, *No sign*, right to the corridor to the vehicle yard – *No sign. He'll have been waiting for a lift to his beat. Len Green!* – and sprinted down the passage, barrelled through the door, to see Green's car, lights on, stuffed with bodies, start towards the gates. A window rolled down, releasing a gust of laughter. 'Oi, halt!' Bourton yelled. 'Len, halt!' He sprinted to the rear door, grabbing the handle as the car started forward, running along-side tugging at the handle and banging on the roof. 'Halt!' It jerked to a stop, Green sticking his head out – 'Don't you dare dent my motor, you big lump!' – as Bourton pulled on the rear door. Someone was holding it shut. 'Open this fucking door or I'll break the window!' Bourton shouted, a voice inside telling Green to drive on. Bourton swung his fist at the glass, saw the shape on the other side flinch, gave the door a good tug and it opened dragging Norris, clinging to the handle, legs in the car, body hanging, 'Bourton, you bloody lunatic, leggo!' Bourton punched the crook of Norris's elbow with his fist, and as Norris released the handle with a shout and his face hit the ground, Bourton grabbed his collar and trouser seat, lifted him so his feet found purchase, and ran him across the yard into the rear wall of the nick.

'Why'd you do it?'

'My face,' Norris trying to push off the wall, 'leggo, ah, my face!'

'Why?' Bourton laid his forearm across the back of Norris's neck and leaned hard, jamming his cheek to the brick. 'Just to fuck me up with the skipper? Why didn't you just burn a hole in my tunic you bastard?' Boots and shouts behind him. He grabbed Norris's shoulder and collar and turned him so they were face to face. The yellow light showed scrapes on his cheek and forehead, patches of blood against his washed-out skin, and I-don't-know-what-this-bastard-will-do-to-me fear in his eyes. 'See this?' He grabbed a fistful of Norris's tunic above his left breast pocket, a button spanging off across the tarmac. 'Not a bloody ribbon in sight, and you have the fucking brass to fuck up mine? Just to fuck me up? It's not just a bit of colour, you bastard.' There were hands on his shoulders and voices in his ear, but he wasn't heeding them. 'I fucking earned that. And you had no right to fuck it up.'

The hands pulled Bourton back a foot or so, giving Norris space, and he looked past Bourton, left and right. 'You see this? He's a bloody lunatic.' He must have got some kind of encouragement because his eyes came back to Bourton. 'You earned it? I heard about you, Imjin hero, but you were nowhere near—'

Bourton stepped back in surprise. 'That old bollocks? I never told anyone I was there, anyone asks me I say I was hundreds of miles away. I was never at the fucking Imjin. All right?' He suddenly grabbed Norris by the throat and stepped in close so the other probationer could feel his spit. 'But I was at some other places, where you weren't, where I got shot at, which you didn't, and I got wounded, which will only happen to you if I stop before I kill you.' Arms were trying to pull him back, but either they weren't trying too hard, or anger was making him strong. 'I was there, you fucker. You weren't. And that gives me the right to wear that ribbon, and does not give you the right to deface it.' Bourton let go.

'What are you doing, Dick?' Roger Leakey. 'They'll have you for this and he's not worth it, really he isn't.'

'We got to keep it down, for God's sake,' Len Green, 'else brass will be down—'

'Have a look at what he did to my tunic.' Bourton realised his arms were shaking. 'Go on, have a look. It's all right, I'm done. Just have a look.' Leakey trotted back inside.

'Got a hanky, Norris?' asked Green. Norris nodded, face uncertain, probably wondering how this was going to play out. 'Then clean yourself up, you idle bugger. You were supposed to be walking Beat Two ten minutes ago.' He turned to check the gates, which were barely visible, then stuck his head around the corner to make sure the doorway in the return was clear. 'No one'll see us from the street. Let's chance a smoke.'

They were just lighting up when Leakey came back, carrying the tunic. He thrust it at Bourton. 'Best get it on and get up there. I think you might even be in civvies for this turn.' Bourton nodded, slipped it over his shoulders, ran a fingertip along the second row of ribbons and the ragged-thread dip halfway down. 'Back in the car,' Leakey told Norris, who seemed ready to give grief. 'Go.' Norris slipped away.

'He's lost a button,' offered Bourton, a little contrite.

'He can find it end of the turn. Worthless git.'

'He did that?' Green, pointing at the ribbons. Bourton nodded.

'Just now?' Another nod. 'Well, I'm not having him in my motor.' He turned to the car. 'Oi, Norris! Get out of my car!'

A rear door opened and Norris's head appeared. 'But I'm due up at Beat Two!'

'You'll have to walk.' He turned back to Bourton with a smile. 'Might let the skipper know he's late. And improperly dressed.' He patted Bourton's shoulder. 'We'll keep mum, don't worry. Get on up. And in the meantime, dream of how it'll feel when you teach him his lesson – out of uniform, mind,' a wagging finger, 'and off the nick.'

★

Tullow was readying himself to do his midnight checks as Bourton stood to attention in front of him, willing him to notice the burn.

'Sergeant. Apologies for being late on parade, Sergeant. Won't happen—'

'No, it won't.' His face didn't show much. 'Anyway, you get a pass tonight. Sergeant Harbison says you helped the late turn on your time, so,' he picked up his bonnet, 'I reckoned you were probably out for the count. And the Dale tip earns you a little leeway.' He draped his cape over his arm. 'I'm on my way. I'll allocate you as we go.'

'Roster, Sergeant.'

'Already marked you present.' *Even though I wasn't. That's properly kind.* Tullow waved his free hand. 'Honestly, got better things to do than treat former SNCOs as recruits.' He smiled. 'Besides, you made me feel happy, perhaps not all over, but . . .'

'Up to your knees, Sergeant?'

Tullow shook his head. 'Can't help yourself.' He started out of the skippers' office. *Never even noticed the cigarette burn. He really is feeling breezy.* 'Anyway, you can get back in your civvies.' Across the landing and down the first stair. 'Sergeant Harbison has a job for you. Memory Lane.' Onto the second flight down, laughter and a couple of 'Top this!' shouts from the main hallway. *Nicking that gang's jollied the whole nick.* 'Check in with CID,' he pointed at the doorway below them, 'and find out where DC Athill's fetched up. A pub or drinking club, most likely, and probably one we're not supposed to go to. With a lock-in.' He clapped Bourton on the shoulder as they reached the first-floor landing. 'See? Get into plain clothes and the rules that order a properly constituted constabulary just disappear. Something tells me it might be your natural home.' He pushed him towards CID. 'Make yourself useful.'

61

The scrap of paper from CID led Bourton to a back room in a damp basement on Lancaster Road, with occasional gloomy pictures and wallpaper that had seen at least five monarchs. The door was opened by a sort of ape, a lean six and a half feet of shoulders and chest topped with jet black hair and slanting eyes. The hand that pulled him in was huge and calloused, at the end of a thick, hairy wrist with an anchor tattoo.

'Come on in, Dick.' Athill was at the end of a sit-up-and-beg couch, glowing with beer and let-off-the-leash. There was a chorus of shouts from the half-dozen others in the room. 'Take your considerable weight off. Might even be in time for some pickled bleeding fish.'

'Rex.' Bourton nodded. A white-haired man, fortyish, square-shouldered, square-jawed, booze-sweat on the cheeks either side of his broken nose, sat beside Athill, smiling at Bourton in a secret sort of way. 'Senkus?'

The man nodded. 'Bourton? Korea copper?'

'That's right.'

Senkus levered himself upright, mostly with the help of Athill's shoulder. 'So, I say thank you.' He stuck his hand out. 'For my live.' Bourton shook. '*Parlez-vous français? Parce que je – je—*'

'Sorry, chum – "*Vous êtes très belle, où sont les allemands?*" is about my limit.'

'So.' Senkus smiled, revealing stained teeth. 'I sink – thank – think,' he laughed, then flicked a middle finger against his temple, 'too much.'

'He means,' a fiftyish man in a much-darned jumper said, getting up from the other end of the couch, 'that he's too pissed to speak English.' He stuck his hand out. *Ulsterman, from his accent.* 'I'm Patrick. And welcome to the Baltic Hearth.'

★

Presence, history, the force of his personality: Senkus ruled the room, even the ape doorman, who might lose to King Kong but only on points. It's energy, Bourton realised, after a few minutes and a mug of some kind of potato spirit, a kind of constant energy that pulls you in, iron filings to a magnet.

'Interesting chap, isn't he?' Patrick asked. The accent might have been Ulster but the language was all BBC. 'Born to lead a revolutionary army, and now he's a foreman in a car factory. Extraordinary.' He gestured at the other men. 'But that's true of all of them. Ilvars,' a small, bright-eyed man in a boiler suit leaning against the wall, 'was a fighter ace, fought for the Finns, now assembles sewing-machines. Vladas,' sober, polite smile, old tweed jacket, 'is Lithuania's greatest writer, now a bookkeeper. Vytautas,' a fat thirtyish man bulging out of a hotchpotch of old battledress, 'listens to broadcasts, but was a linguistics professor with very clever ideas about a common language. Even Toomas,' the doorman, 'was extraordinary in his own way – a topman on windjammers. All exiles. All powerless, whatever they used to be. And all deferring to our man.' He waved Bourton in closer. 'And all guilty they did nothing to stop the invader. So our man,' he nodded at Senkus, who'd opened his arms as if he was looking for someone to give him a drunken hug, 'is their hero. And not because he fought.' He half stood so he could reach to speak in Bourton's ear. 'Because he went back. He was out, he was free, but he went back when it could only end in his death. That's what they admire.'

'But he survived.'

'Exactly!' Patrick slapped Bourton's knee. 'And that's why they suspect him. Did he swap his friends' lives for his own? So they watch him, to see, to decide for themselves the great question of the Lithuanian émigré community – is Vejas a traitor?'

'Is he?'

'Rubbish. Utter rubbish. He's a stubborn bugger who can walk and walk and walk.' Bourton nodded, *Hence the good English shoes.* He put his ear to Patrick's mouth. 'And there are chaps like them all over Europe. America too, Australia, Canada. Clever. Skilled. Blessed. Oliviers or Yeatses or Stanley Matthewses. Repositories of a culture or a language or a country's identity. And they're picking potatoes or laying railway tracks, banished from home and status for the rest of their lives.' He raised his hands. 'And all over the world they'll have created little spots like this. Where they can hear their language, talk about home, help each other get ahead. All over. Extraordinary. Paris.' He waved a hand as if plucking cities from the air. 'Wuppertal. Irun.' *Wherever they are.*

'And why do you come here?'

'Why not?' He smiled. 'I did a lot of work with DPs in Germany after the war. And I did Senkus a favour all those years ago. Never do a refugee a favour, Constable Bourton. Your name is engraved on their heart. One day they're on your doorstep with a knapsack and hopeless papers. Hopeless. So I'm a sort of intermediary with officialdom. Tonight,' fishing a cigarette case out of his trouser pocket and offering a smoke, 'well, this, I suspect, will be more along the lines of interpreting.'

'Do you speak Lithuanian?'

'God, no, fiendish language. No, this is interpreting his English. And French. And his friends'. He'll only talk to the police with friends and drink. Word soup.' A cautionary finger went up. 'But you're never getting him in a court. He thinks, his friends think, it would get him killed. Might even be right.'

Bourton nodded. *Harbison won't like it but he'll have to accept it.* Another thought occurred to him. 'He's always ignored us before.'

'Why now, you mean?' Bourton nodded. Patrick shrugged and took another pull. 'Perhaps he's feeling stronger. Perhaps he wanted to thank you in person.' *Perhaps you've told him he doesn't have to hide from us any more.* 'Or you've got the culprits, so he's feeling safe. Anyway, ask him.'

★

Getting the details of the attack out of Senkus wasn't like a police interview at all. It was more like men explaining a fight to the mates who'd returned from the pub khazi to upturned furniture and broken glass. The émigrés tussled, in whichever languages came to hand, over the events and how to put them in words that these slow English policemen could follow. It was loud and argumentative, punctuated with abuse and irrelevant anecdotes, acting out, and at least two rounds of pickled fish. But it made sense in Bourton's notebook, even if that was down to Patrick's helmsmanship, not the Lithuanian's language skills.

Senkus didn't like not knowing his ground so at the end of each shift he'd find a different route back to Lithuania House. At the beginning of February he'd noticed the Bertram Terrace bombsite and gone in ('I think, I find this place in Germany, France, Annam, Russia, not in England. *Alors*, I look'), found the holes, found a better hole and settled in with a smoke and his flask. There were a couple of prostitutes who wanted to use his hole for business, once he'd disturbed an old man who wanted to be alone like him, and he could always hear the boys playing war ('Bang bang! Brrrrrr! Boom!' Huge laughter), but most of the time he'd be left alone to sit, and drink, and smoke, and remember ('*Copains*, dead, *Indochine*, *Lietuva* – too many dead'). Sometimes he'd even sing. ('Lithuania song, love song, Legion song, Germany song, "Lili Marlene", you know? *Vor der kaserne, vor dem großen tor . . .*' The whole room had sung it through, a German-English medley that only found unison in the girl's name at the end of every verse.)

That day, the day the King died, he'd finished early, and for the first time he'd caught Bertram Terrace in daylight, and seen – well, mostly heard – its regulars. The kids playing war; more kids, playing football; the old man, on his way to work. ('He want to talk, this day.' A shrug. 'He is like me, like holes, I say OK.') Men from the pub, pissing away their beer. As it got dark he'd got drunker, perhaps a little bolshy, and once he'd got his hole back from the courting couple he'd surrendered it to, he'd started to get maudlin, not just remembering other holes and the men he'd shared them with but counting them off, year by year. And so he'd started calling the roll, yelling the names of long-dead men at the sky above the Dale and answering for each with a bellow and a sip. ('*Gefreiter Willig! Hier! Capitonas Ramauskas! Štaî! Sergent-Chef Sweibert! Présent!*') He was halfway through his last company in the forests of Lithuania, with his now-empty flask at his lips ('All my boys, yes, Patrick, same *p'tit rituel* all my boys!') when a bang on his head knocked him to his knees. He'd knelt there for a minute or two, brain numb but skull torn, blood tickling his neck, before he'd passed out.

He came to on his face on the floor of the coal hole. The bombsite was silent. He'd stumbled upright, banged his head on the vaulted roof, gone down again, then crawled out backwards. He'd heard the piano in the Three Horsemen, stood up to climb out and go for help, but by the time he'd found a foothold that could lever him up to ground level he couldn't see any more. A few steps in the wrong direction, the music getting further away, then lights out.

'Did you see who hit you?' Athill, notebook out, suddenly looking like a copper again rather than a bloke still wondering at being paid to drink.

Senkus shook his head. 'Hole. Nothing else.'

'But you could hear? 'Cos you heard the piano, didn't you?' Senkus checked with Patrick and Vytautas, then nodded. 'So did you hear anything, footsteps, voices, before or after you were hit?'

In a minute or so Athill had Senkus replaying the scene, crouched down on an amputee armchair as if sitting on the coal hole's brickwork shelf, with the rest of the room shifting and jabbering as they tried to work out what he might have sensed. He'd been at the end of the shelf, by the entrance to the coal hole, right side facing out, back to the wall, and heard nothing before the blow, sensed no presence, just – bang. But afterwards, on his knees, the scuffling of feet, perhaps someone standing behind him for a few seconds, some whispers, almost squeaks.

'Doesn't one of the coshing gang have a squeaky voice?' Athill asked Bourton.

'Yes. Little one. Bennett.'

'Might have been even squeakier nine, ten months ago.' He looked at Senkus arguing with Ilvars. 'Oi, Jonny, when you were sitting, where was the roof?' Patrick explained and the Lithuanian raised his hand, palm flat, above his head. 'It was about five foot at its highest, so say . . . four six at the walls. And the wall outside would have been . . . Where'd you get hit, Jonny?' After negotiations Senkus parted the hair on his scalp to show the scar. 'Top of the head, right-hand side . . .' Athill turned to Toomas. 'Stick your arm there, sunshine.' He curved the sailor's arm so it formed an arch just above and to the right of Senkus's head. 'See the problem, Dick?'

'No.'

Athill stood slightly behind Senkus, holding an empty bottle in his fist. 'See me, Jonny?' Senkus shook his head. 'This is where the suspect stood. Any further forward, Jonny would have seen him.' He stepped alongside the Lithuanian – 'See me Jonny?' Senkus nodded – and then retreated. 'Any further back, if he swung the brick,' he lifted the bottle, 'he's going to hit Jonny's shoulder,' he brought the bottle down in a high arc onto Senkus's jumper, 'unless he swings it lower to get it under the arch,' he round-armed it like a tennis racket, 'in which case it hits the side of his head, not the top.' The bottle rested just above Senkus's right ear. 'Now include the fact that Jonny says he had his flask to his lips, which brings his head back, and the top of it closer to the wall and the roof. There's even less room to brain him. See?' He brought the bottle down in a high arc and a low, and either way it only reached the front half of Senkus's head. 'What does that tell us?'

The rest of the room was buzzing with excitement. Toomas patted Athill on the shoulder with his free hand. 'They like the Sherlock Holmes act,' said Patrick.

'It tells us,' said Athill, 'that whoever hit him was short.' He looked around the room. 'Vy-taters, you'll be the shortest, take this.' He gave him the bottle. 'Stand here.' He pushed him into place, 'bottle here.' He laid the edge against the scar. 'Raise your arm,' he lifted it in a reverse arc, elbow locked, 'and the brick . . . hits the arch.' Athill pushed down on Vytautas' shoulder. 'Bend your knees, sunshine, and see how far down you have to go before you can clear the arch.' The Lithuanian complied, stopping only when his thighs were at forty-five degrees to the floor. 'Hold it there, chum.' Athill held out his left hand parallel with the top of Vytautas' head. 'Patrick, tell 'em we need a tape measure.'

'This is an illegal drinking club,' drily, 'not a workshop.'

'And it's full of philosophers who now work for a living. Ask 'em.' He nodded at Vytautas, his left hand still in place. 'You're relieved, Groucho.'

Vladas was despatched and returned in a couple of minutes with a neatly rolled paint-flecked tape measure. Athill put one end in his left hand and had Vladas stretch it taut to the floor.

'Four foot ten, something like that. How tall's the shortest lad in the coshing gang?'

'It's Bennett. Over five foot, I'd say.'

'Well, perhaps he was shorter in February.' He reached for his drink and waved as if to say, 'You can clear up my show now.' 'If he wasn't, then chances are, it wasn't them.'

★

Half an hour later they were at the opening front door, Senkus with his arms around both coppers' shoulders ('Thank you, thank you, for my live!'). A rush of cold acid air caught in Athill's throat and he coughed for a few seconds until some phlegm came loose.

'Bloody fog.' He reached for his hanky.

'You talk to Našlėkovich,' said Senkus, happily. 'He help you.'

'And what's he, a ballet-dancing miner?' asked Bourton.

Senkus's smile said, Don't understand. 'Old man, in hole. Našlėkovich. He helps, air,' he put his hand over his mouth and nose and breathed deeply, '*les tuberculeux*, White City, Ealing. He show me, *comme un masque à gaz*.'

'To help you breathe?' *Another bleeding breathing apparatus?*

'Yes, breathe.'

'He's Polish or Russian, this bloke?' asked Bourton.

'No, no,' the smile a little tired now, 'he . . .' He turned and bellowed, 'Vytautas!' down the corridor. The professor emerged from the back room, there was a brief and eventually grumpy exchange, then the professor came up the corridor.

'That's bad. If you mix Lithuanian and Russian, in time, Lithuanian will die.'

'What are you talking about?' Sharply, because Bourton was cold, half cut, and wanted to be on his way.

'Senkus, he has made up this word Našlėkovich, a nursery construct, "Widow" in Lithuanian and "kovich", you know, the Russian suffix for "son of".'

'What's the son of the widow got to do with anything?' More sharply.

'Name!' called Senkus. 'Name of old man! With *masque à gaz! Fils de la veuve!* Widow son!'

He's British, thought Bourton. And then, with a lurch of surprise: he could be the Traveller.

62

This time Bourton asked the questions, in the only part of the Hearth where he could reckon on some privacy – the back garden, away from the route to the khazi. The cold acid air and his urgency startled Senkus and Vytautas into sobriety. This time there was no theatre, just one man, an interpreter, and coppers with the need to know.

That day, the day the King died, Widow son (Widdowson?) had joined Senkus in the hole at about a quarter to four, perhaps an hour after the Lithuanian had settled in. He'd been dressed in an old suit and a mack, about Bourton's height, quite skinny, clean-shaven, in his fifties, with old eyes – Vytautas: 'He talked about the war, working during the air raids, helping people.' He was on his way to work, a TB isolation hospital, Acton, Ealing way. He had his gas-mask device because he was to show it to his employers; he'd been helping people with breathing problems for years, ever since he and a famous surgeon had developed it, and perhaps it might help the tubercular too.

'Why did he show it to you?' asked Bourton.

Half a minute later: 'Senkus had his flask. He said something about what was inside making him feel better. Widdowson said he had his own kind of relief in his case, and laughed. Each showed the other.'

'And the case?'

Bourton knew the answer from Senkus's gestures, even before Vytautas interpreted: 'A square, deep case. Smaller than a suitcase, bigger than a briefcase. Like a salesman carries.' And even though he'd known the answer was coming, once the words were out Bourton's knees sagged and his stomach knotted.

He was under our noses, all this time. Illogical, wrong-headed – they hadn't known about the Traveller in February; still, he felt as if he'd somehow fucked up.

'Dick? Dick?' Athill, coming in close to see better in the mustard-edged night and the kitchen-window glow. 'You all right, chum? Looked like you had a turn, there.'

'I'm fine.' Bourton nodded.

'Take your word.' Athill's voice had his light I-don't-mean-it tone. 'This all something to you?' Bourton nodded. Athill gripped his elbow and led him to the edge of the pool of light so the Lithuanians couldn't hear. 'Your killer?' in a near-whisper. Bourton nodded. 'All right. And he's different from the man the Squad have their eye on?' Another nod. 'OK.' He reached for his fags, embarrassed and awkward. 'And why can't it be the Squad's suspect?'

'The smog.' Blank face. Athill offered Bourton a smoke. 'It's all about the smog.' Bourton couldn't think of how to get across the depth, colour, feel of why the Murder Squad was wrong, and it frustrated him. *He likes hard reasoning. Think simple. Think . . .* 'The victims all have bad lungs. There's a smog on. Opening the front door lets in the air that sets them off. Like you, on the doorstep. Now, the Squad's suspect is a traveller in electrical goods. If opening the door sets you off, why do it for someone selling electricals?'

'Perhaps,' lighting their smokes, 'for some reason we don't know?'

Bourton shook his head. 'I've seen how it gets them, the ill ones, in the smog. They get all panicky, they hide away and cough, wait for the smog to go. If you're like that, you're not coming to the door for a new iron.'

'But you are for a bloke with balm for your lungs?' Bourton nodded. 'That's logical.' A long draw. 'Have you,' more tentative, 'told the Squad about your suspect?'

'Yes.'

'Thank God.' Almost a cough. 'Least you haven't cocked that up.' His glowing cigarette waved. 'Sorry, hardly fair. But half the time with you, I think if I open my mouth I'll fall off a cliff. So,' more businesslike now, 'how do we help the Squad find him?'

For a moment all Bourton could think of was what he didn't know. *If Widdowson is the same man as the Traveller. Or Christie's 'Arthur'. If he's a medic. Or got blue battledress. Or contact with any of the victims. Or offered his breathing apparatus to anyone. Or even if he bloody exists – I've just got Senkus's word for it, and he was pissed when he met the man and had his brain knocked about after.* He shook his head. *You're fitting the facts to the theory. There's nothing solid to any of it. And a court will show it up in an instant.*

But he's out there, I can feel it. Just like that Chinese bloody army.

He sighed. *Do what you can and let the rest sort itself out.*

★

02.35. 'Mr Christie?' Bourton banged on the door a second time. *Bang it hard enough it'll fall in and we can roust him quicker.* 'Mr Christie, it's PC Bourton again. We're sorry to disturb you at this hour but it's urgent police business.' The curtain in the neighbour's bay window parted – *Someone sleeping in the sitting room?* – and Bourton there-there'd with his left. He banged a third time as Athill lit up a Player's. 'I'll keep knocking until you answer, sir. I'm afraid it's too important to wait until morning.' He put his ear to the door but just got paint flakes on his skin. Another thump.

'Give the house a minute or so to recover,' said Athill.

Wait. Call again. A cautious 'Mr Bourton?' through the door.

'Mr Christie, I'm here with DC Athill. We're sorry about the hour but we need your help.'

'You're not coming in.'

'We knew that, as a former colleague, you'd not grudge us getting you out of bed.' Athill mimed spreading something smooth on a piece of bread.

'You're not coming in.'

'Don't want to, sir, we just want to run some names past you, for that Arthur chap from CD.'

'You can try them from there.'

'We will, sir, but you might not hear them through the door, not properly. Could you open it a chink? Sir?' Silence. 'I could always punch a hole through, sir,' cheerily, 'make it like a confessional.'

Silence. After half a minute: 'You're not doing any more damage to my house.'

'Your landlord's, actually, Mr Christie.' Athill's voice was curt and grumpy. He raised his hands in puzzlement. 'Damage to his house?' he whispered.

'He was scarpering so I took his kitchen door down,' Bourton whispered back.

'Bloody hell.' Louder: 'Look, Mr Christie, open the door or the Ambling Alp here will bleeding break it down. Could we just get on with this?'

A key turned in the lock. After a few seconds: 'The door's stuck.' Bourton bumped it open with his shoulder. Athill shone his torch in the gap but lit only dark corridor. 'I'm cold, and not dressed for company,' said Christie, from behind the door. 'This is a liberty, a presumption, at this hour.'

'Thank you, Mr Christie.' Bourton, cheery and unctuous. 'I can see how you got your reputation with CID.'

'What reputation?' whispered Athill.

'Mr Athill, could you shine your torch on my notebook, please?' Bourton pulled out his notebook and turned to an empty page. 'So, we've got some surnames of Arthurs at Paddington CD who might fit the bill. The name . . .' he plucked one out of the air as the beam fell on the paper '. . . Partridge mean anything?'

'No.'

'Higginbotham?'

'No.'

'Macdonald?'

'No.'

'Marlow?'

'No.'

'Widdowson?'

'That's him. Arthur Widdowson. Pardoe Street, Kensal Rise, that's where we first met, autumn 'forty. A medic with Paddington.' The door started to close, then halted. 'A brave man, that Widdowson. Always ready to go in when someone was trapped. Known for it.' Christie suddenly sounded very Yorkshire. 'Good man. And probably doesn't deserve what you've got planned for him. Good night.'

'Good night,' replied Bourton, 'and thank you,' but the door was already shut.

Arthur Widdowson. Got you.

★

'I can see your smile behind me in the night and fog,' said Athill, on the trot.

'Pieces falling into place.' Just staying on his colleague's shoulder made Bourton breathless. *Skinny bastard.* 'My suspect is a CD medic. Has a portable breathing apparatus. A salesman's sample case. Fiftyish. Clean-shaven. Widdowson ticks 'em all.'

'Your suspect.'

'My suspect.' *I'm not backing down on this.*

'Your suspect.' A little lighter. 'And a good one.' *Peace offering.*

Along Lancaster Road, now reduced by fog to just pavement and the odd bit of front garden wall, and into Ladbroke Grove, Athill containing himself so he didn't streak out of sight. The world Bourton could see was reduced to Athill's heels and a few yards of paving. Which started to ramp up – *Must be the bottom of Notting Hill* – and straight away Bourton's legs lost the last of their bounce. *Christ, I've had it. There's nothing in the tank at all.* He found himself alone, hands on his knees to lock them at the end of each stride, thigh muscles twitching, as the paving rolled uphill to an invisible summit. *For Christ's sake, it's only a hundred feet high.*

Athill trotted back into view. 'All right there, Dick?'

'Dunno. Probably too many three-hour nights. Too many coshings. But I just feel all in.'

'Fair enough.' He fell into pace alongside, but he was fidgeting, clearly wanting to get on. 'Tell you what, I'll crack on with the isolation hospitals and you follow at your own pace. See you in CID.' And he was gone.

Bourton rested at the top of the hill, bent over, hands still on knees. *You need daylight, kip, proper food and fewer bruises, Richard Arthur Bourton.* When he reached the nick it felt like a ghost town. *Half the Hill must be on the sick. I should be too.* He took the stairs up to CID one leaden step at a time. He'd sprinted up them twelve hours before.

'Take a pew, Dick.' Athill was pointing to the desk nearest the door, where there was a mug of tea steaming beside the typewriter and a packet of sandwiches sitting on the blotter. 'That's actual corned beef in the sanger and as much sugar as I could cadge in the tea. Get them down you while I make a start on the business.'

He took a sip. The brew must have had four teaspoons in it – *Been raiding the canteen* – and when he bit into the sandwich he could taste bacon dripping under the corned beef. *His wife made this.* He felt so grateful that tears started in his eyes. But Athill had his head down as he dialled. *Leaving me to get myself together. Good bloke.*

He took a deep glug of the tea. *If this can't do it . . .*

63

Manning phones at half past three, the world dead and most people dead to it – but they had more luck than they deserved.

Tony Marling, getting to the receiver after three minutes twenty (operator wanted to pull the plug but Hopalong would need time): 'Christ, am I late on stag or something?'

'I've got a name for you. Arthur Widdowson, medic with Paddington CD in the war, fiftyish – check him. Arthur Widdowson. Will call later. Thanks, chum. Oh, Tony – you might want to stand to. He looks like our man.' The phone went down on his 'What? How?'

The Knights of St John Isolation Hospital, Western Avenue, Acton, the third hospital Athill rang ('Since when does that happen? I reckoned on trying ten or more'): 'Arthur Widdowson is a porter here, yes.' A good man, very sympathetic with the patients, there about two years. Then a sudden 'I'm afraid that's all I'll say on the telephone. Goodbye.' And no answer when Athill rang again.

The Murder Squad (or, rather, the Scotland Yard operator, a clarion-voiced woman whose words carried despite the receiver jammed to Athill's ear): 'The duty officer is a DC Murtagh and he knows nothing of either you or PC Bourton. He says the investigation you refer to has an established line of enquiry.' Athill ended up leaving a message for Nunn and Lloyd, 'But they won't get it,' he told Bourton, 'until they clock on.'

All of which meant that at ten to four Athill stood up and grabbed his coat. 'Yours too, sunshine,' he told Bourton. 'If the Squad aren't going to move on Widdowson for hours, then we have to.' Bourton smiled, suddenly stoked by the sanger and the brew, and his thighs didn't protest that much when he stood. 'Don't think this means I'm satisfied he's the man,' Athill waved a warning finger, 'because I'm not, given you've told me Sweet Fanny Adams and even that seems sketchy. But if he could be, then someone needs to find him now.'

★

Fifty minutes crawling out to Acton in a pool Morris, a journey that would take a tenth of that at 0400 hours on a normal day. They parked in front of the locked wrought-iron gates of the isolation hospital, 'Police' sign on the dashboard, and Athill promptly swarmed over the metalwork as if it were a scramble-net. He was kind enough to point his torch away while Bourton struggled up and over and fell in a graceless tumble that jarred his bones and rattled his teeth.

'Been in one of these before?' asked Athill.

'Nope.'

'Should be white lines, mark where we can go. Everywhere else is out of bounds. Sickies only.' He shone his light on whitewashed kerb-stones. 'Got it. Follow the Yellow Brick Road.' He started walking. 'Should at least take us to someone who's awake.'

The white lines led past several brick buildings, all of them dark, to a block with a well-lit double doorway and a bright corridor beyond. It took two minutes of rattling the door before a matron appeared to peer at their warrant cards through the glass, grumble inaudibly, tap her apron watch and shoo them away.

'This is a murder inquiry!' called Athill, a half-shout, but she was already walking down the corridor. 'Oi! Oi!' Louder. 'Sister! Matron! Big chief nurse-wallah!' She rounded a corner and disappeared. 'Oi! Matron!' He was shouting properly now. 'If you don't come back I'll wake the whole place. How'd you like a little George Formby?' He backed away from the building. '"I'm Henery the Eighth I am,"' singing loud and coarse enough to be by a pub joanna, '"Henery the Eighth I am I am . . ."'

If the Traveller weren't out there probably killing people, this would be a farce. Bourton stepped back from the door. 'We need to get in, not hauled off for a breach of the peace,' he snapped. He ran up and hit the door with his shoulder. There was the sound of wood splintering.

'Then at least – oh, look, smash the glass with your torch, do less damage.'

'I want to break something.' A longer run-up this time. The whole door jarred in the frame and there was the sound of wood splitting by the hinges. 'And I want someone,' he took half a dozen strides along the path, 'to give a damn.' This time he went in with his left shoulder and immediately felt something give above the lock. 'No whining about the rules of evidence or visiting hours.' He stared at Athill. 'Savvy?'

Athill gazed back, in the insulted deadpan that Bourton had first seen shown to Kalvaitis all those months ago, then nodded. 'Savvy.' He smashed in the door glass with his torch, reached in, tried the lock. 'There's a key.' He knocked out the last shards from the frame, reached through to open the door, and headed down the echoing passage. 'She went this way.'

★

'Arthur Widdowson.' Athill, upright in the visitor's chair opposite her desk, Bourton leaning against the doorframe, arms folded to contain his anger. The DC was aiming for formal and respectful, to make up for the door, and for snatching the phone from her fist to tell the police operator no response was needed – Matron Beeston was assisting DC Athill and 491 Bourton in a murder inquiry, and her responses would determine whether they brought her in for obstructing same.

'He isn't on duty.' Beeston was in her mid-forties, a small woman above the waist and a wide one below, long-faced, tired and pouchy; Bourton wondered if they'd disturbed her napping. She was still bitter despite Athill's tone. 'I haven't seen him for days.'

'How long?'

'I can find out.' Athill nodded. She waited for Bourton to step aside – he hadn't stopped glowering at her and she'd got the wind up – then led them down the passage. The building felt completely deserted. *Probably the admin block, only staffed in daylight hours. Might explain why no one's come running.* She opened a door marked 'Administration', turned the lights on and threaded between a jumble of desks with shrouded typewriters to a filing cabinet at the far end. She flicked through the time cards in the top drawer. 'Widdowson . . . Thursday.

Fourth of December. Did the two till ten. Not been in since.' She slammed the drawer shut. 'That enough for you?'

'No.' Athill had his notebook out. 'We need his address, how long he's worked here, what kind of man he is.'

'You want to look at his personal file.'

'Yes.'

'Not possible.' Shaking her head. 'I can tell you what I know of him, no more.'

'Matron,' Bourton trying for honey but his frustration showing, 'you know this is a murder inquiry, and that Mr Widdowson is a suspect. Could you try a little harder?'

'I'm trying.'

A moment of inspiration. 'This killer preys on people with bad lungs in the middle of the smog. When they're at the end of their tether.' She blinked several times. 'People like your patients.' Another thought, calculated to get her on his side. 'If it's Widdowson, he might even have been preying on your patients, not here, of course,' *Butter her up*, 'you'd know that – no, once they're discharged.' He perched on a desk to look less frightening. 'Abusing their trust. People he's known and helped.' She looked pale and unhappy. 'He kills in the smog, Matron. He could be killing now. Now.' She looked at the curtained windows as if the Traveller were standing there trying to peer in. 'So please help us find out if Arthur Widdowson is our man.'

*

'He started in 'forty-eight, just after we joined the Health Service.' The personal file was open on her desk, retrieved from the director's locked office with the aid of a master key.

'Age?' asked Athill.

'Fifty,' said Bourton, scanning it over her shoulder. 'Born on the first of February 1902, Rotherham. Royal Navy 1919 to 1926, medical discharge, rated Able Seaman. Did manual jobs after so can't have been that disabled, joined Great Western as a porter, Paddington goods yard, 'thirty-four, stayed until 'forty-six. Nothing mentioned after. Address forty-eight South Wharf Road, Paddington, married, no children.' He looked up at Athill sitting on the other side of the desk. 'Nothing here rules him out.' *But no mention of a King's Commendation, either, to rule him in.*

'Don't suppose there's a photo?' asked Athill. Bourton shook his head. 'You take a staff photo?' he asked Beeston. 'Something he might be in?'

She nodded. 'In the corridor.' They after-you'd out of the office, but the three pictures – '48, '50, '52 – weren't very big, and Widdowson just looked like a thin-faced man, no longer young, in a porter's coat.

'Is there anything the pictures don't show?' asked Athill. 'Scars, that disability?'

She shook her head. 'He's just a thin, middle-aged man with a Yorkshire accent.' She started back to her office.

'Fair enough,' said Athill. 'What's he like?'

She'd taken refuge behind her desk again. 'Polite. Helpful. Willing, I suppose.'

'Does he spend time with the patients?'

She nodded. 'It's most of his job. They're stuck in here for months on end, in their wards, the common rooms, and they get cabin fever. And they may get on each other's nerves. So, apart from the lifting and carrying, it's his job to play Monopoly, make tea, chat. Cheer them up, occupy them.'

'Which builds their trust,' commented Bourton, thinking, Someone respectable wouldn't let in any old apparatus man – but one who'd been bringing you brews day after day . . . *Respectable. Maybe there is something to that killing-on-your-doorstep yarn I gave her.* He flicked through his own notebook, back a month or so, to a list of the Traveller's possible victims. *One of them was dead respectable, that was what her friend Mrs De Something had said, dead respectable and lost a lung to TB. The house with the Catholic tat. The woman who was always trying out cures to get her through the smog.*

'Could you do me a favour?' Bourton cut through whatever the other two had been saying. 'Could you take this name and address,' he wrote them on a fresh page in his notebook, 'in fact, all of these names,' flipping back and forth, copying frantically in signaller's block capitals, 'against your patient records?' She was about to object. 'All I need is for you to look up these names, tell me if they were patients here. No more information needed. They're all dead, anyway, so we can't offend them.' He looked up at her. She was clearly wondering how she could say no without giving offence. *I really have put the wind up her. Sorry.* 'Unless we don't catch the man who killed them. Then their ghosts might get right narked.' He smiled, tore out the leaf and handed it over. 'You come back with the answer I expect and we'll be gone. There's an incentive.'

He smiled again but a chill swept over him. Suddenly he felt sick. *Oh, Christ, this is real, more real than it's ever been – a link, a real link, between real people and a real suspect.* He felt as if he'd walked in on a murder, not helped to solve one. She must have registered the change in him because she blinked decisively, took the paper and hurried out.

'Do you really think he'd kill someone he was linked to?' asked Athill. 'Wouldn't he risk it coming out? What if she just told a friend, "That nice Mr Widdowson, he's popping in"?'

'That's what I was thinking. But if the death isn't suspicious, he can kill whoever he likes. No one has reason to ask who she saw last. Or think anything of him calling if they do know. Her death, his visit – they're not connected.' The nausea had settled in the pit of his stomach and now his bones ached too.

'Apart from your Mrs Hartham.'

'Apart from Gladys Hartham. And her cocoa, and her shoes, and her Up West best.' He smiled. 'Bert said it was the small things I had to keep an eye open for. Bullseye.'

'Still,' said Athill, 'it doesn't sound like the Traveller.'

'I don't know, Rex.' Bourton creaked into Beeston's chair. Gravity seemed to have him beat. 'Perhaps he just kills people he can.' He closed his eyes. 'But then I'm new at this detection game.'

Beeston opened the door and Bourton sprang up, gravity defeated by some impulse of good manners or obedience to authority. The piece of paper was outstretched and she looked all business as she sidled through to her desk. 'One name.'

'Bénédicte White?' She nodded and Bourton turned to Athill. 'He's the Traveller.'

64

'Take me through it.' Athill was perched on the desk in the admin room, where Bourton was waiting for the operator to put him through.

'The Traveller has a sample case. Mrs White is one of his victims. Widdowson has a sample case. He knows Mrs White.' A voice from the receiver said, 'Connecting you.'

'You do know that sounds thin?'

The Scotland Yard switchboard. 'Murder Squad, DC Murtagh, please.' Bourton covered the receiver. 'That's the *Reader's Digest* version.'

'Murder Squad, DC Murtagh speaking.'

'Mr Murtagh, sir, 491 Bourton, Notting Hill. And before you tell me to buzz off, have you got a direct link between your Traveller suspect and any of the victims? Other than him selling door-to-door on their streets?' There was silence at the other end. *Bleary and hasn't caught up yet. Or 'No' but you won't admit as much.* 'I bet you haven't. However, there is a definite connection between this man I've notified your Squad of, Arthur Widdowson of forty-eight Lower Wharf Road, Paddington, and one of the victims. Widdowson has a sample case, he's been touting a breathing apparatus, he fits the description of the last person seen visiting another of the victims—'

'Which victim?' *Not bleary, then.*

'Captain Bradford, Crawford Street.'

'Never heard of him.' Bourton felt as if he was on the edge of a precipice and his sinking stomach would take him over. *Lloyd said they were concentrating on Mrs Hartham and the Kennington woman as victims. Did that mean they'd struck all the others off their list?* 'So, what's the connection?' Murtagh sounded end-of-the-night-turn – tired, impatient, not necessarily ready to listen.

'It's not with Captain Bradford, it's with Mrs White.'

'Who?'

'Mrs Bénédicte White, up near Marylebone station.'

'Never heard of her, either.' Bourton closed his eyes. *They haven't even got the right victims. No wonder they've got the wrong suspect.* 'Look, Barton, I know you were the chap said Mrs Hartham had been murdered, and we're grateful, but I don't know who these people are, this stuff in your message about breathing devices, this suspect you've got. Look, DS Lloyd will be in in about three hours, I'll do the hand-over and perhaps he'll call. But in the meantime I suggest you get some kip. OK?'

What's the point? 'All right.'

'And look,' said Murtagh, 'if he doesn't call, don't take it amiss. We've got a suspect in custody, we're having a rest before we come at it full on in the morning, and maybe it'll all be done by noon. All right?'

'All right.'

'Good night, Barton.' The receiver was nearly in the cradle when it squawked again. Bourton brought it back to his ear. 'Barton. Look, you'll be a witness when this comes to trial. And if you go down this other-suspect rabbit-hole, it won't change the result, but some brief will say it's your bloke not ours, then the Crown will make you look silly, 'cos he has to. And then you're not a keen young copper with a good eye and a commend from the judge, shoo-in for early CID, but an embarrassment. Keep your powder dry, OK?'

It made sense, was even well meant, but it didn't really register: someone else's neat answer to their own tricky sum. 'Understood, Mr Murtagh. And thank you.' He hung up.

'How come you call him Mr and not me?' asked Athill, lightly.

'Haven't met him yet. He's still got the mystique of CID.' He was pleased to have mustered even that feeble insult.

'True,' said Athill. 'Brush-off?' Bourton nodded. 'Oh, well. We're on our own then.' Bourton opened his eyes, mildly surprised. 'O' course I'm on board. Why else would I nick Widdowson's time cards? If this place is his alibi we'd better be prepared.'

★

'Why's he doing it?' Athill at the wheel, a steady ten m.p.h. down Westway, Bourton minding his watch for the Wood Lane turn.

'Don't know.'

'Do the Squad know?'

'Might do. Not said. One minute. Last I heard they thought it wasn't robbery.'

'OK.' Unimpressed. Seconds of silence. 'Why do you think he's doing it?'

'Don't know.' *He wants more.* Bourton closed his eyes to pull stray thoughts across the marsh of his tiredness. 'Not worked it out, really.'

'Isn't that the heart of it, though? Why?'

'You've done murder investigations, you tell me.' Looking at his watch: 'Three, two, one, mark,' and half right the glow of a copper on lighthouse. Athill turned the wheel and waved at their colleague as they trundled by. 'But this isn't much of an inquiry, as everyone keeps telling me. Sorry. Came out sarky.' He paused. 'Can't work it out, really. Killing doesn't seem to fit with him being a medic. He's not in it for the money. Doesn't seem to be in it for sex. Victims are all different so it doesn't look like hate. And there's no sign of torture so he doesn't get his jollies from hurting people.' *Forgot to check my watch at the Wood Lane turn. Bugger.* 'Nearest I can tell, he's just killing people. And he likes the smog.'

'Thanks.'

The explanation sounded weak. 'Sorry, Rex.' *Eight months in and I haven't got an answer.* 'Probably too worn out to think.' *That's not it.* 'Nah.' He found a thought. 'Been hard enough pushing the murder rock uphill without working out the why.'

'And we don't know how he's killing them?'

'Squad might. No PM was done on any of the victims I found. Their new victim might tell them something.' His eyes wanted to close again. *Drop off if I'm not careful.* 'They might not take much killing. They're all weak and frightened and ill. Stifle 'em. Bit of gas, per'aps. Can't be too obvious or even the doziest of these docs might notice.'

'This is *Alice in Wonderland* stuff,' Athill was shaking his head, 'murder that doesn't show, victims who don't exist, killed for God knows why, evidence that isn't evidence. It's like a riddle.' He pulled over and applied the handbrake. 'And I need to do one thing at a time.' He turned to Bourton. 'Right. Rules of evidence. We want to get him on the scaffold. How do we do that?'

'Rex, I'm too knackered for this.'

'But you're not thinking like a copper.' *Not thinking at all.* 'What happens if we knock on the door and he's not there? His wife will tell him and he'll run. Or we don't knock, we sit outside, wait for him to turn up. What do we pick him up for? And even if he's got his apparatus on him, can we make anything stick? D'you understand? If we get this wrong we lose him – either he shuts up shop or a brief gets him off.'

'Rex,' floundering, 'I want to stop him killing people.'

'What – kill him? Or just bash him up?'

Bourton looked around them, at a fog still so thick they could barely see the kerb they were parked against. 'God alone knows how many people he can kill in the next day or two.'

Athill was silent. A taxi engine ambled past them going west; they never saw the headlights. 'He can't have been.' Voice tight in denial, perhaps even to keep nausea in check. 'Killing lots of people. Each time. Each smog.'

'Captain Bradford, Mrs White, the Kennington bloke, all died the same weekend.'

'Nah.' Athill was shaking his head again. 'He'll find someone, warm them up,' getting stronger, more confident, 'pick his time, knock on their door when he knows they'll be low—'

'Why not kill and kill and kill, each time?' Hard, merciless. 'Foley spoke to four boroughs. And each one – each one – had a suspicious death. Why not one in each of the other boroughs? And that was in November, before the worst pea-souper in a century. God alone knows what he's been doing while we've been flailing about—'

'Come on—'

'Why not? There's been nothing to stop him. Probably the only thing slowing him down has been how long it takes to reach his victims.'

'Oh, God.' Athill bent over the wheel. 'Oh, God.'

Bourton let it sink in. Then he shrugged. 'I'm sure it's not that bad. Probably hard for him to find victims. Probably why he killed Mrs White – run out of everyone else.'

'It would take a while,' Athill talking to the dashboard, 'to get their trust.'

'Though he'd have months to do it in.'

'And God alone knows,' Athill still trying to convince himself, 'it would be hard enough to get around in the smog. All over London, much of it on foot.'

'Let's say one a day,' offered Bourton.

'If he's lucky.'

'Which makes three, four a smog. Six smogs a year? Twenty killings a year? For God alone knows how many years?'

'Ah, Christ.' Athill stared through the windscreen. 'Britain's never known anyone like him. He's . . . bloody Henry Holmes.'

Who? 'I want to stop him killing anyone else,' said Bourton, quietly. 'I just want to get there, and grab him, and do . . . something. So he can't. Make something up. Nick him, soften him up, search everywhere he knows while he stews, or just let him know we're on to him so he stops.' He closed his eyes. 'I'm too knackered to think any more. But you're cleverer than me, more copper than me. Come up with something, would you?'

65

06.20. 'He doesn't know.' Athill on the doorstep. 'Remember that. He doesn't know what we don't know.' He knocked hard, a triple rap.

Bourton could barely see his feet but he remembered Lower Wharf Road from a notification with Bert: shoddy warehouses and canal cottages older and less grand than the rest of Paddington, peering at a canal basin with enough water to make the rubbish dumped in it rot nicely in summer and jab above the ice when London froze mid-winter.

A faint chink of light appeared under the door of number 48. A key turned in the lock. *I'm going to have you.* Bourton put on his copper's blank this-is-normal-business face. *I'm going to have you.*

'I'm low meself, Maggie.' A woman in her fifties, long, thin, dark-eyed face above a floral housecoat held closed over layers of woollies and flannel. 'You're not Maggie.' Glasses from a pocket. 'Who are you then?'

'Mrs Widdowson?'

'I am. Who's asking?' *Yorkshire, just like her husband.*

'DC Athill, PC Bourton, Metropolitan Police, ma'am.' Athill showed his warrant card. 'Could we have a word with Mr Widdowson, please?'

'What about?' Curiosity rather than concern. *She's got no idea.*

'Could we have that talk with him?'

'Not here you can't.' She smiled. 'He's out. Look, it's freezing cold, dears. You look all in. You want to come in for a cuppa?'

★

'Every pea-souper the same,' said Mrs Widdowson, sloshing the pot to strengthen the brew. 'The fog comes down and he's off to do his Civil Defence drills, all over the borough.'

'What drills?' asked Bourton.

'You don't know?'

'Mrs Widdowson,' Athill, very kept-in-the-dark-but-do-what-I'm-told, 'all we know about your husband is his place of work and the fact that he helped one of the patients there.'

'That's Arthur,' proud, indulgent, 'always wants to help. He prepares the air-raid shelters, see. For if they're needed.' She poured the tea. 'I hope you don't mind no milk, but I'm out, really, that's what I was telling Maggie – well, you. I don't even have powder.'

'Black is lovely, Mrs Widdowson,' Athill said.

'Lily, please.'

'Lily, we're at the end of our shift and a pick-me-up is just what we need.' Athill smiled and picked up his brew. 'What was that about the shelters?'

'Oh, the shelters. It's because of his medical training, see.'

'Medical training?' Bourton, hands around his own mug.

'Oh, he was a sick-berth attendant in the navy,' *Been lying to you for a while, then,* 'and they made him all up-to-date in the war, for the rescue squads, see,' she sat down with a brew of her own, 'and he did that, night after night, all through the Blitz and after. He helped lots of people, did Arthur, crawling into the rubble.'

'And the shelters?' Bourton trying again.

'Oh, the shelters. Well, there's the worry, see. About the Bomb.'

'Of course,' Athill, 'everyone's worried about the Bomb.'

'Do you know, I'm not. I thought, all through the war, if it comes it comes and it's the same with the Bomb, we won't know anything about it. But of course people will get frit, and the government has to allow for that, doesn't it? And perhaps we'll have a warning so people can hide like they did before the Luftwaffe came.'

'What's Arthur doing with the shelters now, then?' asked Bourton.

'Testing them, of course.' Looking at them as if they should know, her cup half empty though she'd barely had time to breathe let alone drink. 'They've been working on them, see if they can make them so they'll keep out radiation, and some of the other stuff that might go with the Bomb. Arthur mentioned some peptobismides and other things but it's all just words to me. And they've found out that the smog is like these things, see, the way it seeps in. So when a smog comes on, Arthur gets the call.'

'Here?' asked Athill.

'Oh, no, we're not on the phone, at work,' *No, he doesn't,* 'for him to go down to the shelters and test them, see if there are signs of the air and that getting past the new doors and compartments, and because of his medical training he's the man for the job.'

'He would be.' Athill, approvingly. 'They're lucky to have him. Do you know where these shelters are?'

She shook her head. 'All over the borough.'

'And when would you expect him back?'

'After the fog's gone.'

'Does he not pop back at all?'

'Oh, no. Does his rounds and his tests, sleeps in the shelters, different one every night.'

'Any chance he'll be in touch?'

'Oh, no, he doesn't bother me at work, Whiteley's,' she pre-empted them, 'in the staff canteen, no, he concentrates on a job until it's done.'

'That's our bad luck, then.' Athill with a professional smile. 'The sergeant wanted us to sort this out today so we could move on to other things. We'll have to come back another time. When he returns could you tell him we called?'

'Of course, love. And which station?'

'Notting Hill.'

'And what's it about?'

'A patient from Knights of St John,' said Bourton. 'We'll tell him when we see him.'

She was walking them down the narrow corridor, chatting about the smog, when Athill smacked his head in theatrical stupidity.

'You know what, Mrs Widdowson? We don't even know what your husband looks like. Could we have a dekko at a photo, d'you think?'

His timing was perfect. She was standing by the front parlour door and promptly turned the handle, ushering them in with an apology and a deft flick of the light switch. Bourton's eye skated over the furniture to the photos standing guard on the mantelpiece. *A young Mrs W holding a baby, a long-faced, baggy-eyed young man in naval uniform with 'HM Submarines' on his hat band, a clipping from a news magazine of men in battledress carrying a stretcher over rubble, a wedding portrait centre stage.*

'That will do fine,' Athill was saying, 'won't it, Dick?' pushing a picture of the couple at the seaside, Mrs W about five years younger, in front of Bourton. Widdowson was a tallish spare-looking man with high shoulders, thin cable-like forearms, and a little pot belly under the collarless white shirt. His long face and pouchy eyes were crinkled in a smile. His hair shone. *What fifty-year-old man sheens his hair at the seaside?*

He didn't look like a killer. He didn't look like anything much at all.

'So, what do you have for me?'

The Traveller looked at the blank metal door in front of him and savoured the moment – the moment every morning, every fog, when a fellow would muster, clean shirt, close-shaved, rested, ready to step out on deck and discover . . . Clear skies? A breeze sucking the fog out to sea with the tide? Dry air absorbing the mist, leaving a yellow haze that hid little? Or damp, still air, thick with coal and sulphur and nitrogen, the tang of metals, the sting of acid?

Tongue out. Open the door.

Glowing streetlight, yellowed night, shrouded steps, and beyond – nothing. A whole city, hidden to everyone but him. He locked the door behind him and walked deliberately to the street, breathing past the first acetone tang in the lungs, savouring the tingle.

Five days, and the fog was still not done. He'd never known a pea-souper like it. Every morning the air was thicker, richer, yellower, more metallic. He smiled. The fog was impenetrable. *And it'll be worse by noon. They'll stop the tubes, no one'll drive, no one'll be able to get around. So everyone will stay at home, wave their sick-notes, listen to the wireless, chat to the neighbours, tell stories, wipe fog-grit off their furniture.* And because he knew the fog in his soul and lungs and bones, he'd be free to pedal through empty streets, navigating by what no one else seemed to see: the shadows behind the fog – of buildings, roof-lines, walls, parked motors – and the corners marked by the spaces where the shadows stopped. He put down his case and fished out a cigarette. *Fog's only impenetrable if you don't know what to look for.*

Let's try for five. Mark this fog by making the most of a day. Make up for the dither-day, the widow off Horseferry keeping the freeing down to one. Stay west, with the bike, plot the route, and by the morning . . . Sixteen souls. Lead sixteen souls to the sky. He smiled. *Now that's a proper tribute to the fog of fogs.*

66

07.10. 'That CD stuff is balls.' Every surface in the Morris seemed to radiate cold but Bourton was awake again, fizzing with tea or indignation. 'Just a line he's shot her. CD's barely been stood up again. It's old blokes in church halls practising reef knots and gas drills. As for hiring some old medic like him to test the shelters! Garn. They'd have some surveyor type from the borough engineer's, or a proper scientist.'

'You notice the photo of Mrs W with their dead baby?' asked Athill. 'I thought they had no kids.'

'They haven't, but it was her baby. She had that look – you'll recognise it when it comes. That picture, of his dead kid, was less important than a magazine clipping of him saving someone. Might have been relegated over time – still, who does that?'

'Mr Sun Shines Out of My Arse. And he sheens his hair on holiday. As if he's a lad on the sniff. A fifty-year-old man out with his wife. Who's he trying to pull? Women? Or people with dicky lungs? Here.' Bourton laid his notebook on the dashboard. 'Get out those time cards.' He turned on his torch and flicked through the pages. 'Eighth of January, that was Constance Dean, in the City.'

Athill laid the cards alongside, took off his gloves and started thumbing through. 'All right. No shift between the sixth and the tenth.'

'Twenty-ninth of March. Mrs White, in Marylebone.'

'Nothing between the twenty-seventh and the thirty-first.'

'Though the twenty-ninth was a Saturday, so perhaps he'd have been off anyway.' Athill looked up from the cards. 'My wedding day. Can't forget that.'

'Won't be allowed to ten years on.'

Bourton gestured at the cards. 'Try the seventh of February. Gladys Hartham.'

Athill started thumbing again. 'Clear between the sixth and the ninth.'

'So he was lying to Senkus when he said he was off to work. Lies even to strangers.'

'So where was he going, in a suit and a mack, with his sample case of treats?'

'Will we ever know?' A throwaway. *But it's true.* 'Even if we comb all the death books, whoever it is is just one of them, one of the thousands.'

'We can ask him. All right? We can ask him. He's a bragger. We get him in an interview room and he'll be desperate to show off.' Athill nodded at the notebook. 'Now, who else is in there?'

A tiny fraction of those he's killed, that's who. He put the thought away. 'The two others the same weekend as Mrs White. Captain Bradford, twenty-seventh or twenty-eighth of March, and Frederick Slingsby, found on the twenty-ninth of March, probably died on the twenty-eighth.' Pointing at the time cards, 'Bet those will show him off duty through every smog. How does he do it and not get sacked?'

'Says he's sick? Or he's useful – it's a duff job, they don't know if they can replace him.' Athill put the cards in his pocket. 'I'm not sure I can stand any more right now.' He stared out of the windscreen, as if a sign was going to appear from the soup saying 'Widdowson 2 miles'. 'So where is he? If this CD stuff is balls, where does he go?'

'Dunno,' said Bourton. He shook his head to try to clear it, suddenly unable to think much at all. 'Wherever it is, he'll have left to start another day's killing by the time we get there.' *Another day's victims, and there's nothing we can do.* He closed his eyes, weary but also accepting. *It's going to take another day or two of death before we get close. And that's just the way it is.* He apologised to the sick, frightened souls Widdowson was going to kill today – people who would die because he couldn't do his job, couldn't get his blokes up from where they'd taken cover in the wheat, up to push forward against the lash of the MGs and the mortars and that fucking flak wagon. *Sorry, B Company. It's just your turn.* He sensed Athill looking across as he sank back in the seat, surrendering to gravity.

A hand patted his arm. 'All right, chum. Sleep it off. We'll be at him later.'

★

08.15. 'Oi, Bourton.' DC Martin in the canteen doorway. 'This bloke one of yours?'

Tony Marling was on his heels, rested and beaming in tweeds, torch, Die-hard tie. Bourton was too tired to muster a thought or a greeting and watched him over a banger-laden fork as he crossed to his table. 'Morning, Dick.' He sat down. 'Standing to, as suggested.' He stuck his hand over Athill's plate of sausages and powdered egg on toast. 'Tony Marling.'

Athill introduced himself. 'You the CD bloke? The councillor?' Marling nodded. 'Don't suppose you can get eggs taken off the ration?'

Marling shook his head. 'Can get streetlamps put in, though.'

'Not on toast, I hope,' sniffed Athill. 'Bad enough already.'

Some thoughts joined up in Bourton's head. 'Rex, Tony's been helping me with the CD angle.' A nod of success at making sense. 'Might have something on Widdowson.' He gestured at his second plate of bangers and eggs. He badly needed oomph for his muscles and oil for his joints. 'Mind talking while I eat? Won't be up to anything if I don't.'

Marling got straight down to business. 'If Widdowson is in CD, it's not in Paddington.' *I think I should be surprised.* 'Bertie Humphreys, Paddington's Secretary, Preparedness, popped round to their CD HQ. They've got no record of Widdowson serving in Paddington Civil Defence since it was reactivated last year.' *Line-shooter – wearing a uniform to which he's not entitled.* 'Now, according to the current head of section, Widdowson was in Paddington CD throughout the war – he first met him in the queue to sign up in September 'thirty-nine – first as a rope and tackle man on light rescue, then as a medical assistant. Paddington B. Left the section when it was wound up in 'forty-five. No honours or awards.' He looked up at Bourton. 'So if he's been wearing a King's Commendation he's not entitled to it.'

'Bollocks,' said Bourton. 'All that wasted bloody effort.'

'I don't know about any of that,' Athill said – *That's right, he doesn't* – 'and it sounds like I shouldn't, so I don't have to lie if the brass ask.' He took a forkful of egg and sausage and bit the end off half a slice of bread. 'Course, him not being in CD shows that everything he's told his wife about testing the old shelters is bull.'

'Why on earth would we test them?' Marling, slightly indignant.

They might offer some protection against blast, but as for fall-out . . .' He shook his head. 'Of course, he could be using them, though. The old shelters.' The others stared at him. 'I mean, we're not.'

'Well, blow me down,' said Athill, 'wouldn't that be neat, though?' He seemed to put most of the food left on his plate on his fork and gestured at Marling with his other hand. 'So, Your Worship, where do we go next?'

67

09.40. 'Nobody needed them.' Bertie Humphreys was a trim architect in his late forties, with dark-tinged skin that would bloom brown in the sun, a polio limp and an accent just the scruffy side of RP. His prosperous heavy worsted suit was as out of place amid the municipal leftovers of Paddington Preparedness as a swan in a pit-head pool. 'Some of them the council had title to. Others were just converted from cellars under private buildings. In any case they became redundant for local government purposes as soon as the V2s stopped. We locked them up, handed back the key where appropriate, and walked away.'

'So what happened to them?' Athill, tone hinting at some dereliction of duty.

'Nothing, as far as I know.' He offered them smokes from a cigarette case on his desk and they lit up. 'What would we use them for? They're just windowless spaces twenty feet underground. People certainly don't want to live in them – they'd much rather be four to a room at Mum and Dad's until they get to the top of the housing list.' He took a deep pull. 'Anyway, the shelters under private buildings, I assume the landlords use them, or just locked them up and forgot about them. And with those shelters, I'm sure someone who knows it's there, or perhaps has a key, could put it to their own use.'

'What about yours?' asked Athill.

'God knows. I'm sure there'll be keys somewhere, but I'd have no idea where to start looking. And if I had the keys I wouldn't know where most of the shelters were. I'd probably have to ask Bill Pittock. He was the senior relevant official when everything was wound up in 'forty-five.'

'I can't believe you'd just lock up and walk away,' Athill, verging on rudeness.

'It may sound slapdash,' Humphreys deciding not to take offence, 'but they – we – really were surplus to requirements. Like you chaps, we just wanted to get back to normal. I think we were done even before VJ Day. The stores went into, well, storage, the vehicles got auctioned off, the section posts got turned back into school gyms and council offices, shelters got locked up, the chaps handed back their kit and went home. Within a month or two it was as if CD had never existed.'

'So if someone is using the shelters, how does he get in?'

'Well, you mightn't need keys.' He shrugged. 'Quite a few started out as spaces off tunnels, or boiler rooms, or machine shops, with access that wouldn't work for crowds of people, hurrying, nervous, in the middle of a black-out. So the borough engineer would block or board up the original access, and put in a new entrance that didn't lead past boilers or through sewerage tunnels. If you knew the space before it became a shelter, you'd probably know the original access. Could get in that way.'

'And if you did need keys, how would you get hold of them?'

'I can't think it would be that difficult, frankly. Widdowson would have known everyone in Paddington CD, and probably half the chaps on the squads in the neighbouring boroughs. It made for very . . . very strong bonds, working on the squads. All of them – CD, fire brigade, police – pooling skills, pitching in, with a common purpose, saving life. I'd see it every night and envy them. Tremendous fellowship. Tremendous purpose.' Another pull. 'Anyway, I'm sure you can see how someone like him could get some keys – help an old chum doing the lockup, or sneak about and pinch them. No one would ask questions of someone like him. And what is there to suspect, anyway? Everyone thought the shelters were valueless.'

'So we've got private shelters off tunnels and such,' Bourton's foggy brain made even a basic summing-up hard work, 'and council ones he might have the key to.' He closed his eyes to concentrate. 'Can't do anything about the private ones – if he knows these . . .' he tried to find a word that didn't sound childish but failed '. . . secret entrances we won't, even if we get a list of the shelters. So the council ones, how do we find out about them?'

★

12.50. Twenty minutes of calls around a near-deserted Paddington Town Hall to find a number for Pittock, the official who'd wound up CD in 1945, in retirement in Bexhill-on-Sea. Half an hour waiting for him to return from walking the dog. Twenty-five minutes to explain, then get enough names, departments, cubby-holes, for plentiful alternatives should his first suggestion hit the buffers. Then an hour and a half's search of town-hall nooks and crannies, from Preparedness on the fifth floor to Maintenance in the basement, to produce a card-bound register with 'Firewatch' drawn through and 'Shelters – Disposition' stencilled below. And a single key sitting inside, filling the gap where two dozen pages would once have been, stitched to the binding.

'Could it be a master key?' asked Bourton, half believing this mud-bound chase might finally make it onto good going.

'Not for all of them.' Humphreys shook his head. 'Too many owners, too many old locks. But the brand new shelters – perhaps.'

Two pages: fifty-two shelters, each identified by a simple address and in the next column a set of initials. Fifty-two, half of them probably tucked under buildings whose use had changed, where no one would know about the shelters or let them in, or even have turned up on this red-letter day for skivers. They sat in the deserted town-hall canteen over brews and a near-vegetarian cottage pie, all four looking at the strong, looping handwriting in weak wartime ink as if a genie were due. 'Put a whole turn on this,' Athill said hopefully, 'could do it in about four hours.'

'We don't have a whole turn,' said Bourton. 'And it's too late to snaffle anyone coming off the early and too early to snaffle someone coming off the late.'

'So where do we start?' asked Marling.

They all looked at each other. They're clueless, thought Bourton; I'm just knackered. And smelly. He stuck his nose into his armpit to check if the whiff was him or his shirt. *Me. I need a bath.* A thought actually flashed through the murk inside his head, like a flare set off by accident. *He needs somewhere he can sleep, hang his clothes, wash, because his victims won't let him in looking like a scruff . . .*

'Plumbing,' said Bourton. 'Shelters with plumbing.'

68

Jammed in the Morris, riding the bell through the gloom at a glacial ten m.p.h., Athill behind the wheel, Humphreys grinning childishly from his cranny on the back seat, Marling with Pittock's shortlist of twenty-four shelters, and Bourton with the key. Bouncing from cellar to cellar, looking for blue battledress, a sample case, running water, the signs of someone living rough, in a London which seems to have been forgotten . . .

14.35: Widdowson's old workplace, Paddington goods yard; a shelter given a snooker table and half-decent seating, too busy with skiving railworkers to give the killer a home from home. 15.10: a thirties office building on Eastbourne Terrace, opposite Paddington station; a door warped into the frame, eddies of dust, and while the network of concrete rooms still had benches, partitions, even electricity, the sinks, taps and khazis had all been removed. 16.00: a one-storey brick block like a lecky sub-station, a gap in the terraced smile of pretty Seymour Street, and sixty feet below it, a fifty-by-forty space in Admiralty white, well ventilated, brightly lit, with running water, working WCs and the feel of a cruiser mess-deck. And signs of use: no dust, stray bits of rope, an old hose-wheel with 'LFB' on the drum, everything well maintained . . . But nothing a man would leave behind in a temporary billet.

16.25: regroup. Then a locksmith on Westbourne Grove to copy the key, the nick for another vehicle, a couple of Notting Hill pubs to find off-duty coppers to shanghai, and the Baltic Hearth to recruit come-down-in-the-world muscle – muscle that doesn't limp and isn't flagging on the stairs. Two teams, not one; a five-hour hunt, not ten; the chance of a result before the end of time.

★

17.35. 'I'll take north of Harrow Road, you south.' Athill crouching to stick his head through the passenger window of the nick's pre-war Ford grocer's van, strange booty from some allocation of war-surplus kit. Bourton nodded. The van dipped as Senkus and someone else – Poniak, from the 'Hey, Communist killer!' – climbed in and sparred with Tony Marling over where to put their knees. 'You've got eleven shelters against our nine. Here's our sequence. Humphreys has worked it out.' Athill handed over a scrap of paper. 'Let's RV at the Paddington Green Children's Hospital at twenty-two thirty if we don't meet up before.'

'OK.' Bourton nodded. 'Look – watch it, Rex. He really doesn't have anything to lose. If he's going to hang anyway, killing a copper won't make any difference.'

'And we don't have anything to hold him on so we're a perfect match.' He stood up and banged the roof of the van. 'Off you go, Dick Barton, and nick the bugger.'

★

17.55. 410 Harrow Road, and a shelter in the crypt of St Luke's Church – but a crypt long reclaimed by the vicar and stacked with folding chairs, broken pews, boxes of damaged prayer books, a corner of shapes under a painter's sheet. A sink, but no WCs, or laundry, or bedroll, or toothbrush, or sign that anyone other than vergers, vicars or parish do-gooders had been down there since Hiroshima.

18.20: the Porchester Hall, on Porchester Road. A huge hallway with a sweeping staircase, a cascading crystal chandelier above, carpets, brasswork gleaming in yellow-tinged light, and a maintenance man to show them the way. Two minutes' wait while George Brown and Senkus stoppered the shelter's exit onto Queensway, then Marling turned the key. Bourton and Poniak charged in, a landing, staircase down, a fizz and flare at the bottom as the Lithuanian found the switch, then into a cavernous grey-walled space broken by ranks of brick columns marching on and on and on, lights buzzing into life ahead as their boots pounded down the lanes between the pillars.

'Mattress!' shouted Poniak. 'I have mattress!' Bourton swinging around a pillar to see the Lithuanian booting bedding out from under a dustsheet, registering a figure flitting out of sight far beyond him, calling, 'Metropolitan Police!' and as Poniak looked up, pointing off to the right, 'Over there! Heading that way!' Pounding down parallel lanes, the figure just coat flaps flickering between columns, the sound of shoes slipping on concrete over to the right. 'Tony! He's heading for the stairs!' Hand grabbing a pillar, swinging around to change direction, the coat tails vanishing behind brickwork. 'I see him!' From Poniak pounding somewhere out of sight, Marling crying, 'Widdowson!' perhaps twenty yards away, a scuffle, shouts, yells of pain, blows on flesh, swinging into another lane to see Marling on his back under Widdowson at the bottom of the stairs, arms around his waist, one of the killer's hands pulling up on the banister and the other punching down, and Poniak charged in scooping him under the arms and flinging him on the concrete, fist cocked for a huge punch.

'Wait! It isn't him!'

The man was William John Dooley, twenty-eight, of Sligo, a waiter in the Hall who'd sublet his room in Kilburn to two lads from home over for the roads. He got in and out through the Queensway door ('I changed the lock, didn't I?'), scavenged his meals from Hall leftovers, and every night would pinch the last of the hot water in the neighbouring Porchester Baths by sneaking through a connecting door ('The Queen won't be cleaner! Sure and the boilers come in useful for drying my articles too'). He'd lived this way for nine months without discovery. Bourton couldn't help thinking Dooley would go far.

*

And so they slogged on. A huge cellar under Whiteley's department store, stacked with goods, but with the water turned off and no sign that Widdowson might be camping out beneath his wife's workplace. A wide-fronted interwar office building, all curves and metal window-frames, further down Queensway, and beneath it fifty yards by twenty of emptiness under caged ship's lights and a metal-beamed roof. Electricity off, khazis removed, signs of life: nil. The Society for Distressed Gentlefolk, a double-fronted house with a big porch set behind its own carriage sweep off Bayswater Road, and an arch-roofed coal hole six foot high under the driveway; Bourton dropped his torch, DC Brown banged his head, and all they had to show for it was concrete and puddles. The Union Jack Club off Edgware Road – brasswork and gilt, nice pictures, *Widdowson would love hiding under the feet of ex-officers*, and beneath it another brick-pillared cavern stocked with stacked furniture, prints in broken frames, boxes, trunks with service stencils on the sides; no sign of taps, a khazi, laundry or kit, a little bivvy out of the wet. 'Six shelters down,' Brown's voice scornful, dismissive. 'Sure this bloke exists?'

20.45. Cranmer School, 32 Star Street, W. Out of the van for the umpteenth time, wiping off the last crumbs from the Union Jack's cheese sarnies, the novelty of their posse long gone, Marling struggling but too proud to drop out, while the rest wanted to be away from the chill and the Ford's awful seating. The school shut up and dark, but a blank knobless door in a patch of brighter brickwork in the lee of number 30. Bourton led, a short corridor, corner, stairs in council concrete, suddenly bright as lights blinked on, into a room about ten by ten, a replica space with benches against the walls and yellowed wartime posters, another room, and another, and another, sink on the left, table on the right—

'Someone's had a fire here.' Marling, from the fourth room, perked up by the discovery. 'Perhaps a field stove or something. There's a big vent,' stretching to stick his hand in front of a grille on the wall, 'and it's still drawing. That's probably why.'

'What are these hooks doing in the ceiling?' Brown in the room beyond the sink, pointing at a big timber beam revetting the roof. 'This writing – what's his name again?'

'Arthur Widdowson.'

'AW. "Head of Sect," head of section, "AW, GC." Think that could be him?'

'He's wearing a commendation and a uniform he's not entitled to, why not dream about the George Cross too?' Bourton felt his blood stirring, like cold broth at the bottom of a warming pot. He joined Brown, examined the hooks. *Eight feet apart?* 'He was a matelot. What's the betting they're so he can sling a hammock?'

'Hey.' Poniak calling from the sink room. 'Korea copper. Come see this.' He was bent over the table, fingers tracing something etched in the top. 'You remember in the summer when you ask me to translate in the bombsite?' Bourton nodded. 'I see – saw – this.' He tapped the table. '"Souls soar free." Wrote just once on the wall, not many times like here,' the words obsessively repeated, 'but definitely this words. Then, I think it is about fish. Now, it is about crazy person.'

Brown clapped Bourton's shoulder. 'Not such a wild-goose chase, after all. Even if he might not have been here for months.' Brown started heading back to the entrance, his energy, approval, their little success pulling Bourton behind with a vigour he'd last felt long before this day without end. 'Let's see where he is now.'

Killing someone. The thought put a comma in Bourton's stride. *Or sitting at another table, carving with another knife, resting after killing someone. There's no triumph in finding this bastard – no triumph at all.*

69

21.25. 'Come on, Dick Barton.' Bourton jolted awake from a hot-eyed sleep, as if he'd nodded off on stag.

'Where are we?'

'Three four one Sussex Gardens.' Bourton nodded. *Shelter eight.* A rush of colder air as Brown opened the driver's door. 'Your tail should be up, sunshine. Proving us all wrong.'

Only 339 and 338 Sussex Gardens marked the end of the street – and their occupants said that 341 didn't exist. Bourton's posse checked around both corners to see if another house entrance was tucked into a blank garden wall: no luck. But they did come across a communal garden surrounded by railings, barely visible from the pavement let alone the houses set back down their driveways, where they could line up for a piss. And, in buttoning up and turning away, stumble on guard railings around a staircase in the pavement and above it, an ornate sign saying 'Shelter'.

They trotted down to a heavy metal door wearing a 'Property of the Borough of Paddington. Do Not Enter' sign. Two minutes of work with the key, Brown swung it open and Bourton was through, Senkus on his shoulder searching for a light switch.

Concrete hallway, staircase beyond, four flights with right-angled bends, cannoning off the wall to round each corner, and a closed door sitting at the bottom of the stairs. Twist the doorknob, open and in, Senkus's hand slapping the wall behind as he looked for another light switch, whitewashed concrete wall with WCS ← TEA → in black, 'George, go left!' Bourton running right, into a room twenty feet square, benches, noticeboard, table, doorway left and a glimpse of Brown's coat flitting by beyond, doorway ahead and into an identical space, doorways left, right, ahead, straight on into a third room with a grey blanket hanging over the doorway at its end. Hefting the torch as a club, through the makeshift curtain into room four, three cluttered tables against one wall, electric heater on the floor with a line just above, strung between a table leg and the corner of the noticeboard frame. *Washing line for his smalls.* Another table in the corner behind him, a sleeping bag laid out on top, then following the TEA ↑ sign in black beside a brown-curtained doorway, into the room beyond. Sink left with an enamel mug hanging from a dripping tap, a small stack of food sitting on the draining-board – Spam, cheese, beans, a couple of packets of compo biscuits on top – beside an upturned mess-tin; little field cooker squatting over blackened concrete floor on the right, 'Stove!', yet another doorway on the far side of the room, *A proper rabbit-warren, this.* Brown came through the doorway beside the sink shaking his head. 'Khazi?' Bourton asked.

'No sign of him.' Brown looked around. 'One lavatory's still working. Running water, there are bunks and all on the other side, stove, rations. Electric heater. The wife wants one for home, and here he is camping with it. He's got himself well set up.' He turned to Bourton. 'It's not another Mick waiter, is it? It's him?'

'Dunno,' said Bourton. 'Perhaps there's something in all that clutter next door.'

'Whoever he is,' Brown, 'with that heater and the sleeping bag – he's coming back.'

★

22.05. 'This is like a puzzle box.' Poniak in the doorway with the blanket curtain gathered on one shoulder. 'Twenty rooms, I think. But well built. Not much damp, no big cracks. I can feel air, so – er, no . . .' he mimed choking '. . . for the people. Four WC. Better than my lodgings.' Senkus's voice said something foreign. Poniak smiled, a little sadly. 'Vejas says if he had shelter like this, he will still be in Lithuania killing Russians.'

'Right, gents, we've got an appointment.' Brown turned to Bourton, who was trying to make sense of the tables of clutter – slippers, pictures, jewellery, a couple of hats, as if someone had emptied an odds and ends box. 'You think this is our man?'

'Best bet so far.' He looked up. 'There are only three more shelters, anyway. If Rex hasn't got anywhere, give him our shelters, then come straight back. I'll sit on this one with the others. That way we're covered.'

'Will do. Oi, Poniak,' the Lithuanian reaching out to the clutter, 'don't touch.' Brown called to the others: 'And that goes for all of you. Anything that isn't nailed down – clothes, that sleeping bag, rations, the stove, this rag-and-bone cart,' waving at the table, 'coppers only. *Verstehen Sie?*'

'*Zum befehl.*' Poniak clicked his heels, while Senkus offered a mock salute. Marling looked too knackered for irony.

'You all right with this lot?' Brown was fidgeting, clearly wanting to be off. Bourton nodded. 'Back soon. An hour, tops. Good luck.' He stepped in close, so he couldn't be overheard. 'If this is evidence, he's finished. No way we'd need a search warrant for an abandoned shelter.' He clapped Bourton on the shoulder. 'Nice one, chum.'

★

Waiting by torchlight. Senkus and Poniak outside, against the garden railings, to ensure whoever entered the shelter didn't escape; Bourton and Marling inside, torches only, so Widdowson wouldn't see light on the internal staircase and run. Because the Traveller needed to be nicked inside the shelter, where he could be linked with whatever Bourton might find, rather than outside, before he'd entered, when he could claim he'd just been revisiting old haunts.

Gloves on. Marling to another room, away from the evidence. Start search. The sleeping bag was straightforward British Army surplus, probably condemned because of a huge blue stain over the bottom half. He pulled down the thick zip and opened the bag like a suitcase, passing the torch beam up and down the seams, over the fabric and the label. Nothing apart from specks of earth, a clod of dried mud. He ran his hands over the padding, to see if anything had been stuffed inside. Nothing – though surely the bottom was more padded than—

He moved the sleeping bag aside. Underneath it, flat on the table, was a blue battledress, trousers and blouse, with a medic's brassard on one sleeve and a silver oak leaf sitting above the breast pocket. The torch beam started to shake. *Can't be.* He grabbed the table with his free hand, his heart beating through a microphone. *Evidence. Proper, proper evidence. Nine months and at last something solid . . .*

When his hands had steadied he picked up the blouse. There, inside the collar, stitched to the manufacturer's label, was the legend 'Widdowson A.' *It's his. It's really his.* He shook his head, to try to clear the cobwebs furring his thoughts. *So now there's a link between Widdowson and Bradford – one with a witness, and evidence to put in front of a jury.* He checked the pockets in the blouse and trousers. Nothing.

He turned to the clutter on the tables. Slippers, a scarf, women's shoes, a Bible, a framed photograph, a tie, a hammer, a crucifix, another photo in its frame, Victorian bloomers, a pillbox hat with a veil, a fountain pen, a tin fob watch, a pipe, lorgnettes, a tie, a piece of unfinished embroidery, a hair grip, a brooch with a white enamelled rose, a Merchant Navy 'MN' lapel badge, a thirties seaside snap with 'Prideaux, The Parade, Scarborough' printed across one corner, a china cup, a trowel, a tiny wooden elephant, a lipstick. That was just half the stuff on the first table. *If there's a logic here, it's that of emptying an attic.* But the women's shoes were buffed up and worn down, the hammer handle was discoloured by years of sweat, the brooch looked old but well polished. *Some of these things mattered to someone once.* He played the torch over the heap. *So, emptying rooms, not the attic.*

What might have a name in it? He rifled through the jumble. A wartime ration book in the name of D. H. Willing. A scarf with a label saying 'Lewis's' but no name tag. The women's shoes, also nameless. A white silk blouse with 'A.D.B.L.' stitched on the collar label. The Bible, presented to Enid Batten by the Ebenezer Baptist Church in Tiverton, for Sunday School attendance, complete with neatly penned family tree below. A pewter tankard with 'F.W.S.' engraved crudely in the soft metal. A good fob watch, silver, on a silver and jet chain, and inside the casing 'To Ernest Faccini. With the respect and gratitude of the Board and Directors of Hill, Knowles and Kerr. 14 July 1939'. A Letts Diary for 1933, no name inside the cover. The veiled pillbox, made by Madame Labarra of the Undercroft, Stockport, for Mrs J. M. Dunn. Slippers, no label. Another scarf, this one from Warwick House, Great Malvern, but no name tag. A 1920s cigarette case, no engraving—

The family tree. There was something in that family tree. He cast around until he found the Bible again and opened the cover. Enid Batten, daughter of Charles Jacob and Edith Augusta Batten, née Chilcot, married William Edward Llewellyn Chirk, three children, Margaret Hilda dead in infancy, Jacob William killed in action in 1942, Nancy Maud—

Enid Chirk. Bible down, notebook out, flicking through to November, twenty pages and three weeks – *More like five years* – ago, his conversation with DC Lloyd. Enid Chirk. The new body in Kennington, found dead in her best, of smog-related causes, in the smog not after it – and visited by a traveller just before she died. One of the two women the Squad were treating as a murder victim.

He smiled. *Gotcha. The battledress puts you here. The Bible puts you at Enid Chirk's. And now you'll hang—*

He dropped the torch and notebook, as if they were limbs from a rotted corpse, and stepped back from the table, stripping off his gloves as if they were smouldering, his mind a little slower than his reflexes. *That Bible's a trophy. Which means that cigarette case, those scarves, the tankard, the watch, the bloomers—*

'Dick!' Marling at his shoulder. 'Dick, you all right?' Marling's torch beam on Bourton's face, bringing his hands up to shield his eyes. 'You look like you've seen a ghost.'

'See that,' nodding at the table, 'see all that . . . stuff.' The torch beam complied. 'You know what it is? Stags' heads on a wall. Mementos of the people he's killed. Look at it.' Distaste was turning into anger. 'You see how much there is? How many people he's probably killed? Each one,' he stepped back to the table to find his torch, 'it's like one of them suitcases at Belsen, all stacked up, each one a body or a family gone up the chimney.' He found the switch. 'Three bloody tables' worth. And no one noticed a fucking thing.'

'Bloo-dy hell,' quietly, Marling's beam passing over the clutter, 'each one? Surely not—'

'For God's sake, it hardly matters! Whether it's one each or three each, that's dead bodies!'

'Steady, Dick, steady!' Bemused, offended, protective.

Bourton's knees gave, his hands missed the table and suddenly his bottom hit the floor and he tumbled onto his back. 'And I'm not even drunk.' He sat up. 'Need some sleep. And food. And a little less strife.'

Marling was reaching down with a hand to pull him upright but Bourton shook his head. 'I'm staying down for now.' *Apology in order.* 'Look, I know you helped when no one—'

'I never knew.' His torch beam scanned the tables again. 'I had no idea. I mean, you weren't saying but I assumed it was at least the one, but this . . .' He turned his torch off. 'If this is what you've been after, then yell all you like.' He was silent for a few moments. 'Let's hope he's coming.'

'He is,' said Bourton. 'I just hope he doesn't have more mementos when he does.'

'Yes.' Soft, even elegiac. 'But if these are trophies, they'll get him hanged.'

'Evidence.' Bourton could feel energy returning, because suddenly he knew that, whatever happened, whether Widdowson came back or not, the big guns now had to be on his side. 'Tony. Do me a favour.' Bourton struggled upright and found his torch and notebook on the table. 'Go to a phone box. Call the Murder Squad.' He wrote 'Enid Chirk' and '491 Bourton' on the final page and tore it out. 'Tell them you're the Shah of Shelters an' you're assisting me with the CD part of the inquiry, that there is evidence linking Arthur Widdowson to this woman,' he handed over the page, 'at this spot, as well as evidence of other victims of the Traveller. Tell them I'm waiting for him at this location, and that they are to attend. And if they give you argy – wave your accent. All right?'

'All right. But won't you need—'

'I've got those two bruisers outside, and the others will be back even before you are. Don't worry. We're copacetic.' He gestured towards the curtained doorway with his torch. 'Off you go.'

★

22.25. A few moments scanning the other two tables, wondering which memento had belonged to Gladys Hartham, or Captain Bradford, Mrs Dean, the old bloke Slingsby down Elephant way, before he headed through the blanket-curtain to the benches – to save the torch batteries by sitting in darkness, but more because he knew he couldn't rifle through all those severed lives and the pleasure in taking them without daylight, colleagues, procedure, to protect against I-could-have-done-more. The army had trooped the local worthies through Belsen when they'd found out the scale of what the Nazis had done. Who would they troop through an old air-raid shelter in Paddington? Doctors? Coroners? Coppers? Which of the *i*-dotters and *t*-crossers, who hadn't done their job?

Back against the wall, torch off. He turned it on again to check everything was to hand for when Widdowson came through the door – warrant card, stick, handcuffs in his parka's external pockets, Anna's sap and knuckles inside. Torch off. He closed his eyes, pushing his gloved hands back into the coat's hip pockets. *Think nice stuff, good things, things worth holding on to, store it up against the winter of Widdowson's world . . .*

Anna: probably helping up at College Farm, with the boys, the greenhouse, perhaps even with the ditching or the fences, given her passion for the country idyll. Out and about the village and on the walk to the plague barrows, last of the leaf fall mulching nicely on the copse path – just to clear her lungs, get colour in her cheeks. Frost-brittle grass, morning ground-mist, the pale winter light and a sky of watercolour blues washing away to white – no sulphur, no dawn-less days or dusk-less nights, no grit in the lungs or yellow in the sky or smarting skin. *Whatever made me think London was it?* Anna at their wedding, before illness, London, something unseen soured her; certain, happy, besotted, home. The way she'd looked in September, above Odstone Coombe, sun on her face, mischief in her eyes, blouse askew where she'd buttoned it up wrong . . .

*

Reaching up for the brew, thanking old Mrs Cardew behind the counter as she looks over my shoulder: 'Excellent – more customers. Looks like police this time.' Turn to see a half-dozen Royal Hong Kong Police easing up the path, five Chinese men and a blonde woman, blue eyes, high cheek-bones and, God help us, curves beneath the sweat-stained grey-blue, the rest of the section falling silent at the sight of a white bird under fifty, 'Does the Russian gel drink it black?', making room at the counter so she and the inspector can front up.

'*Thank you, Corporal.*' *A catch in her throat – cigarettes, catarrh, Lauren Bacall: whatever it is I'm hard inside my tropicals, turn to face the wagon so she can't see.*

'*Corporal Bourton, Sergeant. Dick Bourton, 1 Middlesex. I'd salute only I'm hoping to drink this tea rather than wear it.*'

*She laughs. Definitely Lauren Bacall. '*I'm not a real sergeant, Corporal Dick Barton, so no need to add tea to the mud and,' *she gestures at my uniform, '*things.' *Something foreign in her accent, perhaps a bit of Ingrid Bergman; close up, the eyes are almost more grey than blue, and clever, knowing, captivating. The policemen are talking in Chinese, something entertaining, and I'm the butt of it, but if she'll just keep looking at me . . . She talks Chinese back. They all laugh – one of the constables mimes jabbing something overhand. '*They think you have value as an ox, Corporal Dick Barton, if the army is boring. Constable Chen thinks there is no field you could not plough.*'

'*Wearing the traces?*' *Confusion on her face. '*Pulling it?' *She nods. '*And would Constable Chen be cracking the whip or you?*' *Where did that come from? I've never been so forward.*

'*Chen.*'

'*No deal, then, Sergeant.*'

'*Timofeyev. Anna Timofeyev.*' *She smiles. '*Pleased to meet you.*'

The inspector calls something, abrupt, an order. The heads swivel, shapes bobbing over the ridgeline six hundred yards away, more refugees, more infiltrators, the instructions shouted now, jabber jabber jabber, Chink jabber Chink jabber—

Angry Chink jabber. Eyes closed, to keep out the cold, miserable Korea night, the Chinese shrieks of fury, the bloodstained rifle butt hovering above; the end here, bound and a prisoner, in a concrete culvert. Think of home, Anna, her smile when she said yes, Anna Anna Anna, thank God she can't see this or hear what he's screaming—

Nothing. No jabber, no smash to the head, no breathing, no protests. Eyes open. The Chink's gone but the last false starshell moonglow shows the four other survivors sitting here, backs against the culvert wall, hands wired behind so the skin's against the rough concrete, everyone holding their breath, afraid the Chink will come back to his little stash of prisoners. And in the stream, face up, with an eye sitting on a smashed pulpy cheek, kid Coleman, the creak and pop of wheezy chest, blood bubbles at the mouth, the bayonet must have got him in the lungs, the chest still rising and falling, trying to breathe when those head wounds mean he's dead, dead for looking up and catching Comrade Chinky-Chink's eye . . .

That's war, chum. Luck got you through the pass; luck got you killed in the culvert. Luck.

Close eyes again; he won't catch me looking – I've got a bird to marry, a body to know. Cold, dry concrete rough behind the head, feeling every bump against the scalp, the solid throb in the thigh – would slosh out the wound if only people weren't dead in that stream. Cold seeping up from booted feet awash in the current, the wind off the mountains gusting through the culvert, finding cracks in clothing – could change position but then Comrade Chinky will kill me when he comes back. Or the cold could kill me first.

Open eyes to blackness. Forgotten it's still night. Blokes whimpering now, cold and fear getting to them, but no one's talking like before Comrade Chinky came back, no sharing of lives, home towns, what-are-they-going-to-do-with-us – just closed in, waiting, teeth chattering. Malinowsky has fallen silent. He'll be dead by morning. I could cuddle up, be his windbreak, but he's someone else's responsibility. I've got a wedding to arrange . . .

Crab-hop over the water, stumbling between the boots, thigh is numb but still doesn't want to take weight, lump down beside Malinowsky, wriggle to put my back to the wind and front to his side, trying to pass on a little heat. Firing from the pass, everyone breathes in sharply: a ripple of small arms, a cascade of rifles, burp guns, mortars. Silence. Whoever ran the gauntlet will be dead now. The whimpering and teeth-chattering are back.

'Let's sing a song.' I said that? But it's what we need: if we can't cuddle up proper we need to stay awake or the cold will get us. All of us. 'I'm going to teach you all "Roll Out The Barrel". It's what we sing in Britain whenever we've got a disaster, and as you know, we've had a lot of them. We're all going to sing it, even Malinowsky here. Now the first line goes like this . . .'

Third time through the chorus they begin to sing a little. Glance over the shoulder to see a whisper of light behind the mountains – dawn in about forty minutes. 'Come on! "Roll out the barrel, we'll have a barrel of fun!"' Soon there's enough of a ripple in the blackness to see profiles, stances, who's slumped and who's perky, who needs a jolt—

Firing. Close. The singing stops, faces freeze. Wind whipping it away, but perhaps it's two, three hundred yards south, along the road, maybe near where his jeep sits, a charred hump of tin . . . More of it. Voices now, the rustle of Chinks in their soft soles padding through grass.

'Asshole!' From the Yank opposite, head bowed for the executioner—

Blinding light, electric light. But there's no electricity in the culvert.

A British voice. But the lads don't come up and rescue them for hours yet.

'You all right there, friend?'

70

22.55. 'You all right there, friend?'

Eyes open, lights on, a tall figure looking down, face and body in shadow. Bourton jolted forward.

'It's all right, friend. You were dreaming.' Shadow resolving into a suit, hat, mack, a long face, medicinal smell. 'You're awake now. In the old shelter, bottom of Sussex Gardens.' Flat Yorkshire accent. *That's right. I nodded off, waiting for—*

Widdowson.

The shock must have shown because Widdowson brought his hands up, palms open. 'It's all right, I'm a friend. Sorry to wake you. Must have been the light. I didn't know you were here.' Hands down into mack pockets. *Does he have a weapon in there?* 'Though it sounded like you weren't anywhere pleasant.' Bourton's hands gripped the handcuffs and the end of the stick, then relaxed slightly. *He doesn't think I'm a threat.*

'Korea.' *Parka, boots, unshaven, bleary – I could pass for a tramp.* 'Comes and goes.'

Widdowson nodded. 'Sinking sub for me.' Flat statement, sympathetic tone. *He's got no idea I'm a copper.* 'You like a brew now you're awake?'

'You got the makings?' Bourton stood abruptly, a hand up to rub his face, realised he'd reveal the truncheon handle sticking out of his parka pocket and jammed it back, forearm pressing the wood against his hip. 'I saw your kit – I didn't want to disturb it, a man's kit.'

'I know you didn't.' Rueful smile, but something false to it. 'First thing I did when I realised I weren't alone was check.'

'Well, a man would.' Bourton nodded. *You're down, not out, a bit of shame, a lot of self-respect.* 'Saw the sleeping bag, thought, That's another man's, that, bench'll do me.'

'Got anything to chip in?' Widdowson pointedly looked around the room. 'Where's your kit?'

Where would it be? Left luggage? But that would still be open. 'Chum's house. Was supposed to bunk there, but he's locked me out.'

'How'd you know about this place?'

'Courting days.' *Man-to-man smile.* 'Used to see a married woman from the council after the war. We'd meet here or Star Street—'

'The pub?'

'Under the school.'

'How'd you get in?'

'Her key. Pinched it.' *Why would I keep it for so long?* 'Never know when a man might need a free roof in London.' *Would I stand for this inquisition?* 'Look, you want me gone I'm gone, first dibs, swear by it, can head off to Star Street.'

'You're all right, friend.' Widdowson ducked through the curtain and Bourton could hear his shoes cross the concrete floor next door, a pause, then the tap running. *Off the hook for now.* 'Besides, no heads in Star Street. Much better off here.' Bourton stowed the stick inside the parka and pushed through the curtain.

'You've got yourself a right little billet, chum,' Bourton called, 'heater an' all. You running off mains wi' no meter?' He stuck his head through the second curtain.

'Aye.' Widdowson was lighting the field stove. 'And if they switch it off, for whatever reason,' he jerked his head at the wall behind him, 'the shelter generator still works.' He rested a mess-tin full of water on the stove. 'Proper ship-shape.'

Bourton stood by the sink, looking around the room as if he were properly examining it for the first time. *Let's move things along.* 'Sorry, I'm Dick.'

Widdowson looked up from the mess-tin. 'Hello, Dick. I'm Arthur.'

'Good to meet you, Arthur. And thank you kindly.' Bourton stuck his thumb over his shoulder. 'You mind my asking about all that stuff next door?'

Widdowson stood up. 'You look at it?'

Bourton shook his head. 'Another man's kit.'

'Easy to say.'

'Well, I looked at it as I went by . . .'

Widdowson took a packet of tea out of his coat pocket. 'I know what's there, anyway. If you've taken something . . .'

'Honest.' Now it was Bourton's turn to stick his hands out. 'See? Empty.'

'And your pockets?'

Handcuffs and warrant card. 'Only what you need in London at night – a cosh, and knuckles.'

Widdowson smiled. 'Never a truer word.' He threw the packet of tea and Bourton caught it. The label said 'Powell & Sons, 82 Borough High Street, London SE'. *Booty?* 'Anyone could be out in this fog.' He pointed at the enamel mug hanging from the tap. 'Shake a brew's worth in there, would you? I could tell you, the types I've come across, over the years, out and about in pea-soupers.'

'Wrong 'uns?' Reaching for the mug.

'Wrong as they get.' Widdowson shook his head. *Bloody hell, he means it. He isn't one of them – he's sound as a pound and it's the burglars, the coshers, the pimps.*

Opening the tea packet, 'Been reading about those coshing gangs.'

'Little thugs.'

'What they'll do for a lark.'

'Should start National Service at sixteen, that's what I say.'

'Went to sea at fourteen, making of me,' shaking in the tea.

Widdowson smiled. 'Sixteen, me. Trawling?'

'Merchant Navy.'

'RN, me. Well, well. Two old salts in an old air-raid shelter. I never.'

Bourton smiled back, old comrades' club. *This is crackers. But if I try asking about the clutter now . . .* He handed over the mug. 'My brother was in subs,' lying to make common ground, 'Med mostly,' Widdowson going down on one knee by the stove, 'till he got invalided out.' *Make it something about breath.* 'Whiff of chlorine when the battery flooded. Has to live in the country, work casual 'cos the city don't agree with his lungs.' Widdowson looked up, face unreadable. *Have I overdone it?* 'Pension doesn't make up for that, I can tell you.'

Pause. Widdowson nodded. 'Never does.' He looked down at the mess-tin. *Suspicious, hiding his eyes – I have to stay off the things I want to know.* 'So, how long you been out of the army?'

'A year, give or take.' Bourton shrugged. 'Thinking of going back, if I'm honest. Can't seem to settle.'

'It'll come.' Widdowson looked up. 'Just takes a while. War ended and I got bored. Happy not to be in danger but . . .' he shrugged '. . . bored. Took two years, really.' *He's got bicycle clips on. We never thought, a bike.* 'Two years, an' something new, to keep me busy.'

Something new?

The creak of a door opening, *Cavalry*, Widdowson not reacting, Bourton clutching his warrant card, 'Not sure I shook enough tea in' to blot it out, get close. Voices—

'The light's on.'

'He must be looking for evidence.'

They don't know he's here – so he didn't go past Senkus and Poniak. How the hell—

'Dick?' Rex Athill's voice, clear as a bell, Widdowson turning, tensed, hand to pocket. 'Dick, you in here?'

'Expecting friends?'

'No,' trying to buy time, 'just looking for a roof.'

'Sure of that?' Widdowson's right hand out with a switchblade, click, circling behind the stove. 'What are you?' *He must have got in through the back of the shelter or he'd have seen me before he saw his kit.* Bourton shifted towards the doorway to the rear to head him off, Widdowson's eyes flicking from him towards the voices.

'Dick? Dick?'

'They know you, you liar.'

'Dick, the other shelters were clear, this is the one.'

Fear. 'You a copper?' Sidling towards the doorway. *Won't have time to get my stick before he's on me with the knife. Calm him.*

'No, look, I don't know them.'

'Bloody copper!' Voice up in indignation.

Cat's out of the bag. 'Arthur Widdowson,' parade-voice for the others, hand in for the truncheon as Widdowson hesitates, 'you are under arrest on suspicion of the murder of Gladys Hartham and Enid Chirk.'

Brace for the knife but Widdowson turns back, and as Bourton gets the stick out Widdowson reaches down to the mess-tin and up comes boiling water, Bourton ducking away, left arm shielding the face, hot wet cloth on the chest, arm down, *Got to grab him*, stove glances off the forehead, a tug at sodden clothes, falling back, hands flailing for any part of the killer as he runs for the side doorway, out of reach, gone. Up again, 'He's running, he has a knife!' Follow Widdowson through the doorway by the sink, another room with two doorways, *He'll run away from the main entrance*, turn right, another room, doorway straight ahead, through past bunks and WCS ↑, a banging door, 'He's heading for the khazis!' A battery of identical doors ahead. *Cubicles?* Only one has a keyhole, finger in to pull it open. 'Past the khazis!' Corridor beyond ending in a heavy metal door with a lock, tug but no give, parka up to rummage in trouser pockets for the key, goes in reluctantly. *Work work work.* Wiggle and the lock gives, open on a narrow concrete staircase, feet audible at the top, start up two at a time but thighs losing drive, step by step to another door at the top, locked, key in, turn, open, step onto pavement. *This is street level.* Cough as the fog catches, close eyes. Running feet. To the right. *God knows what's over there.*

Whistle. Lift to lips, bolt of cold air across the belly, hand through cloth to skin. *He got me with the knife, blood? Nothing, thank God.* Calmer now, three short blasts; then follow the footsteps, sitting in the air, ahead, somewhere, neither left nor right, hovering against a backdrop of engines, a door slamming, a man's yell. A couple of feet of pavement. *I can see where I am, but not where I'm going. No torch – but no time for it anyway. Just run.* A glow above, steer around streetlight, jolt down from a kerb, stumble, run on, shouts behind. *The lads? No, that's anger at him, I've overrun.* Turn about, headlights ambling ahead, turn left before the kerb, voices: 'You all right, chum?'

'The bastard hit me with his case!'

'Which way did he go?' Into the murk: 'Metropolitan Police, which way?'

'Past me, chum, along Praed Street,' *So that's where we are,* 'towards the station.'

He must know every cranny. 'You all right?'

'Jerry give me worse.'

Remembering the bicycle clips, 'He still on foot?'

'Well, yeah.'

Another voice: 'What you after him for?' Pure London.

'Murder.' Speeding up. *Must get to the station before he disappears into it.* The voices now behind, whistle up to the mouth, two hard blasts, listen through throbbing pulse for a response, an echo from fifty yards away, bellow over shoulder, 'Suspect is running east along Praed Street, heading for Paddington station.' Pavement disappears, jolt onto tarmac and stumble, stationary headlights, sidestep and bounce off a metal panel and slide to the ground, hand clutches, finds a trouser leg.

'Gerroff.'

'Police, where'd he go?'

'That way.' The pointing hand invisible.

'The station?'

'Well, prob'ly,' a hand in front of Bourton's face, grab it and stand, 'only he won't get in, not this side.'

'Why not?'

'It's closed off.' A face, now, up close, forties, heavy stubble, a postie's cap above: 'GPO rail is snafued, all the post for the mail trains is coming by van – we close off the western entrance, run a chain of blokes passing sacks through to the platforms.'

Stepping round him to check ahead and, sure enough, another van, rear doors visible in the headlights – and then silver glow after silver glow, smudged stars in a yellow-tinged night, a convoy of lights reaching into the fog. And curses, angry questions, from further up the line. Onto the bonnet of the van, hands cupping the mouth, big breath: 'Attention, all GPO drivers!' Full bellow: 'Attention, all GPO drivers! This is the police! The man running towards Paddington station is wanted for murder! He is wanted for murder! He is fifty years old, five foot ten, and wearing a mackintosh! He is armed and dangerous! Armed and dangerous!' Slide down, start running along the line of vans, voices and boots behind, a scuffle ahead and a shout of pain. 'Where is he? Where is he?'

Answering shouts – 'This way, guv,'

'Up here.'

'Ran towards the ramp.' A huddle of bodies with a couple of torches focusing low, *They've got him,* a beam in the face, arm up but night vision gone.

'You the copper? He slashed this bloke's arm.'

'Tie it off.'

'We done that.'

'Where?'

'He tried to go down the ramp, got blocked, he headed off down Praed Street.'

To try the southern ramp. A couple of whistle blasts, 'Suspect continuing down Praed Street!' for the others somewhere behind, then 'Can I borrow a torch?'

'Here, chum.' A hand grabbing his and wrapping it around the shaft. 'Come to me after, Dick Bourton, Notting Hill,' shining the beam onto the ground, kerbstone, pavement, curses, shouts off to the right, *The entrance to the Circle Line station*, thread between two vehicles and jostle through bodies beyond, but the station is shuttered. *Of course, no tubes.* Bourton calling, 'Where is he? Where is the fugitive?' listening for responses, more shouts over by the Great Western Royal Hotel on the other side of the road, cut back through the waiting vans. 'Mind your backs! Police coming through!' Torchlight on a black cab stranded by the mail convoy and three men in a finger-jabbing row. *Where's he gone?* Right to the line of vans, trot along them, bellow now a little hoarse: 'Anyone seen a fiftyish man, five ten, mackintosh, case, switchblade, running this way?' Shapes passing him, knocking on windows, rousting dozing drivers. 'Ray,' Athill's voice at his shoulder, 'block off the south entrance ramp.' Figures rushing by, 'Clear a way, clear a way.'

'Rex,' grab the DC's arm, 'where's he gone? He was running this way, slashing, hitting with the case.'

'No sign?'

'No sign.'

'We think he's going for the station?'

'It's got tunnels and crannies he'll know and we don't.'

'Why not slip through, walk quietly into some side street, disappear?'

Why not? Mind like toffee. 'Because – because – because he knows it and . . .'

'And it's our best bet.' Athill looks down towards the south ramp, hidden in the fog. 'If he's running east and can't get in the south ramp, there's no other entrance this side.'

'The tube is closed.'

'He'll have to run half a mile or more, cross the canal, come back half a mile the other side before he can come at it from the north.'

'Long way round.'

'He'll have doubled back.' Excitement in the DC's voice. 'Much quicker. Up Eastbourne Terrace, Bishop's Bridge Road. He can come at the northern ramp onto the platforms or into the goods yard.'

'Run.' Back the way they'd come, Athill immediately lost in the fog but his hard, alien command voice – 'Police coming, clear the way' – creating a wake Bourton's stodgier legs can canter through. Shapes, a sidestep, bobby's helmet, voices. *A PC summoned by the whistles.* 'I'll sort it, Rex, you run!' Athill's heels and parade-voice escaping in the murk. Instruct the copper – description, offences, likely intention – and send him down to the western entrance with a reminder ('Armed and dangerous, chum, all right?'). Start cantering again, five, ten paces, brake, smack head at the stupidity – *Why run all the way round the station when we can run through it? He's the one who can't get in, not us.* Turn again. 'Clear the way!' Trot back past the Great Western Royal – 'Clear the way!' – and the cab still trapped by the vans, *Will have a chance of getting to the northern side before Widdowson too*, aiming for the glow of the lamps above the southern ramp. Down the tarmac into the brick-lined chasm, fog eddying in the stronger light. 'Ray, Dick Bourton coming through,' DC Martin, Poniak, Senkus at the centre of a line of posties cordoning off the concourse.

'Stay here. I'm going up to the northern ramp to close it off.'

Into the station, a cavern of clangs and whistles, engine smoke lacing the acid air. Wave the torch to catch the eye of empty cabs moving towards the southern ramp, sodden slashed clothing around the middle leaving Bourton shivering cold. *Need to run some more, warm up. Or nick this bugger, go home to a brew and a bed.* A taxi, not stopping, the driver in a rush to get home, *And who'd blame him?*, and suddenly the bottom of the northern ramp, curving up towards the black patch where the roof stops and the smoggy night begins.

Wait. The sounds of the station, gone eleven on a week night; puffs from the train with steam up ten yards away, announcements for Oxford, the Fishguard boat train and the sleeper to Penzance, railwaymen's shouts echoing in the rafters, the squeak of a laden luggage dolly being hauled up from the end of the platform. Ask the porter, 'Sorry, chum,' in response, turn back to the ramp to find a taxi rounding the bend above and easing down the last stretch to the platform. One hand out to halt it, the other with the warrant card. Start with the cabby, shake of the head, passenger on the rear seat, a bloke, forties, pulls down the window, anxious face and a hairy tweed. Round the cab to check the luggage compartment, suitcase, no murderer, just the fare in the back, wave the taxi on. Squeaks and clangs, accelerating chuffs, as a train behind the fog eases out of a platform. Black Humber rounding the ramp corner at speed, move to the middle to halt it, brakes hard, step aside as it stops with a jolt five yards onto the platform. Matelot in the driver's seat, two naval officers in uniform in the back, eye over them and the vehicle, ask the driver, no luck, nod the Humber on to see another, more cautious, edging around the bend. Another matelot, more naval officers, no more luck with the driver, wave on.

Rex will assume I'm following him and wonder why I'm so slow. Up the ramp, close to the waist-high riveted steel wall, call near the top: 'Rex, Dick here, I'm on the ramp. Any sign of our man?'

'Not a peep.'

Must be inside already. Or holed up in some back street where we'll never find him. No, Paddington's what he knows. 'Stay there. I'm going to see about a search inside the station.' Down the ramp. *That sounded like an order. Oh, well . . .* Back to the cordon at the bottom of the southern ramp, now a gaggle of heads – Martin, the Lithuanians, Humphreys, Tony Marling. *Good for you, chum, still in there and—*

'DS Lloyd,' blurting, *Say something civil,* 'nice of you to join us.' Bourton wants to say, 'What are you doing here? Your job?' and 'This lot are more use as murder coppers than you and all your chums,' but what comes out is 'You got blokes at the shelter on Sussex Gardens?' Lloyd nods, already handing out Cravens. *Good idea – silence plus fags.* 'That's something, then.' Take a smoke, Lloyd's light, first pull, feel some of the anger seep away. 'I reckon he's got into the station, before we could close off the north or south ramps.'

'Could he have got on a train?' Marling, perked by the chase.

'Could have,' another pull, 'but we've got to do what we can do,' let the smoke sit in the chest, 'and we can't do that.'

'No train,' Senkus is shaking his head, 'no train.' He closes his eyes as he takes his first pull. 'Našlèkovich like holes.' His eyes open. 'He hide in hole, not run on train.'

Bourton nods, knowing he's right, knowing he'd feel it in his gut as well as his head if only he weren't so tired. 'So we need to search.' Exhale. 'Detective Sergeant Lloyd, sir, could you take Senkus and Poniak – Senkus can recognise the suspect – and whoever else you can muster and work up the tracks to the goods yard? Widdowson worked there for ten years or more. Mr Marling, Mr Humphreys, please stay here and maintain this cordon. DC Martin, sir,' another pull, 'we're off to organise a sweep of the station.'

'You seem to know what you're doing.' Lloyd, meaning *So you're giving me orders?*

Close eyes for a moment, to enjoy the smoke and decide which of several different answers he should give. 'Be nice,' he decides, 'if I could say the same about you.'

00.10. 'He's had about twenty minutes.' Looking out at the duty manager Mr Roper, four of his station staff, a dozen posties and four coppers from the Paddington Green turn, faces eager, *Like the first patrols in Korea, before everyone realised they really could get shot.* And then on one side, clumped up, veterans keeping distance from the doomed, Athill's posse: DC Martin, Toomas vast in a blue pea-coat, another Estonian called Erik, spare as Toomas but half the size, and Vytautas, dabbing off sweat. 'He'll have needed somewhere to rest. So we're looking into storerooms, places that don't get used at night that are easily reached from the platforms or the concourse, particularly any old air-raid shelters.' Staring hard at the faces, willing across a seriousness he wasn't sure he had the energy to send. 'He's armed with a knife and is facing the scaffold. Don't take him on. Summon help and we'll run him to ground. Understood?' Nods, flickers of worry, a couple of coppers instinctively touching truncheons, Vytautas checking a pocket. *I hope that's not a firearm.* 'Five groups, each with a copper and a station bloke. Rest of you, allocate yourselves. Mr Roper, please assign search areas. Good hunting.'

★

He's down here. Logic said Widdowson was gone, on a train, or through side streets, or hiding out in the goods yard – places they couldn't reach, couldn't see, didn't know. *But I'm too tired for logic or choices. I've got energy enough to know one thing and keep knowing it until I'm right or wrong. He's down here.*

Door after door: Roper with the key in the lock, looking for the nod to turn it, Bourton on the other side of the doorway with Toomas and Erik on his shoulder, Sid and Irvine the two posties ready to follow on. A nod, open, in, torch in the left hand, stick in the right. Storerooms, pugging spots, empty space. No Widdowson.

Ninth doorway. Bourton stepped into the corridor, leaving behind a skiving drowsy station bloke still tangled in his blanket, passing Roper on the threshold, 'One of yours' – and across the way another door, brickwork around the lintel jutting out past the rest of the wall and 'HELT' painted in white on metal-studded wood.

'Boys.' The men catching the change in tone, Sid the postie – fifties, wiry, stitching scars crawling up from one wrist – immediately slipping into the corridor as if a sentry needed his throat slit. Taking position on the door, the wedge on his shoulder with Sid behind Erik, Roper opening his mouth but Bourton raising finger to lips. Door open, Bourton pushing through, torch beam onto whitewashed corridor, the squeak of metal across concrete from ahead. *He's here*. A jolt of energy pumping knees, into open space, huge crash left and the beam jumping with the shock, shapes slipping past as the hounds caught the scent. A wall of grey-painted metal – a huge secure stores chest on its side barring the entrance to a passage – and just above it a sliver of space below the ceiling, Toomas already swarming up the front, 'Watch it, Toomas!' then wriggling through the gap and disappearing over the other side.

'This door here is lock!' Toomas in a topmast bellow from beyond the chest. Bourton stepped back into the entrance passage to see Roper by the corridor doorway working the light switch, 'Roper, the other door into the shelter, thataway,' pointing as the lights finally sputtered on, 'where does it come out?' The railwayman puzzled, looking at a ceiling light as if to fathom why the electrics were slow. *Try a different tack.* 'What's that way?' Jabbing now. 'Roper!' Eyes coming down, following Bourton's hand. 'There? Aah,' looking around, at the corridor outside the shelter, then back in, 'aah, probably . . . the Praed Street tunnel, through to the Circle Line platforms.'

We'll have to go around. Bourton pushed past, but Roper clutched his parka: 'The tunnel will be closed by the concourse! We won't be able to get through that way!' *Of course, the tube station is shut. They'll have closed the tunnel entrance gates. Which means Widdowson will only have been able to get into this shelter through this door. So if he's escaped through the other one, it's got the same lock. Roper can open it.* The station manager was ahead of him, hurrying down the corridor to the main room of the shelter to see the men barging the chest along the floor creating an opening, Roper stepping around them and through the gap into the corridor beyond with his keys outstretched, Erik and the posties bundling behind, jostling for position. Door open, and a charge into echoing darkness.

A confused chorus: 'Where—'

'What the—'

Foreign.

'Mr Roper!' into the blackness. *The tube station's closed, they've turned the lights off.* Torch on. 'Find someone to turn the lights on, someone who knows the platforms and passages.' He stood back in the doorway as Roper headed past, 'And thanks very much, sir.' Bourton cast around with the beam. White tiles behind, signs for the Bakerloo Line left, Circle Line right. *He's got choices, we'll have to split up, and get reinforcements . . .* 'Irvine, get up to the third floor, tell the copper there Widdowson's in the tube station, bring his bunch down.'

'Right you are.' The postie slipped through. 'Good luck fellers.' *He's glad to be out of this.*

'Sid, you're with me. I've got a sap,' fishing it out of the parka, 'and you look like you might know how to use it. Toomas, Erik, go down to the Circle Line platforms, should be some light from the concourse, see if he's there. Erik, come back if he is. Don't approach him. And here are some knuckles, Toomas,' *I've got the best-armed wife in Britain,* 'just in case he tries his luck.' He shone the torch on the tiles to create a glow to see nods by. 'Sid, follow me.'

★

12.35. Down the white-tiled passage, beam on the floor to light Sid's way, into a hall, dark-painted wood and glass right, *Ticket booths,* warmer brown veneer left, *Escalators, off for the night.* He halted and turned to Sid to get the measure of the man, torch up so the down-glow from the beam on the ceiling would light his features, not blind him.

'Wind's not worrit was,' Sid's eyes frank, 'not twenty no more.' *Londoner.* 'Might not be able to keep up.'

'Done this before?'

'Not this. Was in the trenches, though. Can look after meself, if that's yer worry.'

'It wasn't.' Matter-of-fact nod. *He's got nothing to prove.* 'But that,' gesture at the sap, 'that's only for if he comes at you. I reckon he'll try to escape, so if we see him, you'll be coming back to spread the word, all right?'

'Fair enough.'

A little nod. *Business done.* 'Stay close.'

Stick out, torch by the back leg to show the way, and slowly down the escalator, the only sounds the clump of their feet and fast shallow breaths echoing off tile, brick, wood. A slight stumble on the shallow bottom treads, into a hallway. First passage, on the right. *Southbound platform. If he's running he'll run north, but the tunnels run both ways. So which tunnel?*

Onto the southbound platform, torch arm wide to halt the postie. Torch off. A stillness while the glare fizzed down and eyes adjusted to black. Silence. Then murmurs of sound nudging from the quiet: draught in the tunnel, echo of a distant train, rats on the track bed. No scuffling on the hard core. *If he's in a tunnel he'll need his torch on.* No light. He listened for a thirty count. Fading train echo, pattering rats. No Widdowson. Close an eye to protect night vision, click on the beam, walk to the end of the platform, click off, open night eye and listen to the tunnel. A whisper of a draught. And the stillness of man-made depths when man has gone home. Turn, eye, click on. Walk down platform, check lateral passages, into last twenty yards, 'Danger. Do not walk beyond this point', beam glancing off the dirty ruby of the red light beyond the platform end. Click off, eye, listen. Nothing. Turn, eye, click. Through the hallway, passage to the north-bound platform, arm out to stop the postie, click off. *Let's see if we can catch a rabbit.* Night eye open, Sid's hand on parka tail, shuffle onto the platform, shuffle shuffle shuffle to the edge, look left, darkness, look right, darkness and a slashed silver spot, a quarter-moon seen through the wrong end of a telescope – a torch beam masked by a body, wavering at the edge of the earth.

'Gotcha!' A stage whisper. 'Sid.' Reach back to the postie and pull him in close. 'I'm going to follow him.'

Acid breath with a nicotine edge. 'What you want me to do?'

'Stay here until the lights come on.' *It's crackers to be talking like panto villains but you never know.* 'Then go up and pass the message. Tell them I'm following the suspect north, along the northbound Bakerloo Line tunnel.'

'North, northbound Bakerloo. Gorrit. Hey, here.' A grip on his shoulder, working down to his arm, then his hand, holding it open. 'Your cosh.' The sprung weight settled in his gloved palm. 'Could need it.' A pat on the arm. 'Good luck, Mr Copper.'

'Thanks, Sid,' putting the sap in the parka's right hip pocket and the torch safe in the left. Then, bottom on the platform edge, he dropped down onto the hard core. 'Mind that electric rail!' from Sid somewhere behind.

★

12.50. How do I follow him? Turn on the torch and he'll see me. Don't turn it on, I won't know what's underfoot. Like that electric rail. He looked around at the blackness as if it were a board with suggestions chalked on. Then, blink blink, an answer. *The tunnel must be curved. If it were straight he'd have stayed on the right, following the platform and then the tunnel wall. But his torch beam was on the left. Which means the tunnel curves left – if it bent right I wouldn't have seen it. So if I cross to the left-hand wall, cover the light, keep it low, perhaps he won't see . . .*

Arms out for balance, find the first rail with a boot, step over. *Out of the station so no dead man's pit to fall into.* Second foot over so both are on hard core. *How far is the electric rail – a couple of feet? If I shuffle forward a little, then a big stride, I should step over it – as long as I don't touch the far rail with my right foot and the electric with my left, I should live. No time to haver, anyway.* Shuffle forward, weight on left leg, high step with the right, onto metal, *Get it off!,* and down to gravel as left boot bangs an insulator. *Bloody hell. Could have fried. Villains and railway lines.* Bring the left to join the right, shuffle over to touch the wall. Breathe.

Stay away from that live rail.

He stuck his torch inside his left glove, closed his night-vision eye, and clicked the switch. *Like a glowing udder, waving at the brickwork.*

It'll do. He pointed it down, finding a brick ledge perhaps a foot wide at the base of the wall, *Should be good going,* and stepped up. Truncheon forward, torch by left knee, the glow showing a yard or two of brick causeway, he started to trot – a stodgy rhythm of leaden thighs, low knees, boots hitting brick in a half-skip, but easy breathing, with no acid air or coal particles to catch in the throat, just dust, damp, rat piss. No sign of Widdowson's torch beam. He tried to catch sounds beyond his boot-scuff and breath. Rats, points changing, a leak collecting in fat drops – nothing like a fifty-year-old man running for his life. *Probably a few hundred yards ahead.* Trotting steady, the causeway looping gently to the left, right boot slipping off the brick, stumble, yellow glow behind, *A train,* flatten back against the wall. *But the rails are silent.* Look right, the Paddington platform picked out in deserted detail, *They've turned the lights on in the station,* push off the wall, *He might see me,* flatten again, *But I couldn't see his torch or hear him. I must be hidden by the curve of the wall.* He pushed off, started trotting, *The station light will put the wind up him,* picking up the pace to get away from the glow, *He'll catch my silhouette if he looks back.* The causeway straightened – and up ahead hovered the slashed silver spot of Widdowson's torch, lighting the killer's way.

Two more strides and the light pool from the Paddington platform was gone. A steady rhythm, *He'll be able to hear me if he listens,* a distant train singing down the rails. The silver dot rounding, *Body isn't masking it,* but no flash, *still pointing away,* blooming wider every few paces. *Definitely getting nearer, and quickly – has he stopped?* Instinct pulled his legs to a stumbling halt. He listened to the tunnel, mostly breath above the ringing rail, no footfall from ahead, *Definitely stopped. Two hundred yards? He must have been walking slow if I've come up this quick – no wind? Or just twice my age?* Widdowson's torch glow turned into a short beam against the wall and then a waxy finger, reaching down the causeway, *He won't be able to see me – but stand still just in case.* The ringing rail louder now, backed by a hiss, the burr of an engine, *Must be going north or I'd see its lights beyond him.* Bourton pressed back against the wall. *But the lights'll show me up – get down, as long as you stay on the bricks you'll be all right,* face down onto the causeway and right side falling onto hard core, *Jesus, you're too wide, turn side-on or you've had it,* wriggle to lie face against the wall, grabbing a fistful of loose parka to wedge it in against the brick, *My fat arse better not kill me*, hugging the wall tight. Screaming wheels, light, a tremor in the brick, arms up to cover the head, *Parka will get loose*, and a pressure wave of dust, engine oil, hot metal as the train pounded past. Breathe out. *At least I didn't shit myself.* Bolts of light slotted by on the brickwork feet above. *Suppose it's too much to hope it'll wrap Widdowson around its wheels.* Fish around, find the torch, look along the tunnel to see the train disappearing north and a shape separate from the wall, silhouetted in the rear lights, and start a jerky trot.

Up, eye closed, torch on, *The train will deafen him for a bit*, and Bourton started running full on, boots hitting the brick with a joint-ringing jolt, breathing hard. Widdowson's torch blinked on as the last of the train light vanished, his shape clearly visible behind the beam, a tiny stick figure in a lumpy trot, *Something's stiff*, pounding the causeway, the figure thickening, *Am I too close? He'll hear nothing but his breathing, his pain, it's the light I need to worry about.*

Widdowson's beam swung right. *He's turning round.* Stumble to a halt, switch off, eye open, flatten against the wall, but the killer's silver shines across the tracks, not down the tunnel, washes across a structure and onto tiles, the torch resting chest-height, rolling slightly, *He's laid it down on the platform of the next station.* Grunting and scraping, *He's climbing up*, the torch beam swinging across asphalt and tiles, a 'Warwick Avenue' sign, Widdowson trotting along the platform, *Why go into a tube station? It'll be locked up. He can't get onto the street*, and turning right, out of view.

Hell. Run, or I lose him.

Eye closed, switch on, torch out of the udder to throw a proper beam and sprint, arms pumping, torchlight waving across the causeway, wall, causeway, wall, a sing in the rails. *Another bloody train.* Legs pounding, warm, smooth, *Empire Games yet, hundred-yard dash in ammo boots and the dark.* Causeway, wall, causeway, poster, *Platform should be opposite.* Point the beam right, a brick path across the tracks, the ring, hiss, burr from the tube train engine, *No light yet, safe to go* and run, leaping over the electric rail just to be sure, jump up off the right leg and roll onto the platform, roll again and up. *He took the first passage.* Find the entrance, trot up, switch off, eye open, turn right into the passage, look for light, listen for footfall.

Nothing. Blackness, silence. *Where's he gone? Up into the station? But there'd be a glow from his torch, even if he'd reached a passage at the top of the stairs to the surface. So, through to the southbound platform? Why? He's hardly walking back to Paddington.* He shook his head. *Irrelevant. Find him.* He put the torch back in the glove, closed his night-vision eye, clicked the switch, started moving. Glow on floor and tiled wall, draught from right, *Staircase hallway,* echoing boot cleats, *in passage, light off,* switch, open eye, onto the southbound platform, look right, look left.

Nothing. What the hell is he playing at? Does he know I'm here? Is he lying doggo? Waiting for me to go, or come by so he can finish the job? Or did he get beyond the escalators, somewhere far enough to hide the torch-glow? Still nothing. *Perhaps I'm just thinking too hard, should just move and—*

A faint metallic snick. He dropped flat, face down on the platform, truncheon clattering, heart pounding in his ears. *What the hell was that?* Metallic groans, left, beyond the platform, from the tunnel. *Hinges. Creaky hinges. And before that, that snick – a bolt, pushed home. Christ, I must have thought it was a Jerry putting one up the spout.* A growing rattle and roar from the northbound platform, *The tube coming through, will drown me out. Run.* Up, close eye, torch on. *He's just gone through a door, he can't see the platform.* He whipped the glove off the torch and pounded down the platform behind the full beam jerking back and forth, the train din pulsing through tiled passages, ebbing twenty yards before the platform end, *He's behind a door, can't hear me,* charged past the 'Danger' sign and leaped off the platform, legs churning. Heels together, boots into hardcore, stumble and stagger on, legs tired and leaden again, across the stones and sleepers, torch beam on the wall looking for the door Widdowson disappeared through.

There: metal, gleaming black, a door a few inches ajar, an open bolt. He flattened himself against the tunnel wall, stuck his boot in the gap, let the torch swing from its strap while he put his glove back on and breathed deep, slow, steady. *No guns, please.* A big breath, kick away from the wall, door clangs back on brick, swing body round, torch beam head-height—

No one. A room, oily mats in the doorway, armchairs grouped

around an electric heater, a table with a stack of ashtrays and a match caddy, old tube seats fitted to wooden plinths lining the walls. Hanging from the ceiling: 'Please remember to remove overalls before sitting on the upholstery.' He hustled through, pushing past makeshift curtains to empty space, a concrete floor, a staircase in the right-hand corner. He started up, stick out, torch suddenly dimming, *Don't conk out now*, a light at the top, then gone, feet running above, a door banging open. Up thirty feet, more, into another whitewashed shelter, signs, space, bolted benches all gleaming in the strong overhead glow, feet scraping on steps above, torch and stick forward and through an open door, take the first flight three at a time, a corner, three at a time, corner, a bang from above, *Door to outside?*, three at a time, *I'll have you, you bastard*, corner, cold air, three steps, then stumble as legs lose drive, two at a time, corner, torch beam on a door at the top, *He's left the key in the lock – you're panicking, chum*, and suddenly thighs are driving three, four stairs at a time to the landing and the acid chill of the fog.

72

01.10. Outside, an old-mustard murk blotted out the street and the night, fairy-dusting his skin with grit. *Freezing.* He zipped and buttoned his parka to his chin. *Must be somewhere in Little Venice.* He took a deep breath, held it, closing his eyes, focusing on hearing – trying for a snatch of Widdowson, something that might be Widdowson, anything at all. Blankness. Only with a regular beat under it, a pulse through water, somewhere off to the left. *The only sound. Better follow it.*

Bourton started moving, torch left, stick right, the truncheon outstretched to find obstacles. A fast trot despite legs feeling drained again and cleats slipping on the paving, *If he's panicking he's moving as fast as he can.* The beat now clear, something voiced, a kind of grunt just after the softer sound of footfall, *Like Tony, pain each time one foot hits the ground.* The glow of a streetlamp head-height, a muffled curse. *He's close now, fifteen yards?* Bourton lengthened his stride into a canter, *He'll still have the knife,* jammed the torch into the left-hand pocket and pulled the parka across to grab the sap from the right, a jolt as the pavement disappeared, stumble stumble then fully upright and back into his stride, the drill-square clip of cleats on tarmac, no beat. He slowed. *Has he stopped? Is he hiding? Waiting in ambush?*

If he keeps still I'll never find him.

Halt. 'Widdowson!' Full parade-ground bellow. 'I'm going to have you!' Skittering ahead, like a cat startled from bins, then a muffled yip, *He's moving,* and the sound of heels hitting paving. *Keep him running.* 'Widdowson! You're mine!' Start moving again, a window sash slamming open somewhere to the right. *Keep him frightened.* 'Just me an' you! An' I'm not old, with dicky lungs, like all those poor dears you killed.'

'For God's sake, put a sock in it!' From the window. 'Decent people are trying to sleep!'

'You won't make it to the scaffold.' His stick banged something waist-high. He waved it left, right – emptiness. Bourton stepped in, felt with the heel of his left hand; a smooth squared-off upright, *Railing?* He reached out with his right foot and tapped. Slipperiness, give, *Slick planking – one of the footbridges over the Grand Union Canal? Don't go in.* Goosebumps on neck, chill in the gut. *He's waiting for me.* Edging onto the bridge, sap left, stick right, moving the truncheon in an X, shoulder-hip hip-shoulder, watching the murk in front for a blade point. *Plan to parry, then smack his hand with the sap.* Listening for smooth soles, breath, inhaling to test for sweat, fear, bad breath above the fog tang.

Scuffing feet right, *He's beside me.* He stepped left and lashed right as the knife flashed past his face and flicked back, lashed again to keep the next stab away and turned to face Widdowson. *Out of view.* Truncheon up, sap low, feet spread, make the X. Fog, thumping pulse, breath, a slamming door back in the street. Breathe in, hold, listen. A catarrhal click half-left, sweep with sap, a hit, a gasp, *Leg?* Flick wrist to hit again, jab with stick into space, the knife-point waist-high from the murk, short hard slashes, shrink away and lunge in. *Chest should be* – thump, gasp – *there*. Hustle in, sap hacking, stick jabbing, hits, a clatter, *The knife*, 'Fuck!' from Widdowson. Jab hard at the voice, scuffing feet. *Backing away, now he'll run, keep hold.* Bourton's hands let go the stick and sap to bob from their wrist-straps and reached blindly into the fog to clutch fists of clothing and haul out a shadow, a body, Widdowson's face coming in, eyes wide, arms up, jaws open to bite, *Lift him*, into the air and out of sight but his buttocks hitting something unyielding. A moment to think *Railing* before gravity grabbed and the killer's body was a deadweight falling away, clutching the parka hood, a yank under arms, thighs bang railing, chest jackknifes, boots arc up, a flailing somersault—

Feet first into sudden drenching cold. Limbs scissor, breath hisses fast, boots leaden, parka fills, and hands drag right leg down. *He'll kill me.* Kick kick kick as chin mouth eyes go under, a cold-vice clamps on skull and the taste of oil, rust, chemicals hits the back of the throat, sparking retching that drives out all air. Panicky crawl-stroke, still sinking, *Sap stick sodden kit, don't breathe in*, claws on chest, scraping up to shoulders, pushing off, shoes kicking chest, Widdowson rises. *Pushing me down, the bastard, follow or die.* Clutch a trouser leg, yank down and kick with all might and face is in air, sucking sulphur, grit, oxygen. Hands from behind on parka, pushing down. 'Die, you bastard,' head going under, claws and weight on shoulders, knees in back, sinking out of Widdowson's reach, cleats hitting hardness, *Something on the canal bed, push or drown.* Bourton dipped and sprang but the hard surface broke and the soar became a bob, blunt blows to the face, *His knees, must be close to the surface.* Clutch calves, thighs, pull Widdowson down and clamber up into air, kicking to keep the killer at bay. Flail-crawl, breath hissing, smacking water for anything hard, fixed, to support twenty stone of deadweight, enough air to gasp, 'Help!' Flounder-flounder. 'Help! In the canal!' Bourton's voice a whisper now, a cough. Left hand scrapes down a hard ribbed surface. *Bricks?* Swing right arm over, wool catches – *Gloves still on, Ernie Potter died this way* – as hand hits water. The weight beginning to drag again, legs treadmilling frantic-ally, *Get the parka off*, as claw at buttons, gloved fingers too stupid for subtlety, chin going under, big breath, tear off gloves, hook weapon straps down wrists, over hands, off, arms lifting and chin bobbing clear as weights drop away. Paddle with right hand, numbed left grips zip tab, halts at breastbone, tuck shoulders in and settle lower in water, big breath, chin to chest putting face in canal, hook fingers in hood, work the parka up, jerky inches at a time, zip teeth catching nose, haul the coat over head and flop it onto the surface, breathe deep. Lightness returns, deadweight now just in the boots, *And they're not coming off soon*, slow breaths, slow frog kick, arms paddling as fingers stretch for anything hard. *At least now I'll last long enough to freeze, not drown.*

Widdowson. Drowned? Swimming hard to stay afloat? He trod water, arms beginning to feel the strain of sodden ammunition boots, watched, and listened. Blackness at water level, then a dirty yellow glow a foot or two above, *Towpath streetlamp can't reach any further.* Water sloshed against the canal walls, but no gasps, splashes, breaths. *Sounds like he's had it. And I'm too cold to care.* A lorry engine from the direction of the shelter, the crack of a crow-scarer on the railway line outside Paddington, *Christ, it's close,* the whistle of a train . . .

Whistle. Right hand like a slab of bacon. Lanyard. At the end the freezing hardness of metal. Start blowing as tread water, SOS. *Perhaps Rex will hear it, get to tell me if my Morse has improved any, again and again, or the 'decent folk' man from the street, or any coppers near Warwick Avenue. Sid the postie will have told them – they must have got some people up to the next tube stations in area cars. Just paddle, conserve heat, think about what you've got to lose, like Anna, she'll be sleeping right, getting colour, rubbing Mum up the wrong—*

Splashes behind, hands on shoulders, 'Shut that bloody row' shivered in ear, as weight bears down and head goes under, mouth filling, cough it out, reach up and behind but now face down, Widdowson above, can't reach him, *Swim away,* kick hard, reach deep and pull and the weight hovers and is gone, a thump on left temple, warmth on cold, *I've gashed my head,* pull up and turn to face where the killer might be coming from, break the surface and breathe. Splashes, fingers crabbing up face, grab the wrist with left, haul the slick arm in close as Widdowson's other hand bumps off forehead, cock right fist and hit above and between the arms as hard as a frozen, weary, floating copper can. Fist hitting flesh over teeth, *Cheek,* then down to clutch Widdowson's trapped arm, tug him past, left hand feeling its way to the killer's shoulder, then right hand dragging his forearm high into his back, 'Hold still now,' shivering at him. 'You're under arrest and if you muck around—' Widdowson trying to swim away, thrashes, kicks out, goes under, Bourton's right hand now holding his wrist, yank it, no give, again, no give. Follow the arm with left hand, face in water to reach down to Widdowson's shoulder perhaps two feet below the surface, frantic movement in the killer's back, chest, the captive arm. *He's hooked up.* Up for deep breath, release wrist and duck under, feel along the front of the wriggling body, hit something rigid, with rivets, slick cloth wrapped around, *His mack, he's still wearing his mack,* the movement frantic now, *He'll use up all his breath,* fingers into the wad of cloth, find a fold, grip the edge, boots skittering across riveted metal, set them, flex and push up, lock knees, hips, shoulders, sustaining the pull . . . The cloth parts and suddenly head and shoulders break the surface, another breath, reach under, a leg kicking weakly, follow the tensed body down to the metal, the wad of cloth still in place, torn edges. *Hopeless job. Let's try to get it off.* Feel up the body to the right shoulder and a thick knot of waterproof jammed under the armpit, across to the left, the mack tugged tight enough to have shrunk, *I'm not slipping his arm out of that*, back across the body to the collar, *Let's try the seam down the back*, plant boots, *Will be pulling at the wrong angle, it's all I can do*, heave, collar lifts, takes the strain. *It's caught underneath him.* The body goes slack. *What if he'd buttoned it? Have I just throttled him?* Feel around the neck to the throat searching for a pulse, but all there is, just above the button and surrounding fabric embedded in flesh, is a still lifeless chill.

★

01.30. Harder to paddle now. Every kick more like a sweep, leaden boots swinging legs too numb and burdened to bend, and arm muscles running down as they try to compensate. Breathe in through nose, out through the whistle, a feeble trill, numbed lips clamped to the icy metal. *Have to thaw me out to get them unstuck. At least moving to stay afloat means staying awake until it's time to cop it. Might not be long, now, though.*

Arm brushes something solid bobbing below the surface. Reach, clutch, feel chill stodgy weight, hairs, a sock. *Widdowson's leg.* Push it away. *Would have been nice if he'd lived. Had some questions for that bastard.* A boot thumps something hard. *My foot's in that boot. Didn't feel a thing. Numb enough for concrete.* Widdowson's leg bobs, nudging right arm and shoulder. *Must be above the scrap that killed him, get away, don't want to get caught too.* Kick again and boot hits the metal, skating up over rivets to water too shallow to tread. Lie back to stay afloat, heels bumping off hardness, *Some kind of shelf.*

I could stand on that. Stop my boots dragging me under. Try to muster reasons why it might be a bad idea. *Hope it hasn't rusted through. But floating's going to kill me, so I might as well give it a try.* Soles down, try to stand, knees won't bend, cleats skitter across the metal and bottom comes down on rivets. *Or sit on it. Less chance of it breaking.*

Sit up. *My arse can feel the rivets – good sign?* Upper body out of the water, *Will I be colder in or out? Too knackered to know*, legs already feeling the ease of relief from the boot-weight, and resume SOS. *Some bugger's going to find me, I know it.*

PART FIVE

Dawn

73

Bourton was still sitting up fifteen minutes later when two Harrow Road uniforms followed the whistle to the canal. He was shivering so hard they never got his name, and with his warrant card still in his parka pocket, floating somewhere in the water, they weren't even sure he was a copper. His hands were too clumsy to fasten the rescue rope they'd fished from the boot of a householder's Vanguard; a uniform had to jump in to do it for him, and it took six men – the dry copper, four residents and an insomniac out with a Jack Russell – to haul his deadweight up the canal wall. When he got into the ambulance some time past three – after half an hour being chafed alive by strangers in a Blomfield Road bed, before being hustled to a warm bath and feeling in his toes – he still had a hot-water bottle clutched to his chest.

*

18.20. Bourton's eyes opened to drawing curtains, the smell of antiseptic, and Bert Parkin in his shirtsleeves and braces, upright and snoring on a bedside chair, like a pig spiked for display on a Smithfield slab. He turned, eyes sweeping over a crowded hospital ward before they settled on broad hips and a flat stomach wrapped in nurse's white. *Much better.*

'Fog's broke.' The nurse twitched the curtains. 'Wind came along and blew it away, just like that.' Chirpy as a Blitz survivor in a propaganda picture. 'Could have done that afore.' She bent down. 'So you're awake.' Thirtyish, broad pale face, dark eyebrows, brown eyes, wide shoulders. 'Slept for fourteen hours clear, you 'ave. Must 'ave needed a proper rest.' She pulled out a thermometer. 'How you feeling?' He opened his mouth and she popped it in. 'Prob'ly hungry.

I'll see if I can get you some tea. Kitchens might only run to a sanger and a cuppa.' She checked the thermometer – 'Normal' – and picked up a chart at the end of the bed.

'Can I go home, then?'

'Per'aps in a couple of days.' She started writing. 'You've been in the Grand Union Canal, Mr Bourton. Cuts an' abrasions all over your body. We gave you penicillin and an antiseptic scrub but God alone knows what's in that water and got into you.' She nodded at him. 'Rest an' get your strength up. I'll bring you some food.'

★

'What they give you?' Bert, stirring in the chair.

'Luncheon meat sanger,' over the last Dettol-scented mouthful, 'and a hard-boiled egg.'

'Hard-boiled egg,' Bert doing a face-sweep with his hanky to catch the snotty dribbly debris of his kip. 'If a bed was empty I'd jump in and claim a couple.' He was looking old and tired. 'O' course, every dicky-lunged dear in London is reporting sick. Could both be out on our ears by morning.' He watched enviously as Bourton took a swig of tea. 'Missus is on her way. She'd have been here before but no one knew who you was. No warrant card, not a word o' sense out of you, just "Roll Out The Barrel".' He leaned in. *A confidence is coming.* 'Tell you who you have had, though. While you were out for the count.'

'Who?' Obligingly.

'Mrs Widdowson.'

Blimey. 'With a hatchet?'

'The opposite. See, Harrow Road didn't know he was this Jack the Fog Ripper or that you was Sherlock, they just thought one of you had fallen in and the other was a Good Samaritan. So when they saw Widdowson's ID they notified her and told her nice and friendly that there'd been another bloke in with him and he was in St Mary's. And round she came. O' course, they wouldn't let her into the ward so if she did have a hatchet,' smiling, *Probably picturing an axe sticking out of a handbag,* 'she'll just have had to take it home again. Far as I can tell she wanted to know how her little Alfred came to be in the canal, who was saving who, whether he'd suffered. Did he?'

Trapped, face down in filthy freezing water a foot from air, desperate, terrified. 'Yes.'

'Good. Well done, lad.'

'I didn't kill him.'

'O' course you didn't.' He tapped the side of his nose. 'Smart bit of work, Richard Bourton. This way nothing gets aired in court and no one hears how stupid the doctors and the coroners and the Murder Squad really are. And none of them needs to shoot the messenger.' He stood up straight again. 'Or his SO. Which, given I been shot once already this year, is good news for Vera.' He suddenly reached for his pocket and dropped something heavy and metallic on the bedclothes. 'Widest man I ever saw left this for you at the front desk.' Anna's knuckleduster. 'I'd hide it if I were you.' He looked cheery and hopeful now. 'I need to tell the Squad you're awake and *habeas corpus*. Wonder if I can get a brew too?'

★

19.10. 'Oh, Richard.' Anna sank to the bed, her eyes huge under straying ash-blonde hair, and Bourton could feel his heart step up, his skin flush, his cock stir. *God, you're a fine-looking woman. And you're mine.* 'It's late, I don't know if I'm allowed . . .'

'You can kiss me, girl.'

She leaned in for a peck but he grabbed her shoulders and pulled her tight for a smacker, a you're-mine kiss, only decent. She resisted for a moment, then nestled under his chin. 'You smell of kitchen floors.'

'I think they dipped me in Dettol.'

'Oh, Richard. I am away for two days and here you are. I told you we should not be separated, we are separated, and straight away you fling yourself into danger.'

'Mostly I fell into mucky water.'

'In pursuit of a dragon.'

Bourton snorted. *Widdowson, breathing fire.* 'Dragon half my weight, twice my age, slow enough even I could catch him.' His mood lowered and a lump rose in his throat. 'Still, would have been good if he'd been make-believe too.'

'I know.'

'Vicious old bastard. Kept on trying for me, right to the end.'

Anna gripped him tight. 'You're safe now.'

'I thought of you, you know. When I was in the canal. Held on, thinking of you.'

'I knew you wouldn't die.'

Odd thing to say. 'Wasn't aware it was on the cards.'

Her body stiffened, then eased. 'You were going to look for a murderer, Richard. That is always dangerous.'

'It was the canal nearly did for me.'

'You always rise back up.' Her hand went below the bedclothes and tried to wobble his stomach. 'You've lost weight.'

'Eating badly, not sleeping, haring around London. You seem in the pink.'

'Clean air. All day, outside – the fencing, a new trough in the something field, new slates on the dairy roof. Here,' she brought scarlet chapped hands up to his face, 'proof. Two days in December, I have farm-shaped bruises and scrapes all over. Emptying my lungs. I woke up this morning and the cough was gone, pfft.'

'Like the fog.'

'Like the fog.'

And Widdowson's victims. 'All those people. He had tables of mementos, tables.'

'It was him?'

'Yep. I was right, girl. It was him.'

'He got what was coming to him.'

'I'd rather he'd provided some answers first.'

'Why?' She sat up. 'Who for? The families? Tell them their loved ones' last moments were terrified, inside a mask, being poisoned? When they think they were just ill, it was a matter of time, it happened?'

'Keep it down, girl.'

'This is a hospital, I cannot talk about death?'

'Well, not where everyone can hear.'

'That's foolish. There are people in the corridors, they have the look in their eyes, they know. These ones.' She waved at the ward.

'Don't tell 'em they're dying, for Christ's sake,' he whispered, though some of them probably were: they had the mortuary pallor or boozer's blush that said heart, or lungs, or circulation was near to U/S. 'I think mostly they fell over and banged something.'

'You think they don't know people die here, are dying now?'

'How was Joan? And Fred?'

'You're trying to change the subject.' She shushed him before he could speak again. 'All right, no more death in a hospital full of dying people.' There was the sound of shoes in the corridor. 'This might be my marching orders.' She leaned in, cupped his ears in her roughened hands and kissed him gently on the mouth. 'I am sorry. I always seem to be telling you off for saying things, simple things. I think I have been a mad person for a while.' She looked into his eyes. He wanted to close the curtains around the bed and make love to her until something broke. 'I love you very much. We will be normal again, I know. And I will make our room just right for you, fire and all,' she smiled, 'for when they let you go.'

★

Which turned out to be that evening. They needed his bed.

74

Bourton woke in Elgin Terrace, blankets around his waist, Anna's sticky bush against his bare bottom. A faint glow surrounded the window frames. *Natural light. Haven't had that for a while.* The room had an unlived-in chill. He got up, put on his Hong Kong cotton dressing-gown, walked over to the window nearest the bed, pulled aside a curtain, wiped off the night-time condensation with his sleeve, noted the gritty smog-smear on the frame's paintwork, inside and out. He knelt up on the chest lid below the sill to get a better view. The sun was where it should be, peeking over Paddington, unmasked; a good reddish ball, blinding if you looked at it, burning off the filth of the night. *Hello, sunshine.* And below, chimneys, roofs, the peeling face of Elgin Terrace, parked cars. And movement – a taxi ambling past a woman in a fur hat and blue coat, three suits and a workman hard clipping for the Grove, a fiftyish man with pyjamas beneath his coat trotting back from some round-the-corner errand. *I can see.* He sensed a sound beyond the chilly glass unheard for a week, the hum of a city going about its business – trains, traffic, chats, doors closing, windows opening, feet on pavement, brick being laid and concrete poured. *Now this is London.*

He checked his watch. Seven forty-five. *Will Anna be working?* He turned to the bed but she was already padding towards him, lower legs blotchy with bruising and scrapes, her scabbed chapped hands tugging down the hem of her army-shirt nightgown. *Modesty or the cold?* The rough cloth made her nipples stand to attention.

'You need more of these, girl.' He rustled the fabric as she huddled in. 'They suit you.'

'*Merde*, it's cold, really cold, Richard.' Her hands on his back underneath the cotton. 'How you can stand here in that tiny thin thing . . .' Her kiss tasted of morning breath and sex. His hands rested on her buttocks, already losing heat. 'I will get warmth from you and then I will light the fire.' She ran her hands up his back. 'Really, you are like a hot-water bottle. All winter I should go around naked, wrapped around you.'

'Might cause a scene.'

'I will be warm, who cares?' She looked up. 'Honestly, you need something winter that fits. You are all shoulders and legs and arms in this, a gorilla running out of a laundry. Or something.' She patted his stomach. 'Too cold for chit-chat.' She stepped back, fished last night's knickers from the end of the bed, stepped in, and trotted over to the fireplace. 'Get back into bed. I will light this, then I will join you.' He pulled the curtains half open to enjoy the sun and ran for the bed, dumping the dressing-gown. 'Richard.' Some of the playfulness was gone. 'Sit up. Show me your back.' She clicked the light switch by the door as he complied, then sat down side-saddle. Her fingers traced his skin before she laid her palms against his sides, under each shoulder blade, above each hip, before patting his shoulder. 'Tuck yourself under. I will be back in a moment.' She shrugged on her red coat and trotted out, leaving the door ajar. Bourton snuggled down. *Indulge the girl.*

A rat-a-tat knock below, hushed voices, footsteps, silence, and finally two pairs of trotting feet. 'Richard, be decent, please,' and after a beat Anna came in, Mrs Suchanek on her heels holding a thermometer like a wand. 'Mrs Suchanek would like to look at your back, and we will take your temperature.' He pulled the bedclothes down to his waist and turned onto his front. Cold palms pressed his skin. Mrs Suchanek said something Slavic. 'Mrs Suchanek says you have scars where wives like them – in the back.'

'Didn't know you spoke Czech, girl.'

'I don't. Nouns and a little intelligence, we get by. Turn over and open wide.' He did as he was told. The thermometer went in. They all waited, as if they'd just asked a question of the Omnipotent Oz. Then the women started talking refugee again, the flow stopping only when Mrs Suchanek disappeared next door with the thermometer. *Must have the wrong answer – see? Just fine.* The glass was winter-stream cold when she put it back in his mouth. He closed his eyes. *Wonder if she'll be game for another jump once this rigmarole . . .*

'One hundred and two,' said Anna. He must have nodded off: he hadn't noticed the thermometer being taken out. 'Last time was a little higher.' She twitched the bedclothes. 'Out. Get dressed, get some things,' she and Mrs Suchanek exchanged consonants, 'the colonel will be running us up to St Mary's.'

'But I feel fine.'

'You are not.'

★

'Do you have lots to read?' asked Suchanek from the driver's seat as the Humber pulled into Ladbroke Grove. 'In my experience one never has enough.'

'Not much of a reader, myself,' said Bourton on the back seat, swaddled in layers he felt no need for. A familiar figure sauntered past the Humber in an over-large duffel coat, heading north to the Grove's junction with Holland Park Avenue. *Derek Jeffrey. Haven't seen you about for a while.* 'More one for smoking and contemplating my navel.'

'Ah,' said Suchanek, smiling. 'A philosopher. Somehow I am not surprised.'

Bourton registered the boy's school cap, the satchel, the big circular canteen pouch, *You could water a horse from that thing*, which he probably used for his sangers. *Must get the 52 from Pembridge Road, change on High Street Ken or Knightsbridge for the run down to Sloane Grammar.* He closed his eyes. The clothes were making him sleepy. *Bright boy, that. Keep him in school and he could go far.*

★

He woke on a chair in St Mary's, Anna tugging clothes out of his waistband. *How did I get here, then?* 'Do you see?' She gently pressed his torso forward and bared his back. 'It is hot, and red, and inflamed, and he is already on penicillin.'

'How did this happen?' A tired, well-educated voice.

'Half an hour in the Union Canal.' Suchanek, very clipped. *Yes, sir!*

'Another drunk who fell in in the fog?'

'No, Doctor,' Suchanek, withering, 'a police officer trying to detain a suspect.'

'You gave his bed to someone else,' Anna, 'and now he needs it back.'

'Madam, the fog has filled the wards. Decisions are based on needs. Now . . .'

'He clearly has a bad infection,' an edge to her voice, 'so get him a bed –'

'I need to ascertain—'

'– and much more penicillin –'

'We're very crowded, we may have to try elsewhere.'

'– and make him well.' Anna sounded close to tears.

'Her first boyfriend died of blood poisoning, you see,' Bourton tried.

'Sorry, Richard?' She brought her face down to his. 'Speak up.'

Try harder. 'It's not going to happen again, love. I'm not going to die. Not like him. Not like Éric.' He was running out of steam. 'I'll be around to haunt you.'

'Who?' Her hand stroked his cheek. 'Never mind.' Someone pulled his clothes down over his back. She stood upright again. 'I think he may be a little delirious. Find him a bed, please, now, or I will scream.'

75

Blink, blink. Awake. Daylight. Bustle. Tethered to a drip. Bed on the left, sallow bloke, teeth out, being swallowed by the bedding. Bed on the right, lad, stripy pyjamas, fifteen or so, on his side, reading a comic. 'What day is it?'

''Allo, mister.' Comic down. 'You awake, then?'

'What day is it?'

'Friday. All day. What you in for?'

'Which hospital's this?'

'St Mary's.'

'What am I doing here?'

'You don't know?' Bourton shook his head. 'You one of them 'nesiacs?'

'Don't think so,' said Bourton. 'Just a little groggy, that's all.'

'Well, they'll bring dinner by, 'bout half an hour. They gives yer tea with it. That'll clear yer 'ead.' He nodded at his bedside chair. 'Got a *Dandy* and a couple of schoolbooks, you want something to read.'

'No, thanks,' said Bourton. 'I'll just lie here and try to add two and two.'

★

The nurse who followed the lunch trolley got two and two to make four. 'You had a bad infection in your back so they opened it and drained it.'

'And the drip?'

'Penicillin. Just to be certain.'

'I'm not going to cop it?'

'Not from me, anyway.' An artificial smile said, 'Joke.' 'Though we've had a nice little crop of policemen outside for a day or so. You must be public enemy number one.'

'I am a copper.'

'I know. I'm pulling your leg.' A patient smile, as if he'd let her down by dropping the banter ball. She nodded at the liver and boiled potatoes intact on his plate. 'Eat that up. You need it for your blood. And then they can arrest you.'

★

'What colour do you call that?' Bert Parkin, majestic in uniform, a police box in boots, pointing at Bourton's face. 'Death on a plate.' Glancing at Bourton's dinner, 'Comes of not eating up your liver.'

'You can have it.'

'Don't mind if I do.' The liver disappeared under a hanky shroud and into Bert's fist. 'No one give you cake?'

'Just argy.'

'That's 'cos you ain't a hero copper, like me.' He leaned in, wearing his conspiratorial expression. 'Good to know you're *habeas corpus* – you'll need your wits. Guv'nor Adams is outside, is going to have a word. The brass are feeling generous. You put them on the hook, then you drowned Widdowson and got them off it. Smile, take what he offers, no awkward questions. Savvy?'

'I didn't drown him.'

'Good lad,' archly. *He really doesn't believe me.* 'Just keep mum.' He stood up. 'And I'll go and wake up Anna, bring her by. Poor girl been worrying herself out.' He patted Bourton's shoulder. 'Glad to see you're not dead. You had us worried there for a bit.'

★

'January fifth. Three weeks or so.' Adams, stiff on the bedside chair, cap in hands, a band of sweat running around his forehead, the scar on his lip a red worm-cast under his moustache. With the brown bedspace curtains closed behind him he looked like someone lying unhappily on mud, perhaps while being measured for a grave. 'A good rest and you'll be back full of beans in the New Year.'

'Thank you, sir.'

'Light duties until the medics pronounce, but I'm sure you'll be back soon enough.'

'Sir.'

'You can leave nights to others, now, too. Mrs Bourton says she barely sees you and that needs correcting.'

'Sir.' Bourton smiled. *A month ago you sentenced me to nights until the end of probation. Who's got the upper hand now, then?*

'Good catch, there, Bourton.'

'Thank you, sir.'

Adams turned his hat in his hands, as if opening a valve. He was silent for a few seconds. *Now we're getting to it.* 'Gloucester man, aren't you?'

'County, sir.'

'Food off the ration?'

He's not looking to finger anyone. 'Been known, sir.'

'Good for building you up. And country air would do you good.'

'Sir.'

'Could spend your sick leave there. Mrs Bourton's employer is happy to let her take the time to look after you.' *Who gave you the right to talk to anyone about her?* 'Clean house to stay in?'

He couldn't stop himself. 'Well, my family aren't gyppos, if that's what you mean.'

'No, no.' Awkwardly. 'I meant from the point of view of re-infection. We just don't want to send you somewhere that'll make you ill.'

'Not aware you can send me anywhere, sir, if I'm on sick leave. Unless the doc says.'

'You're right.'

'Least of all to gyppos living in swill.'

'Bourton.' Adams's tone said, Enough. 'I meant nothing by it.'

Pause. 'All right.'

'Sir.'

'Sir.'

'Better.' He sat back. 'Please take your sick leave in Gloucestershire. No one knows about Widdowson yet but the Murder Squad feels it might be better for you to be out of London in case the papers get hold of something.'

Bourton took a moment or two to absorb it. 'Ampney isn't the end of the earth.'

'It's more remote than here. Mrs Widdowson is keen to meet the policeman who tried to save her husband.' He leaned forward again. 'She won't.' A harder tone: This order will be obeyed. 'She doesn't know that the policeman who tried to save him is the same officer who called for him that very morning. And she isn't to find out.'

'Why, sir?'

'Because he's just another unlucky casualty of the fog.'

'Is that what you've decided?' Snorting in disbelief. 'You can't swing that. God alone knows how many coppers and postmen and odds and sods know different.'

'Do they? They've been thanked for their assistance and told the suspect has been cleared of suspicion in any murders – though he has been sectioned, and will face knife charges when pronounced sane.' Bourton closed his eyes. *All this time I've been out of it, you buggers have been writing things in stone.* 'It's best if no one makes any connection between the suspect in your hue and cry, and Widdowson. And that his widow makes no connection between your visit to his house and his death. Because if she does, she is likely to ferret away until she finds out what he was suspected of. And then she'll want to clear him.'

'Let her try.' Bourton opened his eyes again to see Adams staring. 'Man murdered God alone knows how many people. Years of it. I saw those souvenirs. Tables of 'em. She makes a fuss and it all comes out. And what could be better than "Murdering bastard faces eternal justice"?'

Adams shook his head. '"Old man falls into canal and drowns in pea-souper" would be better. Better still if the fact that a police officer was in there with him didn't get out.'

'Better for who? The doctors and the coroners who didn't check when all these sick people turned up dead, just wrote "Died of fog, we reckon"? The Met, which wouldn't have noticed him but for me, or nicked the wrong bloke? Better—'

'Better for you.' An emphatic whisper. 'For God's sake, Bourton, *very* senior officers are ordering me to do things I have never done before, involving someone so junior they should not know of his existence. And they note that Widdowson's death . . . can be explained in different ways.'

'He drowned.'

'When a drowned man shows evidence of a struggle the issue of charges will depend entirely upon the construction placed upon events.'

'But I didn't kill him. And they'd have God's own fight if they tried to say I did.' He shook his head. 'What gives them the right? He'd still be out there killing folk but for me.' *Calm, Dick Bourton, calm.* 'Anyway, that's not much of a threat. First questions anyone asks, about being on another nick's ground, in civvies, knife holes in my kit, lots of cuts and bruises, it'll all come out.'

'Alternatively,' Adams smoothed his moustache, 'you'd been obsessed with the idea of a murderer for months, you identified a suspect, did not have sufficient evidence, and you ended up in the canal together . . . A man twice your age and half your weight. Will anyone believe that a man of your size, your experience, couldn't subdue a wretch like Widdowson?' Bourton opened his mouth to protest but Adams raised his hands. 'That's one way it could play out. For my money,' some sternness, distance, returning now, 'it's nonsense. You chased an armed man when off duty and confronted him, and the rest is the roll of the dice.' He sat back. 'But you're missing the point. The brass know who you are. Which is not healthy for a probationary constable. They want you to do something. And doing it would not be a hardship. So I suggest you do it.' He stood up. 'Go to Gloucestershire. Get well. Come back in the New Year. Widdowson will be history.' He grasped the curtains. 'There'll be another flap on, you won't be in the middle of it, and they'll forget who you are. Understood?'

★

Straight after, a flurry of Hill coppers, many still in blue, making their mark with a Well-I-never or Ain't-you-the-lucky-one, and snippets of who's-nicked-who. Then heads turned and they scattered like minnows at Bert's heavy tread, Anna on his heels, eyes pouchy with sleep and tears and making sure he really wasn't dead. Bert turned for the door even before she'd reached Bourton's bed.

An hour together before the nurses clapped an end to visiting. They mostly held hands and chatted. About December in Ampney – 'It'll be bitter, love, no two ways'; about weeks under his mother's roof – 'We will fight over who nurses you, but I will win'; about the things that his colleagues had left – 'Cigarettes, books with naked ladies, playing cards with naked ladies, what use are they all? You can't smoke with all these dying lung people and you can't play with yourself in a ward . . .' She'd ask if he were comfortable, and suggest another pillow or a brew, and was gracious about Bourton losing the sap ('It did its job. Enough'). But throughout that hour he sensed a silence behind the words, things unsaid, even if he had no idea what they might be. And when she got up to leave and bent down to kiss him, her whispered 'Thank you, Richard Bourton,' seemed meant to say more than Ta. What's that for? he thought, even if his mouth offered an automatic 'My pleasure, girl' instead. She stepped away with a knowing, even indulgent smile. *She thinks I know.* He blew a kiss to her as she joined the other visitors clumping in the doorway. *But I don't.*

76

'Bourton.' Blink. DS Lloyd on the bedside chair, notebook on his knee. The curtains were drawn again.

'What are you doing here? Visiting hours are well gone.'

'Your guv'nor said you were feeling bolshy.'

'Blame the interruptions to my kip.' Lloyd smiled patiently. 'And knowing if you'd listened to me in November, we might have caught him before the big fog.'

'Yes, you were right. Let's move on.'

'No.' Bourton rolled onto his side, propping himself up on his elbow; the tug from the drip line made him grumpier still. 'I call a nurse, you're off without whatever your guv'nor sent you for. Perhaps I should speak out, cost you all your bloody jobs.'

'Point taken.'

A glib answer, insincerely delivered. 'No, it isn't. How many did he kill last week? Half a dozen? More? Do you even know? Will you ever know?'

'Keep your voice down.'

'You listen to me for as long as I choose, or you hop it.' Lloyd's eyes shifted to the curtains, as if he could see eavesdropping sickies beyond. 'I looked up to you lot. When I came in in November, I was embarrassed, the big thick country plod with no proper learning, showing his little investigation to the pros. An' even when I left, I thought, They're going about it wrong but they'll find him. But you didn't. Even when I told you on Monday Widdowson's your man, I got the brush-off.'

Bourton levered himself up on a straight right arm. 'A good plain-clothes of my acquaintance says it's the biggest case ever in British history. The biggest. And where was the Squad? Nailing the wrong bloke. Off-duty coppers, foreigners, posties, that's who it took to get

Widdowson. Borough councillors, for Christ's sake, blokes with polio or one bloody foot, running themselves into the ground. Now,' Bourton tried to point accusingly with his tethered left, 'I just want to scream how bloody useless you all are.'

'Look, Bourton—'

'But I won't. I know it wouldn't change anything, won't bring anyone back. An' I was never the do-or-die type. So I'll bugger off to Gloucestershire like I've been told, if that's what you're here for, and say, "Who's Widdowson?" if anyone asks.'

'Right. OK.' Lloyd looked slightly stunned. 'My guv'nor will be pleased.' He stood up abruptly. 'Look, I'll come back another day, visiting hours, we'll do this properly.'

Bourton waved his left hand to say, 'Don't worry about it,' but the drip turned the gesture into a galvanic twitch from a corpse. 'Nah, let's get it done now.'

★

'Look, for what it's worth,' Lloyd tried, 'I'm sorry. For all of it.'

Bourton nodded, more comfortable now he was propped against the bedhead. 'Lot to be sorry for. I nearly copped it, doing your job on my time. You going to apologise to my missus, say how I'm here because you're useless?' Lloyd looked down, finally showing shame. 'Not all of it your fault. Course, apology be better coming from your guv'nor, but not a chance.' He stabbed the bed with his right forefinger in emphasis. 'But he can't duck this. Whoever you find out Widdowson killed this last fog – they're on him, it's his Squad, his conscience.' A sudden thought. 'And you find out. Don't you dare give up just because it would make you feel bad, because it never happened—'

'We won't.'

'Don't. Because here's a promise. I hear who he killed last week or I tell all. And I don't care what it means for me. You lot need a reckoning. Names. Faces—'

'We'll know.'

'I'm serious.'

'We'll know.'

'Make sure you do,' laughing, a laboured 'Hah' to cover embarrassment – at what, he wasn't sure. 'Christ, listen to me. Be dying
wishes next.' Anger settled into impatience. 'Bollocks to all that. Let's
have what you came for.'

Lloyd nodded, pleased to get down to business, and sat back,
opening his notebook. 'Your statement.' Brisk, neutral, as if the last
few minutes hadn't happened. 'Bit sketchy.'

'I had exposure.'

Lloyd smiled. 'Anyway, you don't mention the sample case.'

'I don't?'

'In fact, there's a lot you don't mention. Like the murders
Widdowson was wanted for. Any reason for that? Apart from the
exposure?'

Bourton recalled that morning in this hospital, thawing in another
warming bath while the dubious Harrow Road PC scribbled away.
'Honest? I thought it might sound daft. He only had my word for it
I was a copper. If I'd started talking about Jack the Fog Ripper—'

'He'd section you.' Bourton nodded. 'So what did happen to the
sample case?'

'Why do you want to know?'

'Why do you think?'

He closed his eyes. 'Can't be worried about someone else using it
– no one who finds it will know what it's for.' Lloyd's silence said,
'Yes.' 'Won't need it to tell you how he did it, a couple of PMs will
do that.' A nod. 'You won't be worried about someone picking it up
and adding two and two, because there's nothing to add, nothing
happened.' Lloyd nodded again. 'Which leaves . . .' *Only one answer.*
'Me. Someone who knows and thinks other people should too. On
my own I'm just a crackpot – but the sample case is evidence, cred-
ibility, right?'

'Right.'

'Which means someone thinks I know where it is. And am minded
to do something with it.' Bourton closed his eyes to think again.

*Lie. Tell them what they fear is true. I've got the case, I'll use it, now
tell the world.*

He shook his head. *But if I had it, and I wanted the world to know,
I'd use it. It's no good to me hidden away.*

Or: I've got it. Tell me what I want to know, or else. But then . . .

He shook his head again. *You're too stupid, or too sick, to work this through.*

Truth. He opened his eyes. 'I never saw it. In the shelter, he must have put it in a room I didn't enter, picked it up on his way out. The last time I know he had it was Praed Street. He hit a couple of blokes with it, so they said. After that – could be anyone's guess.'

Lloyd was looking at him hard. 'Certain?'

'Certain.'

'On the Bible?'

'On the Bible.'

That answer must have come too easily. 'On whatever you hold sacred?'

'Want me to cross my heart and hope to die?' Suddenly Bourton didn't want to play any more. Lloyd might only be doing what he was told but that wasn't enough to earn him a friendly ride. 'I'm telling you the truth. Now bugger off and let me be.'

77

Ampney time. Late reveille to an egg from the coop and bubble on the range, Anna in his mum's pinny with not much on underneath, then upstairs for as much of a jump as his strength and stitches could stand. Kip, dress, a walk – the grass, stone, hedges all bleached by hard frost till gone ten, all month – and perhaps a house call, Anna the star of wherever they fetched up. Dinner, kip in front of the parlour fire, wrapped up warm with the wireless burbling as Anna knitted or sewed or interrogated a paper. Up for tea and Mum's return from the big house, with a niggle if Anna had used the wrong pan or jumbled the jars, and Dad from the workshop; and after, perhaps a visit from a cousin or a chum to bring on best behaviour. Then the pub – Three Tuns with young 'uns, the Crown with old – and home to the wireless, a last brew, and stifled hanky-panky in bed.

And his first home Christmas since '48. Lunch with the Bourtons in Poulton on the Eve, square old men and padded women loading spuds around the new Formica; then Ampney in Ted's new Riley, to the garden and the big house goose and Mum's barren hen, plucking and dressing the birds in shifts warmed by insults, smokes, whisky-and-hot-water. Up to the squire's for booze in better glass, Bourton in battledress out of shame for his suit, Ted with chicken feathers in his turn-ups; on to College Farm Lodge and the Packers' beer and sangers, thirty-odd grown-ups and God alone knows how many scallies seeing in the Day with carols around the joanna, the Ink Spots and Tommy Dorsey on the gramophone, and everyone helping get the tree back up after drunken stumbling felled it in the hall. Christmas morning: Mum to the big house and Bob's Margery preparing the birds instead, the men tiddying themselves for church as if a sergeant major hid by the lych-gate. The ten o'clock service, the vicar brief in the sermon and civil after, nothing forced in his smile or don't-touch in his handshake, then back to Ridge Cottage, the women in the kitchen, the men moving the table and laying up, Bob's boys upstairs playing with the little air force that Ted had stamped out of scrap tin at the works for their Christmas presents. A raucous dinner, Mum stoic at the burned patch on the goose where Ted's tipsy fingers had taken skin as well as quills, an austerity Christmas pud with shredded carrot and perhaps swede in the mix, parlour games, the Queen on the wireless. Then presents at the tree – to include a nicely turned baby's rattle from Bob and Margery, 'Cos you need to crack on' – kitchen defaulters, naps and chat around the wireless, before sarnies and nips of whisky-and-warm sent his brothers and Bob's quartet up the road to their beds. No rows, only two kids' tantrums, and a house full of the fat and happy. After all that, New Year's Eve at the Cirencester Young Farmers was a bit morning-after.

And all of it against the backdrop of the fog. Choked hospitals, backed-up undertakers, gravediggers' overtime – jolts of reality from the wireless or the paper, delivered as if London had never had a pea-souper before. Perhaps Bourton was primed to hear it, perhaps Widdowson had exposed a nerve that would twang at mention of the word – but he didn't think so. After a week or so he shrugged away the stories. The fuss wouldn't change anything. And thinking about it would take time and energy he'd rather give his wife, his family, a soft-boiled egg, butter thick on proper bread, a nice bit of bacon.

So he had resented the hour-long call at College Farm, a few days before Christmas, from Tony Marling – a new Marling, using lawyerly hopscotch to wish Widdowson away. 'Things have changed, Dick,' he insisted. 'I've had some chats, and there's an . . . awareness, even in government, that recent events could not have happened without a general acceptance of the unacceptable. And it's a point that, it has been made clear to me, I will be in a strong position to make.' Typical, Bourton remembered thinking at the time. The copper gets light duties and a country Christmas, while the toff is offered the possibility of power.

Then 5 January, London, and the nick: happy insults and the promised light duties – front desk, storeroom, clerical in CID, silent muscle in interviews and nursemaid in cells, and a lot of kettle work. Near enough three months of it, not one. Three months of the fabric of the nick, the chats, the gossip, the running gags, the Ladbroke Arms at the end of a turn; of tea and sanger runs, of learning the lives of faces from the stairs or canteen or roll-call, gaffers, WPCs, skippers, plainclothes, even guv'nors, and mapping their porkies, gripes, kids, how they liked their brews, their poison down the pub. Three months of early and late turns, chairs when his feet got sore, char and wads when the mood took and a skipper was amenable. And always warm, always dry. Time and again, Bourton would walk in or out of the nick, humming anticipation before a turn or bonhomie at the end of it, and think, *I could get used to this.*

And every day would end with his wife, the woman he'd married, not the silent movie actress made batty by the fog – a woman who took the two two-day pea-soupers of January and February in her stride, with Vicks, and a muslin mask, and a smile that said, 'Do your worst.' Perhaps he'd meet her out of the office at five, after the early worm, and take her to the pictures or – after a late turn – catch her doing her make-up gone ten, ahead of the pub or a palais. They'd get up and go to bed at the same time, eat at least two of their three meals together, and unload, grumble, dissect, plan – togetherness instead of ricochets, for the first time in their London life, with none of the little lies and silences of weeks before. He couldn't believe he'd stood for anything else.

And running on the same clock, they could come over all social. Sunday lunch at the Parkins', five of them jammed around the table in the tiny kitchen, Anna ballasting herself with Vera's roast potatoes ('The best food I have eaten in England. Ever'). Tony Marling's birthday drinks, Dorothy-vinegar-tits nowhere in view; a boozy evening of well-spoken men in suits, ties, and haircuts civvier than Bourton's, but with judies powdered or lumpy beside his missus, and all in thrall to her as knowing ingénue. Foursome pub-and-pictures with Bill Nickerson most weekends, hoping some of Anna's stardust sprinkled on his shoulders as he courted Jen hard. And spare hands at a party for Rex's twins at his semi in Pinner, a lovely Saturday that left Anna broody and Bourton pining for his own patch of suburbia, and wondering how the hell he could get it.

Every now and again, over those two months, he'd look at Anna, or chums in the pub, or the dawn – a dawn he'd woken for, not patrolled – and think, *Mug. Mug for pulling your weight, tightening your belt, doing your bit; mug for being a stranger to your wife, your family, normality. Mug.* Other times he'd just revel in this new life, as if he were scrunching his toes at the bottom of a dry sleeping bag at the end of a cold stag.

So DS Lloyd's call at the end of January threw him. He had to rummage for the man's name, fish it from a corner of his memory stocked with Merchant Navy shipmates and his Home Guard platoon, and write it down, again and again, across the front desk Occurrence pad. There was a gulf between that week in December and Light Duties Bourton, and Lloyd's world seemed far out of reach. But the reason for his call came back sharp as vinegar and miserable as donning sodden clothing: Widdowson's last victims. *The Squad could have ignored me, never called, would have made it even easier for the Met to pretend the Traveller never existed, too.* And as he walked down the nick steps, off to the Yard, he found himself resenting Lloyd for dragging him out of his nice warm hole, just to tell him something he no longer wanted to hear. He smiled. *Blame the bloke you black-mailed.* Then the smile vanished. *And ignore all the poor bloody dead. Richard Arthur Bourton, you're a right one.*

78

'Four,' Lloyd was brisk, businesslike, 'that we could be sure of from the fifth to the ninth of December – i.e., the period of the fog.'

'Four?' A surge of old anger, like bile. 'He could do that in a day.'

'If he had that many targets.' Hand out, to stop a runaway Bourton. 'Anyway, four. And that's taken six weeks, going through the Daily Books just like you did, picking the most likely names and seeing what we can find out. We haven't had any short-cuts, like a diary, and those . . . items. We can only link them to six of our twenty-two probable victims.'

'Twenty-two?'

'That we're pretty sure of.'

'How many "items"?'

Lloyd consulted his notebook. 'Two hundred and eighty-nine.'

Bourton swallowed. 'So isn't your tally a bit low?'

'Probably.' His hand came up again to fend off a fury Bourton couldn't muster. 'But we can't know if they're all mementos, or how many go with each victim, let alone put names on them – most are unmarked. The oldest case we've identified is November 'forty-eight, and that was a fluke. Most of the names thrown up by the Daily Books, there are new tenants at the addresses, or the next of kin don't remember anything being missing when they sorted out the estate – and it's not as if they'll miss stockings, or a scarf, or slippers, anyway.'

'What about Widdowson? See where he takes you?'

'That only gave us two names, both from the isolation hospital. Look,' hands wide, Trust me, 'we've been doing our job.'

'What about patterns from your twenty-two?'

'They don't get us names, just make the names we get look likely.'

'Post-mortems?'

'Professor Simpson at Guy's says we could exhume almost everyone from the Daily Books and we'd get nothing. All the evidence is in soft tissue and that will have gone.'

'But won't poison—'

'He didn't use it. Simpson's best guess is the apparatus was effectively airtight – perhaps a gas mask, with the filters and box closed off. Inside there was some kind of irritant, probably masked by something like Vicks. Widdowson would put it on the victim, hold it tight for a good seal, they'd breathe deeply, get just the irritant, start coughing for air, he'd press their diaphragm to get the last oxygen out and they're unconscious in thirty seconds. To a GP who's been expecting them to die, they look like they've been carried off by a coughing fit. And for us, if we exhume, Simpson says the evidence that has survived could equally point to a coughing fit and a couple of knocks as they went down.'

'So?'

'So we're not going to find everyone. We're looking. We may find more from December, but it's hard – the bodies are stacking up, perhaps four thousand more dead over the last six weeks than usual.'

'Four thousand?'

'Four thousand. Apparently the worst pea-souper in living memory is liable to kill off people who'd have made it through something shorter. You wouldn't believe . . .' He shook his head. 'Anyway, even if only a few of those before his death were Widdowson's, we're still having to wade through over a thousand names. So those twenty-two, we're pretty sure of.'

'Bradford? Dean? White?'

'All the ones you said. You were right, if that's what you want to hear.'

'I'd rather have heard it first time we met.'

'For what it's worth,' slowing, like the sound from a winding-down gramophone, 'I would too. Guv'nor as well. He particularly wanted me to tell you that.'

'Couldn't do it himself?'

'He thought you might take a swing, get yourself thrown out on a discipline.'

'And kick up a fuss.' Lloyd shrugged. Bourton closed his eyes. Twenty-two people. Twenty-two murders, unnoticed. More that might be identified, perhaps tens, even hundreds more that never would. He felt the weight of them all, each souvenir on those tables a fresh shovelful of earth on his chest. *I don't want this to drag me down, weight me with despair. But all those poor, poor people* . . . 'What are they called?'

'Who?'

'The twenty-two.'

Lloyd nodded. He took a folded sheet of paper from inside his jacket and laid it on the table. 'The roll so far. And,' his fingers held it down, 'it stays in this room.'

Names, addresses, dates of death, a trophy if they'd found one, all neatly typed on a machine with a slipping 'n':

Gordon McFee, 67, 88 Ferndale Rd E (Leytonstone), 14 Nov
    1948, engraved watch
Eleanora Micklem, 68, Flat 4 Warwick Mansions, Nevern
    Place SW, 29 Oct 1951
William Wragg, 49, Flat 2 16 Mantilla Road SW, 29 Nov 1951
. Jane Dunn, 60, 8 Whitehall Gdns W, 30 Nov 1951, hat
Irene Gurdon, 55, 18 Old Nichol St E, 17 Dec 1951
Morris Singer, 50, 61 Buxton St E, 17 Dec 1951
Edward Dalley-Smith, 58, 6 Halston Rd SE, 8 Jan 1952
Constance Dean, 70, 44 Fortune House, Pepys Court EC, 8
    Jan 1952
David Willing, 66, 355 Commercial Rd E, 9 Jan 1952, ration
    book
Gladys Hartham, 71, 28 Bewley St W, 7 Feb 1952
Marlene Izbicki, 37, Flat 10 240 Kenmore Ave Harrow,
    10 Feb 1952
Arthur Hurt, 56, 400 Evelyn St SE, 10 Feb 1952
Thomas Bradford, 53, 12 Crozier Mansions, Crawford St W,
    28 Mar 1952, shooting medal
Ethel Faccini, 61, 189 Sutherland Ave W, 28 Mar 1952,
    husband's engraved watch
Frederick Slingsby, 72, 13 Hampton St SE, 29 Mar 1952
Bénédicte White, 67, 39 Boston Pl W, 29 Mar 1952
Enid Chirk, 72, 6 Wincott St SE, 8 Nov 1952, family Bible

William Lynch, 58, Flat 2 18 Cotleigh Rd NW, 10 Nov 1952
Elizabeth Fowlds, 76, 63 Braybrook St W, 5 Dec 1952
Helen Mitchell, 54, 17 Tynemouth St SW, 6 Dec 1952
Daniel Crotty, 61, 8 Abingdon Rd N, 8 Dec 1952
Isaac Morris, 55, 212 Willifield Way NW, 8 Dec 1952

The names filled his throat, a rockfall of dry biscuit he didn't have the spit to swallow. 'Christ, it's a lot.'

'And there are three years between McFee and Micklem.'

'Ah, God.' Bourton pushed the sheet away. 'I can't even . . .'

'I know. When they're names, with lives, homes, people who miss them . . .' He looked tired, empty, worn away, like the medics who'd worked on in Belsen long after Bourton and the other uniformed trippers had buggered off back to their billets. *And I buggered off to my cushy life, leaving him with name after name, death after death, chipping at his soul . . .*

'I don't suppose,' Bourton chose his words carefully, 'we know why he did it?'

Lloyd shook his head. 'Wasn't the usual. Sex. Hate. Jealousy. Financial gain. Once you've ruled them out, it's any man's guess.'

'And yours?'

Shrug. 'Didn't like sick people. Because he could. Fun. Playing doctor. Playing God.' Bleak smile. 'Some men have more than one guess.' The smile wore away. 'And we have nothing to say which one is right.'

'How do you copper after this?'

'If you stopped, you'd do yourself in.' He gestured at the list. 'Just knowing, this is the tip of the iceberg, all those lives – if you walked away without trying to make it right . . .'

'But how do you?' Bourton felt a quick bloom of anger, the righteous edge of weeks before. 'With no one to hang and the whole thing hushed up?'

'We do what they let us. And then, when they say stop, we'll stop.' He smiled sourly. 'You said it. Back in St Mary's, when you gave me what-for. Betty Fowlds, Helen Mitchell, Dan Crotty, Isaac Morris. A teacher's widow, a book-keeper at Arding and Hobbs, a builder, a furrier. The ones we should have saved. That we know about. Think about them.' His smile was easier now. 'When they let you off light duties, and you find yourself wanting to scream from the rooftops or drown your sorrows or jump off London Bridge, think of them. And be as good a copper as you can be.'

79

Three months of light duties and home to the wife; a life others led, one Dick and Anna Bourton could have enjoyed for years.

Then, over two days, it all fell apart.

24 March 1953

'Bourton? You off light duties?' George Brown, leading a clutch of CID down the nick's front steps, Bourton standing back to give them right of way. And then, before he had a chance to answer, 'Might be an idea to bring him, guv'nor,' to DI Knox, twelve o'clock shadow and National Health specs over preoccupied eyes and deep nicotine wrinkles. 'Heavy jobs.' Knox raised a hand in agreement as he hustled onto the pavement, hip swivelling slightly with his sciatica limp. Brown jerked a thumb at the nick. 'Tell the front desk we've borrowed you, then catch us up.'

'Mr Brown.'

'Oh, and have you had your lunch?' Bourton shook his head. 'Good.' He jerked his thumb again. 'Chop-chop. And draw a crowbar and a shovel while you're at it.'

*

'It's Rillington Place.' Bourton halted as the silent knot of coppers turned into the poky cul-de-sac, thinking, Can't be.

'That's where the body is.'

'Which number?'

'Ten,' Brown waving Bourton into a tiny garage without scratching his paintwork, 'ground-floor flat. Chop-chop.' He halted. 'You—' He checked over his shoulder. The other coppers were onto the pavement. 'It's Christie's flat. But you know that, because you were asking about him, in December.' Just audible: 'Was that your Traveller hunt?'

'Yeah.'

'And it wasn't him. We know he had nothing to do with it?'

'He knew Widdowson, from the war, that was all.'

'Thank Christ. At least we're in the clear there.' The rest of the coppers were following Knox into number 10, a group of bystanders on the pavement – five coloured men and a pair of biddies keeping their distance – edging back as if they'd been snapped at. 'You spoke to him?' Bourton nodded. 'Keep mum about it. This business will be bad enough.'

The coloured men made room on the narrow pavement, respectful nods belied by mutinous eyes and muttering. 'Haven't you got jobs to go to?' said Brown, curtly. 'Go on, hop it, there's nothing to see here.'

'He not do it.' A dark brown man, mid-thirties, bigger than Bourton, a pork-pie hat incongruous over a collarless white shirt and braces. He seemed impervious to the cold.

'Who?'

'Beresford.' He pointed at Bourton's burden. 'We see those, we heared he find a dead body, but he still in your station.'

'Beresford just move in.'

'It's Christie kitchen.'

'Gents,' Brown, less edge, 'he's making a statement, no more. There is nothing to see here. Now hop it.' He touched the brim of his hat. 'Ladies.'

If anything, 10 Rillington Place had slumped in the last three months. The front door sagged, the smell of damp was stronger and laced with something rancid and musty, and the attempts to keep up standards – a newspaper Coronation poster tacked above the lintel, the whiff of Jeyes from the corridor floor – felt like bunting on a bombsite.

The CID men were swapping peeks through the far wall of the kitchen, like schoolboys sharing a two-bob peepshow. The room sounded empty, smelt like rancid butter, and was cold enough to condense Bourton's breath.

'Young woman, strangled,' said Knox to his men, 'perhaps a week dead.'

'Smells older,' DC Hume, from the Scotch accent, 'couple of months maybe.'

'Sealed space,' said Knox, 'with external walls, God alone knows. She certainly hasn't been in there since November 'forty-nine.'

'Hell of a shock, guv'nor,' DS Hutton, 'knock a hole in a wall and see that. Enough to turn a darkie white.'

'You'll turn white too,' Knox having none of it, 'if we've hanged the wrong man.' He turned to Hume. 'Jock, we'll need the surgeon, a pathologist, a camera, and some uniforms for outside. And a be on the lookout for Christie, police only, for now.' The DC nodded and hurried out. 'Vic, Ted,' to Hutton and a DC Bourton hadn't seen before, 'we need to know when Christie did his flit and where to. See if that lot outside have got any gen.' He turned to Brown. 'George, take him,' a thumb at Bourton, 'to the wash-house, check there isn't a body or two under the sink or the slab.' Brown must have queried the order with an eyebrow or something. 'I know,' Knox sounded apologetic, 'but that's where they were last time. Go on. Set my mind at rest.'

The door Bourton had broken down was now nailed shut so he and Brown had to leave the kitchen and step outside through the common access door. The return was lined with jumble – a broken chair, old clothing and newspapers, chipped crockery, a single shoe. Brown opened the wash-house door. 'Riddle around with the crowbar,' he told Bourton, 'behind the door, that's where the baby was, and under the sink.'

There was more jumble under the sink but nothing as substantial as a body. 'What's he about?' Bourton asked, as he stepped out of the freezing brick box.

'Not sure,' said Brown. He lit smokes for them both. 'But this Beresford lives upstairs, says he hasn't seen or heard of Christie's missus since before Christmas.' They took companionable first pulls, truants down a brick alley. 'Perhaps the guv'nor thinks she's been done away with too. Or is she in the kitchen?'

'Old and fat,' said Bourton. 'Fifties?'

'So not her, then.' Brown crossed to the low wall separating the return from the garden. 'This,' so quiet Bourton had to stand beside him, 'this body, if she was killed after Evans was nicked, late 'forty-nine, then everyone will say he's innocent – and him,' he jerked a thumb at the house, 'and the DCI, they're the ones served him up to the Crown.' Another pull. 'Someone walks into a Welsh nick and confesses to hiding a body no one knows is dead, who's going to look for another suspect?' He shook his head. 'Good guv'nor. He'll take this hard.' They smoked in silence, looking out at the fifteen or twenty feet of wonky fruit or veg canes, a sagging fence, half-buried corrugated tin and the backs of the houses beyond.

'What do you reckon he grows?' mused Bourton.

'Nothing I'd want to eat.' Distracted: 'If he dug for victory it's a wonder we didn't lose.' He scanned the garden. 'Christ, he's a sloppy bastard.' Suddenly he sounded animated. 'Did you see that door in the kitchen? These canes? That fence?' He gestured with his cigarette. 'Doesn't need it with that high wall, could take it out. Or straighten it out, do it properly. But what does he do? Prop it up with scrap. Idle bugger. Tell you what, wherever he's gone it isn't far.'

Bourton turned to the fence. The closest section bowed and listed, held upright by bits and bobs of wood, a metal bracket, and a table leg with patchy varnish. 'Probably didn't dig it in deep enough,' he suggested. 'Bet those palings are sitting in about two inches of earth.' He drew deep, the tobacco supplanting the scent-memory of Christie's rancid kitchen. 'My dad would have words.'

'Mine too,' said Brown. They smiled at each other. 'Dads.'

'Mine would have done something with that table leg, too.' Bourton pointed at it with his smoke. 'Dab hand with wood, he is. He'd reckon that a criminal waste.'

But that's not a table leg. Bourton stepped onto the filthy earth and squatted. Close to, the varnish looked like muck and the patches areas where mud or layers of London had washed away. 'George,' he said quietly, 'I think it's a bone. And too big to be a dog's.'

'Never.' Brown squatted alongside Bourton. He took a pencil out of his pocket and ran the barrel along one of the clean patches. 'But it feels like bone. Looks like it might have been chewed a bit, too. Thighbone, perhaps.' He stood up and scanned the length of the fence. 'We need to get off here and tell the guv'nor. If it's old he could be off the hook.'

★

An hour later, Bourton puffing through Capstans, still minding the evidence to ensure a dog didn't make off with it, the common access door banged open and men pulling out smokes spilled into the return, as if the credits were rolling on a wife-pleasing double bill. They huddled beside the privy to blot out the smell of putrefaction. Brown lit up and joined Bourton, gazing across the earth and rubble as if over lawns and an ornamental lake.

'You're better off out here. Three,' he said. 'Three in that alcove. Stuffed in, like things in a cupboard.' He pulled his notebook from an inside pocket and handed it over, open on a page with three sketched figures. The cheap paper smelt of death. 'Break your heart. All young women, all strangled, all of them with nothing on below.' Brown took a deep pull and shook his head. 'Tastes of Vicks.' He paused, exhaled. He seemed to be bracing himself. 'First one sitting down, like she was gathering herself to get up, kept upright,' he pointed at his sketch, 'by her bra hooked over the legs of number two – on her back, legs up, saw her and the first thing I thought was one of those health films, you know? Pretty birds in shorts doing that cycling exercise. Number three, she'd been stuffed in on her head, wrapped up and stuffed, like – like . . .' Another pull while he gave up trying to finish the thought. 'None more than three months dead. So, that's the guv'nor on the hook, then.' Bourton had nothing to say.

'Broken stock.' Brown reaching for the notebook and putting it back inside his jacket. 'That's what they looked like. Broken stock, back of a stockroom, get chucked out when the lease is up. Broken stock.'

★

Cordon duty, outside 10 Rillington Place. Housewives, night workers, the jobless, faces he knew to be tarts, a fireman, a ticket-taker at the Regal – forty or fifty mismatched locals, ghoulish one moment, buzzing with anger the next. And, notebooks in hand, three or four men who had to be journalists, who harried the DCI as he left: 'Did you hang an innocent man?' With only four coppers on the perimeter, the crowd was close enough to hear the floorboards come up in the front room, and the cries of disgust when Mrs Christie's body was disturbed.

When the corpses were stretchered out wrapped in sheets, it was their smell, not linked arms or respect for the dead, that kept the way clear.

By five there must have been a hundred people milling around Rillington Place, at least half of them kids; the surge after six seemed to be strangers to the Dale, pulled in by the evening papers. Mostly the crowd was polite, reluctant to chance its luck. There was a tricky moment after half seven, when a stony-faced knot of women paused at the edge of the glow from the streetlight outside number 10, a couple of them bracing each other, and one of the older uniforms said, 'Oi-oi, boys, I think they might be Evans's family, they're local', but the women came no nearer, and the uniform had the wit to doff his bonnet, and after a few minutes they turned and left the street.

'Not our fault, anyway,' muttered Timpson. The other coppers' silence suggested otherwise.

Most of the time, though, Bourton found himself thinking through something he'd seen at about five fifteen – a face in the crowd, a nod, a reminder of December, and a belated adding of two and two. Which was why at the end of their turn, when the uniforms reached the junction of St Mark's Road and Lancaster Road and turned left to return to the nick, he waved goodnight and made a right, deeper into the Dale.

80

'Mr Bourton.' Beryl Jeffrey looked as if she'd expected someone else. 'Is there— Derek's in, honest, we only—'

'I need to have a word with him, Mrs Jeffrey. All three of you, if Mr Jeffrey's in.'

She stepped behind the front door, as if she'd just noticed her housecoat, passable for neighbours but not the law. 'It's very late, Mr Bourton,' her head reappeared, 'the morning—'

'Mrs Jeffrey,' bonnet off, 'if we wait until morning, it'll be official. We'll be taking him out in cuffs and he may not come back for ten years.' After a couple of seconds her hand went to her mouth. 'Is Mr Jeffrey in?'

★

'Why didn't you tell me about Barry Flett and his thug friends?' Derek's face popped up from under the bedclothes, looking guilty. *Reading with a torch or fiddling with himself.* He threw the boy's school blazer, picked up from a hall hook, on the bed. 'You and Don are thick as thieves. He'll have known his brother was up to something – why didn't you tell me?'

'Wha'? Whatcha doin' in my room?'

'You knew people got beaten close to death, and you said nothing.'

'Mum, Dad, what's he doin' in my room?'

'Guilt, I'd say. Something like it, anyway.' A bedside table and bookcase, head-height wardrobe with speckled mirror, gate-leg table as desk, chair with strap over the back – the strap of what he'd thought back in December, while feverish and confused in the back of Suchanek's motor, was a canteen pouch. 'Know what this is?' He picked up the pouch and opened it. It was empty. 'You'll like this. It's a pouch for a drum magazine for the Russian PPSh sub-machine-gun. And that,' pointing to a design stamped into the flap, 'is the badge of the MGB. This,' hefting the pouch, 'is rare as hen's teeth in Britain. Might find a Red Army mag pouch but not MGB. Only someone who'd dealt with the MGB – or killed them – would have this.' He threw it hard, striking Derek in the face. Now he looked shocked. 'Where's the gun?' Derek shook his head jerkily. 'Senkus had a gun. Small, fit in a man's hand, but lethal. Where is it?' Derek shook his head again. 'The man you tried to murder a year ago had a gun and a flask in this ammo pouch. Where are they?'

'You silly bastard,' muttered Peter Jeffrey from the doorway. Beryl was stifling sobs.

'I don't know what you're talking about.' Derek, all grammar school, but the line lacked conviction.

'That's the best your brainpower can do? Keep on with it and you're lost. I've got the pouch and the statement of the man you tried to kill, and he'll pick you out in an identity parade. You'll be convicted of attempted murder, and go away, and when they let you out you'll be young but a felon, can't join up, get a job that goes with your learning . . .' He shrugged. 'Where is it?'

Derek's eyes flicked to his parents, then away, *Looks like he's got no support there*, and settled on the bedclothes. Bourton could see muscles shifting in the boy's face as he thought.

'I don't play in Bertram Terrace,' he tried.

'Who said it happened there?' Pause. 'Besides, that's a lie.' He pointed at the blazer badge. 'That motto, Quam Bonum blah-blah, you scribbled it on the wall of your coal hole.'

'Anyone could have.'

'So it's where Sloane Grammar goes for a smoke, is it?'

'And, anyway, I was at school.'

'How do you know when he was hurt?'

'Common gossip, innit, in the Dale?'

'Fact of Mr Senkus getting hurt, yes. When – only his attackers would know.' Bourton jabbed a finger at the boy. 'Besides, you weren't at school. It was the day the King died. Schools closed at lunchtime, mark of respect.' He shook his head. 'You had a nice way of showing it.' Anger, guilt, pride, all seemed to flash across Derek's face, but then his mouth clamped tight enough for his lips to show white.

Try again. 'What you don't know is that Mr Senkus owes me a favour.' Bourton losing some of the interrogator's needle. 'After you tried to kill him, I saved his life. And he's ready to tear up his statement if I ask.' The boy blinked. *Gotcha.* 'Give me the gun, and the flask, and the ammo pouch, and I'll ask him. There'll be no evidence, no plaintiff, the attack never happened. And in the morning you'll go to school, just like this morning and last week. What do you say?'

Derek's mouth relaxed. He stared at the bedclothes, then glanced at the bookcase. He pointed at it. 'Dornford Yates. The three-in-one Dornford Yates, bottom shelf.' Bourton pulled out the fattest volume and opened it. A palm-sized automatic pistol, .22 calibre or perhaps even smaller, sat in a neatly cut hole in the pages.

'Oh, Derek,' said Beryl Jeffrey, sounding broken.

'It's all right, Mum,' said Derek. 'They're bad books.' He nodded at the bookcase. 'And Edgar Wallace, *The Mixer*, top shelf – the flask's in there. That's terrible an' all.'

Bourton removed the pistol, found the magazine release catch and pushed it. An empty clip dropped out. He worked the action but there was nothing up the spout. He looked at Derek. 'Where are the rounds?'

There was a moment, Bourton could tell, when the boy thought of lying, but he shrugged, as if to say, 'Why bother?' and smiled.

'I fired 'em.'

'Jesus Christ,' said his father.

Derek looked at each of them in turn, to make sure they were paying attention. 'At the wall of Wormwood Scrubs. In December. During the fog. You'd have been proper pleased, Sergeant Bourton. Slinked up, five rounds, bam-bam-bam-bam-bam, spooked back.' His smile turned into a grin. 'No one even noticed.'

81

'Why?' Spooning fully clothed on top of the bed, Anna's voice breathy in his ear.

'Disrespect, he said.' *As feeble from my mouth as his.* 'The day the King dies and there's this Aryan dream singing German marching songs. Or,' a better explanation, 'he had a chance to be a soldier, like the dads.'

'No, I mean why do any of it? A clever boy who will escape from the Dale?'

'Dunno.' Still puzzled. 'School of life? The opposite of books? His mum and dad are dead keen on his learning.' He tucked her arms tighter around his middle. 'I think his dad's away a lot. The driving. The war.'

'But most fathers were away in the war.'

'Perhaps most of their sons are like Derek and his mates.' *A clever-clever answer.* 'Nah. But the papers are always talking about bad lads, the need for more discipline, perhaps there's something to it. Or maybe—'

'It wasn't you, if that's what you were going to say.' It had been. 'He and his friends attacked Senkus before you even met them.'

'But I had it, all the pieces of what happened, back in December, and I forgot all about it. Like the canal wiped it from my mind.'

'Richard, you could have stopped nothing. You are just unhappy because you like everything neat and tidy. But nothing about this is neat and tidy, why he did it, why he *would* do it. Everything is very . . . unsatisfactory. Like life.' He could almost hear her shrug. 'In fact, the only neat and tidy part is the detecting. That is *very* neat. You are very clever, Richard,' she patted his temple, 'even if you now want to tell yourself you are very stupid.'

'Clever,' muttered Bourton, 'bullying a twelve-year-old boy, in his bedroom, in front of his mum and dad. He crumbled right away. Might have wanted to be the tough guy, but—'

'And you know what that shows?' Leaning up and forward so she could see his face. 'He is clever and mostly good. A bad boy would lie and lie and lie, a stupid one would not see the chance you were offering. You have done the right thing. You have. Now, think how to put him back on the right path.'

★

25 March 1953

Side by side, scoffing their last egg of the month – whipped up into Anna's 'scruffy *pain perdu*' – the seven o'clock news as a backdrop to the clatter of knives and forks; 'Queen Mary is dead.' Bourton pushed back his chair as if to stand. *You can't stand to attention at your own breakfast table, you idiot.* 'The consort of King George the Fifth, mother of King Edward the Eighth and King George the Sixth, and grandmother of the Queen, died in her sleep, at Marlborough House, at twenty minutes past ten o'clock last night. She was in her eighty-sixth year and had been suffering from a gastric illness.'

'I'm sorry, Richard.' Concern, sympathy on Anna's face as she spoke over the announcer. 'Is she – was she—'

'Well, she's – you know – the Queen,' he stammered. *This is daft, normal people don't want to stand to attention.* 'She was the Queen when I was born, Queen Mary, and I suppose – well, she was popular . . .'

'. . . the discovery of several bodies in Rillington Place, Notting Hill,' the announcer continued. They both stared at the wireless. 'The Metropolitan Police would like to interview Mr John Reginald Halliday Christie, one of the residents of the house, in connection with the discovery.'

'Bloody hell,' said Bourton, in wonder. 'I never heard my ground on the news before. I meant to tell you last night but we nodded off. I spent the whole turn at Rillington Place, your man Christie—'

'I thought he was dead.' Anna, staring at the wireless, 'I thought you killed him, in the canal.'

'Look,' annoyance and surprise giving edge to his voice, 'I didn't kill anyone. Savvy?' She wouldn't turn to meet his eyes. 'I won't take it from coppers as a joke, let alone my wife meaning it. I am not a murderer.'

'Murder, killing in a fight,' she shrugged, 'just different words.'

'They're not and you know it.'

'Besides, you can't murder a Christie. You put him down, a diseased dog.'

'I didn't kill him, he drowned himself. And it wasn't Christie, it was Widdowson.'

'Who's Widdowson?'

'The Traveller.'

'That was Christie.'

'No, it wasn't. You thought it could be, but it wasn't.'

'But he was.' She nodded at the wireless. 'Or something like it. Did he say a number of bodies?'

'At least five, by the time I came off duty.' *How could she think it had been Christie in the canal?* 'There were three he'd killed in the last two, three months and stuffed in an alcove, his wife under the floorboards, probably someone in the garden too.' *Perhaps none of us mentioned Widdowson's name around her before we were banished to Ampney.* Anna looked sick, skin grey-tinged and tight over her glorious cheekbones. 'You all right, love?'

'You should have killed him,' getting up.

'Christie?' Baffled. Her silence said yes. 'Whatever for?'

She gestured at the wireless. 'This.'

'But – but . . .' He was so astonished he didn't know what to say first. 'I had no – no suspicion, no evidence, and – and this is London, not Shanghai. And what do you take me for? Going around killing people 'cos they deserve it?'

'You were a soldier.' She reached under the bed and pulled out his tin trunk.

'Yes, fighting other soldiers – then. But now I'm a policeman and I uphold the law.'

'Which allows your Traveller to murder and murder.' She stood up, holding the Wehrmacht bayonet in its scabbard. 'And now he is out there.' She stowed the weapon in her handbag. The pommel jutted out. 'And we know he is dangerous. He knows me, so I will go out protected.' She nodded at her plate as she reached for her jumper. The colour hadn't returned to her cheeks. 'You can have my breakfast. I think I will go to work early.'

'But – but . . .' She pulled her red coat from the wardrobe. 'What's going on?'

'I am going to work.' She put on the coat and picked up her handbag. 'You will be home at about ten, yes? Tea will be ready.' She kissed him. 'Have a good day, Richard.'

He watched her walk to the door, pinned to his chair by the freak wave of her logic. *This is like that fight over the fire in December. I've done something and suddenly she's not herself.* 'Love.' She stopped and turned, hand on the doorknob. 'Here.' He willed himself upright, lumped over to the trunk, dug out the British spike bayonet he'd carried pointlessly about north-west Europe, and walked over to the door. 'Take this. The socket handle's not much cop, but it's small enough to go in your bag. Without,' he retrieved the German bayonet, 'a swastika showing. We don't want you run in for carrying an offensive weapon.' He kissed her cheek. 'Mind how you go, love.'

*

Christie must die. All the way from the front door to the Caccia where Christie had entered her world, all the way. *Christie must die.* Coffee, toast, a table by the window, the glass unfogged, a milder day, no need to keep wiping with the sleeve: he can see her, the one who got away, and come in, order his tea, sit at her table or the next and gloat – until she pulls the bayonet from her bag and stabs, quick quick quick, no time for him to know anything other than She is killing me . . .

Christie knows that I lie. So Christie must die.

After an hour or so her mind lets her hear the chit-chat. British reserve trampled, by Queen Mary: I hear she could be a stern one, oh, to bury two sons and one as good as dead . . . By Christie: I hear he worked at the Regal, no, the Kensington Park Hotel, no, he kept the books at Rootes, I hear he used to be a policeman, he never . . . And by long-dead Timothy Evans: He did it all right, good British justice – but such a shame, good people . . .

And the more she hears, the more she understands. He won't be coming. He is on the run, far away, or in hiding; he will not be in old haunts like the Caccia Café on Westbourne Grove, sitting next to mad foreign women with bayonets in their handbags and no plan in their heads beyond kill kill kill. But he will be gloating about the women he has killed, three of whom would be alive today if Anna Bourton had told the truth.

And freed of the duty to look out of the window, she lowers her head, wills tear ducts closed, and thinks, Fool, fool, this secret makes you a fool, a foolishness that others pay for—

'Never mind, dear.' A hand reaches across the gap between tables and pats her forearm – a liver-spotted hand, beautiful pale skin over veins and knuckles in relief, the anatomical detail of the nearly dead. 'It'll be all right in the end, you'll see.' Anna has enough sense of what is required of her to nod. 'And d'you know what? There isn't much in this world that isn't made better by a nice cup of tea.' She nods again. 'Though,' the voice a whisper now, 'there's no chance of that here. So what do you say to a cup of coffee?'

'That would be lovely,' Anna says, looking up into a long, thin face, younger than the hand, and trying for the brave smile you are supposed to offer in Britain when resolved to give up your tears. 'Very kind of you.' The smile comes.

But so does the thought: *Those women are gone, bodies now, nothing I can do, walk on. But my lies . . .*

All he has to do is get caught. And talk. Confessing to attacking me means asking why I went. Telling why I went leads to the lies on my forms. The lies on my forms lead to expulsion, and the war, and the comfort house. And the comfort house destroys everything – Richard, this life, a future. The logic does not fail.

So my lies are still safe. As long as Christie stays silent . . .

★

Late into the office, but composed, with a good lie – heel broke, the austerity shoes in red, finding a decent pair nowadays . . . – to meet the spring rush. Wives calling in before window-shopping, husbands taking time during lunch or out of the office, enquiries or even the odd booking for a summer break from rationing, sooty cities, white-collar suburbia. But in the space between, whenever Anna and one of the other girls are free, the questions: You ever see him in the street and that? Hello, Mr Christie? Ever meet him? Is your Dick on it? I bet the police are worried about that man they hanged . . .

It takes an act of will for Anna to talk about him as if he is a stranger. And all day, even when they are framing a nice picture of Queen Mary – a cascade of jewels, a belle-époque dress all ruffles and crinoline, severe face daring the country not to eat its greens – with black ribbon over one corner, Christie Christie Christie. The day is without end.

And Christie is nowhere to be seen.

★

17.20. She can't mean it. Three hours into another turn keeping the crowd away from 10 Rillington Place, he found himself focusing on the assumption that had pinned him to his chair that morning. *She can't think I'm a killer, can't be angry with me for not killing, can't think I'm some comic-strip avenger, ahead of the law. Can't. Because it's not me. And she knows it. Knows me. Knows—*

But I'd have killed Widdowson.

Only I didn't. He shook his head. *Rather not work out if I'm really a killer.* He scanned the crowd: boiler suits, bowler hats, chars with pinafores, kids with satchels, straw-haired navvies just off the Holyhead boat, biddies in charabanc best. *Roll up, roll up, come and see the House of Death! Nothing to see! Nothing to do!*

'This place,' he muttered to John Absalom, whose scarred face seemed to keep the crowd further from his section of the cordon, 'needs one of them WVS mobile canteens.'

'Christie prob'ly killed all the WVS an' cooked 'em,' Absalom muttered back, rocking up on his toes. 'The ghouls will have to go to Mancini's like everyone else.'

If she knows me, how can she hold it against me for not killing him? It's not as if she'd given me a job to do and I'd forgotten.

Or did she?

'Let me get to my own front door, for crying out loud!' An angry voice from the back of the crowd, where heads were turning and moving aside. 'It's bad enough living in this dump without all you lot—'

'Make some room, ladies and gentlemen,' called Bourton, in his parade-voice, 'or I'll make it, with my big boots.'

Did Anna think that was what she'd sent me out to do – to kill? When she must know I'm not the killer type?

A skinny, thirtyish man in a stained jacket and open shirt was ejected onto the pavement in front of Bourton like spit from a hot skillet. 'Which number do you live in, Mr . . .?' asked Bourton.

'Swinney. Ted Swinney. Just here, number nine,' turning to look at the crowd barring the way to his door, 'ground floor.'

Anna must have thought he was enough of a threat that I'd have to kill him. But how could she know that?

'I'll help you through, sir,' said Bourton. But the door of number 10 opened, and as someone came out, the front of the crowd pushed forward and Swinney fell onto his bottom, then his back, arms up in defence as feet tangled in his legs and gawkers tried not to trip. Bourton stepped over him, chest butting an excursion lady into retreat, arms barring the way to stop him getting trampled, bellowing, 'Everyone back! Everyone back!' Absalom grabbed his left hand, restoring the cordon, adding his own voice to the coppers' chorus. A skinny teenage boy and his bony-shouldered girl were jammed against Bourton's chest, the boy glancing at the barrier of the coppers' arms, then bending his knees as if about to duck under them and get through the cordon. 'Don't you dare!' Bourton bellowed, forgetting their heads were six inches apart. The lad flinched and covered his ear as if a firecracker had gone off.

'Bloody hell, that's a foghorn.' Swinney's voice. 'Wake the dead with that.'

'You all right, sir?' called Bourton, over his shoulder.

'He seems fine, Bourton.' DI Knox's voice. 'Dust you off, sir, good as new,' probably to Swinney. 'All under control, 491?'

'Seems so, sir.' Everyone had found their feet and some space, the boy peering over Bourton's left arm, the girl slightly turned to one side and looking over his right. The lad's wide-lapelled jacket and her tightly tucked white jumper suggested they were out for the evening. 'Couldn't you take her to the pictures?' Bourton asked the boy. 'Because there really is nothing to see here.'

'Bleeding hell,' said Swinney from behind. 'The fog. It was you yelling for Christie in the middle of the night, banging on his door. Barton.' A prod between the shoulder blades. 'Why didn't you arrest him then? Eh?' A jab now. 'Eh?'

'That, sir, is assaulting a police officer.' Bourton looked over his shoulder to see Knox pin Swinney to the doorway. 'I think you need to calm down.'

★

17.35. From the top deck every tenth man looked like Christie to Anna: a little tall, a little thin, a little grey, a little old, a little respectable, a little worn down. *He is London. No one would know what he is. Should I scourge myself because I did not? Yes, because I am not London. London has not known what I know.*

In the beginning her hand tensed around the bayonet handle with each stooping man in a shabby mackintosh or a balding hat pulled too low. But soon she calmed, left her palm loose around the pipe-like metal, and watched. *So this is stag – the sentry, who will keep the enemy at bay, will kill to save the others. Or to save myself.*

'Notting Hill Gate.' The conductor, in a barrow-barker tenor. The evening paper boards outside the tube station shouted both 'Queen Mary Dies' and 'Notting Hill House of Death – Suspect Sought'. But the hubbub was all about Christie. *Decades of visiting the sick and launching ships and smiling smiling smiling, and at your death all your subjects want to know about is a murderer. The wages of service . . .*

Christie. Calmer now about him. She could think, idea following idea in logical sequence. *I can find him. He needs to impress, but who will be awed by this shabby man with his wrong words and airs? The poor, the unschooled, fools who want to believe. And there are twenty places in the Hill and Dale where they go.* She stood up and staggered down the aisle. *If I am to find him, what am I doing on a bus? He cannot have stayed here. But if I don't check the places where he can find silly women like me, I cannot be sure. And night is when he would come out.*

She pulled the request cord at the bottom of the stairs and stepped onto the platform, face in the chilly, petrol-scented air. *I cannot bring those women back. But I can silence him.*

82

18.35. 'He's cooling his heels in a cell.' Knox, drawn and tired, standing by the canteen table, rubbing the bridge of his nose with tea-coloured fingertips. 'We'll walk him home about midnight, crowd should have gone and there won't be any press for him to tattle to. Whether the threat of the assault charge will stop him talking tomorrow . . .' Knox sat opposite Bourton. 'Now, why were you after Christie?'

'That Murder Squad business.' A nod. 'He gave me a lead. I went round during the fog, about three in the morning, to run a name by him. Turned out to be our man, sir.'

'Did you go in?' *How much do I say?* 'Not a time for evasions. Did you go in?'

Bourton shook his head. 'He wouldn't let us past the door, sir.'

'Us?'

Swinney can't have seen Rex. 'Expression, sir.'

'Oh, yes. But I'll come back to that. Did you go in on any other occasion?'

'The day before. A man answering his description had been hawking a breathing apparatus at a local surgery, which fitted the MO of our suspect. Christie was also known to offer this type of assistance.'

'Anyone see you?'

'Mrs Christie.'

'Who's dead. Anyone else?'

Bourton shrugged. 'Visibility wasn't five yards.'

'Anyone hear you?'

'Perhaps.' Awkwardly: 'He ran when he saw me, sir. I thought he was my man. I had to take a door down to get to him.'

'The one in the kitchen?' Nod. 'See anything suspicious in there?'

'I ran through, walked back. It was a Dale kitchen.'

'In the garden?'

'Couldn't see my feet, sir.' Bourton looked at his brew. 'Might have stood where I found the bone later.'

Knox nodded. Bourton could almost hear cogs whirring. 'How was Mrs Christie?' A flicker of a smile. 'Apart from being alive.'

'Happy to see her husband in trouble. They were having a row. He'd collected his cards, said he'd find another job easily. She made some jibe, I heard a smack. Though there was no sign on her when she opened the door.'

'She handed in her laundry on the twelfth, after the fog, so that wasn't the row that killed her. All right.' Knox nodded. 'How was Christie?'

'Shifty.' Bourton fiddled with his mug handle. 'He said he'd run because he'd pinched some money at work, thought I was after him for that. He got cagey when I asked about the breathing apparatus.'

'Did you see it?'

Bourton shook his head. 'Said it was being fixed. Something had broken.'

'Did you push him?'

'Didn't need to. I knew he wasn't our man. He was wrong for it, the fog didn't agree with him, his apparatus was wrong.'

'But you never saw it.'

'He described it, it used a big oxygen cylinder he'd get from Lee's, whereas our man packed his in a sample case.'

'And you believed him?' Bourton nodded. 'Why?'

'He . . . was wrong for it.'

Knox's eyes watered. 'Did you write any of this down?' Bourton shook his head. 'Crime book, formal statement, request for assistance, interview notes, daily action, Incident Book, Occurrence?'

'Nothing, sir.' Defensive. 'It was all supposed to be sort of under the radar, sir,' Knox's focus now more like a stare. 'If it hadn't been, I would have been stopped and we'd never have found Widdowson. I mean, our man. Sir.'

'You'd never have called on Christie, either.'

'And that's now a crime?'

'Some might say that not nicking him then would be.'

'What for?' *If anyone should have nicked Christie, shouldn't it have been you, in 1949?* 'Sir, I was looking for a man who killed people in

their homes, who'd nip across London through the fog like, like . . .'
not a wraith, for Christ's sake '. . . an eel.'

Knox waved it away. 'I'm not after you. But you called on Christie
in the course of a murder inquiry weeks before he murdered at least
three women. You stood in the garden where he buried at least one
body. You spoke to one of the women he later killed.' He rubbed his
nose again. 'All of that could be difficult to explain away.'

★

19.05. 'Who you lookin' for, darlin'?' The man is forty or so, balding,
open face, birthmark on his neck; the question is friendly without
being lewd. He and his friends seem spare, scrubbed, in clean, much-
repaired clothes. *Working men sent out by their wives. Respectable men,
in a respectable pub.*

'Reginald Christie,' Anna says, as she steps around the group to
look beyond it at a gaggle of men over by the fireplace. No prostitutes,
no desperate roof-for-a-night girls: this is definitely not Christie terri-
tory.

The group laughs. 'You an' the whole country,' says the spokesman.
'I'm not sure he's a man with what you might call prospects.' They
laugh so hard their beer starts slopping onto the floor. 'Still,' he raises
his glass, 'I wish you joy of it, young miss.'

Back on the pavement she pauses, looking east along Westbourne
Grove, through a crooked avenue of streetlamps and shop lights and
Londoners leading evening lives. Half a mile from the Caccia Café
but she does not know this ground like the Dale, cannot guess which
pubs or cafés to try. He will not be on a main road, she tells herself,
or near the Dale, or somewhere respectable, and everywhere here
is too public, too proud. Her left hand grips the knuckleduster in
her hip pocket and her right the socket bayonet in her bag. *Time to
walk.*

★

20.50. 'What were you doing in there, then?' Bert nodded at CID,
heaving with coppers working on the Christie case amid a head-height

nicotine haze. The din of typewriters and yelled phone calls was wearing, even on the landing.

'Knox.' Bourton was desperate for an audience. 'Been parked outside his office for two hours, not allowed to talk, shut out of brew runs, listening to CID cross wires and miss clues. Says he wants me where he can see me, where I can't say or do anything that might put me in the witness box at Christie's trial. The neck of it.'

'And you're good in a witness box, you are,' said Bert, cheerfully. 'Don't take it hard, young Dick. Won't be about you.' *But it obviously is.* Bert leaned in and adopted his conspiratorial whisper. 'The brass are headless chickens about something and I bet it's that Christie. They're up in the SDI's office with the door shut, the CID guv'nor's line is permanently engaged, someone's been placing calls with the international operator,' finger alongside the nose, 'and you know who went up to Brass Alley a few minutes ago? The detective super. Now, if the head of F Div CID has got off his chair, then you can bet there's a proper flap on.' He leaned back. 'That Christie. Proper trouble.'

'You know him, then?' Bert looked puzzled and shook his head. 'Then . . .' *Don't go into his logic ambush or you'll never get out.* 'Never mind.' He glanced into CID. Knox was still on the phone, his back to his squad. 'I thought you had Beat Four.'

'I am on a late break, which, being an experienced officer of the law, I expect to last until end of turn.' He leaned in again. 'Is your missus in any trouble?'

'Anna?' *Christ, someone's found that bayonet.* 'Not that I know of.'

'Well, that's good to hear. Fine woman, your missus. You're a lucky man,' nodding. Then silence. *Forgotten what you had to say?*

Prompting: 'Do you think she's in trouble, Bert?'

'I don't know, young Dick, I don't. Only Jack Tullow was asking me about her, what I knew, where she was from and that. I think he was trying to do it on the QT but I wasn't born yesterday. So, with your leave, I was extorting her virtues.'

Bourton, floundering: 'So she hasn't been stopped or anything?'

'No,' Bert said slowly, as if it was a stupid question he couldn't respond to. 'Should she be?' Bourton shook his head. 'Good thing too. Fine woman, your missus.'

'She is,' automatically, because he still hadn't worked out her morning outburst and was trying to avoid a verdict by not really thinking about her at all. 'She is.'

★

22.05. Phone box on the Grove. First call, to Rex Athill in Pinner, to warn him that Knox was on the warpath about their visit to Rillington Place and apologise for saying he hadn't been on his own. 'Just keep your own head down,' advised the DC. 'I'm a big lad, can look after myself.' Next call, to Div, and Norman Gudgeon – a Peel House acquaintance whose typing skills had condemned him to clerical rather than a beat – to find out why the brass were in a flap. He wasn't in, so the third call was to Ma Gudgeon's in Harrow; according to Norm, the last he'd heard at clock-off after the early worm was that the detective super was planning to stay well out of everything to do with Rillington Place, on the grounds that Notting Hill could clean up its own mess.

He put the receiver back on the cradle. *Right. Home. Or I could stay here. Or, like a normal bloke, have a few in the pub, go home, slap her for this morning, wake tomorrow with everyone knowing where they stand.* He smiled. *Or not wake at all courtesy of a bayonet in my ribs.* He bumped open the door with his hip. *Or I could just go for a walk.* He shook his head. *You really don't want to have to decide what to say about this morning.*

'Ah, sod it.' The moment of duck-and-cover had passed. *I want to be home, boots off, feet up, scran on the plate and a sporting chance of a jump after lights out; and if that means a row with the woman I love but at times do not bleeding understand, well, that's marriage.*

Only she wasn't at home. The room was dark, the ring and the fireplace cold, her work shoes and bag missing from the wardrobe; she hadn't been back since clocking off. He briefly mourned the tea she hadn't cooked for him, the warm fug she hadn't built up, the domestic snapshot denied him on walking in; only afterwards did it occur to him to worry about where she might be. Yet as he removed his boots, and remembered how she'd left that morning with a bayonet in her bag and her knuckles in her coat, he realised the worry was misplaced. *You're peeved she hasn't told you, not frightened she's come to harm.*

Thinking makes my brain hurt. And then: *We're all arsy-versy; a wife pissed off that her husband wasn't a murderer, and a husband not worried about his wife. Anyone might think we were supposed to be Bonnie and Clyde.* He put the kettle on, picked up his Rules of Evidence – *Start thinking about promotion early, my son* – and read a little about the Larceny Act 1916 while his brew mashed. But the armchair was too comfortable, and just before he nodded off, with the Rules open on his tummy and his tea still steaming on the Formica, he concluded, as if he'd just staggered to the end of a long and involved argument, *Normal marriages aren't like this.*

83

07.00. A very sorry breakfast, with no eggs, milk or marge; two thick slices of Ministry bread, dry-fried on the ring to create the illusion of toast, with his mum's raspberry jam, so little sugar it's effectively stewed fruit. At least the tea is strong, if the wrong colour. Anna sort-of apologises for the food, says little about last night ('Just walking, Richard, all safe because of your *baïonnette magnifique*'), and doesn't mention his failure to kill someone he suspected of nothing at all. As they sit, supposedly listening to the news, the words 'What was all that about then?' sit so far forward on Bourton's tongue he's afraid they'll flop out every time he takes a bite.

But as the food goes down and the opportunity to speak gradually disappears, he realises he won't ask her, perhaps ever. Because she won't answer? Might say something he doesn't like or can't grapple with? Or because he wants everything to be all right, and there's no way that picking apart a reaction so immediate, heartfelt, *wrong* can end well? Richard Arthur Bourton, he tells himself as he uses a goodbye kiss to check the bayonet in her bag is properly sheathed, niceness will be the death of you.

★

07.50. Marble Arch: penultimate stop. She pulls her stockings away from the rawer parts of her feet, knowing the shoes will bite anyway, before slipping them back on. Bag, strap over shoulder, right hand on the bayonet handle; stand. *I am going to search Christie country in these?* She clumps down the aisle to the stairs, feet rigid, braced for promised pain. *Choosing these shoes was my subconscious saying, 'Stop the hunt,' because London is too big, with too many dowdy places, our paths will never meet. So for all your calm, rational thinking you are still a foolish woman, driven by emotion, the unconscious.*

She steps onto the pavement, already looking for the bus that will take her beyond Oxford Circus and save her feet. *But if I am not to hunt him, what do I do?*

*

10.05. Morning brew-making in the tiny kitchen at Tours and Trains, Tor opening the off-ration tea Pattison junior has smuggled back from India in his Merchant Navy kitbag, Anna warming the teapot. 'Where is the beggar?' Mag sticking her head in to join the Christie chat. 'That's what I want to know.'

'France, I reckon.' Tor. 'That's where I'd run.'

'You speak French.' Mag. 'Will he?' The kettle whistles.

'The papers say he was in France in the first war,' says Tor. Anna turns off the ring.

'So was my dad,' Mag again, 'and all he can say is "*Vin blong*" and "*Voulez-vous mademoiselle?*"' Anna fills the teapot. 'How far will that get him?'

'Mrs Bourton?' Vi, calling in false-genteel. 'A customer would like your help.'

Thank God. 'It needs a stir,' she tells the other two, and slips out.

Vi's customer is on the far side of her desk, a fiftyish man with greying sandy hair, pinstripes and a belonging-tie. He stands and extends a reddened, scratched but clean hand, like a gardener's. 'Patrick Morrow.'

She shakes. 'Anna Bourton.'

'Mr Morrow,' Vi indicates, 'is arranging a trip to visit a friend in Austria and was noting that we seemed to speak a lot of languages here. I mentioned that we even ran to Russian and Chinese and he wondered if you might be able to help with something.'

'Of course.' Anna offers her professional smile. 'My Russian is rather rusty.'

'And your Chinese?' He has an accent – Scottish, Irish, she is not sure. 'My sister's married to a planter out east and this came with her latest letter this morning.' He passes over a folded piece of paper. 'Unfortunately she didn't send a translation.'

Anna opens the sheet. Five lines of ideographs, crudely and unevenly printed in black, with some ink absorbed by the coarse paper, and rough holes in the centre of the top and bottom of the sheet. She immediately feels a chill. 'Where did she get it, if I may ask?'

'One of the trees on the estate. They've been getting a few of them of late.'

'Then I would suggest she move. It is a death threat.' A sharp intake of breath from Vi. 'It is not to them directly – perhaps they have already received those. "Warning," it says.' Anna starts tracking the ideographs across the paper. 'I suppose, "Inasmuch as", this makes no sense but phonetic, it could be "Pork Close" – is her husband fat?'

'He's called Faulkner.'

'Ah. "Pork near". So, "Inasmuch as Faulkner is sentenced to death by the Perak State Committee, Communist Party of Malaya, the Malayan National Liberation Army—"'

'Not "Races"? Aren't the bandits called the Malayan Races Liberation Army?'

'They may be, but that would be a mistake,' she points to two characters, '"*minzu*" can mean "races" but in this context it is "National". This army "warns all running dogs and lackeys of British imperialism that," oh, "association with said Faulkner will expose them to the revolutionary justice of the people of Malaya. Signed, the District Committee."' She hands the sheet back. 'I have seen leaflets of this type before, Mr Morrow, in China and Hong Kong. In my experience they mean what they say. Even if that is a threat to the Chinese people on or near the estate, they probably do want Mr Faulkner dead.'

'Thank you,' says Morrow. He puts the sheet away in a briefcase. 'I think they have all sorts of tough types looking after them.' He looks up and smiles. His teeth seem longer on the right side of his mouth than on the left. 'What luck to find you. You've saved me a trip and endless telephone calls.' He sticks out his hand. 'If ever I am planning a trip to China or the Soviet Union, I shall know exactly where to come.' Anna smiles, knowing he knows it will never happen. A soft-brimmed trilby materialises from under the desk and he shakes Vi's hand too. 'Thank you very much for all your help.'

'Imagine,' says Vi, as Morrow steps into the street, 'finding that near your house.'

'Communists,' says Anna, absently, *That piece of paper has never been on a tree, in a damp climate. Indoors, on a notice-board – an exhibit – perhaps.* 'It is what they are like. Did he book anything?'

'No,' says Vi. 'I'm afraid I couldn't tell him where the Soviet zone begins, which I must look up.' She reaches for a notepad on her desk.

'Pity,' says Anna, thinking, *What was the purpose of that, then?* 'I don't think he will be back.'

84

13.35. 'You decent, Bourton?' He looks up from buttoning his tunic. Tullow's face is severe, his tone clipped. Chat stops. A brace of half-dressed coppers out of Tullow's sight line shoot Bourton looks of concern. Tullow moves close, casts an inspection eye. 'Do up your belt. Hitchcock, pull him round properly and get that lint off his shoulders.' Bourton does as he is told. *This is not good.*

Hitchcock pulls his tunic tight and tucks the excess under the belt at the back. 'You'll be all right, chum,' he whispers. He steps around to brush off the lint, looks into his eyes. 'Die Hard.' He steps back.

Tullow nods. 'You'll do. Follow me.'

On the stairs, Tullow stops, steps aside, as Rex Athill clatters down the flight, sees Bourton, halts, confusion and something tight – anger? – on his face. 'We did the right thing, chum,' as if Bourton has said they didn't. 'I don't regret it. Not a bit.' He sticks his hand out. 'Good luck, Dick.' He nods, then trots down the stairs and into the corridor to the vehicle yard without a look back.

'Come on, 491.' Tullow climbing again.

'Sergeant?' Bourton, stricken, holding on to the banister. *What have they done to Rex? And if they can bugger a DC . . .* 'Am I on the dab?' Despite being blasé about the prospect all those months ago, now he really wants the answer to be no.

Tullow turns, takes pity. 'I didn't tell you to bring your bonnet. That should tell you everything you need to know.' *So they're not marching me in on a formal disciplinary.* Tullow gestures upstairs with his head. 'Get a move on.' Bourton takes the four more flights up to Brass Alley on Tullow's heels, three stairs at a time, anger growing, driving his legs. *Give it your best shot, you bastards.*

Tullow opens the door marked 'Chief Inspector A. C. F. Millichip BEM, Kensington Sub-Division' – a room Bourton has never been into before, home to a man he's met just twice – and announces him. Bourton sees Millichip, straight-backed behind his desk, shoulders squared, *He looks pretty formal to me*, and walks in, a confident half-march, halting at ease in the middle of the floor. 'Afternoon, sir.'

'Bourton.' Millichip's flat country face is stern but there's no venom in his eyes. *Got that famous mean streak under control, then. So perhaps this won't be so bad after all.*

Millichip waits for Tullow to take a chair by the window against a backdrop of one of the Grove's blackened plane trees. He points at his desktop. 'Here there are three documents.' His Yorkshire delivery turns the last word into three. 'One is formal notification of your summary dismissal from the Metropolitan Police' – *What?* – 'for failing to meet the standards expected of the office of constable. One is your voluntary resignation, with immediate effect, from the Metropolitan Police. The third is your attestation to the Malaya Police, in the rank of lieutenant.' Bourton knows his jaw has slackened, that he must look like a drooling fool, but he is trying to keep up. 'This . . . discussion will end your service in the Metropolitan Police. If you resign, your conduct sheet will read "Exemplary". If you are dismissed, it will read "Unsatisfactory". With all the implications for future employment that that might present.

'Resign, and sign this third document,' Millichip pushes it across the desktop, 'you will be on a Constellation to Singapore on the twenty-eighth of March, Saturday,' *That's the day after tomorrow!* 'accompanied by your wife who, according to the Colonial Office, is to be offered a job in government. You may then return to the Metropolitan Police after a period of not less than six months, in the office of constable, your probationary service being deemed complete, and your previous conduct sheet applying. If you are dismissed, or do not sign this document, you will be recalled to the colours from the Army Emergency Reserve for a period of not less than six months and embark, also on Saturday, on a troopship, the *Empire*—'

'I'm not in the AER,' Bourton blurts, fixing on the graze not the wound.

'You are now.'

'I'm in the Regular Reserve,' not letting it go, 'you can't just sign me up—'

'You will embark on the *Empire Fowey*,' Millichip returns to his speech, 'also for Malaya. The posting will be unaccompanied.'

Bourton's mind is gradually focusing on the first shock. 'You're chucking me out.' He's embarrassed he can't think of anything cleverer to say.

'If you choose not to resign – yes.'

'But you can't – I mean, don't I get a hearing, charges, a defence?'

'No. Your probation is being terminated.'

'What for?'

'Unsatisfactory conduct.'

'Which is?'

'Assaulting a fellow officer.'

'Who?'

'Police Constable 824 Norris D. W.'

'When?'

Millichip looked down. 'December the eighth, 1952.'

'That business in the vehicle yard? I barely touched the skiving deadweight.' Anger breaks through the bafflement but Millichip remains impassive. 'And it's not as if I didn't have reason. Sergeant Tullow saw – you saw, Sergeant – what he did to my tunic.'

'Bourton,' Tullow, 'you're missing the point. When you walk out of this room you are out of the Met for six months. That's all. You come back as a fully-fledged copper, nothing on your record, a couple of months before your probation would have been up.'

'If I make it back. They've got a bloody war on there.'

'And probably with a hundred quid in pocket – double the pay, tax free, missus earning . . . Or you might want to stay – a house, probably a maid or a nanny, it's a good life.'

'And if I don't want to go to Malaya?'

'You're going,' says Millichip, flatly, 'on your own, on an infantry sergeant's pay, or with your wife, on a police lieutenant's. Refuse to sign the attainder and miss the trooper, you'll be absent without leave. Which, when the redcaps pick you up, will mean cell time, probably a reduction in rank, and then Malaya. Alone.' Millichip's face softens a little. 'You don't seem the over-the-hill type to me, Bourton.'

Bourton is silent, absorbing part of what he hears; more might get through eventually, but most is running off into a gutter. They are waiting for him to say something, but his mind fixes on Millichip's ribbons, which indicate he's only ever been a copper so has no right to talk about what kind of soldier Sergeant R. A. Bourton MX might be. The best he can do, summoning stray brain cells and knowing it sounds like acceptance, is 'It's done?'

Millichip nods. 'It's done.'

Bourton suddenly finds some nerve. 'This is bollocks. I don't want to go to Malaya and you can't make me.' He winces inside at how childish it sounds.

'We can,' says Millichip, 'and we will.'

'Look, Bourton,' Tullow standing to make his point, 'this can be a step up. There's a job in Special Branch there if you want it. You're intelligence-trained.'

'And the war in Malaya,' a voice from behind, 'is an intelligence war.' Bourton twitches in surprise and turns. A narrow-shouldered man in his late forties, with a large, mostly balding head and clever eyes behind heavy-framed specs, gets up from the armchair tucked into the corner of the room. He sticks out his hand. 'I'm Oliver Hopkirk, Mr Bourton. I look after police issues at the Colonial Office.' Bourton shakes, purely a reflex. 'I'm the man who'd interview you if you came in via the more conventional recruiting path.'

'Mr Hopkirk,' Bourton says politely. *Good manners? Now?*

'You've seen the advertisements, they're crying out for blokes like you.' Tullow. 'You do six months, get experience you'd never get here and you're set up when you come back.' His arms are wide, *You'd turn this down?*, an uncharacteristically showy gesture.

Gears finally engage in Bourton's brain. 'You're sending me to war.'

'Your track record,' Millichip still unemotional, 'suggests you might be suited to policing somewhere you can shoot people.'

'They can shoot me. They give coppers grenades there. Coppers shouldn't need grenades. For Christ's sake, I'm a married man, my wife says no risks.'

'Then don't take any.' Tullow again. 'You can say where you go. My chum in the Branch has a safe job for you,' Tullow continues, 'all office or HQ, using your training.'

'A man to be reckoned with, Superintendent Barratt.' Hopkirk.

'We've talked about you,' Tullow again, 'and he's keen.' Bourton is clearly meant to say, 'Yes, please,' and look eager, because the usually remorseless sergeant seems surprised. 'Look, I mentioned you because I thought it would be a fit, set you up for the autumn, but if it doesn't suit, there's stores, marine police, normal CID—'

'If it's so great, you join.'

'Bourton,' Millichip impatient now, 'it's done. You choose. Dismissal,' he pushes the first form, 'resignation,' the second, 'opportunities,' the third. 'Your call-up papers aren't here but they'll issue them as soon as I ring.' Hand on the phone. 'Do I need to?'

They're bustling me. His rational brain is engaging now and he realises they're denying him time to think, argue, fight. He shakes his head, sees Millichip relax, points to say, 'Nothing's decided, chum.' *Slow them down.* 'Why send me away? Won't the sack do?'

'Your conduct is prejudicial to public confidence in the police,' says Millichip.

'Eh?'

'Your visits to ten Rillington Place, before Reginald Christie is believed to have murdered at least four women, and after he is believed to have murdered another two, put the Metropolitan Police in a prejudicial position.'

'And CID getting an innocent man hanged doesn't?' Millichip and Tullow's expressions do not change. He tries another tack. 'Why six months?'

'There is a feeling,' Millichip sounds as if he's not used to circumspection, 'that the difficulty passes once Christie has been hanged. Six months should be plenty.'

'So this is all because of those two visits to Rillington Place?' Neither will answer. A penny drops. 'That's why Rex is in the soup.' Millichip blinks. 'Because he was with me when the neighbour woke up. What are you doing to him? You can't sack him.'

'He is choosing a secondment to either the British Guiana or British Honduras police,' Millichip, deliberately, 'three months, unaccompanied, with promotion to DS on his return.'

'Send me where he goes.'

'Malaya,' Hopkirk, 'has a State of Emergency.' *So?* 'People who ask questions deemed to be prejudicial to security – such as by querying a police officer's past record – can be detained or deported.'

'So what happens to anyone asking questions about Rex?'

'Nothing,' Millichip, 'but we don't think there'll be any. No one has identified him by name. His secondment is,' he searches for a word, 'more pro-phy-lac-tic.'

'More to the point, Mr Bourton,' Hopkirk again, 'we can only offer you Kenya or Malaya. The Metropolitan Police has asked us, at very short notice, for a favour, and we are happy to grant it. But it must be worth our while. An experienced detective is an asset in any colony's police force. But you are a probationer with . . . chequered police service.'

'What do you know?' Angry now. 'We'd never have got near Widdowson—'

'Bourton . . .' A warning tone from Millichip: *Hopkirk isn't meant to know.*

'And there was Granger.'

'Perhaps,' Hopkirk smiles in apology, 'I have been given the short-hand version of your, what, sixteen or seventeen months as a police officer?' The smile is artificial now. 'However, your army service is exactly the kind of experience that police forces in shooting wars are looking for. Then I understand that your wife reads and speaks Chinese and served as an auxiliary in the HKP. Given the black hats in Malaya are mostly Chinese and government is chronically short of Chinese speakers, my department felt she could be extremely useful.'

'This is nothing to do with my wife.' Bourton stabs the desk with a finger. 'Leave her—'

'Come on, Dick,' Tullow, suddenly familiar, 'after all that time apart, you'll leave her behind?' *How does he—* 'After all it took to marry her?' *Bert.*

'If you're going away,' Hopkirk, 'then Mrs Bourton is very much part of the picture. I think your superiors hope that her being offered the prospect of work of genuine importance would act as an induce-ment to you.'

'And if she says she won't go?'

'You go without her.' Millichip.

'What if she doesn't want this job you've all organised without a by-your-leave?'

'She stays here.' Hopkirk. 'She's only getting in with the government job.' He had the grace to look regretful. 'Emergency regs, I'm afraid.'

Anger is popping up all over Bourton's body, like bubbles in Yank beer, and he focuses his gaze on Millichip, a hard stare. *I want to pull your head off and ram it up your arse.* The chief inspector stares back. Bourton turns to Tullow. *And you – I thought you were all right.* The sergeant remains impassive. Bourton shakes his head. 'You can't play God like this. This is my life, my wife's life. You don't own me.' He knows he sounds as if he's given up, they've won, but the anger has to go somewhere, and he doesn't loathe these men enough to hit them. 'You just don't. You know how long I been in Britain since June 'forty-four? Two and a half years. Out of nine. And now you're packing me off—'

'Bourton.' Millichip, hard, authoritative. Enough. 'It's for your own good.' Bourton snorts. 'Stay and your name will be public property. Swinney can talk to the papers any time he chooses. Christie can talk on the stand. You will be known as the man who could have stopped a murderer before he killed another four women, but didn't. However, if you go where the papers can't find you, Swinney is just another neighbour telling tall stories about the House of Death, and Christie's a defendant lying for his life.'

Bourton can think of nothing to say. The injustice of it is squatting in his mind, pushing out any thoughts other than *No one's sending Knox to Malaya.*

'People will think this because it is true. You *could* have stopped Christie before he killed those women. Did you report he'd admitted to having his own breathing device? Did you suggest anyone try to find out why he was so shifty? No. Once you'd got what you wanted, you forgot all about him.'

'But he wasn't a suspect,' Bourton manages.

Millichip leans forward. His neatly barbered hair glistens. *What do you comb into it?* 'An officer walks into a jeweller's, buys a present for his girl, goes on his way. He never notices the man under the counter pointing a Webley at the jeweller's guts. A few minutes later the jeweller's dead and the shop's ransacked. Should the officer have spotted or stopped the robbery? Letter of the law, no. Copper's law, yes. He should have noticed. The jeweller will have been nervous, perhaps sent some signals. It's the copper's job to notice.'

Now Millichip's face is angry, even slightly contemptuous. 'The only reason the Met would have you back after Malaya is that you are, in police terms, a bloody baby, barely responsible for his cock-ups.' *And there's the mean streak.* 'The Met doesn't set much store by probationers because there's not much there to set any store by. And that, 491, is your salvation. Any questions?'

As many as there are hours in the day. Bourton opens his mouth to start when he realises it would be wasted breath. *I'm finished anyway.* More to the point, questions would be protests, a whining refusal to face a big truth Millichip has understood and he hadn't: *Christie was a wrong 'un. I knew it, and I did nothing.*

'You could just have asked me.' Bourton doesn't know where the thought has come from. 'You didn't need all this palaver. Just to go away for a bit, like in December.'

'No, we couldn't,' says Millichip. 'Everyone knows you're a bloody-minded bugger. You'd've just said no.' He pushes the documents forward and uncaps the fountain pen on his blotter. 'Time is up.' He stands up and offers the pen, barrel first. 'Your choice.'

My choice. He looks at Millichip's face, mostly neutral again, apart from a sour set to the mouth, which probably means contempt. *It is my choice.* There's a muscle twitching underneath Millichip's right eye. *Nerves? Of course he'll be nervous – someone's told him to put me on that plane.* And now he reaps the benefits of slowing Millichip down, because he can see what they didn't want him to, weren't planning he'd have the time to work out – that much of this is bluff. He smiles. Millichip pushes the pen at him.

'I'll resign,' says Bourton, 'looks like I've got little choice.' He takes the pen. 'But the rest of it is balls.' He signs the resignation letter, number, rank and full name, a sudden unwanted act, like executing someone when there's a gun to your head. *So then, Met, kaput.*

He has difficulty swallowing, so the next words struggle to get out. 'As for the Malayan Police,' he throws the pen on the blotter, scattering ink across it, and reaches for the form, 'I'll discuss it with Mrs Bourton. I'm not going to make any decision like that without discussing it with the woman who sailed across the world to marry me.'

'I'll need to sign it too, I'm afraid,' says Hopkirk.

'Then I'll come by your office, like a normal recruit.'

'No.' Millichip. 'Sign it now or you get your call-up.'

'Go on, then.' Bourton's gut feels hollow, as if he's nearing a cliff edge and is about to discover the drop. 'Let's get my call-up.' Millichip blinks. 'I don't think you can. I'm not in the AER and you couldn't fake me signing up, not in twenty hours – and even if you could, you're rumbled as soon as *I* pick up a phone.' Millichip pulls out the drawer. 'Which of the missus' referees do I call? General Horrocks? Can have a word with anyone in Parliament, any time he chooses? Or General de Guingand, Monty's old right-hand man, can call the head of the armed forces any time? Bet they've got more army clout than whoever you or your brass got lined up.' Millichip retrieves a piece of paper. Bourton's gut lurches a little. *They couldn't have managed to fix it after all, could they?* 'They weren't happy the way me and the missus got mucked around last time, and that was the army doing the dirty. Imagine how argy they'll be when they find out it's fucking flatfeet trying it on.' *Disloyal sod – a minute out of the Met, and you're already insulting it.* 'We Die-hards stick together.'

Millichip reaches for the phone. 'Please yourself.'

Bourton shrugs. He's looked over the cliff edge and thinks it's a sloping drop to deep water, with lots of bracken to break the fall. 'Anyway, only Parliament can call up the Reserves and they won't pass a law or whatever just for me.' He turns to Hopkirk. 'Perhaps you could jot down the job, and the department, and the salary you think my wife will find so appealing that she'll agree to move to a theatre of military operations, Mr Hopkirk sir.'

'Of course,' he says. He takes out a notebook and starts writing. 'I'll also jot down the number of a chap who can answer questions, should she have them.'

'That's kind of you, sir.' They all watch Hopkirk scribble, Millichip with his hand on the phone, probably hoping for a way out. Bourton shakes his head. 'How could you think you could pull the wool? Fucking woodentops.'

Millichip looks up from the phone. 'Watch your language, Bourton.'

'Or what? You'll sack me?' Hopkirk tears out the sheet of paper and hands it over. 'Thank you, sir.' Bourton turns to Tullow. 'Thanks very much, Sergeant, for talking to your chum. And as for you,' Millichip is still yet to dial, 'try asking nicely next time.' Bourton folds the two pieces of paper and turns to leave. 'Might get what you want that way.' He pauses, hand on the doorknob. 'You may have the authority to run my life as a copper; but everything else – *everything* else – is up to me. And now I'm not a copper,' he opens the door, 'you've got no say at all.'

85

2.20. The locker room is deserted; the rest of the turn has mounted. *That way Millichip gets me out of the door without much chance for anyone to ask questions.* 'Got anything at home?' Tullow asks, one hand on the kit stack. His face is all business. *A nod that I've been given the mucky end of a big shit-stick would be nice.*

'A spare whistle, but I paid for that myself.'

Tullow nods. 'Right, we'll go up, sign it over, you hand over your warrant card, collect your pay and your conduct sheet, you'll be done.' He picks up the top tunic. 'Here, lend me your scissors.' Bourton opens his mending kit and hands them over. Tullow sits, draping the tunic over his whippet's legs. 'These are yours.' He snips through the thread fixing on Bourton's ribbons, runs a thumb over the silver oak leaf at one end, 'Good that you've got a memento of the Met,' then hands over the fabric block. He does the same with the high-collared number-one tunic; when he hands over the second set of ribbons his eyes have softened a little. 'Don't take this Christie stuff too much to heart. Lots of experienced coppers would have done the same. And if you'd just been asking him about his fiddling the books, you'd still be OK. Just your bad luck, that's all.'

Bourton is present enough to be confused. 'What is?'

'The breathing apparatus.' Bourton is still puzzled. 'You don't know.'

'What?'

'The PMs. Two of the women in the alcove died of carbon monoxide poisoning.' Tullow shrugs, *The bullet could have had my name on it.* 'That's the real flap. Bracing Christie is one thing. Doing it about what might have been his murder weapon, before he used it – well, that's another.'

'Bloody hell.' The reaction is automatic. Then, as guilt, anger, and finally his brain kick in, he tries to throw off the burden he's just accepted. 'Look, this isn't my fault.'

'Enough people know that – you won't be getting the blame. But a lot of grief's coming. Some brass,' jerking his thumb at the ceiling, 'want to make themselves feel better.' Finally his eyes show some of the sympathy Bourton has been looking for. 'The offer is real, you know. You should come back. Job's there if you do. Aide to CID, perhaps the Branch, Information Room at the Yard. And it wouldn't be there if they thought this was your fault. But,' his expression hardens again, 'only if you go to Malaya. If you don't, I don't know what they'll do to you, but the job will be out.'

'We'll see.' Bourton smiles sourly, putting the ribbons in his pocket. 'Wife might take agin the Met. The loyal type. Might forbid me to rejoin even if I want to.'

But Tullow has already moved on. 'Right. Let's get you upstairs.'

Bourton picks up his kit. 'What about goodbyes? There are a lot of blokes—'

'We'll sort something out. Ladbroke Arms, tomorrow night. You and Rex Athill. If,' a warning finger, 'you're going to Malaya. If not, then you'd just be resigning for no reason, and that'll set too many hares running – the brass won't want you talking to anyone.' He raises a hand. 'After you, 491.'

★

14.35. Seventeen months after entering Notting Hill nick for the first time, through the vehicle yard, he leaves it, for good, by the front steps. *I'm not skulking for anyone.* But no guard of honour waves him off, no guv'nors or skippers wait to see him gone, and even the blokes he passes on the way out just muster a raised eyebrow or a 'Hello, Dick.' *Rumour mill not been cranked up, then, not yet at least.* He has too much pride to prompt goodbyes by breaking the news himself. But a big, angry part of him wants to stand by the station sergeant's desk and bellow, 'I nicked the Traveller – you could hold the bloody door for me.' He walks away from what was meant to be the rest of his working life. *That went according to plan.*

He starts marching, anger keeping his back straight and his stride long. *I'm not going back. I won't do what they want. I'm going to find a nice factory job, somewhere west, eight till five with overtime, then home to the missus, a garden, kids. No uniforms, no bull, no duty. And they can take their threats and shove them.*

He turns the corner onto Holland Park Avenue. Traffic is blocked as far as the Coronet picture house; he hears loud voices and sees arms being waved on the pavement up ahead. He smiles. *It's all some other bugger's business now.* He walks past the blockage – a cab and an electrician's van locked across the carriageway, with half a dozen busybodies goading the drivers to blows – and boards an eastbound number 7 bus. He settles back in a front-row seat on the top deck, watching London unspool ahead of him through a new, bystander's lens. He lights up, catching sight of McGahern trying to untangle argy opposite Embassy Row. He smiles. *Feel like a truant.*

The boards for the lunchtime editions outside Marble Arch tube – 'Christie Hunt: Latest' – pop his I-don't-care-any-more balloon. *Christie really could drop me in it. Or his brief, to make Christie look good. Either way the Met won't back me up. And my face'll be in the papers, on the newsreels. They'll stare in the shops, cut Anna dead, stop talking when I come into the works canteen.* He shakes his head. *Getting ahead of yourself. He's got to be captured alive, make it to court, think it's in his interest to mention me or put me on the stand before any of this can come true. And how can involving me help him? After all, it shows he had a breathing apparatus. Or, given I never saw it, that he didn't.*

But the weapon doesn't matter – he had four bodies in his house, two more in his garden. He has no defence.

But what about his character? Perhaps his brief will want the jury to know just how helpful the creepy ex-copper could be.

Bourton leans against the window. *Just this what-if leaves me drained and brain-sore.* It has also torn off the nice little bandage – of anger, false cheer, Never-never Land – stuck roughly over the wound of his ejection. Oh, bollocks, he tells himself, I hope Anna can help sort this out. He feels a little lurch of surprise as he realises that he isn't sure she can. *I'm not up to much deciding right now, love.*

And then, thinking about her strangeness over Christie: *Please don't be too mad.*

86

15.40. 'Hey, An, it's the strong arm of the law.'

Anna looks up from the letter she's clattering out. Richard is visible through the front window, smoke in his mouth, arm up as if he's hailing her across a crowded platform. Then he leans against the frame, solid, purposeful, slightly sad – a thug waiting to take part in a robbery, but one unhappy with his lot, who will be redeemed by the love of a good woman by the middle of the third reel. She smiles as she flips up the typewriter carriage. *Strange Richard, who makes everything, even resting, look like a philosophical choice.*

★

'I am no longer a police officer.' She is holding his hands as they sit on a bench in Soho Square, and she thinks the statement is a philosophical scene-setter for 'Why I am unworthy of my warrant card', so she flinches in shock when he turns their knotted fingers to look at his watch and says, 'As of two hours ago, when I signed the papers.' He registers her reaction and hurries on, 'Don't worry.'

'I am not worried. You have made a decision.'

'I mean, the money.'

'You are a clever man, and loyal. You can find a job straight away.' He smiles, rueful, not sad; she must have said the right thing. 'If you want not to be a policeman—'

'It's not that.'

'You have led men. You can do it in a factory, or a big company – you could even go to night classes while I work, make your paper match your brain, and skills.'

'It isn't my choice.' She is too puzzled to respond. 'Well, I mean, it was jump or be pushed. Look, can you let me tell you?'

So she sits, arms rigid with anger – he thinks it's at him, starts to apologise but she waves it away. 'I hate these little, little men, save the Met, they are saving senior officers' arses' – as he explains how that vile *nécrophile*, with his dangling balls and false respectability and garlic mayonnaise, has lit a fuse. She bites back her first reaction – 'You should have killed him' – and waves the angry devotion that goes with her second – 'They have hurt you.' The expression stays even as her mind goes off down little *impasses*, such as *That man threatens my life and squats in my thoughts and now disorders us too*, and *You fastened your soul to this and now you talk of its end as if it happened to someone else. You are truly wasted as a worth-nothing makee-learn flic*. But after a while she wants to move on – *The police is finished, now, done, enough* – and she squeezes his hands to break his flow.

'My love, I am excited – they are, oh,' she searches, 'fleas, but you have your good conduct paper, we find something worthy of you. But now, look, I told Re a few minutes—'

'They want me to go away for six months.' As abrupt as a stubbed toe in the dark. 'And they want you to come with me.' She is silent, thinking, Like Christmas? No, they do not command him any more. 'They've offered me a job. A good one. Six months, then back to the Met if I want it. They say there's a job for you too, using your Chinese.' He hands over a folded piece of paper. 'There's some info there. Only the jobs are in Malaya. And we'd leave on Saturday – they fly us out, even. O' course, I wouldn't go if you wouldn't.'

And to her eternal shame, her first thought is *I'm free! Even if they catch Christie now, first they will care about the bodies he has left behind, so who will bother with half-a-world-away me?* Eternal shame, because it turns out this good job is dangerous, and is good partly because staying behind is worse – court, newspapers, the holding up of an honest, brave, too-dutiful man to public fury and contempt. A good job that will expose him to danger but free her from Christie, fog, the consequences of her lies, give her a comfortable life with a proper house she can fill with the East. And offer her interesting work – 'Clerical Officer Senior Grade, Federation of Malaya Ministry of Defence' is almost certainly not what it sounds . . .

It salves her conscience a little that she is aware of all of this – aware that although the man she loves must choose between bad or worse, she faces bad or bountiful. So when he starts lining up what he might do if he decides to stay – 'I'll talk to Bob, they need good foremen at Stretton's, or we could try Cowley or Abingdon, Morris are expanding' – she feels appropriately guilty as she cuts him short and says, 'Malaya. I don't care about the government job, I don't care about the money – but I care about you. Malaya.'

★

16.15. Bourton's just getting into his stride on the subject of jobs at home, beginning a swan around the possible – and, yes, they're all look-ats and worth-a-tries against the cert of Malaya, but that's what you'd expect, given until two hours ago he didn't need a new job – when she jams a steel bar between his spokes and stops him dead. *She can't mean it. She wants safety, a home, a future – all right, Bristol's not heaven, it's short of houses too, but bandits don't shoot up trains into Temple Meads, or pop out of the Mendips to kill farmers . . .*

He smiles awkwardly. 'I thought you'd be keener on home.'

'I would be but,' she bangs their hands on his knees in emphasis, 'Christie is *everywhere.*' Her face is alive with energy, enthusiasm, impatience. 'On the bus, in the office, shops, everywhere in London – everyone is talking about Christie. Some people say something nice about Queen Mary, *politesse*, but then they all get excited and talk about Christie, Christie – how many, why, how, where is he, I thought I saw him on the District Line . . . That's what it's like *now.* Imagine what it will be like when the trial comes, when that neighbour tells his story. And if there are official enquiries? If someone else was hanged for his murders, there will be anger, questions in Parliament – who is a better sacrifice than you? If you stay, Richard, everyone in the shops and on the streets and in the cafés and pubs and canteens will talk about Christie, and Bourton, and they will spit on both of you.'

'Steady on, girl.'

'All right.' She releases his hands and lifts hers into the air in annoyance. 'It will not be that bad. But it will be bad. Here,' she taps his temple, 'you know it. Don't you?'

'It could be bad,' he allows, 'but, well, he could top himself, or be found batty, or keep schtumm about me for any old reason or never get caught, even. Which would mean Richard Arthur Bourton would never bother the papers at all.'

'What is the probability that your name will get out? One chance in five?'

'More like one in three, perhaps forty–sixty.'

'And you will bet everything on forty–sixty? Really? When all you have to do for zero–one hundred is go away and be paid more money to live in a proper house and do something you would be good at? Richard, this is a good deal. Forget who is offering it, forget that they are fleas and they have bitten you. Take it.'

'I'm not sure I want to.'

'Richard,' there's a hectoring edge to her voice now, 'what would you stay for? London? It's been spoiled – for me and you. Or are you desperate for grey skies, ruins, rationing? Even if the papers never hear about you, do you really want to find a factory job? When you could easily be something else?' She leans in close and grips his hands more tightly. '*You* found the Traveller. *You* worked out the coshing boys. Even the mystery of the Lithuanian – *pouf*, Poirot. You are good at this, Richard. Men follow you, listen to you, and in Malaya,' a very French shrug, 'who knows what you can do?' She waits for a response but he can't think of one and she frowns. 'Is it because you would be an officer?'

Bourton shakes his head. 'I'm not sure I got that far, love.'

'Because you are clever, you have brown knees, you are a Queen's Bravery Man, all of this they will like. As for teacups and curtsies, well, I will teach you.'

'Not to curtsy, I hope,' he tries, but she is already standing up, looking preoccupied. *If you end this now, you're telling me what to do.*

'Look, I said I would only be a few minutes, and now I must give notice.'

'Come on,' he stands to resist, *you're bustling me too,* 'there's no need, we've only just started—'

'Richard,' stepping in to kiss him, 'I know you will think about this,' kissing him again, 'which is right as it is your decision,' she picks up her handbag and checks the bayonet, 'but you will see that there is really only one choice.'

He offers a humour-you smile despite his acrid unease. *Why are you bustling me?*

She steps away, wiggling her fingers in fake-coy farewell. 'I must pack!' She starts down the path across the square, calling over her shoulder, 'We can celebrate our first anniversary *en route*. Baghdad. Somewhere in India. The mystic East.'

87

16.25. Bourton sits upright in the unit photo pose, hands on thighs and arms straight, as if a little stiffness will put him back in charge. *Well, I wanted her help. Just didn't expect her to jump that way.* He smiles. *It's easier to say boo to the Met than my wife.*

Still not going to do what she wants, though. Control restored. *I'm not going to war again just to save my good name. If it gets mucky I'll change it. Or go somewhere it doesn't mean anything.* He nods, as if this is wisdom he's paid a week's wages to acquire. *Getting shot at to avoid getting shat on is stupid.*

For the first time in, oh, a decade, he has nowhere in particular to be. So he leans back, pulls out his Capstans and lights one. *Don't have to worry about being pegged for smoking in uniform.* He smiles.

Now he's decided what to do he has snapshots of the life he'll be leading: in a boiler suit or perhaps a gaffer's collar and tie, banging shut a front door in Bristol or Gloucester or Swindon at seven-ish every morning and opening it at five-ish every afternoon, boots off as the missus brings in the tea, evenings with the wireless or the pictures or oppos down the pub, and a kid or two or three – the kind of life his parents had before the Depression took the jobs away, the kind of life his brothers enjoy now.

Be a shock when I tell her. She's that keen on Malaya. Won over by sun, food that doesn't come with coupons, air that doesn't make her cough. And here was me thinking she'd want to stay home. Shows how much I know about my wife.

He sits up again. *But I do know a lot about her. For instance: she'd ask more questions. She'd want to know more about Malaya – pay and conditions, what I'd be doing, where we'd be, how much danger we'd face; she'd kick around her government job, call Hopkirk's man. She'd question whether we need to go at all – she's happy here, I know she is, friends, a family, a life. She'd jib at that Saturday departure, because flitting to the other side of the world with two days' notice wouldn't be doing right by the Parkins, the Athills, Joanie and Fred, the people who have taken us in. She'd quibble at least. And she'd ask about the HP on the wireless, the deposit on the room – she'd want to know about leave.*

She'd want to know. And she doesn't. So what the hell does that mean? He can feel the warm cigarette smoke filling his chest, his throat, his mouth. *She wants to go. For her own reasons, as well as for me.* He pushes smoke out to clear space for his next few puffs. *So why jump now, without even trying to find out the first thing about it?* He pulls so deep he fancies he can feel the tickle from lungs to ears. *She must want to go* now.

Why? She was happy last week – happy here, with us, our normal-hours life. So what's changed in the last week?

I got birched with the shit-stick. He lets a plume of smoke out into the soggy air. *But that wouldn't stop her asking questions – it would make her ask more, to be sure Malaya wouldn't be a birching too.*

What else, then?

Christie. He's what's changed. She thought he was dead and found out he wasn't.

And panicked. He takes another pull. *That's what that overreaction was – panic, laced with logic, anger, my-husband-does-not-understand.* He nods. *That's what it was during the fog, too – panic. And here was me thinking she should just tell me her troubles, when she was no more compos than someone with the shellshock shakes. Bastard.*

He closes his eyes for a moment, to push away his marital short-comings and focus. *So what made her panic? The news that Christie was alive. But why should that bother her?*

Suddenly he feels sick. *Because he's a threat to her, Anna Bourton – a threat he couldn't pose when dead.*

What kind of threat? He bends forward, head down, because he can only work through this logic if his face is hidden from the sun and other people. *A physical one – that's why she went out with the bayonet. And that's why she wanted me to kill him – even if she didn't ask in so many words.*

'Oh, God.' His voice is hoarse, squeaky, struggling. *He must have tried it on with her in the fog before I took her to Ampney – and she thinks he wants to finish the job. Those bruises, when she came to see me in St Mary's, they were too old to be from College Farm, like she said. Something else was wrong, too.* He recalls that chat by his bedside, when he'd been able to cry – just a little – on her shoulder. *She said the Traveller's victims had been poisoned. But they weren't. Christie's were. And she thought Christie was the Traveller. So how could she know Christie's victims were poisoned unless he'd tried to poison her, too? He tried it on, she fought him off, she knew he was dangerous so she warned me to be ready for him . . . And she couldn't tell me.*

Why? Because she doesn't love me, doesn't trust me?

He closes his eyes again for a moment. *Leave her, you, out of it. This is about the logic. Nothing must get in the way.* He opens his eyes, registers his Capstan has burned down, and grinds it out on the asphalt. *So, focus.*

If Christie's a threat, why hasn't he killed her? He's had three months. And: why run to Malaya? Now? Fear of Christie might make her want to go away until he's nicked, but she could go to Ampney, return when he's in custody. And in any case my Anna's not a run-and-hide girl, she's a face-it-kill-it, gut-it-like-that-rabbit girl. Why does she need *to go to the other side of the world, on Saturday, for six months? It doesn't make sense.*

Unless . . . Unless he's a threat whether in custody or not. Which means the threat isn't physical – it's something he knows, can tell. Something so important to her he knew, back in December, he could leave her be – even though she could have put him on the scaffold before any bodies had been found. Something that can't touch her if she's on the other side of the world.

Something she can't tell me. Even though he tried to kill her. He lifts his head a little to put a Capstan into his mouth. *You should have told me, love. Whatever Christie has on you.* The hand with the light is shaking. *Or reported the attack.* He gets the smoke lit. *If you had then the women in the alcove would still be alive. And you know it.* He feels a sudden stab of sympathy, as if she's rolled up her guilt in a newspaper and jabbed him in the gut. *No wonder you turned on me.*

He takes a deep pull, *Enough*, closes his eyes. Now something else doesn't make sense. *If Christie hasn't tried again, why does she need the bayonet?*

Oh, Christ. He hunches up his shoulders to his ears, as if to squeeze out the last of these thoughts, bitter toothpaste from the tube: *It isn't to defend herself. It's to kill Christie.*

Suddenly the nausea is back. *She meant it. Every word. When she said I'd done wrong for not committing murder, that was after the shock had gone, of Christie being alive. Cold hard reason. When she sent me off to kill in December, cold hard reason. No panic, no brainstorm, just plain speaking. And when she picked up that bayonet, it was to do the job she'd given me. The job she still thinks needs to be done.*

Oh, Anna. He opens his eyes, as if to watch the life he'd imagined leave Soho Square, perched on the running-board of a rattling pre-war cab. *We can't stay. We really can't stay . . .*

88

27 March 1953

Goodbyes.

Half-of-the-story-honest ones: 'I cocked up,' to his father, stowing Elgin Terrace kit in the little loft above his workshop. 'That's the truth of it, so they're tucking us away until Christie's in his grave.' And then, his father struggling to decide just how bad this sudden squall might be, 'It's cushy, Dad, and I get to go back to the Met, with a month extra seniority,' seeing They-don't-give-that-to-fuck-ups relief on his face, 'in the autumn, and aide to CID if I want it.'

His father manages a smile, and 'Well, that sounds like they're doing right. Just don't do anything to give your mother the willies. You've given her enough of those for a lifetime.' At the ladder: 'A baby or two would make her happy too.'

Or to Rex Athill, in the corner of the snug of the Ladbroke Arms at the wet to wave them off, the DC puzzled that Bourton is going where he doesn't want to do a job that might get him shot: 'It's the papers. Anna's that worried about what the papers might say about me, and I haven't got the heart to fight her as well as them.'

The DC leans in close, face tight, still furious at being banished for good coppering. 'Write it all down. Take what the brass give but don't reckon they won't try something when it suits.'

Disingenuous ones: 'A job suddenly came up there,' to Suchanek in his foreign-trimmed drawing room, Bourton and Anna holding hands on the sit-up-and-beg sofa as if getting the squire's permission to wed, 'and they thought I'd be suited, so the Met is sort of lending me for six months.' And Bourton feels a blush of pleasure when Suchanek smiles knowingly, one old soldier to another, as if to say, 'We both know what kind of job this must be . . .' Or another version

– to coppers at the farewell wet, sceptics who'd see the summons-for-cloak-and-dagger-glory line as a fantasy for ex-probationer Dick Bourton: 'The army means they like me, and the shot at CID means I like them. After all, they still got honest crime, and someone's got to solve it.' A version that pleases Tullow, the smiling string-puller, always within scragging range to ensure no real truth gets told. And a version ripe for mockery ('If you're solving crime then I'm coming to Malaya to commit it') – even as the coppers' laughing eyes signal a little 'You're really doing this?' and a lot of 'Mug.'

Accidental, almost-in-passing ones: 'I've left the Met and joined the Malayan Police,' to Senkus, in the hallway of the Baltic Hearth, where he's gone to leave the man's possessions and been surprised to find him present, sober and drinking scalding tea from a jam jar, 'which means I don't have to either report a certain illegal firearm or chuck it in the canal.' Senkus takes the news and the pouch without surprise, as if flying across the world to fight Communism is what normal men do. He asks where the pistol's bullets are, and where he can get more. 'Dunno,' says Bourton, peeved at his ingratitude.

'No matter,' says Senkus, clapping him on the shoulder. 'You kill Communists.' He sticks his hand out. 'Now I retire me from kill Communists, kill some for me.'

And then goodbyes that are pure Pinocchio: 'It's my idea, Mum.' They are standing at the front window in the parlour, watching Anna console a red-eyed Violet by the gate. 'She wants to stay, but it's too good a chance to miss. I want to give her a proper house, with a garden and that,' this fib-of-the-moment makes him tearful, 'and Malaya means I can.'

His mother, avoiding his eyes, says, 'So why is she so much happier about it than you?' Anna's profile is animated and gleeful; she prompts Violet into a girlish hand-over-mouth giggle.

'I'm leaving more behind,' he tries.

She nods, 'Suppose that's so,' turns, and from the doorway says, 'She should be nicer to you.' He realises she is saying something fundamental about his marriage, something she's noticed that he wasn't aware was on view, but by the time he thinks of what to say ('She loves me, Mum'), she has gone.

Then there are the people he won't lie to: Bill Nickerson, well past one on Saturday morning, in his quarter in Beaconsfield, Bourton having thumbed up half-cut after the wet – his old oppo, whom he can't stand having think him a fool. 'Sounds like you're doing the right thing, then,' Nickerson says, over their third bottle of pale ale. 'And,' the Die-hard aiming for reassurance but nailing maudlin through the bullseye, 'she's worth doing the right thing for.' He walks Bourton to the gate. 'Singapore's supposed to be quiet,' he says, as they shake hands. 'And I hear it's the roads an' jungle that are hairy, so stay off – out – of them.' His other hand grips Bourton's shoulder. 'Can't do anything for her if you're brown bread.'

And Bert, the first bloke he tells, on Thursday night as he comes off his late turn – five hours after Bourton's hurried over to the Colonial Office and signed on Hopkirk's dotted line, three after he's smiled at Anna and told her to pack. Poor Bert tussles with all of it, anxious and old over last orders in the Uxbridge Arms: 'I never heard the like, young Dick, and I don't rightly know what to say. Chucking out a good copper for good coppering. An' then taking him back.' Later, shaking his head, 'This is proper wrong. Not sure I can trust any of these buggers again. Well, four months and I'm done, won't have to. But it'll leave a bad taste.' After a pause, 'Jack Tullow, a part of all this,' sourly, 'clever-dickery.' He straightens up on the settle, looking contrite. 'I should have kept you out of trouble, Dick Bourton, and I did not.'

Bourton smiles. 'You got shot for me.'

Bert shakes his head. 'Met trouble, not villain trouble. We should've told John Foley to hop it but I got tempted, proper coppering, that's what tempted me, and like that Tantalus, the apple fell on your head.' He sticks out his right hand. 'Sorry for letting you down.'

Bourton shakes, saying, 'You didn't, Bert. And we got that Traveller.'

Bert smiles. 'That you did.'

Later, after another round: 'She hasn't done anything wrong, your Anna, she knows that, don't she? She was just wrong place, wrong time.'

Bourton nods. 'She doesn't want the Christie thing getting out,' the nearest to an untruth he can get with his SO, 'and I got to help her.'

Bert nodding, the happiest he gets in their chat. 'You do, young

Dick, you do.' And then, still worrying the coppering knot, 'How do you look those buggers in the eye when you come back? They're making liars of you and them both, young Dick, and you can't copper like that, all of you knowing you're all dishonest. You got to be honest to uphold the law. It's why I won't let CID square up my collars.' A finger stabs the table. 'Honest, honest, honest, you got to be honest, and here you are, playing along with 'em.' Bourton's about to protest but Bert's face shows the arrival of a thought. 'Ah . . . o' course you're playing along. You sat on Widdowson for 'em, what's this Christie palaver after that? And why did you sit on Widdowson? Because your stupid old SO said "Take what they offer an' they'll owe you."' His eyes look stricken. 'I done you wrong, young Dick. I done you wrong.'

'That's bollocks, Bert,' says Bourton. 'Was me decided, not you.'

But Bert is already waving away his words. 'Four weeks' leave an' a few months' light duties. That's what I sold your soul for. Cheap at the bleeding price.'

He seems more at ease after a piss, as if he's decided something. 'You come back, young Dick, an' it's all lies. You can't come back to that, take their orders, respect them, they can't respect you, it'd . . . poison everything.' His voice is quiet and warm, encouraging. 'You give this Malaya a proper go, young Dick. You been in all those wars so the shooting won't bother you – well,' a moment of embarrassment as he remembers Bourton's wounds, 'you'll know about keeping your head down, and,' safer ground now, 'these buggers owe you. If they want to cover your palm with silver, then milk 'em. Milk 'em.' He raises his pint. 'Richard Arthur Bourton, commissioner of the Malaya Police.'

★

28 March 1953

Then the last goodbye of all – to unfinished business and, perhaps, the Dale itself.

Gone seven, Saturday morning, stiff from the gearstick housing of the coal lorry in which he'd ridden back from Beaconsfield and bleary from barely three hours' kip, he's back in the prefab off Latimer Road.

'You like the army so much,' he tells Derek Jeffrey, hunched in his bed, sheet under his chin, 'I'll give you a bloody dose.' He drags the mattress off the bed and dumps the boy in a heap of bedclothes beside his desk. 'Outside, PT kit, five minutes. You don't, I'll tan you.' He marches out of the room, slamming the door behind him. Beryl Jeffrey is standing in the kitchen doorway, arms folded over her housecoat, resolute but unhappy. Peter has a hand on her shoulder. His flannel pyjamas look too good to be anything but a much-valued present. 'Mr J, best if you put something on too.'

He doubles Derek up and down all the way to Walmer Road, barking orders between good-mornings to passers-by. Most sense that he's not playing, and cast curious looks at the skinny schoolboy in white shorts and singlet slogging through shuttle runs in the strengthening light. He pushes Derek through the Rugby mission's double doors and up stairs lined with sixty years of Dale urchins. The boxing gym is a blur of movement as boys warm up and there's already a sweat tang to the air. Jack Bonelli, the former Empire and Olympic middleweight who coaches the youngsters, is walking along a line of seven- and eight-year-olds running on the spot, trying to stop their knees knocking their chins. He turns as Bourton's boots thump the planking and heads over. The two men swap handshakes and hellos while Derek gathers his breath.

'This him?' asks Bonelli, an edge to his voice. Bourton nods. 'I hear you like attacking people when their backs are turned,' says Bonelli. Peter Jeffrey appears in the doorway. 'If you want to fight, young man, you learn to do it fair and square.' Derek looks for support from his father, but Peter is deliberately focused on Bonelli. 'And me and the other lads in this gym are going to learn you how.'

'Derek,' Bourton grabs the boy's attention, 'what you did was cowardly.' A flash of indignation in his eyes, then calculation. 'Even more, it was wrong. It was an unprovoked attack on a defenceless man. He'd done nothing to deserve it. He certainly hadn't tried to hurt you. You understand that?' The boy nods, but it's a please-teacher gesture; his mouth is sour. *Perhaps a little shame will make you contrite.* 'He was just minding his own business,' Derek is looking at the floor, 'when you decided to bash out his brains. What was brave about that?' The boy mumbles. 'What's that?' Bourton prompts.

Derek looks up and his shoulders go back in defiance. 'He was a Nazi, wasn't he?'

'Once – perhaps,' says Bourton. 'If it was 1945, and you were both in uniform holding rifles, you could have had a go. But right then he was just a mechanic, end of his shift, alone in a hole with the ghosts of old oppos. And you,' Bourton is surprised to find his eyes smarting, 'you had no right.'

The boy is stiff-backed and staring him down and Bourton realises he'll need another axis of advance. 'Do you know what a British soldier's job is?'

'To fight.'

'To protect. Protect the people of Britain, and the Empire, and whoever he's sent to protect. He fights, but he fights people who fight back. He fights for a reason, within laws – and if he breaks them, hurts who he chooses without proper reason, he is punished. It isn't fighting that makes a British soldier, but fighting the right way. Understand?' More please-teacher, so Bourton leans in for effect and prods the boy in the chest. 'You will. You will. Because you're going to be taught it.'

Bourton pulls out a folded notebook page. Derek's eyes focus on it. 'You are going to learn to box at this gym. You will do it for as long as I say, because I am the only reason you are not facing years behind bars. You will come as often as Mr Bonelli tells you, and you will do what he tells you. You may feel tempted to go absent. Don't. This,' he gestures with the page, 'is the address and telephone number of the man you nearly killed. A man who's hard as nails. Who's fought in battles that make anything I've seen look like an exercise.' Derek's expression hasn't changed. 'Who hung up some Rootes tyke in a chain, and went off for a brew, just for some lip. A man,' *this'll get through to him*, 'who was in the French Foreign Legion, with the toughest men in the world.' Derek's eyes widen. 'Just like Beau Geste. So if you disobey these orders, Mr Bonelli,' Bourton passes the piece of paper to the coach, 'will get Beau Geste to come and give you a talking-to.' He bends down and starts prodding again. 'And it will be face to face. Understand?'

He leaves with Peter Jeffrey, the man's arms and torso tight, restraining violence or perhaps the urge to sob. 'You think it'll work?' Jeffrey manages, as they reach the street.

Bourton jams his hands deep in his pockets. 'Regular taps on the nose, a lot of right and wrong, you never know. It's got at least as much chance as reform school, and it won't wreck his life.' He shrugs. 'If it works, it'll be down to you and your missus, maybe Jack Bonelli, keeping him in line. Beau Geste won't come even if Jack calls.' Rex Athill gets out of a job Morris parked up twenty yards away and taps his watch. Bourton nods. *Plane to catch.* 'Whether it steers him back to the straight and narrow is up to him.' He can see Jeffrey is warming up to be grateful, and he sticks his hand out, because once a taciturn man like Jeffrey starts he might not stop until they're both embarrassed – but also because he's tired, and half done with the Dale, and is due at Heathrow in less than an hour. 'Good luck. To you and Mrs J.' They shake, avoiding each other's eyes. 'I'll write, see how it's going.' The words sound as feeble as the message behind them.

The Morris strains with people too long for the seats and luggage too big for the boot. He jams a buttock between Anna and her Kai Tak case as she works his kitbag between her knees and the back of the driver's seat. Her eyes are gleaming as if she's off to a favourite granny and her hoard of humbugs. They rattle out of the Dale, past the old kiln, Avondale Park, the Walmer, two matrons scrubbing the steps of St Francis of Assisi. He notices that she never once looks back. He smiles – convincingly enough – and wraps an arm around her shoulders. *Skipping away from our first home with a murderer over our heads and baggage stuffed with lies. So much for new beginnings.*

89

'Anyway, Christie never turned up.' Athill pulls out to overtake a gleaming Riley being driven as if third gear would scratch the paintwork. 'Says the *News of the World*. If you can believe them. They claim a couple of uniforms came along, may have spooked him. But I dunno.'

Anna's excursion mood has popped. Her hand is still but tense on Bourton's knee. He presses it in reassurance. 'And what did Christie tell the paper?' He's trying for a conversational tone but his voice sounds brittle even to him.

'At last, a sign for Heathrow. Just that he'd turn himself in to them, give 'em his story.' He looks up into the rearview mirror. 'He didn't mention you or me, if that's worrying you.' It isn't, but Bourton nods anyway.

'And has he called since the failed rendezvous?' Anna's last word sounds like a Paris assignation, but Bourton can tell the Froggy wink-wink hides concern, perhaps even fear.

'No.'

'But he's still free.' Anna's voice has a quiver, almost a croak. 'He still could call.' *Definitely fear.* He wishes he were less punch-drunk so he could work out what's behind it.

'Even if he did, by the time the paper comes out tomorrow Dick'll be over Persia or somewhere and it all becomes,' he changes down and turns on the left-hand indicator, 'fish-and-chips paper.' They turn, Athill changes up, and then his gaze returns to the rearview, and Bourton can see calculation in his eyes, a jigsaw being spread out and turned over and solved. The DC registers Bourton's eyes on his, but doesn't look away. *I know*, his gaze seems to say, *I know* – but what, Bourton's still too cobwebbed to see.

'All right, then,' Athill says, as if they've just agreed something in the mirror. 'Let's get you on that plane.'

★

Why won't they let us out? thinks Anna, standing in the dormer, looking out at the huge silvered bird with the toast-rack tail. She edges closer to the glass, away from the other four police recruits, a strange macédoine of the can't-settle or won't-settle in which Richard does not belong. *Is this right for him? Or is it merely that staying behind would most definitely be wrong?* She feels worn out by all this thinking and is aware that judicious answers seem harder to find. *Let us get there, and see, and then decide.*

A flurry of noise by the door drags her eyes across, heart revving. *Just wealthy Malaya men doing the fancy-meeting-you-here.* Her heart slows. *Silly woman, no one is after you. Men in bad suits will not come through the door, point, cut through the crowd.*

But Christie seems to want to speak now, before he is in custody – what if he rings the paper, any paper, and tells? Tells a tale that will confuse, obscure, cross wires? A true tale that can ruin a reputation, a marriage, perhaps a life – or, more painful, a false one, that twists the innocent and coincidental, from sick woman and dogged copper, say, to White Russian whore and her bent bobby, blackmailed into leaving her attacker free. A no-smoke-without-fire tale that any paper would print . . .

I will not drag him down. She reaches out and touches his fingers. He smiles stiffly, thankful-but-unmoved – the closer to departure, the grumpier he gets – as she tunes in.

'How much are they paying?' The oldest one, Tom/Tam – Scottish, calloused handshake, nicotined fingertips, coolie's haircut – nods at the happy gaggle in the other half of the room, separating themselves from the shabbies travelling on a government chit.

'One hundred and seventy-five quid one way,' Richard says. There's a chorus of astonishment as he delivers his we'll-be-mates-soon laugh. 'Six months' pay in my last job.'

Tom/Tam turns to Anna. 'So how come they're paying for you to fly with the mucky-mucks when they won't even let my missus get a trooper?'

His voice has an edge even if his smile is polite, and Anna's first answers – 'Because the three-year contract is unaccompanied,' or 'Your wife is useless,' or 'Because they must be nice to my clever husband' – won't do. So she smiles, and in rusty Shanghai says, 'Rickshaw man, take me to Malaya, quick way,' and turns back to the window. *What is keeping them?*

Get us on the plane and all of it, all of it, goes away . . .

★

'Government job,' says Bourton diplomatically. 'She's got a bit of Chinese.' Tam Cooper, the forty-ish ex-Seaforth Highlander clearly on his uppers, snorts – Contempt? Disbelief? Anger? – and stubs out his smoke in the BOAC ashtray. *Change the subject.* 'For six months' pay,' he surveys the other passengers, 'you'd think they could give them more than a gussied Nissen hut and paper flowers.'

'I'd troop it an' take the difference in fivers,' says Cooper. He reaches into his demob suit for his Player's. 'And so would my wife.'

And I'd take a factory job and a prefab but neither of us is getting what he wants. The conversation's already moved on, to things they'd all spend a hundred and seventy-five quid on, and as Bourton scans the others he can't help thinking, *Waifs and strays.* Oram, commercial artist, never left Britain, hoping Malaya means the exotic East; Black, ex-Merchant Navy, too young for the war and looking for Adventure; Cooper, drifting since demob, so desperate for a regular wage he'll sign up for three years' separation and the risk of death; and Fielding, the ex-paratrooper with no active service, who's got the look of a man hoping to get the chance to kill someone. *Romantics, the desperate, the mad – Christ, I'm joining the Foreign Legion.* He feels a surge of helplessness, even shame, because unlike them he's got choices, nothing to prove – and whatever Tullow says, there's no way, in this company, that he's doing anything other than running backwards, to a place he doesn't need to go.

Then a surge of anger pushes away the shame and weakness, because this isn't his fault, this is down to his bloody wife and her bloody lies and lies and lies, and he turns to her mooning at tons of metal as if they're going to sweep her into a saddle and ride off to a fairy-tale happy ending, and steps into the dormer, opening his mouth to say, 'Why couldn't you trust me?' but what comes out, in a barbed whisper, the point of a spear thrown to wound, is 'There never was no Éric de Whatever.' She turns to him, slowly absorbing what he has said. 'Your first swain,' he prompts her. 'When I got that infection, I said I wasn't going to die like Éric, and you didn't know who I was talking about.'

She's caught up with him now, and her holding-action smile appears. 'Richard—'

'What's so bad about your first bloke that you had to invent one?'

The smile resists for a moment, then crumbles, and before she turns back to the window he sees her eyes fill with tears. He reaches out, knowing he's hurt her far more than he meant to, wanting to snatch the words back down his throat, but she steps away, into the corner, and shakes her head.

'Oh, Richard.' He pulls out his hanky but she deliberately opens her handbag and retrieves her own. 'You really do not understand what it was like, Shanghai, under the Japanese. How – *difficult* it was.'

'No,' he said, 'I don't.' He pauses, ready to think of something innocuous that will stitch up the wound, but he realises she's protected one lie with another, and his contrition withers. 'But then you don't either. You weren't there much, were you?'

'Richard—'

'You were somewhere else. Somewhere you could only get back from by killing bandits or something.' She wipes her nose. 'After the Japs surrendered. That's what you said. When you got pissed, that night with Tony and Vinegar Tits—'

'Richard.' She raises a hand to stop him. 'You are between polices now. You can let some puzzles lie.' She dabs her eyes.

He stares at her, wanting to hurt, to heal, to chase something that might eventually be truth, but he doesn't have it in him to make up for what he's done or run her lies to ground. So he says nothing. *It's up to you, love. Where this goes – it's up to you.*

★

Oh, Richard . . . Anna keeps focused on the aircraft. She can't trust herself to look him in the eye because then she'll have to speak and she doesn't know which emotion – rage, pity, love, guilt – will choose her words. *I know this silence, I know this technique, show that I am lying, break up the story-world I have created, then say nothing and expect me to tell.*

She shakes her head. *But for all your detective cleverness, how much can you hear? Which truth would be too much? The Shanghai camp the Japanese put me in, or the Manchuria camp they moved me to? The important man I had to please but could not? How about the experiments he would brag about, or the dead bodies he would fuck? Or the brothel that I lived in – that, probably, would be a fact too far. But if you could stand all of that, why, there's the present this* nécrophile *surely gave me, the girl he couldn't screw. Some little memento of the dissecting table, borne on his fingers, lodged in my lungs, to carry south and home, to bloom in the cold. Against all this, the fact that I have lied, lied about it all, to you and the ministries that allowed me to find a home – that, surely, barely matters. And perhaps the knowledge that I have lied should be truth enough.*

★

'They will be summoning us in a moment, I think,' she says. *So the lies have it, then.* 'You go on ahead. I will make myself presentable for our great adventure.'

'Love—'

'Richard.' The name sounds like a command. Then, softer, 'Go on. I will be fine.'

The other recruits are moving towards the door, Oram touching his sleeve to let him know. 'Be with you in a moment, lads,' Bourton says, eyes still on his wife. She replaces the hanky, pulls out and opens her compact. 'I'm sorry, love.' He's surprised to find he means it. 'Shouldn't have said that.' She waves her free hand. 'It's just . . .' He flails for something that sums up his anger and his love, even what he's doing for her, but his thoughts are creaky and awkward. All he can manage is 'You can trust me, you know.'

The compact snaps shut and she turns to face him. Her eye-liner is smeared and her eyes are blotchy. 'You might want to do a little more touching up.'

She puts on her dare-the-world smile and tosses her head. 'We are leaving home, Richard. It is normal for we weak women to cry when we leave our homes.'

He wants to point out that she seemed happy enough as they left the Dale, but senses that her poise is as frail as her logic, that any more argy could break something brittle but unseen. More than this, he realises, she's never going to tell him – and if she won't tell, neither will he. *Live and let live. A lot to be said for it.* So he nods, as if he believes her, and summoning up his sunniest grin loops his arm. 'Shall we, girl? Our carriage awaits.'

She laughs – *Thank you for letting her find that* – and puts her arm through his. 'Of course.' She pulls his elbow close and kisses his cheek. 'Let us find a new home.'

And hold our breath, thinks Bourton, as they head for the door. And hold our breath.

GLOSSARY

ARP	Air Raid Precautions (air-raid warden)
BEM	British Empire Medal (medal for meritorious service or gallantry, below the George Medal but above a Queen's Commendation)
Blagger	Slang for armed robber (police)
BOAC	British Overseas Airways Corporation
Bonnet	Slang for helmet (Metropolitan Police)
Bren	British Army light machine gun
CGM	Conspicuous Gallantry Medal (military award for gallantry at sea, given to NCOs and men; second to the Victoria Cross)
CPO	Chief Petty Officer (senior enlisted rank in Royal Navy)
CSM	Company Sergeant-major (Senior enlisted rank in British Army)
Dab	Slang for disciplinary proceedings (Metropolitan Police)
DCM	Distinguished Conduct Medal (military award for gallantry in action on land, given to NCOs and men; second only to the Victoria Cross)
Die-hards	Nickname for the Middlesex Regiment and its soldiers (from its motto, 'Die Hard')
DP	Displaced Person (a willing or unwilling refugee of the Second World War in Europe)
Early (turn)	The 06.00–14.00 shift (Metropolitan Police)
Gen	Slang for information or intelligence (military)
Ginnel	Narrow gated alley behind, and linking the back gardens of, a terrace of houses
Glosters	The Gloucestershire Regiment (British Army infantry regiment)

GM	George Medal (gallantry medal second only to the George Cross, given to civilians, or military personnel for non-combat bravery)
Gook	Slang for a Korean – usually a North Korean soldier (UN forces)
Guv'nor	Slang for inspector (Metropolitan Police)
Hogget	A yearling sheep, or the meat from it
HP	Hire purchase
Ike jacket	Short US uniform jacket invented by General Dwight Eisenhower ('Ike')
Imjin	Battle in Korean war in which a British brigade was mauled, and then 1st Bn. The Gloucestershire Regiment effectively destroyed, by a Chinese Army Corps
Int	Shorthand for intelligence (British military)
Kaput	Finished, dead (slang, military, originally German)
Late (turn)	The 1400–2200 shift (Metropolitan Police)
LCC	London County Council, the administrative body joining together London's boroughs
MGB	Soviet secret police (later renamed KGB)
MX	Official abbreviation for the Middlesex Regiment (British Army infantry regiment)
NAAFI	British military canteen and shop
Night (turn)	The 2200–0600 shift (Metropolitan Police)
NCO	Non-commissioned officer (everyone in an armed service senior to a private but junior to an officer)
Ob	An observation task, or post (Metropolitan Police)
OP	Observation post (military)
Oppo	Slang for close friend (military – originally the man you shared your foxhole with, so had to depend on)
PPSh	Soviet sub-machine gun
PRO	Public Record Office
Pug up	Slang for an illicit rest while on duty (Metropolitan Police)
REME	Royal Electrical and Mechanical Engineers – the British Army's mechanics
RN	Royal Navy
Sanger	Slang for sandwich

Sap	Small cosh
Scran	Food
Stag	Slang for sentry or (as verb) to stand sentry (military)
SDI	Sub-Divisional Inspector (Metropolitan Police rank between inspector and superintendent, renamed chief inspector in 1948)
Skipper	Slang for sergeant (Metropolitan Police)
Snafu	Slang for foul up (military, originally 'Situation normal, all fucked up' also used as a passive verb – 'everything's snafued')
SNCO	Senior non-commissioioned officer (Sergeants and Warrant Officers) – the trusted, experienced backbone of an armed service
SO	Supervising officer – an older policeman who would supervise a probationary constable
Square up	Slang for to alter a documentary record (Metropolitan Police); often used to describe the CID practice of massaging crime figures by recording crimes reported by uniformed officers as more minor offences
Stick	Slang for truncheon (Metropolitan Police)
Tiddy	Slang for to prettify or neaten (Royal Navy)
Totter	Someone who collects discarded items in, and often sells them from, a horse-drawn cart
Turn	Slang for shift (Metropolitan Police)
Wad	Biscuit (naval slang)
Waffen SS	Combat element of the Schutzstaffeln, the army of the German Nazi party
Wehrmacht	German army of the Second World War
Worm	Slang term for early (06.00–14.00) shift (Metropolitan Police)
WVS	Women's Volunteer Service
2ic	Second in command

ACKNOWLEDGEMENTS

Breathe took a very long time to write; a lot of people are owed thanks for their help in getting it done.

My brother St.John has always been incredibly encouraging of my writing efforts. He identified which of many plot ideas had the most potential and told me how to approach it; he then steered me to Jim Gill at United Agents as the man to bring it to market. Jim's unerring good taste helped shape the novel and his commercial skill sold it as a partial manuscript; when I promptly fell seriously ill, he took all the strain of missed deadline after missed deadline, leaving me in peace to recover. His superb editor's eye was also invaluable when my first draft came in way, way too long. Finally, he and a former Aegis colleague, Helena Lally, both suggested turning my proposed title of *Breath* – the original inspiration of my wife Kirsten – into *Breathe*; I can't remember who came up with it first so they share the blame.

Nick Sayers at Hodder & Stoughton took a punt on a partial and, I suspect, fought my corner in years of internal meetings when there was no hint of a completed manuscript; when it did come in he was spot on in identifying what needed to be done to make it work better. He has never pressured me, despite having good cause to do so. I've been extremely lucky to work with a consummate editor who also happens to be a proper gent. The next book will be easier, I promise.

That *Breathe* got finished is in part due to four readers who, at different stages, said it was on the right track; my brother St.John, my mother Anabel – a superb writer whose *Destroy Unopened* also visits the shadows of Rillington Place – my wife Kirsten, and Jill Button. Jill read bits of early *Breathe* as individual sheets of typescript before they went on a fire; her unqualified approval made me think it would all work.

Years ago I happened to mention to Michael Shipster that I was writing a thriller whose hero had been a Die-hard in Korea. Unsolicited, he sent me material his father Brigadier John Shipster CBE DSO, who'd been a company commander with 1 MX in Korea, had written about the campaign. I hope I have done it justice.

Almost all of *Breathe* was written around my then day job as a political risk analyst. When I fell ill my employers were extraordinarily generous with paid sick leave and then a gradual return to work – a generosity that kept family, body and soul together at a very difficult time. Thank you very much to Aegis's owners, Tim Spicer, Mark Bullough, Jeffrey Day and Dominic Armstrong, and to the CEO, Graham Binns.

My final and biggest thank you is to my wife, Kirsten. You're a star. You're a pretty fine editor, too. The next one is for you.

AUTHOR'S NOTE

This novel was sparked by a coincidence, and a what-if. Notting Dale serial killer Reg Christie (see *10 Rillington Place* by Ludovic Kennedy) resigned from his final job during the December 1952 smog; given he used a self-made breathing device to kill at least one of his victims, what if he – or someone like him – had prowled London's worst-ever pea-souper, offering relief? Of course, no serial killer did stalk the smog of 5-9 December 1952. Yet one could have done so easily enough, given how blasé Londoners and officialdom alike were about pea-soupers' effects; as for breathing aids, these seem to have been a cottage industry.

I have taken some liberties with the health effects of London's smogs, particularly the issue of whether there was a substantial time lag between fogs and deaths (as anecdotal evidence often suggests). The official Ministry of Health verdict on the 1952 smog was that there were 3,500-4,000 excess deaths during the first three weeks of December (i.e., during and immediately following the smog). Yet as the report itself (*Mortality and Morbidity during the London Fog of December 1952*, Ministry of Health Reports on Public Health and Medical Subjects No. 95, HMSO London 1954) concluded, its verdict was undermined by methodological limitations. If the 1952 smog was appreciably worse than other pea-soupers (as first-hand accounts and Christine L.Corton's marvellous *London Fog: The Biography* show), then it seems to me – as someone writing fiction about events for which there is little data – that hugely increased mortality in December 1952 is not incompatible with delayed mortality after lesser fogs. My account of how deaths were recorded is invented, even if the causes themselves are those identified in the Ministry of Health report. I have also taken a small liberty with vocabulary; the term 'smog' seems to have entered popular currency because of the December fog, rather than being in use before it.

The Notting Hill and Dale of *Breathe* broadly existed. Some of the locations, such as Bertram Terrace and Elgin Terrace, are fictional; others, including pubs, the Rootes factory and Notting Hill nick, are not, and the physical geography I describe is still visible today. (Notting Dale is still much poorer than the Hill, which now seems mostly the preserve of the very wealthy.) While Lithuania House existed, I have moved it a little, and the institution I describe is essentially fictitious. The Baltic Hearth is entirely invented (though its name echoes the Polish Hearth, the Polish exiles' club in South Kensington). The terrain around Cirencester and the Berkshire Downs is also still much as described, though Ampney St Mark and Burleaze Farm are invented.

I have also tried to be faithful to the institutions of the time, particularly the Metropolitan Police and the British Army. The Met of the early 1950s was undermanned, poorly paid, poorly housed, and grappling with rising crime rates, with tension between an often authoritarian, pre-war-recruited leadership and post-war junior ranks. As for the British Army, it was extremely busy (Bourton's service record is not unusual for a regular infantryman of that era). The Middlesex Regiment existed until amalgamation in the 1960s; its nickname The Die-hards was earned in 1811, when its ancestor unit the 57th Regiment, scourged by French fire on an open slope, was ordered by its commander to 'Die hard'. The Gloucestershire Regiment survived until the 1990s. The first battalions of both units served in Korea in 1950-51, and when the Glosters were destroyed at the Battle of the Imjin – over 650 men were killed or captured – the unit was reconstituted with volunteers (like Bourton) from British Army units all over the Far East. For readers unfamiliar with the British regimental system, it is still commonplace for serving or former soldiers of a unit who face real bureaucratic difficulties to try to secure the support of senior members. It is thus entirely credible that Bourton would have tried to enlist the support of Die-hard generals to be reunited with his fiancée, and entirely credible that they should provide it. However I have to confess that while Civil Defence was indeed being stood up again in 1951-2, my depiction of it is entirely fiction, even if based on descriptions of it during WW2.

The Korea material is also broadly accurate. Bourton's nightmares fix on Kunu-Ri, a disaster for US arms directly attributable to the refusal of General Douglas MacArthur – the overall commander of UN forces in Korea – to believe that Chinese forces were present *en masse* in Korea, despite plentiful evidence to the contrary. (See David Halberstam's *The Coldest Winter*.) 1 MX were bystanders at this disaster. Even more of a backwater than the Korean War was the CIA- and SIS-backed campaign by partisans against Soviet re-occupation of the Baltic States. Senkus' experience draws on that of partisan hero Juozas Lukša, or 'Daumantas', whose memoir *Fighters for Freedom* was written in the West before his return to Lithuania in 1950; he was betrayed by a comrade and killed in 1951.

Shanghai's White Russians are another historical oddity. Many of those who fled the Bolsheviks in 1917-21 did so via Siberia and China, ending up in Manchuria or the international settlements in Shanghai. (These were outposts of colonial powers protected by one-sided treaties with China.) These refugees were, like Anna, stateless, and led lives often as marginal as is described in *Breathe*. Many were used as human guinea pigs by Unit 731, the Japanese biological warfare establishment in Manchuria. During WW2 the Japanese interned civilians from enemy states, such as the US, UK, and – bizarrely – El Salvador; conditions were appalling, and deaths due to disease, malnutrition and mistreatment common.

Finally, many of the people referred to in this novel really existed. These range from King George VI and Professor Keith Simpson to the murderers Reg Christie and Neville Heath. Sir Francis de Guingand (Field Marshal Montgomery's chief of staff) and Sir Brian Horrocks were both commissioned into The Middlesex Regiment; my characterisation of the latter (whose career included a stint training White Russian NCOs, like Anna's father, in 1919-20, and ended as Black Rod) is in line with his reputation. Sir Cecil Wakeley was also a real figure, and the author of a foreword to the British Red Cross's *Elementary Anatomy and Physiology Manual No.7* (the copy I used belonged to my wife's grandfather, Dr JAD Wyness, a GP in Stockport, Cheshire). I hope Wakeley's idolisation by a fictional murderer he would never have met is not too great an instance of *lèse majesté*.